A NEW MASTER OF HORROR, GRAHAM WATKINS, HAS STUNNED FANS AND CRITICS WITH HIS SHOCKING VISIONS OF TERROR . . .

Praise for DARK WINDS

"ONE OF THE MOST EXCITING THINGS I'VE READ IN A LONG TIME; books like this don't come along too often!"
—Marion Zimmer Bradley, author of *The Mists of Avalon*

"AN IMPRESSIVE DEBUT . . . *Dark Winds* reminds me in ways of Peter Straub's *Shadowland* [and] John Fowles' *The Magus* . . . HIGHLY RECOMMENDED." —*2AM magazine*

"CHILLING AND PROVOCATIVE!" —Andrew Neiderman, bestselling author of *Pin* and *Bloodchild*

"THE STORY CARRIES YOU RAPIDLY ALONG!"
—*Mystery Scene*

"VERY IMPRESSIVE . . . It has a nightmarish sticky quality, like a demonic brand of Krazy Glue, which bonds your eyeballs to the book until you've finished reading it."
—Graham Masterton, author of *The Manitou*

"A POWERFUL AND TERRIFYING NOVEL . . . exotic . . . erotic and mystifying . . . a must for all readers of horror!"
—Randall Boyll,
author of *After Sundown* and *Mongster*

"A THOROUGHLY ENGROSSING STORY . . . HARD TO PUT DOWN!" —*The Warren Record* (NC)

Now Graham Watkins presents an epic tale of modern passion and ancient terror . . .

THE FIRE WITHIN

Berkley Books by Graham Watkins

DARK WINDS
THE FIRE WITHIN

THE FIRE WITHIN

GRAHAM WATKINS

BERKLEY BOOKS, NEW YORK

**For Peggy—without whom these books
would not exist**

THE FIRE WITHIN

A Berkley Book/published by arrangement with
the author

PRINTING HISTORY
Berkley edition/April 1991

ISBN: 0-425-12647-1

Berkley Books are published by The Berkley Publishing Group,
200 Madison Avenue, New York, New York 10016.
The name ''Berkley'' and the ''B'' logo
are trademarks belonging to Berkley Publishing Corporation.

PRINTED IN THE UNITED STATES OF AMERICA

10 9 8 7 6 5 4 3 2 1

Prologue

News items:

DATELINE: BROWNSVILLE, TEXAS, MAR. 1. (AP)

An investigation is continuing into the bizarre murder of Eligio Reyes, 21. Brownsville police have charged Martin Reyes, 39, father of the victim, with first-degree murder for the apparently ritual slaying, in which the victim's heart was cut out. The elder Reyes told police he and his son had seen an omen, which they took to mean a human sacrifice was necessary. Police are still searching for a motive in the killing.

DATELINE: MEXICO CITY, APR. 18. (REUTERS)

The body of an unidentified man was found by tourists today in the ancient ruins at Teotihuacan, thirty miles northeast of Mexico City. According to the coroner's report, the man, described by police as a dwarf, had frozen to death. Since temperatures in the area were not below freezing, police have opened an investigation.

DATELINE: UNIVERSITY OF CALIFORNIA, BERKELEY, CALIFORNIA, APR. 26. (AP)

Astronomers here today reported an increase in the amount of sunlight reflected from the planet Venus. They had no explanation for this phenomenon, which makes Venus, the morning and evening star, appear brighter than it was.

Part
I

New York City

1

As the cold of a New York winter swept up the hallway, David Hallsten emerged from the elevator and hurried over to the line of mailboxes on the wall. He had to search momentarily to find 4D—he could never just walk up and stick his key in it—and opened the box. Without really looking at the contents, he retrieved the letters and returned to the elevator. The indicator remained stationary on seven; this meant that Mrs. Ebelstein had jammed the door open again so she could carry her laundry, piece by piece, inside.

He rubbed his short beard for a second, then headed for the stairs. Deciding against taking them two at a time—too much work so early in the day—he went up at a leisurely pace, noticing that the gray morning was getting a bit brighter. Maybe it won't be so damn cold today, he thought. He remembered how it had been the previous night; he'd been out late, and had been unwilling to linger in the frigid hallway even long enough to collect the mail, preferring to leave it for the morning.

Idly, he glanced at each piece. Mostly junk, he thought; one bill—Con Edison—he tossed down on the small table by the door and the rest he carried back toward the kitchen. Susan was still sleeping; he poured himself a cup of coffee and sat down to look at the remaining mail.

The first envelope he opened contained a flyer extolling the merits of the latest electronic marvels which he could order from the Updike Distributing Company, at, so the flyer claimed, IMMENSE savings. Only a few measly dollars a month. Which of course added up to a price far in excess of full retail. He glanced at the photos of stereos, TVs, and VCRs with an expressionless face and sipped his coffee. The flyer was tossed aside. The next one was trying to sell them a burial plot upstate; it followed the first.

The last one was blazed with a diagonal ''dated mail—please open immediately!'' Designed to make you think it was important, he told himself. Something exciting. Something useful. Not likely. At thirty-four, he did not consider burial plots or overpriced TVs either exciting or useful. He ripped it open, unfolded the contents.

''Dear David and Susan Hallsten,'' it read, ''you have definitely won one of the prizes listed below. You must claim it in person by''—the following printed with a rubber stamp—''March 15, 1987.'' He glanced down at the prizes. Letter A—all expenses paid vacation to South America. Letter B—complete Nikon 35mm camera outfit. Letter C—set of designer luggage. In smaller print below, the odds of winning each—for letter A, 1 to 999,999. For letter C, 999,996 to 999,999. He grinned to himself. Seemed rather likely to be designer luggage instead of a vacation or camera. The grin spread outward a bit, exposing itself to the world.

He became conscious of footsteps behind him and glanced around at Susan. Tousled hair, sleepy smile; the woolly bathrobe she wore every morning hung loosely on her slender body. He redirected the grin into a welcoming smile.

''Anything interesting?'' she asked, walking past him to the cabinet where cups were kept.

''Bill from Con Ed, rest is just junk,'' he replied. ''Unless you think we're lucky enough to have won a vacation in South America''—he held up the flyer—''at the good odds of one in a million.'' He glanced at it again and grunted. ''Literally.''

Sipping the steaming coffee, she looked at the flyer over his shoulder. ''You must claim your prize in person,'' she read, ''at lovely Tascan Acres homesites, on beautiful Long Island.'' This was accompanied by a picture of beach and sand dunes, which might have been taken almost anywhere on the east coast.

''Maybe we should go out there, David,'' she said suddenly. ''It would be an interesting drive, at least, and maybe the luggage isn't totally trash.''

He gave her a quizzical look. ''You're not being suckered by this thing, are you? You know they don't really give away anything worth anything.''

"Oh no, I know that. I just kinda thought it would be interesting, you know? Most of them are in South Carolina or somewhere; a major trip, you know? But Long Island, that's not far, and maybe it would be a nice trip, you know? We could drive down there Saturday, maybe Sunday, and maybe—" She stopped herself. All this had come out at an accelerating pace, as if she were trying to convince David of the importance of rushing down to this development and claiming their prize.

He watched her, a little surprised. The frequent "you know?" in her conversation, as he had often observed, occurred when she was truly excited about something. Many men would have found this irritating; he found it charming.

He found everything about Susan charming, even after five years of marriage.

They had met when Susan had been hired as a secretary at the office where David worked. For several months they hardly spoke to each other; a greeting in the morning, a few casual words exchanged. But almost from the beginning David found himself fantasizing about her constantly. He would catch himself staring at her, averting his eyes quickly if she looked in his direction. With a certain blindness typical of him, he failed to notice that she was doing the same thing. As he later found out, he was in her fantasies as well.

That unproductive situation had continued until a morning they had found themselves alone in the office, courtesy of a heavy snowfall. Their conversation had rapidly progressed from the casual "bad snowstorm today, isn't it?" to a discussion of sexual preferences, and that same evening found them exploring those sexual preferences in David's apartment. Two weeks later, Susan moved in with him; the next year they were married.

David believed, and Susan had always agreed, that the sexual aspect of their relationship was extremely important to them. Their attraction had been mutual, intense, and immediate; when it had been consummated, both had felt that, if anything, the reality had surpassed the expectation, something new for both of them. Neither was by any means inexperienced; they had spent hours talking, reviewing past sexual exploits. Sexually active since his middle teens, David had long ago decided that he would likely never find a woman who was as intensely interested in sex as he was. But in Susan, he felt that he had. He simply could not believe that many other men had sex lives as full and rich as his was. Most of his friends, when talking about their wives and lovers, seemed only able to recount various disappointments. Or stories of how good things had been at the beginning, only to have turned sour now. In such discussions, David was usually quiet. If he did talk, it was about one of his previous lovers, not about Susan.

He remembered one such incident, only a few days before, when Mike Finch, a co-worker of his, had just finished a long story about his wife, Alicia. Mike had gone into great detail about how enormously fat she had become, and how she'd lost all interest in sex. David had said nothing. It had seemed cruel to him to talk about his relationship with Susan, about how totally different it was. If he had gone on about what a tigress Susan was in bed, Mike would have assumed he was lying. As far as Mike was concerned, the notion of a woman who was a tigress in bed was strictly a porno myth. None such existed in his world.

But she was, David thought, smiling inwardly. Vignettes of their various sexual experiences ran through his mind. All his best times, he reflected, had been with her; all his most exciting times as well, except of course for the Incidents.

That stray thought clouded his upbeat mood. He had not thought about the Incidents for months. Always the word itself was capitalized in his mind, even though it had been more than fifteen years since the last Incident. Susan knew nothing of this side of his past; very few people did. He tried to push these memories away. They were not at all pleasant to him, and he had already spent too many years of his life pondering their possible meaning. This had accomplished nothing; now he simply tried not to think about them, and focused instead on his slightly confused-looking wife.

"Hey, all right, slow down," he said, waving the flyer. "If you really want to go out there, we will, all right? I don't know why you want to, though. You know it's all bullshit!"

"Oh, I don't want to go all that badly," she said, frowning slightly. "I just thought it would be something different." David was grinning at her again, and she flushed.

Moving away from the table, she stood momentarily gazing out the window. Below her was the grimy street scattered with lumps of greasy snow; great heaps of nondescript garbage were piled at intervals along the sidewalk. People, also nondescript, moved among the mounds quickly and purposefully. Her attention therefore focused on one man who moved slowly, his head swinging from side to side. He looked like a dog trying to pick up a scent; knowing something of interest was about, and not knowing exactly where it was. She fancied she could hear him sniffing the air, even though she was four stories up.

The man had now stopped. He turned first left, then around, studying everyone nearby. He seemed to be a derelict of some sort, his clothing ragged and light for such a bitter morning, and he was wearing a battered hat which concealed his face from Susan's view. She sipped her coffee and, interested now, continued to watch.

The man was now scanning up and down the nearby buildings in a rather systematic way. She could not see his eyes, but his head was never still, bobbing up and down, obviously looking for something.

"Hey, David, come and look at this guy," she called.

"What about him?" David asked, coming to stand beside her.

"He's weird, don't you think? Watch him for a minute."

After many years in Manhattan, it required considerable eccentricity for David to consider a person weird. That quality was sometimes so commonplace in the city as to be the norm. He had to admit, however, that the man Susan was watching was behaving in an unusual manner. He seemed to be rooted to one spot, unable or unwilling to move until he found what he was seeking. A mugger or second-story man, David thought; looking for a victim. Probably had done time in prison. He was being too obvious. No one would think he was looking for an address or anything like that.

The man's search pattern had now brought him to their apartment building. His head tilted up in increments until he was looking at their floor, then moved to the left until he was looking right at them.

At that point, his scanning movements stopped. He was so still he might have been a store mannequin someone had left in the street. Looking directly into his face, David realized that the man was much younger than he would have predicted; perhaps twenty-five or so. Regular features, a day or two of beard stubble, and piercing blue eyes. Totally expressionless. He did not seem threatening at all. In fact, he looked very ordinary.

"Hell, Susan, he's looking at us!" David said unnecessarily. "But with the light the way it is, I don't see how he can see us." He stared down at the man intently. "What the hell is he looking at, anyway?"

"I have no idea," she said, pulling her robe more tightly around herself. "He's a little scary, David. Those eyes—he looks like he's looking right into us."

David nodded. It had seemed like that to him, too; the man's fixed gaze was making him uncomfortable. It was just a little too intense.

"You think we should call the police or something?" she asked.

"And tell them what? 'Officer, there's a man looking at our building!' I doubt if they'd take us very seriously."

"I guess you're right," she said in a soft voice. "Besides, he looks so—so—I don't know—perfect is the only word I can come up with."

"Perfect?" he echoed. He looked at the derelict again. "I tell you, Susan, I don't know about your taste in men!"

"Sure, look who I married!" she shot back, grinning. "I don't mean like that. You know, I don't exactly know what I do mean. The word just came into my mind." Her voice trailed away toward the end of the sentence, as if she was thinking about something else.

David studied the man. Still motionless, he continued to stare at the window, his eyes blank and yet not blank. It was as if he was looking at something else; David couldn't imagine what. He glanced over at Susan, noticed that her eyes looked rather the same. She was looking directly at the man, almost as if hypnotized by him.

"Susan?" he said. She didn't respond; she just continued to return the derelict's gaze.

"Susan?" he said more insistently, leaning around nearer the window to look into her face. She still made no reply. She had a kind of half smile on her lips, and a fuller smile in her eyes as she continued to gaze down at the man. She looked much younger than her twenty-seven years—David remembered the last time, only weeks ago, that she had been asked for an ID when ordering a drink—but somehow now, standing here staring at a strange man in the street, she looked even younger yet, almost childlike. He studied her face, her dark, shoulder-length hair. He realized he could just stand and look at her for a very long time, and not be at all bored. He thought about her familiar body, the small high breasts and slim hips, so well concealed by the loose robe—and pulled these thoughts up short. After all, they both had to go to work this morning. He touched her shoulder. "Susan," he said, in a heavier and lower tone.

"What?" She turned to face him, the faraway look slowly draining from her eyes. "Oh, sorry, David. I was just kind of—of—" she trailed off. She glanced down at the street again for a moment, then back to him. An odd expression passed over her face. Turning away from the window, she walked back to the stove, refilled her coffee cup.

He turned to face her. "You looked kinda strange there for a minute," he said. "Like you were a million miles away."

"I guess I was," she said, running her hand through her hair. "You know how sometimes a little thing, like maybe an odor, will remind you of something, something you can't really remember?"

He laughed. "No, I don't know," he said. "Things I'm reminded of, I usually can remember!"

She looked at him, frowned slightly. "No, that's not what I mean. Sometimes I have dreams, I can remember them in the morning, but by noon I can't anymore. Then, some little thing reminds me of the dream, and I can remember that I had it, that I knew what it was that morning, but I can't remember the dream itself. Does that make sense?"

He continued to smile at her. "Yes, I've had that happen," he said. "So?"

"Well, a lot of times I can remember the mood of the dream, even when I can't remember the contents; you know, happy, sad, scared. And just now, looking at that man down there—it was like he reminded me of a dream, a dream I had a long time ago. I can't remember the dream, but I feel it was sad. And somehow, I miss the—the—oh, damn, I don't know! The time it represented, I guess."

"The time?"

"The period of my life, I suppose. I just got a wave of

nostalgia, that's all. But I don't know what I was nostalgic for.''

"Now that feeling I can understand. When I was a little kid, I read a book, and maybe ten years later I couldn't remember what it was, what it was about. Indians, I think. But every time I thought about it, I was nostalgic for the time I was first reading it. Real strange, but strong feelings.''

She looked at him. He was surprised to see her eyes were a little moist. "Yes, that's it exactly. I wonder what it is?''

They walked back over to the window and looked out. The man was nowhere to be seen.

2

DANNY

Sure as hell was a bad morning to be out, Danny Hudson told himself. It was bitterly cold, frozen snow crunching underfoot; and Danny's carefully studied derelict look did not allow him to wear clothing really adequate for this kind of weather. At least the air was moderately clean today. He had problems, especially in the muggy summer months, with the city's endemic pollution. It irritated him to the point of dulling his senses, and for Danny, his senses were everything.

As he watched people moving on the streets in front of him, he noticed a slight violet glow somewhere off to his left. This was a familiar sight to him; he squinted and crossed his eyes a bit. As he did, the glow gradually focused itself on a well-dressed man ahead, a briefcase swinging loosely in his right hand. This man was walking quite fast, apparently late for work in one of the myriad offices in this section of Manhattan. Danny increased his pace until he came up behind him.

In sync now, they covered about half a block before the man reached into his hip pocket and pulled out a handkerchief. As it came out, his wallet spilled unnoticed to the pavement, and Danny's hand covered it less than a second after it hit. Totally unaware, the man stuffed the handkerchief back and hurried on his way, leaving Danny behind.

With practiced movement, he stripped the bills from the wallet and allowed it to slide down his leg to rest on the pavement again. Crossing the street at the next intersection and moving away from the scene, he caught a glimpse of the businessman rushing back, eyes to the ground.

Out of sight now, Danny took the bills out and counted them. Not bad, he thought; about eight hundred dollars here. He didn't feel as if he had stolen it. His rationale was that the man had, on his own, lost his wallet; someone else would have picked it up if he hadn't. So what if his peculiar talents let him know this was about to happen? He hadn't asked for it; in fact when he was younger he had actively resisted it.

He had a vivid memory of being about five or six years old. His playmates had beaten him over a hide-and-seek game. He always knew exactly where the hidden children were, always found them immediately, while he himself could find places where none of the others would think to look. Perhaps the worst of it for five-year-old Danny was the precognitive awareness that he was going to be beaten, and subsequently ostracized from childhood games. The beating itself was by far the less painful of these memories. Knowing it was coming, he had taken no steps to prevent it, for he already knew he had no way of preventing the devastating shunning by his playmates.

As the years went by, Danny had tried two separate tactics for dealing with his gift, as his parents called it. The first of these was to try to suppress it; he quickly found that it would not be denied. Certainly minor things, like knowing the businessman would drop his wallet, could be controlled; but as time went on Danny soon realized he was actually suppressing the awareness of the information, not the information itself. Whenever there was an event of significant emotional impact, Danny discovered how futile these attempts were; at such times the awareness came up from nowhere and engulfed him. He knew that scenario well and had no desire to see it repeated, ever again. The only way to absolutely prevent this was to avoid any kind of closeness with anyone. He expected that his next major experience of that sort would be his awareness of his own impending death, and he tried not to think about that.

And he was thinking about it, he realized. Not a day to do that; he had a good cash stake here, and what he planned to do was find a way to convert this into a great deal more money. All he needed to do was await an opportunity; any of a thousand events could present him with one. Danny had made money at the track, in the stock market, in a hundred different ways, but never too much in the same way. His plan and credo was never to draw attention to himself. He was always the derelict denizen of the streets who hit a moderate winner at the track, who won a modest pot in a back alley poker game. He would never consider winning the state lottery, though he easily could; he knew which tickets would be winners and where to buy them. But what the hell; he couldn't really complain. He had over a hundred thousand dollars in various investments he knew would do quite well. And he was only twenty-three; his father would have been proud. A few more years of this would make him independently wealthy, though no one would ever guess it by looking at him.

He allowed his thoughts to focus on the memory of his father, and for a few moments his face softened, lost its characteristic expressionless look. The image in his mind was very vivid; he could almost see his father standing before him on the cold street, telling him again that he must use his gift for "the good of mankind." Danny could not conceive of a more trite phrase. His gift had only brought three responses from the rest of mankind: fear, greed, and what Danny perceived as morbid curiosity. All the researchers and scientists who had wanted to study him had made him feel like something trapped under a cover-glass on a microscope slide. Well, he thought, to hell with them, and to hell with you; I'm interested in the good of Danny Hudson, not the good of mankind. So fuck off, Pop, he told the image; out of my way. I've got money to make today. But as the image faded away, he found that his eyes were misty. He tried to ignore that, and he began his meandering walk again.

He had long ago learned to pace his wanderings; move slowly, but not too slowly. Slow enough to pick up the vibes, as he called them, but not so slow as to attract the attention of either the city's ubiquitous predators or its less apparent officials. Danny found it much easier to adopt a persona they tended to ignore than to constantly try to read and avoid them. Besides, that took his attention away from the tasks at hand; the acquisition of capital.

And so Danny moved down a frigid New York street looking for the peripheral purple glow which signaled that an event potentially beneficial to him was about to occur.

He was midway down the block when he began to pick up another glow, one quite unlike the first. It didn't seem to indicate any particular advantage or threat, but it was strong, compelling, and completely unfamiliar. Slowing his pace, swinging his head from side to side, he again squinted and crossed his eyes. He could not locate its source, but its power and urgency continued to increase. A cold chill began somewhere in his lower body and rapidly spread upwards, his testicles trying to pull themselves in as if he were looking over a very high cliff. But the complex of emotions he began to experience would not resolve themselves into simple fear; he was feeling the edge of a blind panic, but also a passion, and a certain soaring triumph whose source and object were not defined. It seemed he was smelling an odd odor, familiar somehow, but not precisely identifiable. Images flashed through his mind, but so rapidly he could not define any of them.

"What in the hell is this?" he muttered aloud. Heedless now of being noticed, he began to systematically scan his surroundings, looking at the other pedestrians on the street, following trucks and buses, each for an instant. Failing there, he turned his attention to the canyon wall of apartment buildings to his right, and scanned each in turn, going up in increments, one floor at a time.

On the third building he felt he was getting close. The glow in his field of vision had resolved itself to radiating streaks of black and red. He had never seen anything remotely like this, had no idea what it might mean. His eyes tracked up the building. Stronger, stronger, yes! Finally! At the fourth floor of that building! He scanned left, located the center of the visionary sunburst pattern.

Two people stood in the window, any auric patterns they might have been emanating masked by the intensity of the black and red rays. He opened his eyes fully and uncrossed them; he could dimly see a man with a short beard and an attractive young woman, and they seemed to be looking down at him. He felt a warning flash—his habit of not drawing attention to himself asserting itself—but this was much too interesting. He squinted again, looked at the rays, and had a sudden conviction that he was looking at a focal point for some kind of incredible power. It didn't seem to emanate from the couple; rather it seemed to have converged on them for some reason. Danny had no impressions at all of where it might be coming from.

Recklessly relaxing all his mental barriers, he found himself buffeted by a plethora of odd ideas and weird images; nothing made any sense. He was losing his balance, about to fall; it took a great effort for him to turn his head. Controlled now, he looked back at the window, saw that the couple was gone; interior blackness returned his gaze. He realized that for several seconds, possibly minutes, he had been standing frozen in one position. As the vision began to fade, he moved quickly into a nearby doorway, out of sight of the window. He was left with a hodgepodge of fleeting images and odd, unfamiliar words; they did not sound English to him. One in particular seemed to stand out; something like "chalice" and "wheat," with an associated glimpse of a strange, unearthly landscape. Maybe it was "challenge"; he didn't know. It made no sense to him in any case.

Taking a scrap of paper from his pocket, and trying to be as inconspicuous as possible, he walked past the building and jotted down the address with a pencil stub he always carried in his pants pocket. Not right for a derelict to carry a ballpoint pen in his shirt pocket and an address book, he told himself. Attention to detail made all the difference. Blanking his mind, he tried to pick up impressions from the fourth-floor apartment where he had seen the couple. To an outside observer, Danny would have been merely a somewhat drunken inhabitant of the streets, steadying himself momentarily against the pillar flanking the doorway. He was much more under control now, and very conscious of his image. He closed his eyes and concentrated. Nothing. No impressions at all.

The simple fact that Danny made a very good living from his odd talents would suggest that he had them well under control, but such was not the case. He had learned over the years how to take advantage of the impressions he did get, what the various colors he saw meant; but now he was trying for specific things—names, something about the couple—and he was getting nothing. As usual, he became frustrated and angry with himself, his talents, the world. This almost always happened when he tried to get anything specific. He knew that there was something important about that particular couple, or perhaps about that particular place, and that it concerned some kind of power or energy, but that was all; and in reality, that wasn't much. He didn't know if it was good or evil, positive or negative, beneficial to himself or dangerous; he just knew that something unique was going to happen to or around that couple, and he was intensely interested in what that might be. More than that, he was interested in the exact meaning of these new sensations; Danny had gotten where he was by paying close attention to his impressions.

Making sure that he was not in sight of the window, he glanced across the street. There was a bar, apparently open in spite of the early hour. Carrying his hat in his hand and pulling himself up much straighter than usual, he crossed the street. He did not want the couple to recognize him if they had, in fact, seen him earlier. He preferred to remain anonymous for the time being.

Once inside the bar, he pulled two crumpled dollar bills from a shirt pocket and ordered wine. The bartender put a glass and three quarters in front of him, barely looking at him at all. Danny situated himself so that he could see the door, then sipped the wine and waited.

He had only finished about half of it when a bearded man and a woman emerged from the doorway. He scrutinized them closely; he thought it was the same pair, but it was hard to be sure. Squinting, he picked up reddish-brown color wisps circulating around them and especially between them. This was familiar; when Danny saw this type of color wisps moving from a woman toward himself, he knew that she was his for the asking. This knowledge kept him from living the life of a monk, since he refused to get close enough to anyone to allow any relationships to develop. As he watched, it seemed to him that the colors from this couple were very intense, and they not only circulated between them, but in odd directions as well. Some came off the woman in the direction of a man who rode by on a bicycle; some off the man toward a woman who got out of a taxi and walked down the street away from them.

"Couple of hot ones," Danny muttered aloud, pretty sure now that they were the people he had seen. He watched as they kissed, watched the man move away toward the subway entrance while the woman walked to the curb to hail a cab. When both had gone, he gulped the remainder of the wine and went back into the street.

He focused again on the window, now dark and empty. Nothing at all beyond a faint reddish-brown glow, a similar tint to that he had seen around the two people. This further convinced him that they were the people he had seen; but beyond this, nothing. He sighed. He would have to spend a lot of time in this area to find out anything, but right now he was not questioning whether or not it was worth it. Tomorrow, he thought; tomorrow he would come back, same time, and follow one of them.

3

THE OLD MAN

Out on Long Island, a slightly decrepit trailer sat just off a sandy road leading toward the beach from state road 25A. As winter winds whipped the ocean and waves crashed a few hundred feet behind it, a rusted-out white Bronco pulled up near the door. A man in a blue suit hesitated a moment before getting out. He really hated to go in there. Oh well, he thought; it's what I'm getting paid for, and I guess it could be a hell of a lot worse. He had certainly done a lot worse, and it was hard for ex-cons to find anything that even looked legitimate. This scam looked more than legit, he thought; he couldn't even see where exactly the payoff was for the man. But he was getting his up front, so he didn't really care. You never knew about people; maybe this old guy just got his kicks this way. He considered that for a moment, as the winter ocean chill began to drive the heat from his car. The old guy didn't seem like the kind who ever had a kick or wanted one.

Reluctantly, he walked up the wooden steps and opened the door. Inside, it was cold. "God damn, you didn't turn the heat on?" he yelled. "You're gonna freeze your fuckin' ass to death, you know that?"

To the casual observer, it might have seemed that the bulky man in the blue suit was talking to no one. The room he had stepped into was sparsely furnished; a desk with a lamp and a few scattered papers, a swivel chair behind it, a file cabinet, two other standing chairs, and a battered old couch against the back wall. It looked like an office in one of a thousand used-car lots across the country. On the couch, our casual observer might have noticed what appeared to be a pile of brown blankets.

"An uninvited actor has entered the play." The flat, accentless voice came from the pile of blankets. The bulky man jumped as he always did when he focused on the old man's face.

It had been as if a part of the blankets themselves had spoken. The old man's deeply creviced skin had the same color, and indeed nearly the same texture as the rough blankets surrounding him. Only his dry lips and flat black eyes moved. It seemed as if he would be croaking from that ravaged mouth, but his voice was a strong, steady baritone. The other man thought he sounded like a radio announcer when he spoke. Which was infrequently.

Now over the initial shock, he digested the old man's words. "What do you mean, another player?"

"Just as I said."

"Was somebody out here? Somebody see you?"

The old man was silent for a long moment. "No, Mr. Flores. No one was here." He may have smiled a trace.

"Then I don't get it. You ain't been nowhere, there ain't nobody in the scam except you and me and those people down in Mexico." Flores got frustrated again. He just didn't like it, that was all there was to it. He had seen a lot of scams in a lot of places, but nothing like this; he just couldn't figure it. Who was the mark? Where was the money coming from?

"I know. That is all."

"Well, should we do something about it? Is it somebody who wants a piece of the action or what? Cops, maybe?"

"No. And we will do nothing except be aware. Power does not err; it is not possible. If this new player enters our game, then it is necessary that he be allowed to play."

Sol Flores sat down and looked at the old man. "Don't you think I should know what the fuck we're doing? You know, I know a few things about real estate scams. I know you and your people don't own any land out here at all. I figured you were gonna sell it and cut out, but then you started this prizes business! We don't have no fucking prizes to give away! There ain't nothing"—he waved his arms to include the whole trailer—"nothing here like what you said in them ads. Ads to get people out here and look at the land! If they come here, they might find out we don't own it. And then, to top all"—his face became red—"you only sent out five of them! Five!" He was totally exasperated. They could make thousands if they sent out thousands, and got the suckers to send in down payments.

"It is not necessary. What needs to be done has been done. You are well paid for your efforts, Mr. Flores," the old man said. There was a definite finality to these words, and even Flores could understand that no further discussion would be fruitful.

The old man was right, though. He was being well paid. Twenty-five thousand dollars, of which he already had ten thousand. Several times the idea of taking the ten grand and getting out had crossed his mind, but for reasons he did not understand he didn't think that would be a good idea. These people had connections, after all. They had tapped in to him when he thought that the Desedros family was going to have him killed over that cocaine deal. Desedros seemed to be afraid of them. Then they had offered him this job. Sure seemed all right at the time. He had never met any of them except the woman, Maria, who had walked right into the Desedros's villa outside Guadalajara and told them, "The old man wants this filth." They had allowed him to go with her, and he had been glad enough to get away from Alejandro Desedros and his crazy kids. They had been talking about burning him alive because he had tried—and failed—to intercept a shipment of their cocaine coming in from Colombia. Crazy people. But as Flores saw it, Maria and the old man were crazier still, running some kind of real estate scam in New York, of all places! And to make it worse, the old man, whose passport stated that he was Juan Gomez—Flores was quite sure that was not his name— insisted on coming along. He could hardly pass as a New Yorker, Flores thought. He should have sent one of his boys. Flores was sure there must have been some boys; no way would the Desedros people be afraid of this old codger and the woman Maria. Although he had to admit that somehow both of them commanded a certain respect. There was just something about them.

"Look," he said, "some of these suckers may actually come out here figuring on a prize. We gotta get some cheap shit to give 'em, or they'll know something's up!"

"You need not concern yourself. Maria is responsible."

"But we haven't even seen Maria since we came here. Maybe she's not coming. Maybe something happened."

"Nothing has happened to the—" The last part was unintelligible to Flores. To him, it sounded like "No wall woman." He paid little attention. The old man's pronouncements were peppered with words and phrases Flores could not understand. He assumed they were just words he had never heard before, and since the gist of the sentence was clear—he meant Maria— it really didn't matter much. He shrugged and walked over to turn up the thermostat. How the old man could stand it this cold, he could not understand. Well, he told himself as he shuffled the papers on the desk, if the old man gets pneumonia and dies, at least I got some money out of this deal. At the corner of the couch, the old man was as silent and still as a statue.

4

SUSAN

Lost in her own thoughts, Susan did not notice that the cabdriver was about to make a turn. As a result, she was roughly hurled against the armrest when the car careened sharply around the corner at no less than twenty miles an hour; she would have sworn it was eighty.

She looked down at her coat; it had been pushed aside, and the dirty armrest had left a blackish smear on her blue slacks. She swore silently; every morning she took a cab to work, and every morning there was some disaster. She was quite sure that her demise would occur in one of these cabs. It would be somehow appropriate. She rubbed at the smear with her fingers, but that was only spreading it. God only knows what it was, she thought. You never had any idea with a New York cab.

Looking up, she saw that the cab was headed straight down Seventh Avenue, and currently was passing Thirty-ninth Street. It would be some time before any other major maneuvers were required of the driver. With luck, that meant she had at least a few minutes alone with her thoughts, some time to think about the odd events of that morning. She considered herself to be, these days, a relatively stable person. Susan put a very high value on stability; she had not always had it, and she did not like things she didn't understand intruding into her orderly existence, especially when those things involved her own behavior. It had been obvious that David had felt that she was acting strangely about the flyer; but she herself saw it as much more than strange; downright bizarre, in fact. She had no interest in Long Island real estate. She was acutely aware that they could not afford it even if she was interested. Nor did she believe that she and David were going to win some great prize just for going out there. Yet for a few minutes, it had seemed very important to her that they go. The feeling of urgency had faded, but still somehow she could never quite say that she was no longer interested. She knew that a word from her would cause David to pitch the flyer into the garbage, but she'd been unable to say it.

Her reaction to the man in the street was another matter of concern for her. She had not told David all of it, although she'd had no reason to expect that he'd have been upset. But the fact was, she'd found the derelict both exciting and arousing, that effect combining with the odd nostalgia she had mentioned to David. She could not really understand this in herself; she had reasons not to be attracted to strange men. Specific reasons. Thinking about it, she sighed; even though she had those reasons—which she stubbornly refused to admit to her conscious thoughts right now—she often did find a variety of men attractive, although she didn't act on it. It was the nostalgia that was important to her. So strong, so poignant! She wondered where it came from. Like an old childhood dream, perhaps something lost in the mists of distant memories.

The cabdriver cut across two lanes of traffic, prompting an outrage of horn blasts, and pulled up to the curb. Susan paid him, got out, and was almost immediately bumped by a teenager who rushed by near the sidewalk's edge. She instinctively clutched at her purse and steadied herself against the cab, which in turn started to pull away. Pulling herself up straight, she glanced around, feeling a little foolish. Hell of a day already, she thought, and it isn't getting any better.

The flow of pedestrians seemed like a solid, impenetrable wall. She straightened her coat perfunctorily, and joined the masses moving on the sidewalk. A few doors down, she turned and entered an office building.

In the elevator, she glared at the black smear on her slacks. For some reason, this was much more irritating than usual, though it was by no means the first time she had come to work with some mark the city had left on her. Again she tried rubbing at it, this time moistening her fingertips before she started, but that didn't help either.

Reaching her floor, she walked first toward the ladies' room. Foremost in her mind was what to do about the stain. Once inside, she tried wetting it and rubbing it with a paper towel, but that still only seemed to make things worse. Really enraged now, she considered going home to change clothes but, deciding against it, walked back down the hall to her office.

Looking at the paperwork awaiting her on her desk did not improve her mood. Bullshit, every bit of it, she told herself. She held a memo up and looked at it without seeing it.

"Bad day?" The question came from Jeannie Edwards at the next desk.

Susan swiveled her chair to face the other woman. "Starting out that way, for damn sure," she almost growled.

"For me too. Ron had a fender-bender in the car while we were driving in today. No big deal, but enough to piss you off. How about some coffee?"

"Better than looking at this crap right now."

They got up and walked over to the coffee machine, where Jeannie loaded her cup with cream and sugar before pouring the coffee in. Susan, as she often said, liked only coffee in her coffee.

"So what's doin'?" Jeannie asked. She had a chirpy voice that Susan sometimes found irritating in the mornings. Today she was a relief, a steady friend in an off-center world. "You didn't have a fight with Mr. Perfection or anything, did you?"

"Oh, no, nothing like that." She didn't mind Jeannie's reference to David. Jeannie always referred to David as Mr. Perfection, even to his face. The nickname had been given following an afternoon she'd spent with Jeannie in a neighborhood bar. Jeannie had quite a few too many martinis, and Susan her share, even though she had not really been trying to keep up. She had only wanted to seem available as a friend for Jeannie then; it was during a period of difficulties for her and her husband Ron. A bit drunk, she had talked on and on about what a perfect mate, fine man, great lover, etc., etc., David was. Later she had regretted it—it hadn't seemed the best way to cheer up a down friend—but Jeannie had taken it in stride, perhaps because she and Ron had reached an understanding on their problems fairly quickly. But the nickname remained.

"Well, then, all's right with that world at least," Jeannie said, twisting a curl of her short red hair around her thumb. "Well, talk, girl, tell ol' Jeannie all your troubles!"

Susan's eyes went down to her coffee and she studied the black liquid for a moment. She had decided not to tell Jeannie about the episode with the strange man in the street, but the business with the real estate flyer seemed harmless enough. She told that story in a condensed form.

Jeannie looked a little puzzled. She was a much more impulsive woman than Susan, and if it had struck her fancy to go out and look at Long Island real estate, she wouldn't have hesitated. "So go look at this resort or whatever. What difference does it make?"

"Well, it just seemed strange, that's all. I wasn't interested in it at all, but here I was telling David we just *had* to go out there. I still don't know why I did it."

"Look, Susie,"—Jeannie often called her Susie, and Susan secretly hated it—"it just isn't a big deal. Go look at it, get your handbag or whatever—"

"Designer luggage. Ha!"

"Whatever. Just go get it, enjoy the trip, don't worry about it." Jeannie's greenish eyes suddenly became intense as she brought her freckled face a bit closer to Susan's. "Life's too damn short to worry about stuff like that!"

Susan looked down at her. "You're right, I know," she said. "It just seems like everything's going wrong already today, and it's not even ten o'clock yet!"

"Well, look, I'm sure it can't be all that bad." She patted Susan's arm. "Listen, I gotta get to work. Haven't done a thing yet today."

"Yeah, I guess I do too," Susan said. The paperwork on her desk seemed especially dreary to her today; it just wasn't what she wanted to be thinking about right now.

Back at her desk, she picked up memos and glanced at them without interest. The smudge on her pants caught her eye and she scrubbed at it again, becoming more irritated with it every time she noticed it. Finally, she stopped even trying to work and let her mind wander free for a few moments.

She considered the contrasts between her life now and six years ago. She had a decent job in the advertising department of a small photography magazine; and she had a great homelife with David. Six years ago she had been a journalism major at the University of Wisconsin, and things had not been great at all.

Her difficulties in college were partially an extension of her problems in high school. Even at fifteen, Susan had had a very powerful sex drive, so much so that it was hard for her to relate to many of her girlfriends. While they had been interested enough in boys—it was virtually all they ever talked about—their interest was abstracted and idealized by Susan's standards. She herself was driven by forces which placed little emphasis on going steady or school dances, forces which she found confusing and threatening, but also very exciting. She had sensed, however, that her girlfriends were not so driven, and would not be able to understand her if she tried to talk about it.

Neither could she talk to her parents about it. Classic midwestern small-town folks, staid in their Methodism, they had always been more than clear about the value they placed on her virginity; she could still hear her mother extolling the merits of the "pure" life, and she knew quite well what her mother's response would be if she had ever been able to read Susan's mind. Mostly name-calling, she thought. She could imagine the names: Slut. Hussy. Tramp.

There had been a time, she thought ruefully, when she would have agreed with that assessment. She could remember a discussion with her mother, not long after she had her first period at the age of eleven. Her parents had never talked to her about such things, and the onset of the period had, of course, frightened her very badly. She had been sure that this could not be normal, that she was bleeding to death. Her mother had referred to the periods as "the curse," reassured her that what she was experiencing was indeed normal, and proceeded to give her a lecture on what she called Susan's "marital duties." She had told the girl that her husband would, on her wedding night and periodically thereafter, do "horrible, nasty" things to her. But she also said that it had to be tolerated, since men are very different—they needed it, couldn't control themselves—and this was God's way. She hoped Susan was lucky enough to find a husband who would leave her alone after they had two or three children. She had been blessed in this way, she said, but many of her friends were not, and they did not have happy lives.

The young girl thus began her road to adulthood with a frank terror of men and all things sexual, believing that any girl or woman truly interested in participating in these degrading activities must be mentally ill. Sometimes she regretted that she was not a Catholic; she could have considered becoming a nun.

But as the next few years passed, she found herself undergoing major shifts both mentally and physically. Talking with her girlfriends at first, later reading books, had given her an outlook on life substantially different from her mother's. And to make matters even more confusing, her physical drives began to assert themselves in a way that she found most distressing. Her girlfriends seemed to stop after a few kisses and hugs; her body kept telling her that that simply wasn't enough for her. She found the boys at school quite attractive now, and some of the younger male teachers even more so; and her fantasies persistently refused to stop with the innocent schoolgirl kiss. She began to believe that something was wrong with her. She tried talking to the school counselor, but the woman became so embarrassed by Susan's frank questions that Susan herself became uncomfortable, and the discussion degenerated into awkward clinical descriptions laced with dire warnings about venereal disease and pregnancy. Even this did not stop the erotic daydreams.

So at fifteen, Susan had sought counsel from her local minister, a well-thought-of young family man with three children. Salt of the earth, pillar of the community. She could still hear all the clichés. This fine young family man had counseled the pants right off her during the second session, and by the end of the month she was no longer a virgin. She had experienced orgasms both from intercourse and oral sex, and she knew what a man's semen tasted like. All this had certainly satisfied some of her physical drives, but did little for her confused state of mind. The young minister had told her that she needed to know how unpleasant and degrading these experiences were so that she could subsequently reject them until she married. Her problem was that she did not find these experiences unpleasant, although she certainly felt degraded; it would be hard not to, she told herself now, when some asshole is praying to God while you're giving him a blowjob.

They were only five weeks into the "counseling" when they were caught. The fine young minister's fine young wife had walked in on them in a very compromising position. She had walked out again without saying a word, only to return ten minutes later with a loaded revolver. Fortunately, she was not a good shot; the end of the evening found the minister's wife in jail, the minister in the hospital with a minor wound, and Susan totally unhurt physically. The police—and the church—had handled the situation as delicately as possible. The minister had been dismissed by the church and divorced by his wife. Both had left town, undoubtedly in different directions. Susan never knew what happened to them. With her, however, they were far less delicate. It seemed they held her responsible for the whole situation. They told her parents as much of the story as they knew, couching it in terms of Susan's "seduction" of the minister.

When the next Christmas came, there was no present under the tree for her, and her sixteenth birthday passed totally unnoticed by her parents. She withdrew from them rather completely after that. It became her habit to prepare herself a plate from the family table at mealtimes and take it to her room. No objection to this was ever made. Until she left for college on scholarship at seventeen, she was made to feel like a ghost in her family home; it was rarely that she was ever spoken to. Once out of the house and onto the campus at Wisconsin, she had virtually no contact with her parents at all, and she still didn't.

During her last two years of high school, Susan's social life had been nearly zero. Word of the scandal had gotten around, and she always felt like her classmates were talking behind her back, as indeed they were. She tried to ignore this as best she could, and concentrated on schoolwork to fill the time. But the physical drives within her spent that time building themselves to a fever pitch. It was in this state that young Susan Goss went away to college, with the firm intention of beginning a new life away from her past. She had been determined that the coming four years were going to be better than the last two; she couldn't have known at the time how wrong she was.

The phone on her desk rang, interrupting her reverie. Oh, well, she told herself, it really is time to do some work today.

"Susan?" came a male voice. "Jerry Maxwell." Jerry was her immediate superior, and the single worst aspect of this particular job. "Can you come into my office for a minute? There are some things I want to go over with you."

As long as you don't want to go over me, Susan thought. Then aloud: "Sure, Jerry, be right there."

When she reached Jerry's office, he was sitting, as usual, with his feet propped up on a desk far larger than he really needed. The office was littered with paintings and sculpture intended to illustrate his impeccable taste; in reality, they exhibited his lack of it. But somehow this stuff fits well with Jerry, Susan thought. She looked down at him; paunchy, fiftyish, balding, with an utterly incongruous gold chain hanging around his neck. She stood in front of his desk and rocked on the balls of her feet, wondering if he really had some work to discuss or if he wanted to make another pass at her. Either—or both—was possible. She figured Jerry would like his life to be like a pornographic movie, screwing secretaries over his desk all day. If she had to tell him again she wasn't interested, it would be for the seven hundredth time, she was sure.

"Hey, Susan," Jerry said with excessive heartiness. "I want you to help me decide which picture to use for this ad." He gestured at several 8 × 10 glossies on his desk. "Come 'round here. Take a look."

Susan sighed audibly. Not serious work. This was a familiar routine; she would look at the pictures, decide which one she liked best, and Jerry would use the one he and the advertiser had already picked out. At first she'd been a little flattered, and had taken her assignment very seriously; she imagined that this minor decision making might precede a promotion. But in every case, the hidden agenda was either a pass by Jerry himself, or a thinly veiled suggestion that if she were "nice to the client" they would have a better chance of getting the advertising, and her own fortunes in the company would rise. It had always frustrated Jerry when she gave him her best wide-eyed innocent look and pretended not to know what he was talking about. He was incapable of blatantly suggesting that she become the company's unofficial party girl.

Walking around his desk, she carefully kept herself at a good arm's length away from him. At least he would have to move to try to paw her.

He pushed the photos toward her. "See which one you like," he said, shifting his chair a couple of inches closer.

She glanced down at the four pictures and for a moment her head swam. Jerry had gone much too far this time.

The photos depicted an array of graphic sexual activity juxtaposed with bloody violence; decapitated heads and excised hearts rolled about in a sea of genitalia. She glared at him, her face becoming a furious mask.

Jerry looked back at her with a bewildered expression. "What's the matter?" he asked, sounding genuinely innocent.

"What do you think—" she started to say, waving at the photos and glancing down at them again. What she saw stopped her cold. A red flower, close up. Some windsurfers on a blue ocean. A blond child on a swing. A cat walking on a piano keyboard.

She stared at them without saying a word for several minutes, unaware that Jerry was staring at her. She could not believe it. A moment ago, she had seen something utterly different. There was no sense of a hallucination, nothing but normal clarity in any of her perceptions. It was literally as if the pictures had changed in the instant she looked away.

"Susan? You all right, hon?" Jerry asked, sounding sincerely worried. "What's wrong? Susan?"

"God, Jerry, I don't know. I thought I saw something else. Pictures of —ah—I don't know what!"

"Never seen you like this, Sue. Should I call a doctor?"

Much more composed now, she looked back up at him, and then quickly glanced back at the photos. Still safe, normal Black Star stock pictures. "Oh, no, Jerry, I'm all right now. I've had a bad morning, you know? Just got to me for a second there. No, I'm okay." She paused, looked down at the photos. Still the same. "Yeah, I'm all right now."

"You're sure?"

"Yes, of course."

Jerry slammed himself back into his chair, and Susan realized that she hadn't seen him get up, hadn't been aware of his hand on her shoulder. He probably thinks this was a ploy to divert a pass, she told herself, and now he's pissed.

She considered telling him directly that it was no game, but decided to leave well enough alone. Thinking, however, that she could use a moment alone to regroup, she asked Jerry to get her a glass of water.

"Sure, Sue, no problem," he replied, hoisting himself back out of the chair and lumbering out.

As soon as he had gone, Susan sat down on the edge of the desk, rubbed her eyes, and looked at the photos again. Nothing odd there. What the fuck's going on today? she asked herself. Something in the stars? She picked up one of the pictures and studied it closely, turning it over and looking at the back as well. Perhaps that fat fart Jerry had played some kind of trick? But she rejected that idea a moment later. She knew Jerry rather well; he was neither that smart nor that inventive. He also could not have known about Susan and bullfights and—

"Oh, no, no, my God, don't start on that now," she said aloud. "Don't think about it, something else, please!" She studied one of the pictures intently to drive the unwanted thoughts from her mind. It was a simple, elegant photograph of a little blond girl of seven or eight, taken in some anonymous park. The subject was smiling nicely into the camera, riding a plain park swing, wearing a light blue dress, patent leather shoes held up as the swing came forward. Vibrant color, good composition, excellent subject, a thing of real beauty. She found her eyes misting up. This thing, too, was therefore a homage to herself—

She pulled that line of thinking up short. She had no idea where it had come from, no background experiences to try to relate it to. Now this is a hell of a note, she told herself. The rest of this day has only been strange, but that passing thought was downright weird! She tried to dismiss it as a random eddy, but it persistently stuck itself back in a corner somewhere and refused to go away. Sooner or later, I'll deal with you, she thought, but let it be later; I've got enough problems here.

As she put the picture down, she glanced around the office. She had been in here many times, and had always considered it gauche and overdone. But now she focused on the beauty of various things, many of them mundane a few minutes ago. The grain of the wood in the desk, the geometric patterns in the carpet. At that moment, she could find beauty in almost everything in the room. She was smiling now, the earlier stresses momentarily forgotten. But at last her gaze fell upon the smudge on her slacks.

Earlier, she had been annoyed at this, even angry. But now the sight of the smudge, its imperfection in a perfectly beautiful room, filled her with a cold rage. It seemed imperative that she do something about it. Now.

Having almost totally forgotten about Jerry, she stood up and unbuttoned her pants. A little voice somewhere deep inside tried to remind her, tried to tell her that he would be back any second, but she couldn't hear it. The need to rid herself of the imperfection of the stain overrode everything; she kicked off her shoes and stripped the offending pants off. After stuffing them into Jerry's desk drawer, she looked down at her bare legs, holding them up one at a time. She realized vaguely that she was in a very unusual state of mind; everything seemed so crystal-clear, so utterly focused. And the focus was on beauty. All in her sight must be Perfectly Beautiful. She would not have it any other way.

Her legs looked very beautiful to her now, unencumbered by the slacks. Pointing each foot in turn toward the window, she was struck by the contrast between the skin of her thighs and her panties; this contrast was not Perfectly Beautiful, so she stepped out of the panties. They followed the slacks into Jerry's desk, out of her sight. She fluffed the edge of her blouse against her waist, brushed her pubic hair down where it curled backward at the side.

She had made a decision on the blouse and she was unbuttoning it when Jerry returned.

"Here you are, Sue. I brought your—" Jerry stopped; the glass slid from his hand. It bounced on the rug, not breaking. Susan watched the beads of water catch the light as it splashed, each like a tiny gem, in slow motion. After this display had settled, she looked up at Jerry, and in that instant she did not see his paunch, his crudeness. Instead, she saw only that which was beautiful in Jerry Maxwell, and found that he fitted into her world. Smiling at him, she pushed the blouse back over her shoulders.

Jerry was obviously stunned. He had fantasized about Susan many times, but had resigned himself to her unavailability, even though he kept trying. Now she stood in front of him, naked from the waist down and taking off the rest, walking toward him. He recovered from his initial shock and grinned broadly. His hand found his tie and he started to jerk on it.

At that moment, Susan saw any beauty that he had evaporate. He became even cruder, more lecherous than ever. She could almost see fangs. He seemed to have turned into a monster. But she didn't step back; instead, she pulled herself up straight, and, having finished the process of removing her blouse, raised her hands above her head in a peculiar gesture.

Jerry's hand froze on his tie. Susan looked suddenly very

strange, standing there with her arms upraised like that. Somehow regal, he thought; like a queen. He tried to say something, but his tongue was thick, the words wouldn't come out. His vision blurred and he felt a tremendous wave of nausea; a heavy pain ripped through his chest. Darkness swept over him, and he fell forward on the carpet and lay still.

The thud of his body hitting the carpet seemed to cut through her, breaking the unique mental state she was in. She gasped aloud at the realization of the events of the last few minutes. Calm, calm, she told herself; first things first. Moving as fast as possible, she retrieved her panties and slacks from the desk drawer and dressed, buttoning her blouse as she walked to the door. Once there, and reasonably presentable again, she opened the door and ran to the next office, yelling that something had happened to Jerry.

Vern Jacobs, senior editor, rushed out into the hall. "What happened?" he asked, looking toward Jerry's office.

"I don't know, he just collapsed—"

Jacobs didn't wait for her to finish. "Call an ambulance," he said over his shoulder as he rushed toward Jerry's office.

She went into Jacobs's office and did so. The hallway was filling with the magazine's other employees, as well as the various people who seem to appear from nowhere to gawk at an emergency of any sort. She pushed past a man in coveralls and reentered Jerry's office, where Jacobs was leaning over the fallen man.

"He's alive, breathing okay," Jacobs said. "Anything bring this on?"

"No, nothing. I had a dizzy spell, he got me some water, and when he came back in he collapsed."

"You had a dizzy spell and he collapsed?"

"Well, yes, I guess—well, you know—" She felt confused, on the defensive. For a moment Jacobs was her father asking if she had really seduced the minister, his mind already made up that she had.

"No, I don't know, Mrs. Hallsten, but I'd like you to explain it to me if you can." Jacobs looked directly into her eyes.

"Well, I really can't. I don't know what happened to him, how could I know?"

Jacobs shrugged and turned away from her. He examined

Jerry's head, running his fingers through the ring of remaining hair, then looking at them.

He's looking for blood, she thought; he must think I hit him with something. Jacobs doubtlessly knew of Jerry's constant passes at any attractive woman within his reach, and had jumped to the conclusion that Jerry had gotten a little too friendly, that Susan had brained him with something.

She relaxed a bit. I didn't, she told herself, and they'll find no lump or anything. Yet she was aware that somehow she was, in fact, responsible for Jerry's current condition. She tried to tell herself that she couldn't really remember what had happened, but she could, all too clearly.

It was not as if she had blanked out. She could see every event since walking into Jerry's office with a disturbing clarity. She tried to convince herself that she had been not herself, alien somehow, but she knew it wasn't true. Every thought and action had been hers alone, however bizarre it might seem to her now. But the current situation kept her from dwelling on it; on the floor, Jerry was beginning to stir a bit.

"Just lie still, Maxwell," Jacobs said in a fatherly tone. "The ambulance is on its way."

"Ambulance? What happened?"

"That's what we'd all like to know," Jacobs said, looking at Susan again. "What do you remember?"

"I was bringing her water. I had this pain in my chest. I—"

"Heart attack," Jacobs declared. At this moment the paramedics came in the room and pushed him aside. Jerry was hustled onto a stretcher, an oxygen mask clamped over his face, and he was rushed from the room.

Jacobs turned back to Susan, his manner much more friendly now. "Looks like a heart attack," he repeated. "A real shame, at his age. You might as well take the rest of the day off, Mrs. Hallsten. I doubt you'll feel much like working."

You are sure as shit right about that, Susan thought. "Thanks, Mr. Jacobs, I'll do that."

The taxi ride home was uneventful, and Susan could not have been happier about that, since she did not completely trust herself right now. Back in their apartment, she plopped on the couch and turned on the TV. It was nearly time for the afternoon soaps to start; a "Three's Company" rerun was grinding to a predictable end. She kicked off her shoes and lit a cigarette. She seldom smoked, but this was the time if any time was. As she tried to relax, she realized that she was also in a high state of sexual tension; the morning had given her little chance to think about that.

"David, if you can pick up my thoughts, please come home early today," she said aloud.

She glanced over at the phone, toying with the notion of calling him. Bad idea, she thought, and turned her attention back to the TV.

But she really wanted to make that call.

5

BERTIE AND JOHN

On different highways in different parts of the country, two quite different men drove steadily northward. One of them was pacing his Toyota Celica up Interstate 75 toward Lexington, Kentucky; the other had taken his Chevrolet Citation on what he thought might be the scenic route, using U.S. 301 instead of Interstate 95 between Smithfield and Rocky Mount, North Carolina. One was clean-shaven, wearing an impeccably pressed suit; his Air Force uniform hung in the back of the Toyota. The other wore a full beard, rumpled work shirt, and blue jeans. He had never been in the military, never had a notion of joining. But these two had a common destination—New York City—and awaiting both of them there was a flyer offering free gifts in exchange for their inspection of a new development on Long Island called Tascan Acres.

The man in the Citation looked up in his rear-view mirror to see the flashing blue lights of a North Carolina state trooper's car close behind him. He checked his speed—about 57—and pulled over to the side. The trooper remained in his car for a few minutes, talking into his microphone, before getting out.

"Could I see your license and registration, sir?" the trooper asked. He had less of a Southern accent than the man in the Citation had expected.

The bearded man pulled out his wallet and handed over the license, wondering what had provoked this stop.

The trooper looked at the Florida license. One John L. Goss, of Miami. The registration matched the plates on the car.

"Mr. Goss, it's the law in North Carolina that all front seat passengers wear a seat belt, and you're not wearing yours. I'm going to write you a warning citation."

John leaned back and listened to the lecture, rolling his eyes. Damn waste of time. Why did they have to try to protect him from himself, anyhow? If he wanted to be smashed all over the dash of his car, whose business was that except his own? It might be for the best if he was, he thought glumly.

He waited for a few moments after the trooper's car had pulled away before starting his own and pulling back out on the highway. His idea about a scenic route up 301 had fallen flat and that depressed him, as did all disappointments in his life, whether major or minor. Route 301 used to be the main North-South artery through this part of North Carolina, before I-95 had been built; in those days, motels and restaurants had thrived on the New York-Florida traffic. But like many other places, they had been bypassed; the thriving businesses now centered around the Interstate exits. All along this highway were crumbling reminders of a once-prosperous past.

John had no idea why he found all these downtrodden places so very depressing. The idea of a business going under was not, to him, an inherently sad notion. But always, all his life, the remnants of past glory, however mundane that glory might be, filled him with a kind of a sad nostalgia he didn't understand. Rather the way a young boy feels on the last warm days of summer.

He had just passed a little town called Selma, and slowed down as he saw a closed and battered motel on his right. It had obviously been abandoned to the elements for many years. The little cottages which had once served as rooms were barely visible through the tangled vines which had overtaken the place. He imagined that in high summer it might look something like an ancient Celtic village in ruins. But now it just looked barren and desolate, and he couldn't imagine why the local county officials didn't come and bulldoze it down.

The analogy with an ancient ruin started his mind in another direction. He certainly was extreme about such things, he thought. When he had visited the Mayan ruins on Mexico's Yucatan Peninsula, he had actually broken down and cried. He remembered how flustered and embarrassed the tour guide had become at the time. But the notion of the grand Mayan empire being reduced to a pile of stones—however interesting and mystical these stones were—combined with the incredible poverty some of the modern Maya lived in, had seemed so totally unacceptable, so totally wrong somehow, that it had temporarily crushed his spirit. Afterwards, he had spent the remainder of his visit in his hotel room, and when he finally did leave— his departure having been delayed by Hurricane Agnes, then pelting the Florida coast—the desk clerk thought that he had never in his life seen a sadder man.

John sped up again, trying to put the memories of the Yucatan out of his mind. It seemed that every time he thought about that trip, it just depressed him more, and he didn't need anything more to depress him than this dull, gray section of North Carolina countryside. Apart from the pine trees, there was nothing to relieve the winter brownness of the landscape. No white snow, no Florida greens, not even any colors on the farmhouses and occasional country stores and gas stations. Everything gray and brown. He passed through small towns: Micro, Kenly. Gray; brown; lifeless. He had the distinct impression that everyone here was dead and simply hadn't realized it yet.

"If everyone is dead, there's nobody to let you know you're dead, so you just keep walking around," he said aloud. He often talked aloud in the car. Sometimes, when someone was riding with him, he forgot they were there and still talked aloud to himself, a running commentary on politics, current events, the arts, and especially his own problems. John tended to see his whole life only in terms of his problems. He believed himself to be an anachronism, but thought no other time was better; he believed it was Western society, but his wanderings had shown him no country more suited to him. A self-portrait of John would necessarily be out of focus.

His problems, he believed, centered around the fact that he thought too much, acted too little. He had a vision of himself at ten years old, everyone wanting to know why he sat and stared into space so much, why he cried over things that no one else thought were sad. Even now he could not understand his parents' reactions; whenever he behaved in some manner they considered peculiar, his mother seemed afraid of him and his father became angry. But in the end they simply put up with his eccentricities, which for the most part were harmless enough.

He remembered his sister, his only sibling and his only true friend until he left home for college. Fire to his ice. He had been born crying, she had been born smouldering. He felt like the world had it in for her. She was sure to be crushed by the impersonal forces out there, by the uncaring, the selfishness. He really loved her, couldn't bear to see that happen to her; so when he left home, he cut all connection to her and to their parents as well. Letters were never answered; phone numbers were changed if discovered. Gradually they gave up their attempts to stay in touch with him, and he preferred it that way.

He looked up ahead and saw that he was entering another town, another dingy, dirty city filled with people living the most wretched existences. He tried not to think about them, tried not to think about his sister, or the Yucatan. In short, he tried not to think at all. But as always, he was unsuccessful in these efforts; and his mood sank lower and lower as he drove into the city.

As John carried the weight of the world up a North Carolina highway, the other driver was having a totally different kind of experience. This driver was also in pain, but it was physical, not mental. Periodically he shifted in his seat to try to relieve it, but it would not go away. Perhaps it was just the memory, he thought; he was getting very close to the exact spot where that pain had been inflicted three years earlier.

When he saw the signs for Richmond, Kentucky, his stomach tightened a bit. "Not far now," he told himself. "If I get by the bridge, I'll be okay. That's all I have to do. Get by the bridge." He had done it before, twice. This was the best route for him, and a good highway; it would be irrational to take another road just because of what had happened on this one.

Up ahead, he saw the road turn downward between two artificial cliffs, cut from the limestone to make the highway's descent gentle. Various names adorned the rocks: Eddie; Janie; Sam Jackson '81. He knew this area very well, although he had never seen the town of Richmond. After all, he had almost died here.

The pain he was feeling intensified, and his stomach tightened even more as the Toyota dipped between the two cliffs. The Clay's Ferry bridge was visible now, the muddy Kentucky River far below it. A bridge and a river he had shared a terrible intimacy with.

He blinked his eyes, and relived the accident in a fraction of a second.

He had been driving his Corvette at the time, his beloved yellow Corvette. He wasn't going very fast; if he had been speeding, it probably wouldn't have happened. He wouldn't have been in that place at that time. But the gods decreed, he thought, that the truck had started to pass his car on that bridge at precisely the right moment. As it had pulled level with the front of his car, he had heard a loud bang, had seen pieces of rubber flying from the truck's blown front tire. The truck swerved so suddenly into him that he didn't have time to even think about it, much less try any kind of evasive maneuver. The truck bounced away from him and came to rest against the left guardrail; his car had struck the guardrail on the right and the rear end had come up and over. He could vividly remember the sickening sensation of flying straight out into midair, shot out of the car like a stone from a slingshot. During the fall he recalled glimpses of the yellow Corvette in a slow, almost majestic descent to the river below; then the trees and the muddy water rushed up to meet him at incredible speed.

His next memories were from a room in intensive care at University Hospital in Lexington. "Is your name Herbert North?" he could still hear the doctor asking.

"Yes. You can call me Bertie. Everybody does." A stock line coming through the haze of drugs and pain.

Then they had told him about his left foot, although he had somehow already known. In spite of the long fall through the trees and onto the rocks at the river's edge, he had been remarkably uninjured, except for his left foot. It was missing completely. In its place was a jagged stump terminating right at the ankle bone. Then he remembered a vivid image; a huge, hideous, aquatic monstrosity of some sort, rising out of the river as he fell. He could see the gaping jaws and discolored teeth as it had snapped at him, taking off the foot in one bite. For a year he had seen a psychiatrist about this. If he was not a rational man, he could almost have believed that a dragon-like creature had risen from the depths and bitten off his foot. Of course, all the doctors had assured him that the foot had doubtlessly been torn off in the fall.

Because of the intensity of the vision, Bertie had asked the police and the doctors if his foot had ever been found. All they knew was that it was not in the wreckage of the car. One fat cop told him, "We don't send out no search party for a lost foot, boy. We got better things to do."

As he guided his car across the bridge now, he scanned the waters below. Any time he was near this river he did that. And as always, he chided himself for being ridiculous. This was the Kentucky River, not Loch Ness. Nobody else ever saw monsters in it.

The psychiatrist he had seen had been genuinely interested in this vision. He tried to explain it in terms of symbolism; perhaps the monster symbolized fate, since Bertie was so very aware of the fact that he had had to be in exactly the right place at exactly the right time for this disaster to befall him. So Bertie had tried to dismiss it. But every time he relived the accident, either waking or in his dreams, the thing that ate his foot was a part of the whole story.

Losing a foot had been less of a disaster than Bertie would have believed while he was in the hospital. There were draw-backs certainly; the nuisance of the artificial foot, and espe-cially the phantom pain he was feeling at the present time. But there had been some mitigations. He had gotten used to the prosthesis very rapidly, and he only had a slight limp. But the limp and the story about the wreck had seemed to make him more attractive to women. He had never had any problem in this area, but now it seemed as if he could have his choice of anyone who crossed his path. Anytime he did run into a bit of resistance, an imaginative lie about being a part of the invasion of Grenada and stepping on a land mine worked like a charm. It was a tactic he never hesitated to use.

But usually he didn't have to. His other attributes—the athletic body, which seemed to stay athletic even when he was out of shape, the boyish face, the eyes women referred to as bedroom—these generally got him pretty much whatever he wanted. If he had a problem, it was not because he could not get what he wanted, it was because he did not have the time to indulge all his pleasures to the extent he would have liked. He had been toying with the idea of leaving the Air Force and becoming a professional gambler. His luck at poker and craps was unbelievable; he always won. Last year he had taken a trip to Vegas, and had come away with nearly $9,000 in winnings. This money he had invested in the stock market, and currently its face value had nearly doubled.

Yes, he thought, as the bridge disappeared behind him, I'm a real lucky guy, even with only one foot.

He glanced at his watch; 5:30. The winter daylight was rapidly fading over the gently rolling Kentucky bluegrass country. Though he could easily have driven a couple hundred miles more, he decided to stop in Lexington for the night. He was not at all in a hurry to get to New York, and he knew that his route past Lexington didn't offer an abundance of good, cheap motels.

Taking the U.S. 421 exit, he drove toward the city. He knew of several motels along the beltway which encircled the town. The first one he came across, with a huge horse head logo, had the vacancy sign lighted, so he turned in and stopped in front of the office.

The girl behind the counter watched his slight limp as he walked in. He looked at her critically. Probably no more than nineteen, short blond hair, pretty enough. Acceptable for a stopover. He adjusted his face to what he mentally called his lost little boy look and approached the counter.

"I just need a single, overnight," he said, giving her his practiced crooked grin. It was intended to convey a brave front in spite of internal pain. Normally very effective.

The girl smiled back at him. She took off her glasses and handed him a registration form. As he began to fill it out he noticed her watching carefully, head slightly tilted so she could read his name.

"You're just passing through, then, Mr.—?" she paused on his last name as if she hadn't read it, but he knew she had.

"Call me Bertie. Everybody does," he said automatically.

"Yeah, on my way to New York. I'll just be here the night."
He watched her try to muster courage. He knew she was attracted to him already, and that she knew she had to move fast
if she was going to do anything about it. He decided not to
make it any easier. Let her work for it, he thought. Saves me
the trouble.

She was silent for a moment, then: "Well, listen, can I
recommend someplace to eat or something? I mean, if you
haven't had dinner yet—"

He looked up, caught her eyes directly. "Yeah, that'd be real
good. I don't know this town at all"—an absolute lie—"and
well," he paused. "Hey, I got a good idea. You eaten supper
yet? Maybe you could show me that restaurant. I'm buying."

She reddened slightly. "No, I haven't eaten, but I—" She
stopped and looked down for a moment. "Yeah, hey, I'd like
to. I get off at seven. Mind waiting?"

"Not at all. What's your name, hon?"

"Marcia."

"Nice name. Look. I'll go over to my room and dump my
bag, okay? Then I'll come back here around seven."

"Fine. Sounds real good."

He drove the Toyota over and parked it in front of number
thirty-two. Humming a little, he carried one of the four bags
he had with him inside. Should be an okay night, he told himself. He looked over at the office, saw Marcia dial the phone,
talk a minute, then hang up and dial again. She didn't get off
at seven, he told himself. She's trying to get somebody to cover
for her.

"Eager little bitch," he said. She would not have been attracted to his eyes if she could have seen them now. They were
far too cold.

Just as Bertie was stopping at a motel in Lexington with a
horse head logo, John was pulling in at a somewhat rundown
motel in Rocky Mount, North Carolina. His selection had been
based on price and on proximity to I-95; he'd had enough of
the depressing little towns along 301. For an instant he sat in
his car and stared at the place; it seemed to him it was missing
something. He shrugged, dragged his stiff body out of the car,
and headed for the office.

John was a big man, well over six feet tall and of a rather

burly build. His longish hair and beard combined with his work shirt and jeans made him look like a lumberjack. But whenever he spoke, he spoiled the illusion; lumberjacks did not usually articulate so carefully, so precisely. Words were important to him; he chose them with great attention to their subtle nuances and colorations. Unfortunately, most people were not aware of these nuances, with the result that John was frequently misunderstood. He was at least vaguely aware of this, and like almost everything else, he found it depressing.

The girl at the desk looked up as he came in, but seemed to look right through him. She was very plain, a little overweight, but she somehow seemed like a pleasant person to him. She wore a blue plastic name tag that identified her as Marcie.

"I need a room for one, just overnight," he said.

She didn't say anything, but pushed a registration form across the desk toward him.

"You know any good places to eat?" he asked as he was filling out the form. "I've been on the road for quite a while, and I—"

"There's Hardee's and McDonald's up on business 64," she interrupted. "And there's a lot of good restaurants downtown. Just follow 64 east, that's Sunset Avenue here." She was reading some kind of magazine, and she looked back down at it. *TV Guide*.

What fascinating literature, he thought. Oh well. He pushed the registration form back to her; she gave it a cursory look, then turned to get his key.

"That'll be $28.60," she said, leaning her elbows on the desk.

He got out three tens and handed them to her. Suddenly bold, he asked her point-blank if she would like to go to dinner with him. Then he waited. He sometimes expected that he would be laughed at, but that never actually happened, and it didn't happen now.

She smiled. "Oh, look, I'm sorry, I'd kinda like to, really, but I've gotta work here till eleven, and anyhow, I already ate."

He managed a return smile. No disaster, but again he would eat alone. "No problem," he said, turning away. He left the office and got back in the car, looking at the key. Number thirty-two. A sign indicated that was to his right. He parked in

front of the door and went inside after selecting one of the
cases from his trunk. Not really hungry yet, he told himself.
Actually it was eating alone that bothered him. He turned on
the TV and lay back on the bed, piling the pillows behind him.
A local commercial extolled the merits of a local car dealership
in very strident tones; he was only half aware of it as he began
to fall asleep. The car commercial was replaced in his mind
by images from another place, another time. He smiled in his
sleep, his eyes darting back and forth under closed lids. It was
the first genuine smile of the day for him.

Back in the office, Marcie was talking to a rather oily-
looking young man who walked in only moments after John
had left.

"You see him, Bobby?" she asked. "I swear, I don't know
how I know it, but that guy is on a hell of a heavy downer. I
wish he'd picked some other motel."

"Ah, forget about him," the oily youth replied. "I'll go get
a six-pack. You be ready about seven, you hear?"

"Sure, Bobby, I'll be ready." She picked up the phone and
dialed it.

6

At about four o'clock that afternoon, Danny returned to the
same bar; it was convenient, affording a good view of the entrance to the building, although not, unfortunately, the fourth-
floor window. Again he sat by the window, watching the entrance carefully. He was not worried about being recognized;
he looked like a totally different person. Neatly pressed slacks,
turtleneck sweater, styled hair. He was fairly certain that the
couple in the window had seen him, and he wanted to be sure
they did not suspect him of hanging around, since they would
draw the conclusion that he meant them harm. He didn't, he

told himself; he didn't really care much what happened to them, as long as he was in a position to take care of himself.

He ordered a beer, began to nurse it along; he had no idea when they might come home, and he certainly didn't want to dull his perceptions with alcohol. But then again, two or three mugs of beer wouldn't affect him substantially; he knew that from past experience. As he waited, he began to get a few faint impressions of something from the building. He squinted out the window, paying close attention. The bartender passed in front of him and he averted his eyes momentarily, not wanting the man to notice.

But that had caused him to lose his perception, he thought, and— No! Wait! It was back; much clearer. One of them was already home! This thought came through very clearly, with a certainty that he knew was generally trustworthy. He didn't have experiences of this sort often, but when he did, they were usually reliable. He didn't quite know what to do with the information, though. One of them was home. So what? Was he going to rush up there and ask, "What's about to happen to you?" Good way to get locked up. Besides, they probably didn't know anything about it. So he waited, sipping the beer, hoping for something more.

Twenty minutes later, the beer had gone flat; he had apparently nursed it too long. He stared into the golden liquid and sighed. Hell of a pastime, he thought. Drinking a glass of warm beer and waiting to watch somebody come home.

As he sat there castigating himself for wasting time, he noticed that the beer in his glass seemed to be changing in an odd way. It was getting darker by the second, at least on top. Must be something wrong with it, he told himself. He had a momentary flash of fear; he had already drunk half of it. But he felt all right. Interested, he watched the process, the couple momentarily forgotten.

The surface of the beer continued to darken until it had become quite black. Then it seemed to take on the characteristics of a mirror; he could see his reflection clearly. He looked at the side of the glass. From that angle, it was still normally golden. He picked it up and looked up toward the surface, tilting it toward the window. From below, the surface looked normal. From above, a black mirror.

"Well, now what the hell?" he said under his breath. As he

continued to look, it seemed that he could see indistinct designs superimposed on his reflected face, but everything looked smoky; he couldn't make anything out. But there was an image of some sort there, he could tell. If this is some kind of clairvoyance, it's new, he thought. The image became a little clearer; he could see two sets of lines angling downward, a hundred and twenty degrees between them. They didn't seem to intersect. There was something at the top of each set of lines, a dark shape but with a brightness—

A black tongue, forked, flicked out from below the two lines. He would have sworn it flicked right up out of the beer. The lines and shapes coalesced for him and he realized what he was seeing. He was staring directly into the face of a rattlesnake.

He jerked back. He could see the heavy coiled body behind the head, the uplifted rattles, the whole thing far larger than the mug of beer. The head itself appeared to be too large to fit into the glass.

The bartender walked up at that moment. "Looks like your beer's a little flat, bud. Need another?" He picked up the glass without waiting for an answer, glanced into it, away, then looked back. "What the shit!" he screamed, and the glass smashed to the floor behind the bar. Danny lunged to his feet and looked over. The bartender was looking too; at broken glass and spilled beer. Nothing else.

Danny headed for the door. He had been taking this as some kind of psychic perception, like his colors; no one else could see them. The researchers had told him years ago that he probably didn't actually see them either. It was just the way his mind interpreted information coming in through whatever the psychic channels were, like people who saw powerful magnetic fields as a purple glow. But this was totally different; the bartender had seen it too.

"Was that some kinda sick joke, asshole?" the bartender yelled after him as he ran from the bar.

7

Susan didn't see Danny run into the street. Dressed as he was, she wouldn't have recognized him anyway. She continued to watch the TV, as she had most of the afternoon. David had not, of course, come home early in response to her mental signals, and her state of arousal had not abated at all; if anything it was worse. It seemed to her that everywhere she looked she found something else to turn her on more, generally something she associated intimately with David. Now she was lying on the couch watching Wile E. Coyote come to disaster again in his latest attempt to catch the Roadrunner. At least she didn't find the cartoon characters erotic, she thought wryly. It had not been the same with the afternoon soap operas; she had found them intensely arousing today.

She closed her eyes for a moment and fantasized about meeting David at the door stark naked, attacking him as soon as he walked in. That would be less weird than some of the things she had done today. She smiled with the memory of a day, not long after they were married, when David had rushed home early and greeted her at the door, totally nude, with an erection. There had been some memorable lovemaking that day.

Must be about 4:30, she thought, since she could hear the cartoon show going off. She opened her eyes and looked at the screen. After a seemingly interminable string of commercials, most of them aimed at the after-school children presumed to be the main audience of this show, another cartoon show was announced; "He-Man and the Masters of the Universe." She watched with little interest as the stylized characters moved through trite plots. It just didn't have the class of Bugs Bunny or Walt Disney somehow. But it was obviously appealing to children; one saw plenty of spin-off toys advertised during the numerous commercials, and the toy companies didn't make those if they didn't sell.

She perked up a little as the plot got more interesting. Seems that He-Man's rival had somehow conned him into screwing his sister, and now the morose He-Man was about to immolate himself in a huge fire—

She sat up. What the fuck kind of a children's program was this, anyhow?

Something wasn't right. The figures were not cartoons any more, didn't look like images on a TV screen. They were three-dimensional; the sound was high fidelity. It was as if she was watching this horrifying scene in person. She could even feel the heat of the fire on her face, smell the burnt-wood odor. And more, the man about to jump into it looked terrifyingly familiar.

She tried to say something, but nothing would come out. For a moment she struggled, and at last the sound burst free as a full-throated scream.

8

While Susan watched her TV, David was getting a headache from the roar of the subway train as it barreled uptown, swaying precariously, lights flashing on and off. Sometimes they remained off for ominously long periods. The train was absolutely packed with humanity; he fantasized briefly that he was in one of the cattle cars the Nazis had used to transport Jewish prisoners during the holocaust. The discomfort he felt increased when the lights went off; in the darkness between stations, he fantasized gangs of hoodlums creeping up on him. At such times the idea of driving his car to work in the infamous New York traffic did not seem so bad, and he again considered doing this, starting tomorrow. But the morning trains were not so bad, and he knew he wouldn't do it.

His thoughts turned again to that which had occupied his mind most of the day; ever since Susan had referred to the street derelict as "perfect," he had been having a running fantasy of watching them together, making love. It was obvious to him that the idea of realizing this particular fantasy was fraught with so many dangers and complications that it was not to be seriously considered. He certainly was not about to go out, locate the bum, and invite him up. Even if he knew Susan would welcome it, which he was sure she wouldn't. But in a fantasy, the protagonist can be nonviolent, clean, disease-free, and so on, so all the real world problems don't necessarily apply. And these particular fantasies—watching his wife and another man—were common for him. He had often wondered why, tried to search out the exact dynamic of that, but without a lot of success. He found the notion exciting, though, and didn't hesitate to indulge himself in his imaginary voyeurism.

The subway car took a lurch, throwing his body forward as he held onto the overhead bar. He had not, of course, been fortunate enough to get a seat, and had ridden all the way from downtown standing up. But this was the rule in the afternoons, not the exception. What was unusual was that the train's lateral movement had called his attention to the fact that he had an erection. Surprised, he glanced down at himself, then quickly up again. God damn, he thought. Sure as hell is obvious enough. His face felt hot. The best he could do was try to act unaware of it, but that was small consolation. He tried to think about his work, his car, his bankbook, anything but sex, to get it to go away. Persistently his pants felt stretched. It seemed to him that everyone in the car was staring at him, but he was able to convince himself that no one appeared to have noticed. Yet.

It came as a relief to David, then, when the car's lights went out again and stayed out for a longer time than usual. Even when there began to be uncomfortable murmurings from the other passengers, David privately hoped the darkness would remain for a while longer. But his difficulty showed no signs of abating. He closed his eyes tightly and tried desperately to think of something else, but all he saw was Susan and the strange man entwined on their bed, and he just seemed to get harder.

"This is totally insane," he muttered aloud. He thought the

train might be getting close to his station, and he dreaded the idea of trying to walk through the station and home in this condition.

With its internal lights still out, the train passed through a station which was not one of the regular stops. The station lights flashed through the windows, acting like a slow strobe on the restless passengers. Still trying to be inconspicuous, David let his eyes roam over the other riders. They stopped on a dark-haired girl sitting across from where he was standing. He studied her; she was quite small, perhaps less than five feet tall. Large brown eyes, short dark hair, very full mouth held in a kind of permanent pout. She wore a tight peach dress, visible since her coat was unbuttoned. The body the dress revealed was, to David, very impressive indeed. Even the way she was sitting was erotic to him. He became aware that he was staring, but couldn't seem to help it. The problem erection remained, but was forgotten.

As the train rushed back into darkness, David kept his eyes trained in her direction, even though he could not see her. The lights flashed momentarily, and he saw her jaw working. She seemed to be eating something. When the lights flashed again, he got a glimpse of her throat muscles working as she swallowed. Another flash of light. He saw her bend over and—

Saw her bend over, pick up a cigarette butt off the floor—

Pick up a cigarette butt and eat it—

Eat it?

He told himself his eyes must be failing him, some illusion of the light. He had not seen this outrageously attractive girl pick up a cigarette butt off the floor of a New York subway train and calmly eat it like it was a peanut. He waited impatiently for the next light flash. When it came, he saw her scraping bits of old bubble gum or something from the armrest of her seat and eating the pieces.

His stomach lurched. He couldn't accept what he was seeing. The woman must be insane, an escapee from some mental hospital. Even in New York, this was incredibly weird. He remembered his erection, and to his utter consternation, found that it was not gone! Surely to God the sight of a beautiful young girl sitting there eating garbage would turn him off. Another light flash. Now she had picked up a lump of mud or something similar and was eating that. She appeared to be doing this surreptitiously with respect to the passengers around her, and to be unaware of David's horrified gaze.

He thought he was going to be physically sick. He tried to look away from her but couldn't. The worst hit him a second later; he still found her incredibly desirable! Unbidden fantasies swarmed into his mind, in which this woman was eating his excretions while he watched Susan and the street derelict on the bed. He couldn't believe himself, this was so utterly sick, so perverted! He hadn't even believed in perversion an hour ago. You sure could trust the Big Apple to shake up any nice secure notions you had, he thought.

At last the lights in the train came on and stayed on. He looked at the girl; very demure, very ordinary, except for her beauty. He imagined telling the man next to him what she had been doing. Probably would get him locked up. He looked at the full lips. Again his stomach churned; he wanted to kiss her! The desire would not go away no matter how revolting his conscious mind found it. Maybe I need to be locked up for a while, he thought. He considered telling Susan about this incredible event. Would he tell her he still found the girl exciting? How could he explain that?

The train ground to a halt, its wheels screeching on the metal rails. His stop. Erection or no, he wanted off this damn train, wanted to get away from the woman. Lunging toward the door, he pushed an elderly lady aside to get out. On the platform, he leaned against one of the tiled posts and tried to steady himself before heading for the escalator that would take him to street level. His stomach calmed, and his hands stopped shaking. Several people passing him seemed to notice his erection, but now he didn't care. He just wanted to get home. Maybe have a drink, a rare thing for him. Maybe have several.

As he pulled himself upright and started toward the escalator, the girl walked past him and headed in the same direction. Like a mechanical man, he fell into step behind her, feeling somehow doomed. His self-respect was slipping away from him, and he couldn't do a thing about it.

As they neared the escalator, she dropped something, a piece of paper falling unseen from her purse. David stopped and picked it up; it was just an empty envelope. He looked at the name: Kathryn Phillips. The address was quite nearby. The return address was also familiar—Tascan Acres, Long Island.

Part of him demanded that he rush up and return the envelope, thus opening the possibility of conversation, but he retained enough control to hold back. He doubted he could resist if she made an advance toward him, unlikely though that might be. He felt that a sexual experience with her would degrade him so much he might actually die. Yet part of him wanted her frantically.

Control won out, and he watched the escalator carry her up and out of sight before getting on himself. At last the cursed erection was showing some signs of subsiding; when he reached the street, it was almost gone.

An icy blast of wind seemed to cut right through him as he emerged from the subway, trying to will himself not to look around for Kathryn Phillips; but in spite of himself he did. He felt relieved that he did not see her anywhere, but he did have her address. He tried to drop the crumpled envelope on the street, but his hand would not open.

A disturbance of some sort, directly across from his apartment building, caught his attention; he saw a man who seemed vaguely familiar running out of Vince's Bar. Vince himself appeared in the doorway, shaking his fist and yelling words David could not hear. He wondered if the man had robbed the place.

As he entered his building, he heard a woman's scream from above, faint with the distance. He figured it was coming from outside, perhaps related to the man running away; maybe somebody up above had seen something from a window. Then he realized that it might well have come from the direction of his own apartment. Even though he usually got home before Susan did, the worst possible scenarios presented themselves, and he tore up the stairs.

Bursting into his apartment, he immediately realized that it was, in fact, Susan who had screamed. He saw her on her knees on the couch, clad in blouse and panties, one hand in front of her mouth. She was shaking, her eyes were red, as she stared at the TV. A cartoon show was playing.

He glanced around, saw no clear and present dangers, and rushed over to her. "Susan? What is it? What's happened?" he asked.

She looked up at him, momentarily without recognition. Then she threw her arms around him. "Oh, God, David, I'm glad you're home! You just won't believe the day I've had! I think I'm losing my mind!''

You too? he thought. Then aloud, ''But just now, did you scream?''

''I think so. Oh, God, David, I saw it on television. Horrible—but it wasn't on television, it—it—'' she seemed to be making an effort to calm down. ''I thought I saw something on the TV,'' she said in a forced level voice. ''But it was some kind of hallucination, like looking at a real event—''

Oh good, David thought. You're hallucinating, and I just watched a woman eating shit on the subway. We're a great pair tonight. ''So there's no real danger in the apartment?'' he asked finally. ''Nobody tried to break in or anything?''

''No. No, I don't think so. No.''

He realized the door was still hanging open. No real New Yorker leaves his apartment door hanging open that long, he thought. He disengaged Susan, who released him only reluctantly, and went to the door to close it. Behind him, he heard her turn off the TV.

''David, please come and hold me for a minute,'' she asked, looking very fragile as he came back to her. ''Then I want to make love,'' she said over his shoulder, her voice much stronger.

She slowly released him and took off the rest of her clothes. He did likewise, his erection returning rapidly, welcome now. She was already very wet, and he slid easily into her with virtually no foreplay at all. This was not unusual for them; on many occasions they conducted what many other couples would consider foreplay while already connected. He kept his movements very gentle, sensing that she wanted a close lovemaking as opposed to a passionate one. Besides, he was not in a hurry; he had been fantasizing this, and many other things as well, all day.

As they moved slowly together on the couch in familiar synchronization, he felt the warming of her skin that always occured during their lovemaking; she in turn felt his penis become almost hot inside her. She knew this preceded his orgasm, and she tightened her legs around his buttocks. She hoped he would continue his gentle motion right through his orgasm, and he did. Seconds afterwards, her own orgasm welled up through her; she could feel its migration from her groin area all the way to the tips of her fingers and toes, a special bit of fire reaching her nipples, which were buried in David's ample chest hair. He moved his weight slightly to the right, but did not pull out; she arched her body and relaxed completely for the first time that day.

"I'm going to have a tough time telling you about my day, you know?" she said. "It's really been crazy."

"Well, mine hasn't exactly been sane. You first."

She went through the incident in Jerry's office, leaving out the part about feeling that she had caused Jerry's collapse; that sounded too crazy to her. "I swear to God, David, I do not know what the fuck possessed me to take my clothes off in that man's office. I don't know what the hell I would have done if he hadn't collapsed, you know?"

He listened to this with rising interest. It sort of went along with his fantasies of the day, but Jerry Maxwell was pretty disgusting, and it spoiled the image somewhat. But nonetheless, he found the picture of his little Susan stripping down in the man's office arousing.

She then related her vision of the incest and fire. This he didn't understand at all, and he told her so. She didn't either.

He told her about Kathryn Phillips and her unique appetite, but he left out more of the story; he didn't tell her of his intense attraction to the woman, or about the envelope which was now stuffed in his pants pocket. He did tell her of the embarrassing erection on the train, told her he had been thinking of her; but he didn't quite finish that either. He didn't tell her what she had been doing in his fantasies.

9

The weak winter sun was right in his eyes as Bertie awoke. He glanced at his watch, on the bedside table: 6:15. To his right, Marcia was still sleeping, her back to him. He sat up in the motel bed and rubbed his face. It was time to be back on the road, he thought.

Marcia stirred and rolled over. Her eyes found Bertie's face and she gave him a sleepy smile. Bertie did not return it; his face remained impassive. Perhaps she'll just get up and leave without a word, he thought; it would be the decent thing to do. The sex with her last night had been pleasant enough; she was inexperienced, but very eager to please. He thought she might be entertaining notions of riding on to New York with him. Well, if that were so, he'd end it quickly enough. He really didn't even like looking at her right now. He wasn't horny, and as far as he was concerned, women were only useful when he was. At other times, they should stay out of sight. Cook, or something. He didn't care. He sure as hell didn't want to talk to them.

But Marcia reached over and rubbed his chest with her hand. Obviously, he thought, she wants another one this morning. Well, too bad. He had to go. There was money to be made, places to go, important people to be met.

"Mornin', sweet—" she started, but he had already pushed her hand away and was out of the bed, headed for the shower. She watched him disappear into the bathroom. As yet she wasn't taking his behavior as a personal rejection. Her sexual experience was not vast by any means, but Bertie had been far and away the best she'd ever had. He was so passionate, almost wild, and just rough enough to be exciting to her. He had scared her a little, but in the end everything had been okay. More than okay by her standards. She desperately wanted this to be more than a one-night stand, and at this particular moment, she was sure Bertie felt the same.

After a few minutes he came out of the shower and began rummaging through his suitcase for underwear. He did not look at Marcia; in fact, he behaved as if no one else was in the room.

"I know a good place for breakfast, just up the beltway from here," she said. She had decided maybe he just wasn't into morning sex. She certainly was.

"Fine. I'll try it," he said impersonally, without asking her what the place was or where.

Now she looked worried. "Bert?" she said, walking over to him. "Is anything wrong?"

He looked back at her, and she shrank away a bit. His eyes were so cold. "No, nothing's wrong. I just have to get going, that's all."

"But I thought we—I thought maybe—"

He looked at her levelly. "Don't make more of it than it was. We had fun. That's it."

Her mouth trembled as she turned away from him and began to get dressed. Bertie, in front of the mirror, smiled at his image. He liked his own looks, and was very fond of mirrors.

Within an hour, Bertie found himself alone, dawdling over breakfast and wasting a good deal of time. For some reason, he was hesitant about getting back on the road. He tried to ignore the feeling, but the memories of the accident, and the sense of fate it always provoked, made that impossible. He asked the waitress for a third cup of coffee. She was hanging around his table a lot, but he paid no attention to her. Finally he felt he could not stand sitting in this crummy restaurant any longer, and decided to drive through the downtown part of the city. He did not find this idea unpleasant, whereas the idea of the highway was, at the moment, unacceptable.

He drove the Toyota slowly through the streets of Lexington, telling himself that there was really no hurry, he needn't get back on the highway till he was good and ready. At the moment, he could just kind of cruise around, looking in the windows of the shops, which were just beginning to open for the day.

One of these caught his attention and curiosity. It was, according to the sign, an "Antique and Junque" shop. The owner was setting various pieces of ceramics out in front of the windows, most of them absolutely dreadful statues of dogs and panthers. But one piece piqued his interest, and there was a convenient parking place only about twenty feet away from the store entrance. On impulse, he stopped the Toyota and got out.

When he reached the shop, he was puzzled. The piece he had been interested in was not at all what he thought it was; from the car it had looked like a piece of Indian art; but up close it was a gaudily painted lawn bird. He touched it, then turned and went into the shop. It was always important to him that he appeared to others as if he knew what he was doing at all times. So it would not look right for him to park the car, look at this ridiculous bird, then immediately leave.

It was one of those antique shops where close-set shelves are packed with every conceivable type of useless bric-a-brac, much of it covered with a layer of dust testifying to the years it had remained untouched. Idly, he wondered how the man stayed in business. Whole sections of his merchandise showed price tags that were so old that the ink had faded or been light-bleached, even though the interior of the shop was quite dark. He walked slowly down the aisles, looking at this and that, occasionally picking up a piece and turning it over in his hands. He had no intention of buying anything.

"Help you with something?" a voice came from behind him. Bertie turned and faced the proprietor, an old man dressed in coveralls, his sleeves rolled up in spite of the cold day.

"No, I was just looking around. I thought I saw a Mexican sculpture in here; maybe pre-Columbian art." He was irritated with himself for saying this. To expect genuine pre-Columbian artwork in such a shop was foolish.

"Ah. Pre-Columbian," the old man said. He rubbed his hands together. "I think maybe I have a few things here. Now where were they?"

Bertie's irritation increased. He knew the old man was going to push some made-in-Taiwan crap at him claiming it was pre-Columbian. But he followed, farther back in the semidarkness to the rear of the store, where he watched the proprietor rummage around and finally pull down a large oil painting on black velvet. Blowing the dust off, he held it up in front of him, as if for Bertie to see. It was a fanciful representation of an Aztec sacrifice; the victim looked exactly like a dark-haired, copper-skinned Marilyn Monroe. Her eyebrows were incongruously light. Bertie sighed. The old dude was doubtlessly about to try to pass this shit off on him as pre-Columbian, he thought.

But no, he put the awful painting aside without comment. He apparently was just moving it out of the way to get to some objects behind it; objects on a shelf that had been hidden by the framed velvet.

"Take a look at this stuff. I'm sure you'll find what you want there," the old man said, stepping aside.

Bertie looked. He was truly surprised; there were several small stone figurines that might actually have been pre-Columbian. But it was the group of objects behind them that really attracted his attention.

One of these was a small amulet of some sort. Picking it up and rolling it over in his hand, he could see, even though it was encrusted, a slot cut in the back, as if it were intended to fit on a belt. The other side bore a piece of flat dark stone, set with exquisite craftsmanship into the metal. He rubbed the stone with his fingertip; his reflection shone back at him. He turned his body slightly so that the shopkeeper could not see, then scraped at the metal mount with his nail. The greenish incrustation came away, and bright yellow shined beneath. Gold, he thought. The whole thing weighed maybe two ounces. He was no archaeologist, but he thought this might be genuinely prehistoric as well. As such, it would be worth a fortune.

The other object was equally interesting, and he now turned his attention to it. It was a long knife with a handle that appeared to be of bone. The blade, perhaps eight inches long, was gracefully curved in a perfect arch; it didn't seem to be made of metal. He examined it closely and decided that it was flint, or quartz perhaps. He ran his finger along the edge; it was amazing how sharp it was. You could shave with this thing, he told himself, finding it hard to believe that such a keen edge could be put on stone. The other side, on the interior of the curve, was equally sharp. There were flecks of some darker material on the stone; he picked one off and looked at it stuck to his thumb. It appeared to be dried blood.

Holding it up, he looked closely at the handle, at the intricate carvings on it. He did not recognize all the figures, but the front of the handle was in the form of an open mouth, apparently a jaguar's; this held the blade. At the rear sat a man with a plumed headdress; on his headband, right over his temple, was an unmistakable representation of the small mirrored amulet he had just seen. Obviously, then, the amulet and knife had been found together, were a pair; otherwise the coincidence was just too great.

He picked up both items and considered what to offer the storekeeper for them. He didn't know if the man had any idea of their value. Bertie really didn't either, but he was sure it was high. These things looked genuine. Moreover, they had a *feel*; there were sensations of some sort attached to them, a mood created just by holding them. Bertie liked that mood.

He started to turn back to the man when a glint of light from farther back in the shelves caught his eye. Curious, he moved a couple of large, somewhat battered stone sculptures to get a better view.

What he saw startled him at first. It seemed to be a boot. He reached in and picked it up, pulled it out, and for a moment was speechless.

It was not a boot; the top of it was closed. It was a carved foot.

A carved left foot, just about the size of the flesh and blood foot he'd lost.

It seemed to be made of some kind of stone also, but he had no idea what; it was rather light, just about the weight of a real foot. There were similar carvings on it; jaguars, bats, eagles, and stylized Indians with fantastic headdresses. He noted rings at the top, apparently for straps. This thing was meant to be worn by someone with an amputated foot, he realized. On top of the piece, extending down toward the toe, was a precisely carved mirror of the same blackish stone in the amulet. Obsidian, it came to him, but polished to a very fine finish. He could not find a chip or flaw in it anywhere. He turned it up and looked at the toe itself; there was yet another carving there, and as he looked at it the shop swam momentarily, and he was forced to steady himself.

He was looking at a precise image in stone of the monstrosity of his vision, his personal dragon, the creature which had bitten off his foot years ago over the Kentucky River.

10

It was past ten that morning before John finally awoke, looked outside at an overcast and dreary day. With effort, he dragged himself from the bed. Though he couldn't remember them, he knew his dreams had been pleasant; waking up to the real world was decidedly not. But he had to face it; he had to get to New York by tomorrow afternoon at the latest. If this buyer was interested in his stuff, he would be in good shape financially for the first time in many years.

The dreams still bothered him, even as he downed sausage biscuits, and coffee at a nearby Hardee's. They seemed profound to him, even though he could not remember all of them; something he should pay attention to. They reminded him of childhood dreams, dreams that had fed his notion that somehow the Gosses were not his true parents. There was some little grain of truth that fed this; something about the births of both the Goss children had always been treated in the family as a mystery, perhaps a scandal. But he had never learned what that was.

Before leaving, he decided to check his merchandise, make sure nothing had broken. Stepping behind the car, he opened the trunk; inside were several boxes of items wrapped in newspaper. He poked at them, didn't feel any breakage, and lifted one out at random. Unwrapping the newspaper revealed a beautifully intricate polychrome jar, executed in a pre-Columbian style. The critics had always loved his pottery, he reflected; it had been a deciding factor in buying the place in Florida and going into this business full time. But he certainly hadn't been getting rich at it; he had barely been making a living at all. This trip could change all that. A major chain of exclusive art dealers was going to talk to him about distributing his line. This was the reason for the drive to New York. He had very high hopes for this meeting.

Putting the jar back, he got in the car, remembering the seat belt this time. Soon he was headed out U.S. 64 toward its intersection with I-95; he'd had enough of 301 to last a while.

He had just turned onto I-95 when he first saw the bird. It was swooping and diving in the sky above and in front of him in a very odd manner. It looked very large; he assumed it must be an eagle or a large hawk. It definitely was not a vulture; its flight was nothing like their methodical, energy-conserving soaring. He watched it with some interest, unable to see any details; it was just a black winged silhouette on the gray sky.

As he got closer to it, he really began to wonder what it was. It looked huge, larger than any bird he had ever seen; and he had seen several bald eagles in his travels. He judged this thing to be at least four times the size of any eagle, yet it was diving and cavorting like a sparrow. Odder yet, it was staying in front of his car, where he could see it. Sometimes it dived toward the side of the road, but it always came back to a position right in front of him. He still could see no details of color or plumage, but he was close enough now to see that it had a rather long neck and a very long tail.

"Maybe a heron or egret of some kind?" he asked himself, but he knew there were none that large. Also, those were familiar birds to him in Florida, and the shape was just not right. The scene he was viewing suddenly got considerably brighter. Glancing around, he saw that the clouds had parted in the east; the sun was coming out. He could also see Venus, the morning star, clearly framed by an opening in the gray overcast.

The steering wheel jerked in his hands and he looked back, realizing that he was running off the road. The bird was hovering directly in front of him, closer than ever. John stopped, got out, and for a few moments stood there facing the immense hovering bird, the rising sun at his back, Venus brilliant in the hole in the clouds. Then the bird moved, straight at him. He thought consciously that he should be afraid; the creature was so huge, so fast. But emotionally he was calm. This was right, said a voice from inside, a voice he had not heard since he was a small child. The bird cut its speed only about fifty feet from him, then began to rise. It went directly over his head, very close, the wind from the wings blowing his hair around, raising a cloud of dust. Then it was gone, headed away over the woods to his right. He had never really gotten a good look at it, still didn't know what it was. But as it flew away, he caught sight of a single feather, perhaps four inches long, floating down on the air currents. He stepped forward and extended his hand; the feather fell into his outstretched open palm. It was a brilliant, iridescent, emerald green.

As soon as he had the feather in his hand, the wind began to rise; dust swirled around him and the sky grew dark again. He looked back and saw that the sun and Venus had both disappeared. He looked back at the feather; an odd feeling, a nostalgia, surged up in him. Something from far back, something he should remember. A childhood dream, perhaps? He couldn't be sure. He continued to gaze at the feather, wondering where it was he'd seen one of these before.

11

Susan was more than twenty minutes late for work that morning; she and David both had considered taking a sick day, but they'd decided against it. Nothing abnormal had happened to them for the remainder of the night, and Wednesday morning breakfast was equally mundane. They had agreed to try to put the previous day's events down to a weird alignment of the stars or something, and to get back into the usual flow of their lives. She peeked into Jerry Maxwell's office as she went by; he was not in. That wasn't surprising. Most likely he'd been kept overnight at the hospital for observation.

Squaring her shoulders, she went straight to her desk in a very businesslike fashion and set to work. Naturally, since she really hadn't done any the previous day, she was behind; she threw herself into it and succeeded in concentrating on it alone. Actually, it was turning into a pretty good day for her. By lunchtime, she had gotten quite a bit of the pile cleared and everything seemed very normal.

"Ready for lunch, Sue?" came a voice, cutting into her concentration. She looked up at Jeannie, then at the clock; five of twelve. The morning had gone fast.

"Sure, Jeannie, let me just get my coat," she replied.

The two women left the office building and went to a small café about a block away. This had been their habit for over a year.

When they were seated, Jeannie spoke again. "Look, Sue, you know you really don't have to talk about it if you don't want to, but about yesterday and Jerry—"

Susan put her hand over her eyes for a minute. Could she tell Jeannie what she hadn't told David? Doubtful. If she expressed her belief that she had somehow struck Jerry down, she'd be thought crazy. Maybe she was crazy. It wasn't the first time she'd considered it a possibility.

Jeannie paused for a moment, and when Susan didn't say anything she continued: "I know Maxwell, Susan. He's tried to put the make on me more than once." This was news; Jeannie had never told her that before.

She looked up. "What happened?"

"Nothing much. He just asked me to look at some pictures and grabbed my ass. I told him I'd have him up on harassment charges and he's let me alone since."

Harassment charges! Why hadn't she thought of that? All this time she'd just been dodging him. "But you just said more than once," she observed.

Jeannie colored. "Well, yeah, there was a time before that. I was new here, and I didn't know—and well, he kinda felt me up a lot, and I ran out." Jeannie was physically squirming. She really hadn't intended to get into this incident, Susan realized. She suspected that perhaps things had gone farther than feeling up, and searched for a way to bail her friend out.

"Well, nothing really happened yesterday, you know?" she said. "It's just that—well, I took my clothes off in his office and—" She was aware that Jeannie was staring at her. "No, no, not like that," she said quickly. "I had a dizzy spell, and I asked him to get me some water, and while he was gone I took my pants off. Simple." She gestured with her hands. "I had this stain on them, you know? And, well, it really bothered me, so—'' Her voice trailed away. "Anyway, I think maybe he had a heart attack when he walked back in and saw me standing there with no pants.'' She closed this description with a nervous giggle.

Jeannie looked at her closely, leaning across the table. "That's not nothing, Sue. Why'd you do that?''

Susan's attempt to be light about it failed her completely now, and she visibly wilted. "Damn, Jeannie, I swear to God I don't know.'' She really wanted her friend to understand, at least as well as she did. "It just seemed to me that the stain on my pants was unacceptable, I just couldn't stand to have stained pants—'' She stopped. Jeannie was still staring at her, but her eyes looked glazed and out of focus. "Jeannie?'' There was no response. She reached out and touched the other woman's hand.

Jeannie looked right at her. Susan had never seen that kind of look on her face before. "Yes, of course, I understand,'' she said in a monotone. "You cannot be other than perfectly beautiful.''

Hearing Jeannie's words sent a chill through her. She thought she was being made fun of, but that phrase so closely echoed her own thoughts of yesterday.

"Jeannie? You putting me on?''

Jeannie did not answer. As she gazed into Susan's face, her own was taking on a rapturous expression. Susan became increasingly uncomfortable.

A busboy came by their table and in a very professional manner began to lay out placemats and silver. The last thing he put on the table was a small vase containing a couple of cut flowers; he sat them directly in front of Jeannie's face. As he left, Susan reached out to move them. In passing she noticed that the plants had one bloom each and at least five or six buds. As she took hold of the vase, her fingers brushed against the plant leaves that were hanging over the side, and in the next few seconds every bud on the plant burst into full bloom.

12

Bertie looked suspiciously back at the proprietor of the antique store. He had to have these things, whatever it took. He didn't even consider the possibility that the old man might ask thousands of dollars for them. He just had to have them, that was all.

"What do you want for these?" he asked, trying but failing to keep his voice from cracking.

"Oh, that stuff? Well, lemme see—How's a hundred dollars for the boot, fifty for the knife, and twenty for that there little pin sound?"

God, that was easy. Bertie relaxed. He said, "Fine. I'll take them." He was reluctant to put anything down, but he had to get his money out. At last he shoved two hundred dollars at the old man.

"Funny about that stuff," the old man mused as he counted out the change. "Had it a real long time. An old guy came in here one day to sell it to me, I guess maybe forty, fifty years ago. I wasn't gonna buy it, didn't know what it was, but this man who brought it in, God, I won't forget him if I live to be a hundred. I'm eighty now!" He beamed at Bertie, proud of his age.

Bertie was interested. With the artifacts securely in his possession, he asked the old man about the seller.

"Well, I think he was maybe a Puerto Rican or something. He was real dark and had black eyes. It hadn't been long since my daddy died, and I inherited this place from him, so I was tryin' to be real careful about what I bought. I didn't wanta get stuck with junk I couldn't sell.

"Then in walks this old guy, like I told you. He's got a bag with that stuff in it, and he takes it out and says he wants to sell it. Well sir, I thinks it can't be real old stuff, it's too good;

it'd be worth too much. He'd be sellin' it to some museum or something. So that means it's hot, or some cheap crap. Anyway, I didn't wanta fool with it. But he says, this old guy, you gotta buy it. I swear, he was the oldest guy I ever saw, then or since. Couldn't believe he's up walkin' around. He looks like one of them Egyptian mummys or something.

"But his voice, man, something else! Real deep, powerful, like some movie star—Yeah, who's that guy, Lorne Greene! But somehow bigger. I swear, if that guy said jump, you wasn't gonna just stand there. Anyways, I kept arguin'. But he says I have to buy it, and he looks at me kinda hard. And by God, believe it or not, I had to buy it! I just couldn't say no. The old guy, he says, don't you worry. One day the man who's stuff this really is will come along and he'll buy it from you. And he says, you sell it to him, too. If'n you don't he'll kill you and take it.

"So then I figured the stuff had to be hot. When the old guy left, I felt real bad; I'd only been runnin' the place a few weeks, and I had a load of hot stuff on my hands! Then I thought, hey, while you been standin' around here feelin' sorry for yourself, the old guy left! And you never paid him a penny for the stuff! Now that ain't so bad, is it?

"So after that I stuck it right up on that shelf where you found it. For years I looked for some toughs to come around to get it, but nobody ever did. Nobody ever wanted to buy it either. So now you did! I guess the guy who owned it won't care, he's probably been dead forty years."

Bertie thanked the old man for his story and left the shop. Back in his car, he slipped off his artificial left foot and held it up next to the carved one. Near identical size. He pulled the straps off the old one and fitted them to the rings on the antique. Exact fit, no problems. Breathing a little hard, he fitted it to the stump of his leg. Somehow he was expecting this; not only was it a perfect fit, but even the contours of the upper carving meshed exactly with the shape of his stump. He put it on the floor, not quite believing how comfortable it was. Getting out of the car again, he walked up and down a bit. Never had any prosthesis fit him this well; it was exactly the right weight, and it seemed that— No, he told himself, that was ridiculous! But nevertheless, it seemed like it flexed when he walked, and even pushed off with the toe at the appropriate part of the step.

When he got back in the car, he actually felt like he had his original foot back. Even a casual observer would have seen the difference; Bertie didn't limp any longer.

13

All that morning, from the time he'd left the apartment until he'd arrived at the office, David had been uncomfortable. At first he tried to tell himself that it was just the aftermath of the odd events of the previous day; but increasingly, he didn't believe it. Something was wrong, something much more concrete, more real. He felt he was being followed. There was a man in a long cashmere coat; he had seen the coat outside the apartment, seen it on the subway. He had been searching through the morning commuters, looking for Kathryn Phillips; he had not seen her, but he had seen the coat. And each time he saw it, he never saw a face, because the owner quickly turned away.

He put down the contract he had been working on and walked over to a window. Down in the street, crossing from the other side, the cashmere coat. Too far away for him to see the face. What the hell was going on here? Not only was he being followed, he was being followed by an amateur.

He decided he'd had enough. Time was when he had run away from such things; not anymore. Not ever again. He grabbed his own coat and started down the stairs, reckless about the possible dangers of confronting the man in the cashmere. When he reached the street, he was gratified to see that the man was still there, walking up and down in front of his building. Now he could see the face; bright blue eyes looking upward at the skyscraper. This face is familiar, David thought; where have I seen him before? Disregarding the startled looks

from people on the sidewalks, he ran up behind the man and
seized the collar of his coat.

Damn, this was a waste, Danny thought. He didn't know
one single thing more than he'd known the first day, but he
surely had the impression that whatever was going on here was
a major event of some kind. But what the vision of the rattlesnake had meant he had no idea. If it was a vision, he told
himself; the fact was that the bartender had seen it too, or seen
something. But he was not prepared to accept the idea that a
real honest-to-God rattlesnake had suddenly materialized in his
beer. His concept of the universe might allow for a little pre-
cognition, some clairvoyance here and there, but that notion
was a bit extreme. He shuddered even though he wasn't cold.
His present outfit allowed warmth, at least. But it had also
attracted a little more attention than he liked. There weren't
many cashmere coats on the street.

As planned, he had followed the man from the apartment.
And the man had gone to work. Nothing at all out of the ordinary. Now Danny knew that he worked for an investment
firm that specialized in agricultural products, grain futures,
and the like. That was a big help. Maybe it explained the
impression he had gotten before of the word "wheat," but he
couldn't be sure. At least ten times Danny had walked past and
squinted at the windows of the investment firm's offices, and
gotten no impressions at all beyond the coppery color he associated with concern for money. What the hell would you
expect from an investment firm?

It was getting close to noon. Perhaps, he thought, the man
would do something as he went out to lunch that would give
Danny a clue. If he went out to lunch. The way his luck was
running, he wouldn't see the man again until he left to go
home; then he'd go home, stay there, and Danny would be
back to square one. Perhaps tomorrow he should follow the
woman instead. But that was inherently more dangerous. A
man following a woman around the city was, he felt, much
more likely to be noticed.

Concentrating on the task at hand, he looked up again at the
office windows. Suddenly he got something. Bright red, flooding into his field of vision from the sides. Danger. Warning.
From behind.

Damnation, he thought, now I've done it, I missed this coming, I've had it. He started to spin around, but a strong hand closed on the collar of his coat, jerking him momentarily off balance. He was terrified, sure that some mugger or crazy was about to kill him. His back pushed forward to escape the expected bullet. Turning his head, he looked at David.

"Who the hell are you?" David demanded, yanking Danny around to face him. "I know you've been following me. Why?"

"Shit, man, what is this? Let go of me! I was just walking down the street, I got a right to—" Danny's mind was working fast. He knew this wouldn't wash, could see that David wasn't buying it.

"Don't give me that. I saw you this morning outside my place. On the subway."

"All right, all right! Damn! Just let go, will you, before somebody calls the cops. I'm not gonna run off!"

David released Danny's coat and stood looking at him. He still looked familiar, but where—? Then it hit him. "The bum," he said slowly. "I remember the eyes. You're the bum outside, yesterday morning."

Oh shit, Danny thought. A bright boy here, he's putting it all together. What am I gonna tell him? "Yes, Mr. Citizen, I am a psychic, see, and I saw all this stuff and—" The man would call the cops for sure. Danny didn't need that. He wanted to remain invisible. But maybe that was the best way. Let this guy think he was nuts. Why would he call the cops? It wasn't a crime to ride the fucking subway. He'd just warn Danny to stay away, and maybe he would. This was getting to be too much trouble.

"Let's go somewhere outta the street, okay?" Danny said. "I'll tell you all about it."

David considered this. Having lunch with his shadow was not what he'd had in mind, but in reality, this man didn't seem dangerous; in fact he was kind of likeable. It was also obvious that he was scared, and this simultaneously bolstered David's ego and made him cautious; frightened people could be unpredictable. But what could happen in a public restaurant? A lot; you heard about it every day in the newspapers. Still, he really didn't know what else to do. He was not by nature a violent man, and the idea of beating the guy up here and now was not a serious consideration.

"All right. There's a little restaurant down the street. We'll go there. But I want some straight answers."

"You'll get them."

When they were seated in the restaurant, David studied the man. Danny in turn studied the table top. He wanted to create a sympathetic portrait, wanted David to pity the insanity he was sure would be apparent from the story he was about to tell.

"First of all, what's your name?" David said.

"Danny Hudson." God damn! He had snapped out his real name without even thinking! Jesus, that was stupid!

"Now, why were you following me?"

"Well," Danny began. Make it so straight it sounds really bananas, he thought. "See, I'm a psychic. But I don't make a living reading tea leaves or Tarot cards, I just take advantage of situations. All kinds of situations. Horse races, sometimes. Poker. I know when people are about to lose money and things like that, so I make sure I'm around to find it." Danny felt he was doing well. This even sounded crazy to him, and he knew it was the truth. "So yesterday morning, I see these colors—I see colors mostly, that's how I know something is going to happen. I usually don't know what, just something, and I know if it's good or bad for me. If it's good, I stay close, if it's bad, I get away. So I see these colors around your window, and I don't know what they mean, but it could be good to be around. Well, I don't know if it's good, but anyway, it's real interesting. So I hang around. Then last night I'm at that bar across the street and a rattlesnake appears in my beer. So they throw me out. So I wanta know what's going on, see?" Danny was still studying the table top, and he almost laughed. That was beautiful; the whole truth and nothing but the truth, ma'am, and good God did it ever sound crazy.

There was a moment of silence and Danny looked up. His mental grin faded. David was regarding him very seriously, apparently digesting what he had said—almost as if Danny had been talking about eating a hamburger.

"So you saw these colors. Around us? What were they like?" David asked.

Danny couldn't believe it. This man was taking his story at face value, like it was nothing out of the ordinary at all! In his lifetime he had talked to a lot of people about being psychic;

his parents, teachers, friends, researchers. Always the reactions were fear, disbelief, curiosity, mockery. Never this; acceptance. He didn't know what to do with it.

For the moment, ride with it, he thought. "Red and black, like a sunburst," he said. "Now usually to me, red means danger, and black, well, I don't wanta scare you, but black usually means death or disease or something. I see black when somebody is gonna die. So normally if I see red or black I get away. Far away. But this was a different red and black, and anyway, I never see things in patterns like sunbursts. And it was so strong! Couldn't believe it. Strongest I've ever seen!"

"So what did you get? What'd you think it was?"

"Well, I didn't know. I got a couple of, well, words; 'chalice' or 'challenge' and maybe 'wheat.' Made no sense to me. But I got this feeling of, I don't know, power. Made me feel real small."

"So why'd you follow me?"

"I thought maybe I could find out more about it if I found out about you. But I don't know anything else."

"What could you find out about me that would help you figure this out?"

"Hey, man, like I said, I don't know! I was just waiting for something. But I didn't get it, and I still don't get it, even sitting here across from you."

"Maybe it has to do with Susan, then."

"Is that your wife?"

David looked at his hands. "Yes," he said. "And some weird things have been happening with us too. I'd like to know why. I want you to meet her. See what you get from her, up close. Can you come over tonight?"

Danny stared at him. He hadn't expected this. "Uh, sure, I guess so."

"You know where we live. Make it about seven-thirty."

"Sure man, yeah, I'll be there." He was still stunned, but he knew he would, in fact, be there. With a last look at David, he got up and left the restaurant.

David watched him go, was aware that most people would regard what he had just done as absolutely crazy. But he thought he knew what he was doing; he didn't think Danny was mad. Besides, he had some kind of gut instinct about this man. There was something about him, some reason to keep in touch with him. He didn't know why, but the feeling would not be denied.

14

Since the accident, whenever Bertie crossed any large bridge, phantom pain in his amputated foot made the crossing uncomfortable for him. But today, as he drove onto the bridge spanning the Ohio River, it was actually as if he had his real foot back; the carved stone artifact really seemed to be part of him. He looked down, caught his reflection in the black mirror. It was a little conspicuous, he realized. When—and if—he went back on duty he would have to get a special shoe to cover it. The Air Force would not appreciate an officer who wore a mirrored foot.

This brought him back to the decision he was trying to make, the reason for the trip; whether to stay in the military or leave. He wanted to experience a freer lifestyle for a while, meet some new people, have some fun; maybe run down to Atlantic City and make some money at the gaming tables, anything to relieve the boredom of his current assignment. Few people even knew about the data analysis center in Knoxville, and command was very antsy when their officers socialized too much with the townspeople. Their job was too top secret; they worried too much about little leaks.

He'd been assigned there as a computer programmer shortly after the loss of his foot; the accident had ended any ideas he might have entertained about flying. He'd been fortunate—or so he'd believed at the time—not to have been summarily discharged. But he had a background in systems analysis, and he was still useful to the Air Force. So they'd sent him to Knoxville.

At first, he had wondered why a data analysis center was so top secret. They had not initially told him; and the programs he worked on were only bits and pieces, subroutines, so that he didn't really know what exactly he was doing. But his skills had carried him upward, and eventually he had more information about the nature of the project. If anybody asked, they were doing cost-analysis, and to further this illusion, some of the programs really were. But not the main ones. These had to do with a running probability of all-out nuclear war, of the likelihood of the Soviets trying a preemptive strike. If their information indicated a high probability of this, then the U.S. might try to go for it first. That knowledge had caused Bertie to become uncomfortable with what he was doing. He liked to think of himself as a kind of pure warrior; slaughtering millions of people via computer output was not what he had joined the military to do. In fact, he was no longer clear on exactly why he had joined in the first place, and why, of all the branches he could have chosen, he had gone into the Air Force. The Marines were more his style. He often found himself wishing that soldiers still fought with swords, one-to-one; modern warfare was too impersonal, too technological. A peculiar attitude for a programmer to have, but that was the way he felt.

As he crossed the bridge and passed into downtown Cincinnati, he realized that he was getting hungry; but it was noontime, and most restaurants in town would be crowded. If he waited, he could either stop in Columbus after the regular lunch crowds were gone, or maybe some little country place in between. That idea appealed to him, and he pushed on.

He was not far beyond the city limits of Cincinnati when he saw a perfect place, a little truck stop on a service road alongside the Interstate. A girl in a checkered uniform and white apron stood in the doorway for a moment, then went back inside, out of the Ohio cold. The place didn't seem to get much business; there was only one car sitting out front.

He took the next exit and turned on the service road back toward the diner. Davis Grill, the sign proclaimed. Inside, he sat down in one of the four booths across the front. The car out front must have belonged to the waitress; he was the only customer. She came over to his table, pad in hand. He watched her walk; she was truly beautiful, not just acceptable as Marcia had been. He wished he had been here last night instead of in Lexington.

"Hi," she said. "Get you some coffee or something while you look at the menu?"

"Yeah, that'd be good," he replied. Moments later she returned with a steaming cup. "Looks a little slow today," he commented.

"It ain't a little slow, mister. It's about dead. Been that way all day."

He looked around, didn't see a cook. "You all alone here?"

"Yeah, business has been bad lately. Daddy doesn't know why. It's his place. Fact is, he's in Dayton today tryin' to sell it. It's all right with me. I've had about enough of cooking."

"Well, I'll make this one easy. How about a BLT and some fries?"

"Sure enough. Comin' right up." She walked away and stretched three strips of bacon out on the grill; it began to smoke.

Bertie left the booth and carried his coffee over to the counter. "I know how this sounds, but what's a nice girl, et cetera?"

She looked at him, did not smile. "Just to help out my dad. He couldn't afford any help. My fiancé and I"—she emphasized fiancé—"are going back to Chicago as soon as things are settled. Daddy lives in the house out back, and we have to sell it too, get him settled again and all."

She finished making the sandwich and put it in front of him, and he carried it back to the booth. While he ate, he examined the flint knife and the amulet more closely; he had been unwilling to leave them in the car, afraid someone might steal them. He didn't know exactly what they symbolized, but they were beautiful to him. He glanced up, saw the waitress coming back, and tucked them inside his coat.

"Anything else?" she asked.

He looked up at her. She had a model's face and figure. "No more food," he said, giving her his best bedroom smile.

"What?"

"Look, I'm just passing through. You're here all alone with a perfectly good house out back. We can't let this opportunity go by!"

She gave him a hard look. "What are you trying to say, mister?"

"You know what I'm trying to say. You're attractive, you think I am too, so let's not waste a lot of time. Your daddy might come back or something. I'm not staying here overnight or anything.''

''No, you're wrong about that. I don't think you're attractive. Oh, you look good, and you're smooth, but I work as a model in Chicago, and I've seen lots of smoothies. You thought you were dealing with some hick? You disgust me, mister. You come through here, thinking you're God's special little gift to wo—''

Bertie couldn't believe he was hearing right. Not only was she rejecting him, she was putting him down! A torrent of rage was rising in him. This little tramp had no right to treat him like this; not him, of all people! He just wasn't going to take it, wasn't going to hear any more of it.

Before she had quite finished, he had whipped the flint knife back out of his coat and, rolling it over so that the interior curve of the blade came at her like a hook, struck with all his strength at her throat. The blade was so sharp, passed through so easily, that he nearly lost his balance.

She stood totally still for a moment, an expression of utter shock on her face, blood spurting from her open throat like a fountain. Bertie quickly moved aside so it wouldn't splash on his clothes, but a few drops landed on his mirrored foot. Finally she started to move a hand upward toward her neck, then crumpled to the floor. Bertie bent over her; the blood was just flowing now, no longer a fountain. He felt very strange, looking directly into her eyes, watching her life drain away onto the floor of the country grill. There was an amazing amount of blood; Bertie was careful not to step in it. As her eyes turned glassy, and the pump of the blood slowed, he felt a strange exhilaration, an energy; it was a very pleasant feeling. He didn't notice the curls of smoke rising from the mirror on his foot; didn't notice the pulsations of the flint knife blade. On impulse, he wiped the blade carefully through the open wound, completely covering it with blood. A few moments later, when he started to wipe it off with a napkin so he could put it back in his coat, he noticed without surprise that it was dry. Methodically, he checked his clothes, his coat, for bloodstains; he found none. Outside, he saw no cars but his and hers. All clear.

It was not until he was back in his car and on the highway again that the fact of the murder hit him. Never in his life had he done anything like that. He had no idea what had come over him, what he'd been thinking about.

15

John had just passed a sign which said ROANOKE RAPIDS-19 when he noticed that the traffic had slowed down considerably, and was merging into the left lane up ahead. Joining the flow, he inched forward with the others. Some kind of road work, he assumed. I-95 in North Carolina was a rather poorly maintained road in places; there were a surprising number of potholes for an interstate highway.

As he passed the point of merger, he could see that it was not road work, but an accident. Like everyone else, he looked. A late-model pickup truck lay on its side, half in the right lane and half on the shoulder, its left front fender crumpled down on the wheel. About a hundred yards in front of it was a somewhat older Datsun, standing upright, but with the right rear crushed. It appeared as if the Datsun had cut in front of the truck, which had ridden up its rear and flipped over. There was a small knot of shaken people standing around the Datsun; he could not see anyone near the pickup. The police had not yet arrived, but a crowd of onlookers stood around; several cars had stopped.

There was another knot of people down an embankment beyond the truck. Just as he noticed them, a cry went up from someone in this group, a cry of anguish; it cut right through him. He pulled the Citation over to the side and ran down the embankment to see what he could do.

"Oh, God, somebody help her! She's not breathing!" a woman was yelling as John arrived. He looked down, saw a little girl's body at the bottom of the embankment, but he couldn't see any breathing either. None of the onlookers was even trying to do anything; they just stood and stared. He pushed his way through, and it seemed for a moment as if the crowd was actually resisting him. Once past them, he saw a man and a woman standing nearby, evidently the woman he had just heard cry out. Presumably, they were the girl's parents.

"Don't touch her," a man in the crowd said, yanking at John's coat.

He turned and looked at the man. Pinched face, a cap advertising International Harvester. "I have some medical training," he said coolly, turning back to the girl.

Reaching down to pick up her wrist, he assessed the situation. True, he couldn't see any evidence of breathing, but her body was not twisted in any way, nor were her limbs. There was little blood, only a few relatively minor scratches. She was a very pretty child, blonde, wearing a T-shirt and jeans; her coat had been ripped off and lay up the bank. For an instant he could see her in happier days, on a swing in her light blue dress, patent leather shoes held up to the camera—

Camera?

He ignored that stray thought and felt for a pulse. It was there; weak, but there. Lifting her eyelid, he watched the iris contract in response to the sudden light. Quickly, he began to apply mouth-to-mouth resuscitation. Behind him, he could hear the voices of the people he assumed to be the parents.

"Please help her, mister. God, she's just a little girl." This from the woman.

"She was ridin' in the back of the pickup when we wrecked. We couldn't even find her for a minute," said a man's voice.

John started to give the child another breath when she breathed back into his face; he smiled broadly. Hopefully she didn't have any major internal injuries. It was a toss-up; she'd been thrown quite a distance, but had landed in a patch of dense but soft vegetation, which was brown and dry for the winter. It had broken much of her fall; she'd gone through about fifteen feet of it down the embankment. Her eyes flickered, then opened. Good sign. At least a few things turn out right, he told himself.

The parents rushed up and knelt by the girl, the woman sobbing hysterically. The man turned to him. "Thanks for he'pin' my Amy, mister," he said.

"No problem. Just make her use the seat belt from now on,

okay?'' He thought he saw a flicker of resentment in the man's eyes. It would have helped if he wasn't so damn sure that six months from now, the girl would be riding without a seat belt anyway. But now, she was sitting up, supported by her mother's arm. John looked back at her and their eyes met.

As they did, she gave voice to a tremendous scream, followed by words that made no sense: "He killed me! God, oh Mommie, he cut my throat! I wouldn't fuck him, so he killed me!'' Her eyes grew very wide. She screamed again, an impossibly loud, high-pitched sound. Then, a strange cry: "Aiiii-yii-yi! The Smoking Mirror! The Smoking Mirror!''

John just stared at her, frozen. What in the hell? Her mother was trying to console her and scold her for the obscenity at the same time. The rest of the crowd, including the father, was looking at John in a peculiar fashion. Surely, they couldn't believe it! They were all standing right there watching him; they had seen what happened. All he'd done was give the girl artificial respiration until she came around. They'd all seen that. Hadn't they? What the hell was the matter with them, anyway?

More people were running down from the road, asking what had happened. The pinch-faced man in the crowd yelled out, "The big man down there! With the beard! He tried ta rape th' little girl whilst she was out cold!''

Again John was frozen for a few seconds, unable to believe that the man had actually said that. He had to have seen, he'd been right there—

"Let's get him!'' somebody else shouted. Several men rushed at him. He looked to the father for defense, but to his shock the man said nothing. When the other men were almost on him, he suddenly jumped toward them, bowling two of them over with his sheer weight and momentum. The crowd took a moment to react to this, and John raced up the bank toward his car, reaching it several seconds ahead of the crowd. Jumping inside, he fumbled for the keys, found them, and the engine roared to life. He started to pull away just as a man grabbed at the handle of his door.

Out on the highway again, he saw in his rearview mirror that a variety of cars and pickups were pulling out, apparently in pursuit. At that moment, he wished he'd been a criminal these last few years instead of a medical student, intern, mu-

sician, potter. At least he'd know how to run. As it was, he'd
have to play it by ear. He pushed the Citation as hard as he
could, watching the speedometer rise: sixty-five, seventy-five,
eighty-five. The speedometer peaked out, but he kept pushing,
fervently hoping there were no highway patrol cars about. He
glanced back. His pursuers were there, but well back, too far
to read his license plate. But as long as he stayed on 95, he
couldn't expect to lose them. He had to do something. Up
ahead he saw an exit, and there was a shallow dip in the highway ahead of it. He decided to try for it; for a moment, he'd
be out of their sight, near the exit. If he could swing onto it,
they might just go on straight. A quarter mile from the exit,
he hit the brakes; the car slewed sideways, but he managed to
keep it on the road. He was still doing sixty-five when he
turned; the car leaned heavily, but again he retained control,
sped on down the secondary road at about sixty. A half hour
later, when he'd seen no sign of pursuit, he breathed a sigh of
relief. Apparently it had worked. He hoped they hadn't gotten
his license number.

He stayed on the secondary roads until he was a good hundred miles inside Virginia, then returned to the highway. If
they'd gotten his number, he was going to be pulled over sooner
or later anyhow.

16

Throughout dinner, David and Susan had hardly said a word.
For the second day in a row, their conversation on seeing each
other had centered around the day's weird events. Susan was
particularly distressed; all afternoon Jeannie had continued to
look at her in the strangest way, and had agreed with everything she said. She had the feeling that if she suggested that
Jeannie walk in front of a truck, she'd do it. She reminded
Susan of nothing so much as a little red-haired puppy, so ter-

ribly eager to please, and Susan found it very annoying. Especially from a normally independent person like Jeannie.

She didn't know what to think about Danny's impending visit. It was exciting, if odd; David seemed to accept the man as a psychic with no questions or reservations at all. He had told Susan about his abilities in the same manner as if he had been telling her that the man was a car salesman. She hadn't known David felt that way about the supernatural and such. If she had, she might have told him about her feeling that she had struck Jerry down the previous day. In any case, it had made it easier for her to tell him about the flowers. This he had not accepted so matter-of-factly, though he had seemed really excited, asked her to go over it several times. But he didn't treat her like she was crazy; he appeared not to doubt her at all.

Then there was the thing David brought home. He had to steal it, he said; he couldn't find one to buy. When she first saw it, she thought he had somehow known about her lunch with Jeannie; that wouldn't have been any stranger than some other recent events. But David was being mysterious; he said it had to do with something else. He sat it on the table and refused to talk about it, saying he didn't want to tell his story twice. She looked over at the object; a quite dead, brown, dried-up fern. He said he had stolen it from someone's windowsill on the next block.

Very strange, Susan told herself.

David paced restlessly, carrying a cup of coffee, periodically walking to the window and looking out. He checked the time again: 7:45. Damn, was the man coming? There were things here he felt an urgency about, things he had not really thought about for years; but recent events—particularly Susan's experience with the flowers—had brought it all back to him. When she'd told him about it, he had realized why they had been so intensely attracted to each other from the very beginning; they were two of a kind. And maybe Danny made it three of a kind. A very rare kind, if he was any judge. But he knew that events of this sort had a tendency to race out of control, and he wanted to get a handle on it before it got completely away from him. Like it had once before.

At five minutes to eight, their buzzer sounded; David almost pounced on it. "Who is it?" he asked, speaking into the intercom.

"Danny Hudson. Have I got the right place?"

"Yes. I'll buzz you in." He pressed the button, and they heard Danny come into the lobby. A few minutes later he was in the apartment.

David went through the common amenities, introducing Susan, offering Danny coffee or a beer. Danny took the coffee. He seemed very uncomfortable. David wasn't surprised; he'd be uncomfortable too, in Danny's position. In fact, he wasn't sure he would have come at all, and he wondered why Danny had.

The fact was, Danny was miserable. He had decided that afternoon that he wasn't coming over here tonight. If this dude wanted him, he could come looking; he knew Danny's name. But as the day wore on, he began to doubt that he had the will to resist. It was as if Hallsten had commanded him to be there, and he couldn't fight it. Or maybe his curiosity was just overwhelming him; after all, he had wanted to get close to these people, to find out what was going on. Wasn't this a great opportunity to do just that? And in the end, he had gone, kicking stones on the street as he walked, like a small boy coming in from play when he didn't really want to. Now he wondered what the hell he was doing here. He believed in being invisible, and he wasn't; he felt as if he was being X-rayed.

He watched the reddish-brown wisps of color playing around David and Susan and caught something else, just a shadow. With a start, he realized there was more truth to that than he thought. David was looking into him; this man was like him. Not as developed in some ways—no, that wasn't right—developed in different ways. Maybe repressing it, as Danny had once tried to do. But there was something; he knew it. He started to say something, but shut it off. Let's see exactly what happens first, he told himself. You've already committed a lot, and it didn't work out like you thought, so let's be a little more cautious.

But he didn't know if he could be. He didn't know how much of himself David could see.

For several minutes they sat and drank coffee in silence. At last Danny said, "Well, look, folks, this isn't exactly a social visit. What exactly do you want from me?"

"I want to know what you know. All of it," David said flatly.

"I pretty much told you this afternoon."

"Take a look at Susan there. Do whatever you do. See if you get anything."

Danny looked over at her, sitting beside David on the couch. Very pretty indeed, he thought; smoky eyes. He sighed. Might as well go all the way. He squinted and crossed his eyes slightly, wondering if they were going to laugh.

They didn't, but he really wasn't getting anything other than the persistent reddish sexual swirls he had seen around them before. He grinned mentally. Some of the swirls were moving from Susan toward him; she did not find him unattractive.

"What are you getting?" asked David.

"Not a whole lot. Just the—well—ah—"

"What?"

"Well, you folks are—ah—right sexy people, know what I mean? Ah—with each other and stuff—"

"Okay." David nodded. This was not news.

Danny squirmed. How much could David see? He couldn't tell. It really puts me at a disadvantage with him, he thought.

David turned to his wife. "I don't know if you can do this, but, do you think you can put yourself in the same state of mind you were in at lunch?"

"That's just it, David," she said. "I really wasn't in any odd state of mind. It was just me, like always. Nothing unusual."

"Well, try, anyhow," he said.

Susan appeared a bit annoyed, but she seemed to be trying. David looked at Danny.

"Are you getting anything different?" he asked.

Danny shook his hand. "Not a thing," he replied, wondering what was significant about Susan's lunch.

"Let me try just thinking about what happened," she suggested. "But I'm not really sure what you're after."

"Never mind that right now; just trust me," David said, patting her hand.

As she concentrated, Danny focused on her again. Same old thing. Red-brown wisps of sensuality; neither of them ever seemed to put out anything else. Then, subtly, a shift. Just a little. He tried to catch it, but it was fleeting; he worked harder, and began to see a reddish-brown glow in the middle of her. That was new. Almost like a faint light was shining on her.

"I'm getting something different," he said, flicking his eyes over at David. He started. David had a similar glow in the middle of his body, but his was verdant green. Not the usual greens Danny associated with potentially dangerous emotions like jealousy, but a leafy green; a very pleasant color. He looked back at Susan and saw that her reddish brown glow had gotten much brighter, shifted to a sort of rich auburn shade. He uncrossed his eyes and opened them wide to cut off the vision momentarily. But it didn't cut off. He could still see them glowing with his normal vision, bright lights in the centers of their bodies near the navel area. The colors were now getting brighter than the room lights; there were tendrils of light emerging from the color centers, like fine tentacles, reaching out into the room, some apparently passing through the walls to the outside. A larger number of the green and auburn tentacles were intertwined between them. With a shock Danny realized that several tentacles of each color reached out to him. He looked down, saw a thick auburn tentacle penetrating his own body around his navel. He looked up at their faces, and for just a moment they didn't even seem to have heads. They appeared to be glowing eggs of color with millions of light tentacles flowing around them. Then he could see the bodies again through the light, their faces serene, but their eyes seemingly unfocused.

Danny choked a little, found his voice. "My God," he said. "What the hell—?"

His speaking seemed to break the moment. They looked at him, the colors rapidly fading away, the tentacles becoming fainter and disappearing in a matter of a few seconds.

"What did you see? Something?" David said eagerly.

"God, yes. What did you feel?"

"I don't know; nothing really unusual. I was just relaxed, trying not to interfere with Susan—"

"I didn't feel any real difference either," Susan put in. "As a matter of fact, my mind was kind of blank, you know? At ease."

"I'd hate to see you people any more relaxed!" Danny cried. He tried to explain what he had seen.

"What does it mean?" David asked.

"Damned if I know. I never saw anything like it. I keep seeing things around you people I've never seen before. Look"—he was getting a little desperate—"I'm not sure I really believe you don't know anything about all this. What the hell is with you, anyway? For one thing, you're just too damn cool about it. It ain't normal. Most people would be freaked, a crazy man comin' in here tellin' 'em they look like fucking Easter eggs and all!"

David held up his hand to stop Danny's slightly panicky outburst. "Maybe you're right," he said. "Maybe I do know something. But I don't know what's setting this off again now, and mister, I want to know. I've had enough of this shit to last me a lifetime already."

Susan looked at him. "David? What are you talking about?"

He got up off the couch and began to pace again. "I think all this is coming from me. Somehow. But why now?" He stopped and looked at them; they both appeared to be hanging on his words. "I know you don't know, Susan, and of course you couldn't, Mr. Hudson, unless—"

"Danny," he said.

"All right, Danny. You couldn't know unless you're one hell of a good psychic. But I'm going to tell you what I think I know, and maybe we can figure out something together."

As David was speaking, Danny wondered if maybe he really just ought to get up and leave. He had now seen all manner of odd things in association with this couple, but not a bit of it of any use at all. He didn't even know if he would ever get a satisfactory interpretation of the images; he was beginning to suspect that he wouldn't. The other issue was David himself. Now, the woman was acting right; curious about him, maybe a little scared of him. But David—He just couldn't understand the man. He was treating Danny like a long-lost buddy, including him in the process of trying to solve this mystery like he was one of the family, and it definitely made him uncomfortable. But he couldn't deny he was curious about these people; he sure hadn't seen any others like them. What could it hurt to sit and listen to the man talk?

David started out addressing himself directly to his wife. "Susan, you know part of my childhood, we've talked about it some. I've told you that I grew up on a farm in Nebraska, and that I was orphaned at fourteen by a house fire that killed both my parents."

"Yes, David, I knew all that."

"Well, what you don't know is that I was directly responsible for that fire. Oh, I didn't set it or anything, but I might as well have. It happened because of some things that happened to me, what I've always called the Incidents. Well, I've stopped the Incidents, or at least I thought I had. But now, well, maybe not."

"David, what are you talking about?" Susan asked reasonably.

"I'd better start at the beginning; I can't expect either of you to understand if I ramble around." He paused, cleared his throat. "When I was twelve years old, man, I can remember being happy as a clam. Everything was right in my little world. My dad was a farmer; corn, like most of the neighbors. Every year we got good crops. We always had the money for what we wanted, I had lots of friends, and I did well in school, did well at games, did well. I can still see myself then—not a care in the world. I knew my whole life, it was laid out for me. I'd inherit the farm and grow corn like my dad, marry a farm girl, have lots of kids, grandkids, the whole works. The great middle American dream.

"But the summer after my fourteenth birthday, it all changed. And overnight I knew that the world was not always kind, that everything you expected could be gone suddenly. See, that summer, in early August, we had a drought. Just a simple little drought. Happens all the time. So the crops aren't what they should be this year—all farmers have to ride through a bad year every now and again. We could do it. I remember my dad sitting down and working it all out. It would be no big problem. We'd have a small Christmas this year, but otherwise we'd never notice it. And next year the crops would be good again, and everything would be all right.

"Well, it didn't work like that. This drought dragged on and on. By November it still hadn't rained a drop in our county. The year's crop had been given up. The land, God, I'll never forget it; it looked blasted. Desolate. Just dust, everywhere you looked. You couldn't walk around without raising a cloud of dust. We were dirty ten minutes after we left the house in the morning.

"December came, and still no rain. Then we heard a prediction of a blizzard. Finally, we thought; snow is even better, it doesn't run off so fast. We waited for it. We were going to celebrate it.

"We got the blizzard, but not the snow. For some reason not a flake fell on our farm, or any of the farms around. But we got the wind—howling winds, eighty or ninety miles an hour. The windmill out back fell down. We thought the house was going to go. It lasted all night. It was a night I'll never forget.

"Next morning, we could see what it had done to us. The wind had taken all the topsoil from our farm; taken it somewhere else. Like the dust bowl in the thirties. The same had happened to the other farmers in the county. My dad stood in the back door, I can see him now, that wind still blowing thirty miles an hour, crying like a baby. I'd never seen him cry before. I thought the world had ended, and I ran to my room and cried too.

"Come the next spring, all the farmers scrabbled at the hard surface and tried to plant some seed. But it was no good. Most of the seed didn't even sprout, and what did was dying off at an inch high. I don't know if you can understand the feeling. Every year before I could remember, the fields had pretty, neat, little green rows of healthy plants. This year there was just these pitiful looking things, leaves all brown on the tips. Everybody in our area just walked around like they were dead. I heard my parents talking late at night; sure, maybe we could survive another bad year, but with the ground like that we aren't going to have any more good years. Maybe not ever. Maybe we should give up the farm. Then Mama would cry and Dad'd put his head down on the table. God, I felt bad. Bad for them and bad for myself.

"Then I started having the dreams. At first I didn't pay much attention; everybody has dreams and nightmares, particularly when real life is uncertain. But these dreams persisted, the same kind of thing, night after night. It was like, well, they should have been nightmares, but they weren't. I hated to wake up from them. Or maybe I just hated to get up and look at the pitiful crops outside. I figured it could have been either one.

"But by any standards, these were weird dreams. I became aware of myself in the dream looking down from a great height,

like I was looking out of an airplane window. But I wasn't in
a plane, and I wasn't standing on anything either. It wasn't
even like I was flying. I was just there. I didn't have any awareness of body, just a floating consciousness, at a great height. I
could see the whole county at once. But at the same time, I
could see details on the ground as well. I could even see myself
in bed, having the dream, could see right through the roof. It
was very exhilarating at first. I could see everybody, see what
they were doing at night. First few times I had these dreams,
I just floated around looking.

"But I didn't make anything of it for a while. I didn't talk
to my folks about it. They had other things on their mind. But
then something happened.

"One night I was having this same dream, and in the dream
I was looking into the Elkin house. They were neighbors of
ours. I saw a man break in, saw him cut the screen on a window and climb through. Old man Elkin must have heard him,
though, because I saw him get up, get his shotgun, and go
searching through the house. But the burglar, who was a kid I
knew from the county seat, saw him first, and he had a gun
too; a pistol. He shot old man Elkin dead in his living room,
then ran out.

"When I woke up the next morning, I didn't think much
about it. But you might have guessed already what happened.
Later in the day I found out that old man Elkin was dead, shot
in his own home by a burglar. I was really shook. I had always
taken these dreams as just dreams. I never thought I was looking at real events. I thought I should tell somebody, but I didn't
know how. After all, I knew who the killer was!

"As it turned out, it didn't matter. They caught the kid, the
same kid, the next day. He still had the gun. It was an open-
and-shut case.

"Next time I had the dream, I tried to concentrate on the
corn, which was about to die out completely. I wanted to see
if there was anything I could do. I don't even know what made
me think I could do anything at all. It was just what was on
my mind. And maybe I didn't want to look in the houses, see
any more murders. But what I did see, out there in the cornfields, set events in motion that didn't stop for years.

"I saw a young girl, lying in the fields all alone. She was
about my age—I was fourteen, like I said—and she looked so

sick. It looked like clumps of her hair had fallen out, she had sores and cuts all over. I had never seen her before. But as I looked, she seemed familiar in some way; I still don't know how or why. A runaway, I thought. But what had happened to her? She seemed to be dying. I looked at her closely. Under all the sores, in spite of them, she was really beautiful. It sounds trite, but the only way I can explain it is that my heart ached for her. You have to be fourteen to truly understand that. When we get older most of us don't acknowledge feelings like that anymore.

"I looked at her light blond hair, spread out on the ground. Her eyes were green, and she was staring straight up at the night sky. I seemed to be looking at her from a little to the right. Then I got a surprise. Something happened that had never happened in the dreams before. She turned her head and looked right at me.

"Well, of course, I thought that was just coincidence, she had happened to turn and look in the direction I seemed to be looking at her from. But no. Then it got weirder. She spoke to me.

" 'I'm glad you're here. Please help me. I've been waiting so long.'

"You know how you look around to see who somebody is talking to sometimes, when you can't believe it's you? Well, that's what I did. But there was no one there. She was either speaking to me or the thin air.

"I had never before spoken in these dreams, although I could hear other peoples' voices. But now I tried; I said, 'What happened to you?' And it boomed out across the fields like thunder. I could see little things, I don't know, little scrolls of light flying down across those fields toward her. She rolled over and hid her face. I looked around, and I could see lights coming on in the nearby houses. One house becoming lit up was my own. The view in front of me began to fade, and then was replaced—kind of faded into—a view from inside my bedroom. I could hear my parents downstairs. I listened for a moment. They were asking each other what that loud noise had been! Then it hit me; the same loud noise had caused me to wake up! I was shaking like a leaf. I didn't know what to do or what to think. I got up and looked out the window. Little sparks of blue and green light danced over the cornfields, then faded away.

"The next day was a school day, but I couldn't go to school. I was physically sick, probably in shock. I didn't know what was happening to me. But that night, I determined to go out in the cornfields where I had seen the girl, try to find her again. I didn't doubt she was real.

"So after dinner, I said I was still sick and went to my room, but instead of going to bed I climbed out the window and down a tree, and ran out into the corn to look for her. The place where I had seen her in the dream was not too far, in a neighbor's field, and his land adjoined ours. I could remember the dream images, looking down from above. It seemed like the spot I'd seen her was right in the middle of the county. It was, too. Later I checked that on a map. I don't know if that means anything or not.

"Sure enough, when I got there, she was sitting on the ground in a blue dress, holding herself with her arms like she was racked with pain. She looked up at me as I came to her, said something like, 'I'm glad you came back.' Her voice was real weak. I thought I ought to get her to a doctor.

"I tried to tell her to come with me, we'd go to the emergency room in town. But she shook her head. 'A doctor is no use,' she said. 'But you are here. You can help me.' I didn't know what she was talking about. I sat down on the ground in front of her. So pretty, and so sick! But still I had to ask the question that burned me.

" 'What did you see last night? Who were you talking to?'

"She looked up at me. Her eyes were big and green, real green. She said, 'You. I saw you. Here. You asked me what happened.' Then she bent her head and started to cry. Big tears, I can still see them, dropping from her eyelashes to the hard ground. 'But you know it isn't my fault. I have tried to live. But I don't think I can. It's too hard.'

"For a second I just watched her, hardly able to believe what I was hearing, but not really able to doubt it either. She was crying so much the ground in front of her was wet. It looked shiny, like a snail's track.

" 'But how did you see me? I was asleep in my bed. I wasn't here. It was a dream!' I told her. This seemed to upset her even more, and she threw herself facedown on the ground. Her whole body shook with her sobs. I couldn't stand it.

"I got up from where I was sitting and walked toward her. I was going to try to comfort her or something, I guess. But as I walked, I slipped a little and my heel caught one of the little three-inch corn plants in the row there. One that was still hanging on to life. But as I looked at my shoe, I realized I had uprooted it, crushed the fragile root. It didn't seem important, one little corn plant.

"But she jerked on the ground, just as it happened. I looked, and saw one of her fingers crushed and bleeding, like I had stepped on her finger instead of the plant. She wailed even louder. I was afraid somebody would hear and come out there. And I felt, well, territorial about this. This was mine alone.

"I knew something was real weird here. I said, 'Who *are* you?'

" 'You know who I am. You have turned your face from me, and I will die here on this barren ground. What have I done? Please tell me, so I do not repeat my sins.'

"Then words just came out of me. It wasn't like anyone else was speaking, it was me, but I didn't know what I was talking about. I said, 'It is not your fault'—and here I used a word I'd never before heard, and not since—'Xilonen.' It seemed like it was her name. I said, 'The land has withdrawn its favor, the people do not know how to appease it.' It's hard to communicate this to you now. I kept spouting these things without the slightest idea of what I was saying. But it seemed to make sense at the time.

" 'Then you must tell them, else I shall surely die,' she said. 'Tell them soon, please.' She got to her feet then. 'I must go now. But tell them. At least leave me a little life. For you, it is so easy.' Then she got up and ran away. It was an awkward, limping run, like she had a sprained ankle. But even so, she disappeared into the darkness and I couldn't find her. Finally, I went home and to bed. I didn't dream that night.

"The next day I got up and felt fine. I wanted to find the girl again, but I felt I had a mission; it was like I'd had it all along, but didn't know it. I felt magical. I was going to save the county. Somehow I knew what to do. I still told my folks I was sick. Since I hardly ever missed school, they didn't argue, and I stayed home. Just about noon I went out into our cornfields. I took my pocketknife out and cut my hand, right here where the little webbing between the fingers is. It bled a lot, and it hurt, but I didn't mind. I walked all over that cornfield, dripping blood on the ground. I guess I was in a kind of ecstasy. Every time it stopped bleeding I pushed the cut open again. I must have been out there two hours, bleeding in the cornfield. My hand hurt like hell. Part of me didn't know what I was doing, and it's real hard to explain now, but it just seemed so damn right. Then I washed my hand off and went to sleep for a while.

"I didn't dream that night either. Next day, I got up and looked outside. Both my parents were already out there, wandering around in the cornfield, looking a little dazed. The corn seedlings had only been three or four inches high the day before, and about half dead. This morning most of them were over a foot high, very green and strong looking. I felt strange. I should have been surprised, shocked, excited, something like that. But I wasn't. I was just pleased. Pleased like a normal fourteen-year-old is with a good catch in a baseball game. Nothing less than what's expected of you in the circumstances. That day I went to school, and I saw that it was only our fields that had improved. Everybody else's still looked like they had the day before.

"That night, I still didn't dream, but I woke up for some reason; I remember it was just before sunrise. The sky was purplish gray, and you could already see the fields. Our corn was about eighteen inches average. At that time of year, two feet would have been considered a bumper crop in the making. I climbed down out of the window and walked across the field. There was a little rise back there, off to the east of where the house was. I saw the girl again. She was completely healthy looking as far as I could tell, and she was dancing in the fields. Then the sun broke over the ridge, and I've got to tell you, there's no describing the feeling at that moment. The sun rising, the fields green and lush, and that beautiful girl dancing on the ridge. I just fell down on my knees for a minute. I was crying like a baby. You had to see it to know what I felt. Then the sun was up, and she was gone. I looked for her for an hour, but I couldn't find her.

"The next day, the fantastic growth rate of the corn had come back to normal, but we had a great crop going. I remember feeling really satisfied. Several days passed, and I was not having the dreams. I had looked for the girl every day, but I hadn't seen her again. I believed everything was right with the world again.

"But I was wrong. About a week later, I came home from school and found about five of our neighbors over at the house. I was starting to go in and say hello to everybody—we had considered all these men friends—when I realized this was not a happy occasion. I found out that this was not the first discussion about why our fields were doing well while everyone else was suffering. My dad told them he didn't know, but they thought he was holding out on them. Now it had turned ugly, and this afternoon they were threatening to beat him up if he didn't share the secret.

"Finally they actually did start to beat him. Two of them held his arms, and another was punching him in the stomach. I couldn't take it. I ran up and grabbed at them, screaming that I had done it, I had the secret. One of them grabbed me by the shirt and lifted me right off the floor. I didn't know until then just how desperate they were. When he did, my mother came running, trying to hit him; another one hit her and she went down. It was a nightmare.

"So they demanded that I tell them. I told them that the land needed 'the blood of self-sacrifice.' Even now I have no idea where that phrase came from. It just popped into my head. I expected them to laugh at me and figured they'd lock me up if I tried to tell them the whole story. But they didn't laugh. They just let go of me. I suppose they thought I was crazy, I don't know. But they obviously didn't accept my story, because they told my dad that they'd be back, and he'd better tell them the whole story.

"Then, over the next few days, it seemed that my story had gotten around. I started getting teased about it at school. Our preacher came by and talked to me, but only obliquely referred to my statement. He just wanted to caution me about getting mixed up in satanic ideas. I didn't connect, then, what he was saying with what had happened. It didn't have anything to do with Satan, not as far as I was concerned.

"But of course, it didn't end there. There was a family down the road from us that had two sons, and they were—I don't know—maybe a little retarded. But they had heard about my now-famous pronouncement, and I guess they'd seen too many late shows. What they did was incredible. They decided to sacrifice someone to the land, just in case I was right. So they kidnapped a girl on her way home from school. You have to remember that these were midwestern farmers. They took a .22 rifle and the knife they used to slaughter hogs, and they treated her just like she was a hog; shot her in the head, then cut her throat and drained out the blood. After that they just took it and dumped it in the middle of the field. They buried the body, but right away some dogs dug it up. But still, the police didn't arrest them until three days later. By that time they'd killed another girl in the same way. They really were amazing. The police got suspicious because they were asking around to try to find out who was a virgin and who wasn't. Like I said, too many late shows.

"Well, you can imagine that there was hell to pay. What I couldn't understand then—and maybe not now either—was how I got blamed for it somehow. I never suggested these idiots go out and kill a couple of people. But a lot of people seemed to think I was responsible, and there was a lot of talk.

"There was especially a lot of talk about our fields, and that led to more disaster. One night we looked out the front window and there was a mob coming; just like something out of a Frankenstein movie. Apparently they thought I was in league with Satan or something. I never knew.

"So here they came, some of them even carrying torches, for God's sake. I'm sure they had in fact gotten the idea from a Frankenstein movie. The trouble was, I was the monster. I could see the farmer whose boys had killed the two girls. He and a preacher from some little fundamentalist church were leading the group. It wasn't like they were carrying a rope in hand or anything. I don't really think they knew what they wanted to do. Just something. It had been decided that I was evil. So before they got a chance to surround the house, my dad told me to run away and hide, across the field in the back of the house. I did. As I was leaving, I could see the county sheriff and our own preacher, the one who'd talked to me earlier, drive up. They stood on the porch and tried to talk to the mob.

"What happened then, I don't know. I heard gunshots, screaming; then the house was blazing. I forgot all about the danger to myself and ran back, screaming for my parents. When I got there, the house was an inferno. On the front lawn was the sheriff and our preacher, both of them shot dead. People were milling around everywhere, a lot of them with guns. A few were actually dancing some wild crazy dance. The fundamentalist preacher was up on a car, preaching a sermon, but nobody was listening.

"Then they saw me coming up across the yard. Somebody screamed 'There he is!' and they all started running at me. A couple of men aimed their guns at me, and I was sure I was done for. Dead.

"Those next few minutes, everything was moving in slow motion. I could see, in the light from the fire, one of those men take careful aim at me and start squeezing the trigger. I knew he wouldn't miss. And I thought, maybe if I can speak like I did in the dream, maybe I can stop them. I tried to look down on them a little. I couldn't do that, so I closed my eyes, gathered all my strength, and yelled 'STOP!'

"And nothing happened. Just a scared little boy yelling. I remember sobbing then, saying to no one in particular, 'Please help me. I've got things to do.' What a thing to say when you're about to die, right? I guess we've all got things to do when it's too late to do them anymore. Anyway, I didn't want to give them the satisfaction of watching me cringe. So, probably again from watching too many movies, I pulled myself up to my full height and waited to die.

"Then something happened. The man with the gun looked up, off to my left. The crowd of people rushing at me slowed down, looking off in the same direction. I looked too. There was an old man standing there. God, I couldn't believe it. He really didn't look alive. He looked like the oldest man you ever saw. Legs and arms like toothpicks, wrinkled and sunken. He was very dark, maybe an Indian, I thought. But he wasn't wearing feathers or moccasins or anything. He was wearing some kind of a dress, it looked like. Then I thought maybe he was Egyptian, or something like that. Whatever, whoever he was, he sure did look strange—and imposing—out there in the Nebraska night, lit up by the burning house. He was so deeply wrinkled that the firelight made his skin seem to squirm. He sure wasn't anybody from around there.

"Then the crowd started moving toward us again. He held up his hand as if to command them to stop, and the man who'd been aiming at me took aim at him. Then the old man did something strange. I remember it so clearly, in such detail. His hand was straight up, palm out, in a traffic-cop gesture. He rolled it over, a finger at a time, until it was palm up, fingers pointed at the gunman. Then he closed his fist with a snap.

"And the gunman fell straight forward, facedown, and didn't move again.

"The people in the mob looked at him, backed up a step, then surged forward. Some of them were yelling. The old man extended both hands palms up, closed his eyes, and snapped his fists shut.

"The results were even more incredible. About three rows of people in the front keeled over. They didn't squirm, or jump, or anything, they just went down. I guess it was about twenty people or so. The rest of them stopped, and those who had guns started to aim at him. He did the same thing, but faster. Then there were only a few people left standing. Most of them started to run the other way. The only one left then was the preacher. He was still on top of the car. He started screaming 'Begone, Satan!' or something like that. The old man just pointed at him. He was still yelling, but no sound was coming out.

"Then the old man looked at me. His eyes were absolutely black, and they glittered in the firelight. He didn't say a word. He just turned and walked away in the darkness. I've never seen him again.

"The preacher had run off. There was nobody left moving but me. I went up to some of the people on the ground. These had been my friends, my neighbors. I couldn't find any that were breathing. They all seemed to be dead.

"So I ran off, too, to the gas station about a mile down the road, and called the state police. I didn't know what else to do. When they came out, they found forty-three people dead in our yard. Only four of them had reason to be; my parents, our preacher, and the sheriff. I'll never forget hearing a cop say that the coroner had said that they just stopped living. Then a nightmare of questions, red tape, and more questions. I'm sure they didn't believe my story about the old man for a minute. But they didn't have any good ideas about how all of those people ended up dead. They were absolutely determined to keep it out of the papers, too, and that wasn't going to be easy. All those people dead, all those relatives asking questions,

questions they didn't have any answers for. They figured I was the only one with answers, and they were determined to get them out of me. But I didn't really have any. They put me under hypnosis, called in a professor of some sort from the university, even called in a priest. It just dragged on and on. All this time I was effectively being kept jailed. Finally some psychiatrist suggested it might have been some kind of mass hysteria, brought on by the stresses of the bad crop year. By this time I don't think they cared anymore. They were going to jump on the first reasonable answer they got. That became the official line. The killings of the girls was cited as evidence that this had been coming.

"But they still didn't let me go. I don't know why. I guess they really didn't believe their own line. But my uncle came in from Key West with a lawyer, and finally, after a bunch of court orders, I was released to him, and went with him to live in Key West.

"That was what I consider to be my first Incident."

17

As David was finishing his story, the brightly lighted George Washington Bridge was host to two different cars coming from two different points; two cars among the thousands. The timing was such that the two, a Citation and a Toyota, arrived at the bridge at nearly the same time, the Citation a bit ahead. But the Toyota was moving just a little faster, and it overtook the Citation on the bridge and passed it. It happened that at this particular time, one of the drivers looked to his left, the other to his right; and a bearded man in a work shirt looked at a cold-eyed man in a suit, and vice versa. Though neither could have said why, they noticed each other; each wondered if he'd seen the other somewhere before. Both felt a little odd as their cars approached the western wall of the city. Neither knew why. Both had other things to be thinking of; a matter of a life, a matter of a death. Both thought they might just possibly have been pursued in connection with these matters. They would go from here to different destinations. One would stay at a friend's apartment, an apartment within sight of the bridge. The other would check into a hotel in the downtown theater district. Tomorrow morning, both would find a letter addressed to them; a letter offering a free gift if they came to look at a land development on Long Island called Tascan Acres. Both would wonder how these people had gotten their address so fast, especially since both addresses were temporary. But the lives of both these men, already vastly different from the lives they were each living the previous day, would again be changed forever by this letter. At the moment they locked eyes on the bridge both realized, at least on a deeper level, that they were caught up in events far beyond their control.

Out on Long Island, an incredibly old man wrapped in a blanket was talking to a woman who was known to many as Maria. This was not, in fact, her name. Anyone who looked at her would have guessed that she was Mexican. They would have said she was neither ugly nor pretty, tall nor short, fat nor thin. Just a Mexican woman, dark-haired, dark-eyed, dark-skinned. But if they were at all observant, they would have commented on her imposing presence. She sat now on the floor in front of the old man, her legs crossed, her colorful long skirt spread. It looked like she didn't have legs. The old man had only a face, peeping out of the pile of woolens. The trailer had grown very cold again. Neither Maria nor the old man seemed to notice or care.

"Then all is in order?" he was asking in his cultured baritone.

"Yes. Everything has been arranged."

"Excellent. They are beginning to become aware of themselves in some ways. But the time is very short. They must be in Tlillan Tlapallan on the day appointed in the Tonalamatl. It may be necessary to complete some of their preparations there."

"We can do that?"

"Yes. It is not a problem. It would be far worse if any of them had to be taken to that place against their wills."

"Of course."

"We will therefore continue as we have."

"Yes. It will be done." She got up, a graceful fluid motion that didn't seem to require the use of any muscles. Without another word, she turned and left the trailer. She had no coat, only a thin white cotton blouse and a serape. But even outside, she seemed indifferent to the icy wind blowing off Long Island Sound. There were no stars over the water; the overcast night was very dark here. But she could see without difficulty, if one judged from the sureness of her step. As she started to walk from the trailer to the Oldsmobile parked in front, she noticed the light from the city, miles away, illuminating the western sky before her, casting its light up onto the low clouds. She stopped for a minute and looked at it.

"Such an evil place, a sea of poisons," she said aloud. Her eyes were hard. She paused for a moment, then squatted on the sand where she stood, hiking her skirt up so her knees were exposed. A trickle of water, then a full stream, fell to the sand from beneath her skirt. She held up the cloth with her right hand, and put the left under her; it came out wet. She hurled the droplets of water into the sky in front of her; they seemed to explode in midair like tiny bombs, flashing red and green. She repeated the procedure four times. Feeling much better, she got into the Oldsmobile and drove off.

Only a block or two from the apartment where David was relating his childhood experience to Susan and Danny, Leo Frykowski slumped in an alley, quite drunk on Thunderbird wine. He was thinking about all the different ways he would have to pay for this tomorrow. As soon as he could get up, he told himself, he should be going home; Edie would be waiting, and she sure would be pissed. His train of thought was interrupted by a very pretty dark-haired girl, walking by on the street. She undoubtedly thought she was alone. The street was deserted, and Leo was at rest in shadow. She could not have seen him.

Idly, he wondered if she was scared; she was so very attractive, and very small, very alone-looking. Well, she wouldn't welcome his company, no doubt, even if he was sober, which he emphatically was not. He contented himself with watching her perfect legs as she walked along.

Then she stopped, and Leo thought she might have seen him. She was about thirty feet away. He stayed very still and watched. No, she had seen something in the street, just over the curb; he couldn't see what it was. She glanced around, then reached down and picked it up. As she did, Leo could see it.

A dead sparrow. A sparrow that had been dead for quite a while, he thought. It was almost flat from cars running over it, and not a little dried out, at least on one side; but even as she held it, a small amount of liquid dripped from inside it somewhere. He wasn't quite as drunk, or at least not as aware of it, now. Why had she picked that thing up?

As he watched, she proceeded to eat it like it was Kentucky Fried Chicken.

The next day Leo stopped drinking for good.

18

David stopped, and put his hand over his eyes for a moment. He picked up his coffee cup and took a sip; it was cold.

"David, I never realized—" Susan said, feeling strangely numb, at a loss for words.

"Man, neither did I," Danny added. "I tell you, I was wondering from the beginning why you accepted my story at face value like that. Nobody else ever had. But now I understand. You, my friend, are a loony. You're certifiable. I never in all my life heard a tale like that. Egyptian magicians knocking people dead with a gesture! And that girl! She's supposed to be some kind of a corn goddess, I bet. That's good, man. Real good. I gotta remember this one. I'm leaving!"

David looked at him without smiling. "I sort of expected that kind or reaction from you. Wouldn't have been surprised if Susan had reacted the same. But if you'll wait a minute, I'd like to show you something."

"What? You got a magician in the closet? A goddess under the couch? Virgins slaughtered like hogs! That's sick, man, I tell you."

David did not reply. He went to the table by the door and picked up the plant he had brought home.

"What's that?" Danny asked.

"It's a dead fern. Look at it if you don't believe me. Somebody left it out in the cold and it died. I stole it."

Danny got up and fingered the plant. Dead fern all right. He couldn't argue with that. Pieces of the brittle brown fronds crumbled in his fingers and fell to the carpet.

"Now watch," David said. "Very few people have ever seen me do this, but I still can. At least I could a few years ago."

He produced a sewing needle from somewhere, quickly jabbed it into the tip of his index finger. Susan gasped; two big drops of blood appeared on his fingertip. He put the needle aside and, closing his eyes, pressed his fingertip into the soil around the base of the plant. Within a few seconds, a little greenish color appeared down in the center of the plant and began to spread up the fronds. It looked like someone was painting it green with an invisible brush. But more than that was happening; the fronds were also filling out, the surface of them shifting from the dry brown to a smooth, healthy texture. After a minute or two of this, David stopped. Withdrawing his hand from the soil, he smiled, perhaps a bit grimly.

Danny was speechless. He glanced at Susan; she was standing with her mouth open, evidently as surprised by this as he was.

Finally she spoke, finding her voice before Danny did. "You brought it back to life? Just like that? How? David, I don't understand!"

"Fact is, neither do I. But ever since that time when I was fourteen, I've been able to do this pretty much whenever I wanted to. I don't do it because people get hostile about it. I know that from experience. Or at least they get scared. I'm sure you know what I'm talking about, Danny."

Danny nodded. He still didn't trust himself to speak. But his head was buzzing. "I remember them talking about psychokinesis—mind over matter—when they were experimenting on me in the lab down in North Carolina. I could never do that. I don't know how to ask you, but, well, what else can you do?''

"Nothing that I know of. That's it. My one magnificent, useless talent. I've got a real green thumb.'' He smiled cynically.

"Have you ever tried it with a—uh—an animal?'' Danny asked.

"You were going to say person. No, I can't read your mind, Danny. My only clairvoyance or whatever was in the dreams, and I haven't had any of those for years. But I knew what you were thinking then anyway. And the answer is no. No, I can't; yes, I've tried. With a dog that was run over in the road, a dead fish, so on. Not with a person. But I never could.''

In a way that was a relief to Danny. But he felt a disturbed rumbling down inside himself. Based on what he had just seen, it was not so very easy to discount David's story. And the idea of mighty wizards stepping out of the darkness and killing people, corn goddesses dancing in the fields, did not fit comfortably into his world view. Even if all these events had happened twenty years ago, they seemed mighty close tonight. Danny found the image of the young girl as a corn goddess very familiar, and he didn't know why. Seemed like he'd heard of something like that somewhere before, a long time ago; but he couldn't place it.

"So what now?'' Danny said. "Now we know your big dark secret, and so what? It doesn't help make sense out of anything, and— Wait a minute. You said there were more things like this? Other things that happened to you later?''

"Yes. Several times. I always referred to them in my own mind as the Incidents—maybe I said that already—and a lot of my energy went toward making them stop. But none as dramatic as the first one. I haven't had one for years, unless this is one. That's what I'm getting at.''

"Well, I don't see any association—''

"Well, Susan and the flowers—''

"Huh?''

"Sorry, we didn't tell you about that yet.'' Briefly he synopsized Susan's luncheon, the suddenly blooming flowers. "What I thought is maybe I transferred this to Susan somehow. I was hoping you could find out, with your talents.''

"Sorry. I don't have talents like that. I wouldn't even know what to look for. But I'd guess it's possible. Judging from what I've picked up, you two are real close.''

David looked disappointed and frustrated. He really had had high hopes for this, but it was grinding away to nothing. They really didn't know any more than when they'd started.

Again Danny changed the subject, back to David's references to the subsequent Incidents in his life. Again David tried to pass it off. "It's not germane to what we're talking about," he said.

"How can we know that, David?" Susan put in. "We don't know what is going on. Danny or I might see it from a different perspective."

Mentally David cursed himself. The business about the other Incidents had just slipped out; he hadn't meant to mention them. But now he was trapped, and he'd have to talk about it, in general terms at least. "Well, like I said, I don't know what it has to do with anything, but several times, later on, I saw—ah—I don't know—ah—ghosts or monsters or something." This last came in a rush, his voice fading as he said it.

Danny looked at him calmly. You can't fault a man for seeing monsters when there are rattlesnakes in your beer, he told himself. "What kind of ghosts or monsters?"

"I don't know. I had some more dreams, the visionary dreams, I guess you'd call them. Once in the spring, in Key West, I—ah—there was a monster—actually a man, but he was a monster. I saw him in the dream. I had found those dreams to be accurate before, so why not then? But it couldn't have been real. I would have heard about it, on the news or whatever."

"Dammit, man, what did you see?" Danny demanded.

"Well, I saw this man. He and some others, they—ah—they killed another man. With arrows. Then they cut off his head. Then they—ah—they—"

"David?" this time from Susan. "What was it?"

"All right, dammit! They skinned him. Took off all his skin. At least the poor guy was already dead. Jesus, it was grotesque! They skinned his body and his head, worked with the skin, and then they—they—" He looked away from them, walked over to the window. "This one man, he wore the skin, like a costume. The head was a kind of a mask, and the body skin sort of like a leotard. Oh, man, it was hideous! He danced around wearing this poor bastard's skin. And all these people, they were so happy, throwing flowers and all—'' He paused, wiped his face. ''The body itself, they cut it up, cooked it, and ate it! I remember them saying that the thighs were the best part.''

''Where was this happening?'' Danny asked.

''I don't know. You know, it was funny; when I had the dreams in Nebraska I could always see exactly where I was. But in this one, I couldn't tell. Just somewhere. I remember thinking it was in the East, so if that was right, anywhere up the Keys or in Miami, maybe.''

''What else happened?''

''That was all.''

Danny looked at him suspiciously. He didn't have to be psychic to tell that the man was holding something back. He glanced over at Susan, and was pretty sure she could see it too. ''You said, other incidents. Plural. What else?''

''Exactly the same thing. But for me, particularly bad. I saw the man with the skin for three weeks, every night. The skin he was wearing was rotting on him; it turned a bright yellow color. I could even smell him. God knows, the stench was terrible. It got so bad that I began drinking gallons of coffee, eating No-Doz like candy, trying to stay awake. But I'd always fall asleep, and there he'd be. Dancing around in that nightmarish rotting skin, people laughing and throwing flowers at his feet. It couldn't have been real, surely it would have been discovered and there would've been headlines. It was so bizarre. And another thing; it couldn't have been real because what I was seeing was taking place in daylight, when I was sleeping at night. Of course, it's always daylight somewhere on earth, isn't it? But the dreams always started out with the same feel as the ones in Nebraska; it just freaked me. Finally I got sick from so much caffeine. But about that time, the dreams stopped, maybe because I was sick, I don't know—''

''So you never had any kind of verification of these dreams?'' Danny asked.

''No.''

''What makes you think they weren't just nightmares?''

''I just know, that's all.''

Danny thought about this for a moment. Damn it, that all had a familiar ring to it too; where had he heard of something like that? He just couldn't place it. But the whole thing seemed to dovetail in with the corn goddess David had described earlier. There was something here, but he couldn't put it together. It really irritated him, because it seemed important.

"This corn goddess you saw in Nebraska, David, what was her name again?" he asked.

"Xilonen. You know, I meant to ask you about that. Why are you calling her a corn goddess?"

Danny looked surprised. "Isn't that pretty obvious? She was sick when the corn was sick. When you got the corn going again, she was well, dancing around. She told you she was trying to live and all. She's, well maybe not a goddess—I'm no anthropologist or anything, I don't know the formal distinctions—but at least a spirit of the corn. Don't tell me that never occurred to you!"

David hung his head for a moment. "Well, I don't normally think of myself as stupid, but no, I'd never seen it that way. You're right, too. It's kind of obvious." He looked over at Susan. She was nodding agreement.

"And in these other visions. At first you said, ghosts or monsters. But then you told a story about a man; a homicidal maniac, perhaps, but a man. Why those words? What did you mean?"

"Well, what they were doing was monstrous."

"Why ghost?"

Damn, David thought, this man is sharp and persistent. Unless I can trust him completely, I've got to be careful around him. "Uh—this is hard to explain—but it seemed to me that—that when the man put on the skin, the other man—the dead one—had, well, it was like he'd come back. Like he'd been resurrected."

Danny considered this. A complex mystery, he thought, worthy of some serious consideration. Or a lot of delusions. He looked at the fern; it was greener and more alive than ever. Not all of it could be written off as delusion, that was for sure.

David saw him staring at the plant. "By tomorrow it'll look like something right out of a florist's shop." He smiled. All right, he told himself; he had dodged the essence of the subsequent Incidents. The part he didn't want to tell them, didn't want to tell anybody. He wished he hadn't known it himself, but he did; nothing to remedy that. He had to live with it; the fact that he himself had been the man who danced in a costume of human skin.

Susan rubbed her eyes; she was beginning to get more than a little tired. She had contributed very little to the conversation; she'd been a bit afraid to, lest she accidently wander into some dangerous areas, areas she most emphatically didn't want to talk about. She was still digesting David's story, and the re-markable—to say the least!—ability he had exhibited with the fern. But she couldn't figure out how it might relate to the things that had been happening to them. Her primary interest was in getting the weirdness to stop.

David and Danny were not helping at all, she observed. They seemed to be fascinated with each other. Both had pos-sessed odd abilities since childhood, and neither had really had a chance to discuss it with someone who could understand. Susan, on the other hand, had never, before yesterday, had what she'd call odd experiences. Just odd ideas. Which had themselves led to some unique experiences. But not supernat-ural; they had been very natural indeed. You couldn't get more natural.

Again her thoughts were interrupted as David and Danny raised their voices. They were arguing a point over the nature of gods and goddesses. She wondered what the hell either of them really knew about such things. Absolutely nothing, she decided. Yet there they were, arguing over it, really involved in it, each trying to convince the other of the rightness of his position, neither moving an inch. She sighed. That was so very male.

She looked at Danny, who was waving his arms about vio-lently as he tried to make a point. He was, she was sure, a nice guy underneath his hard-bitten facade. His me-above-all attitude was just a defense against a world he'd found hostile most of his life. David, whose experiences were possibly even more profound, had much more successfully hidden from his abilities. He'd been burned badly, but only for a short time; Danny had been cooked over a slow fire. But she was sure it hadn't gotten to him down deep. She liked him, and although she hadn't known it when she first saw him yesterday morning, she found him sexy as well.

David, on the other hand; David was, at least tonight, the

calmer of the two. Generally he sat with arms folded, nodding occasionally, listening intently. Then he'd make his points, carefully, maybe somewhat pedantically at times. She reflected that David was not always calm; generally he was, but he was given to sudden explosions, the causes of which were not always clear. Often it seemed that these explosions were triggered by something he'd read in the paper or heard on the news. Some absurdity of twentieth-century life. That was something he hadn't gotten into tonight, but it was a favorite subject of his; the insanities of the modern world. She wondered idly if he thought the ancient world was less insane. She knew that of course things had never really been any different. Why, back about three thousand years ago, she had seen—

She stopped, frowning. What had she seen? She couldn't remember what she had been about to think! Three thousand years ago? Ridiculous! She put the thoughts out of her mind and concentrated on watching David. He was speaking again, also using his hands to gesture, but more slowly and methodically than Danny. Periodically he'd pull on his short beard, while keeping his other arm across his chest. This would often be followed by smoothing back his hair at the temples, even though it was too short now to fall in his eyes. She scanned him up and down; he had a dancer's body even though he never exercised. To her, he was very beautiful.

Eventually the conversation began to run down. Danny allowed as how he enjoyed the evening, just as if he was a friend on a social visit; and she realized then that she did consider him a friend. She invited him to come back soon. David concurred. Danny said he would, and left. David looked at her, a suggestion in his eyes, and moments later they were in their bedroom. Again, they were both more than ready, and as David slid his penis inside her, she reflected that Danny had surely been right about one thing, at least.

Just outside the Hallstens' building, Danny stood on the curb trying to hail a cab. Several had already passed him, but his mind was on something else. He still didn't have any good ideas what was going on, but he was, if anything, more determined than ever to find out. He resented David and Susan a little; they had broken into his isolation, in just one evening. He couldn't help liking them. And Susan was so damn sexy, he told himself; moreover, David wasn't a jealous type. He had picked up that maybe David was a bit of a voyeur or something. At any rate, he was well aware that David had seen that Susan and he were at least somewhat attracted to each other, and that had appeared to excite him. But all between the lines. Be careful, Danny told himself. You don't want to stab this man in the back.

But it was the other thing that occupied him for the most part. The corn goddess—what was her name? Yes, Xilonen—and the ceremony of the human skin costume. Familiar, from somewhere. Maybe a documentary on PBS? He just couldn't place it, but it bothered him. There seemed to be some proper connection there with rattlesnakes, but he didn't know what it was.

19

SATURDAY, FEB. 7, 1987

Saturday morning was just as cold as the middle of the week had been, and in ways a less pleasant day to drive. The weather had turned clear, the sky a crystalline blue. The sun, burning down through the windows of David and Susan's Chevy, heated up the interior of the car excessively; David was constantly turning the heat up and down. If he turned it off, it got too cold; when it was on, it was too hot. Bright, blue days ought to be hot, he thought. If it was cold, it should be overcast. He opened his window a trifle; in spite of the brightness, the wind was icy. Closing it quickly, he glanced at Susan. She was sleeping, her dark brown hair hanging over the side of her face. Again, in sleep, she looked very young. A smile played around her lips, and David could see her eyes moving behind closed lids. Obviously a good dream. He smiled at her, let her sleep.

Up ahead, he saw the exit for highway 83; the little map on the back of the flyer from Tascan Acres had indicated that he should take 83 to 25A, then look for the signs. He swung the car off onto the exit ramp and headed north on 83. Susan stirred a bit as the car rounded the turns, but did not waken.

Thursday and Friday had been calm enough days for him, and uneventful for Susan as well. He'd seen Danny for lunch on Friday, and he had no outstanding news either. Actually, about the only thing remaining to remind them of the weirdness of Tuesday and Wednesday was Susan's friend Jeannie, who continued to behave strangely. The other people at the magazine were beginning to notice, Susan had said. Apparently, when Susan wasn't around, Jeannie was perfectly normal; but in Susan's presence it was different. She gazed at Susan for long periods, an almost longing look in her eyes, and tried to stay as physically close to her as possible. David had gone to their office Friday afternoon, ostensibly to pick Susan up so they could go out to dinner but actually to see Jeannie for himself. It was just as Susan had said. He wondered if Jeannie had suddenly turned into a lesbian and fallen in love with her. But one doesn't turn into a lesbian overnight, he told himself. Besides, Jeannie's attitude seemed subtly different from that. She reminded David of nothing so much as a small dog with its master.

They continued to travel up 83 until they reached 25A, then turned eastward again. After driving for a while, they came to a sign indicating Tascan Acres, off to the left. He realized how ridiculous this was; they were much too far away from their work in the city, even if they could afford a homesite. But that wasn't the point, he told himself. It's just an outing, listen to some bullshit and pick up some cheap luggage. He reached over and touched Susan's shoulder to wake her as they turned down a narrow gravel road indicated by the sign. She sat up and brushed her hair back, instantly awake; he received a radiant smile. Best one in a week, he thought, returning it in kind. Behind the smile, his mind turned again to Kathryn Phillips, the woman on the subway. She'd gotten a letter from these people too. What if she were here now? How would he react? He shrugged it off. But her sensual image would not leave his mind.

The road was fairly rough, and they were obliged to travel slowly. It was a very wild area; sand dunes on either side of the road, a few rocky outcroppings, seacoast plants. Gulls clamored overhead. Because of the dunes, they couldn't see very far in any direction. It would have been easy to imagine that they were in the African wilderness.

Finally the road curved past a large dune, and they saw a rather beat-up looking trailer with a sign: Tascan Acres—Office. A single vehicle sat outside, a rather rusted-out white Bronco. David looked around, didn't see anything else in the immediate vicinity. It was really a shoestring operation; he couldn't even see where any potential homesites had been marked off. Strange, he thought. But what the hell. We really didn't come here to buy land. What can it hurt?

He pulled the Chevy in alongside the Bronco; they got out, headed for the office. The steps leading to the entrance were rather flimsy looking; he took Susan's arm as they started up. Before they had mounted the second step, the door opened and a large, bulky man in a rumpled blue suit looked down at them.

"Hi, folks!" he said expansively, loudly. As if to answer, a wave boomed in on the shore behind the trailer. "I'm Sol Flores! Please, please, come right on in! Watch your step there, little lady, them stairs ain't what they should be!"

David decided that he didn't like this man at all. He was determined to make this fast, get out of there.

Inside, he was somewhat surprised at the sparsity of the furnishings. It was a bit cold inside, as if the heat had not been on very long; he could hear the heater fans working. Flores waved them toward a pair of chairs and sat behind the desk. The chairs were not comfortable, and David found himself squirming a bit; there was something about this man, or this place, or maybe both, that made him nervous.

"Well, folks, so maybe you'd be interested in some beach property, eh?" Flores said, putting his hands behind his head.

"We'd just like to see what you have," David replied, hedging. He didn't feel like telling the man directly that they weren't going to buy anything, they just wanted to pick up their gift and go.

"So far, ain't too much to see. You done seen it as you drove up. We're going to divide up the beach out there into lots. But we ain't done it yet."

"How big will the lots be?" Polite conversation. Utterly useless, David thought.

"Well, big enough, friend, big enough." Flores got up and

lumbered over to the window. "Just look at that scenery out there though; imagine yourself here in the summertime. You'll love it, I can tell you that. And the little lady here, why, she deserves no less, no less!" His voice was a little strained. He continued to rattle on about the beautiful beach scenery.

David was beginning to wonder about this. No plots laid out, no model open? What kind of development was this, anyway? "What kind of houses will they be?" he asked.

"Well—ah—nice ones, friend, I can assure you that!" David got a glimpse of his face, and he honestly thought the man was going to burst into tears. He didn't seem to know what kind of houses were planned! Had he been thrown into this with no preparation? Or was it some kind of a scam? He was really suspicious now.

"What's the price range?"

"Ah—cheap! Under—ah—under a hundred fifty thousand! Think you'd be interested?"

"Well, Mr. Flores, it's really hard to say. I don't know where, how big, what kind, or how much. I'd be kind of buying blind, don't you think?"

"Yeah," Flores agreed, looking miserable.

He obviously doesn't know what's going on, David thought. Probably somebody's brother-in-law or something, filling in for the day. Might as well end this. "Well, we are supposed to get a free gift, according to this." He held up the flyer. "And if we can pick that up, I guess we'll be going. Maybe we'll drop back by sometime." This last was just to make Flores feel better. David was beginning to feel a little sorry for him, but of course had no intention of ever returning. He handed the flyer over.

"Sure, stop back. Real good," Flores said, looking as if he'd be just as glad to get rid of them. He stared at the code numbers for a moment, then went over and started rummaging around in a file cabinet which seemed to be almost empty, and came up with an envelope with a number matching theirs. He returned to his desk and sat heavily in the chair. "Okay, friends, let's see what you got here." He ripped open the envelope, looked at the contents. "Well, I'll be shit-faced!" he shouted. "Motherfucker! 'Scuse me, ma'am." He seemed genuinely flustered. "You won the vacation, folks. One chance in a million. All yours!"

David and Susan looked at each other. No, he said mentally.
Too good. What's the catch? He reiterated this last thought
aloud.

"There's no catch, folks. All yours, free and clear. Here's
your tickets, right here." He handed them two envelopes which
had been stuffed in the other. "And"—he picked up a typed
sheet, read it aloud—"you will be contacted at Miami International Airport. Arrangements will have been made to take
you on to South America."

David looked at the tickets. Miami all right, via Eastern,
stopover at Raleigh/Durham. But they were dated for Thursday! This Thursday! Impossible to arrange, he thought. No
doubt this was the catch. Go Thursday or not at all. For most
people, that meant not at all. No cost. But yet—

He had these tickets in his hand. They could go to Florida,
if nothing else, assuming they could set the vacations up.
Weird, he thought. A strange scam, no payoffs really in sight.
They hadn't been asked for a penny yet.

"This is impossible," he told Flores. "We can't go Thursday! We don't have our passports. And what about inoculations?" He ran on down the list of problems.

Flores again consulted his sheet. "You don't need 'em," he
said. "The vacation resort is on a small, privately owned island near Aruba. No passport required. No native people, so
no inoculations, either. No problems, except maybe gettin' off
work. I can't help you with that, haha." The laugh was utterly
phoney.

"Well, exactly what is the name of this place? The resort, I
mean?"

"Uh—lemme see—uh—it doesn't seem to be in here. Just
says it's near Aruba. That's all."

"Great. We're going to go on a vacation, and we don't even
know where we're going. Sure we are. When hell freezes over.
Come on, Susan. Let's got out of here."

Susan nodded agreement and got up. David thought he
caught a glimpse of a little movement in a pile of blankets on
the tattered couch, saw that Susan was looking too. No, he
must have been wrong. Or maybe it was an air current from
the heater. Anyway, it was not important. They had to hurry
home, get all packed for their free vacation. Such a wonderful
prize. If he couldn't get the time, he'd by God quit the fucking

job, he thought. Mr. Flores had made it sound so fine; he just couldn't wait. He looked at Susan and could tell that she felt exactly the same. He frowned for a second; wasn't something wrong? No. All was very well indeed with their world.

Susan was literally bouncing with excitement as they drove away from the trailer. She looked at the tickets again. This was simply unbelievable good luck. They had won the vacation! It was hard for her to really accept that it had happened to them. She'd never even known anybody who won a big prize in any of these contests and things. But here they were, leaving in less than a week for the resort at—at—she couldn't remember. But it didn't matter. Sun and surf awaited, and she was delighted.

David pulled the car back onto 25A and they began the trip back to the city. Only a short distance from the entrance to Tascan Acres, they passed a small sports car going the other way. Susan just got a flash of the driver; a dark-haired young woman, very pretty. David, however, seemed to stiffen when he saw the car; he turned his head to follow it. Far behind, they could see it slowing down, then turning left, apparently into Tascan Acres.

"Was that someone you know, David?" she asked. Her tone did not imply anything, but David jumped nonetheless.

"No. No, not at all. Just looking at—ah—the car."

She didn't pursue it. After all, the girl was in fact very pretty. But that was a little strange for David; he'd always been one to look at an attractive woman, and he was never shy about letting Susan know about it. It didn't bother her. At the beach in the summer, she'd often point out sexy girls he might miss seeing. She wondered why he felt the need to be secretive about this one. But she didn't let it spoil her ebullient mood. If it was important, he'd talk to her about it. He always did.

Sol Flores turned and spoke directly into the pile of blankets. "All right, you old fart! What the fuck is going on? I tell you, I wanna know what the scam is, and right now. I feel like a fuckin' moron! Anybody'd know there's no Goddamn development. And why didn't they even see you? And then, they weren't gonna go for it, but when they left, they—they looked at you—and—" He ran down, finally realizing that perhaps something a bit out of the ordinary had just happened. Maybe

he shouldn't push the old asshole, he thought. He remembered
hearing about the brujos when he was a kid; he always thought
that was bullshit, but felt there was no need in taking unnecessary chances.

"I have told you, Mr. Flores. This is none of your concern.
Now if you will look out the window, I believe you will see
another of our guests is arriving. Please greet her properly.
And do not worry. All is proceeding as it should. Maria and I
will attend to the details." Having said his piece, the old man
again melted into the blankets. Maybe it wasn't really so weird
that the Hallstens couldn't see him, Flores considered.

He walked over and looked as instructed. A small sports car
had pulled in, and a very attractive girl was getting out. This
bimbo is alone, Flores thought. Maybe there's a possibility
here. A fringe benefit. Even if she's not interested, why it's
such a lonely spot; if he could get away just as she was leaving—

"Please do not entertain such thoughts, Mr. Flores," the
old man said unexpectedly. "The lady is quite significant to
us. You would not be allowed to harm her."

Flores turned, started to ask who was going to stop him; but
he looked at the flat black eyes, and he knew the answer.
"Goddamn old shithead. Stop reading my fuckin' mind, all
right?" He turned back to the door. When he opened it, he
was as unctuous as ever.

20

John sat down, popped open a can of Stroh's, and turned on
the six o'clock news. He was, by his standards, in a very good
mood. Things had gone well with the buyers; it looked like
they were going to pick up his line. At least, they had taken
all his samples in exchange for a fourteen hundred dollar check.
This worked out to something like $200 per piece; he had

never gotten that much money for his work before, at least not from dealers. An occasional individual might have paid above that for one item, but this was a new ball game. He was, he felt, being recognized. At last.

Idly he watched the news. As usual, most of it was bad: murders, rapes, muggings, tension with the Soviets, tensions in the Middle East. A West Virginia town evacuated due to a chemical spill; a waitress brutally murdered at a truck stop in Ohio last Wednesday. Police were searching in five states for a man seen leaving the scene, but all they had was that he had been driving a Toyota with Tennessee plates.

John shook his head, sipped his beer, listened to the next story. More of the same: police were searching in six states for a man driving a mid-sized American car, make unknown, Florida plates starting with UTM; he had apparently tried to rape a young victim of a car accident on a roadside in North Carolina. On the screen flashed a composite sketch from eye-witnesses' descriptions.

The beer tipped in John's hand as he stared at the screen, transfixed. A reasonable likeness to his own face, rendered in a police artist's pencil, stared back at him. He glanced toward the mirror, on the wall to his left. The only major difference was that John's fundamental expression was one of sadness, whereas the police artist had rendered his features leering and cruel. He sat stunned. He hadn't gotten away all that cleanly after all. Perhaps he should turn himself in; surely in a trial the girl and her parents would tell what had actually happened. Yet the original accusations, insane as they were, had come from the little girl herself; and the father had not jumped to his defense, possibly because of his remark concerning the man's negligence. The mother was his only hope, and John didn't want to risk his freedom on something that tenuous. He felt it was better to disappear for a while, change his appearance. He couldn't do anything about the car—the Florida motor vehicles department had it down in black and white. Even selling it wouldn't— Or maybe it would, he thought; they only had a partial license number. He could trade the car, here in New York, today. It wouldn't be difficult to find a car lot open on Saturday in the city. But first, he needed to change his appearance.

* * *

Four hours later, he reentered the apartment and looked in the mirror. He would hardly have recognized himself. His long hair was cut and styled, his full beard trimmed very short; he just couldn't stand to shave. Gone was the work shirt and jeans; he affected rather a preppie style of dress. Out in the street, the Citation had been replaced by a Subaru station wagon. He had left evidence, in the form of the motel registration, of his travels up I-95 and 301 in North Carolina. But they couldn't check all the motel registrations in the state. If he could get back to Miami, avoid being detected here, he might never be connected with the incident. But it was time to go. Anybody could have told the police that he was headed north. They'd be concentrating their search here, not in the South. He started to pack his things, then realized with annoyance that he had left his bags in the Citation's trunk. Too much of a damn hurry, he thought. But bags or no bags, he had to get out of here tonight. It was too risky, he decided, to take I-95 back; perhaps the longer route through Knoxville and Atlanta? Hurriedly, he consulted his map. Yes, that was fine; he'd do it.

He put the map back down, noticed the flyer from Tascan Acres lying on the table; it had previously been covered by the map. Too bad, he thought. He was really curious as to how they got his name and address here. He glanced at the list of prizes again. I could really use the luggage now, he thought. But that was hardly of any real importance. What he needed to do was get on the road, stay overnight somewhere in Pennsylvania. It would be safer.

As he stuffed the flyer into his pocket, he felt a slight dizziness; the excitement of the day, in fact of the whole damn week, he told himself. Not too surprising. He took off the new tie, then unbuttoned his shirt. He wanted to go to bed right away; it was important that he get out to Tascan Acres first thing in the morning and get the free luggage. Right after that, he'd head back to Florida.

21

Bertie had spent that Saturday evening in the streets of the city, and as a result, had missed the newscast that had so profoundly affected John. He was no longer really thinking about the murder; he thought it was regrettable, but the girl's life was of no real consequence to him. The main thing was to be sure that it caused him no problems; but he had decided it would not. He'd left no evidence, been seen by no one. The truck stop was so deserted; the only car he'd even seen on the access road was just turning onto it as he was leaving, and that was a good quarter mile from the truck stop. No, he was free and clear. No problems. He could concentrate on the decision he had come here to make.

He found himself outside a little club on Forty-sixth Street, not far from Broadway. Feeling that a drink would be nice, he went inside, ordered a whisky sour, and began to watch the eleven o'clock news, which was playing on the TV above the bar. They repeated the story John had heard earlier. Bertie was very attentive.

Still no problem, he thought. The last hard evidence he'd left of his whereabouts was in Lexington; he could have gone a variety of directions from there. So someone had gotten the make of the car; Toyotas were not rare, even with Tennessee plates. They didn't have a description, like they did of that poor bastard from Florida. And, he hadn't left any evidence at all. He was sure of that. The way he'd killed the girl, he had hardly touched her, and she hadn't touched him at all. He still had the weapon, so what could they have to go on?

His ordered train of thought suddenly stopped. He was staring at the glass in his hand. A thumbprint stood out in sharp relief, the whorls defined by dew from the liquid's chill. He remembered. His plate. Water glass. Coffee cup. Fork. Perfect canvases for fingerprints. All right there on the table, a corpse lying on the other side of it. He could see the scene again, all the dishes accentuated in his vision. Superimposed, a scene of himself, being fingerprinted in the military. Kept on file.

He put the glass down and covered his eyes. How could he have been so outrageously stupid? Maybe it was—what did they call it?—blood simple. He couldn't have left more direct evidence if he'd left his business card with a note on it saying, ''I killed this girl.'' This was bad, really bad, only a matter of time. He had to move.

He left the club, his drink unfinished. There were decisions to be made; get out of the city, or disappear into it? One thing was certain; there was no going back to the Air Force. They'd have him in a minute. They wouldn't know it for a week yet, but in his mind he was AWOL as of this moment. First things first, he thought. Get rid of the car. Then, maybe—maybe go on out to that place, Tascan Acres. After all, he was lucky at gambling. Maybe he'd win the vacation, get out of the country under a bit of cover. One thing for sure, it was safe enough. No one would expect a murderer on the run to be looking at beachfront property. That was good. Tomorrow morning he'd get rid of the car, then go out there. He didn't want to chance driving that distance in the Toyota. He moved on down the brightly lighted street, still cursing his stupidity.

The newscast had not mentioned that the witness had been the waitress's father, or that when he'd walked in and seen her lying there, blood all over, he had gone into a state of shock. He had called the police, but then had mechanically begun to clean up the mess. He was mopping up her blood when the police arrived. Of course they had stopped him; but they had no way of knowing he had already cleared and wiped the table, had even turned on the dishwasher. That restaurant had, at one time, been his pride. He liked to keep it spotlessly clean.

22

About seven o'clock Sunday evening, Danny stopped by the Hallstens'. He knew they had been going out to pick up a gift from some developer, and he was curious as to whether anything odd had happened on that trip. Saturday he'd gone to Atlantic City and picked up a little over three thousand dollars. He could have done more, but why push it? There was always another day. Today, he had relaxed, watched the Knicks play basketball. Nothing unusual had happened.

He rang the bell, heard David answer, was buzzed in. Once inside the apartment, Susan asked if he wanted something to drink; this time he accepted the beer.

"So how was the development? Get some nice luggage out of it?" he asked.

"No!" Susan said. She really looked excited. "Danny, you won't believe it, but we won the trip to South America! The vacation!"

"It's true," David put in. "Hard to believe, but true!"

Danny was genuinely pleased for them. They both seemed so happy and enthusiastic, it was sort of contagious. "Well, now, that's just great! Really great! Where are you going? And when?"

"Well, it's on an island near Aruba. That's off Venezuela, you know. A privately owned resort island. We leave Thursday. This Thursday! Can you believe it?" Susan was almost gushing.

"This Thursday? Jesus, how can you get ready that soon? I mean, you got your passports and all?"

"We don't need them," David said. "Or anything else. That's what's so great. Just pack, and get off work; that's it."

Danny looked at them, their open, happy faces. What was all this? A trip to South America and you don't need passports? Not as far as he knew. "So what's the name of this island?" he asked.

"We don't know. They weren't sure at the developers," Susan said. "We have tickets to Miami. They said we'd be contacted there for the rest of the trip."

"You're going to an island you don't know the name of? By charter plane, or tramp steamer, maybe on pelicans? What is this, guys? You puttin' ol' Danny on here?"

David looked at him oddly. "No. That's it."

"You don't see anything funny about that? Nothing at all?"

"No. Should we?"

"Well, I sure as hell would. I mean, I don't know how these things are set up, but I doubt if this is typical!"

"Oh, Danny!" Susan cried. "You see something strange in everything! Sure, it's been a weird week, but that's over, and some good came out of it. I mean, we found each other as friends, you know?"

Danny couldn't help staring. They didn't see this as strange at all! What the hell was the matter with them? A week ago, he'd have walked at this point, telling himself that these people's problems were none of his business. But he was hooked, caught both by his curiosity and by the fact that he had come to consider these people friends. And Danny cared deeply for his friends; it was exactly the reason he avoided having any.

"David, Susan," he said seriously, "I don't understand. What are you doing?"

"Just going on a tropical vacation, Danny, that's it. We'll be back in—in—" David stopped and frowned. "Susan, how long was the vacation, anyway?"

"I don't remember him saying," she said.

"Well, not long, anyway."

Danny was even more astounded. "Could I see your tickets, David?" he asked.

"Sure." He went to his desk, got the tickets, handed them over. Danny opened the little blue folder, pulled out the tickets and looked at them. Miami, all right. One way. The small alarm bell he'd been hearing had turned into a gong. Something was very wrong here. And for whatever reason, Susan and David were totally blind to it. He realized there was no use trying to talk them out of it; they just couldn't see. Just possibly, this was an extension, a continuation of the week. He made a decision. He was going with them; but he was not going blind, as they were.

"Hey, listen!" he said suddenly. "You got any objections if I tag along? Paying my own way, of course."

"No, that'd be great!" Susan said. "But I don't know. If it's a charter or whatever out of Miami, you may not be able to get on it."

"Well, hell, if that happens I'll just take the next commercial flight to wherever. There's always a way. And I already have a current passport."

"Sounds good, Danny," David said.

"All right. Look, I'll be going now. I gotta pack and get ready myself. Only a few days till Thursday!"

"Right!"

Back at his own apartment, Danny pulled a couple of large suitcases down from the closet. He also got down the special item he wanted to pack: a .38 revolver and four boxes of shells. He didn't like to take any chances.

23

MONDAY, FEB. 9, 1987

Susan arrived at work early Monday morning; she wanted to talk to Jacobs about taking her vacation. There was no question she had the time, but to leave Thursday was very short notice indeed. Normally she would have seen Jerry Maxwell about this, but she figured Jerry probably wouldn't be back yet. She glanced at his office as she walked past; the door was closed. But Jacobs was in, as she had expected. She knocked, was invited in, and began to explain her situation.

"My dear Mrs. Hallsten, why are you telling me this?" he

asked, folding his hands on his desk. "Maxwell is in charge of these matters; you should be talking to him."

"Oh, is he back?"

"Yes. He got out of the hospital Friday afternoon. And I do believe he is in, yes."

She thanked Jacobs and left his office. In front of Jerry's door, she hesitated a moment; she wasn't eager to see him or talk to him about what happened. She sighed. There was no way around it. Squaring her shoulders, she knocked on his door.

"Come," he yelled.

"Hi, Jerry, glad to see you back. How're you feeling?"

He gave her a long hard look before answering. "Fine. Yourself?"

"Oh, I'm okay. What was it? I mean, did they find out?"

Again the stare before he spoke. "Nothing," he said slowly. "Nothing is what they found. Nothing at all. No reason for it whatsoever."

She fidgeted under his gaze, wanting to end this, but not knowing how. "So—um—what do they say?" she asked.

"They say there was no reason for it, that's what they say. You think they're right, Sue?"

I trust they're right, she told herself. I'm not sure what I'd do with a power to strike people down. "I'm no doctor, Jerry," she said. "But if I were you, I think I'd get a second opinion."

"Maybe I will," he muttered. "Anyhow, what can I do for you?"

"Well," she told him, "I've got two weeks vacation coming. I want to take it starting Thursday."

He gave her an exasperated look; the old Jerry was definitely back. "Thursday? Pretty short notice, Sue. I don't know. Let me check." He looked at various papers. Susan knew they had nothing to do with her request; Jerry just liked to look important.

Finally he said, "Well, it looks okay here. But next time, try to give me two weeks notice, willya?"

"Sure will, Jerry. Thanks a lot." She left the office, went to get a cup of coffee. She was not used to being in this early. Jeannie was already there, stirring a freshly poured cup, and Susan groaned inwardly. One more day of Jeannie's doggy attitude and she would strangle the woman.

The redhead looked up. "Mornin', Susan. How's stuff? Mr. Perfection okay?"

"Yeah, we're both fine." She paused for a minute. Jeannie wasn't gazing at her longingly like she had been Friday. Maybe a test was in order: "Nice day out, isn't it?" It was drizzling a cold rain when she came in.

"Nice? You nuts? Well, maybe a weekend with Mr. Perfection makes you feel that way about a shitty day. Must be nice!"

Susan felt a rush of relief. Jeannie was back to normal. Her anxiety melting away, she told her about her upcoming vacation.

"Let me get this straight," she said when Susan had finished. "You really don't know where you're going?"

"No, but I'm sure—"

"You are nuts. What's the matter with you? This deal stinks to high heaven, lady."

What the hell was the matter with everybody? she wondered. It sure was clear enough to her. "Well, you know, I could really use a rest. After last week and all."

"Yeah, right. But, Susan—"

As they sipped their coffee, the discussion continued. Susan was becoming irritated with her friend; at least Danny had understood when they'd explained it to him. Jeannie, on the other hand, was being utterly obstinate, throwing up objection after objection. When they finally returned to their desks, a cool curtain had fallen between them. Susan felt badly about it; Jeannie had always been someone she could talk to, but evidently not about this.

24

Hoping that no one was there, Danny nervously peered through the windshield as his yellow Chevette bumped down the path out at Tascan Acres. He'd had a hard time finding it;

David had only mentioned that it was off 25A, so he'd followed 25A all the way from its inception in Queens, one hell of a long drive. And likely for no reason, he told himself.

At last the trailer was in sight. Danny still didn't see another car; it looked good. He could do some snooping around and, if he was lucky, be gone before the agent—Flores, he remembered David saying—arrived. Pulling the Chevette around behind the trailer, where it couldn't be seen immediately by anyone coming up the narrow road, he got out, peeped in several windows. No sign of anyone. The latch on the back door was an easy one; he slipped his Master Charge card into it, snapped it open. Cautiously, he went inside.

The trailer was devoid of furnishings except for a sparsely outfitted kitchen and the few pieces in the main office. He considered his suspicions justified; it really looked like a fly-by-night operation. Quickly, he rummaged through the desk, the file cabinet. No maps, no contracts, nothing. None of the stuff needed to sell property. In fact, nothing at all except numbered envelopes and a manila folder with what amounted to a typewritten script and a list of names: John Goss; Herbert North; David and Susan Hallsten; Kathryn Phillips; Frank and Evelyn Wasserman. Danny read the list; none of the other names were familiar to him. Pulling a handful of the numbered envelopes out of the file cabinet, he glanced at them, then looked back at the list of names; beside each name was a number. A number that corresponded to those on the envelopes. He held them up to the light. They were all empty, except the one for the Wassermans. That envelope was full, and in the light, he could see the airline tickets. For Miami, he assumed.

Sitting on the ragged couch, he considered this. There was no doubt; whoever was running Tascan Acres was baiting a specific group of people, his friends included, into a trip to some unknown place. There was no land for sale, no other prizes; everyone who came here won the trip, and only the invited ever came. It was not by accident that this place was hard to find. But what was the motivation, the payoff? Not easy to see. Perhaps a bunch of crazies, but usually they didn't have the money to set up something like this. Couldn't be ruled out, though. And that was worse. You could never know what the motivations of crazies might be. He fingered the .38, secure in his pocket. He would hate to use it, but it might be necessary. He intended that he and his new friends would come through this in one piece.

Deciding to check if his talents offered any help; he crossed his eyes and squinted. Nothing around the desk or file cabinet. Nothing anywhere. No, wait. A little red warning glimmer at the right of his field of vision. His head turned.

And froze. His conscious mind frantically asked for the gun, but his body wouldn't move. His bowels and bladder spasmed, creating a terrible mess and a worse stench. Only two or three inches from his own face was the most dreadful face he had ever seen. Definitely human; but old, impossibly old. Canyons carved into mahogany skin. A great hooked nose, with a draining sore on it, so close to his. One eye blind, staring off at a weird angle, popping from its socket; the other black, glittering, transfixing him. A lipless mouth, wide open in a hideous grin, a scattering of teeth inside, teeth coated with a greenish moss; the tongue moved on the floor of the mouth like a snake coiling to strike. Somewhere back in the mouth, perhaps from the throat, a white maggot appeared briefly, writhed around, then vanished. The mouth, already open wider than a human mouth could open, gaped further. It split a little around the corners, draining blood and pus. In that moment, he was sure the thing was going to swallow him like a serpent swallows a rat; but still he remained paralyzed.

The face moved closer to his, the teeth elongating, becoming sharper as it came. Now the huge nose was only a millimeter from his, nearly touching him. He closed his eyes tightly in anticipation of the contact, opened them again when it didn't come immediately. He stared at air, at the wall of the trailer. Nothing there at all.

"What the fuck?" he yelled. He looked down at his pants; the mess was total. He didn't know how he was going to drive back to the city in this condition. He started to get up, but his knees were weak, and he leaned back heavily for a moment, caught in a state of utter confusion.

It took him a few minutes to collect himself, but finally he managed to get up, walk to the trailer's bathroom. Inside, there was no soap, no towel. The shower didn't look like it had been used in twenty years. At least there was a full roll of toilet paper. He took off his pants and underwear, cleaned himself up as well as he could; his shorts were discarded, his pants rinsed out in the sink. He put them back on, cold and wet. He couldn't remember the last time he'd been this uncomfortable. Turning toward the bathroom door, he started to leave, then froze. A huge shadow fell across the doorway; he could hear a scraping or grinding sound of something very large moving in the outside room, heading toward the bathroom. This time there was no paralysis; he pulled out the .38 and jumped to the door, standing behind it the way he'd seen cops do on TV, feeling scared and foolish simultaneously.

The sound stopped; he peeked around the doorframe. Nothing. Stepping out into the narrow hallway, he still saw nothing. His wet pants squished as he went back into the office; nothing there was different from when he came in, except for a wet spot on the couch where he had been sitting. He methodically searched the whole trailer. Nobody. Nothing.

"Am I going crazy myself?" he muttered aloud. Then he started getting another warning red glow, in the left side of his peripheral vision. He spun toward it, raising the revolver. Again, nothing; he was looking at a pile of blankets on the edge of the couch. He took a step closer. Funny, that was the same location he had seen the warning glow before. He cautiously approached the pile, gun in hand.

Just a pile of blankets, he told himself. Maybe something under it? It was big enough to hide a corpse. Reaching down, he pulled off the top blanket; and instantly felt a sudden stabbing pain in his left hand, followed by a burning sensation. He looked, saw the head of a rattlesnake withdrawing into the pile. It just couldn't be! It was far too cold; didn't snakes hibernate in the winter? Looking at his hand, he started to tremble. It was rapidly turning a purplish-black around the two puncture marks, swelling enormously. The pain was incredible. Wildly, he looked around for a phone; there was none. He tried to remember how to treat snakebite; tourniquet, that was it. He put the gun down, stripped off his belt, and started to wrap it around his left arm, but his unmarked left hand caught his attention and he stopped. He stared at it; the pain dwindled rapidly and disappeared.

Picking up his gun, he approached the pile again. He couldn't find anything to use as a stick, but he certainly wasn't going to stick his hand in there again. Indecisive, he paused for a moment. Then, reaching down very gingerly with his finger-tips, he caught hold of the edge of the top blanket and jerked it; it came free. He repeated the procedure with the next. Finally all the blankets lay on the floor; there was nothing else there.

For another hour he remained in the office, but nothing else happened, and he discovered nothing new. At last he left; his pants were a little drier, so perhaps the drive back wouldn't be so very bad. This trip had only deepened the mystery, and he was more determined than ever to go wherever it was David and Susan were going.

"Whither thou goest, folks," he said aloud. "Wherever the hell."

Back at the trailer, the old man sat on the edge of the couch and allowed himself a smile. He picked up the blankets from the floor, wrapped them around himself again. A moment later, no one would have suspected that there was anything there other than the blankets.

25

John was literally hiding out, staying in the apartment as much as possible until Thursday, when he was due to leave for Miami. He'd been stunned by his luck; a free trip to South America at a time when South America was probably one of the best places he could be. In his fugitive state of mind, he hadn't worried about the oddities, didn't care where they were going; if it was out of the United States, that was good enough. He'd return to Florida when things had cooled down. He had already sold the new car and packed his things for shipping. He was sure that his friend, Nikki Keeler, would handle that for him when she returned.

That started him thinking about Nikki. He had known her for years; they were the best of friends. Sometimes, still, they were lovers; at one time that had been a regular thing. He had met her when they both were in medical school at Vanderbilt, both feeling alienated, jazz people in a country music town. The relationship had taken off immediately. Even today, John considered those the best days of his life. He could almost see her right now; the very black hair, dark eyes, slender body. He always thought of her in terms of the song by Crosby, Stills, and Nash. Her name really should have been Judy; it fit her so perfectly, the whole song. Sweet Nikki brown eyes. Every time he thought he had her figured out, nailed down, boxed in, she did something that totally surprised him. At that time, being a doctor was of paramount importance to him; it had been his objective since childhood. When they met, in their first year, he had naturally assumed that she and every other student felt exactly the same; but he had never asked her. In any case, it had come as an immense shock to him when she suddenly dropped out in their second year. He supposed that some cataclysm had brought it on; but he saw her very frequently, although she always insisted they maintain separate apartments. He should have known about a disaster.

It wasn't until quite a bit later that he found out that Nikki didn't spend any nights alone. On the average, they saw each other four or five nights each week; by accident he learned that she spent the rest with other men, sometimes charging for her services. He would never forget the scene that ensued when he confronted her with this information. It had come only a week after her sudden dropout from medical school; he had been spending virtually all his time trying to find out why. All she would ever say was that she had decided she didn't like it. So he had questioned her friends, sincerely believing his motives to be purely altruistic. Finally one of those friends had taken him aside and told him about Nikki's secret life. Naturally, he hadn't believed it; but the friend had directed him to the School of Business Administration, and he had learned that Nikki's name was very well known there. But they hadn't known she was a medical student, and he didn't tell them.

When he went to her apartment and confronted her, he expected excuses, tears, self-recriminations, a sad story of desperate finances. Typically, she surprised him.

"Goddamn whore!" he had screamed, hurling a glass to the floor. "Bitch! Slut!"

She had just sighed. "You know, I always meant to tell you, John, but somehow it was never the right time. I truly didn't mean for you to find out this way."

"What the fuck difference does it make how I found out? Why the hell do you do it?"

"Why not?"

That simplicity had stopped him for a moment. He was totally at a loss for words. He started to issue a moral lecture, which in reality would have come from his fundamentalist parents, then decided that wasn't appropriate. So he started talking about VD.

"But, John, as a doctor you will be—in fact, you already are, in the med center—at risk of getting diseases from your patients. Does that stop you from wanting to practice medicine?"

"It's not the same Goddamn thing!"

"Why not?"

"You fucking well know why not! There's no comparison!"

"Maybe not. As doctors, you and I would probably treat just anybody. I mean, let's take an extreme case; suppose the police brought in a guy who had just killed, say fifty children, and he'd been shot. Your oath, your profession, would require you to heal him. Even if you had no doubt that the guy was absolutely guilty, and because of some legal mess he was going to walk free and do it again, you'd still have to heal him. Right?"

"I suppose. But that has nothing to do with—"

"Wait. I wasn't finished. I don't fuck just anybody. I have to think the guy is okay. I turn down lots of guys."

"Well, good for you!"

"Please, let me finish. The guys I fuck are okay, and for whatever reasons in their personal lives, they need it. And I enjoy it. So why not?"

"What a pragmatist. What an altruistic bitch you are. The sexual healer. Bullshit!"

"I suppose I can't expect you to understand me. But I guess I just don't have a moral sense like most people. And I go my own way. You've always known that."

"I understand you make money hand over fist."

"Not always. Sometimes I don't charge at all. It depends. I

won't turn a guy away because he doesn't have money. But if he can afford a hundred, then why not?''

At that point he had lunged like an attacking panther, hitting her hard across the face with the butt of his hand, knocking her off her chair. When she got up, a trickle of blood was running from the corner of her mouth. She wiped it away with a tissue and sat back down, acting like it had never happened.

He had felt terribly defeated then. ''I never want to see you or hear of you again,'' he had said before he left.

As the year went on, John was unable to keep Nikki out of his mind. It seemed like everywhere he turned, he heard her name; she was becoming legendary: the whore with the heart of gold. Some of the other students referred to her as a national treasure. Her notoriety was such that he couldn't understand how it was that she was never arrested. It was a bitter pill for him. Sometimes he found himself wishing she was dead, then castigating himself for such thoughts.

His wish nearly came true. He found out via the hospital grapevine. He had been told that she had finally made a poor choice of customer, had been badly beaten, was not expected to live. He went to see her in intensive care; and all the old bitterness was swept away. Seeing her like that, he couldn't continue to hate her. He kept track of her progress; she did recover, leaving the hospital after a stay of only ten days.

About a month after that, he went to see her. A car was parked in front. It was not hers, unless she had a new one, so he waited. At last a med student, one he knew, left. He walked up, knocked.

She opened the door and was obviously startled to see him. ''John!'' she squealed after a wide-eyed pause. ''It's you!''

''Last time I looked,'' he said. ''Can I come in?''

''Please. Please!''

''You know, it's none of my business now—I guess it never was—but once you asked me, 'why not?' I followed your progress in the hospital, came to see you when you were unconscious. I guess this is a good answer to that question.'' He looked away. ''Shit. I didn't really come over here to say I told you so or anything. I just had to see you.''

''John, I heard the rumor—that a customer had beaten me. It isn't true. It was a car crash. An ordinary car crash. Nothing to do with what I do.'' She paused for a minute. ''Are you disappointed?''

''No. I'm just glad you're alive and okay.'' He hesitated, then reached for his wallet, took out a hundred dollar bill; he had gotten it just for this. ''I need, Nikki; am I an okay guy?''

She jumped on him, threw her arms around him. She was so warm, so vital. He had missed her terribly. ''You sure are, John Goss. You sure are.'' She told him to keep the hundred, or leave it, whatever he wanted to do. It didn't matter to her.

Afterwards, as they basked in the afterglow, he asked her, ''But how do you know one of your customers—patients, maybe—won't actually do that to you?''

She looked at him and smiled. ''How does a psychiatrist know one of his patients won't carve him up? We all take risks; nuns get murdered in the street. Besides, I'm a good judge of people, if I do say so; I think I can avoid it.''

''I hope so. I worry about you, Nikki.''

''I've been worried about you too, John. I'm glad you came back.'' She rolled over him, took his limp penis in her mouth. Soon he was up and ready again. It went on that way all afternoon, and into the night.

After that they were close again. John told her unequivocably: he still didn't like it. But she wasn't about to quit, and he didn't feel he could do without her. So he accepted, and tolerated. And it continued until his graduation. In those days, he was so very proud of the title: Dr. John Goss. He would sometimes sit and doodle it on note pads. He loved the sound of it, the look of it on paper. He got an internship at Memorial Hospital in San Diego and asked Nikki to go with him. He even offered to help her set up her business there; Dr. John Goss, part-time pimp. But she sadly told him that she felt it was time they parted ways. She planned to move to New York. He begged, pleaded, cajoled, threatened; but when Nikki's mind was made up, there was no changing it. In the end they had parted; to opposite corners of the country.

He considered it now. He still, this very day, didn't know her reasons for the separation. His life would have been very different if they hadn't; he was very dependent on her in many ways. In San Diego, he had discovered that; he'd had to toughen up fast.

And really, in the final analysis, he hadn't been able to. The final days of his medical career came when he was in the emergency room, treating the victims of a sniper. The police had brought in the gunman himself, badly wounded by them. There was little doubt; dozens of witnesses had identified him. The man was unconscious when he came in, and John had been present when the police first talked to him, after surgery. Five of his victims, four of them children, had already died; the charge was to be murder one.

But the police had botched the case totally. They'd failed to read him his Miranda rights—John himself had been a witness to that—and they seemed to have lost the murder weapon; it had been held for evidence, but nobody was able to find it. Finally, he learned that another doctor had been a witness to police tactics of bullying the surviving victims into making a positive ID. John had himself heard the man confess to the crimes; it was uncannily close to the example Nikki had used years before. It got closer when the man hemorrhaged, and John was required to assist in saving his life. During surgery, the man's heart was visible; it was all John could do to resist ripping it out and hurling it against the wall of the operating theater. He took the next day off, and the following day he resigned his internship. He never used the title Doctor again.

There'd been accusations of overreaction; all doctors and lawyers had to face these problems, he was told. But he just couldn't, it didn't seem to be in his nature. Regardless of the pressures on him to reconsider, he left the hospital behind and took up an older avocation; the trumpet. He was an excellent musician, and had no difficulty finding enough work in Los Angeles to sustain himself. Sometimes he visited Nikki in New York; each visit was a sexual revelation. She was always coming up with something new and exciting. He had repeatedly proposed working in New York, but Nikki had always ended up convincing him that his proper place was in southern California. She seemed to be doing well all this time; possibly even getting rich. But she still lived rather modestly in a small apartment on Cabrini Boulevard; the one where he was currently staying.

For several years he continued to work as a musician and had some modest successes. But competition in the music business in L.A. was ferocious; no major breakthroughs came to him or any of the groups he worked with. He made most of his money recording behind major solo artists; it was a living, but getting him nowhere.

When the change came, it was Nikki who provoked it, probably without meaning to; he could never be sure about her. Sometimes he thought she could read minds, see the future. She told him that she usually turned about four tricks a day, yet she never got arrested, never got VD, never ran afoul of any dangerous customers. Either she had some odd ability or she was unbelievably lucky. John was never certain.

One Sunday afternoon she had insisted that he go with her to see an exhibit at the Museum of the American Indian in New York. Remembering how the Mayan ruins in Mexico had depressed him, he hadn't wanted to. Thinking about it, he became aware that it wasn't the ruins that depressed him so, but a certain lack of proper respect by the other American tourists. Their attitude—and his own—he couldn't even pretend to understand.

He was doubly dismayed, then, when Nikki breezed past the North American exhibits and headed straight for the Mexican section; the Aztecs, Toltecs, Mayas. She told him she was fascinated with this material, these people. As he looked at it this time, he came to share her feelings; it seemed to him that their artwork radiated energy. He had learned to throw a pot in college; and now he was becoming obsessed with the idea of producing some new pottery, in a neo-primitive style.

When he discussed this with Nikki, she thought it was a great idea. He already had a few concepts in mind, and she arranged, through a client of hers, for him to use the facilities at CCNY. After he had produced a few pieces, both Nikki and her professor aquaintance told him that he had real talent, that he should pursue it. He had been dubious; he didn't have the slightest idea how to make a living at pottery. Again, it was Nikki who suggested taking the pieces around to various gift shops in different cities, trying to sell them. This he had done, and one contact seemed to lead to another, until, after only a few months, he was making enough money at it to support himself.

During this period, he had stayed with Nikki in New York, his possessions in warehouse storage in L.A. It had been an awkward arrangement; he worked during the days, while Nikki was usually free. Often she slept late. At night she worked, in the apartment, and he was required to make himself scarce. He spent a great deal of time in neighborhood bars, annoying the proprietors because he stayed so long and drank so little.

As soon as he was financially solvent, Nikki began demanding that he leave, that their relationship revert to its previous status. He acceded to this and began looking for an apartment in the city. To his surprise, she demanded that he leave New York, and told him if he didn't, she would. Again they argued fiercely; he just didn't understand her. But as he had learned, it was impossible to change her mind once she had made it up. In one of his travels, he had come across a place for sale, just outside Miami, that had been previously owned by a ceramics hobbyist and came fully equipped. Nikki helped him with the down payment, told him to pay her back when and if he could. So he had ended up in Miami, taking every excuse possible to travel to New York. This she seemed not to mind; she always welcomed him on these visits. All these years, he had few other female contacts. He felt as permanently bonded to her as if they were married; but she always kept it clear and unequivocal that although she loved him, she didn't feel the same. As his pottery business advanced, his visits to New York had become more infrequent, and increasingly he seemed to be living the life of an ascetic. It did not suit him, but he continued, more out of a certain inertia than anything else. It had now been almost a year since he had seen Nikki, and just as long since he'd had any feminine companionship. He'd really been looking forward to this very legitimate trip; but she'd sent him a key to the apartment and a terse little note saying she'd be in the Bahamas. It had been a bitter disappointment, but he'd hoped she would return before he left. Now those hopes seemed futile; he was leaving on Thursday, a man on the run from a circumstantial trap.

He looked up in the mirror and saw Nikki's face, as he had so often seen it in that glass, and wiped moisture from the corner of his eye. He really loved that woman. Always had, always would. To him, a night with her every year was worth a lifetime with any other.

Since the police had no description of him, Bertie felt there were no problems with being seen on the street. Nevertheless, he, too, was planning to take the vacation offered by the people at Tascan Acres. Winning it had been no surprise; after all, he was always lucky, wasn't he? But that wouldn't last, he told himself, not since they had his fingerprints. From the island, he could disappear into South America if necessary. There was always a way.

But in the meantime he planned to enjoy himself, sampling New York's night life and its women. Though lucky with those too, he didn't mind paying for an exceptional experience; he called up an absolutely exquisite prostitute he had seen a number of times in the past, but her answering machine said she was in the Bahamas. He shrugged, let it go. There were plenty of others.

Monday night found him prowling about the Times Square area. Although the vast majority of the women in this area—amateurs and professionals alike—were totally unacceptable to him, he had always liked the scene here. It was, he felt, most deliciously decadent; and Bertie had always appreciated decadence. It added an energy to a place, a spark that set it apart from the more staid districts. Strolling Forty-second Street, he watched the hustle around him, listened to the patter of the local denizens—"money talks, bullshit walks"—watched the Iowa tourists gawk at their Sodom and Gomorrah made reality. A very unpleasant-looking woman beckoned to him from a doorway; he nodded, smiled, and walked on. Not his cup of tea by a long shot, but he felt she deserved respect; after all, she was bucking the odds.

He passed several hours here, browsed through the ubiquitous porno shops, watched the live shows. This particular night, the live shows were real. They weren't always. It depended on the current level of pressure the police and the city administration was putting on the businesses.

About 1:00 A.M., he decided that it was time to call it a night. Entering the subway at Broadway, he planned to ride only a couple of stops uptown. In the station was the usual mixed population one sees every night in New York, especially in this area. Nervous tourists; tired laborers heading home after the night shift; occasional groups of more or less hostile youths; winos sleeping on benches; and the vultures awaiting suitable prey. These staked themselves out at intervals, like sea gulls on a pier. Somehow they all seemed to recognize each other. Bertie walked into this mélange smiling and confident; normally, he bothered no one, and no one bothered him. He was a watcher here, a silent witness. Not one of their own and not suitable prey, the vultures generally ignored him. He walked on down the platform, then decided to play a game with them. He took on their persona, scanning the rabbits the way they did, walking like them. He edged into a position between two of them. Without seeming to notice him, they spaced themselves to give him his hole. He giggled under his breath; he was having a great night. Too bad he had to run away from this for a while. But Bertie was confident above all; he felt he could carve a niche for himself anywhere.

A commotion down the platform to his right attracted his attention. In classic New York style, everyone around him seemed to be totally oblivious to it, burying their faces deeper in their newspapers or craning to look for the train. He drifted toward it, merely curious.

When he reached the vicinity of the commotion, he saw that three Puerto Rican youths—he assumed that was their nationality—had cornered a pretty young black girl and were systematically taking everything of value she had. Periodically, one of the youths would punch her, or another would slice her skin lightly with a switchblade. A sheaf of drawings lay at her feet, spilled from a valise she had been carrying. Although the youths were trampling them, Bertie saw excellent renderings of the Times Square nightlife in pencil, and he was impressed with her artistic ability.

He looked up at the melee; the youths were currently having trouble removing a ring from the girl's finger.

"Hey, man, cut it off if you have to!" one of them yelled.

"Yeah, right!" The one with the knife grabbed her hand and, ignoring her screams, prepared to do just that.

Bertie stepped into it. He seized the youth who had made the suggestion by his hair, slammed his face into a steel post with terrific force. He didn't utter a sound, just slid down to the floor. The remaining two looked up at Bertie.

"You gonna be sorry you did that, chump!" The one with the knife lunged at him, blade straight out. Bertie sidestepped the rush, grabbed the boy's arm, twisted it until the blade pointed up. Then he released him, letting him fall with the point under his chin. Immediately he was up again, his hands flapping at the handle of the knife, which was all of it that was exposed. Strings of blood flew around him like streamers. He was making such a peculiar gurgling sound that Bertie laughed aloud. The boy surged back down the platform, the crowd parting to let him pass. He disappeared from sight, leaving a red trail.

The third youth, who had been holding the girl pinned, looked at Bertie indecisively for a moment. Then he let her go and ran. Again the crowd parted, and he too disappeared. The girl's first thoughts were of her drawings; sobbing, she started picking them up, straightening them out as well as she could. Bertie knelt down, helped her.

"Thanks, mister," she said through her tears. "I thought they were gonna kill me."

"It's nothing. Don't worry about it." Bertie replied.

A man from the crowd which had now gathered came up behind him, clapped him on the shoulder. Thinking he had a new assailant, he turned quickly, then relaxed. The man was just a salesman or something; shabby suit, florid face, wheezing. Harmless.

"Friend, that was great! Just great! You're a real hero!" the man said, grinning. "Wish we had more like you to teach these punks a lesson they won't forget!"

"No, I'm not—"

"Yes, you are! We oughta get a reporter! This should be in the papers. You really handled those guys. You some kinda Kung Fu expert or something?"

"No, I just—"

"Well, I tell you, I ain't ever seen nothin' like it! You wait right here while I go call the papers,''—then as an after-thought—''and maybe the cops.''

''No!'' Bertie almost shouted. ''No reporters! No cops. At least not till I get out of here, all right?''

''But you're a hero, mister,'' the man whined. He seemed to notice the mirrored foot for the first time. ''Hey! What's that?''

''Nothing. An artificial foot. I lost one years ago. But now—''

''Hey, everybody check this out! The man's a cripple, for God's sake! He ain't got no foot! And still he manhandled those bums! I tell you, we gotta call the papers!''

This was getting totally out of hand, Bertie thought. I've got to get out of here, and fast. He turned to the still-weeping girl. ''Look,'' he said, ''now I need help. Can you get us away from here?''

''Sure, I guess.'' She looked up at his face, then down at the foot. ''Can you run? I mean—''

''Yes. Lead the way.''

She got the rest of her things together quickly and started down the platform, Bertie following. The man in the shabby suit came as well, still yelling about newspapers and cops, and a crowd of people drifted along behind them. She moved slowly as they left the station, and Bertie wondered if she knew what she was doing; but as soon as she hit the street, she started running like a gazelle, glancing back to see if Bertie was stay-ing with her. Quickly, half a block ahead, she turned a corner, jumped into a doorway and disappeared in the shadows; Bertie himself nearly missed her. But she hissed at him, and together they watched their remaining pursuers run by and disappear into the crowds.

''That was nicely done,'' he told her when they were sure they were clear. ''Especially considering what just happened.''

''I've hadta run from cops and gangs before. It ain't new,'' she said. ''You're running too. I can smell it. But you helped me, mister, so anything you need.''

She's quite sharp, Bertie thought. He watched her search her purse for money, then sigh. The punks had taken it all. Obvi-ously, she had no way home.

Bertie reached into his wallet, came up with a twenty, handed it to her. "This'll get you home," he said. "Don't argue; I know you're in a spot."

She took the twenty and looked at him, then to the cabs still drifting by on Forty-second Street. She knew she could go if she wanted to. She looked at Bertie again. "I'd rather stay with you, mister. If you want me."

"That's fine too. My hotel's just uptown." He stepped out to hail a cab.

27

Susan had definitely had a bad day. It was four o'clock already, but she had gotten very little done; her mind was preoccupied with the trip, with Jeannie's objections to it. To make matters worse, she'd tried to talk to another colleague about it, and this woman's response had been exactly the same! Susan simply couldn't understand it. She had even wondered if perhaps there was something weird about the trip, something she was unable to see, perhaps something dangerous. Can't forget about Mexico, she told herself; can't ever forget about that. But this trip, she told herself, had nothing to do with the other; yet somehow the conjunction of her ruminations about the two had given her the odd feeling of being somehow unreal, as if she were asleep, dreaming, and had just become aware of it. But she wasn't; she was in her office, at her desk. Just like every other day.

She looked up from the papers she'd been staring at, but not working on, and let her eyes wander. Normal people, going about their normal business. Just another day. Susan took it all in, started to let her gaze fall back to her work. But her eyes went wide instead. Near the window, leaning against the wall, stood a man, totally naked. His penis was quite erect, pointing right at her. She glanced around quickly, then back at him. He hadn't moved. There were people all around, but nobody seemed to notice him. She pressed her hands together, staring at the man. He didn't seem threatening; in fact he was extremely good-looking. Fine chest, face—she stopped herself. This was too bizarre. A naked man with a hard-on is standing in the office, she told herself, nobody else can see him, and I'm deciding he's good-looking! I have gone crackers.

She started to call Jeannie's attention to him; but instead, went to her desk and asked her to look over at the window. Jeannie could not possibly look at the window without seeing the man, who was standing right beside it. Without getting up, the red-haired woman looked.

"What, Sue?" she asked.

Verified. He was a hallucination. Not really there. No one could see him except her. "Just the way the afternoon light is coming in. It's pretty," she said lamely. Jeannie gave her a strange look, turned back to her work.

Moving away from Jeannie's desk, Susan watched the man; his face was impassive as he looked directly into her eyes, and she felt herself becoming sexually aroused. Mustering her courage, she walked to the window and stood there as if looking out. As she came alongside the man, he turned so that he continued to look right at her. She was acutely aware of his erection, which still pointed directly at her midriff.

"Are you real?" she asked in a low voice. Though she'd already decided he was not.

"As any other. You must still come to yourself, Flower Feather," he said. She glanced back; he had spoken in a normal tone of voice, but still no one noticed. "Do not think I am only in your mind." He indicated the other people in the room with a wave of his hand. "You and I are more real than they are."

"What do you mean? And what was that you called me?"

"I called you by your name. And you will know what I mean very soon. You must remember that reality is not what you have been taught. Follow your instincts. They will not lead you astray."

"I used to do that—and it almost got me killed!" she blurted.

"It was not the time. Now it is. We shall meet again, Flower Feather. Look for me." He turned and walked out of the room, his erection preceding him.

Susan leaned against the wall for a moment. Crazy, crazy.

She felt she'd really lost control. Standing here talking to a naked man nobody else could see. Moreover, a naked man who turned her on. She was intensely uncomfortable as she went back to her desk. Somehow, she had to get through another forty-five minutes of the workday.

28

David got home precisely at five that evening. Things had gone reasonably well for him; he hadn't had much trouble setting up his vacation time either. As usual, he took the subway home, and as had become usual as well, he looked for Kathryn Phillips. He didn't see her. But the woman was absolutely haunting him; he had dreamed about her every night since first seeing her, and the glimpse of her out at Tascan Acres had only intensified it. Every dream was sexual; sometimes just him and Kathryn, sometimes a ménage à trois with Susan, sometimes with Danny added. He was daydreaming about her, too. His life these last few days had been a perpetual state of sexual arousal, the only variations being in its intensity. He found himself hoping she too had won a vacation and would be joining them, but realized that was ridiculous; these people wouldn't be giving away multiple vacations. Simultaneously, her eating habits were so very disgusting that he hoped he never saw her again. He refused to admit to full consciousness the little trickles of awareness that this was, for him, a part of her appeal. That was just so utterly perverted.

As he left the station and began to walk home, he dismissed any thoughts of seeing Kathryn that day and tried to concentrate instead on the upcoming trip; but his thoughts were interrupted by a man, evidently homeless, who approached him, hands out. He looked at the man closely; Danny in disguise? No, this was obviously a genuine street person, bleary-eyed from an all-day drunk. David started to wave him aside and go on, but the man was insistent.

"Just a minute of your time, buddy. Just a minute," the man whined.

"No." David tried to get past him, but his way was blocked again. "Would you move, please?" he demanded.

"No. You will listen, Night-Drinker." The man's whole demeanor and indeed his face itself changed. He no longer seemed drunk. Dark eyes watched David from beneath a battered hat. David didn't know whether he was more shocked by the man's abrupt change or by the title, Night-Drinker. He had a quick impulse to tell the man that *he* was the drinker, obviously; but somehow that title—and he knew it was indeed a title—had nothing to do with the consumption of liquor. He felt like it was in fact his title; but that was absurd.

"What?" he asked, somewhat more weakly. "Who—?"

"Not important. Let us just say I am a friend of Xilonen!"

David jumped at the familiar name. He looked closely; maybe Danny's disguises were better than he thought. But no, this man didn't even resemble Danny in any way. "How do you know that name?" he asked, a slight tremor in his voice.

"Again, not important. What is important is this. You must come to yourself, and soon. There is little time for you. Your heart will be sorely tried by what awaits, but do not act hastily. Trust your instincts. They will guide you correctly." With those words, the man turned and walked away down the street.

David just stood there for a moment, then ran after him, losing sight of him for a moment as he turned a corner. When David came around the corner, he stopped short. Standing in front of him, not ten feet away, was the girl he had seen so many years ago, the girl he knew as Xilonen. But something was wrong; she was still fourteen, and in spite of the cold evening, she was dressed in the simple blue dress he had last seen her in, almost twenty years ago. She smiled at him; a beautiful, full smile.

"You must listen to his words, my lord," she said. Her voice was inherently musical; it sounded like she was singing when she spoke.

"You're—you're—" he sputtered, unable to talk.

"Yes. Now I must go. But you will see me again, Night-

Drinker!'' She turned as if to walk away, but almost immediately turned and entered a doorway.

David ran after her, but when he got to the doorway, there was no one there, and the door it led to was darkened and locked. He looked at it for a moment. At some point in the past, this doorway had fallen into disuse, and had been painted permanently shut. He felt a wave of loss, a heavy hard feeling like he'd lost something precious. But he knew it wasn't Xilonen. What then? He didn't know; he just stared at the door.

When Susan arrived at the apartment, she found David in a state of confusion. For quite a while, he was absolutely incoherent about what had happened down on the street, but finally she calmed him down and coaxed the story out of him. When he mentioned the phrase about ''come to yourself,'' she interrupted, started to tell her story; both stories then came out in a hurried and confused jumble. A bystander would not have been able to tell what had happened to whom. One thing was clear, however; both were again in a state of high sexual tension. They stripped off their clothes and proceeded to correct that situation on the living room floor in front of the couch.

Their intercourse was leisurely in spite of the tension; they took a greater pleasure in being coupled than in the orgasm itself. On this particular occasion, David sat on the floor crosslegged and Susan straddled him. He nuzzled her breasts as they rocked together gently, her head on his shoulder. When she felt his orgasm beginning to rise, her own started, and they climaxed almost exactly together, a rare thing for them. As she reached the crest of that wave, Susan had a sense of rightness about what was happening to them. She could not explain it, even to herself, but the feeling was very powerful, almost overwhelming. For a moment it seemed that they shouldn't break the flow of it by going on vacation, but she rejected that idea. Whatever it was would still be here when they got back.

Afterwards they sat, still coupled, David's now-limp penis trapped by their position. She knew that his semen was running out of her and might stain the carpet, but she didn't care. She tried to explain the feelings she'd had at the moment of climax.

''Almost like I, well, I lost consciousness for a moment, and— I sometimes sort of do, when it's real intense, you know? And, well, it seemed that whatever was happening to us should be happening, you know? It's hard to explain—just a feeling, you know?''

"I know, I know. Actually I don't know. But in a way, I guess I have the same sense. All this stuff is weird, but not really threatening. At least I haven't felt threatened by it."

"David, why don't you call Danny up, see if he wants to come over? Maybe he's had some more weird things happen to him. I think he'd like to hear about today, anyway."

"Sounds good. If you'll throw a couple of those delicious TV dinners in the oven, I'll see if I can get hold of him."

"Yuch! But okay. At least it's fast."

But Danny wasn't home; at least he didn't answer his phone. Susan was disappointed; she saw that David was too.

Danny heard the phone ring, but he was still in the shower. It had been a miserably uncomfortable ride home for him, even worse than he had expected. He'd be lucky if he didn't get pneumonia after that long, wet drive, he thought sourly. Maybe riding home with shit in his pants would have been better. Doubtful. By the time he had heard the phone and gotten to it, it had stopped. He figured it might have been David; few other people ever called him at night. He wondered whether he should tell the Hallstens about his bizarre experiences at the trailer, and almost immediately decided not to. Their heads were definitely not on straight about this trip for some reason. There was one thing he would like to ask them, though; that was, were any of the other names familiar to them? It might help dope some of this out. But it might not. So far, nothing was making sense to him at all.

He put the phone back down, pulled up his towel and turned to go back to the still-running shower. He stopped. Facing him, in the bathroom doorway, was a man, standing with arms folded. Danny dropped the towel. He couldn't make out features; the man was silhouetted in the bathroom light. He seemed to be naked.

Jesus Christ, Danny thought. A Goddamn burglar. Maybe a crazy. I'm dead, I've had it. The gun was in his jacket, hanging on the bathroom door, on the other side of the intimidating figure. Danny shrank back against the phone stand, knocking it over. He was sure he was about to die.

"There are worse things than merely dying, Mr. Hudson.

You may soon see some of them, should you continue on your current path." The voice was strong and cultured, with an odd rattling undertone, almost as if two people were speaking simultaneously.

"Who—who are you?"

"Who I am is not important. What I have to say to you is. For others, this path is chosen for them. For you, you yourself have done the choosing, even though you were warned. You are not yet strong, Mr. Hudson. You must be for what you must do, if you are to continue this path. If you cannot be, you must turn back, or you will find out what is worse than death. And then you will find death itself, as surely as the sun rises. You will be tested. Prepare yourself. There are no lessons."

Following this discourse, the figure turned and walked into the bathroom. As he did, Danny could see that he was indeed naked. When he cleared the doorway, Danny lunged for his jacket. Gun in hand, he entered the bathroom boldly. He knew the man wasn't armed. But there was no one there.

Danny woke with a feeling that something was wrong. He didn't open his eyes immediately; he tried to clear the fog from his mind. Oh yes. Naked man in the bathroom who wasn't there. That's what it was. Definitely weird, all right. He realized he felt funny; something was wrong with his bed. He opened his eyes.

And looked up at a brilliant, starry sky. He was lying flat on his back on the grass. Cautiously he looked around. In spite of the considerable starlight, it was dark; he couldn't see far in any direction. He was naked, and lying in a flat area of grassland. He sat up, still couldn't see anything. Vaguely, he remembered searching the apartment for the other naked man, finding nothing. After that, he figured he must have gone to bed.

So this must be a dream, he thought logically. But it was an unusual dream. Everything so well-defined. Not like most of his dreams, which were a hodgepodge of confusing images in which he had no awareness of dreaming. He tried to will himself to wake up; nothing happened.

He tried using his abilities, squinting and crossing his eyes. Nothing. No information. He assumed he had two options; sit here on the grass and wait for something to happen, or go looking for it. Might as well wait, he thought. It seemed a pleasant night. It was warm, summery. Actually it was very pleasant here. This wasn't a bad dream at all.

And then it got better. A woman walked into his field of vision from the shadows beyond. As naked as he was, and very lovely. He had never seen her before; he would have remembered her. She approached to within about twenty feet of him, knelt on the grass and smiled at him. He smiled back, and she gestured for him to come to her. Getting to his feet, he started in her direction.

Then her expression changed. She glanced behind herself, then back at him, pure raw terror in her eyes. He looked over her shoulder and saw the cat, stalking her slowly, methodically. A leopard, he guessed. Maybe a jaguar. But not altogether normal; larger than life, with black mirrors for eyes; he could see the stars reflected in them. He reached for the woman's hand, started to turn to run. She shook her head, pulled her hand away, looked up at him. Now her face was Susan's. Her expression was pleading.

The cat was closer now; it was about six feet tall at the shoulder; to Danny it looked even larger. A part of him demanded that he run away, save himself; but Susan for some reason couldn't move. He couldn't save her; he had no weapon, except the club he suddenly saw lying on the ground between them. A second ago it hadn't been there. He picked it up, and it seemed to vibrate in his hands. It was a very stout stick, about ten or twelve feet long. He was surprised he could handle it so easily; it was more like a log. He backed off a step. The cat was very close. He could smell its breath, hear it rumbling. Susan looked up at him, then put her face in her hands. She looked so totally helpless, and he was very frightened, even if it was just a dream. The cat was so very large. It gaped, showing huge teeth, each one glistening in the starlight. The mirrored eyes regarded him for a moment, then looked down at Susan. He stood frozen in indecision.

"You will be tested." He remembered the voice. It broke his paralysis, and he jumped forward, swinging the stick at the huge cat with all his strength.

But the cat had become a man, and he grabbed the stick with his hand, laughing with a rich, deep voice. Danny watched him, still holding his end of the stick. The man wore a small open vest, and what looked like a short skirt. He looked very muscular, his face coldly handsome. He wore a headband with a shining black mirror mounted just above his right ear; Danny noticed he seemed to be missing a foot. In its place was an elaborate carved one, the top being the same black mirrored glass he wore above his ear; the same as the cat's eyes. Curls of smoke rose from both mirrors. Danny looked at the man's other hand, saw that he held a long, vicious looking knife apparently made of some kind of stone. It was hard to see with only the starlight.

The man twisted the stick deftly, and it crumbled into many small pieces, leaving Danny holding only a short piece about a foot long. Danny stared at it for a moment; the man threw his head back and laughed uproariously.

"It is far larger than your prick!" the man yelled at him. "Therefore a marvelous weapon!" He laughed again, and jumped to a position behind Susan, wrapping his arm around her neck and bending her body backward. The knife was suddenly poised only an inch or two above the pit of her stomach. He froze in this stance, grinning at Danny.

"No! For God's sake, don't!" Danny screamed. He couldn't possibly get to her in time, even though he was only a few feet away. The blade was so close.

"For God's sake?" the man asked. "And what do you know of God or his sake? We should discourse on the question at length. Perhaps I would learn something!" Again he laughed. Weirdly, the laugh was pleasant.

"Don't kill her. Just don't kill her. I'll fight you, if that's what you want. But please don't kill her!"

"I don't want to fight. If I had so desired, we would be fighting, till one of us would be dead on the plain. I hazard it would be you, my friend!"

"What do you want?"

He seemed to consider that for a moment. "What will you give me for her life?"

"I have nothing here, except this piece of stick."

The man made an unbelievably quick movement with the knife and the stick flew off into the darkness. He then returned his blade to its position over Susan's body. "And now you don't have that. So what will you give me?"

"I have nothing to give. You can see that."

"Oh, my friend, you are so wrong. I can see you have a precious gift. And you don't know it."

"Whatever it is, you can have it for her life!"

The sky burst into sudden light. Danny covered his eyes for a moment, then looked again. Still the man held the knife over Susan.

"Turn around," he said. Danny turned; there was a kind of stone altar there, about a hundred yards away. Two black-robed figures stood beside it, unmoving.

"You want my life," he said. It was a statement, not a question.

"Not your life, though you will lose that too, in the process of giving me my gift. Your heart, Danny Hudson. Go to them without faltering. They will take it for me."

He turned and looked at the man, who grinned widely and brought the knife down slowly. It touched Susan's skin, pressed in on it a little.

"You must decide. You choose your path. Hers is chosen for her."

Danny turned without further hesitation and walked to the altar. One of the black-robed figures held his head under the chin and guided his body down across it. Without further ceremony, the other plunged a knife into his chest. The pain was not really as bad as he thought it would be, but bad enough. He felt the blade grate against his ribs as the knife-wielder twisted the wide blade, carving a gaping hole. Blood rose in his throat; he couldn't get his breath. Even so, he remained still. He felt a very strange sensation, a heavy, crushing pain, felt something rip inside him. Then the black-robed figure was holding his heart up to the night sky. It was still beating, pulsating in the hand that held it. Danny seemed to be viewing this from the inside of a deep well that he was falling into. The pain had gone, but he continued to fall down the well.

29

David woke up listening to the phone ring. He looked at the clock and swore; 6:00 A.M. Now who the fuck can be calling at this hour, he asked himself. Groggily, he sat up on the edge of the bed. Susan had apparently heard the phone too; she opened her eyes and looked up at him with a peculiar expression. He dragged himself out of the bed and went to the phone.

It was Danny. "David, listen, sorry to call so early but I gotta know. Is everything okay? Is Susan okay?"

"Yeah sure, Danny, but what's wrong?"

"I can't tell you right now. That is, it's a long story. I'll come over tonight, okay?"

"Is that Danny on the phone?" Susan asked.

"Yeah," David said, glancing at her.

"Let me talk to him a minute." She took the receiver. "Danny, I had the strangest dream last night. You were in it. We were out in a field, at night, and there was a tiger or something after us. You hit it with a big stick."

"Oh, good God," Danny said. "Look, this is real weird. You don't have to tell me the rest. I was there. I'll see you tonight, okay? Just listen; you and David be careful today. I don't like this turn of events. Not at all." He hung up.

"Now that's really strange," Susan said, staring at the phone. "Danny and I had the same dream last night!"

"Exactly?"

"I guess. David, in the dream he died so I could live."

David didn't quite know how to respond to that, so he didn't. He looked at Susan closely. "You don't look entirely well," he said.

"You know, I don't feel entirely well either. I haven't since

I saw that man. I keep seeing him, David. He won't get out of
my head.''

David knew exactly what she meant, except that it was Kathryn who wouldn't get out of his head. ''Well, I think we can
safely assume that he was, in fact, a hallucination of some
kind. Not because you're crazy or anything,'' he added quickly.
He knew Susan was sensitive about this subject, but he'd never
known exactly why. Probably related to her experience with
the preacher.

''Oh, I know,'' she said. ''I don't think I'm crazy.'' She
smiled. ''I'm Flower Feather, remember? I really like that.
Glad I came up with it, even if I did get a vision to say it!''

''It fits you. It really does.''

''Thanks, David, that's sweet.''

They put the subject aside and began the usual morning
routines. David watched her strip for a shower; he still enjoyed
just looking at her. But he couldn't shake the image of Kathryn
that kept intruding.

30

Bertie woke up spontaneously, as he always did. He looked
at the girl lying next to him; last night, he had found out that
her name was Geneva Lewis. Her shock and her minor injuries
had not prevented her from being an exquisite sex partner, he
thought, the best he had encountered in quite some time. As
if she could feel him looking at her, she opened her large eyes.
Nothing else about her moved. She lay on her stomach with
her head turned toward him. He studied her; her short hair,
her dark, velvety skin, still marred in places where her assailants had cut her. Fortunately, none of the cuts had been deep.
Bertie had carefully cleaned all those cuts the previous night;
it had almost become a kind of foreplay between them.

Without a word, she rolled over and got to her feet. All her movements were very graceful, Bertie thought. She didn't bother to put on clothes; she just got her sketch pad, sat down, and began to sketch. He sat up, posing for her. He didn't feel flattered; he knew how he looked. But as he had seen, most of her drawings were of hookers, tramps, and drunks.

"Why me?" he asked.

"Don't often meet nobody like you. You ain't average."

He wondered how he should take that. "How do you mean?"

"I mean, you ain't all there. I'm not talkin' 'bout your foot. I mean, in some way, you're like half a person. But more than most men. Men I've met, anyhow."

"I still don't quite follow you."

"I had a dream about you last night," she mused, seeming to ignore his question. "First, you were wanderin' around the country. Somebody was tellin' you you had to 'come to yourself.' This dude just kept sayin' that, like it was real important. He was a weird dude, too, man. Walked around naked as the day he was born, big hard-on stickin' out. He looked like you. Just kept sayin', 'come to yourself.' Then later, you were dyin'. You were throwin' yourself on a fire, somewhere at some beach. You looked different. You had a beard."

"Well, not me, lady. I've never had a beard, and I've never even considered jumping in a fire!"

"Dunno. Usually my dreams mean somethin'. I dreamed my mama was drownin' two years ago. Then she got pneumonia and died. So it was part right. She did die."

"You can die of pneumonia by having your lungs fill up, it's sorta drowning."

"Yeah. I guess that's what happened. I miss my mama, though." She looked up at him intently for a moment, then back to the drawing.

He assumed she wanted some expression of sympathy. "Everybody dies sometime," he said.

"Yeah, that's right for sure. Around here, mostly sooner."

"What about you?"

"I survive. I got a scholarship—City College—in art. I'm doin' okay."

"Why'd you take the chance, going down to Times Square so late?"

"You wanna draw the people, you gotta go where the people

are. But I was real stupid.'' She looked at her hand. ''Wearin' a chain and a ring. Man, that was dumb. Askin' for it.''

''So why'd you do that?'' He didn't know why he was pressing her.

''Dunno. Guess I just wasn't thinkin'. Anyway, how long you in the city? I know you don't live here.''

''Till Thursday.''

''Two days.''

''Yeah.''

''You mind me hangin' around till you leave?''

''No, I don't mind.''

''Good. Throw that cover off there, would you?''

He did as she asked. She got up, turned the pad so he could see it, set it on the chair. Then she climbed onto the bed and straddled him. She began to rub his penis against her vagina. It started to grow.

''You got the power, man, you know that?'' she said.

31

Susan still didn't feel well that morning, and it was getting worse as the day wore on; she had to literally struggle through her work. This couldn't keep up much longer, she told herself. Short-notice vacations, no work getting done. She figured she'd get fired.

She held her head in her hands for a moment. Although she would be the first to admit that her college days had been a bit wild—maybe even more than a bit—since she and David had become lovers she had had virtually no interest in any other man. David was all she needed or wanted; Jeannie's Mr. Perfection appellation was not too strong. But in the past week she had encountered two more men she had to admit to herself were sexually attractive to her—only one of them real. She felt like she was coming apart at the seams. Although she had told

David she knew she wasn't crazy, in reality she was having her doubts. Now this illness; one would have thought she'd had no sex in four years. Her breasts were hot and tingly, and she kept getting waves of butterflies whenever she thought of the phantom, her name for the naked man by the window. Even the sex with David the previous night, good as it was, only pushed these feelings back temporarily.

She shifted in the chair and realized her underwear was wet. Annoyed, she went to the rest room; but once there, wondered why she'd come. She had had a vague notion about taking them off because they were uncomfortable; but that would cause her to wet her slacks the next time. And that wouldn't do at all. She decided she'd just have to live with it. Looking in the bathroom mirror, she tried to see her face objectively. Various men had told her she was pretty; she'd never really been able to see it. All she saw in the face that looked back were what she considered to be the defects; nose too small, chin too sharp. As she started to turn away from the mirror, she saw behind her, reflected, the phantom.

She whirled around. He was still there, looking just as he had the previous day. Arms folded, not a stitch of clothing on, his penis still erect, pointing at her again. She looked him up and down; he was perhaps the most physically attractive man she'd ever seen, other than David. And his sexuality was purer, rawer somehow, than her husband's; David's had intellectual and emotional components to it. This man represented pure lust in its most fundamental sense.

"Who are you?" she asked him again.

He smiled slightly. "You wouldn't recognize my name, Flower Feather. But as I said: you must follow your instincts."

"I don't—don't know what—"

"Yes, you do."

And she did know exactly what he meant. She pushed the button on the rest room door, locking it from the inside. Moving toward him boldly, she looked directly into his eyes. He didn't move at all. As if she were testing to see if he was hot to the touch, she lightly tapped his chest with her fingertips. He was not hot, and he was very substantial. She scanned the whole of his body, resting her hands on his chest; then, moving them around, explored his entire upper torso, running them up his neck, into his neck, into his hair, down his muscular arms. She started to kiss him, but decided against it; for some reason, that didn't seem quite appropriate. She let her hands drift downward, touched her lips to his chest; her fingers curled around his buttocks, slid down the backs of his legs, and her face drifted down his flat stomach until his erection tapped her chin from underneath. Then, throwing all caution aside, she knelt in front of him and took his penis in her mouth.

The feelings of illness began to dissipate as she took him in, ran her tongue over the smooth surface. Her clothing began to bother her; she began to unbutton her blouse, never releasing him from her mouth. For the first time he moved, helped her remove her blouse and bra. Standing up, she stripped off her pants and underwear, then immediately dropped down and continued to mouth him. All thoughts of her work, the trip, even David and Danny, were far away. At the moment, her entire world was compressed into just the two of them. After only a few minutes, she felt him stiffen a bit more, lengthen a bit; then he was surging into her mouth. She swallowed rapidly. This was not a new experience for her, the hot liquid hitting the back of her mouth. She had done this with David innumerable times, and with not a few men before David. But this was different. As she swallowed it, it didn't seem to go down. Rather, it spread out through her upper body. She seemed to feel it coursing through her arms to her fingertips, filling her breasts, rising to her head, even into her hair. It was enormously energizing for her. She looked at herself; her skin even looked different, smoother, more evenly textured.

His hands touched her shoulders and she looked up at him. He was still quite erect. Pushing her backwards gently until she was stretched out on the bathroom floor, he came over her; she spread her legs to receive him. Gently, slowly, he slid himself into her. Again, her world diminished to a small focus as he moved on her, slow and gentle; as gentle as David, she thought. She hadn't expected that for some reason. Her climax rose, crested; then another was rising, followed by another. Only when she was beginning to get exhausted did she feel the hot waves of his semen inside her. She pulled away from the experience enough to realize that this too was very unusual; normally she could only tell that a man was coming behaviorally, she never could actually feel the semen. But as he continued his climax, she could feel each surge as distinctly as she had a few moments ago in her mouth. And the same thing happened, except concentrating in her lower body this time; the fluid seemed to spread through her, leaving a feeling of intense well-being in its wake. At last he seemed to be finished, and he pulled out of her. She couldn't move; she just lay there on the tile floor. He stood up and smiled down at her. It was the first time she'd seen him smile; a very beautiful smile. Without a word, he turned and walked out of the rest room.

For quite a while after he left she didn't move; she felt satisfied in a way she was just not accustomed to, more than just sexually. All her discomfort was gone.

Getting up and gathering up her clothing, she glanced at the door and grimaced. It had the type of latch that you could not lock as you left; whenever it was opened or closed, the little button popped out and the door was unlocked. She had been lucky that nobody had come in; it would be terribly difficult to explain how she came to be lying there on the floor nude, doubtless with a puddle of semen between her legs. She'd made no attempt to catch it or wipe it away. Then she looked at the door again. It was still locked. That was impossible, she thought; she'd heard him go out the door, hadn't she? She examined the floor. No puddle. No trace of any kind. It was as if he had never been there. Again she stared at herself in the mirror. Perhaps he hadn't; maybe he actually was a figment of her imagination, after all.

32

Trying to while away the hours watching the daytime soap operas was just not working out very well for John. He was still afraid to leave the apartment, and he was desperate to fill the time until Thursday without brooding about Nikki or something else. He knew how easy it was for him to fall into a pattern of this; once commenced, it might well last for days. Pushing the buttons on the remote control, he searched the channels for something interesting. PBS was running a cooking show; he wasn't interested in how to make lasagna. HBO had a children's show, Showtime a rock concert featuring a group he didn't like. The independents were no better. He ran past a religious channel, a preacher exhorting the faithful to send in their money. He kept going. A public affairs piece on seat belt usage. He grunted at that one, kept going. Another preacher show. Keep going.

He stopped for a minute. That last one was a damn weird looking preacher show. He flipped back to it.

This particular preacher looked somehow familiar; John was quite sure he had seen him somewhere before. He stood behind a podium emblazoned with some kind of odd symbol; John was sure he recognized it, but he couldn't place it. It consisted of three concentric circles, a large yellow center disc surrounded by an orange ring, which was in turn surrounded by a narrow white ring marked with pairs of radial lines. Four little white balls were attached to the outer ring, one at each corner. From the center of the yellow disk, five brilliant red streams descended, the outer two shorter than the others. Each of these was tipped with a white volute. He stared at the symbol for a moment. Where had he seen that? It bothered him that he couldn't remember. On each side of the podium were potted plants, but not the usual lilies or ferns of a religious show; these were spikey, long-leafed succulents, and he recognized the kind—the maguey, common in Mexico. Tequila was made from it. Two attractive young women and four equally attractive young men sat behind the preacher, who moved around the stage as if very excited, continuing his sermon in a deep, cultured voice.

"And I tell you, brother," he was saying, "It is not long, no, not long at all until the redeemer comes to take his rightful place on the earth, scattering the sinful to the four winds. It's true. The end is near. When you see him walk among us, brother, you'll know I speak the truth.

"Recall with me now, brother, his story. How the father sent a messenger to tell a young virgin living out in a hostile desert country that she would bear a son, and she did! How a sign in the sky foretold the day of his birth! How he grew into a fine man, giving the people new laws, teaching them new ways, ways that were holy! And how, betrayed by one of his own, he died. And how he was resurrected, yes, brother, brought back from the very dead to bring redemption to mankind! How he rose to the heavens; a magnificent sight it must have been, brother, it must have been!''

John was only half hearing the often-repeated story. He still studied the man's face, the symbol. So very familiar, but he just could not place it. It was really aggravating him. The preacher's voice droned on.

''And how it was foretold that he would return some day, near the end of this world, and raise the faithful, yes, brother, raise them to their rightful place in the world! And I tell you today, as I speak to you, that time is not far off. I have seen the signs, I have read the portents, and no, it is not far off, brothers. We have very few days left. Very few days before he comes again. And if he finds us unworthy, oh, brother, my brother, the fates that will befall us! The one who is many will come from the west, and brothers, nothing will remain. Nothing. As the worlds were destroyed before, so will this one be; not by jaguars, not by the wind, not by the fiery rain, and not by the flood; but destroyed nonetheless. We must praise his name. We must—''

Wait a minute, John thought to himself. All very well; virgin birth, resurrection, flood; but what the hell was that about jaguars, for Christ's sake?

''And now we have only a few minutes left, brother. You must come to yourself. And we must honor the lord of this world, until the one born of the virgin comes again.''

Some men came out and rolled away the podium. Behind it was revealed a stone altar, elaborately carved, slightly curved to form an arch. One of the smiling young men got up, took his coat, tie, and shirt off, and laid down across it, still smiling. Four older men came out and held each of his arms and legs while the preacher stood alongside the stone, extending his arms and bowing his head; then suddenly he lifted a knife above the man's chest. There was a moment's pause, then he plunged it downward. The man on the altar gave a little grunt, but kept smiling while the other twisted the blade, ripping open a large hole in his chest; then the preacher shoved his whole hand inside. He seemed to twist it around a bit, then pulled it out, holding the young man's still-beating heart in his hand. The remaining five youths applauded, and there was organ music from somewhere offscreen. Blood ran from the young man's mouth, dripped on the stage; his smile was frozen on his face. The preacher put the heart down somewhere behind him, then casually pushed the body over the front of the altar. One of the young women jumped up, took off her blouse and bra, and laid down in his place. As the preacher raised the knife, John turned the TV off.

He sat there staring at the darkened TV screen in a state of shock. What kind of a program was that? A fairly normal sermon, followed by human sacrifices? Then he realized; it wasn't a real religious show, obviously. He had tuned into some movie just at the right moment, and it had a sequence in it like that, and he, like a jerk, thought it was real. That was truly stupid. A B movie. Trick knives, fake blood, sheep hearts from the slaughterhouse. He laughed at himself, turned the TV back on. The screen showed only snow. Irritated, he flicked it to another channel; that was all right. Then back to the one he'd been watching, channel 62. Still snow. Damn it, he thought. Just when I get interested, the damn channel goes out. Nikki had the number of the cable company taped to the back of the remote control unit. He picked up the phone; when someone answered, he asked when channel 62 would resume broadcast.

"Sir, we don't broadcast anything on channel 62 except between five and ten at night. You must have made some kind of mistake. Please consult your cable guide for more—"

But he had already hung up.

33

Danny arrived at the Hallstens' early that evening. By prearrangement with David, he bore with him a large pizza; sausage, pepperoni, green peppers, no anchovies. He wanted to tell them about the intruder in his apartment, and the dream as well; but he wasn't sure about the latter. His feelings for Susan were hovering right at the edge of friendship, and he didn't want to create any problems. But perhaps it didn't matter; Susan apparently had an identical dream. He'd let her tell it, though; he was a little afraid of giving too much away. How had this happened? he asked himself as he rode the elevator up. Only a week ago, he was a total loner; now he seemed to have a best friend, and he was falling for his wife. How corny. How trite. How did he get himself into this? Curiosity, he decided. Killed the cat, so the old saw went; might do the same to him in the end. Sure did in his dream last night; he was sure that what he'd had was a real death experience. He'd come up from it with his vision blurred and his chest on fire. One thing he'd learned; it was not true that if you died in your dreams, you actually died. He could now speak from experience.

From the moment David let him in, he sensed that something was not quite right here. Across the small studio from the door, at the table in the breakfast nook, Susan sat with her head down on the table.

"What's the matter with her?" he asked David.

"That's just it, Danny. I don't know yet. She came in with a hangdog look on her face, and now I can't get her to talk about it. I think something else must have happened at work today."

Danny walked over to her, put the pizza down on the other side of the table. "Let's eat, Susan," he said gently. "Then maybe we can talk about it."

She raised her head and drew her hands slowly down across her face. Her expression was curious; her mouth and jaw said "guilty," but her eyes were bright and happy. He was tempted to try to read her, but he didn't. That seemed like an unwarranted invasion of her privacy.

"That's a good idea, Danny," she said. "I'll get some drinks. What do you want?"

"Coke's fine if you got it."

"Sure. David?"

"Same for me." Looking glum, David sat down at the table.

"Look, David, try not to get worked up," Danny told him. "These are not usual times. Or events. You can get a weird reaction now and then.'' Like I'm getting from you about this trip, he thought.

''Maybe you're right,'' David conceded. ''It's just that— well, Susan and I could—can talk about anything.''

Now he looked guilty, Danny thought. What's he not telling? They were both doing that, he knew; not quite telling everything. Since day one. But then again, he was doing the same thing, so he couldn't very well hold it against them.

After they had eaten, they started exchanging stories; David's concerning the drunk and the corn maiden Xilonen; Susan her dream story. It was indeed an exact replica of his, from her viewpoint. The man had not killed her in her dream, so he had kept the bargain. There had been little more after he had died; the man had released her ''for now,'' he had said. She had not seen his face. In the dream, she was then very tired, and lay down to sleep. She said she was crying for Danny, and a beautiful green bird came and sat beside her, sang her to sleep. She awoke in her own bed.

Danny went through the earlier parts of his story; the intruder and what he had said about being tested. He told of seeing the woman in the dream, who at first was not Susan.

''What did she look like, Danny?''

''Very pretty, small woman; short dark hair, rather large mouth, but real pretty. A permanent pouty look.'' He noticed that David stiffened slightly at this description. He decided to ask. ''You know somebody like that, David?''

''No—no—I don't,'' he muttered lamely.

''David, what about the girl in the car out at Tascan Acres?'' Susan asked. Now Danny jumped; they hadn't told him about this. ''I mean, I only got a glimpse, you know, but she was small and dark-haired, at least.''

''No. I don't know her. But I guess she could fit the description. I only got a glimpse too, Susan.'' He sounded distinctly defensive.

''Tell me about this, Susan,'' Danny said.

''There's not much to tell. We just saw this girl, driving there as we left. David almost broke his neck looking at her. She was pretty, in fact.''

Danny ran over the list in his mind; he had memorized the names. He would have bet a small fortune that the girl's name was either Kathryn Phillips or Evelyn Wasserman, and very likely the former, since the Wassermans' envelope was still there when he broke in. He considered throwing the name out, seeing what David did with it, but decided against it. He might get some information, but then he'd have to explain how he knew the name. That would lead to a lie or a Pandora's Box. Not good; at least not now. These women would be on the trip, along with Herbert North, John Goss, and Frank Wasserman. He would have bet money on that, too. The trip might be dangerous, but it sure was getting interesting.

"Okay, Susan," David said, much more firmly. "Now look. I know you, and I know something else happened today. Tell us about it."

"Maybe we'd better wait on this one, David. Maybe I'd better tell you when we're alone."

"Should I leave?" Danny asked.

"No," David said to him. Then to Susan: "Look, Danny's been in on all this almost from the start. God, I've told him some dark secrets of my own."

Not quite all of them, Danny thought.

David continued: "So whatever it is, I think he can hear it."

"I don't know, David. This one's kind of personal."

"So was my story about my childhood. So tell us. Please."

"All right. If you're sure, David?"

"I'm very sure."

"Well, you know the man I saw yesterday? Naked, with the erection?"

"Wait a minute, wait a minute." Danny interjected. "I haven't heard about this yet."

Briefly Susan told him about the man. He rolled the name over in his mind. Flower Feather. Sure did fit her, he decided. But the coincidence of the naked man she saw and his intruder was striking, and he said so. The only difference was that his intruder hadn't had an erection.

"But then I don't look like you do either, now do I?" Danny asked, grinning. She blushed. They compared descriptions of the man; he surely seemed to be the same.

"Anyhow, what about him?" David asked.

"I saw him again today. In the ladies' room at work. He just appeared behind me, or maybe he was waiting for me, I don't know."

"What did he do?"

"He told me to follow my instincts. And, David, it seemed so right at the moment. Follow my instincts. Did I say? He was erect again, just like yesterday."

Danny was looking at David. He remembered their first night. He was pretty sure he knew what Susan's instincts had been. She had peppered her description of the man with flattering adjectives.

"You fucked him, didn't you?" David said. It was, by inflection, about half a statement and half a question. Otherwise, his tone was emotionless.

"Yes," Susan said in a small voice, looking down at her shoes. Then: "Do you hate me, David?"

"No, of course not, Susan. Anyway, you said he was a phantom. How could I be jealous of a phantom? I told you years ago, the truth was more important to me than whatever you do."

Danny noticed that David's voice wavered just a little as he pronounced the last of the platitude. He was not following it himself, if Danny was any judge. And he had made a career out of judging correctly. He remembered that his reading of David earlier gave an indication of maybe a touch of voyeurism, or something similar. He stole a glance at the crotch of David's pants; sure enough. That hadn't been an error.

Susan jumped up and hugged David tightly; at that moment, Danny felt like an intruder.

But David sat her back down. "I want you to tell me everything that happened," he said.

"That's all. We made love, on the bathroom floor, and he left. But then, the door was still locked; he couldn't have left through the door. But I heard him."

"No, tell me all about it." He seemed to have forgotten Danny was there, or else he didn't care.

"I just did. You mean all the details? Graphically?"

"Yes."

"David, I don't—"

"Please, Susan."

She shrugged, and went through all the specifics of the encounter, including her own feelings at various points. It took fifteen minutes; and by the time she had finished, Danny was wishing he had been the phantom. He was aware that he also had an erection now, and David was smiling openly, obviously enjoying himself. Danny also noticed that David kept glancing at him; he had not forgotten that Danny was there. He wondered if that added spice to it. He shifted uncomfortably; he didn't need any more spice. The combination of the dreams and Susan's story was driving him crazy. He considered leaving.

Susan had a different kind of expression now; she could see how much her story had turned David on. Danny didn't know whether she realized that it had done the same thing to him. She seemed to be embarrassed, a little frightened, aroused, and confused, all at the same time. Danny felt he should say something, but decided it was best to stay out of it.

Abruptly she turned the conversation back to the shared dream. David seemed momentarily disappointed, but went along. She asked Danny how it had felt to die in the dream. She seemed keenly interested in this, but perhaps it was just to divert the conversation from the sexual topic. She seemed so aroused that Danny had half expected when she began to talk to him directly that she was going to ask him to leave. Again he considered it; it was obvious that they could make good use of an hour or so alone.

"I feel bad you had to go through that, Danny," she said. "Even in a dream."

"It wasn't as bad as I expected. Pretty bad, though. Have to admit that."

"Where did you say he stabbed you?"

"Right here." He touched a spot on his left chest, just below the nipple. He jumped. It hurt! He hadn't noticed that before.

"What's the matter?" David asked.

"I don't know. It's sore there, for some reason."

"Let's see," Susan said. She came over to him and started to unbutton his shirt.

Oh Jesus Christ! Do not do this to me, he thought.

But she proceeded to open his shirt, pushing it back to expose the area he had just felt. He heard her give a little gasp, and looked down. He had a scar there; it looked very old. The sort of scar one gets from a knife wound. Somehow he wasn't too surprised; it went along with everything else.

"I suppose you didn't have this yesterday," Susan said. She

was down on one knee between his legs looking up at him. She was driving him crazy.

"How did you guess?" he asked flatly. "What's really odd, it doesn't even seem strange, somehow. Like I expected it."

"That wasn't any ordinary dream," David put in.

"I think we already knew that," Danny said.

Susan had not moved. Slowly she arched her neck and kissed the scar on his chest. Her belly pressed momentarily against his erection and she looked back up at him quickly. She didn't appear startled. If he had to define the expression, it would have been as pleased.

She glanced over at David, saw that he was looking at her intently. While they were looking at each other, Danny violated his own tentative rule about not reading them and squinted. There was a broad connecting band of the sexual reddish brown color between them, rays of the same color from Susan to him. Damn it, he told himself. All three of them would probably have enjoyed this, but the risks were just too great to suit him. He gently shifted Susan aside and began to button his shirt. She got up and moved away, her expression unreadable. David looked distinctly disappointed.

David began discussing possible Freudian interpretations of the shared dream, and gradually the moment dissipated. Danny relaxed a bit, but he knew this tension would be present for quite a while. Susan was having a very profound effect on him.

"Obviously, we have some phallic symbolism here. I mean, it's pretty direct, with the guy telling you the piece of the club was larger—" David was saying to him.

"Look, David," Danny said. "You're interpreting this as if this were just a normal dream. Like I had come over and said, 'Hey, I had this neat dream.' But it isn't like that. Susan and I had exactly the same dream, and I have a scar that wasn't there yesterday! No, there's more to it. It's connected to these other weird happenings and to—to—" He bit his lip. He was going to say Tascan Acres, but he wanted to hold that back for a while yet.

"To what?" Susan asked. She looked wide-eyed and innocent, but Danny could tell she had a far more incisive mind than that. One had to be very careful around these two if one was going to hide anything from them.

"To the odd people we've been seeing," he improvised. It

was the best he could do on the spur of the moment. Susan inclined her head a trace and looked at him meaningfully. Damn, this was tough. He presumed she knew he was holding something back, but maybe she thought it was his attraction for her. That was safer at the moment. He just wasn't at all sure how either of them would react to a suggestion that the upcoming vacation had anything to do with the odd events; they had made it very clear that they were expecting relief from these things during the trip. He was sure they weren't going to get it.

The discussion of the dream went back and forth for a while, gave way to a new discussion of Susan's phantom lover—a more clinical, less arousing discussion this time—back to the appearance of Xilonen and the mysteriously blooming flowers. Perhaps obviously, no conclusions were being reached.

In mid-sentence, Danny found himself distracted by a ticking noise at the window. He looked, couldn't see anything. But the noise persisted, quite loud at times.

"What the hell's that?" he asked.

"No idea," David said. All three of them went to the window and looked. The source of the tinkling, ticking sound was immediately obvious; it was a butterfly, beating its wings on the window. A very large butterfly at that.

"A butterfly?" Danny said incredulously. "In New York, in February?"

"That's what it is, though," Susan commented.

"I've seen or heard of one like that," David put in. He reached for the crank and began to turn it, the window swinging inward like a little door.

"You think you should?" Danny asked. Visions of huge cats transforming into men raced through his mind.

"I think I have to," he replied, continuing to crank.

As soon as the window was open, the insect flew inside. They watched it as it soared and dipped gracefully around the room. Though its wingspan was some eight or ten inches, it was still a butterfly, and didn't seem at all threatening.

It flew toward them; they could see it swinging its wings forward to brake its flight. It lit on Susan's arm, the big wings moving slowly up and down. She looked startled, but didn't move.

"It's real heavy," she said.

Danny moved close and examined it. It was jet black, body and wings glistening, almost mirrored. In fact, if it wasn't moving, he would have been willing to testify under oath that it was made of black glass. He watched the coiled tongue extend and touch Susan's skin.

"That's a weird sensation," she said, still not moving. "It feels hot and cold all at once. It makes me feel—I don't know. Different. All over."

Danny looked closer, a little alarmed. The damn thing wasn't injecting a venom or something, was it? No. The long tongue just grazed her skin, like a glass hair being dragged along her arm. Butterflies didn't inject venom anyway, he told himself. It turned its eyes and looked at him. He jumped. Can butterflies do that? he asked himself. But the eyes weren't right; not the bulging compound eyes of a butterfly. They were glittering, catlike, vertical pupils. They drilled into his, and he felt odd too; but how was hard to describe. Once when he was a child, he had been in Cleveland with his parents, and the polluted Cuyahoga had caught fire, petroleum distillates burning on its surface. The way he felt now was the way he'd felt then, when he was six years old, watching water burn.

The butterfly recoiled its tongue and lifted into the air. It fluttered for a moment, then landed on David. It went through the same process, grazing his skin.

"I see what you mean, Susan," David said. "It's heavy, and the tongue feels—really strange."

"By any chance like burning water?" Danny asked.

"Hey, that's really a good comparison. Hot and cold, but at the same time. How'd you know?"

"Just a feeling I get from it."

David brought his other hand around as if to catch it. Nimbly it avoided him, springing into the air with surprising speed. It flew around the room, putting on an impressive aerial show, then zoomed straight through the still-open window. They all jumped toward it, but almost immediately it disappeared into the night.

"Now, what was that all about?" David asked.

"No idea," Danny said, looking at the window. He squinted and crossed his eyes. Off in the distance, to the south, he saw a red and black sunburst dwindle away rapidly. Then nothing.

34

About eleven o'clock that night, officers Sams and Eddison received a call to investigate a disturbance in a section of the South Bronx they knew to be inhabited by Haitian immigrants. As Eddison checked their riot gun, Sams turned off the Cross-Bronx Expressway.

When they arrived, they found a large number of people milling around in the street, totally blocking traffic. An odd structure had been hastily erected, and a bonfire built in front of it. As their cruiser pulled up—they were obviously first on the scene—both officers prepared for a possible assault on their car. But the people in the crowd only gave them a cursory glance; a couple of them actually smiled. They relaxed a little; it obviously wasn't a riot. These people were not destroying property, or otherwise behaving in any hostile fashion. They heard a voice, apparently female, shouting to the crowd. Outside of that, it was a quiet gathering. Sams estimated maybe a hundred fifty people in all.

"You think we should just wade into that mob?" Eddison asked.

"I dunno. They don't seem mad at cops. Let's be cool about this, see if we can find out what's goin' down." Sams was black, and he had originally come from the streets; he felt more kinship here than Eddison could, being a product of the white working-class districts of Newark.

Leaving the riot gun behind, the two officers began to move through the crowd. They were encountering no hostility, no resistance; people moved to let them pass when asked. Before they had gotten to a position where they could see what was going on, they heard the sound of drums from up front. Eddison could have imagined he was in darkest Africa, listening to ominous tribal rites getting under way. He looked at Sams, but his partner's expression was unreadable.

At last they came to a point where they could see clearly. The drums' sounds were soft and languid, but insistent, compelling. Behind the bonfire, which was built of scrap wood and old furniture, they saw that the hasty construction they had noticed on their arrival consisted of five posts standing upright, four around a larger one in the center. Over this, a crude roof had been laid, and inside, hanging from the ceiling near the center post, was a child's toy ship on a string.

The woman addressing the crowd stood just in front of the structure, waving her arms. The drums increased in volume and tempo; a double strike each time, like the beating of a heart. Just a little faster, a little louder. Eddison and Sams looked at each other; both were finding it difficult to concentrate. The people in the front were swaying back and forth to the rhythm of the drums. Eddison listened, but could not make head nor tail of what the woman was saying.

"Damballah Wedo!" she screamed. "Maitresse Erzulie! Legba of the crossroads! And Ogou-Fer! All in this city, all tonight! The Loa themselves, not riding, no, not the divine horsemen this night, no, they are afoot, they are themselves! They sleep, but— They! Are! Themselves!" Each of these last words was accompanied by a sharp strike on a drum. A tremor seemed to run through the crowd; it seemed that these people were definitely getting worked up. Eddison especially looked nervous; Sams not much better. These weren't his people, and he didn't know what was happening.

The drums became louder and faster, the crowd was moving more, and even the officers were getting excited, adrenaline pumping. The woman paused for a few moments, her body twisting and flexing with the accelerating drumbeat. She was young, attractive, dressed in a white cotton blouse and long, multicolored skirt, no coat in spite of the cold night. But it probably wasn't cold behind the roaring bonfire; the officers could feel the heat of it on their faces, and she was much closer than they.

"We will give homage to Damballah Wedo! To Erzulie! Homage and honor, and prayers for the journey they undertake!" she yelled. Without warning she stripped off the blouse and skirt and began to dance around. She was wearing a kind of loincloth, but that was all.

"Okay, folks, now just hold on here," Sams shouted, moving toward the woman. They were about three rows back; but the shoulders in front of them closed up. They couldn't actually see anybody moving to resist them, but they couldn't get any closer, either.

"Move aside, folks! Police!" Eddison yelled. No one moved. He looked over the wall of shoulders; up front, people were throwing food into the structure. The woman's dance was getting wilder and wilder, the drums faster and louder. Eddison felt dizzy and disoriented, wished the drums weren't so loud. He shook his head to clear it, but it didn't help much.

Getting no response to his demands to be let through, he took out his nightstick, preparing to hit the man standing in front of him. Someone behind him snatched it from his hand. He looked around for Sams, couldn't see him either. The crowd was dancing in place, people taking off their coats and throwing them down. Eddison was beginning to panic. He looked back up at the dancing woman. From somewhere, a live chicken was handed to her; she danced around with it for a few minutes, then took its head in her mouth. Her jaws clamped down, the chicken squirmed wildly, and she ripped it backward; it came away headless. She released the body to the pavement, and let it run around the front row, flapping its wings and spraying blood on everyone. Opening her mouth slightly, she allowed the blood to drip to the pavement. The head was tossed in among the collected food.

Eddison figured this had gone too far; he was seeing bare torsos in the crowd around him. These people were having an orgy in the street! His head was spinning, he couldn't see or think clearly, and he couldn't find Sams. His senses were being overloaded; he suppressed a wild urge to join in, felt a flash of anger because of the impulse. Pushed to the edge, he drew his service revolver. It disappeared from his hand just as his nightstick had. Hands came out of the crowd, seized him; he was passed from one set of hands to another, back through the crowd, until he reached the back perimeter, not fifty feet from their cruiser. There he was dumped unceremoniously on the pavement. He looked up at a solid wall of backs, shoulder to shoulder. The wall parted for a moment, and Sams emerged just as he had; sans nightstick and gun, but only his dignity hurt. Again, the wall closed.

Both officers sat and looked at each other for a moment, then jumped up and dashed toward their car.

Eddison was the first to get there. "Call for help!" Sams panted from behind him.

"Right." Pause. "Shit! The Goddamn radio's been trashed! And the fucking riot gun's gone, too! Let's get to a phone, call it in."

"Wait, there's a walkie-talkie. Gone. Damn."

"Let's go, man!"

The starter on the car ground hopelessly when they turned the key. It dawned on the men that the engine had probably taken some damage, too. With a sigh, they climbed out again, walked down the dark street; they constantly glanced backward as if expecting to be chased. No one paid any attention to them. When they were about a block away, a great shout went up from the crowd. The officers never did know what it was about.

They had to walk fourteen blocks before they found a phone in any kind of working order, and it had the earpiece missing. They tried it anyway, asking the operator to call in for their backup. That seemed to work; when they were another eight blocks down, looking for another functional phone, a cruiser with lights flashing picked them up. When they got back to the site of the disturbance, there was nothing there to indicate it had happened except for the trash scattered about and the still-smouldering bonfire.

They searched the area for quite a while, but virtually no one was on the streets. After about an hour, they gave it up, informed headquarters. They had to wait until a service truck arrived to pull in their cruiser, and since they had no guns, the officers that had picked them up waited with them.

While they were waiting, a call came in on the radio, requesting other officers to converge on an old warehouse not far from their current position. Seemed that the two white males, one black male, one hispanic male, and two white females had been found in a dumpster, all dead, all without clothing above the waist; all stabbed once in the chest. Preliminary indications gave no sign of sexual attack, and it seemed that the victims' hearts were missing. Oddly, they showed no signs of having been tied; there were no indications of struggle, no defensive wounds on the hands and arms. The oddest note was the fact that the victims were all smiling in death.

"I tell you, this city gets weirder every day," Eddison noted.

"You hear about that business at Times Square last night?" one of the other officers asked.

"No, what was that?"

"Witnesses say some crippled guy interfered in a mugging. A crippled dude goin' on three Rican gang members, can you dig it? Left two of 'em dead. We're lookin' for him. The guy has only one foot."

"Only one foot? How'd he get away?"

"Witness said he ran."

"No shit?"

"No shit."

35

Earlier that same evening Bertie had taken Geneva shopping on Fifth Avenue for new clothes. Dress, shoes, toiletries, underwear, makeup; all told he had spent nearly a thousand dollars. Geneva was stunned.

When he finally saw her, dressed for a night on the town, he decided it had been well worth it. She looked like the queen of some African nation. He thought they made an exquisite pair, strolling around in the vicinity of Fifth Avenue and Fifty-seventh Street. On impulse, Bertie asked a cabbie to recommend a place to eat; he did, and took them to a Mexican restaurant on Seventh Avenue called Alejandro's. Inside, looking at the stucco walls and exposed wooden beams, Bertie decided it was an excellent choice. The decor was somewhat different from the average; there were no sombreros, no bullfight posters. Everything seemed to refer to an older Mexico, that of the Aztecs and Mayas. Bertie liked that much better.

The waiter brought nachos, hot sauce, and water; took their orders for drinks; and left. Then Bertie noticed a dark-skinned young man at an adjacent table, who was staring at him intently. As was his habit, Bertie stared back. The man, who looked like he could be Mexican, continued to regard him with an amused expression.

Bertie soon lost patience. "Do you need something?" he asked in an icy tone. Across the table, Geneva instantly went on full alert; she was quite aware of the potentialities of the situation.

"I'm just curious," the man said in an equally cool, slightly accented voice. "You going to a costume party, or do you just wear that thing when you come here?"

"What thing?" Bertie's voice was softer, even colder.

"That, of course," the other responded, gesturing at the carved foot.

There was a moment's silence. "It's a prosthesis," Bertie said in measured tones. "I lost a foot in an accident—"

"Oh, yeah. A water-dragon bit it off, right?"

Bertie lost his composure momentarily. "What?" he asked, somewhat weakly.

The dark man laughed. "You mean you don't know the legends? You wear a thing like that, and—and—" The man stopped talking. He was staring at the foot now; unnoticed by Bertie or Geneva, a plume of smoke was rising from it, dissipating into the air. Slowly, the man's gaze came back to rest on Bertie's face. His previously composed expression had shattered into one of pure terror. "Uhhh—I'm sorry—" he stammered, "I—uh—I was just leaving—" He rose from his chair so rapidly he knocked it over; and while everyone turned to stare, he ran for the door.

"What the hell was all that?" Bertie asked rhetorically, looking at Geneva.

She shrugged. "You got me," she told him. "New York attracts all kinds of crazies."

36

Unable to expel her image from his mind, John had begun to search around Nikki's apartment for—he didn't exactly know what for. Perhaps something to tell him where she was. He would have liked to call her, just to hear her voice on the phone, even from the Bahamas. He had had no luck, but he did find a few things he really didn't want to find; two pornographic magazines, one dated 1982, showing Nikki and a very handsome, unsmiling man making love on a bathroom floor. The other was dated 1985, and it featured a spread of Nikki and two men engaged in virtually every ordinary sex act he could imagine. While he knew what she was doing when he wasn't around, it was different to see it in an eleven-page spread in full color. But he also found he couldn't stop looking at the pictures.

Her desk had a locked drawer, and the key was nowhere to be found. He had bypassed this several times, feeling more than a little embarrassed about searching through her things. Bending down, he examined the lock. Perhaps if he used a screwdriver and pried down on the drawer itself, he could open it. He decided to try, being careful to ensure that no damage was done, and to ensure that he left no evidence of his prying.

Another fifteen minutes searching turned up a screwdriver, a battered old tool with initials scratched into the handle: HN. He wondered who that might have been. Probably one of her regular customers. Shrugging, he returned to the desk.

For a while he thought he was not going to succeed. The drawer bent downward quite a bit, but not enough to free the latch. Finally, just when he was about to give it up, it released, and he pulled open the drawer. Carefully he examined the edge; no damage.

Inside, there was a stack of papers, nothing more. He rifled through it. He had almost expected more pornographic pictures, but there were none; in fact there were only two photos in the drawer. One was of another long-haired, bearded man; on the back was the legend, "Elliot, 1969." John stared at it for a moment; he could not recall Nikki having mentioned an Elliot. Again, possibly a customer.

The other was a picture of himself, as he had looked in med school. He hadn't given it to her, and he wondered where she had gotten it. It was a candid shot, taken with a telephoto lens; he could tell because of the distorted size of the setting sun that appeared at the side of the frame. It was an excellent photo, doubtlessly worthy of publication. The sun, setting among clouds and only partially visible, created rays of light and shadow that made him look like he was wearing a head-dress, something with long plumes. It was a very striking effect.

Putting the photo aside, he started to glance through the papers. Perhaps legal documents or investments, he had thought; but they were not. All the papers concerned, in one way or another, himself. He was stunned. How had she gotten these things, and why? His college and med school transcripts; notes on his days as a musician; extensive notes on his pottery business. She seemed to have a record of almost every piece he had sold. A photocopy of his birth certificate, with an astrological chart stapled to it. He looked at this for a moment. He didn't know very much about astrology, but he did notice one thing that he had not previously known. He had been born exactly, to the second if the chart could be believed, on the vernal equinox, a precise Pisces-Aries cusp. He had hardly expected to learn something about himself by breaking into Nikki's desk. The woman was full of surprises.

He dug deeper into the papers and found even more surprising things. Notes on his childhood, his parents. One of these had a big asterisk at the corner; he read over it more carefully. It seemed to be a record of his parents' whereabouts, finely detailed, in the year preceding his birth. Again he wondered where, how, and why she had gotten this material. Some of it he already knew; during his mother's pregnancy, she had remained in Wisconsin while his father had been in the Southwest, working on oil rigs in the fields of Texas and Oklahoma. He came home to stay a year or so after John's birth. The dates indicated that he had been home for a month in November; his mother should have been maybe five months pregnant at the time. There was a note that at that time his mother had spent a week in the hospital and his father had been arrested and briefly jailed; he'd never known about that. He wondered what the circumstances were. Back further in the notes, it seemed that his father had been in the southwest for the previous eleven months, and—he stopped, mentally figuring the dates. If they were correct, he had three choices: he was a five-month preemie at birth, or fifteen months overdue. Or his father wasn't his father, at least not biologically. That was a shock. Perhaps it also explained the hospital stay and the arrest. He was finding this hard to believe. His prim, proper, and devoutly fundamentalist mother would be the last person on the face of the earth he would have suspected of having an affair. But the nature of the notes surprised him more; Nikki knew more about him than he did about himself.

According to the documents, his mother had been in a car accident outside Madison in April, and had been hospitalized then for five months. There was a photocopy of an extensive hospital report and medical records from Madison. She had broken her pelvis, both femurs, and had internal injuries, but had been released in late September. He went over the dates again. That was ridiculous on the face of it; the implication was that he had been conceived while his mother was in the hospital with massive injuries below the waist! One report noted that in spite of the injuries, her hymen remained intact. That report bore a date of July 17. But that was impossible; he certainly remembered enough medicine to know that. Unless he was premature, she was already pregnant by then.

But the report on his birth in March made no indication of his having been premature. That report also indicated that there had been complications, that his mother had had a hysterectomy; and that too, he told himself, was impossible. He had a younger sister; he could remember seeing his mother pregnant with her. There was a clear image of his mother standing in some park, the wind blowing her dress back, defining her large abdomen.

The final report was a psychiatric workup. It seemed that his mother had had a truly wild delusion. The therapist had never gotten to the bottom of it, and he rendered an opinion that it was a defense against the affair, or possibly the rape, that he assumed had gotten her pregnant. He expounded at length on the trauma of a rape while she was hospitalized with severe injuries, clearly what the therapist had decided was the most likely event. He also noted in that report that the rapist must have been very small, since her hymen was not broken. She had told him that she and her husband had not yet consummated their marriage, believing only in sex for procreation, and they had wanted to wait until either he came home to stay or she moved to Texas with him. She said she had been a virgin when she married, and he saw no reason to doubt it. But, wrote the psychiatrist, her delusion was a peculiar one; she said a ball of multicolored feathers had descended on her as she lay in her hospital bed, and that when they touched her breast, they had gone inside of her. She had missed her next period, and was convinced that the feathers had made her pregnant.

37

When Danny made the long drive out to Long Island again that afternoon, he didn't plan to break into the trailer; he just wanted to verify something for himself. As he came to the turnoff, he found that his first suspicion checked out. The sign indicating the way to the development was no longer there. He turned in, drove up to the trailer. Yes. He had been absolutely right. It stood with the door hanging open, all signs which might have identified it gone. Looking inside, he saw that most of the furniture remained, a thin skim of sand on it where a wayward breeze had brought it in the open door. But no papers, no file cabinet; even the blankets piled on the couch were gone. It looked like no one had been in there in five years. Danny smiled grimly. Fake, all right; but what was the point? That he still he couldn't figure. Oh, well, he said to himself, we'll find out in sunny South America, no doubt.

He left the dilapidated trailer and started his journey back to the city. From his car radio, a mournful voice started reading obituaries; he didn't want to listen to that, flipped to another station. A commercial for some Christian TV show was playing; a voice urged him to "tune in to the Word of the Lord" on channel 62. On network TV, the voice continued, "sex and violence were the new Gods."

Danny grunted. "Sex and violence are, and always have been, the only Gods," he said aloud.

It was with a sigh of relief that Susan left her office. Nothing but a perfectly ordinary, typical workday today. No phantom lovers—that was maybe a bit disappointing—but today, her libido was under control. Just hot, not flaming, she told herself. She hailed a cab and began the ride home in the hectic five o'clock traffic. She was really looking forward to the trip tomorrow, glad Danny was planning to go.

As she always did, she looked at the cabbie's picture in the little frame, started to glance up at the driver to see if he matched it. Her eyes never got that far; her attention was captured by a very striking couple on the sidewalk. The cab stopped for a light, and she had a chance to watch the two go by. The woman was a lithe, catlike black girl, expensively dressed. The man did not wear unusual clothing, although she recognized his suit as expensive. His face was what interested her. It was very close to, though not quite identical to, the face of her phantom lover. She watched him closely. Something odd about his left shoe. A mirror on it or something. He turned his head, looked into her eyes. If anything, his face was more beautiful at that moment, out in the fading sun, than the phantom's. He smiled broadly, boyishly, apparently at her. The cab moved on, but she could still see that face for many blocks.

As usual, the subway was crowded, and David was hanging onto one of the overhead bars as he rode home. He was thinking about the trip, hoping that Kathryn Phillips would be there, and fearing the idea at the same time. He gritted his teeth as her image sprang up in his mind yet again.

A schoolgirl was sitting almost right on top of him; he worried about getting another erection. She kept bumping him, and if he did she'd bang her head right into it. The bodies on the train were so packed he couldn't move away. He knew that if he did become erect, the schoolgirl would assume she was the cause of it, not his fantasies of Kathryn. He didn't know whether the schoolgirl was attractive or not; all he could see was the top of her head and blue jeans. She was reading a book, which was lying open in her lap. He looked past the blond hair at the pictures in the book; frescos of some kind, some sort of antiquities. He didn't know what. In his limited field of vision, a phrase seemed framed for him. He read it: ''And they awoke from a dream that they had lived human lives,/ And found themselves to be gods.''

He wondered what that was from. He was trying to get a look at the book title when the train roared into a station and ground to a halt. The schoolgirl jumped up to get out; apparently it was her stop. She forced her way to the door, stepped out of the train, and began walking along the platform obliquely to the train. As the train began to pull away again, she turned, looked directly at him, and smiled.

Xilonen.

At Nikki's apartment, John had practically memorized the documents he'd found. He'd known there had been something odd concerning his birth, but this was just too weird to accept. The information here seemed to indicate that he was the product of a rapist, and an especially cruel one at that; or immaculate conception.

''Who do you think you are, John? Jesus Christ?'' he snarled at himself. There was another possibility: his mother was not a parent of his either. He had always felt an extreme alienation from both parents; perhaps this was the reason. Maybe he had been stuffed in his mother's bed like some cuckoo, which lays its eggs in the nests of other birds. But that still didn't explain his sister, born to a woman with no uterus! He realized very clearly how absurd that was. Then another concept occurred to him; his sister could have been a cuckoo also! But no, he remembered seeing his mother pregnant. Or at least looking pregnant. He sighed; he was going in circles. These problems could not be solved from the documents alone. When he returned, he would have to look into it.

On impulse, and to distract himself from the documents, he turned on the television, switched to channel 62. He was startled; the religious program, or movie, or whatever, was on again! Once more the preacher was pontificating:

"And he will return, soon now, brother, sooner every day! Now I want you to know his earthly sign, for you, brother, to honor it! Yea, brother, he has left signs for us. Signs we can see! Signs we can hear! So look, listen, and tremble in fear! His earthly kingdom will soon be made manifest!"

John thought this was the oddest movie he'd ever seen. It couldn't be a real religious program, not with the—

His thoughts were interrupted by the sound of a rock 'n' roll record, one very familiar to him. Only part of it was being played; a crisp, clean trumpet solo. He knew it well; it was his own playing, a recording he'd made years ago in Los Angeles. As the music played, a curtain opened to reveal a display stand, on which stood one of his pots. One of his best, he thought dazedly; one of his very best, the one with the plumed serpent motif. The remote control unit fell from his nerveless fingers. As it bounced on the floor, it changed the channel. When he switched back to 62, he got only snow.

38

THURSDAY, FEB. 12, 1987

David and Susan were among the first people to board Eastern's Flight 762 for Miami that morning. They were smiling, happy, very eager to be on their trip. Danny had been unable to get a seat on this flight, so he had taken an earlier one from Newark; they were to meet in Miami. It was starting out to be a fine trip; excellent weather, no problems at all. Susan sat reading the flight magazine while David watched the other passengers board the plane. As always, a bewildering variety of people; a soldier in uniform, a businessman carrying two huge portfolio cases he refused to check, a terrified-looking older woman, probably on her first flight. An unusual couple caught his attention; the man was very large and muscular, with moderately long hair, and glasses. The woman with him was extremely beautiful, with a cascade of thick black hair reaching her waist, and large turquoise eyes in startling contrast to her olive skin. Her clothing was especially interesting; her blouse matched her eyes, and she wore a short, jade-green skirt. They attracted a great deal of attention as they walked back through the cabin, taking seats two rows ahead of David and Susan. They began to talk; David was very impressed with their voices. His rumbled low, like distant thunder, hers was musical and light, reminding him of mountain streams in the Catskills. He could hear only a few snatches of their conversation, something about scuba diving. Wherever they were going, they hoped the diving would be good; they'd brought all their gear. David called Susan's attention to them as they twisted around to talk to a stewardess. She found them equally impressive.

Then Susan seemed to jump. She tapped David on the shoulder and indicated a man just coming down the aisle. David looked: a very handsome man indeed. Might have been a movie star, or male model, David thought.

"Look at his left foot!" Susan whispered.

David couldn't see it well, but he seemed to be wearing mismatched shoes, and the left one looked like it had a mirror built into the top of it. Very odd.

"I saw him on the street yesterday," Susan said. "He is almost an exact copy of the man in the office! Almost exact!"

David looked at him again. He didn't feel he was any judge of male attractiveness, but the man certainly looked handsome to him. "What's with the shoe?" he asked.

"Who knows?"

Then, in turn, David stiffened. Several rows ahead of them, a woman was taking her seat; Kathryn Phillips. Surely she wasn't going on the same trip! She twisted around in her seat to talk to the stewardess, looked back at the other passengers. Her eyes found David's, and it was the first time to his knowledge that she had seen him. She smiled at him; a rich, sensual smile full of many kinds of promises. In turmoil, he glanced over at Susan, was gratified to find she was looking out the window. When he looked back, he could barely see Kathryn's dark hair over the seat top; but one small foot extended to the side. Staring at that foot caused him to miss another striking passenger boarding the plane; a big, sad-eyed man with newly styled hair and beard, seemingly uncomfortable in his preppie clothes. Susan was looking out the window, watching them load the plane, and didn't see him either.

The flight from LaGuardia to Miami was uneventful; landings always made Susan uncomfortable, since she was aware that this was the most dangerous phase of any flight. But both landings—at Raleigh/Durham and later at Miami—had been as smooth as could have been expected. As the plane taxied toward the gate, only a few people heeded the crew's instruction to remain seated until the aircraft came to a full stop at the gate. She and David were not among them.

As they came through the tunnel, she noticed David looking around for someone, but she paid little attention. She herself was trying to get another look at the man with the mirrored shoe. He fascinated her; she'd like to hear the story behind that odd shoe. But he was apparently already off and gone. David didn't seem to find whoever he was looking for, either. In the waiting room outside stood Danny, looking a little uncomfortable.

"Hi, folks," he said as they came up. "Have a good flight?"

"Yeah, it was fine," David replied. "You?"

"Good flight, but problems since I got here. How are you supposed to connect to your next flight? I can't find out anything about it. The only flight to the vicinity of Aruba is to Aruba itself, or to the Venezuelan mainland."

"They were supposed to contact us here. I kind of expected some agent to be here to meet us, but I don't see anybody."

"I gotta find out what the name of this place is. I don't have a ticket yet."

Susan watched David look around helplessly. There was no one who even might have been an agent. She noticed the striking couple David had pointed out on the plane; they too were wandering about aimlessly.

Then, a voice over the P.A. system: "Will the following people please come to Gate 52. David Hallsten. Susan Hallsten. Herbert North. Kathryn Phillips. Frank Wasserman. Evelyn Wasserman. John Goss. Danny Hudson. Thank you."

Susan stood there looking around. John Goss? Is that what they said? She asked David if he had heard the same name.

"What? Oh, I don't know. We'd better go. Where the hell is Gate 52, anyway?" He seemed very rattled.

"Danny, did you hear that name? John Goss? Is that what I heard?" She was a little frantic for verification. But Danny was engrossed in something of his own, and hadn't heard her.

"They called my name, too!" he breathed. "What the fuck is this? How did they get my name?"

She turned desperately from one to the other, but neither seemed to notice her. Both had something else on their minds, obviously. At the moment, she didn't care. She ran up to the ticketing clerk and asked where Gate 52 was. Getting the information, she returned to the two bewildered men and pointed down a hallway. They followed her lead.

At Gate 52, she saw the agent from Tascan Acres and the striking couple from the plane. She looked around; no one else, yet. Eagerly she watched the hall outside the low wall that defined Gate 52.

"Hello, people, glad ta see ya!" Flores gushed. "We'll be leaving here just as soon as everybody arrives. Shouldn't be long. Just relax, have a seat."

"What about me? Danny Hudson? They called my name!"

"Oh, yes, Mr. Hudson. You have a confirmed reservation, yes you do. Right here." Flores tapped his pad with a thick forefinger.

"But how did you get my name? I've never even seen you before."

"Well, I don't make up the list, Mr. Hudson. You don't want to go? Nobody's forcing you."

"But—but—no charge?"

"No charge. All taken care of. Relax, Mr. Hudson. You'll have a great time."

Vaguely, peripherally, Susan sensed Danny's discomfort. He was trying to talk to David, but David was paying no attention; he was looking for someone too. All this was unimportant to Susan. She anxiously watched the people walking by outside.

The man with the mirrored shoe came in. Susan stared; he was going, too? Flores scanned his list.

"Ah, Mr. North. Yes sir, good to see you again. Just relax, we got two more we're waiting for."

A very small, pretty girl with dark hair walked in. The girl in the car, Susan realized. Did David know her? His eyes never left her as she went up to Flores and told him her name: Kathryn Phillips. Now Susan paid a little attention to David; he seemed about to faint.

"David? You all right?" she asked, glancing back and forth between him and the hallway.

"Yeah, sure, Susan, I'm fine." He almost sounded drugged, slurring a little. Danny must have noticed it as well. He, too, was staring at the girl intently.

Next, a tall man with a beard came into sight, carrying a battered suitcase that ill matched his expensive clothing. Mindless of the startled stares from David and Danny, Susan ran to him. "John!" she cried. "It is you!"

"Susan? Susan!" he cried. They ran into each other's arms, his bag falling to the floor. He hugged her, lifted her off her feet. Then he set her down again.

"My God, Susan, I can't believe it!" he said, holding her by her shoulders. His eyes were shiny and wet as he glanced at David and Danny, who were flanking Susan now.

"David, Danny," Susan said, wiping her own eyes. "I want you to meet my brother, John Goss."

Danny looked from one to the other, thought he could see a family resemblance. Susan was explaining that she had not seen her brother for years, hadn't known where he was. It was obvious that David had never met the man. Danny was very impressed with John Goss; but he reserved judgment on whether he liked the man or not. The most striking thing about him was the extreme sadness in his eyes; it even showed through the pleasure of seeing Susan again.

He couldn't keep his attention on this, though. Strange as it was, the coincidence of John and Susan meeting again on this trip was trivial compared to the other things. First, the absurd circumstance of his being included on the passenger list. Now there was an event that certainly begged some kind of explanation, and it apparently was not going to be forthcoming, at least not from Flores. The second item was downright weird, assuring him—if he had needed any further assurance—that this trip and the oddities of the past week were somehow interrelated. The girl that David seemed so totally distracted by was very familiar to Danny, too. In the shared dream, she had been the woman who had turned into Susan. He was rerunning that dream in his mind when he got his first good look at Herbert North; and he went ice cold inside. Standing here in Miami International Airport was the man from that same dream, accurate down to his mirrored shoe; only the clothing was different. He caught Danny looking at him, returned his gaze with a sardonic, self-confident smile. He himself had been staring at John Goss. A little wildly, Danny glanced around the waiting room, half expecting to see the two black-robed figures. They were all that was needed to make the cast complete. They weren't there, but it hardly made Danny feel any better. To himself, he admitted it; he was really scared.

David was trying to concentrate on Susan's brother, whom he knew only from a few stories. Susan had always spoken of him with great affection; David just hadn't connected the name. In actuality, he appreciated the diversion. It kept him from staring so blatantly at Kathryn, who smiled seductively at him every time she caught his eye. He really felt he was losing control. He had no idea how he was going to get through the vacation without approaching her. Perhaps, he told himself, it was inevitable; fated by whatever gods controlled such destinies.

"All right, friends, your plane is here!" Flores called out. "Let's get on board, get this show on the road!"

As he moved mechanically toward the gate, David realized that Danny was trying to talk to him. "That man, David! With the mirrored shoe! He's the one from the dream!" he whispered.

"Susan said he looked like her phantom lover," David observed.

"And how did they get my name? David, something is very wrong!"

"It'll be okay, Danny." In his mind he was sure it would be. Concentrating on what Danny was saying, he bumped into the person in front of him; Evelyn Wasserman turned and looked at him, smiled. Good God, he thought. Three women on this trip, every one of them a raving beauty. Must have been part of the selection process.

The gate did not take them into a tunnel; instead, they found themselves outside, being led across the tarmac toward a small twin-engine plane. With Flores in the lead, they mounted the stairs which had been folded out from the plane's interior. After they'd all found seats, a stewardess—Mexican, David judged—checked their seat belts. David was actually a bit relieved when he saw her. She was very handsome, but not a beauty. He was beginning to believe women didn't come any other way.

"We'll be taking off shortly, friends, so just relax. If you need anything, Maria will help you," Flores said from the front of the plane. David felt the aircraft move backward, then out onto the apron, and finally onto the runway itself. Soon they were airborne, a smooth takeoff. Still concentrating on the other passengers, David hadn't noticed that the plane bore no markings identifying it as belonging to any airline or charter service.

The aircraft banked smoothly out over the open Atlantic from Florida, remaining at a fairly low altitude. Flores got up in the front of the cabin and introduced everyone, while the silent Maria served coffee. Everyone on the plane seems happy about something, Danny thought, except me. Even sad-eyed John Goss had a veneer of joy over the rediscovery of his sister, and, as he had put it, the fact that "the world hadn't consumed her."

While Flores rambled on nonsensically, Danny looked out the window at the blue Atlantic. There were no clouds, and the midafternoon sun sparkled on the water. He tried to enjoy it, but he was suspicious about too many things. He decided to try to read Flores and Maria. Flores first; he was standing up there blustering, a perfect target. But Danny soon quit, disgusted. The coppery glow of money-lust, and absolutely nothing else; Flores had no interests other than money and power. A very shallow man.

The strong-looking form of Maria came down the aisle carrying a tray; he tried her. As soon as he started, her black eyes flashed wide open; she looked straight at him. Intimidated, he stopped. Now what's this? he asked himself. She seems to know I'm doing it, and she doesn't like it. Very interesting. He waited until she passed, then tried it again while her back was turned.

Immediately she whirled around and looked right into his eyes. Putting her tray down, she came back to his seat.

"Could I speak with you please?" she asked. "In the back." Danny was a little surprised; she had only a trace of an accent. He got up and followed her to the little alcove near the lavatories. "Please do not do that," she demanded.

"What's that?" he said innocently.

"Trying to *see* me."

"I don't know what you mean."

"Yes, you do. And I will not—"

Irritated, he put his hands on his hips. "Now look," he told her firmly. "I've been threatened enough lately. Now suppose you tell me exactly what's going on here; then maybe I'll—"

She sighed, cutting him off. "You and the others are taking a trip. Going on vacation." She looked directly into his eyes; there was a flicker of amusement in hers. "If you insist, then see me. Now."

He took up the challenge, crossed his eyes and squinted, and—

She wasn't there.

He opened his eyes and looked at her. Perfectly normal. Squinted slightly, and she was gone again.

"How are you doing that?" he asked, a tremor in his voice.

She shrugged. "I'm a nagual. You don't know the word, but you know what it means. Now: try to enjoy your flight. Can I get you coffee?"

This last statement was so utterly incongruous he couldn't believe she'd said it. He staggered back, his hands shaking, and fell heavily into the aisle seat across from Susan and David.

"Either of you ever heard of a nagual?" he asked them.

"No. What is it?" Susan asked. David shook his head.

"I don't have any idea." he said. "But to paraphrase an old joke, I think one is crawling up our collective necks!"

He leaned back in the seat and tried to relax, conscious of the gay chatter around him. There was, after all, really very little he could do about it while flying over the Atlantic. But it certainly was not easy to just forget it.

The ocean water was gradually changing color, Danny noticed. He tried desperately to concentrate on the scenery. There were little islands visible now, white beaches surrounded by green or turquoise water. He looked up at Evelyn Wasserman, whose face was to him, two rows up. Exactly the color of her eyes, he thought. He wondered what the story was on these people. Had they been having odd experiences, too? He would have been willing to bet that they had. After they got to the resort, he would approach some of them and find out. He looked at Kathryn. David might not like it, but he made a decision to approach her first. Maybe more than approach.

Out the window, he saw a wide, flat, featureless green expanse of land off in the distance. The plane was banking so that it was now to his left. He looked at his watch; couldn't be the South American mainland, they hadn't been airborne nearly long enough, though he was surprised by how much time had passed. In any case, it seemed that the pilot was bringing them in, the brilliant ocean waters getting closer all the time. He could not see what land mass might lie ahead, just the crystal waters.

"Are we landing already?" Susan asked excitedly.

"Kinda looks like it," Danny replied.

The no smoking sign blinked on, and the pilot's voice came back to them: "Please fasten your seat belts, we will be landing momentarily." Danny was a little surprised, having envisioned the pilot as Hispanic; the accent was American Southern.

He heard the wheels drop down as the plane continued to lose altitude. At length it passed over a coastline, then some trees; it turned a bit, their path becoming less perpendicular to the coast. Finally it touched down. Danny saw a cloud of dust rise and quickly disappear behind the plane as it gradually rolled to a stop.

The passengers rose almost in unison as the front door opened; tropical sunshine streamed in, as if welcoming them. Following Susan and David, Danny walked to the front of the plane and stepped out onto the stairs.

They were on a dirt runway. No terminal building, no hangars, no tower, nothing but scrub vegetation near the runway and trees farther back. He looked back, saw several men—they looked like Indians—unloading the baggage. Down the runway were three Land-Rovers, moving slowly toward them in single file. There were no other signs of human habitation or presence at all.

"We are in the middle of bloody nowhere!" Danny exclaimed.

Part
II

Tlillan Tlapallan

1

Flores was the last one out of the plane; immediately he began herding the group toward the first two Land-Rovers, which had come up alongside. The third one went to the other side of the plane, and they saw their baggage being loaded into it.

"How far is it to the resort?" Danny asked. It was perfectly obvious it was not just up the road. There was only one road, if it could be called that, leading away from the landing strip. It was in fact only a narrow trail, threading back through the trees. Very little of it was visible.

Flores mopped his brow, even though it wasn't all that hot. "Only a mile or two, not far, not far at all," he said, grinning. "Let's get in the cars, now, friends. No fun to be had around here, and we gotta get this plane going again."

Surrendering to the inevitable, Danny, Susan, David, and John climbed into the first of the Rovers. The other four, moving a bit slower, got into the other. The drivers started off down the path. As they went into the woods, they could see the workers still unloading the plane.

"All right, you old fart!" Flores yelled as the second Rover disappeared into the woods. "Where the fuck are you? I know you're here!"

"There is no need to shout, Mr. Flores. I am here."

Flores turned around; the old man and Maria stood behind him. He looked at the old man curiously. Somehow he didn't look quite so old now. Must be the sunshine, Flores decided. But who gave a shit; he wanted his money and out.

"If you'll just pay me, I'll get back on that plane and you'll never see my ass again." he said. "Damnedest scam I ever saw. You brought all those people here; for what I'll never know.''

"No, you won't, Mr. Flores," the old man said. "Here is your money. Try to take pleasure in it."

"Sure as hell will, you can count on that!" Flores said. He turned toward the airplane, saw that the stair had been pulled up. With a helpless gesture, the pilot closed the door, locked it. Flores didn't understand. For a few minutes he was unable to move. Watching the pilot walk past the windows back to the cockpit, listening to the engines start, he wondered if they planned to keep him here. But why? He was done; he had done his job, been paid.

"What the fuck is going on?" he screamed over the engine roar, then ducked instinctively as the plane began to move, to turn around on the narrow strip. Immediately the pilot started his takeoff run. Flores just glimpsed the rear of the third Land-Rover as it disappeared into the jungle. What was this? How were they going to get into town? He clenched his fists helplessly as the plane lifted off, banked out over the ocean.

Maria and the old man had not moved; Flores turned to look at them. One of the drivers must be planning to bring a car back, he thought. The old geezer isn't going to walk two miles through the jungle, that's for damn sure.

"What the hell is this?" he demanded. "I thought I was done with you people. I was going back to Miami. What do you want?"

"It was never our intention to interfere with the fate of common peoples," the old man said. "We only needed you temporarily, and you had no further impact to make on this world. Maria, please tell Mr. Flores what would have happened if you had not come for him."

"The Desedros brothers would have burned you to death, to set an example for others who would steal from them. But there was to be an error. The body would never be found."

"Well, damn, I told you a million times I appreciate your gettin' my ass outa that mess. Those crazy kids! But what— wait a minute. What was that last part? About the body? What're you talkin' about? I—"

"It will be so," the old man said.

Flores felt a rush of fear. Were the Desedros boys here?

What was happening? They couldn't be that cruel, not to turn him back over to them. They couldn't. They just couldn't.

He looked from one to the other. Then the old man's eyes seemed to glitter and widen. Flores felt warm, looked up at the sun; was it really getting warmer? He tugged at his collar. Damnation! he thought. All of a sudden it was getting downright hot. Then he saw a wisp of smoke rise from his collar.

"What are you doing to me?" he screamed. More smoke rose; he started ripping at his shirt. His chest felt like acid was being poured on it. He tore at his hair; it came away smouldering. A tongue of flame burst from his pants leg; he screamed, grabbed at it. Then his sleeve was burning; the pain was unbelievable. He ripped it away and stared for a moment, unable to accept what he saw, even through the pain. The arm itself was afire, as if it had been doused in gasoline. He screamed again, a high-pitched, tortured cry, and ran straight at Maria and the old man, who were only about twenty feet in front of him. Then they were not; they were at the edge of the trail, two hundred feet away, watching him with impassive eyes. Mindlessly, he pulled out sheafs of hundred dollar bills, waved them at the two people. The flames moved up his fingers to the bills, and they drifted lazily on the air, burning as they descended. What was left of Flores, now blackened and dripping, stumbled toward the two motionless figures. His face looked as if a blowtorch were being held under his chin, but the tortured eyes still seemed to see. Finally they flared and went out. The flaming hulk slowly, almost majestically, crumpled to the ground. A piece, maybe an arm, fell away; flames shot out of the end of it. In a very few minutes, what had been Sol Flores looked like the remains of a small campfire. That is, if one took no notice of the half-burned hundred dollar bills lying about.

The two figures at the edge of the trail turned and started walking away. Somewhere, a tropical bird screeched.

2

At first, Danny had tried to talk to David and Susan, but the Land-Rover made so much noise that they had to yell to hear each other. Eventually he gave it up, decided to wait until they reached—where? They didn't know their destination even now. Resort, hotel, cottages, maybe hammocks in the woods. None of them knew. Yet everybody seemed to blindly accept it; everybody except Danny. As far as he was concerned, he'd be much happier when he had the .38, currently packed in his luggage, back in his pocket.

He turned his attention back to the so-called road. He was riding in front; Susan, David, and John on the inward-facing seats in the rear. They were holding on for dear life as the vehicle rolled through muddy ditches, ground its way up small hills, and forded little streams. On both sides of the road was the jungle, a seemingly impenetrable wall of vegetation; the Rover repeatedly had to push extended branches out of its way, stirring a profusion of blooming plants, vines, buzzing insects, and birds. Occasionally an iguana ran from the road, and once they scared up a peccary, one of those small, bristly, native American pigs. It ran up the road in front of them before going off into the bush. It had no trouble outrunning them; the speedometer on the Rover bounced and jumped around ten miles an hour. Danny would not have wanted to travel any faster on this trail; they were being hurled about enough as it was.

After about a half hour of this, the view opened up on the left, although the brush on the other side remained dense. Danny found himself looking out over a flat plain, the treeline still visible in the distance. This might have been an agricultural field of some sort at one time, but now it was just an expanse of coarse grass, dotted here and there with scrubby bushes. Up ahead, he could see that the right side opened up as well. A pair of impressive looking hills rose abruptly out of the plain, at least a mile ahead.

The road was much better here, and the driver at last shifted gears up from second, although he remained in four-wheel drive. Their speed climbed to about thirty miles an hour. As the contour of the land rose a bit, the ocean, turquoise and magnificent in the tropical sun, was briefly visible on their left. On the right, the forest had given way to plains, and Danny could see a low building up ahead. Yelling over the roaring transmission, he called David's attention to it.

As they came closer, Danny began to feel a little better. Doubtless the airstrip was at the far end of this road from civilization; for the little blur of a habitation had resolved itself into a kind of country store, gas pumps out front. The driver slowed as he approached it. No identifying signs, Danny noticed. The Land-Rover pulled in and stopped at the pumps, the vehicle behind them following suit.

Relieved to stop after such a rough ride, Danny got out to stretch his legs. David joined him; Susan and John remained in the car, talking. A very dark-skinned man wearing a straw hat came out of the store and began to pump gas into the Rovers. Both drivers busied themselves checking under the hoods.

Looking up at the two striking hills, which were much closer now, Danny could see only trees atop the one on their right, but the other seemed to have some kind of structure atop it. He shaded his eyes from the sun, tried to see it better.

"Can you see that up there, David?" he asked, pointing.

"Just barely. Looks like a church."

"Yeah, that's what I'm seeing it as."

The man from the store came up to them. "Sí, it is a church, but in ruins now, señor," he said.

"Ruins?" asked David.

"Sí. The Spaniards had it built, many years ago. It is said that it was one of the first churches the Spaniards built here. But it is in ruins, now. And haunted."

"Haunted?"

"Sí. But it is better not to speak of such things." He turned away, approached the drivers for his money.

"Interesting," Danny observed, still trying to see.

"Yeah, we'll have to go up and take a look if we can. I wonder why it hasn't been restored."

"Who knows? Maybe no money, maybe people are afraid of it, if there's a legend it's haunted."

Their driver was motioning them back to the car. They went, still looking up at the church. From here, it appeared to be huge, a most imposing structure. But that could be a trick of the distance. Danny hoped to find out; again his curiosity had been aroused. They climbed back into the Land-Rover and soon were on the narrow road, heading into the pass between the two hills.

Just as the forest had gradually given way to the plains, they in turn gave way to neatly cultivated little plots and small, well-kept houses set amid scattered trees. The riders looked at these scenes with a bit of puzzlement. All of them had at least a passing familiarity with conditions in the American tropics, the pervasive poverty and atrocious living conditions of the common man; but that was not in evidence here. Occasionally a man, woman, or child was to be seen around one of the little houses; they waved gaily at the passing Land-Rovers. Danny thought they were a very attractive people, strong and robust. None of the listlessness he expected from native peoples, which, as he knew, was often concentrated around the American and European tourist havens.

"Maguey," he heard John say, and looked where he was pointing. He saw a patch of very large succulent plants bearing long, pointed, thorny leaves. A few of them had white flower spikes, towering twenty feet or more into the air. He watched a man apparently collecting something from down inside one of the plants.

"What's he doing?" Danny yelled over the engine roar.

"Collecting the sap," John answered.

"What do they do with it?"

"It's used to make pulque and tequila."

"What's pulque?"

"It's like a beer."

They were getting quite close to the twin hills now. Danny could see that they sloped rather gently, and that both were quite flat on top. He wondered if they were perhaps extinct volcanoes. But the presence of the huge ruined church on the hill to his left seemed to deny that. Unless the crater had filled in, he thought; he wasn't exactly an expert on volcanoes. He looked at the church again. The steeple seemed truly immense, ornate; it loomed over the rest of the church, itself an impressive structure. It was obvious by now that the impression of great size was not in error. Sunlight gleamed through the empty windows. He had the distinct sense that it was looking at him as they drove along.

The hill on his right, as he had seen before, was covered with trees; but through them, he could now see the glint of sunlight on windows. There was a structure of some sort up there, too, but he could not yet see what it was. Whatever, it did not seem ruined and was nowhere near the size of the old church, which dominated the local landscape.

Once over a little rise, they could see that they were entering a small town. No sign at the outskirts informed them of its name, but it was certainly charming and picturesque. Neatly kept shops, vendors of various foods on narrow streets, few signs of any sort. Most of the shops bore no identification at all. He saw one labeled simply, Restaurante, another, Cantina. Very interesting. He wondered if the resort had encouraged or perhaps even insisted on this simplicity; perhaps the apparent prosperity of the little village was due in part to the resort. The roadside could even be a facade, concealing the inevitable poverty behind.

"Do you speak English? Hablo Ingles?" he yelled at the driver.

"Sí, señor."

"What's the name of this town?"

"It is called Tlillan Tlapallan, señor," he yelled back.

"Where is the resort?"

"We will be there, just a little minute."

He sat back and continued to look at the town. He had never heard of it, but that wasn't exactly a surprise. The road, which was unpaved, split into two forks; they took the left one. It appeared that the right one went through the heart of the village. Their route took them through a residential section of quaint little houses with thatched roofs. Then the road rejoined the main one, and they continued on. No traffic allowed in the middle of town, it seemed; but other than theirs, they had seen no other vehicles at all.

Turning at about a forty-five degree angle to the right, they passed a large building constructed on an odd floor plan. The front of it fit the forty-five degrees; the rear extended back into a large warehouse-like area. The roofline was very high, but Danny judged it was one story by the tall, narrow windows. A sign above it identified it as the Teatro. He didn't know what that meant.

"What is that?" he asked the driver.

"In your country, señor, I believe you would call it a—how you say—centro de cívico?"

"A civic center?" he said, smiling.

"Sí. That."

The road turned another forty-five degrees, and gradually began to rise; quickly the slope became steeper. Alongside the road here were stone steps, for pedestrians. Danny looked around to get his bearings, then realized they were climbing the side of the hill which had been to his right. The Land-Rovers chugged up, even though the incline of the road was steeper than any American road would have been. As it leveled off, they passed through a grove of fruit trees, then into a circular drive surrounding a truly magnificent two-story house. Perhaps mansion would have been a better word.

"Resort," said the driver. He definitely was not a talkative type, Danny decided, looking over the place. The resort, which was the building Danny had seen from below, was well-shaded by a variety of trees; little gardens with multitudes of blooming flowers surrounding it. Behind the main house was a garage, doubtlessly housing for the Land-Rovers. An ordinary car would not climb that hill coming up here, he was sure, much less negotiate the trail to the airstrip. It really was, after all, a beautiful place. Off to his left, Danny could see the other hill with the ruined church, the town nestled in the valley between them. The hill they were on was perhaps one hundred fifty feet above the town; the very straight, tree-lined slope went right down to the backs of the buildings he had seen on the drive through. Beyond the other hill and the church, the turquoise sea sparkled in the sun. Apparently the beach was at the foot of the other hill.

He realized something else; except for short alleys, the road they were on had no branches, connected to no other road. They had followed it straight from the airstrip here, except for what was an obvious detour around the center of town, and it ended at the garage doors. Beyond the two hills, there was only a vast flat expanse of forest. No other hills, and no roads; at least none that he had seen. Of course, he told himself, he must have missed it; he rejected the idea that there were no roads out of here, it just seemed impossible. But he made a mental note to ask about it.

The other two Land-Rovers pulled up, stopped in front of the house. Immediately, the drivers began to unload the huge pile of luggage in the rear of the third. Accompanied by a very athletic-looking young man, Maria popped out of the front of the third Rover and came toward them. Danny was still looking around, half expecting a man in a spotless white suit to come out and say, "Welcome, my dear guests!" perhaps accompanied by a midget. The way the place looked, it would have been appropriate.

But instead, the athletic-looking young man came up to them, flashing incredibly white teeth in a broad smile. "Nobody jounced around too much on the ride, I hope?" he said. He too had only the faintest trace of an accent, and somehow it didn't even sound Spanish. "The road's still a little rough— oh, well—it's real rough! One day we'll get it paved. But— you're here! Everybody like the place? Eh?"

There were murmurs of "very nice," "sure," and so on.

Ignoring this, the man went on: "My name is Eduardo Arias. I am the manager"—he executed a deep bow—"of this place. Maria and I are at your service. Anything you need, just let us know."

"Mr. Arias," Danny said, taking a step forward.

"Please, please, Eduardo. Ed if you prefer," he said.

"All right, Eduardo. I'm curious about one thing. We never did find out the name of this island. The driver told me the town was Tippin' Tapplin' or something."

"Tlillan Tlapallan. But what do you mean by island, Mr. Hudson?"

"We're on an island near Aruba, right?"

"No. This is Mexico! Surely you knew that."

Danny looked around; everyone was staring at Eduardo. It was obvious none of them knew that. Susan in particular seemed flustered and upset.

"No, Eduardo, we all thought we were going to South

America. Maria was on the plane with us. Perhaps she can shed some light on this.'' He looked at her.

''I would doubt that, Mr. Hudson. We sent Maria from here to accompany our guests back, since, as you can imagine, there are no commercial flights. We simply received an order from a company on Long Island to book passage and lodging for eight guests. We were, as is customary, paid in advance. A Mr. Flores, I believe. He didn't tell you it was Mexico? That is very strange. Maria, what do you know of this?''

''Nothing other than what you said. I met Mr. Flores in Miami. We took the plane. He went back on the plane. That's all.''

''Flores went back?'' David asked.

''Yes,'' Maria told him.

''Well, uh—not that I want to, but—how do we leave here when it's time? I mean—''

''I understand,'' Eduardo said. ''The plane will return in two weeks. Until that time, we have no way for you to leave unless you want to take one of the Land-Rovers''—he gestured toward them—''and drive out. There is a trail, which eventually leads to a road, which will take you to a town, where you can get on a highway to Vera Cruz. But it is a hard drive, many mudholes, steep hills, washouts. Besides,'' he smiled, ''no one has ever wanted to leave before the vacation ended!''

''So we are on the east coast of Mexico?''

''Yes. That's the Bay of Campeche out there.'' He gestured toward the ocean.

''North or south of Vera Cruz?''

''South.''

That answered that; if the man was telling the truth, of course, Danny thought. Why wouldn't he? An excellent question; but then again, why would Flores have told them they were going to South America when in fact they were going to Mexico? Danny looked around. He had no clues other than the flying time, and the fact that the climate was obviously tropical. They could have been on virtually any Caribbean island, in Mexico, Guatemala, any number of other places. The water he was looking at could as well be the Pacific Ocean as the Bay of Campeche. How could he tell?

''Well, in spite of the confusion, I am sure you will enjoy it here. Juana and Rosa will show you to your rooms. We will

meet again in the dining room for drinks in one hour.'' He
shooed them toward two teenage Indian girls, who were to
show them to the rooms. They had come up behind the group
totally silently.

Alone in his room, Danny found that his suitcases had already been delivered. He threw one of them on the bed, opened
it, and dug around in the piles of clothing for a moment. When
he stopped, he had the .38 in his hand.

"Ah, Mr. Smith and Mr. Wesson, I presume," he said.
"Glad to see you guys. I feel much better with you here!" He
slipped five cartridges into the cylinder, set the hammer over
the empty one, and tucked the short-barreled weapon in his
pants pocket. Only then did he really take the time to look
around the room.

It was truly luxurious. Comfortable but soft mattress, large
windows affording a great view of the ruined church, well-
stocked bathroom, even including three tubes of toothpaste and
a toothbrush in a sealed package. He didn't need to bring anything except clothes, he thought. When he looked in the closet
and bureau, he realized he didn't need those. There were shirts,
pants, underwear; all his size. Sure did know he was coming,
no doubt or pretense about that. By the window were wicker
chairs and a table, accented by a vase of fresh hibiscus sitting
in its center. Beside this vase was a curious item; apparently a
quartz crystal, about four inches long, an inch and a half thick.
He picked it up; his hand seemed to tingle a bit when he
touched it. Squinting, he looked at it again; nothing, no information. But for some reason, he liked it, it made him feel good
to hold it. He put it back alongside the vase and sat down by
the window.

It was getting close to dusk; he could see the sun clearly
headed for a sunset over land. He considered what he knew
about geography and astronomy; it was regrettable he didn't
know more. But this time of year the sun should still set in
the southern part of the sky, as long as they were north of the
equator; the vernal equinox had not yet passed. Therefore, the
sun setting over land, to his left, put the ocean north or east of
them. That fitted with what Eduardo had told them about their
location.

But it really didn't get him anywhere, either. So far, he had
come up with only one hypothesis which might explain the lie,

and it was a very ominous one; his idea was that if anyone in the group had told anyone else where they were going, they would have said "near Aruba." And they were very far from that island. So they could not easily be found; and it seemed that access to this place was very difficult indeed. He had a telephone in his room, but it had a message on a small card indicating it only reached the other rooms and the manager's office. He didn't have any concrete ideas yet about why the Tascan Acres people might want to hide them away, but he remembered hearing stories years ago of people being spirited away to Latin America to make films, films containing death scenes that weren't faked. Then he'd heard that rumor denied. Why would anybody go to all that trouble and risk when such things were so easy to fake? No, it made no sense. And David and Susan, at least, were not rich people; ransom didn't hold up. Hostages? Unlikely; too easy to get them other ways, like hijacking an airplane. He began to get frustrated. None of it made any sense, yet he was sure it was connected somehow to the weird experiences and his initial vision. He was eager to talk to some of the other guests and see if they'd been having odd things happen to them too. John would have been the logical place to start, but the person he really wanted to talk to was Kathryn.

He looked at his watch; an hour had passed. Eduardo had asked them to meet in the dining room for drinks in an hour. As he left the room, he looked back at the old church; he had the damndest feeling he was being watched from that place. On the stairs, he decided he'd have to go up there, check it out for himself.

As it happened, he was the first one back to the dining room. The staff had set out nine glasses. Apparently Maria would not be joining them, since Eduardo already had one in his hand.

"Ah, Mr. Hudson, our first arrival!" Eduardo said. "Please, have some refreshment!"

Danny eyed the glasses; each contained a golden liquid that looked much like beer. "I think maybe I'll just have some fruit juice or something," he said.

Without even looking, Eduardo picked up one of the glasses, handed it to him. "No alcohol in this one," he declared.

Curious, Danny looked over the glasses; they all appeared identical. "I would have thought some of the guests would have preferred an alcoholic—"

"Some would," the manager interrupted. "Mr. North, Mr. Hallsten, and Mr. Wasserman. The ladies, Mr. Goss, and yourself were provided with a fruit—"

"But how could you know?" Danny asked, interrupting in turn. "And how can you tell which is which?"

"I know my job," Eduardo said shortly. He gestured at Danny's glass. "Try it, please!"

Danny shrugged, did, and was a little surprised. It was something like pineapple juice, but better. "Excellent," he said. "Really."

Eduardo gave a little bow. "Thank you. It is our own blend, shall we say, a secret recipe." He turned, smiled past Danny. "Ah, Mr. North! Nice to see you again!"

Danny watched the man with the mirrored shoe enter the room. This dude was something, he thought. Him I gotta talk to sometime, too; try to find out what his story is. That shoe was downright strange—if it was a shoe. He frowned, looking at it. It looked more like— Yes! It was an artificial foot, not a shoe! Stranger still; it was a very conspicuous artificial foot, to be sure.

"Call me Bertie," he said to Eduardo. "Everybody does."

"You a New Yorker, Bertie?" Danny asked him.

Bertie turned and looked at him as if noticing him for the first time. He searched Bertie's eyes for any spark of recognition; after all, if Susan had shared the dream, it was possible that this man had too. But there was nothing like that, at least nothing Danny could see. The face, although the features were the same, was somehow different; this man seemed boyishly friendly, while the man in the dream was cold, methodical, violent. It occurred to Danny that one of these masks could easily conceal the other. He intended to talk to him, see if he had any information that was useful. But he also intended to be very careful around him.

"No, I'm not, ah—Danny, isn't it? No, I currently live in Tennessee. I was just visiting New York, and was lucky enough to win this trip. Nice, eh?"

"Yes. The resort is lovely, no doubt about it," he said. Luck's got nothing to do with this, he thought, except maybe in my case. He didn't yet know whether that luck was good or bad.

"You were the one asking all the questions, earlier," Bertie said, rolling his glass in his fingers.

"Yeah. I still don't really understand. We all thought we were going to South America. How about you?"

"Well, I thought South America too. But I guess it really doesn't matter a whole lot. The place is sure good enough. You know any of our fellow travelers?"

"Yes. The Hallstens are friends of mine, and I just met the big man, John Goss, at the airport. Turns out he's Susan Hallsten's brother. Crazy coincidence, isn't it?"

"Amazing," Bertie said, taking the drink Eduardo was handing him. He took a long sip, made no comment.

"So you're a Tennessean?" Danny persisted.

"Well, not by birth. I was born in Wisconsin. I'm in the Air Force, currently on leave, and I'm stationed there."

"Oh? What do you do?"

"Computers. Cost analysis." He paused, gave Danny a long, penetrating look. "What line of work are you in, Danny?"

"Investments. Various kinds. New York's the place for that."

"No doubt."

Danny felt the man was withdrawing a bit; perhaps he was asking too many questions. He eased off, sipped his drink, tried to think of something innocuous to say. He was relieved when David, Susan, and John arrived.

Susan came to him, took his arm. "Isn't this place beautiful, Danny? All the flowers!" Her face clouded a bit. "I just wish it wasn't Mexico, you know? But it's really great!"

"What's the matter with Mexico?" Danny asked.

"Oh, I took a vacation there—I mean here—well, not here, you know, Mexico City. When I was in college. It—ah—it just didn't turn out well, you know? Bad memories."

He didn't know at all, but he said, "Yeah." From David's curious glance, he assumed that he didn't either. Sometime he needed to figure this out; it wasn't the first time he'd felt that Susan was hiding something, something upsetting to her. He also had to admit to himself that he hated to see Susan's face less than happy; she downright radiated when she was.

Kathryn Phillips walked in, and all heads turned to watch her. She also radiated, Danny thought; he realized that he really did want to get to know her, even beyond his need to find out if she, too, had shared the dream. He glanced at David; he looked so stiff that Danny was afraid he might literally break something. The most likely thing was the glass in his hand, he was clutching it so tightly. It was more than apparent that Kathryn had a devastating effect on him. His eyes literally bored into her. Bertie was also watching her, a sardonic smile on his face. John, however, only had eyes for Susan. It seemed very strange to Danny that they had been out of contact for years; they appeared to be so close.

"Well, I'm a little late, so I'll introduce myself," she said. She had a slightly raspy voice; very sexy, Danny thought. "I'm Kathryn. You must be—let's see, I tried to follow all of you as we boarded, and I'm good at names: Danny right? And—ah— David? John?" She got them backwards. Susan corrected her. "You're Susan, I got that, and this is Herbert, right?"

"You can call me Bertie. Ev—" He cut it off in mid-sentence, let the words drain into a warm smile and a direct look. This guy was smooth and practiced, Danny thought. Could be a real pain.

Frank and Evelyn Wasserman were the last to arrive, and another slightly confused round of introductions took place. Danny was really impressed with Frank's voice. It was amazingly low-pitched and full. Evelyn seemed to be watching Danny very closely; she scarcely seemed to pay any attention to anyone else. It was obvious that Frank noticed this too; he seemed amused by it. He walked over to Danny, addressed him directly.

"Glad to meet you, Danny," he rumbled. "Ev and I are divers. It's our second-favorite activity!" He gave a laugh that sounded like a freight train. "What about you?"

"Yeah, some," Danny replied. "I like it, just never got to do it much."

"Well, then, you'll have to join us sometime. We'll find the best spots around, you can believe it!" Danny noticed his eyes, bright blue behind the glasses. He was about the only person he'd ever met with eyes like his own. Frank's teeth were a little odd, too; his canines were a bit longer than all the rest. It was a subtle thing, but it gave him a sort of a Dracula look when he smiled.

All during this conversation, Evelyn had not spoken; but

unless Danny was making a mistake, she was conveying more information by the way she was looking at him than Frank had by his words. This could be a delicate situation, Danny thought; she would be hard to refuse if she came on directly, and he didn't want extraneous complications. He looked at Susan again. She was now staring at Bertie, while Kathryn and David had locked eyes. This was one hell of a group, Danny told himself; there was no way things were going to get boring!

The small talk continued for a while as they finished their drinks; after this, the staff served dinner. The foods served were unusual; baked fish wrapped in a leaf, a unique squash dish, and several items made from corn. Very good, Danny thought. Over coffee, Eduardo explained how to get to the beach, where to go in Tlillan Tlapallan for shopping, and so on. Some of the expected amenities of resorts were lacking; no tennis or golf, for example. Also missing were the boat trips and excursions usually offered at extra cost. But no one was complaining. Danny wondered why there was a scam of some kind in the first place; from all appearances, this place should be a veritable gold mine, run legitimately. But he still had his serious doubts that their reason for being here was legitimate.

Eduardo continued his little talk on how things were done at the resort, how the meals would be announced by a bell. "Of course, if you are in town or at the beach you may not hear it. Not to worry. You can always get your meal late if that happens. Please," he spread his hands, "the resort and grounds are for your enjoyment. Go where you like and do what you will. Our purpose is to make your vacation a pleasant one."

Since everyone was more or less tired from the trip, the dining room gradually emptied as they begged off and went to their rooms for the night. First to arrive, Danny was also the last to leave. He had wanted to study these people as much as possible; but he really had no new information. Looking at his watch again, he saw that it was about eleven New York time, and went back up to his room.

He sat for a long while on the wicker chair by the window, looking up at the old church. He wondered how the resort happened to have electric lights; he had seen no power lines running in or out. Perhaps there was a local generator. Looking out the window, he could see the light from other windows in the resort building, soft against the nearby trees, and the glow of lights from the town below. He could also see a light in the steeple of the old church, but otherwise—he stopped himself and looked at the church again. Why should there be a light there? Hadn't the driver said it was a ruin, feared by the locals? But there it was; very distinct, shining out a window in the old steeple. It was not bright, and had a slightly reddish tinge, like a sodium lamp. As he watched, it winked out, then reappeared in a window further down. The process was repeated, and finally the light was at ground level. Window by window, it moved back through the church; when it disappeared from the last window, it did not reappear. Danny was sure it was someone carrying a lantern or possibly a flashlight. He wondered why anyone would be up there this late. Perhaps it was a tourist attraction, after all; that would have made sense. Idly, he tried to read the church, got a brief flash of the scarlet color he associated with danger. But it was gone very quickly, so quickly he couldn't be absolutely sure he'd even seen it. Subsequent attempts yielded nothing. He tried to put it out of his mind for the night, tried to get some sleep. But the .38 was under his pillow.

As Danny arrived in the dining room for breakfast the next morning, feeling good and well rested, he found David and Susan already there, just sitting down at the table. Outside, the skies were cloudless, already brilliant blue; it promised to be a fine day.

"Well, it's some place isn't it?" David asked.

"Sure is. I must admit, I've never seen or heard of a prettier vacation spot. I tell you, though, the switch from South America is still bothering me, David. I don't feel like I've found any good reason for it."

David shrugged. "You don't think it could just have been a mistake? Maybe our vacation packages got switched with someone else's?"

Danny considered that, allowed as how it couldn't be ruled out. But he didn't believe it; it didn't explain Tascan Acres. Again he wondered who exactly might have been running that operation, who the presumed conspirators might be. The only person he was sure of was Sol Flores, and he had disappeared. Maria could bear some more investigation, but after the experience on the plane he was a little hesitant to confront her directly. She was indeed intimidating.

Eduardo came into the room and greeted them with what seemed to be genuine pleasure. Danny decided to be bold on at least one issue.

"Eduardo, have you ever heard the word nagual?"

Eduardo appeared to be taken somewhat by surprise. "Certainly. Why?"

"What does it mean?"

"It doesn't have a direct English equivalent. It means a spirit guardian, an animal spirit like a jaguar or rattlesnake. It also means a person who embodies a—ah—shall we say, a set of phenomena—I'm not sure how to tell you. A person who is not ordinary, who in fact is kind of an antithesis to the ordinary. In Indian belief, a special brujo, a sorcerer who had achieved a union with his nagual spirit, and is therefore able to—"

"You are certainly erudite for a vacation resort manager!" David blurted, interrupting his discourse.

"It is not the only job I have ever held," he said somewhat haughtily. "But enough of this. We are here for breakfast, not a lecture." So saying, he returned to his own food, leaving no doubt that the discussion was closed.

Following breakfast, the Hallstens and Wassermans headed for the beach. Susan had asked Danny and John to join them, but they had declined; Danny wanted to take up Eduardo's invitation of the previous night, wander around the house and grounds and see whatever was to be seen. Bertie and Kathryn had left without declaring their intentions, leaving John and Danny lingering over the coffee.

"How long has it been since you've seen your sister, John?" Danny asked conversationally, hoping it wouldn't sound like prying.

John didn't take it so. "Oh, at least fifteen years. I cut ties with my family when I left home. Never really wanted to cut ties with Susan, though. I thought the world would destroy her. But she found David, really a great guy. Really great."

"Sure is. Why'd you think that?" Danny asked, sure now that John would think him nosy.

"Lots of reasons. Susan's just different. So am I. So are you, Danny. I knew that before Susan told me about your abilities. Yeah, she told me. Said some weird things had been happening in New York just before they left, but they didn't tell me all of it.''

"It'd be hard to know where to begin. Maybe we should all get together tonight, let everyone tell their own story. But you said you knew that I was different before Susan said anything. What did you mean?''

"Isn't it obvious? Everyone here is different. This is a real select group, Danny. I don't exactly know what it was selected for, but I'm sure it didn't escape your notice that we have, for example, three women, all of whom are beauties. And the five men all have something unusual about them, too. With Frank, maybe it's only his voice. But that's a rare voice.''

"What's unusual about you?''

John laughed. "I guess it's not obvious, no. Maybe it's that I'm a lunatic. Maybe my father is a ball of feathers. Maybe it's this!'' He pulled a feather from his pocket, showed it to Danny. Brilliant, emerald green. "I found it in North Carolina,'' he continued. "It fell off a bird bigger than any bird I've ever seen.''

"What kind of a bird? When?''

John told him the story of the bird, verifying for Danny that he and the Hallstens were not the only ones having odd experiences.

"I wish I could get a handle on all this. I'm still just drifting around aimlessly here,'' Danny said, as much to himself as to John.

"I agree with you. Something is going on here, and it would be good to know what it is.''

"Got any ideas you want to share?''

"Not really. But the first thing I want to do is get the layout, if you know what I mean. Find out as much as possible about this resort, this house and grounds,'' John replied.

"Exactly what I planned to do this morning. Shall we?''

"But of course.''

"House first, or grounds?''

"House. Less of it.''

They got up from the table and started wandering through the house, beginning at the front and working backwards. There was nothing that was particularly unusual; a large sitting room up front, the dining room, a kitchen, some storage rooms in the back, the manager's offices, bathrooms, a sun room over-looking the town, a workshop. Upstairs, only hotel-like private rooms, a total of sixteen of them, presumably some occupied by Eduardo, Maria, and the house staff. There was a trapdoor above the upstairs hall in the back, but they would have needed to carry a ladder from the workshop to get in there, and they decided it wasn't worth it; probably only led to attic space anyway. In short, there was nothing at all remarkable or un-usual about the house. Unless there was something in one of the private rooms; they also decided not to go breaking into every one.

Outside, they explored the garage. Space for four cars, three of them occupied by the Land-Rovers that had met them at the airstrip. The back part of the garage was about evenly divided into an auto workshop and a storage area for gardener's tools. Again, nothing unusual to be seen.

The grounds themselves were spotlessly manicured; there was a pool, rock-lined and utterly clear. They walked around the entire flat area on top of the hill, perhaps eight acres total. It was a square, all edges descending at about the same angle. The views were very impressive, particularly the ones facing the town and the ruined church. Finally, they sat down in lawn chairs near the pool and considered their progress.

"Well, we learned about nothing. Maybe a little less," Danny observed.

"At least we know what is here. And what isn't," John agreed.

Danny looked back up at the house. The windows facing him opened into the sun room; it was off these he had seen the light glint when they were coming up. Above them were the windows of the private rooms. And above that, enough space for a large attic. Unless there were hidden rooms underground, secret doors, there was no place to hide anything. Danny sighed; it just made no sense at all. Besides, he was getting hungry, and hoped the bell announcing lunch would ring soon. Meanwhile, he decided to just sit and enjoy this pretty place, not worry about it for a while.

Danny and John had nearly finished their lunch when the Hallstens, positively glowing, arrived.

"You two have just got to come down to the beach today!"

Susan insisted. "It's such a perfect place, you can't believe it! And nobody down there all morning except us and the Wassermans."

"They're still there?" John asked.

"Yes. They said they couldn't bear to leave yet, even for a while. They're real water people, those two. Almost never get out of it, you know?"

"Well, we were just kind of exploring around the house and grounds this morning. Just checking it out," Danny said. "For me, I believe I'll postpone the swimming until tomorrow. I kinda thought I'd go into town this afternoon."

"I'll join you, Danny, if that's all right," John said.

"Sounds good to me."

"Anybody seen Kathryn and Bertie?" David asked.

"No. Maybe they went into town this morning. I haven't seen them since breakfast," Danny said.

"Well, we're going back down to that magnificent beach as soon as we finish eating. Right, David?" Susan asked.

"No doubt about it."

After lunch, Danny and John waited for them in the front sitting room; since they had to walk to the edge of town on the way to the beach, they had all decided to go that far together. While they were waiting, Kathryn came in. Danny was gratified to see her alone, not with Bertie.

"Hi, Danny! John," she said as she dropped into a chair. "You guys been to the beach this morning?"

"No, we hung around here and explored the house. You went into town, I guess," Danny said, giving her his warmest grin.

"Yes. A first look around. There's really a lot down there. It's fascinating. I thought I might go back this afternoon."

"That's what we planned to do. We're going with David and Susan as soon as they're ready. They're going back to the beach."

"Well, let me grab a sandwich or something and we'll all go, okay?" she suggested. Without consulting John, Danny agreed.

The Hallstens came back down, eager to go; Susan seemed a little impatient over waiting for Kathryn, but she saw it was important to Danny and did so with good grace. Kathryn didn't take long and a short time later the five were walking down the steep hillside alongside the road.

"This is the only problem here," David commented. "It's okay going down, but if you're a little tired, it's a long walk up again." Kathryn nodded agreement.

Not far from the base of the hill, they encountered a sign with an arrow pointing down a path: "Beach—playa." Here, David and Susan took their leave and proceeded down the path; the other three continued on into town. The village was quite a bit busier than it had been the day before; the streets were full of people. The three visitors strolled along, taking it all in.

"It's kind of weird. Seems like there are no cars here, other than the Land-Rovers. I didn't see one all morning," Kathryn said.

"I guess they don't need them. It *is* a small town, easy to walk from one end to the other," Danny noted.

"But you'd think they'd at least have a truck or two for hauling stuff. I don't know. I'm a New Yorker, and a town without cars is weird to me."

"I know what you mean."

They passed the large Teatro, an imposing structure, equally odd-looking from this vantage point. It seemed to be closed at the moment, all the windows shuttered from the inside. They went around the side a little ways, found nothing of interest. Further on, they passed numbers of small shops seemingly intermixed with residential dwellings; short alleys ran off the main street at intervals. Down the alleys, there seemed to be only houses.

When they came to the split in the road, they took the left-hand fork, the path toward the center of the town. The street widened quickly to the south into a kind of a central square, just past the bases of the twin hills. Although the street itself was unpaved, the square, which was about five hundred feet across, was paved with stone. All around it, street vendors sold foods and various items that Danny took to be souvenirs from handheld trays; others had set up little tented stalls, jewelry and clothing being the most common wares. Again, Danny took it to be souvenir material. These merchants had arranged their stalls to completely surround the square, except for the southernmost edge. There, the pavement rose in a series of steps to a low platform, also paved, but quite empty. It seemed to be reserved; for what, Danny had no idea.

He glanced at the material in the tented stalls from a distance. "Always, any tourist town, the souvenirs. Can't get away from them," Danny said.

"You ought to take a closer look at some of those," Kathryn advised. "I've been here most of the morning, and it's not what you might expect."

Danny and John went to the nearest stall, a jewelry vendor, and looked. She was right. The merchandise offered was a much better grade of workmanship than the souvenirs of Mexico one usually saw. A great deal of it was good enough to be called real art. John in particular was very impressed with it.

Deciding to get a look at the whole town before concentrating on any one area, they continued walking until they reached the area of small farms they had seen on the way in.

"Let's head back, maybe explore some of those shops in detail," John suggested.

"Good enough. But we've run out of town, and I wonder if you two noticed what's really odd here," Danny said.

"It's so clean, so friendly?" Kathryn suggested.

"No, though you notice that, especially coming from New York. No. Think about it. No bank. No churches. No police. You ever hear of a town like that in your life?"

They both agreed that they had not.

They were not quite halfway back when John saw something in a little shop that interested him. Danny and Kathryn started to go in with him, but he told them to go on, that he'd catch up with them at the square. Kathryn was going to object, but Danny guided her up along the street. He was grateful for the time alone with her, thought perhaps John had sensed that that was what he wanted.

"John's a private kind of guy," he told Kathryn, hoping that was true. "He'll join us again shortly, I'm sure."

"Okay. Let's get up there, then. I saw some things in the square I wanted to take a closer look at."

Back in the square, they drifted slowly from stall to stall, examining the merchandise. Prices were a mystery; nothing had a tag on it. Danny was even more impressed than before with the quality of the work. Nothing he looked at had a Made in Taiwan label on it, either.

Kathryn found a kind of a vest in one of the little tented stalls she seemed to like very much, calling Danny over to look at it. Danny was referring to it in his own mind as a vest for lack of a better word. Cape would actually have been as accurate. It seemed to be made from one piece, folded back at the collar so that one of the two flaps so formed fell straight to the back. The front one, shorter, had armholes, but no buttons or other fasteners. It appeared to be leather, with overlays of featherwork, adorned with finely pressed metal ornaments and beads. In fact, it had so much ornamentation it should have been ostentatious, but somehow it wasn't; the maker had managed to harmonize the whole thing into true artwork. Danny told her it was undoubtedly the first piece of clothing he had ever seen that he would consider art. He examined the metalwork closely; it appeared to be gold. The only thing he found disturbing about it was that it was similar in cut to the one Bertie—or rather, the jaguar-man who looked like Bertie—had been wearing in the shared dream. He reminded himself to ask Kathryn about that.

"How much for this?" Kathryn asked the smiling shopkeeper.

"For you, my lady? For you it is proper. Your beauty complements the piece. For you, we say, ten dollars American?"

Danny stared at the man; Kathryn looked stupefied. It was obvious how much time and effort had been spent on it; a hundred dollars would have seemed cheap. And that was considering the metal ornaments to be brass, not gold.

"Ten dollars?" she croaked.

The shopkeeper looked worried; his smile disappeared. "Is too much? Five dollars, then. It should be yours, my lady."

"Oh, no, no, no, ten dollars is not too much. Not too much by any means." She rooted in her purse, came up with a ten. "Please," she said. "I feel like I'm stealing it as it is."

"What is proper is not a crime, my lady," he said, smiling again.

"Do you believe that?" she asked Danny when they had moved on from the man's tent.

"No. That's just ridiculous. I'd say the artist can't be getting more than a penny an hour. Tops."

"Wait," she said. She ran back to the tent; Danny was truly

impressed by the gracefulness of her movements, and by the beauty her brief shorts and thin blouse revealed.

"Señor," she asked the man. "Who made this? I mean, where did it come from?"

"I make it, my lady," he said. "I make all things I sell."

Danny glanced around at his other stock; almost all of it was as elaborate as the vest. "You made it all?" he asked. "You are very talented, a real artist."

"Thank you, señor," he said, executing the very slight, odd bow that he had seen Eduardo do. What made it odd was that they bent the knees very slightly as they bowed. "It is well to be appreciated. There are many good artists in the village. I am only one of many." He gestured around to the other little tents. "Let me show you something, something the lady should possess."

Leaving his own stall unattended, he walked them across the square to another which was very similar. Here, instead of clothing, the wares were jewelry; again, much of it looked like gold or silver to Danny.

The man who had sold Kathryn the vest nodded to the other shopkeeper, a much older man. "Look at this," he said. He held out a golden band, about large enough for Kathryn's upper arm. She took it, looked at it, handed it to Danny. It was quite heavy for its size; a metal band in the form of a serpent coiling four times, the plumed head of the serpent holding in its open jaws a figure of a woman in the process of childbirth. The serpent was not depicted as biting the woman, but rather presenting her. The casting skill was obvious.

"What material is it?" Danny asked, wondering as he did if that were a crude question.

The old shopkeeper who was selling it spoke up. "Here, we call it teocuitlatl. You call it gold, señor." He didn't seem offended.

"Now, I almost hate to ask, but—how much does it cost?" Kathryn said.

"For you, my lady," the old shopkeeper said—Danny thought that sounded familiar—"shall we say, twenty dollars American?"

"Twenty dollars!" Danny exploded. "You're out of your mind!"

This shopkeeper looked worried, too. "Ten dollars, then!"

Danny had a sense of déjà vu. "No, it's not too much, man, it's so damn little! Excuse me, I don't mean to shout at you, but—but—if this is gold—and I believe you—why, it's worth three or four hundred in metal alone! Not to mention the artwork. Which is exquisite."

"It is a proper price, señor. To sell a thing of beauty to a person of beauty is an honor. I dig the metal from the ground, I make the cast, I cast the metal. I see it is good. But it is not truly good until someone proper wears it."

They paid the old man his twenty dollars and moved on. Danny was feeling a little dazed, and he could see that Kathryn was too. The attitude he was finding here was so totally different from anything he'd ever encountered before, it was throwing him off balance.

"I forgot exactly what they said the name of this town was, but so far, I think I have a better one," he told her.

"What's that?"

"Shangri-La. Paradise. I swear to God, this is unreal."

"You can say that again!"

"Okay. Shangri-La. Paradise. I swear to God, this is unreal."

They laughed together and went to see what treasures awaited them in the next little stall.

.

3

John watched Kathryn and Danny walk up the street for a minute. Nice people, he thought. The elation he had felt at seeing Susan again had not dissipated; he was in a better mood than he'd been in in a long time.

"In spite of being wanted for attempted rape," he muttered wryly.

Looking back at the shop that had caught his attention, he saw little more than a hole in the wall, a door with a tiny

display window alongside. The display consisted of musical
instruments; an end-blown flute like a recorder, drums of different sizes; all appeared handmade. He opened the door and
bells chimed, announcing his entry.

"Who comes?" called a voice from the back. John looked,
but couldn't see anyone. Then: "Ah, it is you. Bueno, bueno.
Welcome to my shop!"

John glanced down, realized that the reason he hadn't seen
the man was that he'd been looking over his head. He was less
than three feet tall, his back twisted over into a grotesque hump.
His head, hands, and arms looked normal, but his legs were
very short, and his torso doubled over almost on top of itself.
He walked forward with a sort of a hopping gait, smiling ear
to ear; or so it seemed.

"What can I show you? What do you want to see? A drum
perhaps!" He sort of danced around, very awkwardly, but with
a certain efficiency. "No, no, not a drum for you. Not for you.
Wind. Has to be wind. Of course, of course. A flute? Per-
chance a flute, perhaps a bass flute whose tones can be heard
for miles across the sea! When the sailors hear Orizaba's flutes
sounded, they quake in fear, they believe a tidal wave ap-
proaches! Maybe a flute, maybe a flute. But no. The flute, its
sound belongs to the other. So no flute. But wind, has to be
wind. Ah! Ah! I have it, I have it, just the thing! Now where
is it, where have I mislaid it in this accursed dark shop? I tell
you, I need a window! I cannot work by electric light, it casts
shadows that are not, creates new colors, spoils the real. Ah!
It is here. Yes, yes. I knew it was here all along." The little
man paused in his nonstop patter long enough to climb onto a
rickety stool and tug at a leather bag on a shelf about six feet
up. The bag came loose suddenly, and the stool, dwarf, and
bag all crashed into a corner. A drum rolled out and bonged
against the door, emitting a surprisingly deep tone for its size.

"Are you all right?" John asked, starting to move toward
him.

"All right?" he cried, jumping up. "Of course I'm all right,
a little fall can't hurt Orizaba, not possible, no. I'm certainly
all right. Why, perhaps if I were as big as my namesake—
Orizaba is a mountain peak, you know that?—when I was born,
my father thought someone so tiny should have a big name, a
mountainous name. So Orizaba it was, yes. No, I do not fall

like a mountain, I cannot, else I would cause an earthquake that would level this village, yes. Is this not so? Of course, of course. Ridiculous. But here, here, you will look, this is what you want. Yes, Orizaba is sure of it!'' He thrust the bag at John.

Opening it, John pulled out a trumpet. He stared at it for a moment. How had the little man known he was a trumpeter? But that was less significant to him than the horn itself. Although a trumpet was obviously what it was, it bore little resemblance to any he had seen before. The body curve was more open, more nearly circular; the valves, four of them, of an odd levered rotary design John had never encountered on any brass instrument. But the most striking thing about it was its ornamentation. Every section was carved or inlaid as a sculpture, a work of art in its own right. The bell itself, polished to an extreme finish inside, was cast to resemble the open jaws of a snake; the plumes, the familiar Mexican motif, ran gracefully back along the tubing. Each of the metal tubes connected to the valves was also a plumed rattlesnake, its mouth holding the valve on one end and the rattle coiled around it on the other. The eyes of all the snakes were inlaid with a green jewel, probably jade, though they looked like emeralds to John. The valve levers appeared to be inlaid with turquoise.

But the thing that caught his attention the most was a leather thong, wrapped tightly around the mouthpipe, to which four brilliant green feathers were attached. Feathers identical to the one in his pocket.

''What bird are these from?'' he asked Orizaba.

''Ah, the quetzal, the quetzal. The most rare, most beautiful. None around here. From far to the south, those. They made a long journey, a long time ago, oh yes, such a long time ago. From the south.''

''I've never seen one. How big are they?''

''What a question! What does it matter how big they are? Must beauty be big? Cannot a tiny bird, a tiny fish, a tiny woman, have a great beauty also? Are they sometimes not all the more beautiful, just because their beauty is constrained to such a small part of the world? No, no, there is a fineness to the small, you cannot look on a thing of beauty and say, 'This is badness, it is so little!' You cannot, you cannot. About as big as a crow.''

At first the last line seemed a non sequitur, then John realized it answered the question he asked in the first place. He laughed; the little man was certainly an interesting character, to say the least. He looked at the trumpet again. For all its ornamentation, it was surprisingly light and comfortable in his grip; his fingers fell naturally on the keys, and they required little pressure to engage. When released, they instantly returned to their original position.

"May I try it?" he asked.

The little man stomped his foot, turned away from John, and raised both arms in the air. John noticed how large his hands were, out of all proportion to the rest of his body. He began to shout: "He asks if he can try it! He asks me this! It is not to be believed! If this man were dying of thirst in the desert, and came upon the only water in miles, about to be devoured by the sands, he would ask if he could drink it! How can you answer such? How? How?" He turned around again. "Of course," he said calmly.

John laughed again, then put the mouthpiece to his lips. He sounded a tentative note. The horn played more easily and sounded better than any he had ever seen. He tried a riff or two; it felt almost like the instrument responded to his thoughts, adjusting its timbre without his being conscious of it. He couldn't believe this ornately carved instrument was so much better than the Bach he'd left in Miami, but it was, and there was no denying that. This thing could almost force him to go back into the music business.

"You want it, of course. You like it. You have to have it. With these hands,"—he held up his big hands and looked at them—"I made it. Turned every pipe. Carved every key. Like my own child, it is. Perhaps I should have named it. But now here you come, and you want it. Always, that is the way. But pay for it you will! No doubt! There can be no doubt of that, no!" He glared up at John. "How about fifty dollars American?"

4

Lying flat on her back, Susan looked up at the blue tropical sky. There were a few wispy white clouds out over the ocean; otherwise it was completely clear. She couldn't help but be amazed at the good time she was having. The moment it had become clear that they were in Mexico, she had gotten very nervous; she had such bad associations with Mexico. But this was utterly different, this little village. She knew she'd feel better when she was absolutely sure the place didn't have a bullfighting arena. She had promised herself a long time ago never to get within a hundred miles of one of those things again. But she didn't really believe there would be one here. The town was too small.

She rolled over on her side and looked down at the water. David was idly swimming about, not exercising himself particularly, just enjoying the water. She liked to sun herself after swimming; David had little interest in lying in the sun. Even more extreme were Frank and Evelyn; they seldom came out. She could see them about a hundred yards off to her left, snorkel tips breaking the surface. She wouldn't have been surprised to learn that they lunched off raw seafood collected from the bottom, drank the salt water.

She'd been a little worried about sunburn, but the sun, though hot, was not giving her a problem; just more of the utter perfection of this place. You didn't even sunburn here, she thought. And a good thing, too; it was not easy to leave this beach. The water was calm and clear, the sand fine and of a golden color; there was a scattering of picturesque palms along the upper strand. Besides David and the Wassermans, she hadn't seen a soul down here all day, although a fishing boat, probably from the village, had passed by at a distance. Her swimsuit, the briefest bikini she could find, seemed to be a bit constricting to her, especially under the circumstances of the near total privacy. If the Wassermans hadn't been here, it would have been gone long ago. She wondered if they'd be offended. Evelyn also wore a very tiny swimsuit; perhaps she felt the same. Susan decided to try to talk to her about it. Swimsuits seemed so ridiculous to her, here. She remembered the incident in Jerry Maxwell's office and decided to proceed with caution. You could never tell what was going to happen when you took your clothes off.

She turned the other way and looked up at the ruined church, looming above them on the hill. The sun was beginning its descent into the west, and from this angle that took it down right behind the church roof. Already the light streamed through the old windows, silhouetting the building and causing it to stand out blackly against the afternoon sky. It really was an interesting structure, but to her it seemed so alien in contrast to the resort, the beach, the village. Like it had been dropped here by invaders from some other world. It occurred to her that in a sense it had; it was a Spanish church, built here when these were Indian lands. From the little she knew of the conquest, the Spaniards were certainly alien invaders in every sense of that phrase.

She thought she saw some movement up the hill, near the edge of the level area on top. Looking again carefully, she saw that it was true; somebody was moving up the path that started back near the village, and zigzagged up the hill. She wondered who it might be, considering that David had told her that the villagers considered the church to be haunted. As the person cleared the edge, she caught a brilliant flash of reflected sunlight near his foot and realized it must be Bertie. Pretty bold of him to go up there all alone, she thought. Some months ago she might have dismissed the notion of a haunted church as ridiculous, but after the last week, things didn't seem quite so clear-cut in her world.

She watched him disappear into the low brush surrounding the base of the church, then turned her attention back to the ocean. She thought about John; it had been so many years. So often during those dark days after the minister's "counseling," and later after the Mexico trip in college, she would have sacrificed a hand to talk to him. When she was a child, sad-eyed John had been closer to her than either of her parents; she was crushed when he went away, and again when the family lost touch with him when she couldn't even hear his voice on the phone. In spite of this, she told herself, she didn't blame him. She knew he'd done it to survive. That, in the Goss family, was no mean feat. But it was so good to know now, at last, that they both had survived, and in relatively good shape. Their presence here at the same time was, she thought, such an amazing coincidence. Danny must be right about some conspiracy, some plan. But this sea, this sand, this village made her not want to think about that. She felt she was exactly where she belonged at this time.

Smiling lazily, she stretched her body, got up. Fifty feet away was a bush with numerous bright yellow buds on it; she didn't know what they were, but they were pretty. She walked up to it, and looked for a flower in bloom. There weren't any, so she selected a large bud and picked it. As soon as it came free, it burst into bloom in her hand. She smiled again, put it in her hair. Feeling something against her foot, she looked down; a large snake of some kind had crawled out of the brush and lay across her bare foot, its head and a foot of body coiling up her leg. She smiled at it, too, and reached down, moving it gently away. Then she walked back to her blanket on the sand and sat down, hugging her knees to her chest. She found these events as natural and proper as the fact that the sun shone on her back, that a gentle sea breeze caressed her face.

5

Danny and Kathryn finally left the square, but not until they had explored virtually every stall there. It was getting quite late; Danny wondered where John was. In reality, he hoped John had gone back to the resort alone; he was enjoying Kathryn's company far too much. She had made several other purchases in the square, mostly jewelry and clothes, all at the same absurdly low prices. Danny thought it was a little odd that everyone quoted their prices in "dollars American," never in pesos. Kathryn had only spent about fifty of those dollars, and he had spent nothing at all. He had wanted to buy her something, but he wasn't sure she'd think it appropriate; he wasn't sure about a lot of things, but he'd have to take a plunge sooner or later. Might as well be sooner, he thought.

"Kathryn, you won this trip through a drawing at Tascan Acres on Long Island, didn't you?" he asked.

"Yes. I did. Did I mention it?"

"No. My friends, David and Susan—same trip, same place."

"That's strange. I thought they only gave away one trip."

"So did we. But they gave away at least four. John and Bertie won them, too. And I don't know for sure, but I think the Wassermans, besides."

"How about you?"

"No. I came as a paying customer. But so far, nobody's asked me to pay for anything other than the flight to Miami."

"Doesn't that seem odd to you?"

"It sure does. Now—ah—can I ask you a personal question?"

She looked directly into his eyes and smiled slightly. Even with his normal vision, he could see the reddish wisps moving between them. That made him feel very good indeed; but he had a different question first.

"Ah, Kathryn, this is going to seem really odd."

Her expression changed slightly as she realized he was not going to ask the kind of question she initially expected. He watched her face alter subtly, begin to look worried.

But he pushed on regardless. "Has anything—ah—strange been happening to you in the past week?"

Now she looked angry. "What do you mean?" she snapped. "Just what the hell do you mean by that?"

"Hey, relax; please. I don't mean anything, at least not anything personal. But I—"

"You know about it, don't you? You saw me? Or somebody else did and told you about it? Well, Danny, don't you worry about it. It's fucking well not contagious! And you don't have to soil your goddamn hands with me, I won't force you to! I tell you I just can't—" She stopped, her lips trembling, eyes growing wet. "I can't help it," she said in a tiny voice, dropping to her knees in the dusty street. She buried her face in her hands, the purchases falling to the ground, forgotten.

Danny stared at her, totally bewildered. Her body was racked by great sobs. "Kathryn?" he pleaded. "Kathryn, listen to me. I don't have any idea what has been happening to you. Some weird stuff has been happening to the Hallstens, myself, and John, that's all. I thought maybe it was everybody. Maybe it is. But I don't know about your experiences, no. Kathryn, please listen. I consider us friends already. Whatever, you can tell me about it or not. I'd like to know, because maybe then I could figure out what's going on. But if you don't want to say, don't. It doesn't mean as much to me as you do."

She looked up at him. She had stopped sobbing, but tears were still streaming down her cheeks. "If you knew what I'd been doing, Danny, you wouldn't want to be standing so close. You couldn't stand to touch me. I can hardly stand to touch me."

Good God, he thought. What the hell has been going on with this poor girl? None of the experiences he'd had, even the dream and the fright at the trailer, had produced anything close to this reaction. Hers, whatever they were, seemed to have destroyed her self-respect. If anything, his had increased his self-respect.

He bent down, touched her cheek. "You're wrong. Nothing could have that effect on me. Come on." He started to help her gather the packages, glancing around to see if there was a crowd of bystanders. To his surprise, nobody seemed to be paying any attention at all. He pulled Kathryn up, took her back toward the resort. When they reached the edge of town, he stopped again. There was a low rock wall alongside the road here, and they had a long view both up toward the resort and back toward town.

"I wanted to tell you," he said, "about one of the experiences I had." He had been determined not to mention this one, but her reaction had been so intense, her devastation so complete now, he just had to; it was all he had that might be comparable. He told her about his visions at the trailer on Long Island, stressing, if anything, his loss of bowel and bladder control. He used clinical terms, tried to be detached.

She looked up at him, her face a mask, her eyes pleading

with him for something he didn't understand. "So you shit and pissed all over the place," she said.

"In other terms, yes," he said, flushing.

"Well, Danny, this is my experience, old buddy. If I'd been there, I'd have probably eaten all of it. You'd have been sparkling clean, my friend." She turned her head away; her body shook again.

"What? What do you mean?"

"I mean I've had real odd appetites lately. And man, I mean odd." Her voice broke on this last.

"Just in the last week?"

"No, goddamn it! I've been a fucking human garbage can all my life!" The sarcasm was obvious in her outburst. Then: "No, no. Just in the last week. Started—up—last Tuesday, I think. Danny, you don't know what we're talking about here. You really can't. I've been eating trash, all kinds, I don't mean junk food. I mean trash, like off the street. I can't help it. I get these urges, I see a glow or something around some piece of crap, and I have to eat it. You can't imagine some of the things, and I won't make you sick. It isn't your problem. But it can be just about anything. And when it's happening, it doesn't make me sick. It tastes good. Afterward, I want to throw up, but I can't. It's a fucking nightmare!"

"Has it happened since you've been here?"

"No. I was hoping it was over."

"Maybe it is."

"And maybe not."

"Kathryn," he said, holding her shoulders, "I've got some more things to tell you about. They may sound crazy, but I'm going to tell you anyway. If you think I'm nuts then, and want to run away, I'll understand. But first, right now, even if you've been eating cowshit, this." He pulled her to him, kissed her full on the mouth. At first she kept her mouth tightly shut, then opened it a little in response to his tongue. He kissed her long and deeply.

Finally they broke. "Even after what I told you?" she asked.

"Yes, Kathryn. Regardless of any of that."

"You're kind of an unusual person, Danny Hudson," she said, managing a little smile.

"So are you. Now listen. I want to tell you my life story, capsule version."

When darkness fell, and for quite a while afterward, they sat on the stone wall talking. Periodically they kissed; they were never out of physical contact with each other.

"Kathryn, I do have one other thing I needed to ask you about," Danny said, after they'd finally started back toward the resort.

"What's that, Danny?"

He stopped, looked at her. "Again, this'll sound odd, but, before this trip, have you ever seen me? I mean, is my face at all familiar?"

She considered this for a moment. "You know, it's really odd you should ask me that. Because when I first saw you, I was sure I had. But not really. It was in a dream, a real short one. And really strange. I just saw you—or somebody who looked like you—walking toward me in a field, at night. Then I turned into somebody else. So naturally I don't remember any more." She grinned. "You'd have to ask whoever—"

"I have," he said with a grim smile. "I asked you because I was there, too. I saw you—saw you turn into Susan Hallsten!" He proceeded to relate the rest of the dream.

"But, Danny, how is that possible?" she asked.

He shrugged. "I have no idea," he said.

They started walking again, holding hands. He wondered what it could mean, at least three of them sharing a dream. Very odd. But he still had no good answers, and told her so. Gradually the conversation shifted back to more mundane affairs, like what they were going to do with the evening.

"I'll be ready to go down to dinner in about ten minutes," Kathryn told him as they reached her door.

He kissed her lightly. "Fine," he said. "I'll meet you here."

When they got to dinner, everyone, including John, was already there. Holding hands as they walked through the door, they released each other to sit down at the table. No one had been served yet.

There was a long silent moment. Danny looked around the table. Frank Wasserman looked amused; John looked concerned. Everybody else was glaring; Evelyn and Susan at Kathryn, David and Bertie at him. What is this? he asked himself. The only one who had any possible justification for this was

Bertie, and he had made himself scarce ever since they'd arrived. Danny was particularly vexed by David; he was, after all, the guy who had cut off a potential ménage à trois with Susan back in New York. Maybe that had been a mistake. He knew David was attracted to Kathryn, and actually it seemed that was mutual, but David was occupied. That Susan and Evelyn seemed annoyed with Kathryn, he had to admit was flattering. He didn't usually think of himself that way.

"Well, I do hope everybody had as good a day as I did!" rumbled Frank, his voice so loud Danny actually jumped.

"The water was fine," David said flatly, still looking at Danny.

"Oh, it's magnificent out there! Just magnificent!" Frank said. He started a long discourse about the various sea life he and Evelyn had seen while snorkeling. It was obvious he was trying to break the tension, and his voice was so powerful and commanding that he succeeded in doing so. By the time the food arrived, much of it had dissipated; only Bertie continued to look sullen and annoyed. Danny watched his eyes, remembered the dream, the jaguar with mirrored eyes. But Danny would not have trusted the man anyhow. Even now, his eyes looked like those of a cat about to make a kill.

The dinner they were served was as excellent as it had been the previous night. Afterwards, the Wassermans, John, and Bertie disappeared in different directions, leaving only the Hallstens, Danny, and Kathryn lingering over coffee.

"Have you been into town yet?" Danny asked them.

"No," Susan answered. "We spent the whole day at the beach. You really must join us there tomorrow, Danny. It's really beautiful, you know?" She paused for a rather long moment. "You too, Kathryn," she added at last.

Danny suppressed a grin. Perfectly obvious she didn't really want to invite Kathryn. But these tensions were not helpful; they provided only distractions to Danny's main concern, which was figuring out what this was all about.

Glancing at Kathryn again, he saw that she was talking to Susan a while, holding Danny's hand under the edge of the table. But he also noticed her giving repeated glances at David whenever Susan's eyes wandered away. There is obviously only one solution to this, he told himself; everybody throw off their clothes and have a free-for-all, get it out of our collective systems. Everybody but John, of course; the big man did not seem much affected. Even though Danny liked him a lot, John projected an aloofness that made his own former isolationism seem like sociability. It wasn't that John was cold; it just seemed like the core of him, the dynamic part of the man, was either missing or extraordinarily well concealed. He could not remember ever having met someone like that. Intelligent, warm, friendly, insightful, but no spark, no passion. If Danny was a woman, none of these other facets would be nearly enough to make up for the lack of the central essence, the essence so obvious in the tense interaction between David, Susan, and Kathryn. While they weren't paying close attention to him, he squinted enough to see the air full of the reddish-brown sexual swirls, the unpleasant greens of jealousy, and the crimsons of anger. All mixed up together; a common combination, but a dangerous one.

His thoughts were interrupted by the sound, from outside, of a trumpet being played. Just a solo trumpet, but spectacularly beautiful; the notes seemed to cut right into his soul. He couldn't have named the song if asked; in fact, he wasn't sure he recognized it at all. But he knew it was about a man singing of his love far away, a love he could never fully have. He felt the pain of the situation, felt the despair; his eyes were getting wet and he choked back a surge in his chest. He noticed David doing the same; Kathryn and Susan were both openly crying. It took only a few more bars for David to join them. Danny was the last holdout; at the beginning of the next chorus, he too gave way.

The next morning, Danny awoke feeling better about his life than he had in many years. He looked over at Kathryn, lying beside him in his bed, and he smiled at the memory of the previous evening. They had come up to his room almost immediately after the coffee, and they hadn't left again. He hoped there would be many more such evenings in his life. She was still sleeping, her dark hair falling across her face; his fingertips ran over her mouth delicately. This woman, he thought, was totally unique. At least in his experience. Just as David had, she had surprised him with a matter-of-fact acceptance of his gift. He wondered where people like these had been when he'd been growing up. There had been so much pain in his childhood; just one friend like any of them would have made an enormous difference. He remembered his father again, the fights about what he should do with his talents; the sudden, lethal heart attack Danny had known was coming. He had never gotten over the feeling that since he'd known about it, he was somehow responsible; even though he'd tried, without success, to warn his father. But the man just wouldn't accept it; or perhaps he knew it too, didn't feel he could escape, or didn't want to escape. Danny always saw his father as a man carrying a huge weight around. In his dreams, his father had always carried a big burlap sack over his shoulder, like a skinny summer Santa; Danny never had any idea what was in it. His eyes began to mist. He cursed his own emotions; his intellect told him he hadn't killed his father, but down in the darker areas of his mind he couldn't believe that. Danny had been told he was no good so often that part of him had become convinced of it. He wondered now if he should inflict himself, his problems, on such an exquisite creature as Kathryn. He realized he was in a rapid descent from his earlier ebullience; he tried to recapture it, but it was too late. The memory of his father, the guilt, were just too much.

Kathryn opened her eyes and looked at him. She didn't smile; she had an odd expression on her face, as if she had gone straight from sleep into some highly alert, intensely focused state. She said nothing, just pulled the thin sheet off them, threw it aside, and came up on her knees. Her small naked body in the early morning sunshine was incredibly beautiful to him, but his mood prohibited any response on his part. He thought she might feel slighted. He tried to explain, but he was choked up; the words just wouldn't come. He was going to ruin this relationship, just underway, with the goddamn old guilt, he told himself. Tears were running freely down his cheeks. She held his face, looked into his eyes. Still she said nothing, did not smile. He was on a roller coaster; fifteen minutes ago he'd felt the best he had in years, now he felt the worst.

Lightly and delicately, she moved her face close to his, began to lick the tears off his face. He was surprised; there were a number of things he might have expected her to do, but that wasn't one of them. He watched her as she moved down his body, licking, occasionally nibbling when she found a loose hair or a bit of dead skin. She came back up and bit off several little pieces of his hair. Her throat worked as she swallowed. He felt odd. This was a new experience for him, very unusual; he thought it should have been erotic, but, perhaps because of his mood, it wasn't.

She moved to his armpits, licked around those, then down to his navel, where she pressed her tongue down inside. He saw some small hairs disappear between her full lips. She moved on down, took his limp penis in her mouth; he didn't respond at all. The way she was holding it was not at all like she'd held it the previous night. She laid her hand on his lower belly, just above the pubic hair, and pressed lightly. Involuntarily, he began to urinate into her mouth. He was utterly mortified, tried to move, to grab her head and pull it away, but his muscles would not obey him; he only managed to squirm feebly. She stayed as she was, swallowing repeatedly. Then she rolled him onto his side, and he felt her tongue darting into his anus. Again she pressed on his abdomen, and again involuntarily, he began to defecate. He couldn't see her face, but he knew what she was doing.

At last it was over. He could move his muscles now, could speak, but he remained absolutely motionless. He was horrified at what he'd done. But at the same time, he knew he hadn't really done it; she had. He couldn't see her at the moment, she was still behind him on the bed. She certainly hadn't been exaggerating her odd appetites, he told himself. He actually grinned. It didn't really bother him any, his mood was otherwise so good, he could get past a little embarrassment. Then it hit him. His mood was, in fact, good; even better than earlier. He thought about his father and for the first time, really understood that he wasn't responsible. He had new friends, a new lover, life was good, he no longer felt rejected or different. He'd never realized what a huge bag of guilt he'd been carrying around on his own shoulders until now. Now that he was no longer carrying it.

He literally sprang up. As he had expected, the bed was not soiled. Kathryn sat looking at him, her mouth slightly open and her eyes glazed; she looked very sad. A tear coursed down her face, just one. Then the sad look passed, and her face returned to the odd mask he'd seen earlier. Finally she seemed to wake up.

"Oh, God, Danny, oh no—" she started, looking horrified. "Not again, not with you! Oh, God—"

He grabbed her shoulders. "Wait, Kathryn. You remember what you've been doing?"

"Oh, Danny, yes, I'm so sorry, I'll go away, I can't—"

"No. No. You don't understand, and I think I do. Kathryn, please. Try to get hold of yourself. It doesn't matter what you did. It does, but not like you think. You don't know what a wonderful thing you've just done!"

"Wonderful? Are you crazy? It's not—"

"Kathryn! You've got to hear me out. I—I love you, Kathryn!"

"What?"

She looked totally confused, horrified, excited, all at the same time. But she listened while Danny explained his theory of what had just happened.

6

"Really fantastic, isn't it?" David said as they sat on the beach. It was a beautiful morning, just hot enough to make the water refreshing. Danny and Kathryn had joined them today, and David felt that he had his feelings under control. He was slightly embarrassed about the hostility he had shown toward Danny the previous night. Besides, it was just as well that Danny and Kathryn had paired off; his feelings about her were very complicated. But he wondered if his friend knew anything of her odd eating habits.

"I have to agree with you there," Danny replied. "It isn't at all what I expected when we came here. Can't say I'm sorry, though. This trip has been amazing for me. In ways, more than all the stuff that was happening to us in New York. Pleasantly amazing." He nodded toward Kathryn, who was out in the water with Susan and Evelyn.

David looked at the three women. They seemed to be talking as they floated around about fifty yards offshore. Frank's snorkel was visible far off to one side, nowhere near them.

"David, now that we are all here, and things are so damn good, I want to ask you a question," Danny said, running sand pensively through his fingers.

"What's that?"

"Why did you come on this trip? Damn it, man, it was so crazy!"

"Well, isn't it obvious? Look around you!"

"Yeah, yeah, sure, it is now that we're here. But to pack up and go on a trip, on such short notice, not even knowing where you were going— It still doesn't seem strange to you at all?"

For a minute David felt like Danny had slapped him in the face. Of course, he was dead right. What had been wrong with them? Susan had thought it was a fine idea too; he remembered talking to her in the car about it, driving back from Tascan Acres. Suddenly, it had seemed like the best idea in the world, like it had always been a good idea. He tried to explain this to Danny as well as he could.

Danny sat up. "I kind of figured it was something odd. But you two were so fixed on it, I was afraid to say anything."

"So why'd you come?"

Danny shrugged. "You're my friends. I take that seriously. I've had very few in my time. Besides, I was damn curious."

David looked at him, had an insight. "What else didn't you tell us about?"

Danny didn't even look surprised. He related his experiences in the trailer, and the return trip on which he'd found there was no Tascan Acres.

"So what's the point, then?" David asked, exasperated. "It's hard to imagine people plotting a great vacation for us!"

"True enough. I tell you, David, I don't have a clue. I do know that John had an odd week; and Kathryn has been having a very strange time. I'll tell you all about that when I'm a little more sure of what's going on. Frank, Evelyn, Bertie, I don't know. Then there's Maria." He told David about his attempts to read Maria. "Whatever, it's really odd, and to tell the truth, I'm having a hard time keeping after it. This town, this place, it's just too good. But I wonder if it's not somehow too good to be true."

''But it's here, and I can't see where it's not real,'' David responded. ''Maybe the resort owners just wanted a test group, and somehow we got selected?''

''Why not tell us that?''

''Who knows?''

Danny gazed out at the swimming women. ''If I could come up with just one reasonable idea, I think I'd be satisfied,'' he mused.

David thought he was like a dog with an old bone, chewing it, twisting it every which way. ''Well, Danny, at this point I don't think it can be sinister, whatever it is.''

''Maybe not. There just doesn't seem to be a sinister soul around, unless you count Bertie. Maria, well, she's just strange. I can't see her as threatening.''

''Yes; Bertie. I don't trust him. I don't know why. But there sure isn't anything else around here.''

''Except that,'' Danny said, pointing up at the ancient church.

''Well, look. Susan and I planned to explore the town this afternoon, and—''

''Look out for the high prices,'' Danny said, grinning.

''Yeah, I've heard. But anyway, why don't we go up and check the church out tomorrow? The four of us, John and the Wassermans if they want to come.''

''No Bertie?''

''Well, only if he asks!'' David laughed. ''He just doesn't seem sociable, somehow.''

He saw Danny looking back down at the water, saw the three women coming up toward them. Evelyn was dragging an apparently protesting Frank along.

''All right, we're all here,'' Frank said when the group reached them. ''What is it?'' He sat down, shook water out of his ears.

''We just wanted to tell you all at the same time,'' Evelyn said.

''Yes!'' Susan said gaily. ''We decided to drive you all crazy!''

With that, all three of them stripped off their swimsuits and raced back down toward the water.

7

Bertie sat on the edge of the hill beside the ruined church, unconsciously passing the flint knife from hand to hand. The amulet he'd gotten with them was mounted on a beautifully worked leather band with seashell ornamentation; he had bought it in the square for next to nothing. The mirrored surface glinted from its position just behind his left ear. He watched the three nude women run back to the ocean; probably the best looking trio he'd ever seen in one place at one time. Particularly Susan Hallsten, he thought. She really impressed him, and he was still waiting for an opportunity to get her off somewhere alone. He'd seen the way she'd looked at him, and he was definitely interested. Interested enough to work for this one.

He glanced back up at the old church, which he'd already explored; and again he wondered why exactly he was here. Of course he'd been running from the murder in Ohio, but things were just a little too convenient; there were a few too many coincidences. He really didn't believe in coincidences, not even in the accidental juxtaposition of his car and that truck on that bridge at the same time. Certainly not with respect to the mirrored foot and the flint knife. He looked down at the knife, ran his finger across the razor edge. It almost seemed to flex in his hands, the hilt nestling hard against his palm. Like it wanted to be used, he thought. Perhaps it did. The foot seemed like that too, and the little amulet—almost like they had a life of their own.

He got up and moved out of sight of the beach. There was an open area here, invisible from below, containing an oddly shaped stone. Around it there was little vegetation, just a stiff grassy plant whose thorns could almost be used for weapons. He had received several minor scratches from it when he first came up here. He walked around the stone; it was about seven feet long and maybe a yard wide, bowed upward slightly in the middle, which was about three feet off the ground. He thought it was an artifact; the edges were too square to be natural. But he couldn't be sure. Perhaps it was just an odd configuration.

Without thinking about what he was doing, he began an elegant little dance around the stone, waving his knife in the air. His face was toward the sun, and the visual effect the knife blade made each time it crossed the solar disk was fascinating to him. He felt elated; he'd not been able to dance since losing his foot. In time with a drumbeat in his mind, his feet carried him around the stone. But then it seemed he was actually hearing the drums; the tempo increased, and his dance became more furious. His head turned toward the ocean, then to the church, then up. Suddenly he stopped, looked back at the church. Now it appeared normal. But a moment ago, when he was dancing, it was as if it wasn't there at all; in its place was some kind of a temple, a very intricate and unusual building. He'd seen it as clearly as he now saw the blackish stone walls of the church. What the hell, he thought, sitting on the stone. Realizing where he was, he jumped up as if it were hot. For reasons he couldn't have explained, that seemed like a very bad idea. The knife was still in his hand; it seemed to sing to him, a song he couldn't identify, but knew he'd heard somewhere before.

In his mind, the drums returned, their insistent beat timed with the singing of the knife, harmonizing somehow with the sunlight on the odd rock. He gave himself to the elation again, began to dance once more. Faster and faster, until his steps were frenzied. He collapsed, panting, on the bare ground in front of the rock. Facedown, he lay there, his body exhausted. Opening one eye, he saw no church, no grass. He was lying on a stone floor, and again the great temple had replaced the church. Huge pillars with strange carvings had marked the four directions, each a different color; blue, red, white, black. He felt energy flowing into his body again, felt himself come alive, alive as he had never been before. Moving to the black pillar, he caressed it; it seemed solid under his hands, and he didn't question it. He looked up at the sun, and he thought he could sense its hunger; he was hungry too, but not for any food he could think of. The knife was so active it seemed ready to leap from his hands. On the top of the stone were several long thorns from the maguey plants that grew around the town; he had no idea how they'd gotten there, but it really didn't matter. He went to the rock, knelt in front of it, laid his knife on it. The blade seemed to vibrate at a very high frequency. He picked up the thorns and pierced each of his ears, then drove one into his chest on each side. Pulling them all out, he replaced them on the stone and allowed the blood from the punctures to drip onto the rock. The frequency of the vibration went even higher. His body flexed violently, and he collapsed at the base of the stone. His mind became unclear, filled with images he didn't understand, and he thought he was sleeping for a while. But then, you don't think you're sleeping when you are, do you? he asked himself. He opened his eyes again. The stone was the same, but the church and the grass were back; the moment had passed.

Pulling himself to a sitting position, he looked out at the ocean again. His ears and chest hurt like hell, but he didn't care.

8

All of the guests were present at dinner that evening, and Eduardo seemed very pleased by that; they had been coming in at odd hours, and he seemed distressed that they were never together. He bustled around, giving the serving girls unnecessary instructions, generally making a nuisance of himself; Susan wished he'd go away and leave them to eat their dinner in peace.

She was very pleased with her finds down at the square that afternoon. She had bought a vestlike garment of much the same cut as Kathryn's, but differently decorated; Susan's used intricate featherwork to form floral patterns. David had said it was perfect for someone called Flower Feather, and the shopkeeper had heartily agreed. She had picked up a few pieces of jewelry as well, each a treasure in its own right; shopping the square was as pleasurable as the beach.

Everyone's mood seemed so much better tonight, she thought. The tensions of the previous night had calmed, particularly after she, Kathryn, and Evelyn had talked out in the water. It seemed they had become the best of friends almost instantly. It was actually a little strange, Susan thought. It was as if they were old college chums or something, like she'd known these women a long time ago. They would, she was sure, be friends for a long time to come.

Even Bertie seemed different tonight. Gone was his sullen, almost threatening manner; he was actively engaging the others in conversation, and his quick boyish smile was, she could see, gaining converts. Even the normally suspicious Danny was looking at him differently. He was so energetic, so alive, it was kind of contagious. Quite a contrast to the way he'd been. Last night he'd drifted like a dark silent cloud in the corner of the room. It was this place, she decided. Too nice, too friendly for anybody to remain in a sour mood for long.

"I suppose we'll have to go into town tomorrow," Frank was saying. Susan was still shocked by his voice every time he spoke. "Everybody is finding such great bargains. I just hate to miss a day in that water!"

"Well, Frank, I imagine we have plenty of time. The ocean isn't going anywhere, but then, neither is the town," Bertie said with a smile. He turned his attention to John. "You've spent every day in town, John," he said. "But you haven't shared with us what you've found. Come, come, there must have been something."

"Yes. Well—" John paused.

"What was it, John?" Susan asked. John was still strange to her, even after growing up with him, being as close as they'd been as children. Her great, gentle, loving, somehow hollow brother. "Tell us!"

"Well, I—I bought a trumpet. I was playing it outside last night. You might have heard—"

"That was you?" Evelyn asked. "You played that?"

"Yes, I hope I didn't—"

"John, that was truly magnificent," David said. "Some of

the best music I've ever heard.'' Several of the others murmured assent.

"Well, I used to play professionally. But that trumpet— It was made by a man down in the village, a man named Orizaba.'' He turned to Susan. "You didn't meet him today, did you?"

"No, we didn't.''

"He's a very unusual man.''

"From what I heard last night, he must be,'' said Bertie. "That was like no trumpet I ever heard.''

"Any other musicians here?" Kathryn asked conversationally.

"Well, yes, as a matter of fact,'' Bertie said. "I play the flute. Never professionally, but, well, adequate, I guess.''

"You should see Orizaba then,'' John said. "He also made several flutes. I saw them in his shop. Works of art, really. Of course, I don't know how they play, I'm strictly brass.''

"I'll have to check him out. Where's his shop again?''

Susan's attention wandered as John explained where Orizaba's shop was, and they began to discuss music. She watched the men, how they moved: David, a sensual man obviously; every movement of his was somehow subtly sexual. John, a thinker, dreamer, languid, understated. Bertie, pure energy, passion, life, too much for him to contain, it seemed. Frank, liquid and flowing, immensely powerful, strength in reserve, held in check. And Danny, somehow if you could take equal parts of each and combine them to form a new person, you might come up with Danny. She looked at them again, got a different vision; a quick overlaid image of Danny at the center and the other four around him in a square, Frank and Bertie at two opposites, David and John the other two. Something very profound about that, she thought. Then another image; the four men still in their positions, herself, Kathryn, Evelyn—and maybe another woman, she wasn't sure who or why—at the center; she and Kathryn were holding a tree that Evelyn watered, and the tree was Danny. That was very powerful. It seemed to push away her normal perceptions of the dinner table. She realized that she'd stopped eating, was sitting frozen, staring into space.

"Susan?" David said. "Susan? You all right?"

His voice seemed to break the spell. "Of course," she said.

"Just thinking about the beach." She smiled and took another bite of her fish. But she was still thinking about that image. It meant something to her, something just out of her mind's reach. It was very frustrating.

After dinner, the Hallstens, Danny, and Kathryn lingered around the table talking about the day's events. Off in the distance David could hear John's trumpet; not so sad tonight, just pleasant. The man's skill with the horn amazed him. But in many ways, John was an unusual man, a person of hidden depths. But then, so was Susan.

He looked over at her; she seemed to be very tired, almost nodding in her chair. "Anything wrong?" he asked.

"No, no. I'm just real tired. Maybe a bit too much swimming today. I think I'll go up and lie down. You coming soon, David?"

"Well, I'm not that sleepy right now. I'll be there soon, okay?"

She got up, kissed him, and went toward the stairs as David went to the coffee urn, poured another cup. He sat back down, watched Kathryn and Danny holding hands, remembered how she'd looked at the beach, in the nude. Again he felt a surge of jealousy toward Danny. After all, he'd seen her first, she should be his! But immediately he was embarrassed by such totally juvenile thoughts. Danny was his friend; he should be pleased for him. Besides, the thought of leaving Susan for Kathryn had not entered his mind; he just needed to stop being obsessed by her.

"So, Kathryn, tell me," he said, "What do you do in New York?" He was just trying to make conversation before Danny brought the topic back around to the mystery of why they were there. He was beginning to get a little bored with that; they had talked about it from every possible angle, and no answers had been forthcoming. If there was a plot of some kind, it would show itself soon enough, and they could deal with it then.

"I'm a dancer," she said. Danny perked up and looked at her.

"I didn't know that," he said.

"Well, we didn't get around to everything last night, Danny!" she said, smiling. David felt another pang. Damn it, he thought. I'm just going to pieces here. He made an effort to smile and continue the conversation.

"Where do you dance? I mean, I don't know much about it. I was going to ask if you're in a show or something now."

"Well, I was, just before the trip. An off-Broadway show, not too successful, I'm afraid. The backers pulled out their money and we closed ten days before I left. I'll try for others when we get back, I suppose. But I have a hard time getting parts."

"I can't see why," David said. "I mean, I haven't seen you dance, but—ah—"

"Thank you, David, I'm flattered. No, honestly, I can dance okay. I'm not an Isadora Duncan, but I've had lessons, I do all right. No, the problem is, I'm too small. These directors want tall, willowy blonds, not brunette shrimps."

"Maybe you should try acting instead of dancing. Your size might not handicap you there," David suggested.

"Maybe not. But the competition is, if anything, worse. Until you've been in that business you have no idea how many aspiring actresses, models, and dancers there are in New York."

"I guess not."

"Anyway, something will come along. It always does. I've been ready to give it up two or three times in the last couple of years, but then I get a part. It works out okay."

"You'll have to let us know when you do. We'd love to see you dance."

"You can count on it. What about you, David? What's your real life like?"

That expression hit him strangely. He almost said, "My real life is here," without thinking about it. But of course, she meant what work did he do, and so on, back in New York. Odd. He felt like the city, the firm, was a thousand miles and maybe a thousand years away. He had not given it a second thought since he'd been here.

"Oh, boring by comparison. Investments, down in the Wall Street district. The company I'm with specializes in agriculture, crop futures, and so on."

"How did you get into that?"

"Well, when I was a kid I lived on a farm." He saw Danny look at him curiously. "I always expected to be a farmer myself. But events changed that, and I went to college as a biology major. Then when I was about to graduate, I met this guy, an MBA, and, well, we got to talking about things. Turned out I had a real feel, somehow, for how a particular crop in a particular area was going to do. Eventually he got me in touch with the people I work for now. End of story. Dancing is more interesting, I'll tell you that.''

"Not necessarily. To be honest, most of what I do is yell at my agent about getting me auditions. Of course, it's good when you get a part, I'll admit. But you, David—that really surprises me. I don't mean to offend you, but investments—well, it just doesn't seem to fit somehow.''

"I think my coworkers would agree with you. But, to be blunt, I do well at it. It's all in correctly predicting whether a crop will succeed or not, as I said.''

"So how do you do it? Research?''

"Ah—no—well, in a way. I sometimes go out to the fields, wherever they are. And when I'm there, well, I just know. It's hard to explain it.''

"Sounds like it. You mean like intuition?''

David was struggling a bit now. He couldn't quite explain himself, and he hadn't meant to get this far into it. He looked over at Danny, trying to get a clue as to how much he'd talked to Kathryn so far about the events in New York, about his past. To his surprise, Danny was nodding, his eyes closed, obviously quite asleep. He seized on this as a diversion, told Kathryn to look.

"Looks like he's fallen out on us,'' he said. "Should we wake him, do you suppose?''

"Well, I was going to go outside for a little while. Maybe we should just let him sleep in the chair for now. I'll wake him when I come in.''

"Outside sounds like a good idea.''

Kathryn adjusted Danny's arm so it wouldn't cramp, kissed him lightly; he stirred a little but didn't wake. Then she and David went out to sit by the pool. In the distance, he could still hear John's haunting trumpet. He looked at Kathryn, who was sitting on a woven reclining chair with her legs crossed at the ankles. She wore very brief shorts and shirt tied across the front, exposing her midriff. He could not help staring; earlier at the beach, he'd been at least partially distracted by the equally beautiful Evelyn. Although Susan was not second-rate by comparison, he had practically ignored her, being intimately familiar with her body. Later he'd felt guilty about that.

His eyes came up to her face and stopped there. She was watching him intently.

"You know, I saw you on the subway in New York once, I think," she said suddenly.

He jumped. "You did?" He tried to say this without inflection, but his voice cracked slightly.

"I think so. You—I probably would have noticed you anyway, but you had—ah—"

He sighed. So she'd noticed. He wondered if she knew that he'd seen what she was doing. How the hell could you talk about that? He hoped she wouldn't bring it up; the erection was trivial by comparison. "I remember the day," he said, and tried to grin. He was sure it came out crooked and strained. "Quite embarrassing. I kind of hoped no one noticed."

She laughed. "Sorry. I shouldn't have mentioned it. Sometimes I can be too blunt."

"It's okay. It happened. The fact is, I saw you too. Same day."

A flash of concern crossed her face. So she didn't know he'd seen what she was doing. He had no intention of bringing it up.

"Like I said, I would have noticed you anyway. That day, I thought you were the most attractive man I'd seen in years."

His stomach surged; he felt like there was a moth in there with a wingspan of at least three feet. He tried to tell himself to be careful here. There were many considerations; Susan, Danny. Be noncommital, he told himself. Say something nice but nothing to indicate the effect she has on you. Let this die a peaceful death.

"You wiped me out," he said in a low voice. No! A voice inside him was yelling. Noncommital! Impersonal! "I couldn't get you out of my mind for days. To be honest, I still can't."

She turned her head, looked up at the moon. Her profile was truly magnificent in this light, an edge of brightness running down her nose and across her full lips. Unable to stop himself, he followed the line of brightness all the way to her sandaled feet. Tiny, perfect feet. His eyes started back up; calves, thighs, the dancer's perfection. Flat stomach, breasts pushing at her thin shirt, back up the delicate throat, back to those lips.

"I hoped to see you again, and meet you," she said. "And when I saw you on the plane to Miami, I was hoping against hope you were coming here. But there was Susan. I really like her, David. Already she's a close friend, and I don't usually make friends fast. And there's Danny. He's really a special man. Really special. I think I'm falling in love with him. So fast, so fast. I'm more independent, less impulsive than this. Nobody's ever called me impulsive. Ever." Her tone was dreamy, detached. She appeared to be talking to herself as much as to David.

"Right!" he forced himself to say, but his voice cracked so badly it sounded like a duck imitation.

She looked back at him and laughed. "You okay, David?" she asked. "I shouldn't have brought all this up. I talk too damn much."

"Sure, I'm okay," he said. Then to himself: Danny's okay, Susan's okay, and I'm going to fall apart all over this place. "You've got to know, Kathryn, this is a strain for me." He struggled with himself again. He was split inside; one voice yelling, Susan! Danny! Honor! The other voice was much quieter, a heavy driving force trying to lift his hand toward her. The first voice won out: "It's a shame. But we have to remember them. I love Susan, I really do. And Danny's my friend. Your new lover. Of only one day, for God's sake! What are we doing here?"

"We're just talking, David. Knowing where we are."

Against his will, his hand moved toward her. She just looked at it, didn't move.

"If you touch me, David, I may lose my control. I'm on an edge."

"I know. So am I. I won't touch you." But his hand moved imperceptibly closer, like it had a mind of its own.

"I can't stop you, David. Maybe I can resist touching you myself. But I can't stop you," she whispered.

"I'll stop," he said. There was perspiration on his forehead. "I'll stop it myself." He laid his hand on her forearm; it was like an electric shock. She looked down at his hand, back up to his eyes. He reached out with his other hand, untied the knot

holding her shirt together. She didn't move, she just kept looking into his eyes. It was as if they were locked together.

"The garage. Has to be empty at night," he said, as his
hand found her breast.

"The garage," she said, breathing very heavily. They got
up and ran across the moonlit grass.

9

Susan turned away from the window, sat down on the edge
of the bed. She felt divided; part of her wanted to cry, but
another part felt like throwing things. Though she'd felt very
tired in the dining room, she'd found herself unable to sleep;
so she'd been sitting in the wicker chair by the window, looking
out at the moonlight on the lawn. When two figures had come
out to sit by the pool, she'd initially thought it was Danny and
Kathryn. But then the man had turned his profile to her, and
she'd recognized David. For some time she'd watched them
talking, gradually moving closer and closer to each other. The
final scene had seemed inevitable to her; she knew David well.

"Doesn't take a Sherlock Holmes," she said aloud. She was
trying to control the initial surge of rage she felt. After all,
there had been the incident with the phantom in New York.
But she believed there was a difference between a phantom and
a friend, and she would have expected David to understand
that. She was more annoyed since Kathryn had now become a
friend than she would have been if she had been a total stranger.
But it really wasn't surprising; she'd seen how David had been
looking at Kathryn, and she knew from experience that he
could be very persuasive.

Actually, she told herself, her main concern was with Danny;
he could be terribly hurt by this. She wondered if there was a
way she could shield him from that. Probably not; but she
certainly wasn't going to be the one to tell him, and she would

make any efforts she could to keep him from finding out. As for herself, she planned no tearful or enraged scenes with David or Kathryn; tomorrow would be just like today. But there were some things she might want to do, and any inhibitions she'd had were now very much weakened.

She was still thinking about it an hour later when David came in. She kissed him and snuggled up to him in bed as usual; he was still her husband, the best lover she'd ever had, her stability. And she reminded herself again that she felt no threat to that so far, though a guilt-ridden confession from David would certainly have helped. It didn't come, and its absence left a subtle rift in their relationship, one that might be there for a very long while. Once again, her anger flared, and once again she stuffed it down. She believed that David should have realized how meaningless her encounter with the phantom had been, at least in terms of the two of them. But she didn't know whether Kathryn was meaningless to him or not.

10

Danny and Kathryn ran into John in the hallway the next morning. He looked a little red-eyed, like he'd been up quite late.

"I heard you playing again last night," Kathryn told him. "It's really beautiful, John."

"Thank you. I appreciate that. I hope it's not disturbing anybody. I understand my blues song the other night had a strong effect."

"John, that was without a doubt the saddest sound I've ever heard. Did you write that?" Danny asked.

"Sort of, I guess. I was just playing around, a minor key riff. Thinking about a friend of mine in New York. It just came out that way."

"She must be quite a lady!" Kathryn said with a grin.

John smiled back, perhaps a little tightly. "That obvious, eh? Somehow it doesn't surprise me."

"Do you live in New York, too?" she asked.

"No, Miami. But Nikki, the woman I was talking about, does."

"I know a Nikki in New York," Kathryn said. "Can't be the same one, of course. This one is a really strange lady." She looked at Danny. "I'll introduce you to her when we get back, Danny. Maybe against my better judgment. But she's like nobody you ever met. She may be back when we are. She was in the Bahamas—"

"What's her name, Kathryn?" John cut in, a little sharply.

"Keeler. Nikki Keeler. Why?"

John's jaw worked. He seemed totally flustered. Finally he spoke: "I was staying in her apartment in New York. We've been friends for years."

"Oh, John, I don't think so. It can't be the same. This girl is a—ah, well, ah—she's—"

Danny wondered why she was suddenly so flustered. She seemed to have gotten herself into something she couldn't get out of, and not knowing what it was, he couldn't bail her out. Helplessly, he watched her struggle.

"It's all right, Kathryn. I know what she is, what she does. I fought that battle a long time ago," John said.

Kathryn looked at him closely for a minute. "John, I'm sorry I brought it up. It's an amazing coincidence."

"There are a lot of amazing coincidences here," Danny said.

"How do you know her?" John asked.

Kathryn flushed. "God, this got out of hand quick. Oh well. What the hell. I was out of work, my agent knew her. He sent me to see her. We talked about—uh—going into business together. Her business. But then I got another part and it didn't materialize. Anyway, we became friends then."

"What is her business?" Danny asked.

Kathryn and John looked at each other for a moment, then she shrugged. "She's a prostitute, Danny. I'll explain it to you. She's really a very unusual one." John nodded at this. Kathryn continued: "Like I said, Danny, a professional dancer doesn't always have an easy time of it. I hope it doesn't matter to you too much—"

"Kathryn, if a man wasn't broad-minded he just couldn't be around you, period. Or probably anybody here. We certainly are a strange and motley crew. No, it doesn't matter to me. It doesn't matter what you might have done in the past," Danny told her.

She hugged him; John took his leave and went on down the hall. His shoulders were bent, and he had a very sad look in his eyes when he turned away. Danny saw Kathryn's face shift a bit, the way it had the previous morning. She let go of him and took two steps toward John's receding figure; Danny thought she was going to call to him. Instead, she reached down and picked up a piece of matted mud and leaves that had apparently come off his shoe. Knowing what was coming, Danny tried to look away, but he couldn't; he watched her while she ate it. Then she looked very sad herself for a minute. Down the hall, John's shoulders pulled up straighter and his step became more lively. Kathryn's face returned to normal and she looked at Danny, began to flush again.

But Danny grinned at her. "Like I said, a guy's got to be broad-minded around you. But I'll work it out!"

She didn't say anything, just hugged him again. Oddly, her breath smelled sweet; he realized that it always did.

11

"Are you sure you wouldn't rather I stayed with you?" David was asking. Susan was still in bed, having told him that she wasn't feeling well, that he should go to breakfast and on to the beach without her.

"Sure, honey, you go ahead. I'm sure I'll be okay in a little while. It's just a headache. Too much sun yesterday, I guess."

"Well, if you're sure—" His face showed his concern.

"I am. Danny and Kathryn are going back to the beach

today. You go with them. I just want to sleep a while longer, then I'll come on down. Okay?''

He kissed her forehead, left the room. He looked dubious, but he went. As soon as he was gone she sat up in bed and noticed David's beach bag sitting on the chair. Damn, she told herself, I screwed up. As she brushed her teeth, she wondered if David would come back before going to the beach. He might not; there were plenty of complimentary house towels available downstairs, and they had turned the beach into swimsuit-optional. Still, she decided to wait by the window until she had seen them go. Twice she heard someone walk by in the hallway and jumped back into bed; but eventually she watched the three of them walk down the drive in the direction of the beach.

Getting dressed quickly, she ran downstairs, hoping there was still coffee left. She had no plans for the rest of the day; she just knew that she wanted to be by herself. She had considered telling David that, but elected to beg off as sick so as not to arouse any suspicions. For now, she didn't want him to know what she'd seen last night, and she knew David and his intuitions. If she wasn't very careful, he'd see right through her. The consequences of the scene this might lead to were unpredictable—and therefore dangerous.

Again she wondered about Danny. Last night, she'd forgotten about his psychic abilities; could he see enough to know about this? Based on what she knew, probably not. It was likely that he already knew they were attracted to each other. That philosophical point occupied her mind as she sipped the coffee. She'd known it too; she also knew that there were physical attractions involving everyone there except possibly John, who seemed to stand apart. Knowing this, how much real difference did it make that it had been consummated? Probably, in most ways, not very much. It might be a step toward a rearrangement of some of the more permanent couplings, but she doubted it. Permanency did not come from a single fuck, or even from several fucks. The thing that troubled her was that she knew David would have fought against his desires, considering the complexity of the situation. It might lead to problems, and David hated problems. Therefore, it followed that he had lost that fight; that his attraction to Kathryn had been able to pull him—probably both of them—out of control. That was the factor that had to be watched, the thing that really could create problems for all four of them.

She tried to stop herself; she could easily sit around and analyze the situation all day. It detracted from her time alone; she could have done this on the beach.

"Good morning," a voice from behind her said.

She looked around at Bertie, who'd obviously just gotten up; his hair was combed, but frizzed on the ends. It added a sort of charming casualness to his good looks.

"Morning, Bertie," she said. "You running late too?"

" 'Fraid so. Nights are so nice around here it's hard to go to bed and leave them."

"We've been playing so hard at the beach, I've been kind of falling out at night, you know?"

"Yeah, I know how it is. I haven't gotten to the beach yet, myself. But maybe one day before winter."

"Is there a winter here?"

He laughed. "Probably not."

She smiled, stretched. Both David and Danny had said they didn't trust this man, but to her he seemed utterly charming; she didn't share their misgivings about him.

He returned her smile, watching her. "Doing that, you make me think of a poem I heard the other day, down in the village: 'She seems to me indeed a very goddess,/She is so lovely and so gay.' I don't remember the rest of it."

She smiled again. "Sounds like a nice poem. Thank you, Bertie. I'm flattered."

"So what're you up to today, Susan? Obviously you weren't headed to the beach, since I saw the others already go."

"Well, to be honest, I wanted some time alone. But I really have no plans."

"Have you seen the ruined church yet?"

"No. Have you been there already?" she asked, though she was sure she'd seen him up there.

"Yeah. Actually I've been spending a lot of time up there. It's a fascinating place."

"I'll bet!"

"You want to go up there today? I'll show you the way, or one of the ways. There are actually several."

"That'd be nice, Bertie. Now?"

"Now's as good as anytime."

Forty-five minutes later Bertie guided her up over the lipped edge of the hill and she stood in the presence of the old church. Its imposing appearance from below was nothing compared to what it looked like up close. Standing in front of it, looking up at it, the huge steeple looked taller than many skyscrapers in New York. She realized it couldn't be, that it was partially the setting, the black stone monolith towering over a flat plain of prickly grass atop the hill. It was isolated, framed, out of place here.

The front doorway gaped like the open mouth of some immense creature. The doors themselves were missing, rotted away or removed to be used elsewhere. Neither was there any glass in any of the windows; from the age of the structure, she supposed there might never have been. When was glass invented, anyway? she asked herself, realizing that she had no idea.

They started down the narrow path to the door, being careful of the grass on either side; Bertie had shown her how sharp the thorns were. She wished she had worn long pants instead of her shorts; so far she had avoided any cuts, but it made the going slow and tedious.

Finally they reached an open area in front of the building where the grass didn't grow, and she turned her attention back to the steeple. Under it now, she had to tilt her head far back to see it, looming blackly against the morning sky. She couldn't look at it long. If she did, it seemed it was falling on her. The whole atmosphere around the place was somehow oppressive; she could well understand why the villagers thought it haunted.

Bertie took her arm and led her to the stone steps leading up to the great doorway. There were seven of them, and they were steeper than normal stairs. She could not imagine how the builders expected the little old Spanish ladies she had envisioned attending this church to get up them, and remarked on this to Bertie.

"Who knows?" he said. "Maybe it was a Sunday morning athletic event, the little-old-lady-church-step-dash." He ran nimbly back to the bottom, then came back up, imitating an arthritic old lady, holding his pants as if they were a skirt. It was absolutely hilarious, and she laughed so hard she had to sit down on the steps to be sure she wouldn't fall. He helped her up, laughing himself, and they went inside. The arch above the doorway was a good twenty feet high.

"Are you sure it's safe to go in here? I mean, the place isn't going to collapse on us or anything?" she asked.

"I'm pretty sure not. They made this building to stand here a long time. Don't build 'em like they usta, that's for sure."

Inside the door was a foyer with an iron gate at each side, although the iron was so rusted there was little left of it. Another lower stone arch, also with no door but with rusted iron hinges hanging, was directly ahead. They went on through.

The sanctuary itself was breathtaking, although time had taken its toll on it. The back pews, which were wooden, had rotted away to little more than piles of sawdust; a few pieces here and there revealed their nature. The first seven rows of pews were carved stone, and remained intact. She wondered about the roof; it still looked relatively sound. The beams that held it were wood, but so huge they were still strong even after centuries. Each one spanned the building from wall to wall at a height of at least fifty feet, and appeared to be about four feet square. She couldn't conceive the tree it must have been cut from, or the effort required to get it up this hill and onto the walls. There were twelve such beams, supported by the walls and by stone columns rising from the floor. She wasn't worried about the flooring, since it was solid stone. Up in the chancel were great piles of sawdust, much of it covered with fungal growths; probably what remained of the wooden pulpit.

"Look at this," Bertie said, calling her attention to one of the stone columns. There was a carved face on the pillar, barely visible. It seemed to have been covered up with mortar or something, which had been partially chipped away.

"What is it?" she asked.

"Indian carvings. I'm no expert on this stuff, but I've always liked it, as you can see," he said, gesturing at his foot. "I chipped this crap away myself, yesterday. I believe this column was originally part of some Indian temple, and they just covered it over with plaster and made it part of their church."

"How in the world did they get it here?"

"That's what's really interesting! Look at this." He showed her that the floor was carved and fitted precisely to the base of the pillar; he had uncovered more carvings in the floor stones around it. She didn't understand what he was driving at, and said so.

"What I'm thinking is that they didn't bring it here—it was

already here. This was originally a native temple. The Spanish conquistadores came here, found a huge old temple on top of this hill, and probably burned it. They usually did that, if I remember my history correctly. But after the fire, these stone walls, floor, and pillars were still here. Being practical, they rebuilt it into a church rather than pulling down the stonework and starting from scratch.''

"I thought the Spaniards pulled down all the Indian temples they found."

"So did I. But maybe not here. Who knows? It was those steps out front that really convinced me. The Spanish would never have made them that steep. As you said, too many little old ladies to come to church. After the territory was pacified, of course."

"Oh, of course. Got to pacify all those bloodthirsty savages, like those down in the village," Susan said. "Those people in the village, they don't seem to be Europeanized at all. Not like the Mexicans I've seen before."

"No, I think they're pretty much pure Indian."

"What else have you discovered here, Bertie?"

"I'll show you." He led the way up toward the chancel, poked around in the sawdust and rotted wood. She could see a stone dais of some kind under it, covered over long ago.

"I don't know what that was," he said. "It'd take weeks to even start clearing it. But it was here before, I'm sure of that."

Moving off to the left of the altar, they passed through a doorway into another large chamber. Various kinds of decaying trash lay scattered about, virtually all of it unidentifiable. He showed her an alcove in the back of that room; inside was a squarish hole in the floor, where stone steps, steep but not nearly so steep as the ones out front, went down into blackness. He pointed out old rusted hinges and latches attached to the stone around it.

"Covered over by a trapdoor of some kind," he said.

"What's on the other side of the altar?"

"Not much that's interesting. But there is one thing. Let me show you."

They reentered the sanctuary and crossed over to the other side, the side nearest the ocean. There was a door leading back outside, more steep steps down to another area free of grass, with a beautiful view of the ocean. In the center of the cleared area was a roughly rectangular stone, arched somewhat in the middle. She could see he'd been at work again, cutting away at the mortar used to cover over the carvings, which were now becoming visible once again.

She walked over to the stone and touched it; it was cool, smooth. "I wonder why they didn't just throw it over the hillside," she said. "It would probably have rolled all the way into the sea." Her voice was low, throaty.

"This is why," he said. He indicated the base of it where he'd cleared away centuries of silt and dirt. It was continuous with what appeared to be a stone floor under it.

"That's why the grass doesn't grow here," she murmured, glancing around. "The stone." The clear area must have been about two hundred feet square. Immense, if it was all one stone.

"It's raised about a foot from the flat plain out there where the grass grows," Bertie told her.

"I'm surprised they didn't break it. Considering what it is," she said, caressing the hard rock.

"What do you mean?" Bertie asked her.

"It's a sacrificial stone, Bertie. For human sacrifices. Don't ask me how I know, I just know."

"I know what you mean. I had that feeling about it too, when I first saw it. But it doesn't really look like one," he said, his voice almost a whisper. "I've seen pictures. Aztec sacrificial stones were more pointed, more like a tree stump—"

Almost as if keyed by their conversation, the sky darkened above them. They looked up; a huge black mass of clouds was rolling in from the west, moving fast.

"Looks like a thunderstorm," Bertie told her. "We might want to go back to the resort."

"Good idea," she said. Then the wind began whipping up the dust, and a few huge raindrops fell around them. "On the other hand, it may be too late to do that!"

"It may be," Bertie said. It seemed the thunderhead agreed, because they saw a sheet of torrential rain moving their way, pounding the grass flat as it came.

"Shelter from the storm," Bertie said, leading her back up the steps into the church. "If only the roof doesn't leak."

They had barely gotten inside when the storm hit with tropical fury. Sheets of rain whipped by the glassless windows; water swirled inside, forming myriad tiny pools inside the church. Bertie's hope for the roof was in vain; it leaked in a hundred places. But the room nearest the sacrificial stone stayed relatively dry and comfortable. They were going to ride out the storm there.

Near the door leading outside was a small narrow window; Susan stood by it, watching the rain outside. The storm had cooled the air considerably, and she was a little chilly, wearing only shorts and a brief halter top.

The effect of the sheets of rain driven past the window by the high wind was rather hypnotic. She could no longer see the ocean; in fact, she could barely see the stone outside. But she kept getting glimpses of things she knew weren't there; after all, she and Bertie had been out there only a few minutes before. But now she seemed to see a huge black pillar beyond the sacrificial stone. She kept trying to get a better look, but couldn't through the driving rain. The clouds were so heavy that it was somewhat dark, and that also hampered her view. But it was ridiculous, she told herself. She'd just been out there; she would've walked right into that pillar.

There was a brilliant flash of lightning so close she jumped. In that instant of bright light, she saw the column clearly; it was there as surely as the stone was. Jet black, glistening in the rain, with the figure of a man carved into it. A man who appeared to be missing his left foot.

"Bertie," she said, "come over here and look at this. See if you can see it."

He came from somewhere behind her, leaned into the narrow window, his left hand coming to rest on the bare skin of her side. "What, Susan? I can't see much of anything out there except rain."

She told him what she was seeing, and he looked again. As he did, he pressed his body a little more tightly against hers. She didn't take offense. He seemed very comforting, a warm friend in the cold rain.

"No, Susan," he said after a moment. "I don't see it." Neither did she, now; it seemed to have melted in the rain. "But I have to admit, I'm enjoying looking. Anything else you want me to look at?"

She looked up at him; he gave her a dazzling smile. He

really was an amazingly handsome man, she thought as he pulled her a little closer. She didn't resist him, didn't want to. His eyes shone, but they were soft, warm, friendly; a lot like the eyes of her phantom lover, except that the phantom had been distant, detached. Bertie did not seem at all detached. He was very real. His other hand came up, traced a delicate line down the side of her face. For her, it was much as it had been with her phantom; everything in her world except their contact faded into total insignificance. She realized something she never would admit to David; in that moment, she found that she loved Bertie North with every part of herself, totally and utterly. But at the same time she understood that this would not last beyond the rainstorm, beyond the next few minutes.

Reaching around, he untied her halter, let it fall to the floor. His touch on her breasts was gentle, delicate, sure. She clutched him to her body, running her hands through his hair, down his arms, across his back. Totally involved, she wasn't aware of how they'd gotten the remainder of their clothing off, but they had. Kissing passionately, they sank to their knees on the soft layer of sawdust covering the floor. Seconds later they were horizontal, side by side. She guided him into herself; his movements began like David's, slow and gentle, but he seemed more sure somehow, stronger. Then his pace began to accelerate almost imperceptibly. Over the next few minutes it increased steadily until he was no longer slow and gentle; he was fast, hard, energetic. Precisely tuned to him, she followed him step by step, climaxed a moment before he did. Then she waited for the energizing flow she had gotten from the phantom. But it didn't happen. That seemed logical to her; Bertie was, after all, a man, not a ghost.

For a very long while afterward, they remained on the floor in a loose embrace. Neither of them said anything; he just played with her hair, stroked her body. She studied him in detail; every muscle, the little mirror on his headband, the way the stump of his left leg melded so perfectly into the oddly carved mirrored foot. When she'd first glimpsed the foot after their passion, it seemed to her that the mirror had been smoking, but she was sure that was just another illusion of the strange light the stormy skies cast inside the old church.

"Bertie—" she said at last.

"Yes?" His voice was tender, loving. She still felt very

strong emotions toward him. He was so powerful a personality; she envisioned him a knight, a warrior, brave and chivalrous.

"Perhaps it's personal, but why the mirrors?"

He looked at his foot. "You know, I would tell you if I could, but I'm not sure myself. I found them in a little antique shop, and the foot fit perfectly, better than any I'd ever had. To answer your unasked question, I lost my foot in a car crash, years ago."

"That must have been terrible for you."

"It was, until I found this one. Now, I hardly notice. But as I was saying, I found these two things and one other item, like a set. It just seems proper to wear the little mirror, I don't know why. Makes me feel good."

"You said one other item. What was that?"

"This." He reached over to his pants, pulled out the ornately carved flint knife. The lighting made the curved blade seem to glisten like a red flame.

For a long moment she just stared at it. It was certainly a beautiful thing in one way, artistically carved. But to her it looked terribly functional, vicious. Besides, any association between knives and lovemaking, no matter how peripheral, was enough to bring her close to panic. Memories of another time in Mexico started to rush back; with difficulty, she pushed them away. There was yet another issue here, so strange it overpowered her fear of the knife. She'd seen it before, seen it held against her chest at a time when she couldn't see the person holding it. During the shared dream. And hadn't Danny said that the man in the dream, the one who was originally a big cat, looked like Bertie?

"Would you put it away, Bertie?" she asked him, keeping her voice calm.

He looked a little surprised. "Certainly," he said, stuffing it back into his pants.

She sighed. "I'm sorry, it just made me uncomfortable."

"No problem."

She glanced up at his face, impulsively asked him if he'd ever seen her before the trip.

He grinned. "Yes, I did. Hard to forget a face like yours. In a taxi, in New York. I was walking with a friend. I saw you in a taxi. Weird coincidence, eh?"

"Any other time?"

He gave her an odd look. "No," he said. "I would've remembered."

She actually felt relieved. So he didn't remember the dream, hadn't shared it. She took this to mean that Bertie was not the man in the dream, that he only looked like him. That was a relief; the man in the dream had been dangerous, intimidating. Bertie was not. He was, she decided, a nice guy. She liked him.

12

Down in the village, standing at the window of a little house near the beach path, Danny also watched the rain. He, Kathryn, and David had taken shelter there when the storm came up. They had been trying to make it back to the resort, but the storm had come up much too quickly. As they reached the edge of the village, a man had popped out of the cottage and invited them inside. He had warned that they would be drenched before they could get even halfway up the hill. They had gratefully accepted his offer. His wife, a tall, strikingly beautiful Indian woman, had brought them tea. She was now engaged in a conversation with Kathryn about the crafts offered for sale in the square, while David and the man, who had introduced himself as Patecatl, discussed the often violent tropical weather.

Danny just watched the rain. He had immediately picked up a difference between the Kathryn of today and the one he'd known before. At first, he'd been unable to understand; then a very different David, one who refused to look him in the eye, met them at breakfast. A quick read while they weren't looking verified his suspicions. He'd known of their attraction; it should've come as no surprise that they had slept together as soon as the opportunity presented itself. But there were two things that bothered him. One, were they going to try to pretend it hadn't happened? And two, Susan. He was concerned about her; his developing relationship with Kathryn had not diminished his own feelings for Susan at all. While sitting on the beach, he'd considered telling her about it and proposition- ing her; then he'd decided that was petty. If he and Susan ever did anything like that, it should be because they wanted to, not to lash out at David and Kathryn. But he did feel he should do something, perhaps at least tell Kathryn he knew. Otherwise, he'd begin to feel like a patsy, and that he couldn't tolerate.

He turned away from the window, watched her talking to the Indian woman, whose name was Mayauel. Kathryn was so very beautiful, he thought; such a special woman. He had told her he was broad-minded, and while that was true, he was also certain that she was going to test whatever limits he might have.

His musings were interrupted by a tremendous crash of thunder; the cottage was glaringly illuminated for a moment. Danny looked out the window again, glancing around to see if anything nearby had been hit. He didn't see any evidence of fire, and was about to turn his attention back to Kathryn when he thought he saw someone out in the rain, halfway up the hill where the old church stood.

Putting his face close to the glass, he strained to see. There was indeed the figure of a man standing on the slope, although not quite so far up as he had first thought. Who in the hell is crazy enough to stand out in this rain? he asked himself. The water was gushing down the hillside in such torrents that he imagined it would be difficult just to stand there. But there he was, wearing a long, blue cloak, waving his arms around, his face turned up to the sky. Danny couldn't understand how he could breathe; his mouth and nose must be filling with water.

The rain eased off for a few seconds, and in that instant Danny had a much better view. He could see the thick-rimmed glasses, incongruous with the cloak. Frank Wasserman. But what the hell was the damn fool doing out there in the rain? Dancing, it appeared. Some kind of a wild dance on the rain- slicked hillside. What an absolutely crazy group of people, Danny thought. Perhaps this was some kind of mental asylum experimenting with new therapies, and they had been chosen as the wildest and craziest of New York's abundant population of crazies. He thought wryly that it was just about the most reasonable idea to explain their presence here he'd come up with yet.

He watched Frank dance across the hillside. His right arm was extended, bent slightly at the elbow; his hand was open, palm up. There was something peculiar about his hand, Danny noticed. It seemed that there was more water pouring off of it than was falling into it. But that, of course, was obviously impossible. On the other hand, the energetic dance he was doing was almost equally impossible, out there on that muddy slope. The man's skill was really quite remarkable; he never seemed to slip, never missed a step. Then, to Danny's utter amazement, lightning struck Frank's outstretched hand; another jarring crash of thunder followed, so close and loud that Danny was almost stunned for an instant. He was about to cry out to the others, but then he realized that Frank was unhurt, that he was continuing his dance. As if by instant replay, Danny saw the event again in his mind, saw clearly this time that the bolt had gone upward. It had not struck Frank at all; rather, it had erupted from his outstretched hand!

He stared, speechless, unable to accept what he had just witnessed; a man generating a full bolt of lightning from his hand! Yet he had, if his senses could be believed. His head swam for a moment as he considered what was becoming commonplace: people who could resurrect dead plants or make flowers bloom instantly, shared dreams, a woman who could take away guilts and bad feelings by eating someone's garbage. But the magnitude of this brought it home. As he watched Frank stroll casually down the hill, he seemed to know that more was coming; his notions of the very nature of reality might be radically altered before this trip was over.

"I wonder how long this is going to last," John muttered, standing at the doorway of Orizaba's shop.

The dwarf came up beside him, looked out into the rain. "You are in such a hurry to leave?" he asked.

"Well, no, not actually," John said, his fingers working the valves of the trumpet.

"Then it does not matter, makes no difference. It is dry in here, the crops need rain, let it rain. No harm, no harm."

John smiled down at him. He had become quite fond of the little man. They went back to Orizaba's workbench, where he was making a kind of flute, an odd double instrument which was, he'd explained, to be played normally on the one side while the other side was droned. Either side could be played; Orizaba had explained that the sides were "red" and "black," but actually the whole thing was of wood and gold, natural in color. For hours, John had been fascinated by the play of the man's fingers over the nascent instrument. He was very fast, his touch very sure.

"You were going to explain to me what you meant by the 'black' side and 'red' side," John said. "Do you plan to paint it?'"

"Oh, no, no paint! Paint would ruin its spirit, no, it cannot be painted! That is not what red and black means."

"What then?"

"The red serpent and the black serpent. Can you not see the flute as twin serpents? Perhaps Orizaba's work suffers, perhaps his hands and eyes grow too old, too weak. Aiiii! If the serpents cannot be seen, then—"

"No, Orizaba, I can see them, very well done. You are still a master craftsman. I simply don't understand the meaning."

The dwarf looked at him intently. Putting down the flute, he turned his whole body on his stool and pulled up one leg. "It is important that you know this," he said. "Soon it will be critical. I am very surprised that you don't already, but perhaps it is your background, your life in the United States. A very deprived area in some ways." His manner of speaking had changed quite suddenly; his peculiar accent, which was not quite like Spanish, gone.

John suppressed the urge to laugh at him. The dead seriousness, the formal, lecturing tone seemed so incongruous, coming from the small, twisted body. "What are you talking about, Orizaba?" he asked, grinning.

The dwarf looked at him, his dark eyes very serious. Then he looked away and continued. "Don't take it lightly, my friend. It isn't a joke. Now you tell me. What do you know? What do you know of power?"

John's grin grew even broader. "Well," he began, "I'm not an engineer, but—"

"I don't mean that kind of power. I mean personal power."

Forced to acknowledge that Orizaba was serious, John dropped his mocking tone. "Well, I've heard of the concept,

I guess, assuming that's what you're talking about, in anthropology class back in college, and in a few books, but actually, just about nothing.''

"Power is all around us," Orizaba told him, waving his hands as if to include everything. "All living things have some power. If they don't, they can't live. But you, or most anybody, can collect it if you wish, concentrate it in yourself. Then you can use it, you see. Of all the people in this Fifth World, you yourself cannot afford to be unaware of this! But I suppose it's just because of the way you've lived, your veneers—''

"I'm sorry, Orizaba, I don't understand anything you've said. Veneers? Fifth World?''

"Power," the dwarf continued, ignoring John's questions, "can be collected in only one way, and that is through a union of opposite things. These opposites can take many forms. Here, in my flute, the opposites are the red side and the black side, that is, the feminine and masculine sides. They complement each other, you see. The one is not whole without the other.''

"So the red and black serpents represent masculine and feminine?''

"Yes. As well as other polar opposites.''

"Like good and evil?''

Orizaba smiled up at him, almost slyly. "Well, yes, possibly—but consider that those are relative words. You cannot define good except in contrast to some evil, so good cannot exist except in the presence of evil, and vice versa. It is ridiculous to favor one or the other, since you can only increase the polarity; if they are unified both cease to exist, like positive and negative charges.''

"You surprise me, Orizaba. You're quite the philosopher.''

"No, I am not a philosopher, I am only a logical man, and you must be too. You have to understand those opposites which can be unified without destruction. We call such a thing an 'obsidian butterfly.' Tell me, do you understand the image?''

"No, I don't. I mean, I can visualize a butterfly made of obsidian, but I can't see the meaning.''

"The butterfly is a light spirit, ephemeral, delicate. Obsidian is permanent, heavy, dark. Do you see?''

"Perhaps. A union of opposites again.''

"Yes. But I mean the obsidian butterfly that flies, that moves and breathes. The ephemeral that is cast into permanence.''

"Not possible, Orizaba."

"Ah, there you are wrong. The world we live in is the proof. The world is ollin, movement. The flux between opposites. Everything we see is created from the tension between them. Consider the dualities of spirit and matter, fire and water. Spirit is meaningless without matter. It must move into matter, form a union with it, must redeem itself! This union is called atl-tlachinolli, burning water. I cannot overemphasize that all we see of the world is this movement. But as time goes on, over many centuries, these movements slow down. And if they were to stop, you see, well, there'd be nothing. It would be the end of all the worlds that have been or might be. Not a pleasant prospect for those of us who live in one!"

"Well, this is all very abstract, but at any rate, I believe I at least follow the general idea. But why do you think it's so important to me personally?"

"Perhaps for no other reason than that you are a conscious human being, a luminous creature. What that means is that you are yourself an incarnation of spirit—consciousness—into matter. The task of your life, then, is to redeem, to purify, and strengthen that fire incarnate in you. If you don't, your life is a waste, and the spirit will be weaker in its next incarnation. But for you, I do not think that's the only reason. The spirit incarnate in you, my friend, is rather special!"

"That's rather flattering, Orizaba. But I'm afraid my special spirit still isn't really following you very well!"

Orizaba sighed. "Consider the dualities of intent and power. You,"—he pointed a finger at John—"are only intent. Your intent is very good, very strong. But that by itself isn't enough. You need more than that!"

"Are you implying I'm incapable of action? That I have no power?"

"As you are now, yes."

"I don't think that's—"

Orizaba smiled. "Yes, it is. I can see a person, a woman. You would have her close to you, but she is not. Your intent is excellent, but you haven't the power to bring her to yourself."

John seemed to fold up on himself; he felt even smaller than the dwarf. "How do you know, Orizaba? Is it that obvious? Even when I haven't said anything about it?"

"Obvious to anyone who truly listens when you play."

"What can I do?"

"Today, nothing. I cannot give you all the answers. But when the time comes, and you will know when it does, remember what Orizaba has said to you today. Find your power and seize it, do not hesitate too long! It will come; a time when you are thirsty, and to quench your thirst you must deny yourself water. But understand this, too; all the opposites are just reflections of the basic one, the final one. If you are thirsty, and someone gives you water, then she has less water! Or maybe no water at all."

"But Orizaba, what is the basic—"

The dwarf jumped down off the stool and hopped around the shop. "*So* many questions, what do you expect? Am I the oracle? Do I exist here only to satisfy your curiosity? I am a craftsman, I must carve, file, sand! Time is short!" His voice and attitude were back to normal.

For at least an hour, John tried to recreate the mood that had caused Orizaba to tell him about intent and power, but the dwarf was having none of it. He went back to his flute, and eventually started throwing tools at John whenever he asked a philosophical question. Finally John asked him about a lapidary technique he was using on a jeweled insert; he grinned and talked about it interminably.

Within an hour after the rain stopped, the entire group, except for John, had found their way back to the resort. Most were a little tired and the steps coming up the hillside had been slicked with mud and leaves, making the walk a bit treacherous. Late afternoon found them all in the front sitting room, enjoying the coffee Rosa had brought in.

Frank was still dressed in the long blue cloak Danny had seen him in earlier. He would really have liked to talk to that man, get his side of the astounding events he thought he had witnessed on the hillside. But it was difficult to walk up to someone you didn't know all that well and ask him what the hell he was doing pitching lightning bolts around. Danny had almost convinced himself that he'd been mistaken about it, but there sat Frank in the blue cloak. He hadn't been wrong about that.

Frank and Evelyn were telling the group about their trip into the square; Evelyn had apparently found as many bargains as the other women had. She was showing them now; one, which she was wearing, was a very short skirt, made of jade strips with leather bindings to hold it together. Danny thought she really had a predilection for that kind of skirt, since she'd worn a similar one on the plane. Actually, he told himself, they were only superficially similar; this one was another piece of fine art. She had also purchased a vest, similar to the one Kathryn had bought the other day, also with jade inlay, and was wearing it over a T-shirt. All three women were wearing upper-arm bands they had bought, each different and each seeming to fit the personality of the woman who wore it.

Evelyn sat down again, and Danny noticed with only slight surprise that the jade skirt was not long enough to totally cover her, and she wore no underwear. This made her pubic hair quite visible when she was seated. In New York, he might have considered this a tasteless display, but things like that were becoming quite normal here.

"It really looks good on you, Evelyn," Kathryn was saying. "But now you need to go find a shirt to go with it. The T-shirt just doesn't work."

Evelyn looked down at her chest. "You're right," she said. "Not at all." She stood up and took off the vest, and Danny wasn't even startled when she took off the T-shirt. Putting the vest back on, she sat down again; it had no means of fastening in the front, so her breasts pushed it apart a little. He could not deny that the view was pleasant.

"Now! That looks right!" Kathryn cried, clapping her hands.

Danny had to admit that it did; she and Frank looked to him like something straight out of ancient Egypt. Except for the glasses. He wondered what was happening to the Wassermans. When they had first arrived, they had seemed to be the most ordinary of the people there, in spite of Frank's unusual voice and Evelyn's obvious beauty. The extent of their quirkiness at that time was their extreme fondness of water. Now, suddenly, they seemed to be running ahead of everybody else in weirdness. Perhaps, he thought, Evelyn wasn't really being all that weird; the women had, after all, decided to dispense with swimsuits at the beach. But there was a difference between the beach and the resort house, wasn't there? Evelyn's dress now was purely decorative; it didn't conceal much of anything. Eduardo walked through the sitting room and greeted everyone.

He didn't seem to notice Evelyn, and she was unfazed by his presence. Danny had an impression that she planned to dress this way all the time from now on; here, in the village, everywhere. If there were police she'd probably have been arrested.

Danny pulled Kathryn aside. "Have you talked to Evelyn or Frank much since we've been here?" he asked.

"No, very little," she said. "Except for out in the water, yesterday, when we all decided the swimsuits were ridiculous."

"So you don't know if they were having any kind of odd experiences before we left to come here?"

"If so, she never mentioned it. And I haven't talked to Frank at all."

"I think I'm going to be bold about this and just ask him directly. I still want to know what is going on here!"

"So do I, but I swear, Danny, I can't see why you go on about it so much. Aren't you happy here?"

"Well, yes, I am, but—"

"So maybe we should leave well enough alone. In spite of the weirdness, my appetites and so on, I don't think I've ever been so happy. I feel like I've come home."

"Well, I'm happy too, Kathryn, especially about you," he said. Assuming I can keep you and David apart, he added silently. "But I don't really feel like that. Maybe I'm just overly attached to filthy old overpriced New York. But that's home to me."

"You go ahead and talk to Frank. But as far as I'm concerned, this vacation can go on forever. If somebody is out to get us, they're killing us with kindness, that's for sure."

"Yeah," he said. There were times when he felt she was right. Why mess with it? But he told himself that just trying to find out wasn't really messing with it. At least he could talk to Frank.

But when he looked up, Frank had disappeared somewhere, as had Bertie. Susan and Evelyn were talking, David just relaxing in his chair. A moment or two later, Susan and David left the room, and Danny thought he might as well take the opportunity.

"I'm going to go ahead and talk to Evelyn," he said to Kathryn. "You want to join in?"

"No, I'll leave this to you. Let me know if you figure out anything."

He walked over and sat beside Evelyn. She turned toward him, her long hair shifting, covering one breast, uncovering the other. This could be difficult, he told himself. Try to concentrate on the subject at hand. She looked directly into his eyes; her own were fascinating, intensely turquoise.

"Your eyes are incredibly blue," she said bluntly.

"Ah—thanks, Evelyn," he said. "Look, I wanted to talk to you about a few things I'm curious about. I hope you won't mind. I—"

"Oh, I don't mind at all. But I was going to go for a walk outside. Please join me, we can talk there."

He looked at Kathryn helplessly, but she just smiled and tossed her head. Not what he had in mind, but what could it hurt? They got up and left the room, Evelyn in the lead, her jade skirts shifting as she walked; he had difficulty not staring at her as they went outside. He hoped Kathryn hadn't noticed.

"So what are you curious about, Danny?" she said as they walked toward the pool.

Briefly, without going into detail, he told her about the various strange experiences, the strings of coincidences. "And what I was wondering was," he continued, "well, uh, did anything happen with you and Frank? Anything odd, I mean?"

She sat down in one of the lawn chairs. The skirt fell open across the front, completely exposing her pubes. Danny tried to focus on her face, which really didn't help much.

"I tell you, I was trying not to think about it anymore. But yes, some things did happen. Very odd things."

"You mind telling me what they were?"

"No, not really." Looking from one of his eyes to the other, she smiled. "I'm sure I can trust you."

"Thanks," he said, returning her smile in kind, even though he was wondering why she said that.

"Well," she began, "it goes back a week or so before we left. The first thing happened the day we received the notice from Tascan Acres telling us we'd won a prize. We never dreamed it might be the vacation."

"That's very familiar. Kathryn and the Hallstens, same thing."

"Anyhow, Frank and I—as I guess you really couldn't help

noticing by now—we're just such total water people. We met at the beach, can't ever seem to get enough of it. Either of us. We talked about the possibility of the vacation, and I guess decided we just had to be close to an ocean, any ocean. So we took a vacation day, just skipped out, went down to Fire Island. All the way down we talked about Tascan Acres. Of course we'd like to buy beachfront property, but that place was a disappointment when we finally did see it. Totally disorganized.

"But to get back. We went out on the beach, just walking, listening to the waves. I love that sound, I could listen to it for hours. And we ended up staying out there a lot longer than we meant to. When we finally started back, we hardly got anywhere at all before we started having car trouble. It was already too late to try to get it repaired that day, so we had to stay over.

"We got a room at a beachfront motel, no problem. This time of year, the beach is really dead. We had to eat at a McDonald's—okay by me, but Frank hates fast-food places—and the day was just turning out really badly for him. He went to bed early, but I couldn't sleep. I just sat at the window, looking out at the ocean. I can do that for a long time without getting bored.

"There was this soft old chair in the room. I was sitting in it, looking at the ocean and listening to the waves, and to this stupid heater fan, which was making a lot of noise. And—I know it's crazy, but I guess I was about half asleep—I started hearing voices. It seemed like they were just under the volume level of the fan. I could hear them, but I couldn't make out what they were saying. But as I kept listening, it started making sense. Or no sense. First off, they were calling my name, Evelyn. Then a lot of mumbling, nothing distinct. Suddenly, there was a really clear voice. It said, 'Come to yourself!' three times. Then a word I didn't understand, but it was clear enough, something like 'weet-el-ee-kway' at the end. I still don't know what that might have been. Anyway, I guess I must have been dreaming, but it didn't seem like it. I thought I was awake, alert, listening to these odd voices.

"By then they were chanting, saying, 'Come to yourself, O Lady of the Jade Skirts!' And I thought that was really appropriate, because all my life I've liked turquoise and jade-green clothes." She paused, looking down at her skirt, but made no effort to adjust it. "I guess it's even more appropriate now," she said.

Looking up at the moon, she continued: "I started seeing things then. First just shapes, blobs of color. But then a clear-cut image, and really weird. I was in some kind of a palace, a huge tower overlooking this beautiful city. But I was dying, and the city was dying with me. Flood waters were covering it. I felt like the floods were everywhere, all over the earth. I had been killed, assassinated. And I saw my killer, standing over me, looking down at me. Lord, I'll never forget it. It was a leopard, Danny, but huge, and with black mirrors in place of its eyes!"

Danny jumped. "Are you serious?" he asked.

"Yes," she said, looking at him with an odd expression. He decided to tell her later, let her get on with the story.

"So then I decided it was a dream. I tried to open my eyes, but they were already open! I was seeing two images super-imposed on each other, like a double exposure. I was looking out the window of this motel, and at the same time out the window of my palace, watching the world die. Then I was seeing yet a third image; and this one—I tell you, you're going to think I'm really strange on this one. But I'm not, at least not in that way.

"I was lying on a stone, and a man was going to stab me. The oddest part of it was that I was going to let him do it. For some reason it was absolutely necessary. Necessary for me to—as I was thinking then—I don't know what words to use— I guess christen is as good as any—a bottle of some kind with my blood! Besides that, the man who was going to stab me looked just like—"

"Let me guess," Danny interrupted. "He looked just like Bertie North, right?"

"Yes! How did you know?"

"Because I had a dream in which he had my heart torn out. And before he was himself—or looked like himself—he was a giant jaguar with black mirror eyes!"

"Are you kidding me?"

"No! But—any more in your experience?"

"Not then. After that, the images and voices just faded away."

"Any physical evidence left from it?"

"No; why do you ask?"

"Because I have a scar, right here"—he indicated his chest—"that I didn't have before I had the dream."

She leaned forward, unbuttoned his shirt, touched the scar. Then she kissed it, her breasts grazing across his knees. Damn, he thought, I've got to stop showing this to attractive women unless I mean to back it up!

He started to push her back, but didn't. "You said a couple of incidents. What else happened?" he asked, fighting for control; she was having a very profound effect on him.

She lifted her head and looked at him, then off into space. "I'm not so sure I want to tell you about the other one. I don't like remembering it."

"Well, of course you don't have to, Evelyn."

She got out of her chair and sat on the ground beside him, resting her chest against his thigh, her right arm around his lower legs. She laid her head in his lap, her hair falling all the way to the ground. He could not resist stroking it. Vaguely, he wondered what Kathryn or Frank would say if they walked out here now. But that seemed less important than the story she was about to tell.

"The other thing, well, it was just a program on the TV. It happened late one night, about three days before we were going to leave to come here. We'd had a fight, about Nikki. Nikki is this hooker Frank had been to see a few times, and—"

"Who?" Danny asked, interrupting her.

She sighed. "That's what I said. Why am I telling you all this? Just opening right up. Oh, well. Nikki. She's a hooker. She—"

"That's really strange. Both Kathryn and John know a hooker in New York named Nikki. Nikki Keeler, I believe."

"I don't know this girl's last name."

"Still, quite a coincidence. I'm beginning not to believe in coincidences. Anyhow, continue."

"Well, like I said, we had another fight about Nikki, and I told Frank I wasn't going to go with him. He thinks things like that are trivial. If he fucks somebody, he just says, 'a stiff prick has no conscience.' It's his favorite proverb. His, I have to tell you, doesn't. Nikki wasn't the first, and she won't be the last. I have no illusions. So for me, sometimes I do what I want to do too. Maybe I would even if he didn't. Who knows? He isn't going to change, so I'll never know. What pisses me off is he tries to get by with things, then when I find out, he says, 'Oh, I meant to tell you, but it wasn't important and it slipped my mind.' Which is bullshit, he knows it's important to me. So once a couple of years ago I set up this thing with a guy I knew. Man, it was a dirty deal. If it had been anybody besides Frank, somebody would've gotten killed. I set it up so Frank would catch us in bed, right in the middle of it. The guy didn't know a thing. So Frank comes in and we're hard at it. The poor guy was so scared he was retching. I thought he was going to throw up on me. Right up to that instant I'd not given this poor bastard a thought, I was just using him. Man, I felt so bad! I still do, thinking about it now. But anyway, Frank just laughs and says, 'You fuck pretty, dear,' or something like that, and he sits down to watch! But there isn't anything to watch except this guy running out carrying his pants. Frank thought it was hilarious. Man, I was so pissed. I lost a friend, never have felt as good about myself since, and he thinks it's funny! He just laughed and laughed, and the guy told me later he thought he was going to die from the sound alone. You know how Frank's laugh is.

"Anyway, we had the fight about Nikki. And Frank went on to bed, but that night he wasn't laughing. I'd gotten to him. Again I couldn't sleep, I was so pissed. So I turned on the TV, and went around the dial trying to find something good. I saw this show on, I don't know, one of the upper channels, 62 I think. It looked kind of interesting. There was this jungle explorer or something; you know, pith hat, khakis and all. He was on an expedition to find someone, and ended up in a half-ruined stone city, lost somewhere in the jungles. He went in there, and found a temple or something that wasn't at all ruined. Inside, there was a woman, and she was apparently the person he was looking for.

"The actress playing the part had long hair, a lot like mine, and the explorer called her Lady of the Jade Skirts! Remember? From the dream, or vision, or whatever? Naturally I was really interested now. But then it wasn't like I was watching the TV at all anymore. The edges of the screen had disappeared and the picture was three-dimensional. I was there, in person. I hadn't noticed it change, only that it had. Anyway, the explorer was telling her that things had changed a lot; I couldn't figure out what he was talking about. Then there was a series of disconnected scenes. One was of a lake which was terribly polluted, dead fish floating on it and a factory belching filth into it. Then out at sea, I was watching a barge dump garbage. Next, I saw a swamp somewhere in the South that a chemical company had turned into a toxic waste dump. By this time Our Lady was crying, and I discovered that I was crying too.

"Then the scene changed again, and the explorer was gone. Our Lady was standing in a kind of a shrine built in a river marsh; there were reeds and cattails all around. A real pretty place. She was naked, nursing a baby and there was a jaguar lying next to her with a hummingbird perched on its head. Then this monstrosity came up out of the water. It had huge fangs, and—this must be Freudian or something—it was wearing thick-rimmed eyeglasses! But Our Lady and the animals didn't seem to be afraid of it, and it came up on the bank and sat behind the group. A nice family portrait: mother, father, baby, and the pets!

"Our Lady was telling the monster about all the pollution, and she was just furious. She said it would be proper if there was no water at all in the world, that people just couldn't appreciate how valuable it was. And just like that, the rains stopped and the rivers and streams began to dry up. The whole countryside was turning into a desert. I could feel the heat and dryness. But there was this little oasis that didn't dry up. The monster seemed to be able to make it rain there.

"I was looking down through the trees at them. Then I wasn't. I was looking up at Our Lady from real close, and I had her nipple in my mouth! I was the baby! Our Lady looked down and said, 'You have to come to yourself.' I remember gurgling at her. Then she said, 'You are not my child, Evelyn, you are me!' I still thought it was a movie in spite of everything, and I thought, Evelyn? But that's my name! Anyway, the woman was telling me something about how I was supposed to remember what was going to happen next, that it was important. They put me on a reed raft out in the water. Then the explorer turned up again, but he looked totally different. He was standing on the opposite bank, wearing a fancy costume and headdress. His face was painted black, with five white spots arranged like a cross. Our Lady stood up, right at the edge of the water, and held up her arms. All of a sudden he threw a spear at her! Hit her right in the heart, went right through her. For a minute she just stood there, her blood pouring out. Then she fell on the bank, and the rain-monster pushed her body into the stream. It became a full-flowing river, and I was carried away. Danny, I felt like my own mother had been killed in front of my face! The jaguar and the hummingbird were crying. Then I couldn't see them any more. A black snake came up out of the water beside me, it seemed to have green feathers growing out of its head, and it had five white spots on its face too. It told me I had to go on the trip, or my death was for nothing. Not my mother's death, my death! Then it flew away! After that, everything speeded up, like time-lapse photography. I saw the raft land and some people take in the baby. The people were my parents, my real parents. I saw my whole life pass by on that screen right up to where I was sitting watching the screen. It had turned back into a screen, I didn't know when. I sat there for a long time. Then I called my mom, and I just asked her bluntly, was I adopted? I never had a notion, not one thought in my whole life that I was. She started to cry on the phone, and she said no, not legally. She told me that— that—sorry, this is still fresh. It isn't easy.'' She looked up at Danny, her cheeks wet, her eyes red-rimmed. He stroked her thick hair gently.

"She told me her baby had been delivered by a midwife,'' she said flatly. "Born dead. Daddy was all broken up, and he went out, just walking, down by the river. I was born in Lumberton, North Carolina, and our house was only a few hundred yards from the Lumber River. Anyway, he heard crying and found a baby in the cattails. Me. They paid off the midwife, buried the dead baby, and raised me as their own. Fucking unreal. Unreal. Things like that don't happen in real life, do they?'' She began to cry; Danny tried to console her. He was stunned.

13

Long after the rain ended, John continued to talk to Orizaba, periodically trying to get him back to the philosophical topics he'd discussed earlier. But it was all in vain; Orizaba simply wasn't going to talk about anything other than the techniques he was using in the manufacture of the double flute. He appeared determined to finish the flute that day, and John was so fascinated with the construction it was hard for him to leave.

Shortly after dark, Orizaba held up the double flute and pronounced it complete. It was truly a thing of beauty. In Orizaba's own words, it had "heart."

"Are you going to play it now, Orizaba?" he asked.

"Why? I know it will play well, yes, it will conjure many images! The flutes of Orizaba always play well, there is no need for a test, no need, no." He seemed ready to hang it on the wall with his other instruments, unplayed.

"But Orizaba, I would love to hear it played. Maybe I could try it?"

"Oh, no, no, not you, not a flute! And I don't know, don't know if you can accept the playing of this special flute, no, oh, it is special indeed! It can't just be played, no, there must be a reason! But perhaps—perhaps there is. Perhaps too much reason is the reason? Yes, I reason that too much reason can be a reason!"

John laughed. "Not bad, Orizaba! But I think I can stand—"

"Oh, I know you can stand reason. But remember, there are two sides to the flute! If you hear the one, you hear the other. Can you stand the side of unreason?"

John smiled at him with genuine affection. "You play, I stand here and listen, okay?"

Orizaba shrugged his shoulders, glanced up at John quickly,

then away again. He wore a mischievous smile. "Then I play, my very good friend. But always remember, you yourself in person asked me to."

He put the complicated flute to his mouth and sounded a pair of tones, an open fifth. The flute had a weird, unearthly, but very appealing sound. He played a little riff on the right-hand side, the left droning. John was aware that all sounds from outside had stopped; it seemed that even the night birds and insects had stopped to listen to Orizaba play his double flute.

The dwarf began playing a melody, very complex but strangely beautiful. Still playing, he went to the door and outside, never missing a note. John followed him; a group of villagers gathered around to listen to the impromptu concert. Orizaba continued the melody, and John noticed that he was feeling a little funny. It was like he was hearing the flute directly with his brain, not with his ears. His eyes were locked to the dwarf's fingers, flying over the right-hand keys. John's mind seemed to suddenly snap clear; it was as if a veil of fog had been lifted. Never before in his life had his mind, his senses, seemed so sharp. He looked around the street in front of Orizaba's shop; every detail of the street, the buildings, the people, was totally clear to him. The scene in front of him was like a photograph enormously enlarged on very fine grain paper; he could step back and see the whole, or step forward to see the fine details. Actually he didn't even need to step; all he had to do was shift his attention slightly. Similarly, he could focus his hearing on the whole melody, or on individual notes, their exact pitch and timbre. He felt he was being overwhelmed, it was so far above, so superior to, any sensory experience he'd ever had. He dreaded the moment when Orizaba stopped the song, sensing somehow that he would return to normal.

But the dwarf didn't stop. The song shifted slightly, a simple counterpoint coming in from the left side instead of the bagpipe-like droning. Even with his heightened awareness, he couldn't see how Orizaba was doing this, it seemed that ten fingers simply were not enough. He looked at Orizaba's hands and realized he was right; the dwarf had twenty fingers. But the only thing he found strange about that was that he had not noticed it before.

Gradually, almost imperceptibly, the melody line shifted from the bright-sounding right side to the dark, rich left side. As it did, John's perception of the scene in front of him changed. He couldn't quite pinpoint how the changes were coming about; there was still a group of people there, still a street, but they didn't look the same. With a shock, he realized that the group of people were standing in front of a pyramid similar to those at Teotihuacan; but it wasn't a ruin, it was alive, part of a living city. The light was being provided by torches and by a huge fire off to his right. And the people were dressed differently now. He noticed that the Americans were in the crowd; he could see all of them except for Danny. Where was Danny? he wondered. He assumed they must have heard the beautiful music, come down to listen. But they were so oddly dressed; Bertie and the three women all wore only vests and skirtlike garments, Frank a long blue cloak, and David— he couldn't tell what it was David was wearing. Some kind of untanned leather, with a leather ski mask. Really strange. He couldn't see David's face, only lips and eyes, but he knew it was him. He was amazed at the boldness of the outfits in general; the women might as well be wearing nothing at all. John looked at his own body and received another shock; he too was wearing a vest and skirt, very like the one Bertie was wearing. He didn't understand; when he'd been in Orizaba's shop, he'd been wearing blue jeans and a T-shirt.

Someone, a villager, came up and handed John a hat. It was conical, peaked, made of soft fur, whitish with dark spots and streaks. He assumed it was ocelot skin. He hated furs, the whole fur industry, and never wore anything made of natural furs. Yet at the moment, this hat seemed very fine to him. It was his hat, no doubt about it. He put it on; it felt good.

Now wearing the ocelot hat, he looked at the assembled group before him. They had arranged themselves into two lines, standing before the roaring fire. He knew that the fire had been there several days, knew that it had been burning for four days.

But he'd been here just this afternoon. There was no fire— And the flute played on.

At the head of one line was Bertie, behind him Kathryn, then Evelyn. At the head of the other, Frank, then Susan, then David. He looked at Frank more closely; did he really have fangs? There were two men between the two lines; he couldn't see them well. He wanted to ask someone what was happening, but couldn't speak. He could only watch, a mute spectator.

The two men between the lines came up to the front, a solemn procession. John had never seen them before. The first was dressed in the most gorgeous clothes, bright blues and greens; a huge gold gorget hung around his neck. He wore a crown of green feathers and gold, and seemed very solemn as he carried a tray toward the fire. One by one he held up items he carried on it—five emerald-green feathers, like the ones he had in his crown; a number of perfectly round pellets which glinted like gold in the firelight; some long, sharp objects, shaped like thorns, carved from pieces of coral; and gemstones: emeralds, rubies, diamonds. Even from here John could see the quality of those stones; worth a fortune. There were also lumps of a dark substance John recognized as copal, an incense, but he had no idea how he knew that.

With a dignified, solemn gait, the man, walked to the roaring fire and threw everything in. The fire leaped and roared even louder for a moment, then calmed back down. John could smell the aroma of the burning copal as he watched the man put the tray down and back off until he was about twenty feet from the fire.

Now the focus of attention shifted to the other man still standing between the lines. He looked sick, and as he came up into the light John could see that that was indeed the case; he wore only a garment like a loincloth, and he was covered with sores, most of which were oozing blood and pus. He limped as he walked; it seemed there were problems with his joints as well, and he was missing an eye. He also carried a tray, and like the first man, held up items one at a time. A bundle of hay; reeds collected from some riverbank; thorns with what at first looked like a dark red paint on them. John realized they had been dyed with the man's blood.

And still Orizaba played.

Limping badly, the second man approached the fire. He too hurled the contents of his tray in, and again the fire leaped and roared. Backing off, he stood beside the well-dressed man.

Bertie stepped forward, pointed the tied bundle of reeds he was carrying at the rich man. "Tecciztecatl, enter the fire!" he cried in an imperious voice.

The man called Tecciztecatl ran forward toward the fire as if he was going to run right into it. But as he got close, he stopped, put his hands over his face. "It is hot, my lord!" he cried.

Kathryn stepped up behind Bertie. "Tecciztecatl, enter the fire!" she yelled. John was amazed at the power and authority of her voice; so large a voice for so small a woman.

Tecciztecatl drew himself back, made another run at it. This time his knees gave way halfway there and he fell on his face. He lay there for a few minutes without moving, then dragged himself to his feet and looked back at the line. "My lords, I—" he began.

Evelyn now stepped up and ordered him into the fire. Once more he made a run at it, and again he failed. He sank to his knees and cried openly. He looked up at John, who realized that all the assembled people were looking at him, waiting for him to do something.

And the flute continued to play.

"Tecciztecatl, enter the fire!" he said, in a calm voice. He was amazed. He hadn't intended to say anything of the sort. He tried to tell the man he didn't mean it, but the words wouldn't come. Tecciztecatl drew himself back even further and made another run at the fire, screaming as he went, his arms flailing. But he stopped short and stood still, his shoulders down. He cried freely.

"My lords, I have failed, and the darkness is upon the world!" he blubbered.

Now, from the other line, Frank stepped up. The combination of the glasses and the fangs made him look very strange indeed. He held his arms out, billowing his cloak.

"Nanahuatzin, you will be the one to enter the fire!" he bellowed. His voice boomed out, so loud that Tecciztecatl lost his balance and fell over.

Keeping his eyes tightly closed, the poor man rushed forward exactly as Tecciztecatl had. But unlike the previous man, he didn't stop; he ran right into the flames and stood in the center of them, his arms upraised. The fire roared again, the body fell over, and the crackling sound nearly drowned out Orizaba's mournful music.

But the dwarf played on.

Tecciztecatl took his hands from his face and looked into

the fire, where the body of Nanahuatzin lay roasting. With a cry of total despair, he lunged into the flames himself. He flailed around and screamed briefly, then fell alongside the previous man. There was silence as the bodies burned. Not knowing why, John turned to face the east; he did know that Kathryn was facing the same way, and that no one else was.

Then it seemed the night was over. The first rays of dawn broke over the city. John could not believe he had been standing here all night; it had seemed only a short time. He saw the sun, just over the horizon. It was more brilliant than ever, impossible to look anywhere close to it, much less at it. Besides that, it had stopped rising, up only a degree or so, and wobbled around erratically. The group expressed consternation at this, began talking among themselves. But they were interrupted by the rising of a second sun, as brilliant as the other, alongside the first one. John just stared at the never-before-seen phenomenon; two suns in the same sky. He wondered if somehow Orizaba had transported them to another planet, one circling a double star.

Orizaba, unfazed, continued to play the double flute.

Someone in the line cried out in a voice filled with rage. His cry was echoed by all the others; John wondered what they were so angry about. They began to mill about, shaking their fists. Then someone threw something, a brown object; John watched in utter amazement. The object was like a fired missile, headed straight for the suns. He lost sight of it in the brilliance. Then suddenly the second sun went dark. He looked again and saw that it wasn't a sun at all, it was the familiar moon, barely visible in the glare of the just-risen sun. But still the sun did not continue to rise. It wobbled this way and that, sometimes sinking back toward the horizon. The crowd seemed dismayed, held a hasty conference.

"We cannot live! We cannot live!" Evelyn cried.

"We must surround him, it's the only way," David said.

All the people in the lines, as if on cue, began stripping off their clothes. From beyond the fire, the villagers ran up to receive them. Soon everyone in the two lines stood nude before the fire.

Someone out of the crowd, an unfamiliar face, walked up to John. This man handed him a strange red mask; it had eyeholes in the normal place, but the bottom of it projected in a beaklike tube. It was very delicately carved, but very grotesque. John looked at it for a moment, then put it on. He wondered why he'd done that; he hadn't intended to. It had no string or other means of attachment, yet it stayed on his face like it was a part of him. The man was offering him something else; he looked and saw that it was a sword, six feet long and very heavy. It appeared to be wooden, edged with finely carved obsidian. He knew it was unique in that it had a point; like the edges, sharp as a razor.

And still, he could hear the flute.

He tried to make himself give the sword back but he couldn't. Holding it in his right hand, he stepped toward the crowd; they didn't shrink from him. He drew back the sword as if to swing it.

"NO!" he screamed at himself. But no sound came out, and he continued, against his will, to advance on the group. The Americans were out front, Bertie the closest person to him.

"My brother," Bertie said, smiling. John swung the sword downward with terrific force, a far greater strength than he thought he had. It struck Bertie across the left shoulder, split his body down to the middle of his chest. There was an explosion of blood, showering him and spattering Kathryn, who stood directly behind. He pulled the sword back up and swung at her horizontally. She was still smiling as it split her completely in two; the bottom half remained standing for a moment. He looked briefly at the top half of her, lying on the ground. Still she smiled, even in death.

He could hear the flute, hear his breath resounding in the tube of the mask. Evelyn knelt before him as he approached, and he struck off her head with a single blow. The spouting steam of blood looked like a snake leaping from her open neck. He moved around it as she collapsed, advanced on Frank.

"Oh, God, no, make it stop, please," he said, but again there was no sound. He brought the sword down vertically on Frank's head, splitting it in two. Jerking it out again, he swung at David, and his head flew from his body and across the street. He paused, breathing hard. Susan was standing directly in front of him. She smiled richly; he was astounded by her beauty. She held a flower, beautiful, red.

"My brother, my heart overflows with love for you," she said. Surely, he thought, I can't—

He held the sword horizontally and ran it completely through her chest. The flower went flying. He lifted his sword; her body hung on it, blood streaming down it. She was still smiling, looking at him! Then her life faded; he shook her body off the sword and went through the rest of the people in the crowd, a deadly machine, the sword rising, falling, thrusting. Heads flew, bodies were dismembered, the entire area became a charnel house of blood, bodies, and body parts. Finally there was only one man left, and he backed away. He too was wearing a mask—a dog face—and, unlike all the rest, he was still dressed, in black robes.

"I will *not* die with the others!" he screamed. He turned and fled, John after him in hot pursuit. He could still hear the flute, as if Orizaba was running after them both.

Down through the streets they ran, John gaining on him gradually. He turned, pointed his hands at John; fire flashed from his fingers like they'd turned into blowtorches. John slowed, blew very lightly at him through the tube in the mask. The man was hurled backward, screeching like a cat. He jumped up and ran again; then, spreading his cloak, he rose into the air. He glided for a while, landing in a cornfield just outside the village. John ran among the rows, searching. He slowed down. He saw nothing except the cornstalks, all in neat lines.

He looked down at the roots of the corn, that little exposure of them at the base of the stalk. Down the row he went, looking. All normal. But wait, that one—he looked more closely. There were two sets of roots sprouting from a single stalk. And, it was just slightly out of the neat row.

He drew back the sword to swing it at the cornstalk; and suddenly the man in the mask stood before him. Howling, he leaped high into the air, a prodigious leap; John's swing encountered only cornstalks. He looked up, saw the sorcerer glide overhead, land in a patch of maguey plants up ahead. He ran in that direction, still listening to the wild music of the double flute. He looked around, but couldn't see Orizaba anywhere. He was glad; if he'd seen him, he would have killed him, he was sure.

In the maguey, he was confronted with the same problem.

All he saw were ordinary maguey plants. He wondered why he didn't just hack them all up, and another part of his mind told him sternly that it wouldn't be right; they were innocents.

And Susan was not? he thought. David? Kathryn? The flute's sound was insistent, close.

He searched carefully among the maguey plants, looking for double roots. Finding none, he patiently started over. Then he saw something he'd missed before; not a maguey with a double root, but two magueys from the same root! "Ah!" he said. "Mexolotl!" He wondered what that meant. His arms drew the bloodstained sword back, prepared to strike. Again the masked man leaped into the air, but not so high this time. He landed in a pond only a hundred feet or so away, disappeared under the surface. John ran up to the edge of the pond, laid the sword down and knelt by the water's edge.

There was a little creature swimming away, very pale and delicate looking. A salamander, but with a flourish of red, feathery gills behind its head. John smiled, reached into the water; he caught the creature in his fist and brought it out, held it up. "Axolotl!" he said. Then his fist closed like a vise. He could feel the body of the tiny animal give way, bones collapsing under the pressure. He laid it on the ground; it wavered, and then it was the masked man lying there, his body crushed and bleeding. John looked into his dying eyes.

"Xolotl, my brother," he said. "My heart overflows with love for you." Then the life was gone from the sorcerer, and John stood up, gazing at the still wobbling sun. He gathered all his strength, his chest expanding like a great bellows, and blew through the pipe in the mask, straight at the weaving solar disk. The sun seemed to flatten a little, bounce. He stood for at least an hour, motionless, while the sun rose normally, like it had every day of his life.

He was suddenly aware that the sound of the flute had stopped. He looked down at Orizaba, who smiled at him. Then he realized it was dark, and they stood in front of Orizaba's shop in the village. In the street, people went by on whatever business they might have this evening; all was as it was.

"What did you do?" he whispered.

"Unreason. I played its song," Orizaba said, and laughed.

An illusion, a vision. But God, so real! He ran his hands up his face, and they collided with the tube-mouth mask. He took it off, stared at it, ripped the ocelot hat from his head and began to shake. Without another word, he was running back toward the resort, Orizaba's laughter echoing behind him.

14

For the better part of an hour, Danny had been sitting with Evelyn's head in his lap. She had cried for quite a while; he'd stroked her hair, her face, told her that it obviously was not possible that her TV vision was a factual representation of reality. Gradually she had calmed down, but it was more than obvious that the whole affair had had a major impact on her. He wanted to talk to her about this afternoon, try and learn if she knew anything of Frank's strange behavior on the hillside; but he wasn't sure how to approach it. So, after she'd stopped crying, he'd made small talk about the trip, the village, the beach. He liked Evelyn very much; like Kathryn and Susan, she was charming and intelligent. She was also very sexy, very scantily clad, and making him very uncomfortable. He wished he could find a way to get her off his lap. He was acutely aware of every movement either of them made, since her breasts were rubbing against his legs. For a while, he'd found himself hoping that Kathryn or Frank would come out and interrupt this; but by now he'd given that up. He wondered why the hell Kathryn had not come out here with them in the first place. Then he thought about her and David; now it was making him angry. Was he in this position so she could have another tryst with David? Did she care about him or not? Yesterday he'd been so very sure she did, but doubts were starting to set in.

"So you've made your living as a psychic," Evelyn was saying. "Real strange, Danny. Real strange."

"It seems so damn ordinary right now, considering everything else that's been happening."

"Oh, you aren't ordinary, Danny. Not by a long shot. I knew that the first time I saw you."

"You can tell these things at a glance?"

"I'm not psychic like you. But I can judge people." She raised her head and looked at him. "And you, Danny Hudson, are a special man. There's no doubt about that."

"I thank you for the compliment," he said, grinning. Damn those eyes, he thought. They are just about impossible to resist. He hoped he wouldn't have to try.

"You know I'm very attracted to you," she said.

"Oh, shit," he said, involuntarily. "I'm sorry. That was a hell of a response. It's just that, well, you're married to Frank and I'm involved with Kathryn, and things are getting so damn complicated!"

"Attractions between friends aren't complicated," she said. "Unless we make them that way. I made Frank's affair with Nikki—if you can call it that—complicated. Maybe that was a mistake. But you and me, Danny, that's no mistake. I know that."

"What are you saying?"

"That I want to make love to you. Tonight."

Well, she couldn't be more direct, he thought. Of course, the answer had to be no. If Kathryn found out, she'd assume it was just to get revenge; if Frank did, he'd assume Evelyn was doing it because of Nikki; and maybe she was. There were a lot of things that had to be taken into account, that was for sure. He lifted her head, looked directly into her turquoise eyes.

"I want you too," he said. "So bad I can't stand it."

"Now, then. Where can we go?"

Weren't there problems? he asked himself. Complications? He tried to think, but when he looked into her eyes he couldn't remember what they were.

"The garage," he said. "Nobody's there at night."

They got up and walked across the lawn toward the garage. It was all he could do not to take her hand and run.

Sometime later, they came back across the lawn, arms linked. He didn't even care if they were seen, and she didn't seem to either. He was in love with her. Of course, he was in love with Kathryn too. And Susan as well; hadn't he been willing to give up his life for her? He felt very confused, but very good about life in general. On another level, his mind churned. Everything is such a fucking mess, he told himself, how can you be so happy? He cheerily told that part of himself to fuck off. He'd never had such good times in his whole life.

As they neared the pool again, he heard the sound of running footsteps and John came roaring up the path. He was moving at full speed, his eyes wild. He stopped in front of them.

"Danny!" he panted. "Have you seen Susan? In the last hour? Is she all right?"

"What the hell are you—" Danny started to say.

John seemed to notice Evelyn standing there and looked at her strangely. Then he relaxed visibly. "Evelyn. God, it's good to see you. You're all right. Maybe everybody else is, too."

"What are you talking about, John?" Danny asked. He noticed that John was carrying a strange, grotesque mask with an extended mouth, and a little conical cap of some fur.

"An illusion, a vision, not real," he said. He stopped to catch his breath. "At first I thought so, but then I wasn't sure. I've got to see Susan, though. Be sure she's okay."

"Fine, good, we'll go find her now," Evelyn said. "Just try to calm down, everything is—"

He scanned her body up and down. "What the fuck are you dressed like that for?" he screamed at her. "You little bitch, you trying to make me crazy? Tell me!" He grabbed her shoulders and shook her so hard her teeth clicked sharply.

"Stop it, John!" Danny yelled. "She isn't doing anything! What's the matter with you?"

He let Evelyn go, looking a little dazed. Danny heard footsteps; Susan and David, having heard the commotion, came running up.

John looked at her. "Susan," he said. "Susan." He started to cry, huge tears rolling down his face.

Susan held John while he sobbed. When he was under control, David asked him about the mask.

"The face of horror," he said flatly. "My face. My other face."

15

The next morning, Kathryn got up before Danny did. When he awoke, she was already out of bed and getting dressed. He watched her rummage through her clothes, wondered if she had any idea about him and Evelyn. Of course, he had counter-accusations he could hurl, but he didn't want to get into that; he'd decided that it was safer to leave things alone. After Susan and David had taken John up to his room, Kathryn had been very affectionate with him, and again he was feeling good about things, if confused. The most peculiar thing was that he could not find it in himself to feel guilty about making love with Evelyn; it had seemed so very right at the time. Was it possible that Kathryn felt the same about David? He didn't know, but right now he didn't care much either. He was just taking things as they came.

Kathryn turned around to face him. He laughed, not really believing she was planning to go down to breakfast dressed like that. She was wearing the vest she had bought in the square, open-fronted, just like Evelyn had worn the night before; it left her breasts completely exposed. Below the waist, her outfit made Evelyn's look modest. Again, all the items were from the square. She wore sandals, and on her lower legs a kind of a leather legging that extended from just below her knees to her ankles, terminating in a finely beadworked little flap of leather. Her skirt was very short, and bore a design of crescent moons whose horns pointed upward. It was dark blue on the left, white on the right, and split down the front so that it only closed when she was standing up and still. When walking or sitting, the front opened so that her body below the waist was totally exposed. Danny had to admit it was very attractive and interesting, but not exactly the kind of thing one normally wore to breakfast.

She sat in the wicker chair beside the bed. "Let's go, Danny," she said. "Time for some coffee, isn't it?"

He chuckled and climbed out of bed. After he'd finished in the bathroom, dragged on a shirt and pants, he asked her to cut out the playing around, get dressed for breakfast.

"I am," she said, glancing down at herself. She gave him a little bewildered look.

"You seriously plan to wear that downstairs?" he asked.

"Sure. What's wrong with it?"

He was at a loss for words. "Well, nothing's wrong with it, Kathryn, but it'd sure get you arrested in New York! You think it's appropriate here? I mean, these villagers, who knows what their sense of decorum is—"

Now she laughed at him. "Did you see anybody yelling at Evelyn last night?"

"As a matter of fact, yes. Like I told you, John seemed to be very upset."

"That was different, you said he had some kind of weird vision. Maybe Orizaba slipped him a mushroom, I don't know. But I do feel this is the appropriate dress for this place and time. Actually, Danny, I think part of me can see it through your eyes, and I know it probably looks weird and maybe even brazen. I can't explain it. When I saw Evelyn dressed as she was, it seemed so—so correct. Look, I tell you what; if nobody else is dressed like this, then I'll come back up and change. The men aren't seeing anything they haven't seen already at the beach. As for the staff, I'll risk it."

When they got downstairs, the Hallstens and the Wassermans were already there. Danny was startled; not only were Frank and Evelyn still dressed as they had been last night, but Susan had joined in. She, like the other two women, wore an open-fronted vest and armbands; her skirt was long and had a flowery pattern, but it was split up both sides all the way to her waist, and it was not wide enough to close. Danny could not help but admit that the three of them together were nothing short of spectacular.

David was still dressed normally, in shorts and a loose shirt. Danny pulled him aside. "I know they look good, David, but don't you think there could be problems with this? I mean, I think they intend to dress that way all the time," he said.

"I agree. I argued with Susan for a half hour this morning,

but she just wasn't having it any other way. She said it was right for the time and place. And they do look right somehow, can't you see it? Really, it's you and I who are out of place."

"That's what Kathryn said, too. But I don't know. We may start a riot if we go strolling down into the village with them dressed like that!"

"I guess we have to risk it. They aren't giving us a whole lot of choices."

"I suppose not."

Changing the subject, David began to discuss John's unusual behavior. "I think we should all go down to the village today and talk to that dwarf," he concluded. "What's his name?"

"Orizaba."

"Yeah. See what he did to John last night."

Somehow Danny didn't feel that it was going to accomplish a lot, but he also couldn't see where it would hurt to go and talk to the man. He agreed.

As they sat down to eat, Bertie came in and joined them. His appearance made Danny's coffee cup freeze in midair, halfway to his mouth. He too had adopted the odd dress of the others, the vest and a skirt-like, or kilt-like, garment. A heavy, intricately carved knife hung from a loop on the skirt. He now looked exactly like the man in the shared dream, the man who had forced Danny to sacrifice himself for Susan.

By ten o'clock, a total of six of them had descended the hill from the resort and were on their way to Orizaba's shop. Susan had felt that David's suggestion had been a good one; she'd also believed that everyone should go, and had said so. John, however, was still sleeping, and Bertie had surprised her by flatly saying he didn't really consider it any of his business. Frank hadn't been very upset about John's behavior, but he tagged along, saying he couldn't resist the scenery.

Walking through the village, Susan noticed that the women's new costumes got them admiring looks from various men, but otherwise no comments. Her mind seemed to be split; part of her was thinking how totally unbelievable it was, that three American women could walk in broad daylight through a little Mexican village with their breasts and genitals exposed and attract scant attention, but the other part saw it as natural and normal. They were properly dressed now; they hadn't been before, except perhaps when swimming nude. It seemed to her that Frank was also properly dressed, but David wasn't; his slacks and shirt annoyed her. Danny, on the other hand, who was similarly attired, was dressed correctly for him. She was not able to adequately explain that to herself, though.

Arriving at the dwarf's shop, she could see the man inside, busily puttering with something on his workbench. He looked up, smiled broadly, and hopped over to the door.

"Good morning, my friends!" he said. "Please, please, come in! I have been expecting you, yes, expecting your visit!" He stood back from the door and ushered the Wassermans inside, then David, Susan, and Kathryn. But he held up his hand to Danny as if to stop him.

Susan took great exception to this; she put her hand on the dwarf's shoulder before anyone had a chance to say anything. "He is with us," she said imperiously. "He will be allowed inside!"

The dwarf looked up at her, smiled, and shrugged. Danny came inside with the rest.

"So. Who speaks for this group? Never mind, never mind, not necessary. Orizaba knows what you have come about, you want to know about last night. Your brother, he was upset, oh, very upset. But he asked Orizaba to play the double flute. I was not going to do that, no, but he said, 'play!' and who am I to say no to such as him? Not possible, is it? Of course not. So I played. I played the right side of reason, I played the left side of unreason. That is all, nothing else."

"Double flute?" David asked. John had not mentioned this.

"Yes, yes, yes, didn't he tell you? I made it yesterday, just finished it, just yesterday, well, last night." He hopped over to the wall and took down the flute, showed it to Susan. She touched it lightly; it was a beautiful thing.

"Then what happened?" she asked the dwarf.

"Oh, he just stood there for a while and stared into space while I played. It was funny, you should have seen, should have been here." He looked up at them with a crooked grin. "But then, if you'd been here, you wouldn't have been laughing, oh no. Not laughing. You and you and you and you and you"—the string of "you's" covered everybody except Danny—"have yet a long way to come. But I can see you are all getting there. Yes. Getting there. It is good, there is not much time. It is good, good—" He trailed off.

"Perhaps you should play the flute for us now, let us judge for ourselves," Susan told him.

Orizaba laughed. "All together? Not a good idea, my lady, not now. One at a time, maybe. But all together? That would invite a disaster, and Orizaba would not like to see disaster; no."

Something stirred inside Susan. She felt the same as she had about that spot on her pants, in Jerry Maxwell's office; the same rage was building now, with Orizaba as its object. Things were very clear to her; the dwarf had no right to refuse her when she asked for something, not her! She made an odd gesture toward him, crossing her arms across her breasts, then spreading them again.

"You deny me, Orizaba?" she said coldly.

The dwarf's mocking expression changed abruptly to one of sheer terror, as if she had pointed a loaded gun at him. Her hands and arms were moving, her voice was speaking, but she had no idea what she was about to do or say. It made no sense at all. She saw her own hand reaching out, palm up, toward the dwarf.

"No, my lady!" he screamed, cringing. "You don't know what you're doing!"

"Susan?" David's voice cut into her concentration. "What's going on?"

"He denies me, my lord," she said. My lord? she thought. David was her husband, not her lord. What the hell was wrong with her?

"Well, I guess he has a right to," Danny put in. She turned, distracted by Danny. The best one, she thought, the very best. He seemed radiantly beautiful to her; she felt like he was her son. But no, that wasn't quite right. She glanced around at the others; they were all beautiful too, but that was to be expected. With Danny it was not, and therefore of greater value. She walked over to him, put her arms around him, and hugged him; he looked startled.

"If you say he has a right, he has a right," she said, slightly amused at the bewildered look on his face. "We may as well go," she told the others. All of them agreed except David, who also looked confused.

"What the hell—" he started to say. She saw the dwarf catch David's wrist, shake his head.

"You stay. Let them go. I have to talk to you, now, very important," the dwarf said to him.

Susan took Danny by one arm; Kathryn took the other. Followed by the Wassermans, they left the shop. David stayed behind.

David looked down at the dwarf. Gone was his mocking, joking manner; he was very solemn and serious.

"Can you explain to me what the hell is going on around here?" David demanded. "I've never seen my wife act like that. You were clearly afraid of her, right? Why?"

"No, I am afraid I cannot explain everything to you. But perhaps I can help you to understand. As to your wife," he shrugged, "she is beautiful and loving, but sometimes, when she does not get her way, she can be dangerous. It is just that way."

"I really don't see Susan as dangerous. She doesn't have a mean bone in her body. Dammit, I should know!"

"For you, no, she doesn't. She will love you, even after your adultery. It will not matter. But—"

"My adultery?" David said. "What are you talking about?" He was blustering at the man, but he had a sinking feeling that somehow, Orizaba knew about Kathryn.

"You are right, of course," Orizaba said. "Do not be shocked. No one else will be. There will be more than this to come, oh yesss." He rubbed his hands together and hopped around the shop, some of his old ebullience returning. "These are matters that we need not speak of. They will take care of themselves. Power has made the correct alignments. But for you, my good friend, there is a problem. Just look at you! You look like a tourist from Iowa. Why don't you have a Nikon hanging around your neck? One of the self-focusing ones?"

David was surprised that Orizaba knew anything about cameras, much less brand names and features. This place, these people, continued to surprise him, more every day. Not as much as his fellow travelers did, though.

"I will close the shop. We will go to see Mayauel and Patecatl. Perhaps together we can find a way to help you. Otherwise, there will be problems, oh yes, problems for you, problems for all of us!"

Orizaba was shooing him out the door, closing up the shop.

They went back through the village to the cottage where they had taken shelter from the storm. The dwarf hopped up the low steps and knocked on the door.

"Ah, Orizaba!" said Mayauel, opening the door. "I see you brought him. He is getting to be a problem, isn't he? Well, come in, both of you! We need to settle this."

David entered the neat little house, wondering what she was talking about. How was he a problem to them? He'd only met this couple once, briefly talked with Patecatl about agriculture and so on. He was becoming a little annoyed with the treatment, being shoved around by the dwarf. But his curiosity made him hold his peace; there would be time enough.

Patecatl came up from the back of the house. "No need to come in. I believe we need to go out to the fields, stop wasting time. There is so little left, and he," he indicated David, "is so stupid."

"What the fuck do you mean, stupid?" David snapped. "I think I've had about enough of—"

"Please." Mayauel held up her hand. "Patecatl is right, there is no time to waste. But he should learn to hold his tongue as well!" She glared at him; he just grinned.

"Patecatl is right, though," Orizaba said. "Let us take him to the fields; now, this minute."

David tried to be angry with them, but it was hard to. They were such personable, attractive people; even Orizaba, in spite of his deformities. David rolled his eyes in frustration and agreed to go with them.

Patecatl ran back into the house and returned with a goatskin David assumed was full of water or wine, and they set off on the beach path, Mayauel leading the way. At first David was concerned about the dwarf keeping up, but he seemed to be having no problems, sometimes walking with his awkward gait, sometimes hopping along as he did in the shop. All three of them seemed in a very good mood; they pointed out scenic spots, flowers. Any observer would have thought the four were out for a picnic.

Near the edge of the beach, they left the path and walked across a rocky field. Iguanas of various sizes darted in front of them, often startling David.

"Excellent eating, good meat," Patecatl observed.

They moved up the shoreline, skimming the edge of the hill

topped by the ruined church. Now there was a definite path; David could see that it ran in toward the village on the far side of the hill. They had merely taken a shortcut from Patecatl and Mayauel's house. They continued to walk for quite a long distance; David assumed they were probably back farther than the store and gas station on the outskirts of town, but he couldn't see it. Neither could he see the ocean anymore; the path ran alongside a cornfield on the left, and off to the right was scrub brush dotted with the spikey plants John had earlier called maguey. Many of these were quite large, leaves perhaps eight feet long; not a few had huge flower spikes, towering fifteen feet or more into the air.

"Those are huge," he commented, pointing to a trio of large plants.

Mayauel smiled at him. "Little ones, just little ones," she said. "Perhaps today you will see a really big one. Perhaps not."

They continued to walk; soon David began to get a little bored, and more than a little tired. They had come quite a distance, and he was acutely aware that they had to walk back. Judging from the sun, it was getting near noon.

"Is that water?" he asked Patecatl, indicating the skin.

"No, but if you are thirsty it will do," he said, slinging it off his shoulder and handing it to David. All four of them sat down at the edge of the path, as if a secret signal of some sort had been given.

"Two swallows is a cup," Mayauel said, laughing. He wondered what she meant. He lifted the skin, swallowed twice.

And almost choked. It wasn't water, and it wasn't wine either; to David it tasted horrible, yeasty and thick. But he kept it down, realized from the warm reaction that it was apparently alcoholic.

"What is this stuff?" he asked.

"Pulque, made in the old way," Mayauel said. "I know it tastes dreadful to you right now. But give it a minute. It is what you call an acquired taste."

A moment or two later, he was considering that she might be right. The stuff stank horribly and tasted worse, but it was having nice effects. His head felt light, but pleasantly so, and he was getting a warm rush in his stomach. Alcoholic definitely, but not like he was used to; different, better. Much better. Steeling himself against the odor, he took two more gulps of the stuff.

"Two cups," said Patecatl, grinning.

"Anybody else?" David said expansively, holding out the skin. Had to share with one's friends, he thought. Patecatl took the skin and swigged, swallowing only once. Mayauel did the same; Orizaba declined it with a wave of the hand. He remembered passing joints in college; there was always somebody who didn't toke. He took the skin back, swallowed four times. Wiping his mouth, he handed it back, watched Patecatl and Mayauel take one more swallow each.

"Four," Orizaba said. He kept looking at David like he was expecting something.

David could not deny he was feeling very good, but he didn't feel drunk. He wondered if it was going to catch up with him, knock him flat. What the fuck, he told himself; my good friends here will take care of me. He took the skin back, raised it to his lips.

"Only two more swallows," Mayauel cautioned. He did as she said, handed the skin back. Patecatl put the stopper back in and slung it back on his shoulder; obviously they were through drinking. David was a little disappointed. He was really liking it now.

"Only five cups may be taken," Mayauel said. "Ten swallows. That is the rule of the maguey."

He looked at the maguey plants off to the right of the path. There was a medium-sized one, leaves perhaps four or five feet long, only a few paces away from him. He strolled over to it.

"Nice plant," he said. "You make some good shit. Ow!" He had patted the plant as he spoke, and punctured his finger on one of the sharp thorns that lined the edges of the leaves. He looked closely at the leaf, touched the needle-like spike at the tip.

"Bastard bit me," he said, sucking his finger. "I guess it's justice."

Patecatl laughed uproariously; Orizaba and Mayauel were grinning at him. He realized he was weaving, but he didn't really care.

"Be careful there, don't fall into it!" Patecatl yelled. "You might be killed. We don't want that!" This seemed to be a huge joke. Mayauel bent over laughing; Orizaba literally rolled on the ground.

"Oh, no, no, no, no!" Orizaba cried, tears of laughter streaming from his eyes. "He's not in season!"

Again they all cracked up. David stared at them; he didn't get the point. "Private joke?" he said, plaintively.

Mayauel's face softened; she got up, came over and put her arm around his shoulder. "Come over here and sit down. We do not mean to be malicious. It is the only way. Try to remember that, during your stay in Tlillan Tlapallan."

"But now, we have something to show you! It will astound you! It just may open your eyes a little!" Patecatl yelled, jumping up.

David tried to focus on him. He seemed to be seeing two scenes at once, two movies projected on the same screen. The effect was unsettling; for a moment he thought he was going to be sick. Then it seemed to clear up, and he was watching Patecatl bound around out there in the field of maguey. He really didn't seem to be doing much of anything, just running around. He ran across the ground, up on the leaves of the maguey, stood on the points and spread his arms. Then, still running, back down on the undersides of the leaves. A little voice far back in David's head was telling him there was something wrong here, but he couldn't figure out what it was. Patecatl was merely showing off his skills at getting around in difficult places, nothing more. He was enjoying it as he might enjoy any good display of remarkable physical ability, like a good dancer or gymnast.

Out of the corner of his eye he saw Mayauel get up. She had been wearing a long dress, brightly colored in reds and blues. With a single motion she dropped the dress to the ground and walked nude into the field where Patecatl still leaped and cavorted.

"Hey!" David yelled. "Can't any of the women around here keep their clothes on for ten minutes?" Again Orizaba fell on the ground laughing.

Mayauel went up to one of the larger plants, leaves ten feet long or more, each one lined with thorns. With no hesitation at all she climbed into the middle of it, and nestled down as if it were an easy chair. David goggled at her. He had felt the bite of those thorns, only a moment ago. There must have been fifty or a hundred of them piercing her body all over, yet she shifted around casually inside the plant, smiling out at him. Patecatl rushed up to the plant with a roll of hemp twine, started to wind it around the leaves. Vaguely, David wondered where he had gotten it. But his main concern was poor Mayauel, her slender dark body still shifting around inside the murderous looking plant. Then he realized what Patecatl meant to do. He tried to get up, stop him, but he was unable to move.

Patecatl now pulled the hemp string, walking around the plant as he did so, pulling the stiff leaves up, the thorns pointing inward at Mayauel. He continued until the whole plant was closed, pointed at the top. It didn't seem possible; the leaves looked too stiff to bend like that, it looked like they'd break, but they didn't. David's last glimpse of Mayauel showed her still smiling at him; he couldn't understand how that was possible, either. Patecatl ran around and around the plant, beating on it with his fists; then he began to unwind the cord. David didn't want to look. He expected to see Mayauel fall out of the plant badly injured, her body pierced and cut in hundreds of places.

But as the big leaves dropped back down and Mayauel came into sight, she didn't seem to be visibly hurt. She still moved languidly inside the plant. Finally she climbed out, motioned David to come to her. His paralysis was gone; he got up and moved easily.

"Look at the plant," she said. She seemed fine; he could see no blood. Impossible, he told himself. She just came out of a natural iron maiden. He felt the thorns as she indicated; except for those at the leaf tips, they were much like rose thorns. Not long enough to kill, probably, but certainly sufficient to pierce human skin.

"Now look at me, at my body," she told him. He turned to her, at first distracted by her beauty. I should be used to this by now, he thought. No ugly women around here, it must be against the law. "Touch me. Find the wounds from the thorns," she urged. He did so, running his hands over her thighs, her belly. Her skin was silky smooth, unmarked; no wounds at all. His hands ran up her small breasts, one in each hand; no punctures, no cuts. He went higher, encountered the next pair of breasts; nothing but smooth skin and tiny, slightly wet nipples here. He tasted her nipples; the wetness was not milk, but the same pulque he had been drinking earlier. Still searching upward, he checked over the next pair of breasts, and the next; his head swam, he felt peculiar. She encouraged him to keep looking for punctures, and he kept reaching, feeling, kept encountering what seemed to be an endless series of breasts; large ones, small ones, ones that were conical and tight, ones that were round and soft, large flat nipples, pointed nipples, tiny nipples, all the varieties of breasts and nipples he could imagine. Yet he couldn't see her body as deformed or indeed unusual in any way except for its pleasing proportions. From somewhere behind him he heard raucous laughter and the sound of counting, Patecatl's voice: "—two hundred, two hundred two, two hundred four—"

Finally, however, his hands felt collar bones, then shoulders, and he looked into her face. It too was unmarked. His hands ran across her cheeks, her very smooth skin. Her eyes laughed at him, but not maliciously. In spite of his confusion, he laughed with her, then stepped back and looked at her; she appeared very beautiful to him, but very normal. Two breasts. Two legs. All parts in correct numbers. He turned to see both Patecatl and Orizaba rolling on the ground, choking with laughter.

"Come," she said. "We are not yet done for the day. We have something else for you to see." She took his hand and led him across the path into the edge of the cornfield.

Patecatl ran ahead of them and plucked a ripe ear of corn from one of the plants. His attitude was no longer one of merriment; he seemed very solemn. Carefully he shucked the ear down, exposing the golden yellow kernels. Holding it in the palms of his hands, he showed it to David. Mayauel put her arms around David's shoulders, helped steady him when he weaved. He clutched at her waist, noticed she hadn't bothered to put her dress back on.

Orizaba came over and carefully plucked a single kernel of the corn from the ear. Almost reverently, Patecatl turned and laid the ear on the pile of husks he had previously removed from it. The dwarf held up the kernel like a gem, between thumb and forefinger.

"Waste of time," David said, slurring his words slightly. "I'm a farm boy from way back. I've seen corn before. Lots of it."

Then Patecatl was beside him, pulling at David's shirt. With minimal help from him, Patecatl and Mayauel undressed him, leaving him standing—with Mayauel's help—nude in the cornfield.

"Why do I gotta be naked to look at corn?" he complained.

Orizaba looked up at him, very solemn. "Because of that. We didn't want you to hurt it." David looked down and saw that he was completely erect.

"I can't have a hard-on, I'm drunk!" he said. He saw them struggle to remain solemn, but they failed. Both men doubled over laughing, and he felt Mayauel shaking beside him.

Orizaba controlled himself with an effort, then knelt down. Patecatl followed suit, and Mayauel guided him down next to them. With great care, the dwarf dug a little furrow with his finger and put the kernel in it, covering it with just a small amount of dirt. David could still see the yellow of the kernel showing through.

Then he began again to have the sense of watching two movies projected together. In one, the kernel swelled, burst; the first rootlet broke out, then the leaf. The shell of the corn, the yellow, lay discarded alongside the growing seed. Like time-lapse photography, he watched it grow, then break through the surface.

In the other movie, he saw a man, very sick; or at least he seemed to be. He had sores and fungus-like growths all over him. Then the man's skin began to split, starting right over his heart and progressing in both directions. When the split got to his face, David realized that someone was cutting open his skin with a knife while he lay in a shallow furrow in the ground. He couldn't tell who it was, couldn't stop them. When the split was complete, the knife-wielder began pushing the skin back at the sides of the bloody incision, peeling it away from the muscles. He wanted to scream, but he couldn't, or wouldn't. He understood clearly the necessity of this, why he had to be skinned alive. He felt the skin being ripped off his arms, inside out, like taking off a sweater; when the skinner reached his hands, he cut them off at the wrist. Then the skin of his head was pulled inside out, a little grating scrape on the skull was required to loosen the scalp.

Moving his head a little, he saw Mayauel stand up holding his skin. She turned it right side out, held it up like a suit, like some kind of grotesque halloween costume; the eyeless holes in the face stared at him as he writhed in the agony of exposed muscles.

Then the pain began to fade, and it seemed something was happening to the red rawness of his muscles. His legs and feet turned pink, his hands and chest green. He felt strength rushing through him. The sunlight pulled, he felt a great surging joy, and he stood up, spread his arms, and screamed with the pure pleasure of life, the sun! He looked at Mayauel, who still held the rapidly rotting skin, which was now turning a golden yellow. She held it out like a coat, and he put his arms inside. The stench was awful, but he didn't care. She laced it up across his torso, pulled the head back down over his face like a ski mask. He started to dance a little, his eyes peeping through the holes in the mask, his lips sticking out through the dead lips of the skin. It was getting tighter and tighter as he danced; just when he thought it would slip and fall away, it didn't seem to be there any more. He looked at his arms, green a moment ago; now they looked normal, ordinary living human skin.

Stopping his dance, he staggered; Mayauel supported him. He saw Patecatl and Orizaba standing on either side of a new and resplendent corn plant where there had been none a few minutes ago. It was about six feet tall, gorgeously green, little pinkish roots like tiny toes thrust into the soil. He turned to Mayauel, hugged her tightly, and laughed uproariously. Then the world began to spin, and blackness closed in on him.

16

All morning, Bertie had been prowling about, trying to walk off his problems. His attitude distressed him; he had tried not thinking about it, but nothing was working. All his life, he reflected, everything had come easy; he'd formed no real attachments to anyone. As far as he'd been concerned, friends, especially women, were to be used, then discarded when used up or no longer desired. For women, that usually meant one night. He never found a woman as exciting the second time, and usually deemed it not worth the effort. There was always another, fresh, around the corner, and he had no difficulties attracting them.

But now, suddenly, things had changed. First, he had committed a murder; and although that was not his previous life pattern, it didn't bother him as much as what had happened in its aftermath. He had spent several days in New York with the catlike black woman, Geneva, and enjoyed every minute of it. That was in itself not too bad. She was unusual. So what? There had to be a few like that, and it hadn't bothered him to leave her behind at the airport, knowing it was unlikely that he'd ever see her again.

But now, the change was drastic, and profoundly disturbing. His encounter with Susan had started simply enough; an attractive woman, get her alone and seduce her. But in the midst of the seduction, everything had changed. Susan had affected him deeply, probably permanently. He could not stop thinking about her, about her body, her face. He went cold, had adrenaline rushes whenever he saw her, felt like he was living for the next time he could get her alone. In short, she was haunting him. He had even considered another murder; if she was dead she wouldn't have this effect on him. But he knew he was kidding himself. As soon as he saw those eyes, he would be lost.

On the edge of the hill, behind the resort, he sat down and sighed deeply. He had to admit it to himself. He was in love with Susan Hallsten. He believed he could kill David, but it wouldn't help; he'd have to deal with Susan then, and he didn't have a clue about building relationships. Besides, it would hurt her, and he couldn't stand that. Something had to be done. He couldn't be like this! He needed strength, some way to repel his emotions. Hands clasped behind his head, he rocked violently back and forth. He had no idea what to do, no experience in these matters.

He rocked a few more times, and the edge, weakened by the previous day's rain, gave way. He went tumbling head over heels down the hillside, branches and rocks smashing him, mud pushing into his mouth. About halfway down, he caught hold of something and stopped his fall. He hung there momentarily, cursing and pounding on the ground with his free hand. At least no one was around to see it; making a fool of himself was his greatest dread.

He looked to see if what he'd caught was strong enough to pull up on; the hillside was very muddy and soft. It was a perfectly cylindrical piece of stone, jutting straight out from the hillside, parallel to the ground below. He stared at it for a moment without comprehension. What the hell was it? It obviously wasn't just a rock, it was much too regular. He tugged on it experimentally. It didn't budge.

Pulling himself to a half-sitting position, he glanced around the immediate area, and saw another identical piece of stone about six feet away, level with the first. The area of hillside between them looked slightly sunken, although he would never have seen it from either the top or bottom of the hill. A large tree with drooping branches, something like a willow, grew at the top of the sunken area and effectively hid it from any angle. A person had to be within about ten or fifteen feet of it to see it at all.

He squirmed over to it and pushed on it; it felt spongy. He pushed harder, and the whole section collapsed inward, leaving him staring open-mouthed into a rectangular doorway, stone-lined, about six feet wide and ten feet tall. The two stone posts extended from the upper corners; he thought they might have held a door of some sort once, but he couldn't see how it would've worked. Inside, partially covered by soil and roots, he saw a stone stairway leading down and out of sight. There was broken, rotted wood down there too; apparently there had been a cover of some sort, which, rotted with age, had given way to the rain and his final push.

He arranged the tree's drooping branches to hide the opening, then started back up the hill. It was slow going, but at last he reached the top. Not wanting anyone to see him in his current disheveled state, he crept along near the house, made it to his room unseen. After cleaning up, he found Rosa, asked for a flashlight, and set out again for the hillside. Going down should have been easier, he thought, but actually it was, if anything, more difficult. After a few near falls, he reached the opening and, turning on the light, went down the stairs.

He picked his way with caution down the steep, narrow

stairs; the litter from the collapsed door was strewn down quite a ways, making his descent treacherous. The walls and ceiling, he noticed, were formed from huge blocks of stone, the edges irregular but perfectly fitted together. The perfection of the fit was attested to by the lack of animal life; he would have expected spiders, insects of all sorts, maybe bats and snakes. Except for a few insects around the entrance, he had seen none at all, not even cobwebs. Apparently, until the door collapsed they just couldn't get in. He was sure the invasion would now be rapid and intense.

For what seemed a very long time he walked down the stairs, seeing no end to them. At last, he could see a level corridor ahead; he figured he must be at ground level or below. Stopping at the base of the stairs, he shined his light down the corridor; it was featureless, interlocked stone on all four surfaces. There was a bend to the left, about fifty yards down. Cautiously, he went ahead. The stone was cool and dry, not damp as he would have expected. He'd assumed the tunnel to be an antiquity, but maybe not; it was so clean and dry he began to feel it might currently be used. Or at least used not long ago.

He rounded the bend and stopped. Ahead was a series of wide, tall, stone steps, descending again; he couldn't see the walls. Assuming it was a room of some kind, he stepped onto the stairs.

And jumped back immediately. A reddish light, glowing faintly somewhere far above him, gradually gained intensity until the entire area was illuminated. Peeking around the doorway, he saw that it was a room of vast dimensions, lighted by some unseen source at least a hundred feet above. On all four sides, the walls rose vertically for about twenty feet, then angled inward; there was a flat roof above. It dawned on him that he was seeing the outline of the hill on which the resort house stood. The four odd ridges on the sides of the hill reflected the corners of the walls, and the edge of the hill was where the flat ceiling connected to the tops of the walls. They were constructed of the fitted stone he had already seen. He knew then that the hills on which the resort house and the ruined church stood were not in fact hills at all. He should have realized it sooner; they were too regular, and there were no other hills around.

Not hills; pyramids. Flat-topped pyramids in the style of those at Teotihuacan, but larger, he thought; he wasn't sure how big the Pyramid of the Sun was. This one was immense, a major architectural feat. Except for five huge carved columns, one in the center and one at each corner, the walls stood free. Bertie was astounded. He had never heard of a pyramid like this; those at Teotihuacan and in Egypt had passages in them, but they certainly were not hollow like this one! He wondered if the one under the ruined church was hollow too; surely it was a pyramid too, since it also had edges and four ridges.

He stepped forward again, onto the steps leading down to the main floor. There were numerous stairways around, only a few of which led to doorways; he thought this must have been some kind of an amphitheater. He wondered how old it was, marveled at the engineering; all the dimensions here were colossal.

He thought he caught a glimpse of movement out of the corner of his eye and spun toward it. All around the walls, standing about ten feet in front of them, were carved steles about ten or twelve feet tall. They didn't connect with the sloping wall above, and they were not regular in their distribution; in some places they were quite dense, spaced only a few feet apart. But in other places there were few; there wasn't one within forty feet of the exit steps. It was in one of the dense areas that he thought he'd seen movement. Studying the area closely, he saw nothing. He was just turning away when he heard a most unpleasant wet scuttling sound from the same area. He looked again, saw an approximately man-sized shadow move slightly. Then something darted from one group of steles to another, closer to him. He only caught a brief glimpse of a dead-gray body, moving very fast. Judging the distance back to the doorway, he felt he could reach it ahead of whatever was hiding among the steles, and started moving slowly in that direction. But another gray shape darted to a position behind the stele nearest the steps, much closer than he was. He froze, wishing he had a gun. Taking out his only weapon, the flint knife, he moved toward the door, watching the steles carefully, eyes darting from one to the other. Glancing down, he saw clearly that his artificial foot was smoking; at the moment that was only a curiosity.

He was still sixty feet from the door when the creature nearest him came partially out from behind the stele. It had arms basically like a man, but its hands were cat paws; the long, heavy claws were extended, scraping the floor. It seemed to have a man-sized head as well, but the face was anything but manlike. Large eyes peered at him under heavy, straight brow ridges; its snout was extended, about eighteen inches long, and terminated in a collar-like structure from which a number of jointed members like insect legs issued. Each of these was heavily clawed. Behind the collar were four or five curving spikes on each side, possibly teeth, although he could not see anything like a jaw. The overall effect was somewhat reminiscent of the head of a shrimp or lobster. The creature made no sound other than the scraping of the claws on the stone, a chilling sound like fingernails on a blackboard. It looked right at him, crept fully out into view. Its hind parts were built like a man's body hunched over, with abnormally short legs; it seemed to be wet. Every time the rear legs moved, they made a squishing sound, like sponges pressed onto the stone. Bertie watched it closely; then the other one, identical to the first, emerged from the steles on his right. He glanced around, looking for a way out, having no confidence in his ability to kill these creatures with his knife. He had no idea how much damage those peculiar mouths, or snouts, could do; but the front claws alone looked sufficiently lethal.

The one nearest him crouched, stamping its hind feet like a cat judging the distance to its prey. Bertie's nerve broke, and he turned, preparing for headlong flight. The sound of laughter from behind him caused him to stop short, look around again.

"Look at him!" one of the things said in a voice heavy with contempt. "He runs like a rabbit!"

"Doesn't matter," said the other. "He has nowhere to run." They were speaking flawless English, but their mouths weren't moving. Bertie wondered if this was a ventriloquist's trick.

"Isn't he supposed to be a warrior?" asked the first.

"I thought so. I was looking forward to a good fight with a fine warrior."

"We can't just let him go, though. We have to kill him." The creature gestured at him. "Hey! What are you, anyway? We thought a warrior was coming down here!"

Bertie was speechless. Even if ventriloquism accounted for

the speech, these things were an impossibility already; their speaking English seemed ludicrous.

"I—I'm a man. From the resort," he said almost timidly. Damn! he cursed himself. He didn't like to feel timid, even in front of nightmares.

"He says he's a man!" mocked the other creature. "I think not. Men don't run away like rabbits!"

"No. He isn't a man, that's for sure," commented the first.

The other turned to its companion. "So? Shall we kill him now?"

"Yes, I suppose. Let's do it quickly, though. It won't be any fun."

"You're right about that." Fixing their unblinking eyes on him, both creatures crouched as if preparing to pounce.

"Wait a minute!" Bertie yelled. "Why do you want to kill me? To eat me?"

They straightened up; at least he had forestalled the attack for a moment.

"We don't eat disgusting things. What do you think we are?"

"I have no idea what you are!"

"Well, you might show a little respect when you don't know what you're talking to!"

They seemed really insulted if he could judge from their tone of voice. The grotesque faces were as immobile and unchanging as the faces of insects.

"So what are you?" Bertie asked.

"Killers of rabbits," the first one said seriously, leaning slightly toward him. "Now, warriors, that's different."

"How so?"

"What difference does that make? You'll never leave here alive anyway. Only a warrior can do that!"

"Maybe I am a warrior!"

They both hooted at this. It was a desperate attempt on Bertie's part, anyway. "A warrior doesn't try to run away like a rabbit!" the first one cried. "A warrior says, 'it's a good day to die,' and he fights until he can't fight anymore. Then he smiles and says, 'you are as my own beloved father.' And he keeps smiling as he dies. That part is important, you might try to remember it!"

Something came into his head, part of the poem he'd recited two lines of for Susan when he'd seduced her. "I shall fight!"

he cried. "I, myself, in person, order and decree that it shall
be so!" he was reciting from the poem, oddly familiar to him.
"I am the warrior youth, shining like the sun, with the beauty
of the dawn!"

"Isn't he supposed to say that to the woman?"

"Well, yeah, but all these years—a few things always get
fucked up. At least he said it. You want to kill him, or should
I?"

"You go ahead. Just make it quick, all right?"

The second creature came down the steps toward him, flexing its huge claws in and out. Bertie felt he'd gotten all he
could, one of them instead of both. He held the flint knife up
in front of him and waited for it.

Without warning, the creature lunged at him, coming up on
its hind legs, the front claws out at both sides. Bernie could
see the snout-appendages extended like a multitude of scalpels,
aimed right at his head. He was amazed at its speed, but even
more amazed at how fast he assessed the situation and reacted.
He saw that the thing meant to grab him with the claws and
impale him on the spikey snout; he went down like a baseball
player sliding for home, out of the circle formed by the arms
and snout. As he did, he raised the flint knife, hooked side
toward the creature, and slashed into its underside. It felt like
he was cutting into a marshmallow. The thing screeched and
jumped into the air, its blood drenching his arm. The blood
was downright hot, almost scalding. The creature landed behind him, spun around.

"Not bad for a rabbit," it said. The voice was ragged; Bertie was sure he'd hurt it, but could see no more blood. Then it
was coming again, like a projectile; it was running on three
legs, one paw poised to hook up under him. Bertie saw it
coming and twisted to avoid it; he managed to avoid the claws,
but the arm smashed into his ribs with terrific force, knocking
him sideways. He slashed at it frantically, missing. Struggling
to get his breath, he watched the thing circle. This was only a
matter of time, he thought. The thing would wear him down,
get hold of him, and very quickly that would be the end.

He let his head fall a little, like he couldn't catch his breath.
The horror laughed at him, circled closer. Bertie let his hand
droop, looked like he was going to drop the knife.

"Well, almost done," said the creature, giggling. "The rabbit's worn out, it seems. What do you say, rabbit?"

"I am a warrior," Bertie told it, panting more than he needed to. He gauged the distance as the thing moved in.

"Whatever. What do you say?" it insisted.

"You are as my own beloved—" Bertie started. The creature was close enough. It was now or never. He erupted from his crouch, chopped with all his strength at the thing's neck. The first blow cut halfway through; one more finished it, and the thing's head rolled free. The body didn't even twitch, it just sank down.

"Victim," Bertie finished, smiling.

"The proper word is son," said the other creature, still sitting at the top of the stairs. " 'You are as my own beloved son.' The proper line for the conqueror."

"Now you?" Bertie snarled, looking up at the thing.

"Not necessary. One is enough; you have passed the trial here. You may pass this door freely, from now on. What about him?" The creature indicted its fallen comrade. "You want him to stay dead?"

"I don't want to have to kill him again!"

"You won't. Now we are your allies. Until someone else defeats us, at least. But we can't go against you again."

"So what happens if I say he can live again? You gonna resurrect him?"

"I can't do that, I'm not a god. Just put his head back on his body."

Bertie did as the creature asked. The head seemed to instantly bond to the neck, and the creature sat up, looking at him with cold eyes. It made no move to attack.

"So you're my buddy now, too?" Bertie said to it. His hand gripped the still-bloody knife tightly.

"Of course. As Ihuimecatl said."

"So answer, buddies. What the fuck are you?"

"We are the guardians, the first trial." It peered up at him. "You haven't remembered anything yet?"

"Remembered what?"

"Obviously, he doesn't," the creature said, swinging its head toward the first. "What great luck for us, eh? What great good luck!" Its voice was heavy with sarcasm.

He decided not to pursue this, it wasn't getting him anywhere. "So what now?" he said.

"That's up to you. This place is now yours; out here, at least. In the other corridors, well, that might be different. But you got this room, the big room. All yours. Whatever."

"Let me put it a different way. If you were me, what would you do now? Leave?"

"I'm not you, never will be."

"Assume, for the sake of argument."

"Well, I'd probably go and read what's written on those steles."

He walked over to the first stele on the right side. The creature walked with him; the first remained in the doorway, looking out as if for other intruders. The stele had carvings all over it, some kind of hieroglyphics or picture-writing; no words.

"Shit!" he said. "I can't even begin to read this stuff. I don't know if anybody living could."

"There are people in the village who can interpret it," the creature said.

"Who?"

"Almost anybody. Orizaba, Maria, Rosa. Lots of others."

"How do you know all those people?"

The thing shrugged, a near-human gesture. "I know a lot of things," it said.

"Can you read the stele?" Bertie asked.

"No. I can't do that."

"If I bring, say, Rosa down here, will you nightmares kill her on sight?"

"Not if you don't want us to, if she's with you. Otherwise, of course. That's what we do, all right?"

"All right. Let me explore around a little, then I'll go get somebody to come down and read this stuff to me."

"Whatever. Don't go down any corridors. If you pick the wrong one right now, that's all for you."

All of their pronouncements were stated in a disgusted tone; it was beginning to irritate him. Ignoring them, he spent the next couple of hours exploring the main room; there really wasn't anything there except the carved steles and columns. Some of the walls were painted in murals; he barely glanced at these at first. Then something caught his eye and he looked again. Settling on his haunches in front of the mural, he studied it intensely. Much time drifted by.

17

David opened his eyes. His shoulders hurt and his mouth was dry as cotton. He looked at the window; it was obvious he was back in Patecatl and Mayauel's cottage, but he was viewing the window from an odd angle, like he was standing on a ladder. Glancing up, he saw a ceiling joist almost right in front of his face. When he tried to move, he started swinging back and forth.

"Back with us?" asked Mayauel brightly, somewhere behind him. She walked around to where he could see her.

"What's going on?" he said thickly.

"We hung you," she said; then, noticing his shocked expression, added, "Not like that. In a harness, by your shoulders. We had to keep you out of contact with the ground for a while."

"Damn right!" said Patecatl, entering the room. "Otherwise, you'd have taken root! What would we tell that sexy wife of yours if your root had taken root?" He roared; Mayauel giggled. "Why, it would probably have taken both Orizaba and me to console her!"

"Could you let me down, please?" he asked.

"Why not?" Patecatl said. He walked around behind David, worked with the rope for a moment. David was dumped unceremoniously on the floor. Patecatl came back, looked at him.

"You're in a sad state, my friend. Don't you know better than to drink five cups?"

"But you told me—"

"Well, you shouldn't have listened! Actually, that isn't true.

But I can't help giving you people a hard time. You Americans are so full of yourselves, you can't see what's important!''

"All I can see right now is I got smashed on that stuff, had some DT's or something, and now I've got a miserable hangover.''

"You don't remember anything?''

"Not a whole lot.''

"You don't remember fondling my wife's tits out there? You sure spent enough time doing it. Why, Orizaba and I fell asleep, we got so tired of waiting for you to quit playing with her tits!''

David turned red. He did have a memory of that, but it was odd in ways he couldn't really define. "I'm sorry, Patecatl,'' he said. "I guess I made an ass out of myself.''

"I guess so! First-class one, at that! But now to business, David. We've got things to do today. You've heard a saying that clothes make the man? Well, it's got some truth to it. That's what started all this in the first place. You strolled into Orizaba's shop with a bunch of rightly dressed people, and you were dressed like an asshole.''

"But Danny and I weren't dressed all that different—''

"It's right for him. Not for you. Now, get yourself up. We are going down to the square, get you a proper outfit. But you have to pick it out. We can't.''

For the first time, David realized he was still totally naked. "All right, whatever,'' he said. "Just give me my old clothes, I'll get dressed, and—''

"Sorry. Not possible. We burned them.''

"You what?''

"We burned them. No use to you. Seemed logical at the time.''

David put his head in his hands. Lunatics. He'd gotten mixed up with lunatics. "Okay, okay. So they're gone, burned. So lend me something to wear, okay?''

"Why?''

"Why? I can't go into town like this! Besides, where's my money? From the pocket? Don't tell me—''

"Afraid so. Burned. Don't worry about it. Your credit is good here.''

"I still can't go to town stark naked!''

"You can and will. You should not wear anything but proper

clothes now. I don't have any for you. So you have to go to town and buy some. No other way. That's it.''

''Well, I'm not going to do it!''

''What are you going to do, then?''

''I'll go back up to the resort, get some clothes—''

''No. You're still weak from the drink. If you don't come with us, I'll hit you over the head, carry you to town, let you come around in the square. That'll be more embarrassing. I assure you, I won't hesitate.''

David looked at him, convinced that he was telling the truth. He felt trapped. Might as well get this over with as soon as possible and get away from these people. He still had only vague recollections of his experiences out in the fields, but what he could remember was very disturbing. It made little sense, and as it came back, it made even less sense. He had the most upsetting memory of Mayauel cutting him with a knife; and although he had no cuts, he simply couldn't be sure it hadn't happened.

''Okay, Patecatl. Let's go, get this over with.''

''Now that's more like it!'' Patecatl yelled. ''Let's do it!''

Of all David's experiences since the weirdness began, leaving the cottage and beginning the walk into town most closely mimicked nightmares he'd actually had. He could remember a number of them; he was, for unknown reasons, out in public without clothing. Here and now, that was reality, undeniably so. He was walking down the dusty main street of a little Mexican village, whose name he still hadn't gotten straight, wearing only his sandals. Though the villagers had hardly reacted at all to the women's near-nudity, such was not the case for David. People gathered, laughing and pointing; he tried to keep his eyes straight ahead. A young girl, thirteen or so, ran boldly out and patted his rear; Mayauel chased her away, but they were both giggling.

Before they reached the square, they encountered Orizaba, apparently waiting for them. He waddled out, faced David. ''Well, certainly not overdressed, are you?'' he said.

''Don't make it worse. These idiots burned my clothes, and they won't let me go back to the resort. I'll bet you helped them, too!'' He glared down at the little man.

''Helped them? I? Do I look like a crazy man? Do I go around burning people's clothes? You ask these villagers. You'll see!'' He hopped over to the crowd at the side of the street and came back with a girl in tow, perhaps the same one that had patted his rear a few minutes ago.

''Now you ask her. You ask her!'' Orizaba said. ''Fourteen years she has lived here, ask her if she ever heard of Orizaba doing anything of the sort! Ask her, well, what are you waiting for?''

''Well?'' David demanded.

She didn't say anything, just grinned at him. She was looking at his crotch, not his face.

''Could we just get on with this?'' David asked miserably.

The girl jumped forward and touched his penis, then ran back to the crowd; the people roared like it was a sports event, and it turned into a game. Orizaba, Mayauel, and Patecatl flanked him on three sides, while the women and girls from the crowd darted in and out, trying to touch him. When one did, the crowd yelled its approval, especially if the touch was scored on his genitals.

''I know what to do,'' Mayauel suggested. ''I can walk along backwards and hold onto it. Then nobody can touch it. How about that?''

''Just don't start feeling up her tits again,'' Patecatl said.

''Get me to the square, please,'' David said, gritting his teeth.

After what seemed like an eternity, they entered the square. As they did, the crowd melted away. The three natives steered David from stall to stall, their mood more serious now. He sensed that for them, fun time was over. Again he wondered why his attire was so important to them; but right now, he just wanted to get something, anything, to put on.

''Don't rush it,'' Mayauel insisted. ''It has to be right. Choose, don't just grab the first thing.''

Trying to be patient, he examined the clothes offered, though he hated to stand and browse in this condition. The market was very quiet; everybody seemed to be watching him. Mayauel and Patecatl followed him around, but they made no suggestions; they too just watched intently as he picked items up, put them down again. It didn't take long for him to find something that interested him.

It was a full leather garment, with sleeves that came halfway below the elbows. The shopkeeper handed him the garment,

showed him how to put it on. It was very soft and supple,
made rather like an infant's one-piece suit, golden yellow in
color. The back was partially open, with lacing in two places.
He slipped it over his head like a pullover sweater, pushed his
arms into the sleeves. The bottom was free, hanging down the
back; he pulled it through and tied it in front, leaving his legs
bare. There were two flaps hanging from the ends of the
sleeves; he paid little attention to them. He actually liked it
very much. It was comfortable and attractive; the edges had
all been neatly scalloped. Pushing the sleeves out smooth, he
turned to face the others, smiling.

"Very nice," Mayauel said. Her approval pleased him in
spite of everything.

The shopkeeper interrupted. "This goes with it," he said,
handing David another piece of folded leather, exactly matching what he wore. David pulled it out; it was rather like a ski
mask, but again open in the back, held together with lacing.
There were eyeholes, a hole for the mouth, a hole for the bottom of the nose. Very realistic ears; real artwork. He tried it
on, liked it. The square was now very quiet. He looked down
at his arms and torso through the mask. Then it hit him; his
Incidents—this suit was an imitation of a flayed human skin, a
skin like he'd worn in the dreams of his childhood. Whenever
he'd thought of those dreams, he'd been horrified; but now, it
seemed to him that it only made this suit more appropriate for
him.

"How much?" he asked the shopkeeper.

"Twenty dollars American," the man said. "You bring to
me, yes?"

"Yes, of course. You can count on it." The flaps at the ends
of the sleeves caught his attention and he looked at them closely
for the first time. They were in the form of perfect human
hands, turned back from the ends of the sleeves. Well, if it
was an imitation of a flayed skin, that figured. His head was
buzzing; somehow this was related to something that happened
out in the fields, but he couldn't quite remember yet. He was
going to ask Mayauel, but when he looked around again, she,
Patecatl, and Orizaba were gone. He shrugged; it didn't matter. He really liked the suit.

He began to stroll back up to the resort, examining the hands
that hung off the sleeves. Really remarkable work, fingers,

joints, fingernails, everything. He could have almost believed they were real.

18

Susan walked away from John's bedside and looked out the window again. Still no sign of David. She was beginning to get worried; it had been over six hours since they had left him at Orizaba's shop. She knew he had planned to stay and talk to the dwarf for a while, but she couldn't imagine what had taken this much time.

She had spent a lot of it trying to get John to make some kind of sense. His attempt at an explanation of what had gone on the previous night had been disjointed, to say the least. She had gathered that he'd had a vision of himself murdering all the guests from the resort, herself included. One strange feature of this was that she had, in his judgment, wanted to be murdered, and he had merely accommodated her. That sent shivers up and down her back, and brought back memories of another time; another place, but a place not so very far away. It was still Mexico. She covered her bare breasts with her arms as if to protect herself. Mexico, she thought; its flag should be blood red. John's story, nonsensical though it was, would have caused her to suspect that she was in Mexico even if they'd still believed it to be South America. The memories of her college days, the trip to Mexico then, flooded back for a moment; again she pushed them away.

She tried to concentrate on her feelings for Danny instead; her thoughts about him in Orizaba's shop had confused her. She had felt he was perfection incarnate—for his kind. She had no idea what that meant, but she knew it meant his kind as opposed to David's, or John's, or her own. As if they were somehow superior to him. Where had such arrogance come from? And worse, both Jeannie Edwards, for a while, and yesterday Orizaba had treated her as if that was to be expected, was perfectly justified! The dwarf had seemed to be terrified of her, and that was just absurd. Or maybe not; she had apparently struck Jerry Maxwell down in some inexplicable way, and wondered if Orizaba recognized in her powers she herself was wholly unaware of. Perhaps she too should go and have a talk with the dwarf. Things did seem to be centering around him.

John, who had been sleeping, coughed and rolled over. She looked at him, saw that his eyes were partially open, looking back at her. She sat on the edge of his bed, thinking that he definitely had a problem; whatever had happened to him, he wasn't getting over it quickly or easily.

He looked up at her with slitted eyes, and smiled. Good, she thought. For the first time today, he seemed to be coming back to some semblance of normalcy. She felt he wasn't quite awake; she remembered that when they were children, John had always come out of sleep reluctantly, as if his dreams were preferable to the real world, and she'd been very sympathetic to that view. She patted his chest and started to speak.

Still smiling, he reached up and put his hands on her breasts. She was shocked, but said nothing.

"Nikki," he said. "Nikki."

She understood then, and gently pushed his hands back down. "No, John," she said in a gentle tone. "It's Susan, your sister."

"Susan?" He seemed to snap awake. "Oh, damn, I'm sorry. I was having a dream, and you just—well, you just blended with the person I was dreaming about—"

"I know. Nikki. I wish she was here for you, John."

"Thanks. Oh, well. It seems there's enough here to keep me busy anyway." He sat up, looked around.

"You feeling any better?"

"Yes, actually I think I am. It just had to sink in, I guess, that what I saw last night was a hallucination. Everybody's still alive. I suppose somebody must have given me the mask and hat while I was spaced out. But I tell you, Susan, it's a terrifying thing to watch your body killing your loved ones and be unable to stop it. Maybe that's how some mentally ill people feel. It really is bad."

"It must be. But it's this place, John. I've had some really weird thoughts too, not like yours, but some I don't feel very good about. Danny's got to be right. There is something going on, something with a pattern to it. But none of us can see what it is."

John got up and stretched. "Where's David?" he asked.

She explained about their journey into town to confront Orizaba. She confessed that she was beginning to worry some about her husband's whereabouts.

"Well, I hope you didn't push poor Orizaba too hard," John said. "In spite of everything, I think he's a good man, a good friend. After all, it is true, what he said. I insisted on hearing that damned flute."

"You really think it was the flute?"

"Who knows? You yourself said my playing on the trumpet he made caused all of you to cry. Orizaba is a master. I'm not sure what effects he can create with those instruments he makes. Right now, I wouldn't put much out of his reach."

"You don't think he'd do anything bad to David, do you?"

"Oh, no! He's not a mean or violent man. I'd bet on that. Whatever happened, he didn't mean for anybody to get hurt, and in reality, nobody did. And I got this beautiful mask and hat." He picked up the ocelot hat, put it on. "I really like the hat, don't you?"

She had to agree. Although it was definitely not a hat she would have visualized him wearing, it somehow looked right on him, although the rest of his clothes clashed.

He sat in the chair by the window and looked out. She studied his face; so gentle, sensitive, yet strong in some indefinable way. She realized, looking at him now, what an enigma John had always been to her. Although she'd always loved him dearly, she couldn't pretend to understand him.

"This woman Nikki," she said at last. "You want to talk about it, John?"

He smiled at her. "Maybe I should, Susan. I don't know. I've never been really able to get her straight in my mind."

"Don't take offense, but I understand she's a hooker?"

"No, no offense taken. That's true, she is. Probably quite an unusual one. But maybe not. I don't know very many ladies in that line of work." His laugh had only a little bitterness in it.

"It's good you can laugh about it," she said.

"There was a time I couldn't," he told her. "But that was years ago. I really love her, Susan. Every time I think about it, I realize how much. I can accept what she does, even if I don't like it. And in a way, I've really kind of come to terms with it. I worry about her health and safety a lot more than about her morals, or lack thereof."

"Seems like a reasonable concern."

"I've always thought so. But for whatever reason, she doesn't seem to have those problems. It doesn't seem to worry her."

"I guess if it did, she couldn't do that."

"Probably not. As she told me a long time ago, doctors face some of the same problems, and they rarely worry about it."

Susan shifted uncomfortably. She was thinking about the phantom, about Bertie, about Kathryn. She thought she might understand how Nikki felt. The possibilities of disease or maniacs had not really entered her mind. And for her, the idea of maniacs was never too terribly far away, coloring her life in many ways. Idly, she wondered what her life might have been like if she had not taken that fateful trip to Mexico City with Janey. Very possibly a lot like Nikki's, except that it had never occurred to Susan to charge for it. For her, it would be like charging someone for the privilege of serving her a drink. She giggled mentally at the thought. Her sexual appetites had put her through hell, but hell had not burned them away. Just pushed them down a little.

"Penny for your thoughts," John said. "Maybe a dollar. One dollar American!"

"That buys a lot around here," she said, crossing her legs and smiling at him. "You offer much for mere thoughts, good sir."

"Thoughts are worth a lot," he said seriously. "Especially yours, I'd hazard."

"I was thinking about your friend, her life. Between you and me, in a lot of ways I wouldn't mind living that life. Not that I'd do it. But perhaps if certain things hadn't happened—"

He watched her closely. "What things, Susan?"

"Not anything I want to talk about. Actually, I don't mean it like that. I can't talk about it, not now. It brings it back. I would've killed to have had you to talk to then, though."

"I'm really sorry I couldn't have been there for you."

Suddenly she flared. "Why the hell couldn't you? Oh, I know, very well, what Mom and Dad are like, and I can't blame you a bit for getting as far away from them as possible. But you left me all alone! You bastard, you know how that felt? You could have found some way to stay in touch with me! You don't know how I looked up to you, how I needed you, you were my friend, the only one—" She broke off, her anger turning to tears.

Awkwardly, he tried to console her. "Susan," he said, "abandoning you like that is one of the worst things I've ever done. It was purely selfish. I was sure they would destroy you. And your good old asshole brother didn't want to see it. I couldn't watch it, couldn't stop it either. It was a living hell for me. You were sensual and beautiful even when you were a little girl, and Mom was taking it as her God-given duty to drive it out of you, whatever it took. I could see you fighting it, and there just didn't seem to be any answer except destruction." He hung his head, and Susan's anger faded a little.

"You had no confidence in me," she said in an accusatory voice. "You thought I was weak. But I wasn't. You heard about the preacher?"

Head still down, he nodded.

"You know I was treated like a ghost after that? Shunned? I swear to God, you would have thought we were a family of fucking Puritans. But John, trials like that can make you stronger. It did for me. I had to be. Or you would have been right, I would've been destroyed."

"I wish you'd tell me about that!"

"Well, I can't. And right now, I'm not very interested in letting you off the hook. You're right. You were a selfish bastard then. And even up to last week, you still hadn't tried to contact me!"

He raised his head, looked in her eyes; his were wet. "You're wrong about that, Susan. I did try. I even called Mom, more than once, and you know how hard that was for me. But you'd done the same thing I did; you'd disappeared. After college, you seemed to have vanished from the face of the earth. I did find out you'd moved to New York. I tried calling every S. Goss in the New York phone book. You know how many there are? But no luck."

"Of course not, I'd married David."

"Of course I didn't know that."

Her attitude softened a little more. It was perfectly apparent to her that he had suffered from his own demons, over this and over Nikki. And she'd carried this resentment with her for a very long time. Ever since high school.

There was a knock at the door; John called out for whoever it was to come in. When it opened, a very strange looking figure stepped inside; Susan jumped when she saw him, a little alarmed. The man's legs and feet were bare except for sandals. On his torso and arms he wore a golden leather body suit that looked utterly bizarre to Susan. He was also wore a mask, only his eyes and lips visible through it; but she could see his smile.

"David?" she asked incredulously.

He took off the mask. "Me, all right," he said. "Mayauel and Patecatl helped—ah—convinced me to get it. What do you think?"

She started to tell him it was hideous, nightmarish. But before she could even get the words out, it was as if something snapped in her mind, and her perspective changed; it was like looking at one of those optical illusions, which change from two faces to a vase as you look. It was as if her view of David had changed in that way.

"David, it's beautiful!" she said. "I can't believe it, it's just perfect for you! Don't you think so, John?"

She turned to look at John; he had a serious expression on his face, and he was working his jaw. Susan remembered he did that when he was upset about something.

"I think it's very odd," he said slowly, "that David is wearing a costume that looks exactly like what I saw him wearing in that vision last night!"

"Really?" Susan asked. "But how—"

"Orizaba's doing, somehow," David said unexpectedly. "He was with us when we picked this out."

"Where are the clothes you were wearing?" Susan asked.

"You wouldn't believe it," he said. "Don't ask, okay?"

"You know, in spite of the vision, I do think that fits him, somehow," John put in. "I think of David as very earthy— maybe because of his job, the farm background—and that get-up, well, it goes along with soil, growing plants."

"Yes, it does," Susan said. "Why, exactly, I don't know."

"It makes him look like a seed!"

Both of them started to laugh. David looked irritated for a minute, then he joined in. He pantomimed a growing plant, bending down and coming up slowly, spreading his arms. Susan tried to laugh, but it choked off. What he was doing suddenly became serious, no laughing matter. She heard John's laughter stop as well, as David, his originally clownish expression now dead serious, finished his gesture.

"David, that was really beautiful!" John said. "I mean, I know it started out as a joke, but it became like a ballet; really stunning!"

"Yeah," David said. He shook his head, as if to clear it. "I meant it as a joke, but it wasn't at the end." He sat on the edge of John's bed and stared at the window. "I wonder what's happening to us," he said in a distant voice.

"I don't know," John responded. "Doesn't seem like anything bad. I had that horrible vision, but there's no way such a thing could become real." There was a long pause. "Is there?"

"Oh, John, of course not!" cried Susan. "There's no way you're capable of anything like that!"

"I agree," David said. "I've seen no violence in you."

"Well, Evelyn, last night—"

David waved it off. "Yes, yes, I know, Danny told me. But, John, you were upset. And even so, you didn't hurt her."

"No," he said thoughtfully. "Actually, I've never hurt anybody. Never even hit anyone. You know, I never thought about that until just now, but it's kind of odd, too, isn't it? I mean, most kids get into fights from time to time. But not me. No one ever picked on me, I never bothered anyone. Not ever. I have never—never—" He stopped talking. His face seemed to be getting longer by the minute.

"What?" David asked.

"That's a lie," he said heavily. "I did. Once. Nikki. I hit her, I remember. She had blood coming out of her mouth."

"I can't believe that, John!" Susan cried.

"Oh, it's true," he said. "The day she first told me she was a prostitute."

"Must have really racked you," David said.

"It did. But that's no justification for—"

"Look," Susan said, "Obviously that was a long time ago.

And just as obviously, Nikki has forgotten it, or forgiven you. You should give yourself the same break!''

He stood up, paced. ''Hard for me to do,'' he said. ''I'm not very familiar with guilt. I usually don't do things that make me feel guilty. But when I do, like what I did to you, Susan, I have a hard time letting myself off the hook. Same with Nikki, the way I treated her, hit her. Unforgivable, as far as I'm concerned.''

''You're too hard on yourself,'' David said.

''Perhaps. But I have high expectations for the world around me. How can I if I can't control myself, if the world can't have high expectations for me?''

''The world ever live up to your expectations?'' David asked.

''No,'' John replied, in a low voice.

''Well, there you are!''

19

Finding himself stiff and sore, Bertie cursed, held his back, and walked around a little. He'd been crouched in front of the long wall mural for too long. He glanced at the monstrosity he had killed; it now sat passively beside him like an overgrown dog.

''Do you things have names?'' he asked it.

''Yes, of course. My name is Toltecatl,'' it said. It continued to stare, the snout-appendages writhing.

''What about that one?'' Bertie indicated the other, which sat as still as a stone statue, watching the door.

''Ihuimecatl,'' Toltecatl said.

''How can I tell you apart? You look alike to me.''

''I have this red scar running all the way around my neck, where someone cut my head off. Ihuimecatl doesn't.''

Bertie grinned at it. True enough, he thought. He still felt a certain exhilaration from that battle, now more than two hours old.

"Can you explain to me what it is that you are? I mean, I'm being pretty blasé about all this; two impossible monstrosities that talk, one of which I killed and now lives again."

"Like we said, we are your allies. We don't have to look like this. How would you have us appear?"

"Let's try human?"

"Male, female, old, young, fat, thin?"

"Anything!" Bertie cried.

The creature stood up straight as it had previously when attacking him. It seemed to shimmer and shift; then in front of him was a young Indian man, very muscular. And quite naked.

"How's this?" he asked.

"Fine, but what about clothes?"

"Well, I can't change into clothes! You'll have to get them if you want them."

Fair enough, Bertie thought. "Do you have to stay down here, or can you go into the city?" he asked.

"We can do whatever you want us to do," Toltecatl said. "We are your allies, yours to command."

Not a bad deal, Bertie thought. Now exactly what am I going to do with them?

For the moment, he put it out of his mind; the mural was more interesting, more important. In it were numerous figures drawn in the stylized manner of the Aztec or Maya, almost cartoons by today's standards; but their clothing made them recognizable. He had seen a figure dressed as he was, matches for all three of the women's costumes, and one with Frank's blue robes; that one even appeared to be wearing glasses. Another wore an ocelot hat and a long-faced red mask like the ones John had. David and Danny he could not identify, since neither of them were wearing distinctive clothing. There was, however, another major figure, one who wore an odd costume with hands hanging off the sleeves, and a kind of a ski-mask. It would be interesting, he told himself, to see if either man turned up with an outfit like that.

But the pictures as a whole were very confusing; the figures appeared repeatedly, engaged in a variety of odd activities. Some were not so odd. The image which had initially caught his attention was of the figure which was dressed like himself: missing foot, mirrors, and all, having intercourse with the woman in the long flower dress, obviously Susan. Most of the remaining scenes eluded him, however. There were many suggestive things; for example, a picture of him—or the man dressed as he was—having his foot bitten off by a monster coming out of the water. That hit him hard. But most were too stylized. A picture of the man in the ocelot hat, four Frank Wassermans surrounding him, holding out tree branches. A picture of the man with the mirrored foot standing over the headless body of the woman dressed like Kathryn. And so on. Many of the pictures were violent; virtually every one of the people whose dress he recognized were shown dead or dying in at least one of the panels, including the man with the mirrored foot. That he didn't like. He puzzled over them, even striking the mural with his fist as if to force it to make sense.

"If I may," Toltecatl began.

"Yes, what?" Bertie answered testily.

"The real problem is you are not strong enough. Oh, you had the strength and skill to defeat me, but you can be stronger. It has been a long time for you."

"How can I get stronger?" he asked, interested. He hardly heard the rest of Toltecatl's pronouncement.

"We will help. Tomorrow, if you wish. Tonight, bring us clothing so we may walk among the villagers unnoticed."

"But how do I get stronger?" he demanded.

The thing in human disguise told him. At first he was horrified; but he knew instinctively it was right.

20

Danny and Kathryn were already seated in the dining room when David and Susan arrived. Danny did a double take at David's new costume; the association with David's Incidents was immediately apparent. He considered asking about it, but decided that perhaps this was not a good idea. Maybe later, when they were alone. At this point, all the guests had come in; dinner was in the process of being served. Looking around the table, Danny saw that only he remained dressed normally; John still had on a T-shirt and jeans, but he wore the peculiar little peaked ocelot hat. Nobody, including the serving girls, seemed to see anything strange about these costumes. Danny thought they were very strange.

They were just about finished eating when Eduardo came in and stood at the head of the table. "My friends, I have an announcement which I'm sure will interest all of you!" he said enthusiastically. "There will be a ceremony in the village tomorrow night, like nothing you've ever seen! At eight o'clock, in El Teatro! Uh, the big building near this end of town."

"What sort of ceremony is it, Eduardo?" Frank asked.

"There are two, actually. You won't want to miss either! First comes the crowning of the king of the city. The whole populace will participate. Next, the ceremony of the new corn. This pageant has very old roots in Mexico. It was practiced many, many years ago. You have the unique opportunity of seeing it as it was, as if you could take a time machine and travel back, before the conquest, even before the Aztecs! This simple, beautiful little ceremony has been unchanged since then, here in Tlillan Tlapallan! You must see it!"

Danny grinned; Eduardo sounded like a barker at a carnival. He asked what he thought was a logical question. "How much does it cost?"

Eduardo looked like he had been physically wounded. "Cost? Cost? My friend, these ceremonies—one political, the other deeply religious—are a part of the lifeblood of this village. Everyone here at the time is expected to attend! Of course, there is no charge! No cost at all!"

"What do you think?" he asked Kathryn.

"Sounds fine to me. Might be interesting."

There was general conversation around the table; eventually everyone had agreed to attend except for Bertie, who seemed preoccupied with David's new costume. Danny wondered why. He'd also noticed that when Bertie came in, he seemed a little stiff; he would have liked to have known what the man had been up to today.

"So, David, tell us about the new duds," Danny asked, with an attempt to be light. He hoped his concern remained hidden.

"You remember Patecatl and Mayauel," he responded. "They helped me find it. Nice huh?"

"Oh, very nice, very nice. So what have you been doing all day?"

"Just talking to Patecatl, Mayauel, and Orizaba. Interesting folks."

"So I understand."

The conversation trailed off, and at the end of it Danny had learned nothing at all. He sighed; he'd been hoping that David would pick up something useful from Orizaba. If he had, he wasn't talking about it. He considered the possibility of going to Orizaba's shop himself tomorrow, to see if the dwarf would talk to him. He didn't have high hopes for this, considering the way Orizaba had treated him today. He had already talked to Susan, and was convinced that she didn't know why the little man had been so terrified of her. Everyone was acting so strangely, he didn't know what to expect next.

After coffee, Danny, Kathryn, and the Hallstens went outside to sit by the pool and enjoy the tropical night. For Danny, this remained almost pure pleasure, the company of friends in the warm, clear night. Though he still wasn't pleased that neither Kathryn nor David had yet said a word about their tryst, he was hardly in a position to throw accusations around. All he could do was try not to think about it.

As they talked, Danny made no further attempts to discuss the day's events; as long as he didn't, David was as open as he'd been in New York. He had by now wholly discarded his prohibition about reading David and Susan surreptitiously; and as he did so tonight, he saw that they were, at least as far as he could tell, basically the same. The only real difference was the frequency and intensity of the reddish-brown wisps that signified sexual desire; they now came from everywhere and went everywhere. Except, again, for John; closed-down, aloof John. As on previous nights, they heard his trumpet in the distance, beautiful as ever and not at all sad tonight. Danny heard him play an odd little riff, very complex but really pretty. It had an odd effect on his three friends; they went glassy-eyed for just an instant before returning to normal.

After a long period of pleasant conversation, the little group broke up. Danny and Kathryn went back to his room; he watched her undress, noting that any striptease effect was totally eliminated by the utterly revealing clothing she wore. Actually, he wouldn't have minded, except that she and the other women kept him moderately to totally distracted all day long.

Kathryn took a little pouch out of her vest pocket and came to bed, a small naked figure. She sat on her heels in front of Danny, looking down at the leather bag.

"What's that?" Danny asked, pointing.

"David brought them from Mayauel, gave some to me and Evelyn this afternoon," she said. She reached in and pulled out a handful of dark brown items, showed them to him. They were thorns from some plant; each one was perhaps two inches long, but very thin, shaped like a sewing needle except at the base, where it became much thicker. "He didn't say what they were for," she told him. "But I know. It's real funny, just a certain knowledge in your head and you don't know where it came from."

She looked at him, as if expecting something from him. "Well, what are they for?" he asked. He had no idea.

"You don't know?"

"No. But I know what you mean about a certain knowledge, and you don't know where it came from. That's the way some of my abilities work. I just seem to know. But I'm not getting anything from these. So you tell me."

She looked down. "I was hoping you'd know, too. It would verify it for me. This is outside my experience, Danny."

"Well, take it from me, if you have an absolute certainty about something, it's probably right. At least you should check it out."

"You think so?"

"Sure. Why not?"

"Okay, well, here goes. They are for—ah—purification."

He just looked at her for a moment, not comprehending. Then it hit him. He glanced at the thorns again; before, they had looked delicate, small. Now they looked enormous, vicious. "You aren't serious, are you?" he asked pleadingly.

"It just came into my head, as soon as David gave them to me. I saw Evelyn's face. I'd bet she had the same idea."

"Why don't we wait until tomorrow, talk to her and see?" he begged.

Kathryn shook her head. "I feel I have to do this, Danny. But I can't insist you do it. I can understand if you don't want to watch; I'll go down to my room, be back in half an hour or so—"

He put his hands to his head. "No—no!" he said. "That's not necessary. I just don't understand. There's a lot of things I don't understand!"

She smiled and kissed him, then became very serious. Picking out six thorns, she tested the points of each with her thumb, laid them out neatly on the bed. Eyes closed, she adopted a yoga-like posture, her legs crossed in the Amerindian style, not in the Oriental lotus. She picked up one of the thorns, put the point of it against her left earlobe and slowly pushed it through, stopping before the thick part went in. Her expression didn't change. Leaving it where it was, she repeated the procedure with her right earlobe.

This wasn't so very bad, Danny thought. She, like most women, already had her ears pierced for earrings. The only difference from a normal ear-piercing was in the speed.

After a short pause, she picked up another one, placed it against the inside of her thigh, about an inch down from the top. Danny inhaled sharply, but couldn't look away. Very slowly, she pushed it in about an inch. He looked at her face; she was frowning slightly, which didn't surprise him at all. Picking up another, she just as carefully and slowly pierced her other thigh in the same place.

There was another hiatus; she closed her eyes and seemed to concentrate. Gradually the frown left her face. Danny glanced down at the remaining two thorns on the bed, hoping she meant to put them into her arms. She opened her eyes, looked into his briefly, then picked up another. It was what he dreaded; she put the sharp point against her left nipple and started pushing it in. Her face was contorted now, and he wanted to stop her, but was sure that wouldn't be appreciated; he had to sit here and let her go through with the whole thing. Her nipple folded inward under the pressure, then the point sank in, rather suddenly. She trembled, but kept pushing until it was about an inch deep.

He still held onto a forlorn hope that five would be enough, that she wouldn't force the last one; but she set its point against her other nipple. This time she held her breast with the other hand before starting to push, but still it ran into her once started rather suddenly. She let out a little cry, dropped her hands and sat there, her expression very pained.

As she sat unmoving, her face gradually cleared, her tightly closed eyes came open. We're not done, Danny thought; she still has to get them out again. After what seemed to him to be a very long time, she reached up and slowly pulled out the ones in her earlobes, starting with the one on the left. A single drop of blood, bright red in the subdued light, fell onto her shoulder. She laid those two back on the bed, then removed the one from her left thigh; there was no blood from this one. Her right thigh produced another single drop. She paused for a moment, then reached for the one in her left breast. Do it fast, he thought, it'll hurt a lot less. But she didn't; very slowly she pulled on it, the nipple stretching a bit as it came free. Again, there wasn't much bleeding, only a drop or two. She repeated this for the last one, pulling on it perhaps even more slowly. Finally it came free, but this one bled profusely, tracking a red line down the lower half of her breast, across her belly and onto the bed. She just watched until it stopped.

"Are you okay?" Danny whispered.

"Yes, I think so. It really hurts. But it was necessary. I'm sure of it. I don't know why, but I feel more in tune with myself, with this place. I don't know. I never would have considered doing this before."

"I hope you don't plan on doing it again any time soon. It's not easy to watch."

"Don't be disappointed in me, Danny, but I'm sure I will be doing it again, and soon. I'd also bet the Hallstens and the Wassermans did the same thing tonight. I just feel it."

He hated to ask the obvious question, but he had to. "Do you feel I should do it too?"

"In a way, I do. But if you don't, then don't. Maybe it's not right for you, for some reason. But here and now, it was right for me."

He reached for her and they embraced, smearing her blood on his chest. He was afraid, afraid for all of them. Things were getting out of control. They progressed from the embrace to lovemaking, and again things went out of control, but pleasantly so this time.

21

An hour before dawn, Bertie's eyes popped open; he was instantly totally awake. Rising from his bed and dressing as quickly as possible, he left the room and the resort, encountering no one on the way out. He made his way across the moonlit lawn, then started down the hillside toward the opening he had previously found. With him he carried a bundle of dark cloth.

Ihuimecatl and Toltecatl were waiting for him at the doorway; they appeared as young, muscular Indians, one man, one woman. By the scar he knew the man was Toltecatl. He handed them the bundles.

"I bought these on the square yesterday. I hope they won't be too conspicuous," he said.

"They'll be fine, just fine," Ihuimecatl said. She unfurled the cloth to reveal a long, dark robe with a cowl.

"Oh, great," Bertie said when she put it on. "You look like something off the late show. Real good. The only place you wouldn't be noticed is at a witch's convention."

"So why did you buy these things?" Toltecatl asked, slipping into his. It was identical.

"Damned if I know. I had the fucking things in my hand and my money out before I knew what I was doing."

"No, these are good. You followed your instinct and, as you should know, if you do that you can't go wrong."

He nodded, though he couldn't have said he really understood. "Well, we have things to do. Shall we go?"

"Yes. You go to the Pyramid of the Black. You should purify yourself and wait for us. We will be there before dawn."

They all clambered down the side of the pyramid and went

their separate ways, Bertie up to the ruined church, the transformed nightmares into town. He paused briefly to watch them walking down the road in the dim light. At least they hadn't put up the cowls.

Once atop the other pyramid, Bertie ritually pierced his body with the maguey thorns; his earlobes, thighs, and nipples, letting the drops of blood fall on the sacrificial stone. He then stroked the blade of the flint knife in the drops, smearing blood on both stone and blade. The blade absorbed the drops; the mirrors on his foot and at his temple began to smoke again. He felt a kind of pure excitement. He couldn't remember ever having sensations like this, yet simultaneously it was an old familiar feeling.

The sky in the east was gradually changing from black to gray as he walked around the stone several times, too eager to be still. Walking out toward the edge, heedless of the thorny grasses, he looked down the path. Three figures were coming up. One of them was being held by his hair, and seemed very passive. Bertie almost drooled.

As they topped the ridge and came onto the flat top of the pyramid, Bertie saw that they had brought a young man from the village; a boy actually, perhaps eighteen or nineteen years old. He seemed almost drugged as Toltecatl led him along by the hair.

"You understand?" Ihuimecatl asked Bertie.

"Yes," he said. He offered her his curved flint knife, but she shook her head.

"That one is not appropriate for what we will do today," she said. Reaching inside her cloak, she pulled out another knife, held it lying flat on her two hands for Bertie to see. This one had a carved greenstone handle in the form of a crouching warrior wearing an eagle helmet; his hands held an elliptical blade that looked like chipped black glass. He touched the edges, the point; they were like razors. The blade was about six inches long, two inches wide at the widest point. Very efficient-looking. Very right for this particular job. "Obsidian," Ihuimecatl said, but he knew that already. Obsidian, like his mirrors.

He walked to the eastern edge of the cleared area, stood between the sacrificial stone and the place where the sun would soon rise. Facing the stone, he crossed his arms over his chest, and waited. Ihuimecatl took her position beside the stone opposite him, and raised the cowl over her head; Bertie could no longer see her face.

Toltecatl led the young man to the stone. "You are as my own beloved son," he said to the boy.

"You are as my own beloved father," said the boy in reply. "Does my father have any messages he wishes to send?"

"Yes. Say that you are power incarnate, and should be received with respect and love."

"I will say this."

With Toltecatl helping him, the boy stripped off his clothes and lay down on the stone, nude. Toltecatl was very gentle with him. He moved to the boy's head, at the north of the stone, and pushed his arms out straight. Then he waited.

Ihuimecatl watched the sky; Bertie thought she was looking right through him. Then he saw the first rays of the rising sun strike the stone, casting his shadow on it; the shadow looked huge, like it was being cast by someone over ten feet tall. Ihuimecatl's face was visible then, shining red in the sun's first rays. Looking ecstatic, she raised the obsidian knife high in the air, brought it down hard; the shiny black blade sank into the boy's chest about an inch below his left nipple. His face went tight, his body rigid, but he didn't cry out. She cut downward toward the stone, then twisted the blade; blood poured out of the wound, flowing onto the stone. Ripping the blade out, she thrust her hand into the bloody hole she had dug in the boy's chest, pushing it in beyond her wrist, then immediately pulling it out again. The boy made a little noise, and opened his eyes; Bertie could see he was not dead yet. But Ihuimecatl held his heart, torn blood vessels hanging from it, in her red-stained hand. It was still beating violently as she held it aloft. As she started walking toward Bertie, the heart actually jumped out of her hand, like it was trying to get back to the boy's body. Deftly, she caught it before it hit the ground, and continued to come toward him. He saw that the smoke from his foot had increased.

His excitement rose to a fever pitch as she came close. A part of him, far back and distant, wondered how he knew what to do, why he was doing this on the say-so of these impossible creatures. But consciously he knew this was right; it was just an absolute certainty for him. He looked at Ihuimecatl, and opened his mouth widely.

She stuffed in the still-beating heart. He bit down hard; the muscle was rubbery and hard to tear, but he was managing. The pieces were still squirming as they went down his throat. Blood spouted from his mouth, ran down his chin and onto his chest, onto the ground. Ihuimecatl continued to push the bloody organ into his mouth until it was entirely consumed, then went back to the stone. Bertie could see the boy's head turned toward them, dead eyes open, as if he had been watching Bertie eat his heart in the last few minutes of his life.

"Your gift has been received with respect and love," Bertie said. Ihuimecatl and Toltecatl picked up the body by the arms and legs, carried it to the edge of the pyramid, and unceremoniously threw it over. Bertie didn't move. He felt the sun on his back, tasted the blood in his mouth, felt an odd sensation flowing from his stomach to all parts of his body, like someone was rubbing warm oil on him. The silky, pleasant sensation spread to his fingers and toes, then receded. It seemed to split in two, contracting until part of it was in his head, the rest residing immediately behind his navel. He knew he could bring it out, use it, whenever he wished. For whatever purpose he might see fit. He turned, saw the risen sun, saw the boy's body lying crumpled, halfway down the slope. *Good man*, Bertie thought. He really felt a love for him.

22

As evening drew near, Danny thought that the day had, by comparison, gone rather smoothly; there had been no major incidents or upsets, nothing weird had happened. He and Kathryn, along with the Wassermans and the Hallstens, had spent the day at the beach. Danny had noticed that Kathryn had been quite right about the thorns; not only about the other women, but David and Frank as well. Even Bertie; he had missed breakfast, but at lunch Danny had seen the punctures in his earlobes. Only he and John, apparently, were holdouts. And Danny felt John was slipping away; he'd given up the T-shirt and workshoes, his uniform since he'd arrived, for native sandals and one of the vest-like garments. His blue jeans he retained, however. If he gave up those, Danny would be all alone. He didn't know what significance there was to these odd outfits, but it was more than clear to him that there was something.

Dinner was served early, as Eduardo had said it would be, so that everyone could attend the ceremonies in the village. Danny was surprised to see Bertie planning to go with everyone else; so far, he had kept something of a distance from the rest of the group. As a matter of fact, he seemed somehow different today. Maybe it was illusion, but Danny would have sworn he was physically larger. He rejected that, but was still left with an impression of Bertie as changed in some way.

A little after eight, Eduardo and Maria came in and announced that if everyone was ready, they would all go as a group to El Teatro. Danny studied Maria carefully. He had seen little of her in the past few days, and she was still very much an enigma to him. A nagual, she had said. He still wasn't clear on the meaning of that, in spite of Eduardo's attempted explanations, still felt he needed to know more about her. But she had not done anything else to indicate that she was unusual, and so she had not occupied his thoughts much. Too much else had been happening.

Like children on a field trip for school, the group allowed Eduardo and Maria to herd them down the hill toward town. The servant girls, kitchen help, and the drivers tagged along a short distance behind. Apparently Eduardo had not been exaggerating when he said that the whole town was expected there for the ceremonies tonight.

When they reached the building, the doors were not yet open, and a large crowd had gathered out front. Orizaba, Patecatl, and Mayauel joined them; David behaved as if these people were old and dear friends. Danny had thought they were nothing more than casual acquaintances. He also noticed two striking people, a man and a woman, wearing full-length black robes with cowls; he had never seen them before. The general mass of villagers paid no more attention to them than they did to the three semi-nude women. Danny could not understand it; none of the women in the village dressed like that, yet they didn't seem to think there was anything unusual even in Kathryn's dress, which was largely nonexistent, or at least non-concealing.

At last the doors were opened, and the townspeople began an orderly migration inside. They were near the back of the crowd, but even from that distance, Danny could see festive colored lights and banners of various colors and designs inside. The building consisted of one large room, as would be necessary if everyone in town was going to crowd into it.

As it turned out, the place was so large it really wasn't going to be crowded at all. It was pentagonal in shape, the doors opening across one of the points. The sunken floor was made of fitted stones, arranged as a series of tiers leading down to a central pit area in many gradual, long steps, then rising abruptly to a stage on the far side of the room. This stage took up the entire wall across from the doors, and was backed by blue and white curtains running the full length of it. These, and the banners Danny had seen earlier, hung from the ceiling, which was quite high. Apparently there was a backstage area behind the curtains, since Danny could see people coming and going through it, attending to various chores evidently related to the evening's festivities. Five pillars held up the ceiling, arranged as four in a square with one in the center. Each of the pillars forming the square was painted a different color; blue, white, black, and red. These stood very close to the walls, perhaps three feet away. The center pillar was painted black at the bottom, red higher up.

Down in the pit, the floor was mosaic tile, obviously forming patterns, perhaps pictures, but Danny couldn't make out what any of them were. They were too large, and there were already too many people in the room.

The group of Americans found a place to themselves about a quarter of the way back from the stage, affording a good view of both it and the sunken floor area. Patecatl, Mayauel, and Orizaba joined them; Eduardo and the others from the resort seemed to have disappeared. They settled in to wait while people filed in, scattered themselves around the great hall. Their colorful clothing, and for that matter the colorful dress of the Americans, made quite a scene; Danny wished he had a camera. No one had one, he realized; that was most peculiar. But it was so trivial compared to the other oddities that he didn't really think about it very much.

At last it seemed as if everybody who was coming in was in, and the doors were swung shut. Then they were barred, which made Danny a little uncomfortable. But the bar was inside; perhaps it was just to keep out stragglers. Up at the front, he saw Eduardo standing center stage. He raised his arms, waving his hands for quiet, and the crowd became still.

He stopped waving his hands and held them in that position, his arms up and spread, for several minutes. He had obviously done a quick costume change after he'd left the group, because he now wore native sandals and a dark red robe, which fell a little below his knees. Gradually, he let his arms drop. The audience was silent, waiting for him.

Two men emerged from behind the curtains. One of them carried a pottery bowl full of water which he placed on Eduardo's left. The other carried a brazier, which he placed on Eduardo's right. These men were dressed only in loincloths, and their bodies appeared to have been oiled; they gleamed in the reddish light. After depositing their burdens, they retreated to a position behind Eduardo and stood with their arms crossed.

Eduardo lowered his head for a moment as if praying, then raised it, scanning the crowds. "The end of the sun is near," he said softly, solemnly. "It is time that Tlillan Tlapallan's king is restored to it. We have known this time approached!" he cried, suddenly and loudly. "And yea, some will hold dread in their hearts, as well they might! For like the flower in the field that dies before blooming, they will leave no seed. They will leave no seed." His voice faded down on this last. "But you must not despair, for the seed is in the earth. And even if not one flower blooms, the seed remains. It remains.

"For many years, we here have awaited this night. We wait no more. For our king is among us, though he does not know himself. We will show him who he is. And he will know, he will know.

"Let him then come, from the sky-blue land of waters,

"Let him then come, singing like the quetzal.

"Though our flowers die and our fires burn low,

"Our hearts are golden.

"Let him then come, that he may know this,

"Let him then come, the essence of jade.
"We do not despair,
"We look in the west, in the White Land.
"We do not despair,
"Our hearts are golden.
"Let him then come, multicolored like the quetzal,
"Let him then come, shining like the sun.
"Let him then come, the essence of jade."

Eduardo hung his head again for a few moments, then took a step back. He gestured across the audience, including everyone, and called for suggestions as to who the new king should be.

So it seemed to be a sort of election. But perhaps there was some prearranged person who would be named by acclamation; Danny waited to see.

"I name and suggest the man in the ocelot cap!" yelled Patecatl, jumping up and pointing at John, who looked totally surprised. Danny grinned; this king had to be a purely honorary ruler with no real powers.

"I name and suggest the man with the mirrored foot!" came a cry from the back. Danny turned and saw the black-robed man standing, pointing at Bertie.

"Are there others? Any others? Others?" cried Eduardo. "No? Then it will be so. Please, the two men named will come to the front!"

Bertie, solemnly, and John, with a shrug and an "I'll be a good sport" grin, got up and went to the stage, where they stood on either side of Eduardo. He snapped his fingers, and from behind the curtain two men emerged, each carrying a large pottery urn. Each urn had three legs and stood about two feet high; the top was flared and had a turned down collar of spikes. Near the base were vent holes. After an urn was placed in front of each nominee, each of the bearers took some balls of dark material from a bag and dropped them in. Eduardo stepped forward, touched the brazier; fire flared from it, though Danny could not see how it had been ignited. The attendants then lit small torches from it, and in turn lit the material in the urns.

As both torches were extinguished in the bowl of water, dark gray smoke began billowing from the two urns. After a few seconds Danny caught a whiff of an incense-like smell that

soon became overpowering. Both John and Bertie took a step
backward from their heavily smoking urns. Eduardo kept looking from one to the other, as if he expected something to happen. After a while, he produced a handful of green leafy
material; meticulously he divided it in half, threw half in each
of the smoking urns. A small burst of flame issued from each,
then more gray smoke. Danny caught another odor, that of
burning marijuana, and grinned. There was another smell,
barely detectable through the hemp odor and the incense; this
one was unfamiliar to him.

Suddenly, the smoke began to change. As Eduardo watched
it closely, the smoke from Bertie's urn became dark, finally
black; that from John's became lighter, turned white. Danny
thought of the method of selecting the pope; very similar. He
was sure, of course, that Eduardo had rigged it in John's favor,
slipping something into the handfuls of hemp leaves that would
cause the smokes to change as desired. Then it occurred to
him that he didn't know if it was in John's favor; here, black
could just as well be the favorable color.

"The decision is made!" Eduardo cried. "Our king is chosen!" He turned to Bertie. "It is decreed that you," he said,
gesturing to Bertie, "and all of you out there, shall subordinate
your wills to the wisdom of our king, the king of Tlillan Tlapallan!" With a flourish he turned to John and made an odd
gesture, a bow combined with a slight crouch. The entire audience, except for the little knot of Americans, stood as one
and made the same gesture. Up on the dais, John grinned,
obviously embarrassed; Bertie glowered at him and stalked off
the stage. It seemed he was taking the whole matter too seriously. After all, John wasn't a real king, Danny thought. It was
just an honorary title, possibly not even that; it might just be
a game to entertain the tourists.

The two men who had brought out the urns now took them
to opposite edges of the stage, where they continued to smoke
in black and white. Then they disappeared backstage, only to
return carrying a magnificently carved wooden throne, which
they placed center stage. Eduardo indicated to John that he
should sit in it, and he did so. Then, with much ceremony,
Eduardo presented him with a scepter, sickle shaped with seven
inlaid gems, and an odd little round cotton bag, which had a
cloth handle, an embroidered cross in the center, and four little

whisks of cloth attached to it, almost like arms and legs on a fat little body. The last item was a gorget made from a seashell cut crosswise; this Eduardo hung around John's neck.

"Behold our king!" Eduardo cried. He motioned, and John stood. The crowd erupted in wild cheering.

After the noise had subsided, a man came out of the crowd, mounted the steps and executed the crouching bow in front of John. He turned to the crowd and motioned for quiet.

"My lord!" he said to John. "We have for you your first decision as ruler!"

John grinned, obviously playing the role. "And what is that?" he asked.

"Those two!" The man pointed at the man and woman in the black robes. "What is your verdict and sentence on them?"

"What have they done?"

"Nothing yet, my lord! It is not what they have done, but what they are!"

"And what is that?"

"They are demons, my lord! Should not demons who come among the people, in the city, be put to death?"

John grinned again. "Have them come forth," he said loudly.

Without any urging, the two black-robed figures moved down through the crowd and stood at the base of the stage, looking up at John.

"Now," John said. "Are you two demons?"

"Yes, my lord," the woman answered. Danny glanced at Bertie; he was grinning his teeth.

"Well, at least you're honest demons!" John laughed. "Okay. Today only, we've got a general amnesty on demon executions. You're free to go. But stay out of trouble, all right? No scaring the kids and the old ladies."

"No, my lord," the woman said. They turned, walked back to their original place in the crowd. Their accuser shrugged his shoulders, went back to his place as well.

"Okay," John said. "New business? Old business? Good. I declare the official meeting over. Let's get on with whatever festivities are planned. A new corn ceremony, I understand?"

The crowd roared its approval. John got up from the throne and, getting no argument from Eduardo, returned to his friends.

"Very nicely done," Danny said. "You, sir, are a kindly and beneficent leader."

"Why, thank you, Danny, but look, bow and scrape a little, willya? After all, you're talking to royalty!" He laughed again. "I wonder what they would have done if I'd said, all right, burn 'em at the stake!"

"Doubtless built a fire," Danny said jokingly. "After all, you're the king, you know. Your word is the law."

"Well, it was fun, anyway."

The crowd seemed to be getting somewhat restless, but quieted down immediately when a group of people came out from behind the curtain carrying a wooden idol. Obviously the idol represented the corn goddess; she was depicted with a corncob necklace, a kind of a miter headdress, and curiously, the same kind of vest and skirt the American women were wearing. With great reverence, they sat the statue on the stage and left it. There followed a few moments of silence; the villagers seemed to be contemplating the idol. Eight more men now came from behind the curtains, moved to the sunken floor. They were beautifully costumed, green ponchos, yellow feather headdresses, red sandals, green and gold kilts. They took up positions at the edges of this area, as if they were guards.

Danny was beginning to have a little trouble focusing on what was going on. Smoke continued to pour out of the urns which remained on the stage, and although the room really wasn't getting smoky, Danny felt he might be getting a little high; the whole scene was taking on a sort of unreal character. He glanced at his companions; most of them looked a little dazed, especially Kathryn. He nudged her, asked in a whisper if she was all right. She nodded, but continued to watch raptly.

Another man, costumed like the others, came out leading a pretty teenage girl. Clearly she was an impersonator of the goddess whose wooden image stood on stage; her clothing and ornaments were identical to those on the carving. Her hair was tied up in the back, fastened around a bright green feather that bobbed when she walked. On her ankles she wore cuffs of bells, which tinkled with every step. This pair came to the center of the sunken floor, and with a gesture, the man presented her to the hushed audience. Then he moved away, leaving her alone. She turned like a dancer, lifted her face to the crowd; Danny could see it very clearly now. Out of the corner of his eye, he saw David sit up stiffly.

"What's the matter?" Danny whispered to him.

"That girl! Danny, I can't believe this!"

Susan leaned in to hear also, from David's other side. "What?" she asked.

"You're going to think I'm crazy, but that girl! Except that her hair is dark, that's Xilonen! Exactly! Xilonen from my childhood!"

While the girl remained posed in the middle of the sunken floor, five more men came out onto the stage, carrying a variety of musical instruments; drums, flutes, conch-shell trumpets, and others Danny didn't recognize. They took positions to the right of the brazier, and set up to play. Two of them started with drums, two with flutes, and one with a group of rattles. They were simply dressed; white kilts below their waists, nothing above. Each wore a cloth headband, the end loose and trailing down.

The music started with a series of sharp strikes on a tall drum with cutouts at the base; the sound was surprisingly loud and deep. The drummer then began to play a slow rhythm, predominated by a double strike, almost like the beating of a heart. After a few bars, he was joined by one of the flutists; this sound was startling, like a heavy wind coming up, rising and falling. A second drummer, playing a long thin drum carved like a snake, joined in; the lights began gradually dimming as they played. It was a fascinating picture, the colorful figures in a tableau on the floor, the drummers' arms working over the drums, glistening redly in the fading light.

The other two were swaying with the rhythm, but they'd not yet joined in. Four other men came from behind the curtain, each one carrying a banner on a pole. Arraying themselves behind the musicians, they moved the poles in time with the music so that the banners unfurled first to one side, then to the other. These banners were the same colors as the four outer columns, and each had a stylized design embroidered on it. The first was black, with a figure of a jaguar. The second, red, with a green and yellow picture of a growing plant, probably meant to be corn. The third, blue, with zigzag lines in red, yellow, and white, surrounded by many purple teardrops. And the last, white, with the familiar plumed serpent done in greens, reds, and yellows. This one was the most striking of all; as the man moved the pole, the serpent seemed to writhe in rhythm with the music. Even though it was highly abstract, there were times when it took on an appearance that recalled the snake Danny had seen coiled in his beer, back in New York. It seemed to him then that those events had taken place at least twenty years ago; they were actually dim in his memory. He rubbed his eyes and watched the banners, thinking he must be high from the cannabis. Not only was the serpent writhing, but the jaguar on the black banner was jumping like a playful kitten, the corn plant was growing, and the purple teardrops and zig-zags had transformed into realistic rain and lightning. He was fascinated, transfixed.

The drums increased their tempo slightly and became some-what louder as another flutist joined in; his small, ocarina-like instrument produced a light, high sound like the voice of a bird. Finally, the man with the rattles started to play. Then the tempo took a jump as the drummer playing the log drum, which sounded different pitches depending on where it was struck, seemed to take charge. Faster and faster he pushed it, finally breaking into a different rhythm, a two-count. The oth-ers followed, and a very contagious beat resulted. It was hard not to move to it.

Danny tore his eyes away from the spectacle and looked around at the audience. The other Americans all appeared to be as absorbed in it as he was, rocking back and forth or tapping their feet to the beat. The villagers were doing the same; many of them wore an almost ecstatic expression.

One of the musicians put his flute aside, and sounded a mournful tone on a conch-shell trumpet; he varied the pitch by putting his hand inside. The drummer playing the large drum stopped the double beat momentarily, went to single strikes, deep and resonant; the others continued as they had. The mu-sic was intensely evocative, almost hypnotic. Danny was taken by it again, watching the banners, the soft subtle movements of the musicians as they played. Down in the pit, the girl and the eight guards remained as they were, their bodies moving a little to the irresistible beat.

The man playing the conch shell sat down with yet another drum. With a little flourish evidently designed to call attention to himself, he began to play a complex counterpoint to the existing rhythm. Danny, who knew only a little music, could not tell if he was beating three against four or what, but the effect was unusual; the tempo hadn't increased, but it seemed so; the two rhythms intermeshed, wound in and out of each other, impossible to follow. The drummers' oiled bodies looked like they were perspiring heavily as their hands flew over the drums, making it all look so easy, so effortless. Again a double beat from the first drum predominated, an undercurrent to the contrapuntal drums. Danny was startled to notice that his own heartbeat was synchronous with the double beat. Momentarily confused, he wondered how the drummer had known his heartbeat; then he realized that the drums had pulled his heart into alignment with themselves.

The first drummer broke his rhythm and hit four strong, hard beats in a row, causing Danny's heart to jump. Down in the pit, the young girl made a sudden movement, throwing her arms straight up and thrusting her left leg forward, out of her split green skirt. She knelt on her right knee, brought her body and arms forward until her hands touched the floor. The drums returned to the original rhythm, and the girl rose slowly. She began to dance, moving around the pit area while the eight guardians remained in place.

At first her dance was languid, her movements understated and smooth. She glided around, sometimes running, incredibly graceful. Danny was very impressed, wondering how long she'd practiced for this. He glanced over at David, who watched her with a stony face. Danny had dismissed the idea that this could be the Xilonen of David's childhood—that was, after all, impossible—or even the girl he'd seen in New York. He chalked it up to the associations with the corn and a teenage girl. This, he assumed, made David—who was probably also a little high— see her as the same. But he did remember David's description of the beauty of Xilonen's dance, the morning he'd seen her in the green fields. He believed he might understand that a little better now.

The drums again increased their tempo, and the girl's dance became more frenetic. Danny was himself getting somewhat excited, and didn't know exactly why; then he realized his heart rate was still synchronized with the drums, and therefore speeded up.

He marveled at the dancer's grace and stamina as she executed a series of perfect leaps across the floor in front of them. He'd been to the ballet in New York, and this girl's dance seemed more graceful than many he'd seen there. He also realized he found it highly erotic, and chided himself for that; the girl was little more than a child.

She stopped moving around the pit and was dancing in place, right in front of them. He could see her face clearly. She didn't seem tired, she smiled up at them. No, that wasn't exactly right; she was paying attention only to David. Lifting her arms to him as if in supplication, she went down on her knees, leaped into the air, all the while looking at David, smiling at him. Danny glanced over; he was as if paralyzed, staring at her. But his eyes startled Danny. They were on fire, it seemed; burning holes in the dancing girl. He didn't even look like the David Danny had known; his intensity was overwhelming. Danny thought that if David had been like that when he met him—considering Danny's attitudes at the time—he would have been terrified of him. He looked like a volcano ready to erupt.

The girl down in the pit was executing some movements obviously meant to suggest the growing corn, kneeling repeatedly and rising slowly, spreading her arms. Still she watched David. Danny had a weird sensation that she wasn't representing a corn plant, she *was* a corn plant. She seemed to have leaves, roots. He had the oddest sensation that his mind was swaying. Not an idea that had ever occurred to him before. Almost frantically, he stuffed it down, regained a measure of control over himself. But the combined effects of the music, the spectacle, and the cannabis in the air were taking their toll. His control was on a fine edge, an edge he felt he could fall over at any time. He looked at David again and wondered if he was already over that edge. He looked so wild, so intimidating.

He was distracted from this by a general movement in the crowd. Many of the village women normally wore their long hair bundled up on the backs of their heads, and had appeared so tonight. As if on a silent signal, all those who did were now undoing it, letting it fall free. Those who didn't were running their hands through their hair, spreading it out. Danny looked around; every woman in the building except the dancing teenager had her hands in her hair. He was surprised to notice that Susan, Kathryn, and Evelyn did too. But he assumed they were just following suit; there was no way they could have known about this.

The music became wilder, more insistent. The girl moved around the perimeter of the floor again, leaping high into the air. Her smile was so contagious, Danny could not help smiling back each time he saw her face clearly. Finally she moved to the center of the floor, slowed as the music did, and knelt. She became still, only the green feather in her hair bobbing back and forth.

Four more men emerged from the back, carrying a litter which was piled high with produce of all kinds; corn, peppers, squash, and so on. The litter was a plain wooden platform built on two beams, the ends of which extended to accommodate carrying it. There were rails about three feet high on each of the long sides, like fence sections; the front and back were open. The bearers were dressed only in loincloths and sandals, and their bodies, like the others, were oiled. Walking slowly, they brought the litter to the front of the stage, put it down in front of the statue. One of them picked up the water bowl and took it offstage, while the other three unloaded about half of the produce, piling it on the stage. The fourth bearer returned, and they picked up the litter and carried it down to the floor of the pit, where the girl still knelt. They put the litter down right behind her and stood at the four corners; the girl didn't move. Through all this, the musicians continued to play on, at a somewhat less frantic tempo and a lower volume. Still, Danny found that his heartbeat remained in sync with them.

Three more costumed men came out; one wore a magnificently feathered headdress, supported by a gold framework like a tiara; his face was covered by a mask of beaten gold, depicting a bearded man. He wore long green and turquoise robes, which dragged on the floor as he walked. The other two wore robes of red and gray. They were not masked, but wore headdresses made of corn leaves and tassels. Both these men carried smoking censers, which they swung in front of them as they walked.

They came down into the pit area, approached the kneeling girl. The censer bearers waved their smoking pots over her while the masked man approached her, extending his hand. He led her back to the litter, helping her as she stepped lightly onto the pile of vegetables. When she was in the center, he lashed each of her wrists to the side rails with a leather thong; obviously symbolic, since it was very loose. For a moment, she stood there, holding on to the convenient rails, while the other two waved the censers in front of and behind her.

Picking up the litter, the bearers began carrying it around the pit area. Danny was a little surprised at how easily they did this; with the heavy wood, the food, and the young girl, the whole thing could scarcely have weighed less than five hundred pounds. Yet they picked it up lightly, hardly tipping it at all, and made a complete circle of the pit area, walking very slowly. Meanwhile, the three costumed men mounted the stage steps and waited.

Eventually the litter and its cargo were brought back around to where they stood. The bearers stopped and turned the litter in place, backing up so that the girl's head was on the same level as the masked man; she faced the audience, away from him. The two censer bearers were two steps higher, waving their pots about.

The masked man stepped forward, one foot on the litter, and pulled from his cloak a shiny black knife. Danny's stomach tightened; he heard a gasp from someone near him. Quicker than he could have reacted, the man swung the blade. Danny relaxed as he held up the green feather, still tied into a lock of hair that he had cut off. He thought that if this really was an ancient ceremony as Eduardo had claimed, this part might originally not have been so innocent as the cutting of a lock of hair.

With great dignity and ceremony, the masked man presented the lock of hair to the statue, loudly giving thanks for the new corn. The audience joined in, also offering thanks; not a few were crying real tears. Danny was experiencing feelings of unreality again; for a moment, he forgot they were in a building, had an impression that they were outside. The incense pouring from the censers was apparently adding yet another drug to the already heavy atmosphere. He fought for control of his senses, and succeeded, at least for the moment. He wondered how the others were doing with this problem.

The bearers picked up the litter again, with the girl still on it, and began another slow circuit of the sunken pit area. The people near the front cried thanks to her as she passed; she smiled at everyone, a bright, happy smile. When they had come all the way back around again, the bearers mounted the steps and put the litter down so that the girl was facing the audience. The masked man undid the leather thongs on her wrists, but she remained standing on the produce, holding on to the rails. Standing in front of the idol as she was, Danny noticed how closely she resembled it. Perhaps, he thought, some artisan had carved it expressly for this ceremony, using her as a model.

The music played on, the girl just stood there, and Danny's feeling of unreality kept increasing. Again, he had a fleeting impression that they were outside. These things were becoming more frequent as the evening went on, quick shifts of scene into some totally different place, but a place where the same ceremony was being conducted. He rubbed his eyes, but it didn't seem to help. He hoped the ritual would be over soon, and thought it might be, when the music abruptly stopped.

In silence, people from the crowd started trickling down toward the stage. A wooden tub was brought out, placed at the edge of the stage in front of the girl. Danny wondered how long she could stand there like that, delicately balanced so as not to crush any of the vegetables. Her face showed no signs of strain.

Although the costumed men remained at their stations, they made no effort to stop the orderly lines of villagers approaching the girl. At first, Danny could not see what they were doing; he shifted his position slightly for a better view. Although he could see now, he didn't understand what was happening. Each villager carried a little pouch, bottle, or box, and each dusted some flakes of a dark material into the tub, bowing in the curious crouching manner before and after they did so. The girl acknowledged each of them with an almost imperceptible nod. For what seemed like hours, this went on. Danny was unable to figure out what the dark flakes might be, and after a while he became somewhat bored. Again, when his mind was not totally on the ceremony, he realized that things were strange; he kept seeing sky above him, and the wooden idol in a stone shrine, a flat-topped pyramid visible behind it. Try as he might, he could not stop these images from reappearing, but he felt he was more in control when he concentrated on the ritual.

It was almost over; the last few people presented the offering, whatever it was, and finally the last one passed. The two costumed men again swung their censers around the girl, and she sat down amid the produce. The music started again, and people in the audience were laughing and joking, shuffling around. Danny thought it might be at an end, but when he looked back, the huge stone doors were still barred shut. The moon and stars above were very bright, visible in spite of the torchlight that illuminated the square in front of the pyramid, which loomed above the stone walls surrounding this ceremonial area.

It no longer occurred to Danny to question his environment. To him, everything was perfectly logical; they had come down to the ceremonial area in the square, in front of the Pyramid of the Sun, had been here since the ceremony called Hueitecuhilhuitl had begun. All was well with his world, and he was happy. New York, even the resort, seemed very far away, seemed more like a dream he couldn't quite remember. He leaned over to Kathryn, put his arm around her. She smiled up at him radiantly.

The four men who had been the litter bearers came carrying baskets of fruit, tortillas, and so on, and distributed them to the audience. Few people remained sitting; it had turned into a party of sorts. The music became light and happy, although Danny felt that the first drummer, who obviously set the pace, did not release his heartbeat from control. Little jugs of pulque, along with cups, also were set around, and the villagers were eating and drinking, obviously in a happy mood. But the resort guests held back, unsure of the propriety of joining the festivities.

Another set of eight men appeared from behind the curtain. They came down to the pit area, which was still fairly clear of onlookers, and began a dance. Their costumes approximated the symbols on the four banners that were still being waved up on the stage. Danny noticed these again, amazed at the stamina of the men who stood like German clockwork robots, waving and twisting those flags. On the floor, the dancers formed a ring on the floor, began a two-step circle dance, moving slowly in a clockwise direction. The music again became louder and faster, and the lighting dimmed just a little more. At intervals, one of the dancers dressed in the jaguar costume and one of the plumed serpents rushed to the center and fought a mock battle, carefully choreographed with the rhythm, using dummy weapons with cotton-edged blades. Alternately the jaguar or the plumed serpent did a ballet-like death scene, the other dancing a wild victory step; then both would rejoin the circle. The plant-men and the rain-men, who were eagle-feathered, never joined this. Danny felt like he understood this dance, its symbolic meaning, but somehow it remained just out of the reach of his mind. He didn't care, though. He looked up at the stars, the pyramid, and he was a happy man.

Some women from the first few rows moved into the pit area and joined the dance, the costumed men spreading out to make room for them. When the circle contained about twenty or so people, the original eight men who had taken positions around the perimeter of the pit area moved for the first time. They began a new dance in front of the stage, a line that moved back and forth in serpentine fashion; the men from the crowd rushed to join it, while the women now had formed a double ring, the outer moving opposite to the inner. The dances were very precise, the dancers light on their feet, as if they were hovering over the floor and touching it with their feet, rather than dancing. Spontaneously, a third, clockwise-turning ring formed; then a fourth, turning counterclockwise. It was an amazing display. Everyone danced the same, everyone totally intent on what they were doing.

The masked and costumed man who had helped the girl onto the litter approached the resort guests, cutting through the lines and rings of dancers without disturbing their patterns. He went to John, motioned for him to come along, and took him to the center of the innermost ring. He was left there, turning slowly and smiling at the rings of dancers, who periodically turned inward as if to pay him homage.

There were still large numbers of people who hadn't joined the dance, who continued eating, drinking, and celebrating. Danny noticed that Bertie seemed to have disappeared; he looked for him, but couldn't find him. It was difficult for him to orient himself; the bodies moving in lines and rings, the waving banners, created a mosaic of color and form that made it hard to focus on any one thing. Danny glanced at his companions and was amazed to see that only David and Kathryn remained; the rest of them had disappeared. He looked for them, and located Evelyn fairly quickly; she had joined the circle dance, moving as if she knew the steps exactly. Frank was in the serpentine lines, doing the same thing. As he looked, Danny caught sight of a couple of villagers on the floor behind the fourth ring. When he saw them again clearly, just for a moment, he could see that they were making love. He was astounded; right out here in public?

The moving rings shifted again, and he saw Mayauel. She had stripped to the waist, and Patecatl was milking her breasts into the little pulque cups, which were then being passed around. Danny watched this for a while; her breasts were rather small, and didn't look at all full, yet she kept filling cup after cup. A teenage boy ran up and took one of her nipples in his mouth. Patecatl let him suck it for a minute, then pushed him away, not roughly. Danny just watched the scene, feeling like his consciousness had fallen over a precipice.

Now there was Susan, strolling around between the first and second rings. A young couple, villagers, were sitting there, holding hands. She touched them on the shoulders, smiled, and walked on. As soon as she left them, they began kissing passionately, tearing at each other's clothes. Soon they too were making love on the floor. Susan, a quarter of the way around the ring, touched one of the men dancing. He immediately stopped and knelt in front of her. She walked over to a woman sitting alone on the stone steps, touched her and pointed to the man. The two of them rushed into each other's arms. Susan walked on, never looking back.

"What the hell is she doing?" Danny asked David. He didn't respond. He sat there like a stone statue, only his eyes alive; he had put on the ski-mask, and the eyes looking out of it were terrible in their intensity.

"David?" Danny said. "Are you all right?" Still he didn't answer.

A young woman from the village came up in front of David and knelt. "My lord," she said, her head down. "You will confer your blessings on us this night?"

Still he didn't speak, but he nodded, almost imperceptibly; to Danny's utter shock the woman untied the bottom of his leather costume, pushed it back to expose the lower half of his body, and began caressing his penis with her hand, then licking it. Soon he was fully erect, and she had him in her mouth.

"I don't believe I'm seeing this," Danny said, dazed.

"Kathryn, do you—" He glanced at her. She was watching intently and her own hand was on David's leg.

"Oh, yes," she said in a dreamy voice. "Yes, I do!"

Danny was speechless. He could only stare at her, at David and the woman. Another village woman ran up, and the two of them began to switch David's penis back and forth. A minute later, they were joined by a third.

He glanced back at Kathryn, and was again shocked; she had two fingers in her vagina and was actively masturbating. Someone handed him a cup of the pulque, or perhaps Mayauel's breast milk—he didn't know which—and he drank it quickly without thinking. Immediately he realized that had been a mistake. It hit him hard, whatever it was. The floor seemed to tilt up crazily, and he was unsure of whether the dancing rings were moving around him or if he were spinning. He could only see what was in front of his face; the three village women busily working over David, and Kathryn squirming and masturbating, stroking David's leg.

She turned to him. "Danny," she said in a rather breathless voice. "Take off your clothes, Danny. Hurry, I can't wait!"

"You mean here? Now? Kathryn, I mean, I know some of the—"

She gave him no opportunity to argue further, jumping up and tugging at his pants. He tried to resist, but it was useless; she had them off very quickly. He had serious doubts about his ability to perform under these circumstances, but she touched his penis lightly with her fingertips and he immediately began to grow erect. As soon as he was, she straddled him, and he felt himself slide into her. She began moving on him, as she pushed his shirt back over his shoulders.

Out of the corner of his eye, he saw David's body jerking in obvious orgasm. The village woman held him in her mouth for a moment, then carefully allowed his semen to drain from her mouth into a cup. The women executed a squatting bow to David, who seemed not to be aware of them; he still stared at the teenager who sat on the pile of produce, watching all this. Laughing and giggling, the women ran off, approaching other women as they went. Most of those immediately raised their dresses to their waists and smeared a drop or two from the cup on their abdomens. The three would then run on to the next woman. Finally Danny forgot about them, forgot about everything except Kathryn.

After what seemed like only seconds, he was climaxing inside her. She got off him; he could see his semen running down the inside of her thighs. He began to lose his erection, but she kissed his penis lightly, and instantly it started to come back up. Moments later, she was back on him and he was absorbed in her again. He had a vague thought that this was not possible, but at the moment it wasn't bothering him.

In front of him, past Kathryn's face, he could see the dancers; their faces were only a blur to him now, he couldn't focus. He climaxed again, Kathryn came off again. As before, she touched him lightly, with her fingers this time, and again he was erect, again she straddled him. The dance was faster, the music louder. Several more times he climaxed, and the process repeated; they continued their lovemaking. Kathryn's legs were now covered with semen, gallons of it, it seemed. It formed a white pool underneath them, slowly flowing down to the next level on the tiered floor. Danny didn't even think about how this was possible. The drums, the smoke, the spinning colors, had complete control over him now.

Kathryn pulled her upper body close to him, her head over his shoulder. He held her tightly, continued to move with her. She'd done this several times before; but this time he felt something touch his back. He pulled his head back and saw her lips wrapped around the penis of a village man who was standing behind him. A wave of jealousy flared up in him; he started to say something, but she turned her eyes to him, and they seemed to glow for a second. Suddenly, it didn't matter to him. The man climaxed, Danny watched her throat work, and the stranger disappeared into the swirling crowd. Danny himself climaxed, and she came off, touched him, got back on. He'd lost track of how many times. Another villager, a teenage boy, approached them, this time in his full view. She quickly took his penis in her mouth, and only seconds later he was jerking in orgasm. Danny couldn't understand why this seemed so proper to him, but after she'd given him that look, it did.

He saw Susan run by. She looked at them and smiled, continued on her way. Frank danced into their view, laughing his thunderous laugh. Danny could not recall ever, in his entire life, having felt like this. It was a wild, primitive, uninhibited moment, and he was fully part of it. If he had understood before what it entailed, he would have assumed it impossible for him.

Up on the stage, the four litter bearers had taken up positions alongside the girl, who was now standing again on the jumble of produce. The two censer bearers stood between her and the statue, the masked man in front. He held up his hand as if requesting silence, and the drummers hit four sharp blows. Abruptly the music stopped. Danny was only half aware of this at first. Kathryn was still bouncing on his lap; she seemed to be in a near trance, her eyelids and lips swollen, her breath coming in gasps. But the cessation of the music caught his attention. Assuming there was no chance of silence in the place, he turned his attention back to her and ignored the man.

But to his total amazement, the place did calm down. No one got up and got dressed, but all activity gradually ground to a halt, everyone looking at the stage. Even Kathryn slowed and stopped; she turned her head to look, Danny still erect and inside her.

All the costumed dancers moved to the steps leading up to the stage, and arrayed themselves in two lines across them, leaving a gap right in front of the girl. The censer bearers walked back and forth, waving their smoking pots over the girl and the statue. Her head was down; she seemed to be waiting for something. Two of the litter bearers took her gently by the arms, laying her down on her back across the pile of vegetables so that her head was facing the audience, hanging over the wooden tub that the dark material had been dusted into. Each of the bearers held an arm or leg, and with a flourish the masked man ripped away her miter, her necklace and vest, her skirt. The clothing came away so easily, it must have been designed to do that. She lay naked on the pile of vegetables, a full, rich smile on her face. And with no further preliminaries, the masked man began to saw at her throat with the obsidian knife he had previously used to cut her hair.

Blood began spurting into and around the tub, spotting the colorful costumes of the men. Danny was stunned, stricken; he couldn't believe it. He glanced around for the other Americans, saw Susan, John, Evelyn; all were staring at the stage with horrified eyes. No one seemed to be able to move. The villagers appeared to be in an emotional frenzy, but Danny could see no horror on their faces.

The man kept sawing; blood was gushing now, the blade sliding deeply into the girl's throat, her legs and arms jerking against the restraining hands. Danny could see her face; there was pain there, but no surprise, no terror. Her eyes rolled back in her head as the knife-wielder bore down hard, severing the bones. One more quick cut after that and her head came free. Carelessly tossing it onto the produce pile, he helped the others restrain her twitching body. From the stump of her neck, a red river continued to pour into the tub.

Kathryn turned back to Danny; tears were streaming down her face, and she buried it in his shoulder. He saw Susan drop to her knees, covering her face. David was up on his feet, moving like a strange robot toward the stage, calling out "Xilonen!" in a strangled voice. The men on the stage ignored all this. They picked up the tub and hurled the blood onto the statue and the produce around it. There was an enormous quantity of it; Danny could not believe how much. The body, still lying on the pile, continued to jerk spasmodically and drip onto the stage. The costumed men now turned their attention back to it; they quickly cut out the heart, then rolled the body over and began cutting down the center of the dead girl's back, starting at the stump of the neck.

John was the first to break out of his paralysis. He leapt forward, pointed to the stage and bellowed, "You will stop this!"

Instantly the men stopped what they were doing and looked at him. "But, my lord," said the one holding the knife, "the ceremony requires—"

"I don't care! This will stop, now! I, myself, in person, do decree and command that it shall be so!"

"But, my lord," the man on the stage said. "If we do not complete the ceremony, the crops may not—"

"The crops will be fine! But hear my words, my decree, my command. From this day forward there will be no human sacrifices in Tlillan Tlapallan! This poor girl shall be the last! I so decree!"

"Then what shall we sacrifice, my lord?"

John looked flustered. Danny watched him struggle with this, realized he was desperately improvising. "Butterflies!" he cried at last. "Henceforth, the sacrifice will be butterflies, and sea snails! Not humans. Not humans!"

"But, my lord," the man persisted, "will you then personally, yourself, in person, guarantee our crops?"

John managed to look imperious and frantic at the same time. "Yes!" he said finally. "I will!"

Uh-oh, Danny thought. If the crops aren't great and we're still here, we could all be in deep shit for this one.

"What shall we do with the—the—" the man on the stage was asking, gesturing at the now motionless body of the girl.

"Cremate it. Tomorrow, on the square, with the produce. So that all may know it is the last one, the last one in this city!"

"Yes, my lord," the man said, executing the squatting bow. They gathered up the body and head and placed it on the litter, still piled high with produce.

John turned and walked toward the doors. He gestured to the other guests, saying, "Let's go. Let's get out of here!"

Only then did Danny realize he still had no clothes on. He couldn't find them; they had disappeared somewhere in the general chaos of the wild orgy. But walking back to the resort without clothes seemed minor right now. He wanted to find a phone, call in some outside authority. Regardless of John's apparent control of the situation, the fact remained that they had all just witnessed a cruel, cold-blooded murder. And Danny did not intend to let that pass.

"We got to find a phone and call the police," David mumbled to him. Danny felt a bit of relief; at least he wasn't all alone on this. As they exited through the now-opened wooden doors and started back up the path to the resort, Eduardo and the other staff members followed them at a distance. Bertie was nowhere to be seen.

Back up at the resort, Danny hurriedly cleaned himself up, put on clean clothes, and went back down to find Eduardo. Kathryn remained in his room; she seemed to be in a state of shock. On his way down, he encountered David. Gone was the odd leather suit; David was dressed in sport shirt and slacks. They looked at each other; Danny knew their intent was the same.

They found Eduardo in the sitting room, sipping a cup of

tea. He didn't seem at all disturbed. John was already there, standing in front of him, glowering at him.

"No, John," Eduardo was saying. "I can assure you, after what you said, there will be no more human sacrifices, either in or out of your presence. Remember, you are now the king."

"You mean they take it that seriously?" he demanded.

"Oh, absolutely. Go down there, order that somebody be executed. No, I suppose you wouldn't do that. Order someone imprisoned. It will be done immediately."

"What I want immediately is a telephone," Danny interrupted. "To hell with all this king crap. There's been a murder, we all saw it. I don't give a shit if it's the custom here, that murderer is going to be brought to justice!"

Eduardo looked up at him, his calm unruffled. "I am so sorry, Mr. Hudson, but there is no outside telephone at the resort. In fact, there is only one single telephone in all of Tlillan Tlapallan."

"Well, where is it? We want to use it!" David said. He was still very agitated.

"The telephone is down at the store, where we stopped to fill the tanks on the way in. All conveniences of the outside world are funneled through the store there."

"Can you have a man drive us?"

"Surely, but it will do no good. The storm the other day— the telephone line is down. I understand it will be repaired, but I cannot say when."

"What about a radio? Shortwave?"

Eduardo made a helpless gesture. "There is none, at least that I am aware of."

"You mean we're totally isolated here?"

"Until either the telephone line is repaired or the plane returns, I am afraid so."

"When will that be?"

"Not for nine days. Your vacation was to be two weeks."

David fell silent, obviously fuming. He moved toward Eduardo as if he was going to attack him, but stopped himself. "Now look," he told the manager, "we can't just forget about this. There has been a murder! I assume you witnessed it too." Danny sat down in front of the still impassive man. "Regardless of how isolated this village is, these are modern times. You can't just go about killing innocent people like that!"

"Please, my friends, sit down," Eduardo said, gesturing to them. "You must forgive me if I do not understand what upsets you so. John has forbidden more sacrifices, and as I was telling him, that will, for all the villagers, end the matter. There will be no more. Why are you so insistent on calling in the authorities?"

"Because," Danny said, "none of that undoes the murder that happened. There must be some kind of justice!"

Eduardo touched his fingertips together, almost in an attitude of prayer. "Let me try to explain something to you, something of the way we think here. Perhaps it will set your minds more at ease."

"The only thing that will ease my mind is that murdering bastard on a gallows!" David snapped.

"Even that is possible," Eduardo said. "John, here, has only to command it, and it will be done. But will it serve the just cause you seek? I think not. Listen to me for a moment. You, all of you, are from the United States, a proud nation, in many ways a definition of what is modern. You see yourselves as moral leaders in the world, though your national morals shift from time to time. You expect countries like Mexico to emulate you. But here in Tlillan Tlapallan, we do not do that. Here, things remain as they were. Here, we follow a path with heart.

"None of this has upset you until tonight, when you witnessed a ceremony involving the sanctification and sacrifice of a young girl. Now, you have forgotten all you have learned about us. You see us as bloodthirsty savages. Am I not right? I can see by your faces that I am.

"You know that death is a natural thing, like eating, like sex. As you have seen, we have no shyness here about eating, and no shyness about sex, or the human body, either. The fact is, we have no shyness about any aspect of the natural world. Thus, there is no shyness about death. The death of this girl was not hidden; it was performed right in front of you. And you are offended; you wish to see your own definition of justice imposed. Doubtless if the Mexican authorities were to learn of this, attempts would be made to bring that about. It is quite certain that many innocents would be irreparably harmed were such an attempt to be made.

"But I stray. The point is this: in your United States, you

put people to death in the electric chair, by poison gas, by hanging, and by shooting them, is this not correct?''

"Yes, it is," said Danny. "But you are talking about convicted criminals, people who have themselves committed some inexcusable act, like murder. Not innocent girls!"

"How do you know the girl was innocent?" Eduardo asked. "I do not recall any one of you asking that question. As far as you know, could she not have murdered her parents with an axe?"

"Did she?" Danny asked.

"No. The fact is, you are right. She was an innocent. I am simply pointing out the fact that you jumped to this conclusion with no facts at all. In this case, you were correct; but many other conclusions of yours may be very wrong.

"Now consider what you have witnessed tonight. That young girl knew the full nature of the ceremony before she began her ritual impersonation of the goddess. She was not kept in a jail cell, nor tied to a post. If she had wanted, she could have left the village, not come to the hall, many things. But she knew that the ceremony was necessary to ensure the growth of the maize without which the village might well starve. Therefore she came, and the ceremony terminating in her death was carried through. This is the important point, my friends. She died for a reason: the well-being of her people. And when she died, she was full of their love. As those people presented her the offerings of their own dried blood, each called her daughter, told her how proud they were of her, how much they loved her. Her death was not a waste, not in vain. She is, and shall remain, sanctified in our hearts, sanctified in Tlillan Tlapallan. We call this a 'flowery death.' The people in the United States waste human lives. We do not. We strive to make each person's life, and death, meaningful.''

"All these are simply justifications, excuses!" David snapped. "You may have brainwashed that girl into going to her death to satisfy some stupid, primitive superstition, but that doesn't make it right!"

Eduardo regarded him with an expression like amazement. "How can you, after the experiences you have had, dismiss these things as stupid superstitions? Didn't you once make your own crops grow with the blood of your own self-sacrifice? Your father worshipped a god whose son was reputed to have died in self-sacrifice, yet you can still say 'superstition'? Remarkable. Just remarkable.

"There is another point. You have lived in a country that has pursued a scientific technology that has already allowed some of your people to randomly destroy thousands of human lives from a distance, just by pressing a button. None of the people so destroyed even knew they were going to be, much less agreed to it. But this science destroys all in its path; your enemies, and hundreds if not thousands of innocents as well. How many young girls like that do you suppose were in Hiroshima? Nagasaki? Did it matter? Did their utterly involuntary sacrifice accomplish any lasting good? Did it end your global wars, and the threats of another, even worse, that may come? Here we are talking about one girl, who knew what she was doing and did it for the love of the people. Where is your sense of proportion?"

The three men fell silent. Danny felt he was being had, but he could not find an effective argument to counter what Eduardo had said. Worse, he could think of many other examples in his society where life was taken cheaply and meaninglessly. And it had been more than obvious already that the people here held each other, as well as the strangers, in high regard. His outrage was not silenced, but his logic was; he had no good answers. Apparently, from the frustrated looks on their faces, neither did David or John. Shoulders down, they all simultaneously got up to leave the room. Danny felt terribly defeated.

"John, there is another matter to discuss," Eduardo said.

"What's that?" he asked, his voice sounding very tired.

"Tomorrow, you must go to the fields. It is expected. You have taken personal responsibility for the well-being of the crops. Will you discharge your responsibility?"

"Yes," John said. "I'll tour the fields tomorrow, okay?"

"One last thing. Your friend here," he indicated David, "has said that he wishes to see the killer of the young girl hanged. If that is your wish, you have but to command it. It will be done."

"Who was the killer?" John asked. "The man in the mask?"

"I was." He looked at John unwaveringly.

"I'll have to think about it," John said. He looked at David and Danny, both of whom seemed to have no ready answers anymore. "Right now," John continued, "I'm very tired."

Danny realized that he too was utterly exhausted, drained. The three men trudged up the stairs like laborers returning from hard work. When Danny reached his room, Kathryn was already asleep. He didn't really even remember lying down beside her.

23

John spent a restless night, haunted by the image of the girl being killed on the stage. Every time he started to fall asleep, he saw the blade digging into her throat, her valiant attempt to smile in spite of the pain. When daybreak came, he had every intention of remaining in bed until at least noon. But only moments after daylight had flooded into the room, there was a persistent pounding at the door. He tried to ignore it, but it quickly became obvious that whoever it was wasn't going to go away. He got up reluctantly, opened the door; it was Eduardo.

"It is light," he said. "We must go to the fields. There is much to be done today."

"I don't suppose we can do it later?"

"It is expected of you. Please dress appropriately. I will wait."

Closing the door with a sigh, John dragged himself into the shower. As he dressed, his mind was still in a fog; he was only half aware of what he was doing. He put on his sandals, vest, occlot hat, and the cut seashell pendant, the wind jewel. He also donned a loincloth and kilt; it didn't occur to him to wonder where they'd come from. Carrying his scepter and the cotton incense bag, he went out to meet Eduardo.

As they entered the village, they were met by a group of young men Eduardo identified as John's acolytes. These silent, serious youths fell in behind him as they headed for the fields, going first to the area west of the village. Here, the crop was primarily corn. He walked among the plants, touching the broad green leaves, the silks like blond hair on the ripening ears. It looked to him like a very good crop indeed. John hoped there would be no problems with this, at least for the duration of their stay.

The farmer who tended this field came up to him, executed a squat, and told him that while the crop was good, it would be well for the villagers if the individual ears of corn could be larger. John's first thought was that the man was being excessively greedy, that he just wanted a better price for his produce; but he looked into the man's clear dark eyes and knew this was not true.

"You must fertilize this field with the juice of the thorny grasses," he said, startling himself. "If you do that, and your intentions are for the well-being of the people, it will be as you wish it."

The farmer smiled, nodded; he executed the squatting bow again and went off, probably to collect the grasses. John watched him go, wondering why he had said that. He had no idea what the properties of the fertilizer he had specified were; he hoped it wouldn't act as an herbicide. But somehow he couldn't be worried about it; he just had a strong impression that it would be all right.

The next field he was led to was tended by an older man who grew cotton. He met John at the edge of the field, and began to describe his farming methods. Again, the fields looked good to him; he made a mental note to ask David to take a tour through here, indicate any problem areas. He was annoyed with himself for not doing that in the first place; this was David's area of expertise, not his. And it was important that if these people were to continue to forego human sacrifices, their crops do well in the absence of them. Right now, it was a little more nebulous; the sacrifice had been made, but the ritual interrupted before its conclusion. He was afraid that any setbacks in local agriculture would be seen as a sign that he was wrong; perhaps they would even depose him. Knowing what was often done with deposed kings in early European cultures, he didn't want to risk that. Not just for himself; he felt there might be a risk to all of them. These people were gentle and friendly, but it was obvious that they had a strength, a determination of purpose, that might lead them to do almost anything if they believed it was in the best interest of the village. He didn't want to see how far that might lead them.

The cotton farmer was explaining his problems, showing John a ball of the pure white fiber; his wife and daughters spun it into thread, dyed it for cloth. But much time, he explained, was spent in the gathering of the various materials to make the dyes, and it was not a safe procedure; his own mother had died from accidently inhaling the fumes from one of the dyes.

John thought about this for a moment, then began to talk. He had meant to outline safety procedures for the handling of the toxic dye materials; instead, he found himself describing a complex procedure involving the use of Murex snails from the sea, extracting their natural purple dye and mixing it with the maguey's honey; the ratio, he was saying, would determine the color. This was not, however, to be used as a dye, but rather as a soil treatment. Once a section of soil was so treated, the cotton planted there would grow in colors!

The farmer squatted, thanked him profusely, and told him he'd prepare for a collecting trip to the ocean immediately. As he went away, John was really concerned. Not only had he never heard of any such procedure, but as far as he knew, there was no way it could work; cotton did not, could not, grow in colors. He decided he'd better start making some other plans, like how they were going to deal with it when these things failed. Even if they all left safely, his teachings would be discredited and the sacrifices would start all over again. It was very important to him that that not happen. He promised himself he would make no more such pronouncements; this one alone would doubtlessly cause enough problems.

Yet in spite of this, he did make more pronouncements, many of them.

24

Up at the old church, Bertie paced back and forth, trying to sort out his feelings. Ihuimecatl and Toltecatl sat on the ancient stone steps, as still and silent as if they were a part of the stone. He had been up all night. The sacrifice had not, of course, particularly disturbed him; in fact, it had seemed appropriate under the circumstances, a fitting climax to the ceremony. What he was upset about was the naming of John as the king, even though he believed this to be ridiculous. He held the populace of the city and his fellow Americans responsible in some odd way, even though the naming had been done purely by Eduardo, or possibly by the two men who brought out the urns; obviously they had put something in there to cause the smoke to turn color. Still, he felt a strange urge to take vengeance on the villagers.

Worse, when he had suggested to Ihuimecatl that they repeat the daybreak ceremony they had performed on the pyramid yesterday, the creature had informed him that it was quite impossible, since the king had now forbidden it. He had raged at them, finally saying that he would do it himself, alone; but he realized that for some reason, he simply couldn't. He felt shackled; as long as John was the king, and the prohibition therefore in effect, he was bound at least by the letter of the edict. He could not for the life of him understand why that was so, but it was.

"I could kill him," Bertie said aloud, as much to himself as to the cloaked monsters. "That would solve everything."

"Yes, it would," Toltecatl told him. "If you can. But I suspect you would be prevented. He is never alone now, and the others have their means as well. But this has happened in the past, and if you succeed, then of course you would be the king. You could set your own laws and edicts."

"You mean there have been other kings of the village?" He felt stupid having asked that question. Of course, there must have been. He was interested in the fate of the last king, and asked Toltecatl about it.

"It is a story indeed, my lord," the creature said. His manner became oddly formal. "You would hear it now?"

"Yes. Why not? What the hell else have I got to do?"

"Yes, my lord. The last king to rule here ruled in the days of the conquest."

"The Spanish conquest?"

"Yes."

"You mean to tell me that John Goss is the first king named here since the fucking conquest? I can't believe that!"

"But, nevertheless, it is true. Listen, I will tell you, for we were here. We were witnesses."

Bertie sat cross-legged on the ground and listened to the creature talk.

"The king in those days was the Hummingbird from the Left, a proud and honorable man. If he were alive today, I am sure you and he would have been friends. For many years he had reigned here, the city was proud, sitting out in the sun, not like you see it today, hidden. These two pyramids, ah, they were sights to behold then! This one, black and gleaming, so black it looked like a hole turned upside-down. The other red, as if blood-soaked. And blood-soaked they were, every day. There were many villages about, and the sacrifices were plentiful. Willingly and gladly they came here! Their hearts were eaten, and the Hummingbird waxed mighty. Men, women, children, all mounted these steps, looked their last at the world, and entered the World of Flowers. They were happy as they died for the glory and power of the Hummingbird, and the living villagers were happy, as was the Hummingbird. Ah, he was a sight to behold then, all decked in blue feathers! Truly a magnificent man. Truly. As we are your allies today, we were his then. We delivered the sanctified souls to the Flowery Land for him, collected their power, and delivered the power to the Hummingbird. We would have done the same for you if the edict had not been enunciated last night.

"Then came word that the strange ones, the Spaniards, were on the coast. That year, like this year, was Ce Acatl, the year of prophecy, and the Hummingbird knew it. Soon after this word came, a message from his disciple also came, asking for his help and blessing. This disciple, his name you know. He was Moctezuma, king of the great Aztec nation. But the Hummingbird had known of their arrival, had sent warnings to Moctezuma. When the message came, he stood atop the pyramid and cried, in a woman's voice, 'O my sons! We are lost! Where can I take you?' He sent a bird and some men, strange men, to Moctezuma so he would understand. He would send no help. Their day was done. So the Hummingbird sat on top of the Pyramid of the Black and stared into the distance while his godchildren, the mighty Aztecs, died deaths most foul at the hands of the Spaniards.

"Then it was over, the great city of Tenochtitlan leveled and cast into Lake Texcoco. And the Spaniards spread out. More calls for help came, but the Hummingbird was seized with a paralysis, a fever. He could do nothing. His mighty Eagle Knights exercised in the courtyard below. In battle, one of them could have killed a thousand Spaniards, yet they did nothing but exercise. A word from the Hummingbird would have sent them on their way, but the year was Ce Acatl, and he said not the word. The Maya fell, and the Inca in Peru, and Tlillan Tlapallan still sat in the sun, isolated, waiting for a word from the Hummingbird. He never spoke it, he could not, for the year of their coming was Ce Acatl.

"Then, at last, they came here, to Tlillan Tlapallan itself. The day they came, a dark day, never to be forgotten. Down that road they marched, riding their horses, carrying with them the stench of useless death and decay. Gold was what they sought, and gold they would find here. Even as they marched into the city, the Eagle Knights waited on the pyramid where the Hummingbird sat in his chair. They awaited his word to fall on the invaders and kill them all, a most easy task. We stood beside him, waiting, but waiting in vain. The Hummingbird grew thin and weak, and he spoke not. Down in the streets, the Spaniards slaughtered the men, raped the women, and the Eagle Knights were ready, yet they could not move, not without a word from the Hummingbird. But they had come in the year Ce Acatl, and he could not speak it. So the slaughter went on. Ah, the waste, the tragedy! The precious blood of human life running free in the streets, unwanted, trampled by those crude, uncaring men!

"Finally they came up here, to where we sit at this moment. The Eagle Knights were assembled here, waiting for the word if it should come, which it did not. The Spaniards fell upon them and slew them all. They offered no resistance. All that was left was us, and the Hummingbird. We are not knights, and it was not required of us to stand and die. So we did not. When the word did not come, we changed into bats and flew away. This so terrified the Spaniards that they quit the pyramid, and did not return again that day. The Hummingbird never made a sound. He looked very old, very frail. His people no longer nourished him, and he required that. He was wasting away.

"The next day, with their priest leading them, they mounted the pyramid again. The priest was crying commands addressed to us, meant to scare us away. But we just watched as they approached the Hummingbird, who still sat in his chair. They could see him only from the back as they approached. When they walked around the front and looked, they saw the Hummingbird's fine blue feather cloak draped on a dried skeleton, wisps of gray hair clinging to the skull. During the night, he had aged beyond all reason and had died. A tragedy! Incomprehensible, unbelievable! He was so very young, so much younger than many of the others, a recent arrival, a mere babe. How far he had fallen, how his might had faded! Once he had been invincible, but that was before the year Ce Acatl.

"And even in death he received no respect! They pushed him off his throne, over the edge of the pyramid, just as they had done with his image in Tenochtitlan. Picked him up by his feet and toppled him headfirst. He and his weapons rolled on the floor of the square.

"If those were the black days, then they were to get even blacker. The Spaniards tried to throw down the temples atop these pyramids, and they succeeded with the Pyramid of the Red; the temple fell into the forest and its pieces now lie buried there. But at the Temple of the Black, which the Hummingbird had claimed for his own, the great columns would not fall. So they conscripted all the men and women they could find to change the great Black Temple into a church to their own god of war. In our bat-forms, we watched them as they forced the people to work, day and night on end. Many dropped from exhaustion and died where they laid. Others committed suicide. Those women who had children in those days suffocated them as soon as they were born. But from the blood and sweat of the people, the great spire you see above us was raised, the columns were covered with clay, the stone pews carved. The huge temple was transformed into this huge church.

"More Spaniards came, and with them plagues and poxes, and the people died in even greater numbers. There were nights when the sea was full of bodies. The smell of death hung over everything. But we watched, and we waited. We knew that even though the Hummingbird might be dead, there were other, older forces, which would not long allow this abomination, this temple to a strange god, to stand on the sacred Black Pyramid. But we wondered, for soon there might be no people left, and without people, how can a city stand?

"Even more of the Europeans came, built houses upon the plain, and climbed up here to pay homage to their god. Then they went down and wasted more of the people's lives. We lived in the steeple, hanging upside down by day, flying at night. We could not, on our own, kill more of them than we needed for food. For we are allies, not movers. It is not for us to make those decisions. So we could do no more than wait, and wonder if perhaps we should also take our own lives, for the city was dying. Only a few of the people remained, only a few of the thousands!

"Then, when it looked like all was lost, the Old One of the Fire arose from the heart of the Pyramid of the Red. The Spaniards thought the pyramids were solid; they had not discovered the concealed entrances. But on that day, the priest of the church had found the entrance to the Black Pyramid, the one under the trapdoor. He had brought workers to open it. We knew the sacrilege was then too great, and that is why the Old One of the Fire arose from his sleep.

"He walked between the pyramids on the street down there in the night, and we flew to him. We did not test him, we knew he was the Old One, long honored, long known. He wore a cloak of dark red, and his face was terrible to behold. We flew above him as he walked up the side of the Pyramid of the Black. The next day was a Sunday. We were eager in our anticipation, knowing the Spaniards would gather in the church and pay homage to their god.

"At night we three entered the church. He told us that the

next day, when the Spaniards were all in the church, he would appear to them. We were to allow only one person to escape alive, to bear the message. For us, the night was very long. We had purpose again, we had the word! We could fall upon them and kill them.

"Next day, they all climbed up the side of the Pyramid and entered the church. We watched from the rafters. We knew we could catch as many of them as we wished before they could quit the pyramid. When they were all in their places, their priest began the mass as he did every Sunday. We could see their faces. None of them thought anything was amiss. They were blind, arrogant fools! And that was the day they were going to learn what fools they were.

"The Old One of the Fire had already killed their priest and assumed his form, but none of them could see that. So as they sat awaiting their priest's words, he transformed into the image of their own Satan, just as they would have expected to see him! They were such fools, we laughed and laughed. They all began to scream and tried to run away. But he caused their flesh to catch fire and burn. Only a few, fifteen or so, managed to get out of the church unburnt. Others came out flaming. Human torches were all over the pyramid, rolling down the sides. We were a little sorrowful that there were so few left. But as instructed, we fell upon them in our bat forms and tore away their throats. Finally there was but one remaining, a girl of tender years. She ran to her house, but we followed and caught her. For a moment we feared she might die of fright, so I went outside and transformed myself into a man, came back in as if to save her. Ihuimecatl flew away as if in fear. It was a poor charade, but it worked. The girl did not die. We brought her before the Old One of the Fire, who now had taken on the form of a kindly old man. He put her on a horse and told her to carry the message to the next town, that the Spaniards should never again set foot in this area. Their day was done.

"But the Spaniards did not listen to the girl's words of wisdom. We made sure she safely reached the town, taking several forms to do so. But they came again, a whole army of them, with black-robed priests. They were intent on a confrontation with their devil. They brought the girl with them. They had tortured her, believing her to be a witch, and she was near

death, but they forced her along, demanding that she call up
the demons that she had previously talked to. The Old One of
the Fire bade us retrieve her, not killing any more of them than
necessary to do it, and bring her to him. We looked into their
minds. I took the form of a dragon therefrom, and I attacked
them from the air. They scattered in blind fear, and I picked
the girl up and flew her up to the church here, where the Old
One was. This time there was no risk of her dying of fear
alone. Her sufferings at the hands of the inquisitors had tough-
ened her spirit, though her body was very weak. The Old One
healed her, and we all waited for their priests and soldiers to
mount the pyramid, as we knew they would do. In my dragon
form, I sat near the edge where they could see me. Their courage could not be faulted; they came to the attack! The Old One
remained with me at the top, and Ihuimecatl in the form of a
giant bear with saber claws circled behind to ensure none would
escape. Up the side they came, their priests shouting commands, soldiers waving swords and firing their guns. The Old
One, again in the form of their Satan, appeared to them, and
caused them to burn. They wavered in their courage and went
to flight. I myself killed nearly half before they could get off
the pyramid. Ihuimecatl caught the rest down on the road. We
left not one living.

    "The Old One told the girl she had done well, and asked
her what she would do. She told him that she would stay with
us, since she was thought accursed by her own people. We
were surprised then. We thought the Old One would just send
her to live with the remaining people, but he did not. He made
her his personal companion and took her down into the Pyramid of the Red. We stayed above for many years to watch for
more attacks by the Spaniards, and there were several. But
eventually they stopped sending soldiers. After all, none ever
returned.

    "The city had been almost emptied of people. There were
barely a hundred left of the thousands, but left to themselves,
they prospered, and soon their numbers began to build. When
they were strong enough, we ourselves went into the Red Pyramid, where we became its guardians. For centuries, we remained down there, and there was no disturbance. We can
sense such things. Then, only two hundred years ago, outsiders
again discovered the village. Again we surfaced. These people

were not the same, but they bore the same threat to the city as the Spaniards had. We came to them in the night, after letting them see us carrying lights in the old church. We killed several. The remainder went back with tales of a haunted church in a cursed village. Again we had to stay up, because they kept coming, and we kept killing them. Then there was another long period when we stayed underground. The people covered the pyramids with earth, planted trees on them, so that seen from a distance they looked like hills. Still, the village is sometimes seen by sailors passing by on the seas, sometimes from airplanes. But any outsider, anyone who does not belong here who comes, sees lights in the church by night. If he does not heed that warning and go, then we kill him. The city remains undisturbed.''

"But what about us?" Bertie asked. "How do we fit in? Aren't we intruders too? If all you say is true, then why were Eduardo's bosses allowed to build the resort here?''

"Eduardo is from here. He has no bosses. As to the resort, and the presence of the seven, that is different. Nothing like it has happened since the Hummingbird from the Left died.''

Bertie counted mentally. "But there are eight of us.''

Toltecatl regarded him steadily. "Yes, there are. One extra. It is interesting, yes? We do not understand this ourselves. But then, we do not have to. We are no longer under the commands of the Old One of the Fire. Now we are yours.''

"This extra one. Which of us?''

"It is not for me to say. I should think it would be obvious to you by now.''

Bertie pressed the creature a little, but he'd already learned the futility of that. So he asked them a different question. "This transfer of allegiance you referred to; that means you no longer follow the instructions of this Old One, right?''

"Yes, just so. Now we follow you. Your instructions.''

"So you would not attack strangers who found their way in here?''

"Not unless you told us to.''

"And the extra person in our group. What about him? Or her?''

"He was warned, and he did not leave. Possibly he didn't understand the warning, but that is no concern of ours. We would have killed him, but you came to us and defeated me in fair combat first. So we did not. And will not, unless you tell us to.''

Bertie considered all this. Best to leave the status quo until he had all the facts. He didn't consider it outside the realm of possibility that he himself was the extra person who had missed a warning. If he told Ihuimecatl and Toltecatl to go ahead and kill the person, they might immediately leap on him.

''All right,'' he said at length. ''These are my instructions: don't kill this extra person. Let's wait and see. As for other outsiders who might wander in here, what I want you to do is try to scare the shit out of them, scare them away. The bat forms you mentioned, maybe. If they don't scare, then kill them.''

25

When Susan opened her eyes, she saw David sitting up in the bed, staring out the window. She touched his arm, stretched. ''Oh, God, David, I had the most horrible dream—'' she started to say.

He looked around at her with haunted eyes. He didn't have to say anything; she realized it had not been a dream. They had actually witnessed a young girl's murder by decapitation. She struggled to control herself, but her eyes filled up.

''Oh, that poor girl!'' she cried. David held her for a long time. Finally she pulled back, looked him in the eyes; she could see how upset he was. Last night had been a totally outlandish experience in virtually every way. ''Mexico,'' she said. ''Always Mexico. This country has a curse on it, David. I never would have come if I'd known we were coming here. Always blood and death. We need to leave. Today, if possible.''

He shook his head. ''We talked to Eduardo last night,'' he said. ''We can't leave. Unless we want to take a Land-Rover and head across the countryside. The only phone is out, there is no radio, and the plane won't come back for nine more days."

"You mean we're stuck here?"

"I'm afraid so. Unless they fix the phone line sooner. In Mexico, I understand, that isn't likely."

"No, they never fix anything here. That phone might be down for years. David, I don't know if I can stand it! There may be more ceremonies, more sacrifices."

"Eduardo assures us not. Apparently they take that king business seriously. John ordered no more sacrifices, so according to Eduardo, there won't be. But you heard him take personal responsibility for the crops. I sure as hell hope nothing goes wrong in the next nine days, at least. As soon as I can find John, I'm going to go out and look over those fields. You know I have a talent there. Maybe I can put it to good use."

"Yes. That's good." Her words faltered and she fell back across the bed, crying bitterly. Again David held her, tried to console her. She appreciated it, but she knew it was impossible for him to understand.

"Mexico!" she screamed, pounding on the bed. "I should have known, should have known—"

She realized David was looking at her strangely. "What is this, Susan?" he asked her, not unkindly. "I remember, you said when we first got here you'd been in Mexico before, and I meant to ask you about that. Did something happen to you here? Something bad?"

She'd said too much. Ever since she'd seen those photos in Jerry Maxwell's office, this had been rolling around in the back of her mind. She didn't want to face it, didn't want to remember, certainly didn't want to talk to David or anyone else about it. But there just didn't seem to be any escape from it. The pictures, ending up in Mexico again, the purification rituals with the maguey thorns; her sore nipples and ears would not let her forget about those! Now, last night, the sacrifice of the girl. There was no longer any way to stop thinking about her previous trip to this country, a time she wanted to forget but couldn't.

"Susan?" David was asking, "What is it?"

"There are some things I suppose I should have told you about a long time ago," she began. "But I wanted to pretend

it hadn't happened. I guess I should have told you and Danny
the same night that you told us about the death of your parents,
but it didn't seem relevant, you know? Now, it's too late. We're
stuck here. I don't know, maybe it has nothing to do with
anything. But for me, Mexico is, and always will be, associated
with blood, knives, violence, and death. Even more so now. I
never want to see this country again, never!"

"Tell me about it, Susan," David coaxed. "I know you're
upset about last night, but—"

She looked up at him, her eyes tortured. "I know people
die, David. I know they get killed, sometimes horribly. I just
don't usually have to see it right in front of me. Only in Mexico. Only here.

"You remember what I told you about my high school days,
my family life? And how when I got to college I kind of went
wild for a while? Well, it has to do with all that. I only told
you a part of it, the better parts."

"I remember all those parts as being damn sexy, Susan. No
violence, nothing like that."

"Of course. Because I didn't tell you about the trip to Mexico. David, that was the worst time of my life. Worse than last
night. That was just a reminder of it, that's all. There's no way
you can understand until I tell you the whole story. After that,
if you want to leave, and have nothing further to do with me,
I'll understand. The only conclusion I've ever been able to
draw about that time was that I was insane, or perverted, or
both. It was horrible, horrible. I never thought I would tell
anyone about it after it was over."

"Susan, I love you," David said. "Why are you always
saying things like that? Even without hearing it, I assure you
it won't have any effect on the way I feel about you."

"I love you too, David, but—"

"No buts. Tell me about it. Now. I want to know."

She took a deep breath. Here was a moment she'd dreaded
for years, having to tell David this story. It couldn't be dodged
any longer; might as well get it over with. But she knew it
wasn't going to be pleasant, knew the memories were going to
come back full force.

"I guess it started when my friend Janey Stuart and I decided to make a trip to Mexico. We saved up our money for
spring break. We'd planned to make several stops, but we went

to Mexico City first, and as it turned out, last. Last stop for us.

"So there we were in Mexico City, which is a crowded, dirty place, but can be really beautiful, too. It depends on where you look, you know? We were classic tourists, running around to all the shops, carrying our cameras, taking pictures of everything. Later, I destroyed all those pictures. I didn't want to remember that trip at all. But then, we wanted to take in all the sights. Neither one of us had ever been outside the U.S. before. We spoke only a kind of a pidgin Spanish, but we got along. It was turning into such a great trip. We weren't sick or anything, which we'd been warned about. Everything was great.

"Then we decided we'd have to see a bullfight while we were there. You have no idea how much I regretted that simple little decision. Worse, it was my idea. Let's experience everything, you know? Go check it out, what can it hurt? Oh, I know, I didn't like the concept of a bullfight either, a helpless animal being killed by a swordsman. But it's part of the culture. Just like last night, I guess. No real difference, except the bullfight doesn't always turn out like everybody expects it to.

"So there we are in the bullring, and they let a bull out. At first he didn't seem aggressive at all. He was just running around the ring like he was looking for a way out. And well, I guess you know how it goes. The picadors ride their horses up and stick these spears—I forget what they're called—in its shoulders. The first time one of them did that, the bull just kind of jumped and ran away, you know? But the next time, he turned and charged the horse. The horse and rider both went down, but the man got up and ran away safely, while the bull gored the horse. Well, I can tell you, we weren't prepared for that. We'd expected a thing of beauty, even if the bull did get killed, but there was nothing beautiful about the bull goring this poor old horse to death, which is just what happened. And people were cheering! We couldn't believe it. What kind of person cheers when some helpless animal is being killed? We thought we were going to be sick, you know?

"Then another picador went after the bull, but that horse didn't get killed. The bull was busy chasing these other people out there in the arena—chulos, they call them—and just never went after the horse. After that, the banderilleros came out, they were sticking these darts into the bull, who was chasing them all over. Sometimes they stuck in a dart with a firecracker attached, and it exploded right on the bull's skin. I was really feeling sorry for the animal, and Janey was crying, but we were determined to stay, just so we could say we'd seen the whole thing.

"Finally the matador came out, and I thought, we can watch a few of those passes with the cape like you see in the movies, and then he'll put the poor animal out of its misery. In that sense, he was like a hero, where the picadors and banderilleros were like cowards. Oh, I know it takes courage to face the bull, but the poor thing didn't know what was going on. And they were tormenting it so.

"So the matador was making his passes, and he was very good, too, very graceful, like a dancer. I remember thinking that this would have been better if they just did this a few dozen times. No deaths, no blood. I could smell the blood from the dead horse, and it was making me feel funny. But anyway, the matador is making his passes, and finally he gets his sword out and gets ready for the coup de grace. He waved his cape, and the bull charged, and he was getting ready to step aside. I was rooting for the bull. And the matador seemed to slip in the sawdust, so that he didn't step back as far as he wanted to. The bull's horn caught his arm and just ripped it wide open. The sword went flying across the arena, the cape was ripped and fell on the ground. The matador fell down too and the bull was right there, looking him square in the eye.

"Well, he was scrambling to get up, and the chulos were running in and yelling like mad, but the bull just ignored all that and went straight for him. It drove its horns right into his belly and shook him around. I can still see the blood flying in an arc away from him. The bull tossed him, then went for him again. He was still trying to get up, and he made it just about the time the bull got there. It hit him so hard one of the horns drove all the way through him and came out the other side. Then the bull was trotting around again, the man still hanging on his horn. He was obviously dying; I couldn't see how he could still be alive. It was really horrible, but it got worse when I realized what it was doing to me.

"David, I was really excited! I mean sexually. I wanted a man, any man, and right there and then! Later I found out that happens to some women at bullfights even when the matador isn't killed, but then I felt like, this is crazy! And Janey was getting all upset too, she wanted to leave, and I wasn't in a mood to argue. It was hard for me to sit still. So we got up and left.

"When we got outside the arena, these three guys came up to us. They were tourists too, from Florida I believe they said, but I'm not sure. They were really coming on to us, and I didn't need much convincing. They seemed to be good-looking, nice guys. Janey was a whole lot more cautious, but she was turned on too, we could all tell, and we kind of talked her into it. And that, David, is where my guilt is, because I was the one who convinced her. I wasn't thinking about anything except how horny I was at the time, and these guys seemed perfect to me. I mean, we were talking in terms of let's have a beer, but everybody knew, you know? So we went off with them to their hotel. I can see now how reckless that was. Such a mistake.

"Well, we finally got to their hotel, but it took us a while. Traffic in Mexico City is really ridiculous. And by the time we got there, Janey was getting cold feet, and, well, there were three of them and only two of us, you know? Anyway, we started trying to back out, and the guys got mad. Then we really realized what trouble we were in, in a hotel somewhere in Mexico City, we didn't know where, with three guys who'd expected to get laid, but now thought we were teases. They told us there was no way we were getting out of there without 'putting out,' as they said. I mean, we were trapped. I had no idea what to do, except maybe give them what they wanted. One guy especially was getting real mad at us.

"So I said, well, okay, let's do it. But Janey sort of panicked, and she started yelling. One guy, the one who was so mad, hit her and knocked her down, but she got up screaming. Try to understand how this makes me feel, David. Janey was my best friend, I'd talked her into doing this. Now this guy is jerking her around, hitting her, while the other two are tearing my clothes off me. I'm yelling too, and Janey's still screaming. It was just a mess.

"Anyway, for just a few minutes, I was turned around, and I couldn't see what was happening to Janey, but I could still hear her yelling. When I saw her again, the guy had ripped her clothes off, and he was trying to rape her. She was fighting like mad, beating on his head. Then, all of a sudden, she quit screaming. She—she was making little moaning sounds. I thought—I thought—'' Susan stopped for a minute, wiping her eyes. She glanced at David, then stared down into her lap, struggling for composure. The memories were so terribly vivid.

"What, Susan?" David asked, after an interval. His voice was very soft; he rubbed her shoulder gently.

She looked back at him for a moment, then away again. "I thought maybe—maybe she'd gotten into it. Those little noises sounded like—like someone—like a woman who's making love—'' Again she broke off, cried for a short time. "I'm sorry, David, this is very hard. When I could see her again, the guy—I thought—I didn't know what he was doing. He was hitting her in the chest. It took me a minute, then I could see the blood, the knife. He was stabbing her, David. Stabbing her and trying to rape her. Oh, God, I can see it just as if it were yesterday. All that blood! Oh, David—'' She stopped talking, buried her face in her hands.

"My God, Susan, what a nightmare! But it wasn't your fault, these guys went crazy. I mean, maybe you were a little reckless; maybe a lot reckless, but—''

She found a reserve of strength somewhere, raised her head and looked into David's face. She continued, her tone of voice flatter: "Wait, that isn't all of it. By this time, they'd gotten all my clothes off, and this guy who'd just killed Janey came at me like he was going to kill me too, but one of the others stopped him, said it was okay, that I was going to cooperate. For me, this is the really horrible part, even worse than watching my friend getting killed. I looked at her. She was lying there dying. And it was like I had two minds; one of them was crying and screaming, no! and the other, David, the other was more turned on than ever! I just hated myself, I didn't want to exist. I started kicking and fighting and told them they might as well kill me too. And just as calmly as if I'd asked for a drink or something, this guy says, well, okay. Two of them held me down and the other, the one who'd killed Janey—he got his knife and he was leaning over me. I knew it was all over. I just waited to die, I wanted to die. But just like in the movies—just like in the movies—somebody in the hotel had heard us and called the police, and they were banging on the door. The two guys holding me just panicked and ran off somewhere. The third one seemed to be determined to kill me at any cost, and in the state of mind I was in, I was going to let him. It seemed like the only way for me to get rid of the guilt I had, for being turned on when Janey was killed. So I just laid there and looked at him, told him to go ahead and do it, what was he waiting for. It seemed to rattle him, and he hesitated for a minute. In fact, as I remember it now, it was more like he was frozen or something. Like a statue, hovering over me, holding that knife. I could've sworn somebody else was in the room, that he was looking at somebody else, but there couldn't have been anyone else there.

"Then the police broke the door down. They didn't yell at him to stop or anything, they just shot him, it seemed like a hundred times. His blood spattered all over me, and he fell on the floor. I was hysterical, screaming at the cops, but in English, and they couldn't understand. I was screaming at them to shoot me too. Of course, they didn't. One of them was helping me up, and the others ran after the other two guys. There were more gunshots, a lot of them. All three of those guys were killed.

"Then they took me down to the police station, and after a while they found somebody who could speak English, to take my statement. The red tape and all, God, it took forever. They told me I couldn't leave the city, but I booked a flight out immediately and they didn't catch me. When I got back, everybody at school wanted to know all the details, but I couldn't talk about it. I withdrew from everybody, told myself I was swearing off sex forever, it just caused too many awful situations for me. I considered killing myself, but I couldn't quite do it. Once I sat in a tub of hot water with a razor on my wrist, but I just couldn't force myself to move it. Janey's parents called me. They wanted to know exactly what had happened, but I couldn't talk to them. I just cried. For months, it seemed like I couldn't do anything but cry.

"All these years, I've tried not to think about it. But last night it all came back. If you hadn't been here, David, I think I'd have come apart completely."

David reached over and held both her hands. "Susan, I understand. Well, maybe not totally, but remember, I feel I'm responsible for my parents' deaths; but you aren't responsible for Janey's. Sure, you both took some chances, and it turned out horribly. But I don't love you any less, Susan.''

Tears running down her face, she clutched his hands. "But David, I don't understand myself. I've never felt like I was totally in control, never in my whole life. And getting turned on to blood and gore, that's so sick! But I'll tell what's especially bad, what I can't get by. It's the feeling that I should die, then or maybe now, to prevent me from doing something even worse in the future. It would have been better if it had been me up on that stage!''

''Not for me!'' David said emphatically. "I mean, it really got to me, especially with that girl looking so much like Xilonen. But still, it may sound callous, but better her than you!''

''I don't know, David. Danny must have been right. Something's happening to us, something bad. And we're trapped. There's no way out except to see it through.''

''And we will. We'll see it through together. We'll make it. You'll see!''

She looked at him; his face belied his words. He didn't seem nearly as confident as he was trying to sound. The important thing, she felt, was keeping herself under control. Like never before, she felt that was essential, perhaps to their very survival. All the associations with blood and death had to mean something; it couldn't be random. She felt at that moment like a shipwreck victim hanging in a lifejacket, watching the sharks circle closer and closer. Whatever this was, she was convinced that it had been hovering around them for a long time, and finally it was going to make a move. Very soon now.

26

Danny had hoped that the shock of the ceremony would erase all the influences of the village on the group of Americans. But he soon found out that this was not so. Bertie did not seem to be affected at all, and John continued to wear his costume, insisting that it "was expected of him." The others had returned to normal clothing, but only for a short time. Before the first day was over, Frank had gone back to the blue cloak. Evelyn was back to her costume the next morning, and by noon, David and Susan were too. The following morning, Kathryn did likewise. At that point Danny was the one feeling weird, since he was the only person who dressed normally. The day after that, Kathryn resumed her purifications with the thorns. She was not the only one; even John was into it, as Danny could see from the telltale punctures. All his attempts to dissuade Kathryn, Evelyn, and the Hallstens from this fell on deaf ears. Knowing that they were still isolated from any kind of modern medical help, he was concerned about the consequences of infections. But he simply could not get anyone to listen to him; nor were any infections developing. He put this down to dumb luck and hoped it continued.

About this same time, he noticed that Bertie had acquired a contingent of followers in the village. He encountered them one afternoon; Bertie and a group of about two dozen young men, all of whom were dressed in uniforms—they looked like leotards—made of jaguar skins, the open mouths of the animals forming a kind of helmet. At the base of the hill just outside of town, the two cloaked figures stood watching Bertie and the young men, who were apparently studying military maneuvers. Danny walked up to the cloaked figures and boldly introduced himself.

They looked at him curiously, said their names were Toltecatl and Ihuimecatl. They didn't say anything else, just watched him, their fixed gaze making him quite uncomfortable.

"So what's he doing down there?" Danny asked casually.

They looked at each other, then the woman spoke. "He has created a caste of Jaguar Knights, and he is training them. It is very appropriate."

"Jaguar Knights?"

"Yes." She seemed unwilling to say more.

For a while Danny watched Bertie and his men learning sword techniques, using wooden swords. He was no expert on such things, but they all looked highly skilled to him. Certainly he would not have wanted to go up against any of them with a sword.

Danny had always been impressed by the friendliness and openness of these people; even when they'd cruelly sacrificed the girl, they'd seemed guileless. But as he looked into the fierce, determined faces of the Jaguar Knights below, he wondered if Bertie was not changing that somehow.

He finally left the hill and went back toward the square, where he'd earlier seen John. John also had a group of disciples, whom he referred to as his acolytes; apparently Eduardo had used the term first. He found John sitting cross-legged in the square, talking to them. A number of other people had gathered around to listen; he was talking about art and its relationship to life. Danny only heard enough of his discourse to realize it was very esoteric.

When there was a pause in the discussion, Danny approached John. He wanted to talk about potential dangers from Bertie and his knights, but John just shrugged this off.

"If he wants to do that, and the people he gathered want to learn, it's his business," John said.

"You trust him now, John?" Danny asked.

"No. But then again, what exactly can I do about it?"

"Perhaps as the king, you could stop it."

John gave him a gentle smile, and Danny was suddenly aware of how much the man had changed since the night of the sacrifice. It made him feel very strange, as if John were no longer quite human. He tried to shake that absurd notion off, but he couldn't deny the facts: there was now something very different about both Bertie and John, and it frightened him. The Hallstens had changed since their arrival here also, but not nearly as much.

"I can't do that, Danny, it wouldn't be right. It is his privilege, as long as no harm comes to anyone."

"By then, it may be too late!"

"You have your gun, don't you? Do you think they could stand against that with wooden swords?"

Danny was shocked. "How did you know?" he asked. He'd been careful to keep the gun well concealed. No one, not even Kathryn, should know about it.

John smiled again. "I know many things now, Danny. Don't worry. Bertie's knights are no threat to any of us, or to any of the villagers."

"But—"

John smiled at him, waved his hand as if to indicate the matter was closed. Danny was not satisfied, but the most surprising thing to him was his own reaction. It seemed to him that he should have found John's almost imperious manner irritating, but he didn't. He found he had an extraordinary degree of confidence in the man, in his wisdom. He wondered why.

Danny walked away to the edge of the square, turned, crossed his eyes and squinted. Only a second or two was required. He could clearly see the red and black sunburst superimposed on John's head. The same as he'd seen back in New York, at the Hallsten's apartment, that first day. But this one gave John the appearance of wearing it as a crown.

27

The morning after Danny's discovery of the Jaguar Knights, John asked David to tour the fields, see how the local agriculture was going. David was a little hesitant to do this; they still had three days before the plane was due to arrive, and he'd thought it best not to even potentially rock that boat. Besides, he felt he was having enough trouble just hanging onto his sanity. More and more every day, he and Susan had found themselves doing things they'd had no intention of doing. Just yesterday, a woman from the village had approached Susan with her daughter in tow, telling a sad story of unrequited love; the poor girl loved a young man who did not return her affections. In a whisper, David had advised her not to get involved in things like this, but she'd promised to see the young man. She had, and they'd later discovered that the young man had professed his undying love to the girl. David had asked Susan what she'd done to him.

"Nothing really," she'd replied. "I just told him the girl was good for him, that they'd make a good pair."

After that, couples began to come to Susan to ask her to bless their marriages. She'd done so, and they'd gone away happy. This seemed harmless enough, probably a lot more harmless than the matchmaking. The crops were the real worry; if they went bad, things could change very quickly. He'd gone out once before, and at the time everything had looked good. But in spite of his misgivings, he felt he had to honor John's new request.

Accompanied by two of John's acolytes, David set out for the fields, taking the same trail he'd been on before, with Patecatl and Mayauel. When he tried to remember those events clearly, it made his head hurt. Whatever had happened that day, it certainly hadn't been ordinary.

Looking down the trail, he was a little surprised; the cornfield was much closer than he remembered it. Already he could see the tassels, the broad green leaves. Looked real good from here, he thought. As they walked, he began to realize something was a little strange. When he'd been in this field before, the plants had been about three feet tall; now, he could see, they were at least six. They walked on, and on. He began to be aware that the field was, in actuality, exactly where he'd thought it was; its apparent closeness was an illusion caused by the size of the plants.

When he reached the edge of the field, he stared at the corn in utter disbelief. He'd never seen anything like it in his life, giant varieties notwithstanding. The plants were at least twenty-five feet tall, with huge ears, no signs of any damage or disease. Each ear had to be a good two feet long, some larger than that. And they weren't even fully ripe yet. The delighted farmer said he had had to buy an axe to harvest them.

David went into the field, pressing his fingers into the soil around the base of the plants. He always could get a feeling for the quality of the soil that way; this soil absolutely vibrated with life. Totally new to his experience.

Slightly dazed, he suggested that they move on to another field, and was told that down the trail was a crop of squash and pumpkins. They went there, and it was the same. Again he stared; squashes five feet long, but not at all woody, lay in profusion among the vines. A little further along, the pumpkins. He saw one that was nearly perfectly round, and well over seven feet in diameter. Perfect for Cinderella's coach, he thought. He couldn't believe what he was seeing; it was just not possible. Off the top of his head John had come up with a weirdly formulated fertilizer, and these were the results? It was just impossible! Repeatedly he touched the huge fruits to make sure they were not an optical illusion of some sort. They felt very solid, very juicy. Excellent quality. First-class.

It became a repetitive litany of the impossible, the outrageous. Tomatoes, peppers, cucumbers, all enormous. If this technique could be brought back to the U.S., it would absolutely revolutionize farming there. Okra pods eighteen inches long, not yet ripe. Sweet potatoes pushing up out of the ground like small volcanoes. Eggplants that must have weighed a hundred pounds each. Watermelons you could use for a garage. His vision blurred and he felt lightheaded.

The last field they visited was cotton, and as they approached it David was relieved to see that, while the plants were very large, they were not monstrous. He went into the field, pulled open one of the bolls, and stared at the bright blue cotton. He pulled another, from a different plant. Scarlet. Another was verdant green, then a purple one. The farmer told him he'd followed John's instructions exactly, showed him a pile of Murex shells. David just nodded; he didn't trust himself to speak. Even the huge edibles had been easier to accept than this; cotton that grew in colors! He wondered if John had a formula to make a cow give chocolate milk. Giggling inanely, he started back toward town. He had one hell of a report to make.

28

Having spent much of the day by himself in the village, Danny returned to the resort late that afternoon. He'd wanted to buy Kathryn some little gift, and he had found a pair of earrings bearing the crescent-moon symbol she seemed to favor so much now. As he came up the drive, he saw Susan sitting alone.

"Hi, lady!" he called, glancing around. Not seeing Kathryn anywhere, he asked Susan where she'd gone.

"Some people came up from the village. There's a woman down there about to give birth," Susan replied. "They asked Kathryn and Evelyn to come down, and they went."

Danny was surprised. "Why?" he asked.

"They seem to think Kathryn is good luck or something, where childbirth is concerned. Who knows? They seem to think I'm the infallible matchmaker, and they've been asking Evelyn to sort of baptize the children, with water. It's hard to refuse them, Danny. I can't say why, it just is."

Danny sat down. "Damn!" he exclaimed. "Now what? The weird stuff has stopped, but now these villagers are giving you folks delusions of grandeur. Did you know that Bertie is training a paramilitary group of some kind? Jaguar Knights, he calls them. And John, like some latter-day Christ, sits in the square lecturing his followers. I tell you, in a way it's even stranger!"

"But harmless, I think," Susan told him. "Besides, I get the most peculiar feelings around John these days. Like all that stuff he's saying, he's right, you know? Don't you feel it, too?"

"I'm not so sure about Bertie and his knights," Danny grumbled.

"Oh, I think we've misjudged Bertie. He's okay. I've talked to him. Remember, he's not the man in our dream!"

"Maybe so. I hope you're right. By the way, where's David?"

"John asked him to tour the fields today, see how the crops were doing. Now don't make something strange out of that, Danny. That was the job he used to have, back in the states."

"Yes, I know. But I—wait a minute, Susan, did you just say the job he used to have?"

"Yes, I guess so. I—"

"What does that mean? He quit his job to come here? I thought this was a vacation!"

"No, he didn't quit his job. I don't know why I said that. For a minute there, this place just seemed so permanent. But it's only three more days, isn't it? Just three more days until the plane arrives, and we can go.''

"You happy about that?''

"Well, to be honest, I'm of two minds about it. Part of me wanted to get the hell out of here as fast as possible, ever since the night of the ceremony. But the other part feels at home here. And it's not just me. I know that David, John, Evelyn, and Kathryn all feel the same way. What about you?''

"Not me! I'm of one solid, unrelenting mind. Out. Back to New York. Everyday muggers and break ins. Forget this shit. I don't know whether I'm coming or going here!''

"Neither do I, but sometimes I enjoy it,'' she said. "And then, sometimes I don't. I've always hated Mexico, maybe I'll tell you why someday. But I will say this, Danny. When those villagers come up here and ask me to bless a marriage, the feeling I get from it can not be described. It's—it's—well, totally fulfilling. The way women usually talk about having a baby. That marriage or relationship I've blessed is my baby, you know?''

"You sound like you take it very seriously.''

"I guess I do. But in another way, it's all crap, and I don't know what the fuck I'm doing! I think, hey, is it a play or something? Hidden cameras, you know? If it is a play, I wish to hell somebody'd show me the script!''

"I know what you mean, Susan. Half the time I've been here, I've been obsessed with the whys, and I haven't had a good idea yet!''

"Oh, you've had some good ideas, Danny. I know you have.''

"What do you mean?''

"Well, Kathryn and I were talking, you know? Now, how can I say this? I don't want you to get your feelings hurt. I wasn't going to tell you, but, did you know that David and Kathryn slept together?''

Danny watched her for a minute. So matter-of-fact. He'd assumed she'd be devastated. "Yes,'' he said carefully, "I did. I wasn't going to tell you. I didn't want you to be hurt. How did you find out?''

"I saw them. Out on the lawn, running off to the garage. Just like you and Evelyn did.'' She smiled at him.

Danny colored. "That too, huh? Uh, well, obviously I knew about that! I swear, Susan, I—"

She held up her hand. "Danny, there's no need to explain. Around here the usual rules of behavior just don't apply very well. Now, as to how I knew about that, well, we women have been talking a lot, you know? And we've gotten to a point of being real direct with each other. Maybe you can say it's our female intuition." She laughed, beautifully, Danny thought. "But whatever, we feel strongly that there are certain things that should happen, before we leave. And one of those things, which we all agreed on, even Kathryn, is that you, my good friend, should sleep with each of us at least once. Somehow, we think, it's necessary to protect you, but I'm damned if I know how, or from what. But that's our opinion. So. You've already slept with Kathryn and Evelyn. Does that give you any ideas?"

"Ah—Susan, I really don't know. Ah—there's David and all. Are you sure Kathryn was in on this?"

"David won't be back for quite a while, and anyway, this has nothing to do with him. It has to do with you and me. Remember when I first saw your scar, back in New York?"

He remembered that vividly. She stretched, causing her bare breasts to stand out.

"Damn it, Susan, I—"

She looked at him. She was so warm, so bright. He'd wanted her so much that evening in New York, but he'd pushed her away. Now, he just couldn't; she was literally irresistible to him.

"You really want to fight it, Danny?" she asked, leaning over and touching his arm lightly.

"You know I don't. Where?"

"Your room. Let's go!"

Another drill over, Bertie left his Jaguar Knights and walked up the hill to where Ihuimecatl and Toltecatl were sitting. He was very proud of his knights; they had come far in a very short time.

"Well, how'd it look from up here?" he asked.

"Very good. Shortly they will be the equal of the Hummingbird's Eagle Knights. It has been a very long time," Ihuimecatl said.

"What are your plans when the training is complete?" Toltecatl asked him.

He glanced around, lowered his voice. "A coup, of course. Overthrow the king."

"You cannot," he said flatly.

"And just why can't I? His acolytes are like monks. They're not fighters. My knights can handle them easily."

"You might be surprised. We've told you; they have means you are not aware of. Take my word for it. We are experienced in these matters," Ihuimecatl reminded him.

He turned to face her. "But I'd win. I know it!"

"Yes," she said. "Possibly. But it would indeed be a hollow victory for you. For if you do this, the conflict that will result will destroy this village completely. We know. We have seen conflicts of this nature. You would be king, but in name only. You would rule over ruin."

"Better than not at all!"

"Perhaps. But there may be a better way. The way of guile, of treachery. He has set up codes of behavior for himself far in excess of what he asks from the villagers. Have you not seen this?"

"Yes, I have. So?"

"If you can find a way to cause him to violate his own

codes, he will be destroyed in his own eyes. You will be able
to take the kingship unopposed.''

"How can I do that?"

"Ah, the plan must be yours. We can only go so far, else
you become our ally! And I don't think you want that!"

Bertie didn't quite know what that meant, but he didn't like
the sound of it. "No, I don't want that. You keep your place.
But thanks, anyway. I'll think about it."

Down below them, a villager was walking across the open
space where they'd been practicing, weaving a little. Toltecatl
pointed at him. "Four cups," he said contemptuously.

"Yes, hundreds of rabbits," Ihuimecatl said.

"One more cup, that's four hundred," replied the other.

"What are you talking about?" Bertie asked them.

"Merely a saying," Ihuimecatl said. "When a man is totally
drunk, we say he's had four hundred rabbits."

"How quaint."

"Of course, that is ordinary pulque. Not the brew Mayauel
makes. That, of course, is totally different."

"Mayauel—I remember her, at the ceremony, right?"

"Yes. She distributed some of her special brew. Your friends
drank some. They were confused." Ihuimecatl laughed.

"Yeah, I do remember. Danny drank a little bit, and five
minutes later he was balling the hell out of that girl in front of
everybody. I didn't think he had it in him."

"It is always surprising what desires and knowledge may
emerge when five cups of Mayauel's brew is drunk. Even a
little can have a profound effect."

Bertie rolled this over in his mind. He was getting a germ
of an idea. John had not drunk anything that night. If he could
get him drunk, set him up—maybe to kill somebody? No, too
hard to arrange. But perhaps there was another way. An idea
began to crystallize in his mind, and he explained it to the two
creatures.

"An excellent plan!" cried Ihuimecatl.

"I cannot see how it could fail!" added Toltecatl.

"Well, I can see how it would fail. The bastard might refuse
to taste the stuff. But if he does, I've got him, right?"

"Right!"

"Right!"

Bertie looked at them. He was a little suspicious; they were agreeing too readily, and he usually had to fight with them. Still, he could see no harm in trying.

The three of them paid a visit to Mayauel and Patecatl. She didn't seem terribly happy about it, but she gave them a skin full of what the creatures had called her special brew.

As they left, Bertie could faintly hear her talking to Patecatl. "Maybe I shouldn't have done that," she was saying. "Maybe this time, it should have been different. So much suffering. So much."

"No, Mayauel," Patecatl told her. "You were right. It is the way it must be. And you know what we have to do—"

Bertie didn't really understand what they were talking about, but he really didn't care, either. He had what he needed. He was formulating the details in his mind, exactly how he'd go about it. He'd need a mirror, and a little help from Ihuimecatl.

30

Operating on automatic, David found his way back, some-how, to the center of town. He was still feeling a little dazed by what he'd seen in the fields as he approached the square. As he had expected, John was there, the peaked ocelot cap on his head, talking to a group of about fifty villagers. Orizaba sat right beside him. It seemed to David that the dwarf was almost a part of him now. Whenever he left the resort, Orizaba was there.

As he came closer, he could hear John lecturing the group on the nature of sin. To David, that seemed like an odd topic indeed. Like many of his peers, it was something he seldom thought about. As far as he was concerned, it really was not a very meaningful word.

"And it's true, I think, that what we call sin must be atoned for, must be properly expunged," John was saying. "And the more sins that have been committed, or the worse they are, the harsher the atonement must be."

"But," someone asked, "how can one truly know what is a sin and what is not?"

"It's very simple, really: so simple it's usually overlooked. Just as beauty is in the eye of the beholder, sin is sin only in the mind of the doer. If it isn't, then it isn't sin. In other words, what is sinful is whatever a person believes to be sinful. Because there is only one true sin; the violations of one's own intent, one's true will. If a man or woman believes, really believes, that sexual relations without a socially ordained union are wrong, and engages in them anyway, then that is sin. If a person believes that celibacy is wrong, a violation of natural processes, then that person is committing a sin by not engaging in sexual relations if opportunities are there. Both are violating their intent, violating themselves. The nature of true sin is a highly personal thing."

"What about the human sacrifices?" someone asked. "You have outlawed them. Does that not now make them a sin?"

"Not at all! You're confusing sin and law: two very different things! At least they should be. No. For me, if I conducted a human sacrifice, then I would be committing a sin, because that's contrary to my nature. But there are others for whom that is not wrong. They would be in violation of law, but not sinful, if they conducted them here in Tlillan Tlapallan now. Such violations of law do not have to be expunged as sins do. The law itself may exact a material payment—even one's life— but that's beside the point."

"I'm still not sure I understand," the questioner persisted. "Why must one atone for sins at all? After all, they only damage the person committing them, his own development."

"No, that isn't really true. What we're talking about—these violations of intent—they harm the whole fabric of the natural order. By going against your own will, you drain energy away from everyone and everything else. It should be obvious that we are all connected. By atoning for sins, you give that energy back. And you leave yourself clear for further advancement, so everyone benefits. It's simple, really."

No one seemed to have any further comments, and a long, but not uncomfortable, silence settled over the gathering. John rose from his cross-legged sitting posture and walked over to David, Orizaba tagging along as if he was attached by a string.

"You're quite the philosopher," he said when John was close. "I'm impressed."

John shrugged. "Weird. They seem to hang on every word I say. I try to get them to think for themselves, but most people aren't used to doing that. Not even here."

"Don't I know it. It's something that always amazed me, how people always want someone else to make their decisions, and tell them how to live."

"Well, I just won't do that. But these acolytes, at least, they're a cut above that. They've really surprised me."

"That little essay on sin was quite interesting."

"Think so? Maybe I'll send it to the *Christian Science Monitor*, see if they'll publish it."

They both laughed for a minute. "So what's sinful for you John?" David asked. "If that's not too personal."

"Oh, rape, murder, incest, Canadian seal hunts, nuclear weapons. A lot of things, I'm sure. I never thought about it much until after that ceremony."

"I'm not sure I ever thought about it at all. But it was provocative, John. I will now, I'm sure. Under your terms, I'm not exactly free from that type of sin myself."

"Few of us are. You know, that's odd, but I do believe at least one of us here is, and that's Kathryn. I'm not sure why I think that, but I do. Somehow it seems she's not capable of it."

"Lucky her."

"To be sure. Your encounters with her are not so innocent on your part, David."

David flushed; he was sure he was bright red. "You told him, Orizaba?" he said to the dwarf.

The dwarf jumped back as if David had physically threatened him. "Me? Who, me?" he cried. "Oh, no, not I, I would never do such a thing, no, never! May I be struck dead this moment if I do not speak the truth! No, he told me!"

David looked at John again. Was he angry? After all, David had been unfaithful to his sister. But John's eyes were mild, he didn't even seem to be rendering judgment. "How did you know?" he asked, wondering if that was really important.

"I don't know how I know, I just do. That's true with many

things for me now, David. Sometimes it's a little scary. Like the crops. I know your report already. But back to what we were discussing: The problem for you is not what you've done to Susan. You haven't done anything to her at all. It's to yourself. You believed it wrong, but did it anyway. Even though she might be annoyed with you, she really doesn't think such things are wrong, so she wouldn't consider you sinful. But it'll eat at you, David. You have to change either your intent or your actions, they're not in harmony. And they have to be, you know.''

"Yes, I believe I do know. That's not just lip service. I think the time will come when I'll have to pay for that, somehow."

"Probably so. But you have a strong inner core, David. You'll do all right in the end. I know that, too."

"You're quite a guy, John, you know that? Most people wouldn't even try to understand."

"I don't feel you deserve any less."

"Thanks. I needed the talk, I think. But I think I'll be going back up to the resort now, I—"

"Not yet. Stay here for a little while longer. I have a few things to do, and then I do want to hear about what you've seen in the fields."

David shrugged, and John put his arm across his shoulder, steering him away from the road leading up to the house. David didn't see Orizaba and John wink at each other.

31

Late that night, Danny woke up in a cold sweat. Instantly fully awake, he looked over at Kathryn as she lay sleeping peacefully; no problem there. Rubbing his hands down over his face, he tried to identify what had alarmed him. There was no obvious threat in the room, and it hadn't been a dream. No, this was something coming in from the periphery of his consciousness, insistent and urgent. But he was unable to get a handle on it; it was just a sense of foreboding, a feeling that something was terribly wrong.

Carefully, so as not to wake Kathryn, he climbed out of bed. His hands shaking and his stomach queasy, he sat in the wicker chair by the window, gazed out at the moonlight on the lawn, at the stark outline of the ruined church. In his mind, he ran over everything that had been happening to them, and where it could be taking them. Why had they been gathered together? Some kind of destiny, karma? Something that had pointed all these people to this place at this time? But where did that lead? He had always thought in terms of the bottom line; who gets the payoff. Perhaps that was why he'd never solved this mystery; he'd been looking for some kind of material payoff, when in fact the thing might well be vaster than that. But he had a sick feeling now that this did not bode well for his friends or for Kathryn, who was now much more than a friend.

But the problem was, what was he going to do about it? It was not the kind of thing his gun would be of any use in combating. He felt lost, drifting, helpless.

In frustration more than anything else, he stared at the ruined church and tried to read it, as if demanding some kind of answer from it. His body shook with the stress, the intensity of his effort. Then, like a movie fade-in, he began to see something. A scene superimposed itself on the image of the church. The hill was no longer a hill, but a pyramid, gleaming in the sun. He saw a man who looked like John, and he was dead. The others; Frank, Evelyn, dead; there were people mourning. David, Susan, Kathryn, all dead; more mourning. He could barely hear snatches of words, faint and incomprehensible. Now he saw Bertie dead as well, heard it being said that it had all been caused by something John and Susan had done. Everyone dead, caused by John and Susan? He strained to see more. This wasn't illusion; he knew it. It was real information. Unless something or someone intervened, everyone there was going to die.

The image faded and he was left looking at the ruined church again. He never got a notion of what it was that they had done. But he was very sure that they had to be prevented, somehow, from making that fatal error.

32

During this same time, John sat in his room, deep in med-
itation. He found himself doing this frequently now; it was the
only way he was able to get in touch with himself, the only
way to communicate with that part of him that knew about
such things as the ritual fertilizers. According to David's report, the crops were growing beyond all reason, yet John found
it impossible to be surprised. It was as if he had two minds,
but only one personality. The other mind was not alien, not
an intruder; he understood that it had always been there, he'd
just never been in touch with it before. And as the days passed,
he continued to marvel at the amazing knowledge this other
mind seemed to possess. Slowly but surely, he was reaching a
full contact with it, and he was beginning to expect some revelation of truly cosmic import. Images swirled in his head; the
huge bird with its snakelike neck and green feathers, Venus so
brilliant in the morning sky. Images that were somehow so
familiar, so tied together; but their meaning still eluded him,
hanging just out of reach of his struggling mind. He had discovered a technique of rejecting the obvious, refusing to accept
the rational, physical world; when he did, the other mind rushed
in, filling him with strange and wonderful ideas. He did that
now, and was on the verge of entering the desired state, when
he was interrupted by a knock on his door.

He sighed. "Come in," he called loudly.

The door opened; it was Bertie. "I saw your light and
thought I'd stop by and talk for a minute," he said with an
ingenuous smile. "We haven't talked much since we've been
here, and well, I thought maybe it was time we changed that."

John tried to rearrange his thoughts to accommodate a guest.
In fact he was not at all sorry Bertie had dropped by. They had
hardly exchanged two words since the naming of John as the

king, and he wondered if Bertie, as the unsuccessful candidate, would harbor any ill will. He was sure they could deal with it if he did, though. This man was so strong, so dynamic; John felt that he had an enormous amount to offer if his energies could be controlled. But they weren't, and thus Bertie was unpredictable in his behavior.

"So, Bertie, I'm glad you stopped by," he said finally. "Tell me, what have you been doing with yourself lately? I've seen very little of you."

"Oh, not much. You heard about my Jaguar Knights. Those boys seem really interested in that, and I get a kick out of the drills and all. It's no big deal, just a pastime while we're stuck here."

"Sometimes I don't quite understand you, Bertie. You're obviously so capable, but you don't take anything very seriously."

"Sure I do, sure I do. But you, John, you take things entirely too seriously, and man, it's beginning to take its toll on you. You're beginning to look an old man!"

"Oh, come on, I'm sure—"

"No, really. I've been very worried about you. For example, my friend, there are all these women here, some really beautiful ones down in the village. Have you made yourself available to them? I'd bet not. Sitting up here meditating all the time. All work and no play makes John a very dull dude, you know. And we just can't have a dull king, can we?"

"Okay, you're right about the women. In fact, I've gone without for—for—good God, nearly a year! I had no idea myself it was that long. Since I saw Nikki last—"

Bertie stiffened almost imperceptibly, then relaxed as if he didn't want John to see; but John had. Was it possible that Bertie knew her, too? That pushed any possibility of coincidence right out the window.

"Yes," John said, reflectively. "Nikki Keeler. Ever hear the name, Bertie?"

"Can't say that I have."

John recognized the direct lie; he considered his hypothesis verified. That was something he really wanted to think about, Nikki's role in all this. Too many strange things, too many coincidences. Again he sighed. All that just brought her back to the forefront of his mind, made him realize how much he missed her.

"Must be quite a woman, John," Bertie said solicitously.

"Oh, she is, that she is. No doubt about it." As if you didn't already know that, he thought. Convinced that Bertie had been a customer of hers, he felt an anger welling up in him. But he considered it unworthy and stuffed it back down, hoping his face hadn't given him away.

"But I tell you, John, you gotta do something or you're going to get sick. Just take a look at yourself, right now, when you're not posing for your bathroom mirror." He whipped out a black obsidian mirror the size of his hand. Without thinking, John looked into it.

And saw reflected the image of an old, sick man. The eyes were rheumy and tired; crevices marked the cheeks. The man in the mirror, he realized, was not going to live much longer. Stunned, he moved his head, and watched the image follow. Every new angle made it worse. He was falling apart before his own eyes! A deep sadness overtook him; he was going to die; sick, old, and unwanted. But he still had so much to offer his people. So much. He looked again, it was worse still. Deciding to verify it in the bathroom mirror, he jumped up.

He could not possibly have seen, as he walked toward the bathroom, that the image in the mirror stayed there, watching him go. Neither did he hear Bertie whisper, "Ihuimecatl! Go!" He didn't see the black shadow rocket by him, low to the floor. But when he got there, the image in the bathroom mirror was the same. Tears began to roll down into the crevices on his cheeks. Lifting his fist, he smashed it into the mirror, not noticing how the image got smaller as his hand arrived, curling itself into a corner of the breaking glass. He stared at the pieces lying in the bathroom sink, then picked up a handful and hurled them. They stuck in the doorframe, a thousand pieces of crystal, reflecting the light in all directions. Still weeping, he staggered back out to Bertie. His tears blinded him; he could not see the satisfied smile on the other man's face.

"What am I going to do?" he moaned. "I had no idea—no idea—"

"Well, John, as a matter of fact I have a few suggestions." This time John did notice a wisp of smoke disappear into Bertie's mirror as he put it away, but he paid no attention. He was much too miserable with the knowledge of his own deterioration.

"The first thing is to get you to relax a little," Bertie told him. "Now here I have something to help you with that." He pulled the goatskin off his shoulder and, seemingly from nowhere, produced a cup. Filling it with the milky liquid, he offered it to John.

"No, Bertie, I don't think so. I'm not much of a drinker. I mean, maybe a beer every now and again, but—"

"Now look. This isn't like whisky here. It's pulque, it's like a beer. But it has a real mellowing effect, really a surprise. You know how beer sometimes makes you feel rotten a couple hours later? Well, this stuff never does."

"No, really. I've tried pulque when I was in Mexico before, and I didn't like it. I think I'll pass. But thanks anyway."

"John, you just stick your finger in it, give it a taste. If it's like the pulque you had before, you say so and I'll drop it. Okay?"

John looked at him closely. He was suddenly so friendly, and he'd seemed so angry the night of the ceremony. Maybe he'd had a change of heart. He figured he'd give Bertie the benefit of the doubt. What could it hurt? Besides, he did find the local pulque a little intriguing. David had said it was positively amazing. "Okay, Bertie," he said. "Just a taste, okay?" He stuck his little finger into the cup, licked it off.

It totally astounded him. Never had he tasted anything like it! Fantastic! And already he felt better, although that had to be an illusion—nothing could work that fast! "Let me see that mirror again," he asked.

"Sure enough." Bertie pulled out the mirror, and John looked. It was incredible, but true; even after just a taste, he looked a little younger, a little less sick.

"Sure looks like you were right about this," he said, picking up the cup and draining it in one swallow. The warm glow rushed through him; he felt a lot better. Damn, this was nice of Bertie! He didn't understand how he could have been so suspicious of the man. "Could I have another, please?" he asked.

Smiling broadly, Bertie poured the cup full again, and when John downed it, quickly refilled it. This time John sipped instead of gulping. The effects were fascinating; it was loosening him up like alcohol, but without the fuzziness he associated with alcoholic drinks. He tested the stuff in his mouth; alcohol, but something else, too. It was utterly unlike any pulque he'd ever had before.

"Where did you get this stuff?" he asked Bertie, as he finished the last of the third cup.

"You know the woman Mayauel? Friend of Orizaba's? She makes it. Like nobody else, eh?" As he spoke, he filled John's cup again.

Again John sipped it. Bertie was grinning very broadly at him. He grinned back, and both men fell to laughing, John almost spilling the cup. Bertie helped him right it; not a drop hit the floor.

"Last time I had anything to drink, I was in Nikki's 'partment, drinkin' a beer," John said, slurring the words a little. "An' you know what? I saw myself on TV. Crazy, crazy situation. Little girl I give artificial respiration to, after a car crash. She woke up and said I killed her. Called me the Smoking Mirror." He looked at the wisps of smoke coming up from Bertie's foot and broke out laughing again. "See there! She was wrong! I'm not the Smoking Mirror! You are!" He finished the cup and laughed even harder.

Bertie poured the cup full for the fifth time, laid the skin on the floor. He looked at John directly. "Perhaps I am," he said quietly.

"Bertie, my friend, don't think I'm being personal or anything, but why the hell does your foot smoke, anyway?" John laughed again, took a sip from the cup, the fifth cup.

Bertie looked at the foot, the wisps of smoke. "I'm not sure, but it does, doesn't it?"

"Maybe you should take it to a stop smoking clinic!" he said. Again he broke up laughing. The cup was nearly empty. He looked at Bertie; he seemed to have face paint on, black horizontal bands across his forehead, chin, and nose, yellow across his eyes and mouth. Looked good on him, too. John realized he hadn't felt so good in a long time. Not since Nikki—he stopped his thoughts; his mood shifted almost instantaneously from happy to morose.

"Nikki," he moaned. "I wish she was here. She always seemed to have all the answers."

"I'm sorry she isn't, John," Bertie said soothingly. "But you have friends here: myself, David, Danny, and Susan, your sister—"

"Susan!" he cried suddenly. "Has she ever tried this stuff? Well, she's gotta try it. I'll go get her, I don't care if it is the middle of the night!"

"No, wait, John," Bertie said. "You just relax, finish your cup. I'll get her. She'll be so happy to see the change in you. You're almost back to your old self, my friend." He got up with a single fluid motion and went to the door. "Now don't go anywhere," he said, waggling a finger. "I'll be right back in just a minute."

John had no intention of going anywhere. He sipped the remainder of the cup, watched Bertie go out the door. He had turned out to be a hell of a good friend.

Susan was having an incredibly good dream. She was running through fields of beautiful flowers, everything was perfectly beautiful for her. At intervals in the field were loving couples, caressing or kissing, and she often stopped to bestow her blessings. She felt so alive, so happy; then she was seeing David running toward her. Or was it Danny? Maybe Bertie? It didn't matter. They were all so beautiful, each in his own way. She was awash with pleasure. Nothing could be wrong in her world, except for that insistent tugging at her arm; she wished it would stop. But it didn't, and finally it woke her up. She opened her eyes and looked at Bertie, crouched by her bedside. Quickly she glanced at David; he was still sleeping. Now what the hell—?

"Shh!" Bertie whispered. "Don't wake David up. Just get up and come with me. John wants to see you. Just you."

"What for?" she whispered back.

"He's disturbed about something, I don't know what. He needs you, Susan."

She carefully swung herself out of bed. She was still foggy, didn't really understand why she shouldn't wake David, but maybe there was a reason. Standing up slowly, so as not to shake the bed, she started to reach for her clothes.

"Never mind," Bertie said. "Just come on, to John's room. Hurry!"

She hesitated a moment, then thought, well, what the hell. Her clothes didn't really conceal anything anyhow. Nude, she followed Bertie out the door.

Bertie smiled at her as soon as the door closed. "Perhaps

when we're through talking to John, you could delay your return a bit?'' he asked.

She smiled back. "Perhaps,'' she said. He kissed her lightly, caressed her breast. His touch felt almost fiery. She began to get aroused, but they continued on toward John's room.

She found John sitting cross-legged in the middle of the floor, swaying slightly. He looked up at her, his eyes a little unfocused. "John, what's the matter?'' she asked, concerned. "Bertie said you needed me—''

"Yes, and he was right, yessir, good ol' Bertie, by God!''

"John?''

"Listen, little sister, you know that stuff David told us Mayauel gave him? Well, it's great! Just great! You gotta try it. Here.'' He poured the cup full and handed it to her, spilling a little in the process.

"John, I really don't—''

"Look, I'm your big brother, right? And besides that, I'm your fucking king! So drink it. Ah, at least taste it. It's amazing!''

She looked at the milky liquid in the cup. To her, it looked like a cup full of semen. She glanced up at Bertie, who nodded. Shrugging, she sipped it.

And, true to John's predictions, found it really good. David had been ranting about the effects of the stuff, but he'd said it tasted awful. She didn't think so, not at all. It did, in fact, taste a little like semen to her, but that was a taste she'd never minded. And there was more; a creamy richness she'd never before experienced in a drink. She took a larger sip, then finished the cup. The effects were astonishing. She felt it flow through her, almost exactly the same way the phantom's semen had done. It energized her, made her feel incredibly good.

"Well, you weren't lying, brother of mine,'' she said. "I do believe I'll have another!'' This time Bertie poured since John's hands were not at all steady. She started drinking the second cup.

"Well, I told you you'd like it,'' John said, smiling. "Worth getting out of bed for?''

"Definitely. But Bertie, the louse, conned me. He said something was wrong with you, so I came running. All things taken into account, though, I forgive you both.''

"Well, that's good," Bertie said. "I'd hate to remain a louse in your eyes."

Again she smiled at him, realizing she'd rather be making love with him right now. But that would have to wait, at least for a while. "No, it's okay, Bertie. I see the point," she said, watching John sway.

"No, he was in a funk," Bertie told her. "Until he drank some of this brew. Fixed him right up. Everything he needed."

"Everything but Nikki," John said morosely.

"Now, don't dwell on that," Susan said. "If you want, I'll try to talk to her when we get back to New York." She finished her second cup; Bertie poured her another. This one she emptied quickly, and again Bertie filled it.

"Would you do that?" John was saying. "I don't know if it would make a difference, but—"

She finished the drink, watched Bertie refill her cup for the fifth time. "Of course I will, John, you can count on it."

Her vision was going; the drinks were beginning to hit her hard, and she decided that, good as it was, this would be the last one. She was becoming impatient with John, wanting to finish with him and get Bertie alone. John was lying down on the floor now, his eyes closed; she found that she really couldn't see him very well.

Bertie, she realized, was sitting beside her. "Looks like John's passed out," he said as she drained the last drop of the delicious fluid. "I imagine he'll be out for quite a while."

"You sure, Bertie?" she asked. It looked to her like John's eyes were open. She could almost see something else, too—a shadow at his ear—and it seemed to be saying something to him, although she couldn't understand it. Stupid, she thought, it's the drinks. Shadows can't talk.

Bertie took off his clothes and reached around her, touching her nipples. She arched her back into him, her head against his cheek.

"But Bertie, John is still—" she said, although she felt like she was losing control. There was something strange—another person in the room, a woman? Telling John her name was Nikki? But that was not possible, there was no one else there. She tried to see John clearly. How had he gotten naked, and why did he have an erection? She tried to ask Bertie, but he answered her by pressing his own erection against her and running his fingers down into her pubic hair. Well, she thought, John must have passed out, he wouldn't be lying there watching this and not say a word, would he? She reached around and fondled Bertie's penis. He moved her body around, raised her up a little. Then she felt the pressure-and-release of his penis pushing up into her. She gasped, began moving. His hands were everywhere; it seemed like he had four of them.

Quickly her orgasm rose. She paused for a moment and started again, feeling another not far away. Beautiful, she thought, deep down inside where a piece of her mind remained clear. Just beautiful. There was no one else here; she'd been wrong. The only peculiar thing now was that she kept hearing Bertie call her "Nikki." But the onslaught of the next orgasm drove any analysis from her mind. Their lovemaking continued until she was nearly exhausted. Then she felt, as she had only felt with the Bertie-phantom before, semen exploding inside her. A final, shattering orgasm overtook her, and she lost consciousness.

John opened his eyes the tiniest bit and saw the gray morning sky, the light making dappled patterns across the windowsill and chair. He was on the floor. Obviously he had slept there all night, and had awakened to the first overcast day since they'd been there. For a moment he didn't try to move. He expected he would be hung over; after all, he'd passed out drunk. But he didn't have a headache. In fact, he felt fine. Weird stuff. He sensed a weight on his left arm and tentatively turned his head in that direction.

Ice formed in his stomach as he saw Susan's beautiful face, childlike in sleep, nestled on his left shoulder. He looked down; they were both nude. A dried film of semen covered his penis, and she had a similar streak on her thigh. He remembered the vivid dream, at least he'd thought it had been a dream, of making love with Nikki. But it had been no dream, and it had not been Nikki. He felt physically ill. For several minutes he was utterly unable to move.

Finally he pulled himself together enough to carefully shift Susan's head off his shoulder and get to his feet. He didn't know what to do. Utter chaos, utter degradation. His own sister! Never had he felt even remotely like this before. Dressing without showering, he carefully tried to pick her up without waking her. She seemed to be sleeping soundly. He wanted to get her back to her room, but didn't see how he could do that without waking someone. So he put her in his bed, wet a cloth with warm water, and wiped the dried semen from her legs, tears running down his face. How could he have done this to her? She wouldn't have gone along with it, he was sure of that. The scenario in his mind was that she had passed out drunk, and he had callously used her unconscious body to satisfy himself, before he had passed out himself. He was at the bottom now; there was no way he could sink any lower. Silently he apologized to her, hoping that she would never find out what had happened here last night. Hopefully she would just assume that she'd passed out and slept in his bed. Feeling the ''other side'' of himself reaching out to him, he knew he had to open himself to it fully, find what he had to do. His immediate urge was to borrow Bertie's flint knife and end his miserable existence now. But that might not be right. He still had faith in the meditative techniques he had been developing over the past few days; he needed a way to concentrate and focus, and thought he knew how. Collecting his mask, staff, trumpet, incense bag, and wind jewel, he left the room and began a long walk down to the square, where he knew his acolytes would already be gathered. He had a job for them.

The same gray light that had awakened John also fell on Danny's face, but he returned to consciousness a little more slowly. Beside him, Kathryn slept on; he didn't wake her. He needed to see John and Susan right away. It had been hard not to awaken them in the middle of the night to discuss his impressions, and he couldn't wait any longer. They were the key, he was sure. As quickly as possible, he showered. Kathryn raised her head as he began to dress.

''Danny? What's up?'' she asked in a sleepy voice.

''I've got to see John about something. You can sleep a while if you want,'' he replied.

''Sounds good to me. Think I will.'' She stretched, rolled over, and closed her eyes again.

John's room was only a short distance down the hall, but Danny had to suppress an urge to run. Though he felt a terrible urgency gnaw at him, he forced himself to walk, and finally he was knocking on John's door. There was no answer, so he knocked again. The door swung open. Danny peeked in, then stepped inside.

John wasn't there, but Susan was, sleeping nude on the bed. Susan?

He touched her shoulder; she didn't rouse. He shook her a little, and she finally opened her eyes and smiled at him. She looked very sexy at that moment.

"What are you doing here, Danny?" she asked.

"I was just about to ask you the same thing."

"What do you—oh!" It was as if she just realized she wasn't in her own room. "Damn!" she said. "I must have passed out!"

"Passed out?"

Briefly she told him about Bertie's midnight visit, the pulque. Nothing about sexual encounters was mentioned.

"You can always trust that Bertie," Danny said sarcastically.

"I think you're too hard on him, Danny. I told you, he's okay. John thinks so too."

"Speaking of which, where is John?"

Vaguely, she looked around. "I have no idea," she said. "Maybe he's already gone to the square. He's there most of the time now."

Quickly he gave her a synopsis of his vision. She looked a little frightened, assured him she'd let him know before she and John did anything out of the ordinary together. He didn't find that totally satisfactory, but it was the best he could do. He kissed her cheek and struck out for the village, asking her to tell Kathryn where he'd gone.

This day, he noticed, had a totally different feel from every other day since they'd been here. The heavy gray sky drizzled a little rain, and the wind had a cold bite to it. As he came into the village, he saw the people, usually so cheerful and happy, walking about with long faces. He didn't understand, but it made him nervous. He hurried on down the road.

As he came to the edge of the square, he found Orizaba, Patecatl, and Mayauel watching some men, some of John's acolytes, building a box of stone slabs. It was about seven feet long, three feet wide and high. It looked like a large stone coffin.

"What's that?" he asked them.

Mayauel looked at him, her pretty face contorted, her eyes red. "Our king has so ordered it," she said.

"But what is it?"

The dwarf looked up at Danny, tugged at his sleeve. "You will find him there," he said, pointing out a stall. "Mayauel cannot talk to you now. She feels too badly, as do we all."

Danny could not now resist running. Filled with a nameless dread, he sped across the square, ignoring the mournful stares of the shopkeepers.

He found John sitting in the stall of a feather merchant, wearing a beautifully made headdress. He kept his eyes on the ground, even when Danny greeted him.

"John, they said you ordered that stone box. What for?" he demanded.

"I must meditate in complete isolation," John said without raising his head. "Then I will know what's to be done."

"John, what has happened?" Danny pleaded.

"I must not say. Danny, take care. Be very careful of Bertie."

"But I thought—"

"I must go. It is done." Heavily he got up and walked across the square. The people were crying openly. Ignoring Danny's protests and questions, he climbed into the box; four acolytes placed a lid on it. For a minute, Danny could only stare at them. Then, fear giving him energy, he took off at a trot for the resort. He had to see David and Susan. A disaster was brewing. He could feel it.

Even before he was fully awake, David knew something was wrong. He had spent the last couple of hours squirming around in the bed as if trying to escape from it; in his dreams there was something nebulously threatening behind him, he had to get away, run. But he couldn't escape a threat from within. Eventually he opened his eyes, glanced at Susan's back as she lay turned away from him, and quickly jumped out of bed. He almost ran to the bathroom, barely making it there before he lost control. Dumping the contents of his stomach unceremoniously into the toilet, he hung over the rim, retching.

Susan's hands touched his back. They felt cool. "What is it, honey?" she asked, concern in her voice.

"Dunno," he gurgled. "Sick."

Eventually the surging of his stomach stopped and she helped him back to bed, where he collapsed. He looked at her, really for the first time that morning. Her eyes were slightly red, the way they often were when she didn't get enough sleep. But they had gone to bed early the previous night.

"You okay?" he managed to ask. "Doesn't look like you slept well."

"No, well—ah—I was restless," she said, looking away.

Now what? More hidden things, evasions? Order of the day. But quickly his mind turned back to himself. He didn't feel at all well, beyond the nausea. There were several places on his body where red welts were rising, each of them very sore. He called Susan's attention to them, and she examined them.

"I don't know," she said at last. "We'll get John to take a look. He's an M.D., even if he doesn't practice."

David sat up, tentatively. The nausea was abating, but he still had a pretty bad headache, and his whole body felt weak. He was all too aware of their isolation, at least for a couple more days; if he had some fast-moving tropical disease, it could be bad news, no doubt about it. He searched Susan's face, and hoped she wouldn't catch it, too. More than one of them coming down with something could mean a total disaster was imminent. Maybe it was anyway; above and beyond his illness, everything seemed changed somehow this morning.

There was a knock at the door, and Susan, unconscious of her nudity, opened it. Danny rushed in, started talking rapidly and in confusion. He was clearly out of breath, and not making sense. He stopped when he saw David.

"Jesus Christ!" he said. "What's the matter with you?"

"Sick," David croaked. "Can you get John to come up here and—"

"No! That's what I'm trying to tell you! John has had himself sealed in a goddamn stone coffin and he won't come out!"

"What! Why?" Susan cried.

"Damned if I know," Danny told her. "Something's happened, I don't know what. But it's bad, I can feel it."

David mustered his strength and got out of bed. "Well, sick or no, we have to get down there and get this straight. Enough fucking around. I need him, and this silliness can't go on!"

Susan helped him dress—the leather outfit, of course—and put on her vest and skirt. They went down the stairs, she and

Danny supporting David. As they came to the dining room, they found a morose group waiting for them; Mayauel, Patecatl, and Evelyn. It was hard to say who looked more upset.

"Now what?" Susan asked.

"You need to know," Patecatl said. "Your brother has abdicated the kingship. He has, as you already know, sealed himself in a box to meditate without disturbance. His last command as king was that it not be opened for four days. The new king—the other candidate—has stationed his Jaguar Knights at the box to ensure this is carried out to the letter."

"Four days!" David said. "But that's impossible! The plane comes in two days!"

Patecatl shook his head. "I fear the plane will land and leave again with no one to meet it. The Jaguar Knights have closed the road. No one can come or go."

"The hell you say!" Danny raced back up the stairs, was gone for a few minutes, and came back down waving a .38. David was really surprised; he'd had no idea Danny had it.

Again, Patecatl shook his head. "Please, Danny, take our advice and do not try to use that. The results may be an even further disaster."

From the stairs came Kathryn's voice. "Danny, please. For some reason, I think he's right. I don't understand it, but I do."

Danny looked up at her. "I've always thought Bertie was a madman. Now look. You cannot expect me to stand by and do nothing."

Yet another voice now cut into the conversation. "So, what will you do?" Bertie asked, leaning in the doorway and smiling. Oddly, David felt relieved; he didn't look crazy at all.

Danny swung around and pointed the gun at him. "This good enough?" he snapped.

"Oh, very good. Fine. But, Danny, they're right. That could create a disaster. I'm afraid I'll have to ask you to give it to me, now."

"Sure. Bertie. When Hell freezes over."

Bertie sighed. "Toltecatl," he said.

As they all stared, a huge creature stuffed itself through the door; a jaguar, three times life-size. No eyes; obsidian mirrors instead.

"Give me the gun, Danny," Bertie said. The cat moved toward him. "The gun, and he won't harm you, or anyone."

David watched Danny's face. He really didn't seem scared, even though his nightmare was now confronting him in broad daylight. Rather, he seemed to be calculating the odds.

"Even if it kills me, I gotta try," he said. He aimed at the cat's head and pulled the trigger. They all jumped at the thunder of the gun. But the cat had no wound. He couldn't have missed. The cat crouched, as if to spring.

Almost simultaneously, all three women jumped in front of Danny. "You'll have to kill us first!" screamed Susan.

"Well," Bertie said. "Can't have that. But Danny, you can see that the gun is useless to you. But it can cause some danger to all of us. May I have it, please?"

"No. I won't have you using it on us."

Again Bertie sighed. "Difficult. So difficult. I wonder why. Ihuimecatl."

A black shadow came through the door like a rocket. It touched Danny's hand; the gun sagged, became rubbery. Danny and David both stared at it. The barrel was bent down at a crazy angle and the cylinder seemed to have melted. Then both the shadow and the cat were gone, and the two black-robed figures stood near the door.

"Now you can keep it," Bertie said. He started for the door, then turned. "The sun does not shine today. Things must change. Please try to understand." He looked at Susan; his eyes, so very cold, softened. "Know that I love you," he whispered. Then he and the robed figures left.

Discarding the now useless weapon, Danny ran after Bertie and the two robed figures. Kathryn screamed at him to stop, but he ignored her. He caught up with them on the lawn. They seemed to be paying no attention to him.

"Bertie!" Danny yelled. "Will you stop? I want to talk to you!"

Bertie stopped and turned; the other two stopped as well, but Bertie motioned them on, and they went without protest.

"Yes, Danny?" Bertie asked. He was almost friendly.

"Look. I know you have the upper hand, but I just want to know. What do you want from us? Why do you want to keep us here?"

Bertie looked surprised. "Keep you here?" he asked. "Who told you that? I don't want to keep you here at all. You are free to go when the plane arrives. Oh, I see—the knights on the road. They won't stop you, don't worry about it."

"What about John?"

"Well, of course that is impossible. John left instructions that the box was not to be opened for four days. When he did that, he was king. So we must honor it, you see? But the rest of you can go. I'll be honest; I thought about insisting that Susan stay, and I'm planning to ask her to. But even her, if she wants to go, well—"

"You've got to be crazy if you think for a minute the rest of us are leaving without John! And what about you, Bertie? You planning to stay forever?"

"And rule a kingdom? Oh, it's possible, Danny. It has its advantages. I had some—uh—problems in the states, anyway. For me, this may be an ideal solution."

Danny shook his head. At that moment, it seemed unwise to ask what Bertie's problems in the states were. There was no use in taking unnecessary chances; considering the outlandish events that had just taken place in the house, this confrontation had been risky at best. But Bertie didn't seem to be taking any offense.

"Maybe I can get the plane to wait," Danny mused. "Or come back. If so, you have any objections to John leaving when he comes out of the box in four days?"

"No, none at all. The only thing I object to is him trying to reclaim the kingship. He'd have to fight for that, and somehow I don't think he will. So you do what you want, Danny, and don't you worry about it. None of my plans affect you. But I'll warn you of this. There are some things that will happen now, that you and the others won't like, or understand. But you interfere at your own peril, you follow me? Ihuimecatl and Toltecatl, as well as the knights, would take exception. And you've seen with your own eyes what they can do."

"Yes, I suppose I have," Danny said slowly. "Unbelievable. Who—or what—are they, Bertie?"

"Just as they said the night of the ceremony," he said casually. "They're demons." With that, he turned and went on down the hill toward town.

Danny watched him go, wondering exactly what that meant.

Literal demons, like from Hell? Sure had to be considered a possibility. This whole thing had suddenly taken a different turn, and now was plainly out of control. Still, Bertie seemed to be able to command the demons, and if he was being honest, there was still a chance for them to all get out more or less in one piece. Assuming David was not too sick, assuming John came out of the box okay and on time, assuming he could get the plane to come back two days later. A lot of assumptions. But the thing he had to do was meet that plane, regardless of what was happening. It was their only way out. Only reasonable way, anyway. He looked over the forests off to the south. He sure wasn't interested in trying to go cross country, but it might come to that. At least he had to be ready for it.

When he got back to the house, a weeping Kathryn fell into his arms, castigating him for taking such risks. Susan and Evelyn also seemed very upset. After they were assured he was all right, he faced a barrage of questions as to what Bertie had said. He explained, and a long silence fell on the room.

"We shouldn't have a problem getting the pilot to come back, or at least radio in for us," Evelyn observed. "But we can't fail to be there when that plane lands."

"No, we can't." Danny agreed. "Number-one priority. Number two, do what we can for David. There's one more thing: Susan, Bertie said he planned to ask you to stay here with him. Is it safe to assume you wouldn't think of it?"

"No! Absolutely not!" she said vehemently. "I—uh—I have no idea why he thinks it would do any good to ask!"

"Maybe he doesn't, but he probably will. I think he's going to get used to having his own way very quickly." Danny had not missed her hesitation; he was sure now that there'd been more between Susan and Bertie than she'd talked about.

David, however, didn't seem to notice. "With those two things at his disposal, I'm sure of it," he commented. "Demons! Yet I guess we can't reject it out of hand. Unless we had a mass hallucination!"

"There's more here than we're seeing. For instance, why did John abdicate and shut himself up in a box for four days? Everything was going well for him as king. Anybody got an idea?" Danny scanned the faces; everyone seemed bewildered except for Mayauel and Patecatl. He looked at them, addressed them directly. "Look, if you two know what's going on, please tell us. We need to know. That should be obvious."

Mayauel looked genuinely pained. "We just can't, Danny, partly because we're not sure ourselves how everything is going to fit together. Believe me, we'd like to. But we can tell you this: what he meant about things happening you wouldn't understand, or like. The sacrifices, Danny, they'll start again, very soon."

Danny stared at her; Susan started to cry. "Who?" he whispered.

"None of us, at least not yet. The villagers. They will go willingly. They understand."

"God damn!" Danny yelled at her. "Understand what? I admit I don't understand, so tell me! Explain it!"

Patecatl shrugged. "Your friend John tried to find his strength from within. This one won't. He needs power, and he will get it from blood, from hearts, from lives. Really, it is so simple."

"So why did John abdicate?" Danny asked him.

"Also simple. His intent was perfect, but he lacked power. Power cannot come only from within. If it does, the person becomes drained. That's what happened to your friend. This one will be different. He knows how to gain power, but he doesn't always know how to use it. His intent is not focused."

"Doesn't sound good. Too bad they couldn't have gotten together."

"Yes. Together they would have made an obsidian butterfly."

Danny grinned, for the first time today; a tight grin, but there nevertheless. "Can't say we weren't warned, can we?" he said to David and Susan. Evelyn asked him to explain. He did.

33

The next day most of them stayed near the resort. Even Mayauel and Patecatl seemed to have moved in there. They didn't see Bertie at all, but there were rumors. And Patecatl assured them it was true, that sacrifices had already taken place up at the old ruined church. Danny had every intention of bringing the entire Mexican army in here if necessary, to see Bertie brought to justice. Even as he consoled himself with these ideas, he wondered how that army would stack up against the likes of Ihuimecatl and Toltecatl; his gun hadn't done much. But these people couldn't be abandoned to the mercies of a madman forever. He felt like tearing out his hair in frustration. He thought about John, the day he would come out of the box. He wasn't sure whether he would want to hug him or hit him.

The women, especially Susan, were very morose. They did not want to hear anything about the sacrifices, preferring instead to pretend they weren't taking place. The villagers still came to them for blessings, however, and they still conferred them, even though they didn't go down into the village.

Shortly after lunch, Danny went down to the square to check on the box, see if there was any possibility of getting John out early. One of the acolytes again assured him there was none. Glumly, he stared at it; there was now a contingent of six Jaguar Knights and six of John's acolytes guarding it, and their common purpose was to prevent it being opened before it was time. Orizaba, looking sadder than Danny would have thought possible, sat atop it, refusing to speak.

Returning to the resort, he found that David's illness had changed its course. In some ways he was better, not in as much pain and able to get around. But in other ways it was much worse. The sore spots he'd complained of had swollen and burst, and now formed suppurating sores; he had at least a dozen of them. Nothing they were doing helped in the least, and no one had any idea what it might be. But one thing was clear; he was losing his strength rapidly. Danny and Susan tried to talk him into flying out as soon as possible, but they had no success. He insisted on staying with the others, saying he couldn't leave Susan, and she in turn couldn't leave John. As far as he was concerned, the issue was closed.

34

The next day, Danny and Eduardo set out with one of the drivers for the airstrip, two full hours ahead of the plane's scheduled arrival time. They waited there until sunset; but no plane arrived.

35

For most of the evening, and the next day as well, Danny hounded Eduardo, demanding that he do something to help. Finally, the manager gave in. He agreed to station a man full time at the strip in case the plane was late. Standing at the edge of the hill, Danny watched the Land-Rover, camping gear in the back, wend its way through the now-muddy streets of Tlillan Tlapallan.

The next couple of days dragged by slowly; everyone was waiting for the plane to arrive or for John to come out of the box, whichever came first. Meanwhile, David grew more and more ill; Danny was beginning to fear for his life.

Early the following morning, Danny, Susan, Kathryn, and Evelyn all went into town. It was time for the opening of the box, and they wanted to be there when that happened, if in fact it hadn't already. This morning, the sun was out, although dark clouds hung ominously around the horizon.

As they walked into the square, it became obvious that changes had taken place in Tlillan Tlapallan. There were things for sale that had not been before; a slave market had appeared among the tented stalls. They stared in disbelief. It seemed so utterly alien to anything they had seen here before. Four men and six women, all nude, stood on the auction block, tethered by ropes. The sellers indicated the sizes of the men's genitals, and proclaimed the women virgins. The three American women huddled close to Danny, even though there was no apparent threat to them. Watching one of the slave women dance and sing, Danny wondered how these unfortunates had become slaves; perhaps he should talk to Bertie again, try to get the new rules straight.

When they reached the box, Orizaba and the acolytes were already unsealing the heavy stone lid. Danny noticed with surprise that two of the acolytes were women; he had assumed they were an all-male group. With primitive chisels the mortar was chipped away until the lid was loose. Then, grunting, they heaved it off. Orizaba held up his hand at Danny's attempt to help; apparently, the acolytes were supposed to do this alone.

At last they were finished, and the four Americans could see John's motionless form lying in the box, still wearing his feathered headdress and the extended mask; his staff and whisk lay across his chest. Danny was afraid he was dead, and Susan just stared, wide-eyed. But then he stirred, sat up, and took off the mask and feathers. When he looked at them, Danny thought his eyes did look dead. Very slowly he got to his feet and stepped out of the box. With a halting step, as if his legs were still asleep, he came toward them, followed closely by Orizaba. The acolytes reached into the box and removed his trumpet, some jewels nobody seemed to know he'd had, and several pieces of pottery he'd apparently made while in Tlillan Tlapallan. All these things they gave to Orizaba, who stayed very close to John.

He stopped, turned, and gestured to the six acolytes. The Jaguar Knights then stepped up behind them, cut their clothing away with knives, and tied ropes around their necks. As soon as this was done, they were led away to the slave block. Danny felt a chill. So this was the initial source of slaves. Who was next? He felt an increased urgency about the plane, about getting out of this now threatening place.

When John reached them, they bombarded him with a multitude of questions, all of them speaking at once. "I will talk to you all at the house," he said, raising his hand to quiet them. "We will go there now. Please, my friends, my sister. Be patient." His voice sounded very weak, very sad. Walking slowly, like a very old man, he led them back to the house. As they went, people stared at John; some bowed, others cried. He still, it seemed, commanded considerable respect here. Danny was thinking that this fact could be used to their advantage. It was risky, but it was possibly their best option if the plane didn't come. Perhaps John could be convinced to reclaim the throne from Bertie. Once he heard about the sacrifices, maybe—just maybe—

36

"I know," John said, looking at Danny and the others, "that you cannot possibly understand what has happened, and it is my poor fortune that I cannot explain it to you—if I did, an innocent would be harmed. You'll have to take my word for this. I had to meditate, had to find an answer, had to discover what I have to do. You've seen how the village has changed; overnight, it seems. My fault, all mine. I thought I knew myself better, but I didn't. Now, I have one more thing to do. I have to go to the divine sea, and I have to go alone. It's very important. Please, you must accept my word on this."

"No disrespect, John, but there are other matters here,"

Danny said firmly. "First, as you can plainly see, David is sick. You're the only doctor around. We need you. Second, Bertie is playing hell with this place. You saw your own acolytes taken into slavery. Also, we understand sacrifices have begun again, Bertie himself conducting them! I was hoping—"

John held up his hand. "I know all this. But for now, I can do nothing. First, I must go to the divine sea. The sun is calling me."

Danny jumped up and shouted at him. "Damn it, John, this is serious! Can't you see David could even die? We need to cut all the mystical crap for a few minutes and—"

John gave him a look that silenced him. Mystical it might be, but certainly Bertie's pet demons weren't crap. Maybe John knew something he didn't. He sat down, slowly. "How long will you be there?" he asked.

"Not long. Danny, these things are beyond your comprehension right now—and mine too, I'm afraid. But you will have to be a little tolerant." His voice was very gentle. "Now, I want to give you all these things," he said. He began passing out the trumpet, the jewels, the pottery. "It's necessary that I give these things away," he told them. "It's part of a penance I have to do. All of you now understand that, except you, Danny, and I'm sorry, but I can't help you there. You take the trumpet," he said, handing it to Danny. "Keep it. Maybe play it sometimes. It almost plays itself."

When all the items had been distributed, John stood up. "The sun calls me. I must go. Orizaba will accompany me. You are all my dear friends, and I love you all." Carrying his feathered headdress and mask, he left the room.

Danny looked at the others after he had gone. "Well, shit!" he said. "I suppose there's not a thing we can do but wait some more. I tell you, though, I've had about all of this mysticism I can take."

"You were the one," Mayauel said calmly, "always trying to figure it out. Now what? Any answers, my friend?"

He wondered if she was trying to lead him to something. He fell quiet, thinking, running through all the strange events since he first saw the red and black sunburst on the Hallstens' apartment window. He noticed that Susan and David appeared to be doing the same thing. A considerable amount of time passed while the entire company remained immersed in thought.

"Oh, God. Oh, no." Susan started to say. "Danny. David. Oh, God, no. Remember me telling you? Early on? The television show that wasn't? The man on the beach, the fire?"

"Yes, I remember," Danny replied. "So? He-man, right? He'd been tricked into—into—" He stared into her eyes; they were very wide. He saw her on John's bed. His vision. Hers. It crystallized in his mind, and he saw the realization dawning in hers. "Susan, how can I ask, but did you—"

"No!" she practically screamed. "It was Bertie, we were drunk, it was Bertie! I'm sure it was. I— Oh, no—no—no—"

"What the hell are you guys talking about?" David asked.

"No time!" shrieked Danny, jumping up. "We've got to get down there!"

He and Susan ran for the door, ignoring the startled looks from the others. Explanations could wait; now they had to move. When they got onto the lawn, they could see the plume of smoke, as if from a very large fire, rising from behind the other hill.

"Oh, God, Danny, *no!*" Susan screamed, and began to run. He followed, his stomach surging. At breakneck speed they flew down the path, into town. The few people they passed seemed to be praying; it seemed like the world was ending. Susan and Danny took the beach road, sliding in the sand a bit, but still making good time. When they topped the little rise, they saw John, wearing his feathered headdress and his mask, standing in front of a huge fire. Orizaba, a tiny figure, sat off to the side, his face buried in his hands.

Seeing John still safe, they slowed just a little, panting. As soon as she could, Susan called out, "John! Wait! Please!"

He seemed to glance up at them, but maybe he was looking at the sky. Thinking about it later, Danny could never be sure. The whole scene was so clear. The bright blue skies, the first they'd seen in several days. The white sand, the fine green vegetation, Susan running beside him, her hair flying. Stark. Clear. The huge fire, already he could feel the heat. Such a pretty day. So vivid. John so colorful in his little vest and kilt, his feathers brilliant greens, reds, blues. His mask, bright red, long-faced, almost ducklike, grotesque. A frozen moment in time.

Then, in what looked like slow motion, John hurled himself into the flames.

"Nooooo!" Susan screamed, her voice incredibly loud. Danny slowed, but then saw that there was a real possibility that she'd follow him right into the fire. Speeding up, he grabbed her. She fought him, still screaming, her words unintelligible.

"Oh, no, no, no," she sobbed, sinking to her knees on the sand, Danny following her down. He was stunned, not yet really reacting to it. John was still standing upright in the flames, his arms raised; there was a furious crackling, a terrible odor. Then, slowly, almost majestically, the figure collapsed. The crackling reached a new peak, and it seemed that Susan's sobs were in rhythm with the hideous snapping and popping.

Hearing a noise from above, Danny looked up. In his arms, Susan, her face wild, looked too. Birds, thousands of them, dipping and soaring around the fire. He couldn't believe it. He could see the quetzals, bright green; and wasn't that a condor? A golden eagle? Hundreds of colorful parrots, finches, woodpeckers, ducks; all manner of birds. They seemed to be watching the fire. Suddenly the flames died down, and a plume of ash rose. Danny stared at it, transfixed. It looked like gold dust, rising and spiraling into the air, drifting on the currents, forming rings, streamers. He could feel Susan's gaze following his. A bright light caught their eyes, and in the western sky they saw Venus, the evening star, huge and brilliant, sinking into the horizon. Not possible, Danny thought, dazed; it wasn't evening. The light of the star glinted on the ash that looked like gold dust; the birds raised a huge clamor; the fire was dying. From the sky, a single, emerald green feather drifted down, right in front of their tear-streaked faces. Lightly it landed on the sand in front of them, and as Susan picked it up, a small whirlwind stirred the dust.

For a long time, they knelt there in silence, watching the fire gradually burn down. The flocks of birds had dissipated; a pile of ash and the lonely figure of Orizaba was all that remained. Like mirror images, they looked at each other. There was nothing to say about what had happened. Recriminations, hindsight, were unnecessary and useless.

After studying Susan's tortured face, Danny asked, "How can we tell the others?"

"I don't know, Danny," she managed to say. "I don't want to be here. Please—I can't get up by myself." She appeared ready to cry again, but she was dry, no tears left. He helped her up, and they hesitantly walked to Orizaba.

"You know there was no way to stop him, no. No way at all. None. Absolutely none at all," Orizaba said as they came close. He didn't look at them.

"Will you come back with us, Orizaba?" Danny asked.

"No, no, not now. I will sit here. Still I see his visage as he stands here, still I hear his trumpet in the wind. I will always, you know. Always, as long as I draw breath."

"I understand, my friend," Danny whispered. He'd thought Susan was dry, all cried out, but she started again. As she sagged against him, he wondered if he had the strength to hold her up. But he had to be strong enough for all of them. Back up at the resort, David was still gravely ill, and that was the issue that had to be addressed now.

After a walk that seemed to take forever, they entered the sitting room, looked at the stark questioning faces. Except for Mayauel and Patecatl; Patecatl looked away, Mayauel wept openly.

"You knew what he was going to do," Danny said flatly to her. "Why didn't you tell us?"

She nodded, wailed. "He couldn't have been stopped. Maybe for a minute, an hour, a day. But not forever."

"Yes, that's probably true," Danny agreed lifelessly.

"Danny, what's happened?" Kathryn asked, her face a study in anxiety.

"I'm sorry. John has committed suicide. We were too late. He's gone," Danny said, his voice emotionless.

"Oh, God, no!" Kathryn cried. Evelyn began to cry; David looked stunned. Frank's jaw worked, and without a word he got up and walked outside. Danny watched him go, realizing that he had no idea what Frank's relationship to John had been.

"What about the body?" David said finally. "We've got to give him a decent burial, we—"

"David, I'm so sorry. I know how close you'd gotten to him. But there is no body. He—he burned himself."

They stared at him for a moment in disbelief, but then the tears returned with new vigor. Susan sagged against Danny again, crying in great wracking sobs. "It's all my fault," she moaned.

Danny turned to her quickly, wiping his own wet eyes. "No!" he said forcefully, well aware of the danger of this. "I think I know exactly how it went down, and it was Bertie, not you. Understand me? Not you!"

She nodded hesitantly, her fists working helplessly. She was tearing Danny's heart out. The pain, watching her like this, was worse than the literal pain he'd felt in the dream.

"Look," Danny said to all of them. "We've got to concentrate on the living, get ourselves out of here. Mayauel, Patecatl, you're coming with us. Things have gotten pretty nasty here, and we've got to hang together. Your grief will have to wait."

"Danny," Kathryn said. "You won't understand, I know. You've got to tolerate this, though. You're the strength for all of us right now. But everyone else will agree, we have to do a purification, now, for John."

Everyone nodded agreement. Danny opened his mouth to yell at them, but decided against it. It didn't matter that much. There was nothing to do right at the present moment anyway.

"Danny, please," Evelyn said to him, "will you get Frank for me? I'm not sure I can, and I need him with me to do this."

"Of course." He passed Susan to David and went out to look for Frank.

Danny didn't see him anywhere. Damn, he thought; where had the man gone? Splitting their group up right now seemed like a very poor idea. He wasn't sure he wanted Susan out of his sight at all today. Irritated, he began to search the grounds, but a complete circle around the area yielded nothing. Frank Wasserman was nowhere to be found. Not knowing the man all that well, Danny didn't know how profoundly John's death might have affected him. But he knew how Frank loved the beach and the sea. It seemed reasonable that he might go there. He went back inside, checked on everyone else, then told them he was going to the beach to search for Frank. Evelyn agreed that was the likely place, but she looked very worried.

"I'll come with you, Danny," she said.

"Fine. David, I know how sick you are, but don't leave Susan alone, you hear me?" Danny said. David nodded, held her close.

In the kitchen, Danny armed himself with the largest butcher knife he could find. Maybe it was worthless, but it made him feel better. He no longer wanted to go into or near the village unarmed.

On reaching the beach, they found Orizaba still sitting there, just as he had been when Danny and Susan had left. There was no sign of anyone else. Avoiding the remains of the fire, they approached the dwarf, who did not look up at them.

"Have you seen Frank Wasserman?" Danny demanded.

For the first time, Orizaba turned his tear-stained face toward him. "No. He has come to himself, my friend, and he is not here. Up there," he pointed to the ruined church, "up there. You will find him there."

"Why is he up there?" Danny asked, really surprised. "That's where Bertie is, and the two demons."

"Yes." The dwarf turned back to gaze at the ashes, his face a mask of pain.

"Now what?" Danny snarled. "Why would he go up there? Asshole! As if we didn't have enough problems!"

"Please, Danny, he is my husband," Evelyn said, "and he may be in trouble."

"We may be too, going up there," Danny growled.

"We've got to," she pleaded.

He sighed. "All right. Listen, you go back to the resort. I'll go up, see if I can find him. Okay?"

"No! I'm coming with you. Let's hurry, Danny. I have a terrible feeling about this, terrible!"

Danny looked at her. The fact was, he did too. He decided not to argue with her anymore, and they started out for the trail which led up the other hill. As they neared the base of it, they started catching whiffs of an incredibly foul smell. This became more and more obvious as they came closer; at last they rounded a bend in the path and saw the source of it. Evelyn gave a little cry, and again Danny felt his insides turn to ice.

At the base of the hill, just off the path, was a rotting pile of bodies. All were the same; a gaping wound in the chest, arms and legs dismembered. Danny counted; eight men and three women, two of the men being former acolytes of John's. The vegetation on the hillside was broken in a path all the way from the top to this pathetic little pile. Clearly, the bodies had been casually pitched over after the sacrifice had been performed. Danny looked up the hill, saw a flash of movement at the top.

"Look," he said to Evelyn. "Please reconsider. Let me go up alone. I stand a better chance."

"No, Danny. For better or worse, he's my husband. I've got to go with you!"

"All right, all right! But we can't just stroll right in. Let's go around to the beach side and go up that way. Maybe we can see what's going on before they see us."

"Okay, fine. Let's go."

They circled the base of the hill, started up. There were plenty of small trees to hold on to; it was not a difficult climb. After a short while, they reached the top. Danny peeked over; the knifelike grasses were in front of them; they could not cross here. Working their way along the edge, they finally found a narrow path leading through the grass up to the black stone walls of the old church.

Danny looked back at Evelyn; she was nearly naked, and the path was quite narrow. "Be very careful," he whispered to her. "This stuff will cut the hell out of your legs."

"Right!" she whispered back.

Keeping low, they made their way down the path. When he reached the wall of the church, Danny flattened himself against it and looked back; Evelyn had negotiated the path without injuring herself, and she quickly came up beside him.

"What now?" she asked in a low voice.

"We work our way up to that corner, look around, and see what's happening," he told her, pointing.

Slowly, carefully, they started forward. There was only a narrow area alongside the building that was clear of the grasses, so the going was still slow. As long as they kept their bodies against the stone, however, they encountered no problems.

Reaching the edge, Danny carefully peeked around. Evelyn sidled up underneath him so she could see too, and for a moment they both stared at the scene in front of them without comprehension.

The sacrificial stone was now dark brown with the blood of the victims they'd seen at the base of the hill. At one end of it stood the robed figures of Ihuimecatl and Toltecatl; across from them was Bertie, standing so still he looked like a statue. Beside him was Frank, his arms spread straight out, eyes staring through the thick-rimmed glasses. He wore his long robe, but what caught Danny's attention was his mouth. There was something very strange about it, as if he were holding something in it. The overall effect was to make him look like he had huge tusks or fangs hanging over his lower lip, pushing his upper lip into a high volute. It made him look quite inhuman, like a monster of some sort.

Evelyn made a little mouselike noise. He pushed her back, held his finger to his lips for silence.

"What?" he whispered.

"Danny, the vision I told you I had, the monster! Frank looks just like that now!"

They peeked back around. The only other person on the hill was a young woman with a baby in her arms, standing in front of the stone. Danny recognized her; he'd seen her in the village many times. She was facing them, holding the child's face against her shoulder, showing no particular sign of fear. Which was odd, considering where she was.

Ihuimecatl and Toltecatl lowered their cowls, and the former took the baby from the woman's arms. Toltecatl led her to the stone, pulled her dress off, and laid her down, nude. She offered him no resistance. Danny ground his teeth. He was sure he knew what was about to happen, and he felt helpless to stop it.

"Why is Frank just standing there, watching this?" Evelyn asked vehemently, raising her voice above a whisper.

"I have no idea, but please be quiet, Evelyn. We don't want them to see us."

With little preliminary, Toltecatl drove his obsidian knife into the woman's chest. She cried out once as her blood spouted upward. The cowled figure twisted the blade, then thrust his hand into the wound. Ripping her heart free, he quickly brought it to Bertie, who opened his mouth as the creature carrying the still-beating heart drew near. Danny could not believe what he was seeing. Toltecatl pushed it into Bertie's mouth, and, blood spattering his chest as he bit into the tough muscle, he began eating it. As the last of it disappeared, he seemed to go into some kind of ecstasy. Danny was struggling to control his stomach. He felt Evelyn's body spasm beside him, knew she was doing the same.

Toltecatl lifted the woman's body as if it weighed nothing at all, hurled it over the side. It went crashing down the hillside to join the others rotting at the base. Danny was already foaming with rage when Ihuimecatl laid the infant on the stone.

"Oh, no," Danny murmured. "He couldn't. Not even Bertie—"

The baby was crying. "A sign of good rains," Ihuimecatl said. The cries ceased abruptly as she plunged her dagger into the small body, ripping it savagely. She pulled out the tiny heart, beating so fast it looked like it was vibrating instead of pulsing, and carried it to Frank.

He couldn't believe his eyes. Frank's mouth gaped, the fangs glinting in the sun. Ihuimecatl shoved the little heart in, and he swallowed it without chewing. He too looked ecstatic.

"*No!* You fucking bastard!" Evelyn screamed. She shot out from behind the wall, running straight at her husband. She had moved so suddenly that Danny had no chance to stop her. Holding the knife firmly, he took a deep breath and went after her.

Toltecatl intercepted her before she got halfway across the cleared area. While he held her, Ihuimecatl tossed the baby's body over the side and turned toward Danny. He waited for her, holding his blade straight out.

"You don't want to fight with her, Danny," Bertie said. "You'll lose, and this time she'll kill you. I won't be able to stop her."

"Tell him to let Evelyn go, then," Danny said, holding his ground.

"Surely. Toltecatl, release the woman, please."

Toltecatl let go of Evelyn's arms and turned away. He seemed indifferent. Their confidence in their control of the situation was by far the most frightening thing to Danny.

But Evelyn ignored them, turned to her husband. "Why?" she screamed at him. "How could you do that? Are you really a monster?"

"He can't answer you, my dear," Bertie said. "He has fully come to himself, and he only did what he knew was absolutely necessary. He needs the strength, and unfortunately for your sensibilities, that's the way he gets it. But we are not cruel, not unnecessarily so. You will admit we took the mother first. She did not have to watch it. Even as aware as these people are, that would surely have been distressing to her."

"You're all heart, Bertie," Danny snarled. "Of all the sick, vile things I've ever seen, this is the limit, the absolute—"

"I told you there were things you would not understand, or like. I do wish you had not come here with her. Now there will be, for you, more unpleasantness." At last he broke his statue-like pose, came over to Danny. "Some come to themselves earlier than others. Perhaps some never will. But Frank has, completely, it seems—" Bertie stopped, passed his hand across his face. "You know, I do wish I could explain the whole thing to you. Because if I could, I could explain it to myself." His face took on a haunted look. "It's like I have two sides to my head, one I've lived with all my life and another I've just become aware of. It's the other that's pushing me around right now. Half the time—no, more than half the time, now—I myself don't know why I'm doing what I'm doing. But yet I have to, it seems there is no other way; none. I know what happened to John. If it helps any, I know he felt the same way. Just like Frank does right now. Look at him! He doesn't even look human anymore!" Bertie actually looked scared; his cocksure attitude was completely gone.

Danny relaxed a little. At that moment, it seemed that Bertie was in as much trouble as any of them. He wondered if the man was possessed somehow. He'd never believed that possible, but then he wouldn't have believed that creatures like Ihuimecatl and Toltecatl existed, either.

Frank broke his frozen stance and walked toward the bloody stone. He walked right by Evelyn, didn't even glance at her, didn't seem to hear when she called his name in a small voice. Ihuimecatl stepped up beside him, and he knelt by the stone, rather stiffly. Danny had a horrible feeling, one of utter helplessness and terror.

His feeling was immediately verified. Reaching down, Ihuimecatl picked up a sword made of wood, with edges carved from black obsidian. It looked just as efficient as a steel one.

Frank's neck was extended over the stone in a most suggestive manner, and Ihuimecatl raised the wicked blade.

Both Danny and Evelyn screamed, "No!" almost at the same time and started to move. But Bertie caught Danny's arm, and Toltecatl caught Evelyn's. They had no second chance. Ihuimecatl brought the blade down across Frank's neck; an explosion of blood sprayed the whole area. His head, grotesque with its fangs, bounced on the stone and rolled over it onto the ground. Stunned, listening to Evelyn's high-pitched, long scream, Danny watched it roll. Oddly, Frank's glasses didn't fall off; they seemed to be a part of his face.

Still staring, Danny was hardly aware that Bertie had taken the knife from his hand. Glancing down, he saw that he was unarmed. Bertie was smiling at him. As Evelyn stood shaking violently and crying, Ihuimecatl dragged the body and head away from the stone and out of their sight. Danny was unsure of what to do; he just stood and watched.

Bertie put his hands on Evelyn's shoulders, locked her eyes with his. She stopped crying almost immediately.

"What are you doing to her?" Danny yelled.

"I am helping her come to herself. It is time. Ihuimecatl, restrain him."

The creature didn't touch Danny; she just stood close to him. But he knew if he tried to move toward Bertie, she would.

Even from here, Danny could see Bertie's eyes blazing with some incredible energy. Every time Evelyn moved at all, he whispered something Danny couldn't hear. Several times she started to speak, but each time he silenced her with a word.

"Evelyn, get away from him!" Danny cried. She didn't respond. For another minute she looked into Bertie's eyes, then finally glanced back at Danny.

"Danny, I'm so sorry. I don't fully understand, but now at least I know what is necessary. I'm so sorry you're here."

"What are you talking about? Please, we need to get back—"

"No. You need to." She faced him, her expression calm and distant. "Please, Danny. Go back to the resort. They need you there."

"Not without you!" he cried.

She looked at Bertie. "Can't you send him away, make him go?"

"No," Bertie replied. "But we must proceed, you understand?"

"Yes, I guess I do. Danny, I'm sorry."

She climbed onto the stone. Danny screamed at her to get off, but she ignored him. He started toward her, but was restrained by Ihuimecatl. It seemed he had two choices; stay and watch, or go back. He was nearly foaming at the mouth, yelling at her.

"I need to purify myself," she told Bertie.

"Yes," he replied, handing her a bundle of objects. At first Danny thought they were the maguey thorns he had seen Kathryn use. But they weren't. These were larger, perhaps six inches long and a quarter of an inch thick at the base. They gleamed whitely, as if they'd been carved from bone.

Kneeling on the stone, Evelyn removed her skirt and vest. As Danny gnashed his teeth, unable to look away, she pierced each of her earlobes, then spread her legs. He expected the next ones to go into her thighs, as Kathryn's had done before. But instead, she pressed the point of the next punch against her lower abdomen, just inside her leg. Slowly, her face tightening with the pain, she pushed it all the way in.

Danny groaned. He cried out for her to stop, but she ignored him, inserted another on the other side. A little trickle of blood ran from around this one, mixing with the drying blood already on the stone.

Without pausing, she touched the fifth punch to her left nipple, started to push. Her breast folded in from the pressure, but finally the point broke through. Biting her lip, she continued until only the round head of the spike was visible. Blood ran from around it, staining it, dripping down to join the rest on the dark stone. She watched it for a moment, then did the same thing to her right nipple. Danny was yelling that they were too long, that she'd puncture her lungs, but she couldn't seem to hear him. The seventh spike was used to pierce her tongue, from the bottom up. She pulled this one back out, and sat with her mouth open, dripping blood on the stone. Her breathing had become very labored; Danny was sure her lungs were damaged. He could see flecks of blood around her lips, had seen them even before she'd pierced her tongue. He tried to struggle toward her, but Ihuimecatl held him fast. He could only shriek, but his cries were having no effect on Evelyn.

Slowly, she lay back on the stone, spread her arms to the sides. Bertie stepped up to her, the red-stained obsidian knife in his hand. Her turquoise eyes looked up at him calmly, expectantly.

"No, Bertie, please, don't do it!" Danny cried. But again he was ignored. Evelyn nodded to him, and he put the point against her body just below her breastbone. The other victims had been stabbed hard and fast, in the chest; this was different. Perhaps it was only symbolic, perhaps he wasn't going to, Danny thought wildly. Bertie was just standing there, the knife-point dimpling her skin.

Then, as Danny watched in absolute horror, Bertie began to push on it slowly, not violently. Her stomach was only pushed in for a moment; it was obvious that the knife was very sharp. Her face tightened again and her head went back as a little red pool appeared where the point was pressing. Then the glossy black blade disappeared inch by torturous inch into her body. Danny couldn't believe she was simply lying there and allowing Bertie to do this. But, except for some twitching of her hands and feet, she didn't move, and she didn't say a word in protest.

As the widest part of the elliptical blade passed into her, her blood began to surge out, pouring over her body onto the stone, onto the ground. Bertie pushed it in a little further; then, just as slowly, pulled it back out. After helping her to a sitting position, Toltecatl handed her a bowl; she held it in her lap, tipping it so that the blood ran into it. The flow seemed to be slowing; Bertie picked up his knife again and pushed it back into her, working it around inside. Blood gushed, filling the bowl and overflowing onto her legs. Tears streamed down her face as she struggled to breathe, but still she held the bowl in place. When she started to fall, Toltecatl rushed around to help support her. She pressed the bowl hard against her open abdomen, causing another gush of blood.

She raised her head with obvious effort. "I'm—sorry—Danny," she whispered. Then her head fell limply forward on her chest.

Danny was crying openly. He remembered her vision, but he couldn't understand why she'd made it reality. "Bertie, somehow, some way, I'll see you dead, you bastard!" he cried. Bertie just looked over at him and smiled.

"It was what she wanted, actually what she needed, Danny. You saw that. You just can't accept it." He put his arm around her back, taking her weight from Toltecatl, who stepped back. Gently he lowered her to the stone again and, after extracting the six bone punches she'd left in her body, stabbed his knife into her chest. Her body spasmed once. Danny found himself unable to look away as Bertie sank his hand into her, searching for her heart.

"You hypnotized her or something!" Danny screamed. "You tricked John and Susan! You son of a bitch, I'll find a way to kill you! I promise you that!"

"Maybe you will," Bertie said, stroking Evelyn's still form gently. "If it is so decreed, you will. None of us are totally free agents here." Taking out his flint knife, he quickly cut off her head with it. Toltecatl held the bowl full of her blood under the stump, but it could hold no more and overflowed. Almost delicately, Bertie placed her head with her discarded clothing.

"This is for the knights," he said to Toltecatl, pointing to the headless body. The creature nodded, picked it up carefully, and went off down the hill. Ihuimecatl remained, still holding Danny in a vice-like grip.

"Go back to your friends, Danny," Bertie said. He sounded friendly; Danny was astounded at the hypocrisy he felt he was hearing. Bitter salt tears ran into the corners of his mouth. Too late for John, too late for Frank, too late for poor Evelyn. Why he was being spared, he didn't know, and at the moment he didn't care. Blinded by tears, he started back down the hill toward the resort house: as he left, Bertie gave him his knife back.

37

When Susan, David, and Kathryn returned to the sitting room, no one was there. Apparently, Susan thought, Danny and Evelyn hadn't gotten back yet. She wondered where Mayauel and Patecatl had gone; they had left them there when they'd gone upstairs to perform their purifications. Now that that had been done, she felt a little better; she had really been savage with herself, driving in the thorns as if they could push out the massive guilt she felt. But they hadn't, not really. The only thing that was different was that the pain distracted her a bit.

The terrible truth was right there in front of her; it couldn't be denied. She had slept with her own brother, both of them drunk and not really knowing what they were doing. But that didn't change the facts. John had realized this; he'd killed himself over it. And it was all her fault. She knew that Bertie had played a role in it, but couldn't bring herself to believe that he'd create a situation like this deliberately.

David had questioned her as to the events of that evening, and so far, she'd been unable to tell him; all she'd been able to do was cry. But she believed that he had figured it out. He tried to tell her it was all right, that she wasn't responsible, but that only made her feel worse. She hadn't even told him about her lovemaking with Bertie, even though she knew David wouldn't have held it against her. It only added to the massive ball of guilt she was carrying around. It felt like her whole body was full of it. She looked at David's ravaged skin and felt that, as bad as he looked outside, she was even more rotted inside. It wouldn't come out with the tears, wouldn't come out with the blood of the purifications. Right now, she felt anything but pure.

The sound of the outside door banging interrupted her thoughts. She looked up to see a haggard Danny just coming into the room. She didn't see Evelyn or Frank, but she did see the look on his face, the tear lines down his cheeks.

"Danny, what's—" Kathryn began.

"Frank and Evelyn," he said, his voice choked. "They're both dead. Bertie killed them." He fell heavily into one of the chairs as all three of them began to ask questions simultaneously. In a flat, emotionless voice, he explained what had happened on top of the other hill.

Susan listened to this and wept for her friends. But as Danny described Evelyn's death on the sacrificial stone, she found herself wishing it had been her instead of the other woman. At least she would be free from this guilt, from her responsibility for their deaths as well; if she hadn't slept with John, he'd still be the king, and none of this would be happening. She looked at her hands, feeling like Lady Macbeth. The blood would never come off.

"Look," Danny was saying. "There are only two answers for us. Either we've got to get out of here, or we've got to do something about Bertie. I mean, if we don't, we'll all eventually end up on that damned stone!"

"I agree, Danny, but how can we get out? Unless the plane comes, I mean," David said. "I have my doubts about going cross country—"

"Yeah," Danny said. "So do I. And even if we get rid of Bertie, we still have the problem of you. You're sick, and we have to do something about it. I wonder—do you suppose there's a doctor in the village?"

"I don't know. We were waiting for John." His voice broke a little. "And I don't think anybody even asked."

"Mayauel ought to know," Danny said. "Where are they, anyway?"

"We don't know," said Kathryn. "They weren't here when we finished the purification. You didn't see them outside?"

"No. Perhaps they went back to their cottage, although I don't think that's such a good idea. Well, I'll go find Eduardo, ask him." He got up and disappeared into the back of the house. The others sat quietly, each lost in their own thoughts, each wondering how they'd gotten into such a strange situation.

For the third time today, Danny trudged back down the hillside. His emotions were in an absolute turmoil; fear, sorrow

for his dead friends, shared pain with Susan and David, anger
at Bertie, and now irritation with Patecatl. He was, according
to Eduardo, the local physician! And all this time, he had not
said a word about it! Danny was going to find out why, in no
uncertain terms. He had already searched the resort for them;
their absence must have meant they had gone back to their
cottage.

As he came to the bend in the road which would lead him
into town, he saw a group of about six of the Jaguar Knights.
They were just standing around in the road, apparently doing
nothing, but he ducked into the bushes alongside. The knights
were talking among themselves, and Danny paused to listen
for a moment. The villagers all seemed to speak English, but
he had always assumed that their native language was Spanish.
But listening to these men talk now, he began to realize the
reason for the odd accents he'd been hearing since they'd arrived, the reason for names like Orizaba and Patecatl rather
than Miguel and Pedro. The language these men were speaking
was not Spanish; it was altogether unfamiliar to Danny. But it
had a flow to it, lots of words beginning with a "sho" sound,
others ending with an "atl" syllable. Within the context, he
realized that names like Patecatl fit right in. Then he heard
another word; *chalchihuitl*. Clear and definite this time, not
like the last time he'd heard that word, that first Tuesday morning in New York. Repressing the urge to rush out and ask the
knights what it meant, he continued to slip past them through
the bushes. Making a mental note to ask Patecatl about it, he
returned to the road after he was well past them, and went on
to the cottage.

Reaching their door, he knocked, and after a short delay
Mayauel opened it. She leaned against it as if she was very
tired, and he noticed that her dress was crooked; perhaps she'd
just thrown it on to answer the door. He wondered if he'd
interrupted her and Patecatl in bed. But right now, he felt that
wasn't important. He needed to see Patecatl, and he told her
so.

She sighed. "Come in, Danny. I suppose he should have
told you he was the physician, but—"

"Well, where is he?" Danny asked.

"He's in the back. But please, Danny, sit down."

"No, I want to see him, right now, Mayauel. David needs help."

"Danny, it would not do any good. Patecatl had no cure for that. There was nothing that he could have done." She was speaking very softly; Danny had to listen carefully to catch her words. "Please, Danny, let me—"

"Don't speak in the past tense. David isn't dead, and he isn't going to die, either." Danny spoke with a confidence he didn't feel. "Now, once again, I need to talk to him. Patecatl?" He moved toward the back of the house. "Patecatl?"

"It would be better if you don't," she said in a near whisper.

Danny ignored her, pushed aside a curtain that served as a door, and started to step through. "Oh, no," he whispered. "No." The room was awash with blood. Patecatl lay across the wooden table, his throat cut and his body opened from neck to groin. He was quite dead.

Letting the curtain fall, he turned back to Mayauel. "Bertie and his people have been here," he said. It wasn't a question.

"No," Mayauel said simply.

"Then who—"

"He did it himself. Part of it. He knew his time here was done, he was needed elsewhere." She held onto the doorframe, her body bent forward. Danny looked at her face; she was very pale. His eyes drifted downward, and he saw she was standing in a pool of blood. Splotches of blood led to the door and back.

"Mayauel, my God, you're hurt!" He jumped toward her, caught her arm as she started to sink to the floor. Her dress, which he now realized she'd been holding out away from her body, fell back against her stomach and immediately soaked through, bright red. Danny swore. He knew what she'd done to herself, or what Patecatl had done to her before he died. She looked up at him, her eyes unfocused.

"I wish I could tell you—" she coughed, causing the red stain to spread rapidly. "But I don't have time. All I can say is, keep your courage. All is not what it seems to be, Danny—" With a shudder she relaxed in his arms. He looked at her face, peaceful now in death, and began to cry, great sobs as if his body was going to tear itself apart. So much death, so suddenly. Yet in a way, perhaps he could understand why these two had committed suicide. Their way of life, their village, had changed so much since Bertie had taken over. That's where the responsibility was, and he intended to make the man pay for it somehow, someday.

As he approached the hill where the resort stood, Danny was dreading the climb. But he didn't have to make it; just as he started up, he encountered Kathryn and the Hallstens coming down. They were very excited, almost frenzied. He tried to tell them about Mayauel's and Patecatl's suicide, but never got the chance.

"Danny!" Susan said, breathing hard. "Danny, I don't know how it's possible—I mean, I know what we saw, but—we just saw John! Alive, somehow alive!"

"What?" he cried. "Where? When?" Then reason took over. That was just not possible, period. He remembered the body collapsing into the fire. But wait, he was wearing the mask, wasn't he? Was there a way—?

"We all saw him. He was walking up the south path, on the other hill, Orizaba following him. We're sure it was him!"

"Going up the other hill?" Danny had a surge of fear. "Why? Why would he do that? Unless he means to—!"

That idea had already occurred to them. John must be planning to challenge Bertie directly! All three of them had armed themselves with kitchen knives, poor equipment against the demons, but they would have to do. As they crossed the road toward the other hill, Danny broke the news about Mayauel and Patecatl. This provoked more tears, more anguish; but now they had a mission, and they were set in their intent.

As they climbed, Danny warned them about the sharp grasses at the top, remembered how he'd previously warned Evelyn, and felt his eyes growing wet. He wished that her only injuries had been a few cuts from the grasses. Climbing this hill again, with Susan and Kathryn this time, naturally made him uncomfortable. But there was nothing he could do about it. He was well aware that they would not listen to any suggestions that they should turn back, and he didn't even bother.

As he reached the top, he saw a small form lying near the edge. Motioning the others to wait, he crept forward; then he could see that it was Orizaba, and he rushed to him.

Not again, he thought. But it was so. He rolled the dwarf's

body over, saw that he too was dead. Unlike the others, he did not seem to have been stabbed or cut; his body was cold, very cold. There was frost on his eyebrows. He seemed to have frozen to death. It seemed utterly impossible, that he could have frozen in this climate. Yet the evidence was clear.

Moving the small stiff form into the grass, they pushed on. Danny had a sick feeling as they imitated almost exactly the movements he and Evelyn had made earlier, moving single file down a narrow path beside the wall of the church. Reaching the corner, he again peeked around. He was thankful he didn't see John standing as Frank had earlier. In fact, he didn't see anyone. Cautiously, he stepped into the clearing and looked around. Nobody. He motioned for the others to come out, and they did.

They searched the area for a few minutes; Bertie and his companions were, for whatever reason, not up here. But neither was John.

"Maybe inside?" David suggested.

"And maybe not up here at all," said Danny. "Are you people really sure of what you saw?" They had, however, found Orizaba's corpse, so they must have seen something. He still wasn't quite ready to admit it was John.

Out of the corner of his eye, he saw movement in the shadows of the doorway. He whirled, his pulse pounding, and saw Maria step out of the church. "What the hell are you doing up here?" he asked. "And where's Bertie?"

"In the village," she answered. "He'll be there for a while. There is no danger here. Listen!" They fell silent for a moment, heard the sounds of a flute being played. "That's him," she said, "playing the flute. As long as it sounds, you are safe up here. He takes four of the village girls to wife tonight, and that will occupy him for a time. Long enough."

"I know it sounds stupid, but you haven't seen John up here, have you?"

She smiled at them; somehow she looked quite different. Always before she'd seemed so stern, so aloof, but now she acted almost friendly. Perhaps it was because so few of them remained alive.

"I know what you seek," she said. "And now it is time. I can help you, at least in a way. I can show you where to go."

The other three began clamoring for her to do so, but Danny

was suspicious. "Why now?" he asked, his eyes narrowed. He still didn't trust this woman at all.

She shrugged. "Why not?" she said simply. She turned and went back into the church, and the others followed her.

Danny marveled at the size of the place as they entered. They crossed in front of the ruined altar area, to a small room alongside the main sanctuary. Inside, she showed them an open trapdoor, steep stairs leading down. Danny thought this was perhaps an old wine cellar.

"Down there," Maria said. Danny looked down. He saw light, flickering and reddish, like torchlight. That certainly said somebody had been down there recently.

"What is this?" he asked her.

"The entrance to the Temple of the Black," she answered. "There's another to the Temple of the Red. Remember what you've seen, Danny!"

He remembered; the red and black sunburst, the feeling of power. He had something of that same feeling now, looking down this hole.

"That is what Tlillan Tlapallan means," Maria said. "The Houses of the Black and Red." It seemed to Danny that her accent, her manner of speaking, had changed subtly.

"Maybe you can tell me one more thing," Danny asked her. "A word; I've heard it twice now. Chalchihuitl. Do you know what it means?"

"Yes," she said, smiling at him. "But it isn't simple in English. It means jade, the most precious stone, or sometimes turquoise. A bright red jewel placed in the mouths of the dead kings of the Aztecs and Toltecs before burial was also called a chalchihuitl. But what it symbolizes is more important. It symbolizes the most precious thing, the chalchihuatl, the precious water, the blood of sacrifice!"

She turned, started down the stairs. "You're going too?" Danny asked her. Somehow that surprised him.

"Yes," she said. "You have a few surprises waiting for you down there. I can help you a little, at first. Then you'll be on your own."

They followed single file down the spiral stairs. The steps were cut very steep, like those at the front of the church, and they were very narrow. Danny was quite nervous at first; if anyone stumbled, it could easily take all of them careening out of control down these stairs. But as they continued on down without mishap, he relaxed a bit. It seemed to him that the stairs went on and on, incredibly far down into the hill.

When they had reached a point where, as near as Danny could tell, they were at the level of the town, only a few feet above sea level, the stairway suddenly ended. There was a doorway in front of them, topped by a fitted stone arch. Above it was carved the figure of a bat, large sharp teeth protruding from its mouth. It seemed to him like a guardian of this place.

"Are you sure John came this way?" he asked Maria, as she peeked around the doorway. She motioned for him to be silent. He tried to look too, but before he really got a chance she went on through the doorway. He stepped up to it and was totally amazed.

He was looking into a huge room, walls rising about twenty feet, then angling in on three sides to a smaller square top, which was supported by several large pillars. There were carved steles, and brightly colored murals on all the walls. The entire room was lit with a bluish light of indeterminate origin. With a shock, he realized that he was looking at the inside of the hill, probably from about ground level, and he realized that it was a pyramid, and a hollow one at that. He knew then that he should have realized there was something funny about these hills; they were exactly alike, and there were no other hills around. This explained it.

The others came in, and there was a brief discussion about the place and what it could mean. Susan told them about Bertie's discoveries in the old church above; all things taken together seemed to indicate they were inside a structure of great antiquity, probably one unique in the New World.

"You need to concentrate on other things right now," Maria said curtly. "Somewhere around here is the guardian of the gateway to Mictlan, and it will not let you pass unchallenged!"

"What are you saying?" Danny asked her.

"You need to go there"—she indicated the opposite side of the room—"but there's a force here that will try to prevent you from doing that, at least in your current state."

"Current state?"

"Yes. Never mind trying to work it out now. Come with me."

Slowly and carefully, trying to keep watch in all directions, they began to cross the room. There was a wide stairway, leading down to a huge floor, then another going back up. Just as they reached the center of the open area, Danny heard Kathryn give a little cry, and looked around to his left.

He could scarcely credit what he was seeing. A manlike creature stood watching them from about fifty feet away. It was jet black in color, with gangly arms and legs, fingers terminating in talons. It had the head, face, and teeth of the bat he'd seen carved over the door, and it was at least fifteen feet tall. Its eyes stared at him, glittering in the odd light; its ears twitched, and he could hear it breathe, even from this distance.

"The guardian," Maria said unnecessarily.

"Now what the hell do we do?" Danny asked her, trying to remain calm. His knife seemed so tiny in comparison to it; each of its talons was larger than his pitiful weapon.

"We run for the door!" David cried.

"No!" Maria snapped. "You're here now, in its place. You'll never make it. It will tear you to pieces from behind if you run!"

"So what? What?" Danny pleaded. "We can't fight it—"

"You must," she said calmly. "But not with that knife. You are going to have to wrestle it, and defeat it. It's the only way."

"Are you a complete lunatic?" Danny asked incredulously. "Look at that thing! I wouldn't stand a chance!"

"Not so. You don't stand a chance any other way. You, or David, but I'm sure David is too sick. So. It waits for you to set the terms of the combat."

Danny just stared at her. This was crazy, crazy. That thing would kill him in a minute, it was just impossible. He had a sick feeling that Maria had just led the rest of them into a deathtrap. Quick and easy; they all died here, Bertie had free run of the town.

"You are wrong about me, you always have been," she said, as if reading his mind. "I share this risk. If you lose, I'll die here with the rest of you."

"But how can I do this? It's insane! I'm bound to lose!"

"No you aren't. You have a gift, a talent. You have to use it. The guardian can be defeated. It could even be defeated with that knife, but only by a warrior, and you aren't a warrior. Use what you have; your mind."

"We can't run for it?"

"That's suicide for all of us!"

Danny sighed. "All right, all right! How do I tell it I've decided?"

"Throw aside your knife and take your shirt off. It'll take that to mean you want to wrestle. You take away its best weapons that way. It can't use its claws to tear you."

Great consolation, he thought. He wavered for a moment, considering running in spite of what she had said. But its legs were so long, it would have twice their stride. Unless it was very slow-moving, it would indeed catch them before they could reach the door, and one or more of them would die if it used those claws. Left without a choice in the matter, he flipped his knife aside and stripped off his shirt.

"Danny, you can't!" Kathryn cried.

"Looks like I have to," he said, stepping forward to confront the horror.

Stunningly fast, the creature rushed toward him, its huge hands seizing him and jerking him into the air. He managed to get one arm free and flailed helplessly at the thing as it bore him to the floor. Once down, it held him with one hand and put the other around his neck, the distorted face only inches from his. The hand around his neck tightened, and he couldn't breathe. Remembering Maria's suggestion, he crossed his eyes and squinted. Looked at this way, the creature was like a huge black seed, so black it looked more like a hole than an object. It was quite uniform, except for a few things hanging out the middle of it that looked like black threads, very fine and thin, waving around like the tentacles of some small sea creature. Not knowing what else to do, he worked his hand down toward them, realizing that if this didn't work he was dead. Already he was getting lightheaded from lack of air, and just a little more pressure would crush his windpipe. True to Maria's prediction, though, it wasn't trying to use its claws, which could have put an end to this very quickly.

He finally got his hand down far enough and grabbed the tentacles. They felt like fine wire; he wasn't sure how he was feeling them, but he pulled on them, hard. The pressure on his throat relaxed, then disappeared, as the thing reached for his arm. It was then twisting the arm, and in turn he twisted the fine tentacles; the horror made a mournful, low-pitched sound. The other arm, holding him pinned to the floor, released him, and he grabbed a handful of tentacles with his other hand. Now the thing was trying to get away, but he stayed with it, tugging at the tentacles. It was a standoff at best, though; he was controlling it, obviously hurting it, but he had little chance of breaking the tentacles; they were far too tough for that. Still squinting, he scanned it for any other vulnerable spots. The only thing he could see was the spot where the tentacles or threads came out. Although it was black like the rest of the creature, it seemed to pulsate slightly, and to Danny it looked soft.

He released the tentacles with one hand, and, clenching his fist, drove it with all the strength he could muster into the spot. The thing screamed, so loud he almost let it go. He hit it again, and again it screamed; a third time, and it collapsed in a heap on the floor. When he returned to his normal vision, he saw the thing on all fours, trying feebly to creep away from him.

"You've won, Danny. You can let it go," Maria said from behind him. "Don't worry, it won't bother us again. You've won our right to be here, to pass through this place."

Tentatively, he released his grip on the fibers. Remaining tensed, he watched for the monstrosity to attack him again. It didn't; it crept away and lay on the floor, as if trying to recover its breath. The whole fight had taken less than two minutes.

"You're sure?" he asked her.

"Yes. Now we must go. Come along."

"Danny, that was fantastic!" Kathryn said. He just shrugged, as if he did this every day. He was getting a real lift from having defeated the creature. Then he remembered Evelyn, Mayauel, and the rest, and came back down. Silently he followed Maria across the stone floor. From somewhere ahead, he was hearing a sound like heavy machinery operating, and he wondered what it was.

Maria led them through the forest of steles toward the far wall. He glanced at the steles as he passed and noticed several depictions of a man wearing a mask much like the one John, or whoever had impersonated John, had worn when he had jumped into the fire. He wanted to look a little closer, but Maria kept hurrying them along.

She went to a door which had an odd carving over it, a depiction of a stone trilithon like the ones at Stonehenge. The sound he was hearing was much louder within, and she disappeared inside, the others following. The passage bent to the right, then back to the left; the ceiling here was very low, about six feet high, and the passage quite narrow. Finally he saw an opening on his right, about fifty feet down. As he came to it he realized it was not a doorway.

The full view made him gasp. The floor of the narrow passageway had become a ledge near the top of an enormous cliff. Looking down caused him to press himself back against the stone wall, and the others did likewise; the ledge here was only two feet wide. Below was what seemed to be a vast natural cavern. The floor, perhaps five hundred feet down, was strewn with reddish rocks, and the other side was so far away he could barely see it. There was a river, crossing the cavern floor perpendicular to the ledge they were standing on. It seemed to disappear into the cliff. He saw some movement down there, and looked. He could not be absolutely sure of the identity of the person, but a man was walking among the boulders, accompanied by a small dog. From here, it sure as hell did look like John. He was wearing John's feather headdress, and carrying what appeared to be the mask. Susan cried out to him, but it was much too far, and the man didn't look up.

Maria told them they should continue; they did, all using extreme caution along the perilously narrow ledge. Just a little farther on, the ledge turned back into the rock face, becoming a passageway again. The machine noise was now very loud. They pushed on, and finally the walls of the passage curved outward, opening up into a room. On the far side was a door, and the obvious source of the machine sound.

Danny was very unsure that it was in fact a machine, although he couldn't figure out what else it might be. Just beyond the door, two huge pieces of rock, which seemed to be suspended from a third piece—the Stonehenge trilithon—were clashing together, repeatedly. They were either cut to a perfect fit, or had worn themselves that way, because when they closed, there was virtually no space at all between them. The period of the clashing was generally about two seconds between strikes, but once in a while, apparently at random, they closed up more suddenly. The floor of the room was littered with skulls and other human bones, many of them partial or crushed. Danny looked for another exit, but found none; he had a sinking certainty about what Maria was going to say before she said it.

"We must pass the gate," she told him calmly.

There was a storm of protest. She shrugged, told them they could easily go back if they wished. But this was the only way to go on. They all stood silent for a moment, watching the massive rocks swing out, then crash closed. No question of surviving if they didn't make it cleanly.

"There's absolutely no other way?" Danny asked her.

"None whatever," she said emphatically. "All who pass this way must come through here, must pass this barrier."

"So how do we do it?"

"As seems right to you. For each it may be different."

"So. All right." He drew back, tried to judge the timing on the clashing stones.

"Wait; I'll go first," Maria said. She walked up to the gate, studied it for a moment, then scooted through cleanly. On the other side, she turned to face them, encouraging them to come ahead.

Danny stepped up, planning to try to imitate what she'd done. David and the two women were close behind him, watching him carefully. He timed the clashes, was startled by one out of sequence. This, he felt, these random closures, was all that was really dangerous; two seconds was plenty of time otherwise. Of course, that assumed one didn't trip or anything. Ignoring Maria's exhortations for them to hurry, he watched the stones for a while. His idea became clear; from what he was seeing, it seemed good enough.

"Wait for one of the random clashes," he told the others. "Then zip through. They never seem to be very close together."

Taking his own advice, he patiently awaited one of the randoms, then ran into the gap. It was not far, and he cleared it easily before the stones swung shut again. But he was worried about the others, and immediately turned back to the gate.

On the other side, he could see Kathryn preparing to try it next. There was no way he could help her, and silently he prayed for her safe crossing. She also waited for a random clash, then ran through safely, and fell into his arms on the other side.

Now it was Susan's turn, and she stood looking at the gate; then, without waiting, or even really timing it at all, she just walked into it. Danny drew a quick breath. He thought he understood; the guilt she felt was making her take unnecessary chances. But still, the stones never touched her; she walked through like it was an open doorway. Only David was left now, and he waited patiently, trying to time it as Danny and Kathryn had done. Immediately after a random clash, he hurtled into the opening; perhaps a little too fast. His shoulder hit the retreating rock, and he bounced forward, ending up on the ground between the stones. His scarred face was a study in terror as he clawed wildly at the ground, trying to get through. Danny grabbed his arms and put all of his strength into a mighty jerk. Susan and Kathryn were screaming, he could see the stones falling, they were moving.

There was a hesitation, then a release. As they tumbled backwards together, David screamed; Danny saw blood spurting from his foot. They had not quite made it. Quickly, Danny assayed the damage. David had lost a piece of his left big toe. Not a fatal wound, but one that would surely make his continued participation in this quest difficult. Danny tore off a piece of his shirt and made a bandage; a few minutes later they got the bleeding stopped, at least. It was more than obvious, however, that David was in a lot of pain.

"You are going to have to leave me here and go on," he said through clenched teeth. "I can't walk with this, there's no way."

"No way we're leaving you, either," Danny said firmly. "Not even if we have to carry you along!"

As David tried to stand, Danny looked around, and found a branch to use as a makeshift crutch. It didn't occur to him to question what a tree limb should be doing down here, where there were no trees. This seemed to work, and they continued on again, although at a much slower pace.

They were now in an open area that looked like a natural cave. Danny could not understand how it was lighted, and he asked Maria about it. She only shrugged and told him they had to be able to see their way about. This was not exactly a satisfactory answer, but it seemed to be all she had for them. They were following a rather well-defined trail among the big red boulders. Except for the weird bluish light and total lack of any vegetation, Danny felt they could have been in the western desert. The ground varied, sometimes rocky, sometimes sandy. They were generally moving downhill, a gentle slope that he assumed would end at the river they'd seen earlier. Gradually, the sound of the clashing gates was fading away behind and above them as they descended toward the cavern floor.

The slope finally seemed to stop. Danny could look back up and see, quite far away now, the doorway through which they'd come. They had seen no life, nothing moving, since they'd seen John—if it was John—and the little dog walking across the floor. Danny strained to see ahead, trying to pick out the river, but he still couldn't see it.

Suddenly Maria stopped, looked around. She seemed very alert, maybe a little frightened. He'd not ever seen her like that, and it frightened him in turn.

"What is it?" he whispered. The others gathered up close to them.

She held up her finger for silence and continued to look around. Finally she focused on a spot on the ground and her eyes went wide. Danny looked; he couldn't see anything. Then he did; the sand was being pressed into shallow footprints. Something he could not see was coming toward them.

38

Bertie stopped playing his flute and looked down at the girl sitting at his feet. Attractive, but not Susan, he thought. He frowned. Except for her, he pretty much had everything he wanted; it had all gone his way. Yet he felt a discomfort, a vague unease, and he didn't know exactly what was wrong. He'd given up the idea of Susan a while back, hadn't even bothered to talk to her again; his feelings for her were dangerous. He hadn't really planned to use her in his plot to humiliate John; but the way she'd fallen into it so nicely—John himself had suggested going to get her, he hadn't even had to work for it!—had probably ended things between them, especially when

he and Ihuimecatl had taken full advantage of the situation.
Now he had taken these four young village girls, decreed that
they were his wives. All should be well; why wasn't it?

Toltecatl was standing alongside him. "Problems?" he
asked.

"You know, I really can't answer that. For some reason, I
feel uneasy, but I don't know why. I mean, most of my enemies
are dead, and David will die soon of that disease he has; I'm
sure of that. And Danny, why can't I just kill him? I keep
letting him walk away. But he isn't a real threat."

"No, he isn't."

"So why do I feel so—tense? Like it's about to fall in on
me?"

"Because you never look ahead. You always repeat the same
errors. Always."

Bertie stared at him. "What are you talking about?" he
asked.

"The suggestion we made the day we met you, down inside
the temple. Read the steles. You didn't bother. You looked at
a few of the murals and went on with your foolish plans."

For a moment, Bertie felt like Toltecatl had hit him. He had
forgotten all about it! The murals, showing two alternate king-
doms—one with the masked man overseeing, the other with
the man with the mirrored foot in charge—had such a profound
effect on him that he had been determined to immediately shift
the real circumstance to the version he liked best. But now he
clearly remembered the two creatures advising him to read the
information on the steles.

He stood up, knocking the girl at his feet aside. "Still time
to do that," he said. "Might as well be now." He looked down
at the girl, who cringed away a little. "You!" he snapped.
"Can you read that—that—" He stopped in frustration; he
didn't even know what to call it.

"Yes, my lord," the girl said, bailing him out. "I can read
it."

"All right. Let's go down there now, see what we have!"

A short time later, Bertie sat cross-legged on the floor of the
huge room while the girl crouched in front of one of the steles.
Ihuimecatl and Toltecatl had resumed the forms they had when
Bertie had first seen them, but the girl didn't seem at all disturbed.

Quite a bit of time passed while she read bits and pieces from a variety of the steles. If it didn't seem to have applica= tion, Bertie told her to move on. Most of the material re- counted a number of myths and anecdotes involving the vast pantheon of the Nahuatl gods. But so far, nothing seemed rel- evant. He was beginning to wonder if the creatures were lead- ing him astray when he caught a drift of what the girl was currently reading.

"And when he was king, the corn grew huge, the cotton grew in all colors," she read. "Then his old enemy, Tezcatli- poca, who wore a smoking mirror in the place of the foot he had lost to the water-monster Cipactli, brought him a mirror the size of a hand's span, and bade him look. And he did, and he was afraid."

Bertie perked up and listened. This, of course, was very interesting. At the moment, he wasn't going to question the whys or hows; he just wanted to hear the story.

She continued: "Tezcatlipoca then offered him a drink of the pulque of Mayauel of the four hundred breasts, and he refused. But Tezcatlipoca insisted, saying, 'taste it!' So he did, with his little finger. And finding it good, he drank four cups, then a fifth cup. Then, being with four hundred rabbits, he called for his sister Xochiquetzal."

Bertie stopped her. "Are you serious?" he asked incredu- lously. "It actually says that, there on the stone?"

She trembled. "Yes, my lord," she told him.

"Look, Toltecatl, is this right? She's not putting me on?"

"No. That's what it says, all right."

He stared for a moment, then told the girl to continue read- ing.

"So he bade Xochiquetzal, she of beauty, love, and flowers, to try the drink of Mayauel. And she did. She drank four cups, then a fifth cup. Then she was with four hundred rabbits—"

"Rabbits—I've heard that before—" Bertie said, interrupt- ing.

"It means they had lost their sense to the drink, my lord," the girl explained.

"Dead drunk," Bertie said. "Okay. I remember now. Con- tinue."

"And they laid down and loved each other. And when he awoke, he saw what he had done, and cried his woe to all the lands. He bade his acolytes build a stone coffin, and he rested therein four days and four nights. Then he arose and divested himself of all his worldly valuables.

"And he went into Tlillan Tlapallan, and to the shore of the divine sea. Whenever a sorcerer asked, 'where goest thou?' he answered, 'the sun calleth me.'

"At the divine shore, he built a great fire. He put on his feathers and his mask, and cast his mortal body into the flames. While he burned, all the rare birds of the earth came to watch. Then he went to Mictlan, the land of the dead.

"And eight days later, he arose from the dead like a flaming star, lord of the dawn. And his old enemy, Tezcatlipoca, was vanquished and broken into four hundred pieces."

She was at the bottom of the stele and stopped reading. There was a very long silence in the room.

"Goddamn!" Bertie said. "I don't understand—"

"Your people have a saying," Ihuimecatl said. " 'Those who forget the past are doomed to repeat it.' "

"So what can I do? Everything happened again, exactly the same! And I lose out in the end! Tell me, how can I stop this?"

"All you can do is to go to Mictlan, try to prevent his fire from being lit in the underworld."

"The land of the dead? If I have to die to get there—"

"You don't. There's a way. Through the House of the Black. You've seen the entryway already."

Bertie knew exactly what he was talking about.

39

Remembering the earlier fight, Danny tried to read this creature. When he did, he could see it clearly; and he would have preferred not to. It was covered with mottled brown feathers like a bird, but its body and tail were somewhat catlike in shape, its feet and legs rather like those of a camel; clearly, it was built for fast running. Its head was round, with an extended snout almost like a bird's beak, but the snout was filled with numerous chisel-like teeth, so large they hung outside its mouth. When it moved its jaws, sparks flew from where its teeth clashed together. Its eyes were large and catlike, gleaming green in the odd lighting. A bright red, pointed tongue licked in and out as it moved slowly toward them, its back legs bunched under it as if preparing to spring.

"Maria," Danny said slowly, "Now what, Maria? What do we do?"

"I have no good answers," she told him. He could hear fear in her voice, and it increased his own. He held his knife out, waiting for the nightmare to come at him. Risking a glance around, he saw no hiding places, no place to run. Besides, the likelihood of outrunning the thing was remote at best, judging from its appearance.

As he glanced around, he caught a glimpse of Maria. Before, he had been unable to see her at all under heightened vision; but now she appeared as a slender, attractive young woman with dark hair and eyes, evidently a North American like themselves!

Unfortunately he had little time to dwell on this; the creature was moving toward him. He heard Susan's voice in his ear, asking him what it was. She could, obviously, see the approaching footprints, but she could not see the beast.

"End of the road for us, I'm afraid," he said grimly.

She put her hand on his shoulder, and he felt a shock. "I can see it!" she cried. "Danny, I can see it through your eyes!"

He started to shake her off, at least give this fight his best effort. But she grabbed him with both hands, held him.

"Damn it, Susan—" he began.

"Wait," she said imperiously. "That creature, I find it ugly. It shall not exist in my world, in any of my worlds. I, myself, in person, so decree it!"

Danny started to ask her what the hell she thought she was doing, but then he noticed that the creature had become transparent, ethereal, Stunned, he stared at it. It seemed to get less and less substantial, like it was turning into smoke. Finally, the last wisps of it disappeared, and he watched sand slide into the footprints. There was no trace of it left.

"What the hell did you do?" he asked Susan.

"I don't know. I just—"

She looked very confused. The moment had passed, that much was obvious. But he now had an idea why Orizaba had been so fearful of her when she talked like that. Jerry Maxwell, it seemed, had been one very lucky man. He wished Susan could get into this state at will; it would have been helpful earlier if she'd denied Bertie's existence in the world.

He turned his attention to Maria. "I saw you, as you wouldn't let me see you on the plane," he said to her directly. "Don't you think I deserve an explanation?"

"Not yet, Danny. We haven't the time. We all have things to do down here, important things. And right now, what I look like is not important at all."

He decided to accept that, at least for the moment. "What the hell was that thing?" he asked, looking back at the vague outlines of its footprints.

"A quail," she said. "Fortunately for us, only one. Most of the time, they move in packs."

He gave her a hard look. "A quail?" he mimicked. "That sure as hell didn't look like any fucking quail I've ever seen!" Now that she'd mentioned it, though, it did seem that the feathers on the thing had been like those of a quail.

Maria grinned at him. "You've never seen quail down here before, that's all. They're different, obviously. You had an advantage. You could see it from a distance. Usually they become visible just as they attack, and the fright alone can be fatal. And," she continued, her voice becoming soft, "they gnaw bones, of course."

Danny just grunted. If she wanted to call them quail, well, what difference did it make? He just hoped they wouldn't come across any more of them. Glancing around at the stark landscape, the red boulders and reddish sand, he told himself that this whole place didn't make sense in any case. None of it.

"We'd better go on," David said in a weak voice. "We can't let John get too far ahead of us."

Danny looked at him, saw the spectre of death hanging over him. He tried not to let it show, but he had no idea how they were going to manage to save David. He looked like he was falling apart.

They pushed on, down the dusty red trail toward the river. Distances were deceptive here. Long after they felt they should have reached the river, it still was not in sight. Finally they began to see a misty area ahead of them.

"Looks like that's probably it," Danny said, wondering exactly what they were going to do when they got there, how they were going to determine if John had gone upstream or down. From what he'd seen from above, there was no question of crossing; it was simply impossible. They entered the mists, and almost immediately the landscape began to change. Before there had been red rocks and sand illuminated by the weird blue light from above. Now everything was in shades of bluish-gray, a twilight world where even the ground in front of them could not be seen clearly. Around them, the red boulders had given way to stark white stumps of bushes and trees, all devoid of leaves, devoid of any semblance of life.

The soil underfoot became soft and wet; the river could not possibly be much further. Walking became more and more difficult, especially for David, whose makeshift crutch kept sinking into the ground. Danny helped him along, listening to his labored breathing. David certainly shouldn't have come down here, but leaving him alone, at Bertie's mercy, was an equally bad idea. Danny looked at his face; his eyes were swelling. More problems. Just getting David out of here alive after they'd found John—assuming that they did—would be no mean feat.

Concentrating on these problems, he bumped into Maria, who had stopped at the edge of the water. Dead water plants, something like cattails, lined the bank and extended far out into the water. Maria was looking up and down among them, as if searching for something. As Danny had expected, a path ran alongside the bank through the weeds. Now they'd have to make their choice.

He let Susan support David and stood beside Maria, watching the slow current move from left to right. He tried to look across to the other side, but it was too misty, or too far, or both. He could only see the dark water, stirring a little in an even darker area about a hundred feet offshore.

Suddenly, the water exploded upward in a geyser. A huge head broke the surface and continued to rise, supported by a massive neck. It was long-jawed like a crocodile, with triangular, saw-edged teeth. And it was impossibly huge. The jaws alone were forty feet long. How large the animal itself was could only be a matter of conjecture, since all that was visible was the head and about eighty feet of columnar neck, which kept the head waving about, far above them. It turned and seemed to fix its gaze on them, its eyes black and cold, like obsidian mirrors. Hastily retreating from the bank, Danny hoped the thing was fully aquatic, that it could not come out of the water. In any case, it certainly could easily reach them where they had been. As he helped David back, pushing the women ahead of him, he noticed that Maria was ignoring the monstrosity.

"Maria!" he yelled. "Get away from there!"

She turned and looked at him, her back to the massive reptilian creature. "There's no danger," she said. "It can't touch us unless we step into the water."

Danny looked very doubtful. "Are you sure?" he asked. She was certainly risking her own life on it.

"Yes. It is Cipactli, the guardian of the river. It will watch us, but it can't attack unless we leave the bank."

Cautiously he walked back to her, keeping an eye on the huge head towering above them. All it had to do was dip its neck and it would have them, but it stayed where it was, swaying and watching.

"What are you looking for?" he asked her, still looking up at the creature.

"We have to cross," she told him. "I'm looking for a little red dog. It's the only way."

"A little red dog?" he repeated. Then he heard a female voice calling from a short distance downstream.

Still watching the monster, they followed the path in the direction of the voice. Danny was shocked to see a rowboat, a very small one, sitting on the water as if waiting for them. In it sat a red-haired young woman wearing U.S.-style clothing, holding an oar.

"Hey, Susan!" the woman called. "And damned if it isn't Mr. Perfection, not looking quite so perfect these days!"

"Jeannie?" Susan asked, bewildered. "What are you—how is it—"

"Never mind all that. You wanna cross, I'll row ya."

"Now wait a minute," Danny said. "This is suicide. That thing over there—"

"Will not touch her boat. Don't you remember how Susan said she acted?" Maria asked. "Like a dog?"

A little red dog; Danny remembered. Jeannie from Susan's office. But how—?

"We'll have to show them," Maria said, climbing into the boat. "Let's go." Jeannie pushed away and laboriously rowed the boat out. Soon they disappeared into the mists. The water-dragon just watched them go.

After a few moments, Jeannie came rowing back alone. David and Susan climbed into her boat.

"It's usual to pay the boatman, isn't it?" Jeannie said, grinning. "I mean, we are talking the River Styx here, aren't we?"

"Jeannie, how did you come to be here?" Susan asked again.

"Hell, I'm not here. I'm home in bed. This is a really wild dream," she was saying as Danny lost the sound over the water.

One more trip for Danny and Kathryn and they were all on the other side. "Well, bye," Jeannie said cheerfully, climbing back into the boat. "See you when you all get back from your vacation." She laughed. "What a hell of a dream!" Then she was gone, swallowed by the mists.

"Wait a minute!" Danny cried after her. "How do we get back, with that thing out there?"

"Too late, Danny," Maria told him. "You can't go back now. Not that way. Not ever."

"There is another way out, then?" Danny demanded.

"Yes. Up through the House of the Red. But we have a great distance to cover before we can do that."

Danny clenched his fists as if he were going to hit her. But that would do no good; here they were, and they might as well try to make the best of it. He reasoned that even if they'd had this information prior to crossing the river, they would have crossed anyway. Their mission was to find John. What else were they going to do? Sit in the resort house waiting for a plane that might never come, until Bertie decided to send them one by one to the stone? No, it was just as well. Perhaps if they found John, he'd know how to help David. It was the only hope they had.

At Danny's insistence, they rested for a while about a hundred yards from the riverbank. Even though the huge water-dragon had behaved exactly as Maria had said it would, it seemed silly to trust it more than necessary. Maria did not argue with him; one resting place was as good as another.

"Maria, I'd really like to know exactly who or what you are," Danny said to her as they sat resting.

"Is that really so very important?" she asked him.

"To me it is. Look. We're in an impossible place, confronting impossible creatures. Five of our friends are dead already, and for all I know, John may be too. David here is in serious trouble with his health, and I consider it only good luck that the rest of us are still in one piece. So, either you're trying to help us, or you're not. If you are, we deserve to know who you are and what you know of this insanity."

She considered this for a moment. "I am trying to help you," she said at last. "I've been trying to help some of these people for a long time. But here is my problem. A certain pattern of events has to take place, not all of them pleasant from our point of view. But necessary, I assure you, in a much larger scheme of things. For instance, it was absolutely necessary for the woman you knew as Evelyn to first fill the chalchihuitl—a vessel used to hold the chalchihuatl, the precious water, is also a chalchihuitl—with her own blood. Absolutely necessary. If you had known that, you would have taken steps to prevent it. And if you had succeeded—and we have tried not to underestimate you, Danny, you might have found a way—the consequences, well, they are unknown. We just couldn't take that kind of risk."

"You mean you knew in advance that Bertie was going to kill her, and you did nothing? Said nothing? You Goddamn bitch, I'll—"

"Wait, please. Think about it. You witnessed the whole thing. Was what you saw a murder, with an assailant and a victim, or was it a mutually agreed-upon act?"

"He hypnotized her or something, he—"

"No, he didn't. The shock of what the other, the one you knew as Frank, did, readied her to realize what she had to do. The man with the knife was only a tool. If he'd not been there, she would have asked you to do it for her."

"I can't accept that, I can't! Why? Why would she kill herself?"

"In a way, she didn't. She woke herself from a dream."

That silenced him for a moment. He'd heard that phrase

recently, but he couldn't recall where or when. And something else. Jeannie, back at the boat, had clearly said that as far as she was concerned, she was dreaming all this!

"What is all this about dreams?" he asked.

"For some, this is a place of dreams. They come here when they dream. It's as simple as that. Almost no one ever comes here as we have, walking in under our own power, with choices to make." She looked at him directly. "You haven't realized exactly where you are yet, have you?"

He had an idea of what she meant, but he rejected it, assuming that Jeannie's remark about the river had keyed it off. "No, I haven't," he answered finally.

"Yes, I believe you have. Various peoples have legends about this place, Danny. If you come out alive, you can contribute to them. It is most commonly called Hell, but we call it Mictlan."

"That was the honest-to-God River Styx then?" he asked sarcastically.

"One name for it, yes."

"How very interesting," Danny said.

"It is, isn't it?" She laughed out loud. "Seriously, Danny, I am trying to help you all I can. But to tell you all I know right now, well, it could lead to a disaster of proportions you can't conceive. I say could. We don't know."

"You keep saying we. Who's we?"

"My mentor and I. He is still on the surface, but he will be here soon, no doubt. For now, Danny, you will have to trust me."

He looked at her directly, made a decision. "I can't do that, not anymore, Maria. You're going to have to tell me what you know, or—or I'll—ah—"

She laughed at him. "You'll what? Hurt me somehow? I doubt that!" She leaned toward him, tipped her head far back. "Cut my throat. You have a knife, I won't stop you, I won't move. Go ahead!" She held that pose for a moment, then brought her head back down. "No? Of course, you wouldn't get information if I were dead. Torture, then! Proceed. I don't have a very high tolerance for pain. Surely I'll talk soon!" She sat silent for a moment, smiling at him. "Not even for your own life could you do that, Danny," she said.

"Damn you!" he snapped. But he knew she was right. He

just didn't have it in him. That left him with only two options; to trust her or get away from her. Perhaps, if she seemed imminently dangerous, he could kill her; but he was far from that right now.

"We need to move on," he said heavily, and pulled himself to his feet. They all helped David up. He seemed very weak. Soon they'd have to make some kind of a stretcher to carry him on, but for now he was still mobile, and they started off through the dense river mists.

Part

III

Mictlan

1

They had walked for quite a while before the river mists started to dissipate. The trail they were following led into an area of sulphur-yellow sand dunes, a most desolate place. As they entered it, they saw footprints going ahead of them, and everyone assumed these belonged to John; their spirits rose a little higher. Perhaps this was not an exercise in futility, after all.

But after many minutes of struggling along in the soft yellow sand, which was fine as dust, Danny began to have his doubts. David was having almost insurmountable problems, and again Danny and Susan had to support him. There was no end to the stuff in sight, and Danny didn't know how long they could continue. Worse, he had no idea what was beyond. Maria would only say that the Yellow Desert, as she called it, was by far the easier path. There was another way they could go, she said, but there were obstacles on that route that they could not pass; one of these was a wind of flint knives. In any case she knew this desert, and seemed to imply that with the proper skills, one could step in and out of the surface world from here. Giving Danny a knowing look, she suggested he try to find a way.

He considered this idea, then entered his heightened vision state. Far off to his right, he could see what looked like a wall of fog, much denser that the mists around the river. He asked Maria if that meant anything to her.

She seemed to be very excited, and asked him to point it out to her. He did, and at the same time he tried to look at it with his normal vision. He was sure he was looking at the right spot, but there was no wall of fog there.

"That's it, I'm sure!" she said. "From the surface, you look for it on your left, so naturally it'd be on the right here."

"What if we were coming the other way?" he asked reasonably.

She looked at him oddly and laughed. "Well, try it, Danny! Turn around, take a look!"

He did, and the wall was still on his right! He moved his head around. It moved with him, always remaining on his right.

"It's some kind of illusion," he said uncertainly. "It moves when I do."

"That doesn't make it an illusion," she explained. "If you're riding in a car, looking at the moon, it seems to move along with you, right? It's not really moving. Nevertheless, it isn't an illusion. It's an effect of the relative distances of the objects. Well, this is the same thing!"

"I don't understand."

"I know. Look, the one is because of relative distances. This is because of relative states of reality."

"Huh?"

"The wall is moving with you because its reality is relative to you. You can stop it, if you want, and walk into it. Of course you have to see it to do that. Now try it! Turn to face it directly!"

He realized he'd already done that a few minutes ago, when he'd believed it to be fixed. He still didn't fully understand, but he tried to face it now. It moved. Concentrating on holding it steady, he snapped himself around. Now he was directly facing it, and it was much closer than he'd thought it was; just a couple of steps would take him into it.

"Go ahead!" Maria urged. "Try it! Concentrate on some specific place, and walk into it!"

Uncertainly, he did as she said. He was aware of the others watching him closely, but he felt if he spoke or moved his head he'd lose it. He stepped inside, couldn't see anything. Then he stepped through, and into his room at the resort house.

He whirled around, stared at the door. No wall of fog. What the hell? He was out, but Kathryn, Susan, and David weren't; he had to go back! Glancing around the room, his gaze fell on the quartz crystal lying on the wicker table. He hadn't paid any attention to it since the first night, but he remembered it had made him feel good to hold it. Picking it up, he slipped it into his pocket and walked to the window, looked at the ruined church. Did he have to go back down that way, face the monsters and the river, the clashing gate, all over again? Maybe not. Maria had said the wall was a two-way affair. People went there from here, through it. On his left—

He stood so he was facing a blank wall and went into his heightened vision. For a moment, nothing, then—yes! He was getting it, off to the left. He tried to do the same thing, but the wall moved with him, and he turned helplessly in the middle of the floor. He concentrated, pushed, and the wall held. Once more he snapped around to face it, stepped through.

"Danny!" Kathryn yelled. She ran up and hugged him. "We didn't know what had happened!. You just disappeared!"

He looked around at the yellow sand. Perfect, he thought. In and out in seconds. "No, I'm all right!" he said to Kathryn. "Let's see if we can find John. I can get us out of here!" He had a moment of doubt, felt in his pocket. But the crystal was there. It had been real. He looked over at Maria.

"Very well done, Danny," she said, her dark eyes intense. "Most people take years to learn that!"

Patiently, he answered Susan's and Kathryn's questions about what had just happened. He felt a little better. But David was too weak to even ask questions, or take much interest. He just sat on the sand, a pathetic figure in obvious pain.

"We have to move," Danny said firmly. He and Susan got David to his feet, and they continued their trek through the dunes. Periodically Danny checked to see if he could still see the wall. It was still there, moving along with them, just like the moon from a moving car.

The trail they were following started downward, as if they were descending a hill. Ahead of them were more mists; they could not see very far into them. At least it appeared they had successfully crossed the Yellow Desert; no small task, according to Maria. The trail became steeper and steeper, and the going more and more difficult. The sand was very soft, and the footing here very poor. All of them were now trying to support David, who was fighting just to keep his feet. Finally they reached a breaking point; the whole group began a head-long slide down the dune. They separated as they fell, disappearing into the mists.

Almost immediately after the mists cleared around him, Danny dug his fingers into the ground and stopped his slide. Another body came flying into his field of vision. He reached

out and grabbed an arm, realized it was Kathryn. They struggled up, stabilizing themselves. The slope here was not that
bad; it had been the momentum that had carried them downward. They were in an open grassy field, a trail going across
it, light mist everywhere. Not seeing any of the others, he and
Kathryn called out for them, but there were no answers; only
the sound of their own voices in this flat plain of short grasses.

2

David was unable to catch onto anything, and so continued
his slide unabated. He felt the sand turn into grass, then the
grass into soil. Parts of the costume he was wearing snagged
and were torn away. At last he came to rest facedown, in a
plowed field. Soil filled his mouth, and for a few minutes, he
couldn't do anything except lie there panting. He wished the
pains wracking him would stop just long enough for him to
catch his breath; but they didn't. The sanding he'd received,
the tumble over the grass, had all made it that much worse.
His foot throbbed unbelievably, and he felt as if he didn't have
a square inch of skin left that wasn't hurting.

With a great effort, he rolled over and sat up. All he could
see was the bare soil, disappearing into the mists. He called
out for Susan, for Danny. But his voice was not strong, and no
one answered. He seemed to be all alone.

He cursed himself, his condition. It had been foolish of him
to try this quest, as sick as he was, but he hadn't felt all that
badly when they started. The main problem then was the skin
cruptions. But now, besides the foot injury, he was having
problems with his eyes. In fact, he could hardly see at all out
of his left eye. Gingerly, he felt it; it was so swollen it was
protruding. He could hardly bear to touch it, the pain was so
intense.

He realized he had only two choices now. He could either

try to get up, get moving, or lie here and die, alone in this field. Considering how he'd lived his life, that was not the most inappropriate of all possible deaths; but he was not ready to give up yet. He looked around for the stick he'd been using as a crutch, and cursed again. It was gone, nowhere to be seen, and there was nothing he could substitute. There was nothing at all except for the soil.

He tried to stand, and at first he couldn't make it. Continuing to struggle, he finally came to his feet, wobbled for a moment, then took a tentative step. He managed about three of them before he fell again. Cursing, he tried it again, managed to get up once more. From a standing position, he could see a canal or drainage ditch off to his right, and he headed for it. After several steps, he fell again, and gave up his attempts to walk. Proceeding on hands and knees, he finally reached the edge, looked up and down it; both banks formed perfectly straight lines. It was about eight feet wide and four feet deep, lined with stone, the water in it crystal-clear. Definitely a man-made canal. He splashed the cool water on his face, drank some, and sat up beside it, feeling a little better.

Hearing a sound behind him, he turned quickly. A young girl, barefoot and dressed in a simple cotton dress, was standing looking at him, her blue eyes sad.

"Xilonen!" he cried, his voice only a little stronger. "How did you—"

She pushed back her blond hair, smiled at him engagingly. "I told you, in the place of poisons, we would meet again soon!"

"But where are we? Where were you?" he asked. He knew he wasn't making a lot of sense.

"You needed me," she said simply. "And so I came to you. I will help you, if you'll let me."

"Yes, of course," he said. "Do you know where my friends are? I lost them when we fell down the sand dune."

"No, they are not here," she said. "There is only you and I, and the soil, and the water, and the sun."

"The sun? But we're deep underground. The sun can't shine here." He realized then that it seemed to be shining after all, through the mists. The bluish light that pervaded this place had given way to natural sunlight.

"For us, there is always the sun!" she sang, jumping up and

dancing around a little, just as he had seen her do when he was a youth. She looked exactly the same now as she had then. Her dance ended, she returned to sit beside him, began tugging at his leather clothes. "First the water," she declared. He started to protest, but then relaxed and let her do what she wanted.

She jumped into the water herself and stood chest deep, her dress swirling up around her. Lifting her arms, she held out her hands to him, clearly wanting him to come in with her. That didn't seem like such a terribly bad idea; the water had been refreshing a minute ago when he'd splashed it on his face. He swung his legs over the edge and, holding onto her hands, jumped in.

The cool water was initially shocking, but after he'd adjusted to it he had to admit it felt good, like he was absorbing it through his skin. Xilonen stood in front of him and smiled. She looked dazzling. Holding his face in her hands, she pulled him to her, drew his head down to her chest, pressed herself against him. The problem was, of course, that her chest was under water. He could hear her saying something, but couldn't make it out; she was speaking in air, and his ears were under water.

A moment later, it became obvious that she didn't intend to bring his head up. His lungs were starved for air. He began to struggle with her, but she held him under the surface with surprising strength. He struggled more vigorously, and she finally let him up. Gasping for air, he clutched at the bank.

"Were you trying to kill me?" he panted.

She looked sad. "I hoped the water would take you," she said. "It would have been the easiest way for you. But now, no. I can see, that was wrong." She jumped nimbly back up on the bank, reached out her arms, and helped him out of the canal.

Laboriously he crawled out and lay on his back, panting. Xilonen moved a few feet away and sat cross-legged, watching him.

"Now, the sun," she said.

"What do you mean?" he asked her. But he knew already; the mists had cleared above him and the sun's full rays beat down on his body. This felt very good indeed, he realized. The wetness from the canal began to evaporate, and it seemed to him that the sun's heat was drawing the pain out of the sores that covered his body. He relaxed, gave himself up to it; he was incredibly tired, and he fell asleep.

He didn't know that much time had elapsed when he finally awoke. Xilonen was still sitting in the same place, smiling at him. Feebly, he smiled back. He felt better, in the sense that he was not in as much pain, but if anything he felt weaker.

"You will give yourself to the sun?" she asked, sounding like she hoped he'd say yes. He didn't know exactly what she meant. He tried to sit up, and when he moved his arm it cracked.

Still lying down, he stared at it in horror. It had cracked open at the elbow, and blood was flowing out onto the soil. He tried to speak, but he had no voice; when he moved his head, little cracks developed around his neck, cracks he would both hear and feel. He felt terribly dry, like the sun had pulled all the water out of him. Even the blood flowing from his arm seemed thick.

Xilonen came to him and delicately kissed his head. With a concerned expression, she looked into his face. "You will give yourself to the sun?" she asked again, and this time he knew what she meant.

"No!" he croaked, forcing out the sound. "No. Help me, please. I need to sit up."

Quickly she put her hands in the water and ran them over his body, poured a couple of handfuls into his mouth, past his parched and cracked lips. Then she helped him sit up. His body cracked in many more places as he did so; he had no idea he could feel such unbelievable pain. He looked down at himself with his one remaining eye; he hardly looked human anymore. A mass of sores, cracks, burned skin, and blood. He moaned, deep in his throat.

"You have not given yourself to the water or the sun," Xilonen said, a pleading note in her voice. "Now, the thief will come. You will not give yourself to him, will you?"

He didn't understand this, or much care. "Xilonen, I'm in such pain. I need help, Xilonen, please—"

She backed off from him and started to cry, big tears rolling down her cheeks. "I am trying, I really am," she moaned, "but the thief—"

He looked around and stopped talking. He was looking at a crow, an ordinary crow. Except that it was enormous, standing fifteen feet at the head. Dazed, he wondered how it could have come up without him hearing it.

It hopped toward him, cocking its huge head to one side. He scuttled around to face it. Every movement was an agony, but he had no choice. Xilonen had backed off; she was not helping. The bird pecked at him, catching his shoulder in its beak. He flailed at it with his arm and it jerked away, taking a chunk of his flesh along. Dipping its head, it pecked again. The beak drove into his stomach like a pickaxe, and he felt something inside him tear. He pounded on its head, and again it backed off. But then it was coming again, this time getting a good grip on the knee of his good leg. He screamed in spite of his ravaged throat as his bones were crushed. Frantic, he drove his fist into the bird's eye. It released him and hopped away, but circled around, came back from the other side. The eye he had hit seemed to be glazed. It cocked its head and struck again, and for a moment he couldn't move. The tip of the beak had closed on his hip, and he felt it crushing his pelvis. Screaming again, he struck at the bird's other eye; he connected, and once more it jerked back. Through a haze of pain, he saw it hop away, take wing, and disappear.

"Xilonen," he panted. "Xilonen, oh, it's too much, too much—" The pain was all-encompassing, his whole world. He wondered in a detached way why he didn't lose consciousness. Sick, drowned, burned, attacked. He'd had all he could take. His leg turned crazily out at an angle, the bones crushed at both knee and hip. As his head fell back to the ground, he felt an agonizing pain in the back of it. Now what? he wondered. How much more could there be? This new pain was incredible, overshadowing the crushed bones in his knee and hip, running in a straight line from the crown of his head all the way down to the base of his spine, a line of pure fire. He squirmed against it, but was forced to stop by the violent agony of his knee and hip every time he tried to move. Suddenly, he realized what was happening to him; his skin was splitting away, rolling back like a piece of cellophane released from a package. The exposed muscles of his back were lying on the ground, and the pain was utterly incomprehensible. He'd had no idea there could be pain like this.

Through a red haze, he saw Xilonen's concerned face bending over him. "Will you give yourself now to the earth?" she asked him. It struck him then, what she was trying to do. He had to die, he knew that now; all the pain he was undergoing was being caused by his resistance, his stupidity.

"Yes!" he said, in a stronger voice than he thought he could muster. "Yes, now!"

Xilonen raised an obsidian knife over him. He had no idea where she'd gotten it. She hesitated just for a moment, then stabbed it into his chest. He was surprised; the pain of this was utterly trivial compared to what he'd been experiencing. Working hard, she opened the wound, then slid her slender arm inside him. He felt a deep, wrenching pain, watched her hand come out holding a bloody, squirming mass he realized was his heart. Clutching it in her hand, she kissed him, and held him tightly while he died.

3

"Well, now what, I wonder?" Danny mused, as much to himself as to Kathryn. They had wandered around the field for quite a while, but they had seen no sign of Susan, David, or Maria, nor had anyone answered their calls.

"Well, I think we know they aren't on top," Kathryn said, gazing at the sandy slope leading back to the Yellow Desert. "We were all together when we started to fall. And considering David's condition, I can't imagine him climbing back up there."

Danny looked up at it too; he couldn't either. In fact, he wondered if he himself could climb it. He had looked for the wall of fog, but for whatever reason he could not generate it down here on the plain. If they wanted to leave that way, they would have to climb the dune, and that was not going to be easy.

"Seems like we tend to get pushed farther and farther down in here," he observed.

"Do you think we should continue on the path?" Kathryn asked.

He looked glum. He was loath to leave the area without having found Susan or David. Particularly David; he might well be lying around somewhere injured, unable to answer them. For that matter, so could Susan; broken bones from that tumble were not impossible.

"No. We can't, not yet. We'll have to search up and down here, try to find them. We can't go on when they might be injured."

She agreed. Picking a direction at random, they started walking along the edge of the dune. A little ways down it turned into a near cliff, which looked very hazardous to Danny. Sand crumbled continuously from the top, and they kept a distance from it. It looked like it might collapse at any moment.

They had not gone far when they hit an obstacle; a stone wall, clearly man-made. It towered a hundred feet or more in the air, but in the mist they hadn't been aware of it until they were almost on top of it. It was very smooth; the stones fitted together perfectly. Climbing over was out of the question. They followed it for a while, until another wall converged on them, turning the plain into a roofless corridor about twenty feet wide. It remained misty, and they couldn't see where they were going. But, being given little or no choice, they trudged on down the path.

The ground surface began to tip downward again, and the walls seemed to be getting even higher. Danny could now see something up ahead, a change in the monotony. Soon it became definite; a great stone archway under which the corridor ran. Above it, he could faintly see through the mists what looked like a fantastic array of towers and pyramids. As they neared the doorway, it seemed they were entering some fairy-tale castle, except that it was built on a monstrous scale. Finally they were at the opening, which was about twenty feet wide and fifty feet tall. Inside, there was plenty of light, but it was different, more purplish. They stopped and looked inside. Nothing there to be seen, just a huge corridor like outside, but roofed over now. The floor at the threshold also changed from grass to stone, the same fitted stone they'd seen so much of down here.

"I don't like this," Kathryn said, pressing herself up to him.

"Neither do I, but we don't have a lot of choice," he responded. Cautiously they went under the arch, walked on down the vast hall.

Rounding a wide bend, they saw a wooden door, lighted torches hanging on either side of it. Danny approached it cautiously. It didn't seem to be locked or barred, and it moved slightly when he touched it. He pushed a little harder, intending to open it only a crack and peek through, but when he did, it suddenly swung free on its hinges and opened widely, banging back against the stone. He was looking into a hall filled with people, all of whom turned and looked at them.

Kathryn made a little frightened noise and they both started to back off. Danny was thinking fast; to run seemed absurd. There was no place to go. Behind them was the walled corridor leading out to the Yellow Desert, whose dunes they had already failed to climb.

At least twenty men were advancing on them. Danny imagined they looked like Aztec warriors: feathered headdresses, vests similar to those John and Bertie had worn. Several of the ones in the lead were wearing helmets in the shape of eagle's heads, the men's faces looking out through the beaks. They were armed with spears, bows, and long knives. He considered trying to talk to them, but assumed they wouldn't understand English.

Then one of the ones in the eagle masks spoke. "Who are you?" he asked, pointing at Danny. "Why have you come here?" His English was perfect.

"We are looking for friends of ours, who may have passed this way. We mean no harm." Danny hoped this was good enough; the man's spear was up and ready for action.

"This friend; he was accompanied by a dog?"

"Well, yes, as a matter of fact, he—"

The man lowered his spear and smiled broadly. "Welcome, then!" he said. "You will of course pay your respects?"

Danny didn't have any idea to whom or to what, but he nodded. It seemed safer that way.

"Good. Come forth to the stone, then!"

Thinking of the sacrificial stone at the ruined church, Danny hung back a little. "How is it you speak English?" he asked.

"Language is of no consequence in Mictlan," said the other.

"You understand English, so that is what you hear. I understand Nahuatl and this is what I hear."

"You mean you hear me speaking to you in Nahuatl?" he asked.

"Yes. Long ago we learned of these things. But it is not of importance. Come, pay your respects to the old king."

The mass of people had fallen back into two lines, and they were led between them, down toward a dais which was raised in seven steps. Atop this was what appeared to be a coffin, its lid lifted. There seemed to be a bluish glow around it. Slowly, patiently, they moved toward it, while all the assembled people watched them go. Danny realized then that the men hadn't taken notice of Kathryn. They had looked at her, knew she was there, but had addressed no questions to her. He assumed this was simply the male-orientation of the society. She was, by their standards, his woman; thus he would speak for them both.

Reaching the dais, the warrior started up. He mounted the steps with great dignity, and the two Americans followed suit, pausing on each step before proceeding to the next. At the top, Danny saw two armed men flanking the coffin. He had neither seen nor heard them go up. He was wondering if he really wanted to see whose body the coffin held.

Finally they ascended the topmost step, and after a suitable pause, Danny and Kathryn looked into the ornate box. He breathed a sigh of relief. The man inside seemed perfectly preserved, as if he had died only today, but he was not anyone they knew. He wore a gold headdress shaped like a hummingbird's beak, decorated with small green feathers. His vest was also green, with gold ornaments, and his shield was adorned by five tufts of white feathers in the form of a cross, some long yellow plumes, and four arrows. Across his chest lay a blue staff, carved in the form of a serpent. His kilt and sandals were also blue, and his forehead was painted this same color. Clearly this man had been a warrior; beside him lay an obsidian-edged wooden sword and a heavy bow.

His face was dark, but he had been a very handsome man. The regular features and aquiline nose were very striking. Danny had a rush of emotion for the man; he seemed so young, so powerful, it was tragic that he was dead.

After what seemed a suitable interval, he turned to the man

who had led them here, searched his face; he didn't know if it was appropriate to speak. "Who was he?" he asked in a hushed tone, taking a chance on it.

"He was the last king of Tlillan Tlapallan before your friend. He was known as the Hummingbird from the Left, Huitzilopochtli. When his people died, he died with them. I was there; I am Cuecuex, Eagle Knight of the Lord Huitzilopochtli."

Although it sounded silly following such a title, he said, "I am Danny Hudson, and my companion is Kathryn Phillips." The man executed the peculiar squatting bow they had seen in the village, and Danny returned it. He noticed Kathryn did not, and that worried him for a moment, but Cuecuex seemed to take no offense.

"I remember the name, Huitzilopochtli, from school, I think," Danny said, almost idly. "War god of the Aztec, I believe."

"Yes," Cuecuex said simply.

Danny looked back at the man in the coffin; he must have been quite highly regarded to have been named after a god. He wanted to ask how these people all came to be here, what this place really was. Naturally, he didn't take Maria's statement that this was Hell in any sense other than figuratively. He held off his questions, though; it seemed he never got any straight answers anyway. And it was obviously important not to say or do anything to offend this group of armed men.

"You will want to see the stone, now," Cuecuex said. "Follow me."

Again, the stone. But he'd said "see" it, so maybe it was all right. Still uncomfortable, Danny followed him across the dais toward an area concealed by black curtains. Kathryn hesitated a moment, still looking at the body, then followed. He glanced at her; her expression was peculiar.

"What's the matter?" he whispered to her.

"That man in the coffin. I feel like I know him, like I've seen him before somewhere."

"Where?"

"I don't know. I can't place him."

They reached the curtains, and with a flourish, Cuecuex pulled them open. Inside was a small alcove with two elaborately embroidered cushions, one on the floor and the other on a small stand which appeared to be made of gold. The upper one held an obsidian mirror, much like the ones he'd seen; but it was larger, and seemed to be of a higher finish.

"The tezeat," Cuecuex said in a reverent tone.

Danny wondered why the reverence over a mirror. Cuecuex indicated the cushion on the floor; evidently Danny was supposed to sit on it and look into the glass. He did so. Kathryn looked over his shoulder. At first, the mirror showed only a smoky reflection of their faces. But then, suddenly, it cleared, and he was no longer seeing reflections. He looked deeper, spellbound.

4

When Susan finally stopped rolling, she found herself lying on the flat, grassy plain, having gone far enough that she could no longer see the dunes of the Yellow Desert through the mists that surrounded her. Calling out for the others accomplished nothing, and she was unsure of what to do next. At least she was not injured; she had not suffered even a scratch in the long fall, though her long skirt was ripped.

Eventually she got up and began to wander. She had no idea of where she was going or why; it just seemed impossible to sit still anymore. The rigors of the trip, her concern for the others and especially for David, had helped keep her mind occupied, kept her from thinking about recent events. And events not so recent. But now everyone was gone, and at this moment she didn't know if she'd ever see any of them again. She'd tried so hard to catch hold of David as they'd begun their long fall, but she had failed. Like she'd failed at everything, failed everyone, she told herself. The totality of her despair overcame her, and she sank to her knees on the grass, crying bitterly. She felt terribly alone, and even worse, felt like she deserved to be. She was such a disaster, no one should have to put up with her.

The crying spell passed, and she began to walk again. There was a sameness about the landscape that made her wonder if perhaps she was just going in circles. People lost in the desert did that, she remembered. She might just walk until she died of hunger or thirst, but that was a long way off. Right now, she wasn't hungry or thirsty at all.

Finally she saw something ahead, and she quickened her pace. It turned out to be a stone wall, very high and smooth. No way to cross over it, but at least it relieved the monotony of this plain. Pressing her hands against it, she assured herself it was really there, that it was solid. Again she called for David and Danny, but only silence answered.

She began to walk alongside the wall in a direction she thought would take her away from the Yellow Desert, and after a time, had to remind herself that a wall could not just go on forever, that it had to have an end. She told herself that she would surely find David and the others there, and that things would get better for her. But even as she tried to convince herself of this, she knew it wasn't true. Her problems were greater than the plain and the wall.

Lost in her thoughts, she was taken by surprise when she came to an arched passageway in the wall. She had almost walked right past it. It appeared to be a tunnel in some larger structure, bending off to the left some thirty feet inside. The light coming from around the bend was reddish, not the pervasive blue out here on the plain. Looking up, she found that the wall was so high now that its top was lost in the mists, invisible to her. Shrugging her shoulders, she entered the passage.

Once around the bend, it became obvious that the reddish light was being generated by torches set in holders at intervals along the wall. The fact that they were lighted meant that there were people of some sort around; and maybe, she told herself almost desperately, those people had seen her brother. That was all that kept her going, that glimpse of him on the side of the hill, the idea that he was not really dead after all. She needed that, needed it to save her. Otherwise, she didn't know what was going to happen to her. Her thoughts turned to David; she was sure, just positive, that he was with Danny and Kathryn, that he was all right. When she found John, he would know what to do about David; he couldn't die. She could not stand that, refused to admit even the possibility to herself.

The corridor expanded a little, and she could see there were two rooms, one on each side. Each had a wooden door identical to the other. Beyond them, the hallway continued its twisting course to an unknown destination. Stopping in front of the doors, she made a snap decision, pushed on the one to her right. It offered no resistance, swung inward easily. Without hesitation, she stepped inside.

She found herself in a small, dark anteroom. There was another door directly across from her, and it too opened easily. Light from torches mounted on the far wall spilled out as she went it.

Standing in the doorway, she looked around; there was no one there, and no other exits. In the center of the room stood a familiar object; an almost exact copy of the sacrificial stone that stood beside the ruined church. At her left was something that appeared to be a large, overstuffed mattress. On her right, opposite the mattress, was a carved stone block resembling an altar. On it she found a pottery jar and bowl, both painted with beautiful designs, and a ceramic box with a lid, also artistically painted. Lying beside the box were a number of long, thin items that looked sort of like awls. They were carved from bone, and they had very sharp points.

She was about to open the box when she sensed a movement behind her and turned quickly. A man was standing in the doorway naked, his erect penis pointing at her. "Bertie!" she cried. But then she looked closely at him, realized it was not Bertie. "You!" she exclaimed, staring at him.

"Yes, I am here," the phantom said. He came across the room and stood close to her, and in spite of everything, she felt herself responding to him physically. She hated herself for it. It seemed nothing ever changed for her.

"I'm looking for my brother. Do you know who he is?" she asked. It seemed like a nonsensical question; how would the phantom know John? He wasn't even real. But she kept talking, kept trying to push back the physical impulses she was having.

"Yes, I know who he is and where he is," the phantom replied in a gentle voice. "You need not trouble yourself. He is coming here, soon, to this very room."

"He is?" she cried. "Then he's all right? But where is he now, I have to see him."

"No. You must not. If you leave this room, you may miss him. So you must stay."

She considered this, her emotions in turmoil. She certainly didn't want to go wandering off if it was certain that John was coming here. But she didn't like the idea of staying here with the phantom, either; his resemblance to Bertie made her especially uncomfortable. She tried to demand of herself that she find him repugnant, considering the disastrous consequences the last time she'd believed she was having sex with Bertie, but it didn't help. She still found him as arousing as ever; and after all, a voice inside her said, he wasn't Bertie. They were similar, but not identical. This man, for example, had both his feet.

"Remember what I have said to you," he told her. "You have to follow your instincts, all of them. Now more than ever. You should try not to think at all. Just feel, act, and react."

"But you don't understand. I can't do that anymore. I've caused so much pain."

"I do understand what you think you've done. But I say again, you should try to stop thinking. The other can then take control."

"The other?"

He didn't reply. Taking another step toward her, he gently took the lapels of her vest and pushed it back over her shoulders, undid the clasp on her torn skirt and let it fall to the floor, leaving her totally nude except for the gold bands on her arms. Taking her in his arms, he held her to him, his erection pressing into her stomach.

"No," she said miserably. "I can't do this, every time I do, something bad happens to somebody!"

Immediately he released her and stepped back. He looked at her, and she felt like his eyes had grown to occupy most of the room, like she was sliding sideways, out of control. Struggling with herself, she tried to look away from him, but couldn't. Again he stepped forward, put his hands on her breasts. She tried to tell him no again, knew he'd back away if she did, but the sound wouldn't come out. She was fighting a fierce battle within herself, but she was losing.

Gently, he fondled her. She continued to try to resist, but she still couldn't speak. All it would take was one word, and she couldn't get it to come out! His hands were on her shoulders, pushing her down; hers hung limply at her sides. Part of her wanted to use them to touch him, the other part wanted to push him away, and in concert they accomplished nothing. She was utterly passive as he pushed her to her knees.

Slowly, he moved his hips forward until his penis touched her lips. She pleaded with herself to keep them closed, but found that she couldn't. As she opened them, he pushed into her mouth. She didn't move her lips or tongue, just held him loosely. He moved a few times, just small movements, then ejaculated. She tried not to swallow, and succeeded momentarily; part of his semen ran out of the corner of her mouth and onto her chin. But she lost that battle too, swallowed the remainder, and felt the same sensation as before; an energizing flow, concentrating in the upper half of her body. He pulled back, still erect, and helped her to her feet. Then he was guiding her toward the mattress, and she felt helpless to resist. He laid her down, gently pushed her legs apart, and entered her. Again, she didn't respond to him, didn't move at all. For a long while, neither did he; it seemed to her that he was melting into her at the point of their connection. He began to move just a little, but it didn't change the illusion of unity. Her passivity notwithstanding, she experienced an explosive orgasm, and as she did she felt his seed spraying inside her. Closing her eyes, she felt the energy flow through her lower half, and for a moment, she didn't feel bad. Her orgasm, this incredible rich flowing sensation, was all that mattered. Then it was passing, and she opened her eyes.

And looked into John's face.

She screamed like a wounded animal, wildly flailing at him. He got off her, and she rolled to her feet.

"How could you—" she shrieked. "How—how—" Then she looked at him again. It was not, after all, John. But the man looked a great deal like him, just as he had, moments before, looked a great deal like Bertie.

"It's still you, isn't it?" she said incredulously.

"Yes," he replied simply.

"How could you do that? Why—?" She broke off, started to sob.

"The one you await arrives soon," he said as he left, his voice completely emotionless.

For a long time after he left she continued to cry. She had no idea how or why he'd done that, but it had brought her indiscretion with John home with a heavy force. She wasn't even sure if she wanted to see him now, didn't know what to say or do. But gradually her reason took over again, and she felt such relief that he was alive that the massive guilt started to fade away.

She was still thinking about it when the door swung open. Looking up, she began to cry again, tears of pure joy this time. From the doorway, John gave her a wan smile. Really John this time, no doubt in her mind. He stepped into the room, and was followed by another figure, a gaunt old man in black robes. He didn't seem threatening, and John didn't seem to be afraid of him, so she paid him little attention.

"John," she whispered, "John." She started to run to him, but stopped herself. After all that had happened, she was unsure about embracing him in her current condition; nude, with semen on her face and legs. But she wanted to, desperately.

"Susan, I didn't know," he said. "And I couldn't have spared you if I had," he was saying. His voice sounded peculiar, like he was speaking from a barrel.

"Oh, John, please forgive me!" she implored. "It was all my fault, the liquor—" She stopped; he was shaking his head sadly. John had always looked sad, but never like this. "No, it'll be all right now," she continued, sure that it would be. "We'll work through this, at least you're alive, oh, I thought you were dead!"

"Susan!" he said rather loudly, interrupting her. "I am dead!"

She stopped and stared at him, shocked. "Of course you're not, you're standing there, we're talking—"

"No. Things here are not always what they seem. I have a penance, and I have only done a part of it!"

"John, you aren't dead!" she insisted. "Please, please say you forgive me, we can—"

"Susan, dearest sister, I cannot do that. Our faults were equal. I was allowed to speak, and now my time is at an end." He turned to the black-cloaked figure. "Mictlantecuhtli, I am ready," he said. The old man reached out a finger and touched him; in front of Susan's eyes his form became indistinct, crumbled into a pile of dust on the floor.

She could only stare at the dust, stunned, as the black-robed figure turned and left the room; she didn't even notice the small dog that trotted after him. For several minutes, she was paralyzed; when she finally came out of it, she gave voice to a high-pitched, protracted cry, then fell on the floor in a faint.

Consciousness returned; someone was patting her face. Her eyelids fluttered, opened, and she was again looking at the phantom, who looked like Bertie. She let him help her sit up, feeling the weight of her guilt like a ball of lead, somewhere in the middle of her body. She looked at the dust pile; it was still there. As the phantom pulled her to her feet, she really saw him for the first time, saw that he was dressed. She glanced at his left foot. Artificial, mirrored, and smoking.

"Bertie," she said, slurring the name. "How did you get here?"

"Susan," he murmured. It sounded like there was genuine concern in his voice. "I have bad news for you. On my way here, I found this." He pointed to a human skin, flecked with dried blood, lying near the door.

"Horrible," she said. He picked it up, insisting she look at it. For a moment it made no sense; then the face, the short beard, registered. "Oh, noooo," she said in a very small voice. "Oh, God, it's David. Oh, he—he's dead. Not you too, David. You too? Oh, Daviiiiiid!" She lost her strength and sat down hard on the floor. The worst of it was she had no tears left, no tears for David, her love, her life.

"I'm really sorry," Bertie said, kneeling beside her.

"What did I do?" she asked. "What can I do now?"

"I think you know the answer to that, Susan." She wasn't even really aware that it was Bertie talking, just that it was the voice of a friend. He was holding something out to her, the painted box from the altar. The lid had been removed, and inside was a ball of some fibrous material like straw, another carved bone awl, a red flower, and one of the familiar obsidian knives.

Taking the box from him, she examined each item in turn. The flower, the object she recognized as a bone punch, and most closely, the knife. It looked so beautiful to her now, and she understood what the phantom had meant.

Like a sleepwalker, she got to her feet and went to the

stone. She knew exactly what she had to do, knew that there was no other way. Bertie was here with her, and Bertie was her friend; he could help her. Oddly, she found that she could not hold him responsible for what had happened. He was merely following his nature; it was they who should have known better.

Climbing onto the stone, she sat up straight with her legs folded under her, her knees in front. There had to be a balance—she could see that now—and only one way that balance could be achieved.

As Bertie stood beside her, she regarded him coolly for a moment; he had undergone numerous transformations in her eyes. He had been exciting, threatening, despicable; her lover, her betrayer, her friend. But now he was her servant, here only for the purpose of catering to her whims. This was her place, her time; what happened after this moment was of no concern to her. Only the now mattered, this perfect crystal moment, the summation of her life. All events that had any importance had led her directly to this moment. Anything not contributing to it had no significance for her whatever.

No, perhaps there was an exception to that. Danny had not led her here in any way, but he was significant. She allowed herself a moment to consider him, to see his face in her mind. But only a moment. Then she was back to her unswerving, perfect intent. Bertie was obviously waiting, but she didn't care. He would wait until she was ready.

"I will do my purification now," she said, sounding rather distant. Bertie brought the punches and the box from the altar, then stood waiting for her again, watching her. She was completely within herself, hardly aware of him at all.

Selecting the two thinnest punches, she pushed them through her earlobes, left them in place. They felt the same as the maguey thorns had, and she had expected a difference. But it was too soon to judge; these were only a preliminary. Picking up another punch, she touched its point to her thigh. But somehow that didn't seem right to her now. She moved it up until it was pressing against her body, just inside her leg. Somewhere in that area was a perfect spot, a spot that was waiting for it. Moving the point around until she found it, she began pushing it in, up into her abdomen. A fiery pain spread out from it. Resisting the urge to push it fast, she kept an even, slow pressure on it until the rounded head rested against her skin. After pushing one in on the other side in the same way, she paused for a moment, watching the blood trickle from around them. They formed twin foci of pain that spread in an arc over her entire lower body, following, it seemed, paths laid out previously by the phantom's semen. But that was no surprise to her now.

Her fingers found another of the bone punches, and she pressed its point against her left nipple. From her experience with the thorns, she knew this was not easy. Supporting her breast with her left hand, she began her even pressure again. The skin resisted, but when the point finally broke through it sank into her very quickly. Blood welled out around it; the flare of pain almost reached her other arm. She continued to push slowly, and it sank on in with almost no further resistance. There was another, deeper pain, but she paid no attention, kept pushing until only the head was visible, then did the same thing to her right nipple.

Definitely different, she thought, and definitely better than the thorns. She was aware of deep pains in her chest, a difficulty in breathing, but none of that mattered. Still, she sensed a need for something else. Taking the single punch from the box and extending her tongue, she pushed it through from the bottom up. This one she pulled out, and, tilting her head forward, allowed the blood to drip on the stone in front of her. That, she knew, was correct, was exactly what had been needed.

Reaching into the box again, she extracted the flower and put it in her hair. For several moments she remained in total concentration, watching the slowly subsiding flow of blood from her nipples. Then she picked up the obsidian knife, and, holding it with both hands, pressed it flat against her chest for a moment. Turning it inward, she touched the point to her skin over her solar plexus. But then she found she couldn't force her arms to increase the pressure. It didn't seem proper for her to do this alone; she needed a tool, some other way.

"Bertie," she said softly, "help me, please."

He reached out to her, covered her hands with his. She looked at him, then back at the knife, and nodded. He began to push; he was very steady, very strong. The point passed into her skin, and a little trickle of blood appeared, accompanied by a small pain. He maintained the same pressure, and the blade began to slide on into her body. She felt a heavy, dark pain. Her face tightened, tears ran from her eyes. But she continued to watch intently as the blade sank steadily into her. There was little bleeding until the widest part of the blade had passed into her, but as soon as it did the blood started to pump out furiously, flowing over her hands and onto her legs.

Bertie released her hands, and she in turn released the knife. The blade could hardly be seen. The pain was a dark mass inside her, and already she felt weaker. Bertie reached for it as if to pull it out; he too was crying, and she wondered why.

"Leave it," she told him, her voice still soft. "I need the bowl." He took his hand away, quickly brought the bowl from the altar, put it down in front of her.

"Now," she said, and he immediately began to pull on the knife. Holding her hands flat against her body on either side of the blade, she watched him carefully slide it out. Then she pressed the bowl against her abdomen, just below the bottom of the wound, and let the blood wash into it. As it filled, the pain lessened; a numbness was spreading over her. She became aware of his arm around her back, supporting her, and she looked up at him. But he was looking at the bowl, and when it was almost full, he took it from her, put it aside. She no longer had enough strength to sit up, and began to collapse backward. Her field of vision was getting smaller, and sounds seemed to come from far away.

Bertie leaned over her, helping her lie down. He looked into her eyes; she knew what he was asking, nodded, and he quickly stabbed the knife into her left breast. She felt almost no pain at all, only a twinge, but she was aware of how her legs stiffened, how her toes curled back. He thrust his hand and arm inside her chest, and she felt an odd tearing sensation, then a peculiar emptiness. She looked; he was holding her heart, showing it to her. Her vision was now only a little circle ahead of her eyes. She saw him take out his flint knife, felt it cut into her neck, felt it as if through a thousand layers of cotton.

As darkness closed over her, her last thought was that she had finally done something exactly right.

5

Bertie finished the task of severing Susan's head and put it down on the blood-soaked floor. Abruptly, he returned to himself as he had been months ago, and his stomach churned at the sight of the headless, mutilated corpse on the stone, the coagulating blood in the bowl, the now-still heart lying in a shallow depression in the stone, a depression that seemed to be made for a human heart. Like everything else, he told himself; it was not possible that it was coincidence, not possible at all. He had found David's body, his skin removed, and had brought the skin directly here, knowing somehow that Susan would be waiting, waiting to die, waiting for him to provide the final catalyst for her death. Not once had he considered going into the other set of rooms across the hall. His other half, the part that was gradually taking him over, knew exactly where to go and what to do. That part was dormant now, for some reason, and Bertie was totally lost. He had no idea where he was or what to do next. Looking at Susan's face, relaxed in death, he began to cry openly, tears running down his cheeks. Throughout his life, he had not been the most altruistic of men. But all this blood and death, that was alien. At the moment, he was unable to accept some of the things he'd done, yet he'd been casual about them when he was doing them.

Why in the world, he asked himself, would a group of eight relatively normal people suddenly decide to indulge themselves in a bloodbath of burnings, knifings, and beheadings? He had personally killed three of the people he'd come here with, not to mention a number of villagers. And, he realized, Susan and Evelyn had wanted him to do exactly what he had done! It was incomprehensible. Sado-masochism could not account for it, though he did recognize a certain symbolic phallic component in the use of the thorns and bone punches in the purifications, but those weren't exclusive to the women, all of the men except Danny had done this too, himself included. The obsidian sacrificial knives were also phallic, but knives always are. No, there were no real answers there. The part of himself currently in control had expected chagrin and embarrassment from John and Susan over the incest, but hardly the violent reactions that had occurred. It all seemed so very extreme, so very twisted. None of the villagers they'd sacrificed had uttered one word of complaint, and none had tried to run away, though the opportunity had been there. Everybody wanted pain, and he was cast in the role of the provider. Much as he disliked that, he would have liked any of the other roles less, and he was not hesitant about acknowledging that.

He considered the two sides of himself. He wanted to see the now-dormant side as an invader, a demon possessing him; but he could not, it just wasn't that way. Rather, that side was truly him. The other was a socialized, Americanized veneer he could almost remember constructing as a child. His energetic self, the natural Bertie, was not a person who could exist very well in a twentieth-century world. But that still left unanswered the questions of why he was doing these things, and how he knew what to do.

He held his head in his hands. A voice inside him, insistent, pounding, was demanding something of him. It appeared that the time when his other side was quiet had ended. He didn't feel like he was being taken over; it was more like a feeling of responsibility, the need one feels to get up and go to work on a rainy morning, when staying in bed is so clearly the better alternative. But with this sense came knowledge, things he had to do, places he had to go. He only knew that there was a real possibility of John returning from the dead, and it would be very bad for him if that happened. He began looking around for a pike he knew would be somewhere in the room and when he found it, he impaled Susan's head on it. Then he picked up her body, the pike with the head, and David's skin. Thus weighed down, he tottered out of the room and down the hall. His body seemed to know where he was going with his grisly load, but he had no idea. The peculiar thing was that with every step, Susan's corpse seemed to be getting heavier. And it wasn't getting cold.

For a long time he walked down the long, twisting hallway.

He didn't feel at all tired, but it seemed like his burden kept getting heavier all the time. Finally he found a doorway he knew was right, and he entered a small, torchlit room.

In the center of this room was a low table, a chair like a throne sitting at one end. Otherwise, it was totally empty. Bertie stood the pike in the corner and laid Susan's headless body on the table. With David's skin still draped over his arm, he stood near the throne chair and waited. He had started to sit on it, but that felt wrong to him.

He didn't have to wait long before two Indians entered the room and executed the squatting bow. One was naked except for a loincloth; he looked quite unhappy. The other was dressed equally simply, but his body and limbs were painted with narrow vertical red stripes; he carried a bow, a quiver of arrows, and a shield, and he wore a feathered headdress. It was clear that the first man was his captive.

"And you are?" Bertie said, coldly, imperiously.

"Ah, now it is you who have forgotten me," the painted warrior said. "The last time we met, it was I who could not remember you! I am Mixcoatl, my lord. Some also call me Camaxtli. The name of this other is of no consequence, as he is a vessel only."

Bertie started to ask what he meant, but decided against it. The door opened again and two men dressed as warriors, heavily armed with spears and bows, came in. Without speaking, they took positions at either side of the door. Another man walked through. He was very richly dressed, a huge gold solar disk on his chest. He was old, and seemed feeble.

"Our Lord of the Fifth Sun, Tonatiuh!" one of the warriors announced. Mixcoatl bowed deeply. But Bertie smiled at the old man.

"My friend!" he said warmly. "It is good to see you!"

The old man raised watery blue eyes to meet Bertie's and managed a crooked grin. "It has been a long time, a long time indeed," he said. His yellowish skin gleamed in the light of the torches. "And a long time since I have been in Mictlan. I must see this place again soon enough. I would leave as soon as possible. We must be about our business here."

He gestured, and one of the warriors approached Bertie, who handed him David's bloody skin. Working together, the two warriors trimmed the skin into a body suit and mask like the one David had worn for the past several days. They then helped the nameless man into it, lacing it tightly across his back, fitting the head skin over his face. While this was going on, Bertie watched Mixcoatl rather closely. The man bore a certain odd, but undeniable, resemblance to John, even though he was quite obviously Indian, or part Indian. Bertie had a feeling that there was a reason for this, but he could not understand what that reason might be.

As soon as the skin was securely in place, the warriors guided the nameless man to a position at the foot of the table where Susan's body lay. Bertie stood at her left, Mixcoatl on her right, and Tonatiuh rose from the throne chair at the head of the table.

"Xipe!" Tonatiuh said loudly. Bertie jumped a little. "Are you with us?"

There was no response from anyone. Mixcoatl looked a little impatient. The nameless man hung his head and said nothing.

"Xipe Totec!" Tonatiuh called again. "Xipe Totec!" His voice was like a command.

The nameless man raised his head slowly. The eyes peering through the mask were lifeless, dull; but then, as Bertie watched, they took on depth, light. "I am here, myself, in person," he said. Bertie jumped a little. The character of the voice, although not the intonation, was exactly David's.

"We will proceed," Tonatiuh said. "We are the guardians." He looked at Bertie expectantly.

For a second Bertie was lost, drifting, and had no idea what to do. Then he looked at the body on the table and received a severe shock, although he was careful not to let it show. Susan's corpse had changed in two very profound ways; first, it was breathing, slowly and regularly! Bertie could only stare at it for a minute. How could it breathe? There was no head, no heart! But it was, nevertheless. The air whistled slightly, in and out through the severed windpipe.

The second change was equally profound. Susan's stomach, flat and mutilated when he'd picked up the body in the other room, was enormously distended. More, there was no evidence of any wound in her abdomen. She looked pregnant, and due.

With a sudden clarity, he knew what he was expected to do. Taking out his flint knife, he began cutting into her distended stomach, layer by layer, never going very deep with any one cut. Blood spurted, spraying all of them. He glanced back at her chest; the hole through which he'd extracted her heart was still there. How could blood spurt with no heart to drive it? He had no idea, but he continued cutting, finally breaking through the abdominal wall. He and Mixcoatl grasped the tissues, ripped the wound open, and looked at the surface of the uterus. With one sure cut, he opened it. There was a rush of blood and fluids; then they reached inside and extracted an infant.

He let Mixcoatl take the baby and stepped back. There was a moment of silence while the man worked to clear the baby's nose and mouth, then the characteristic newborn wail filled the room.

"It is well," Tonatiuh said. "Take him now, Mixcoatl." The hunter left the room, carrying the baby. Gradually the infant's crying sounds faded into the distance.

Tonatiuh sat back down on the throne, rather heavily. Bertie looked at the body on the table again; the breathing had stopped, and already the skin was growing cold to the touch. With a shock, he realized it wasn't Susan's body at all! This was the body of a taller, more voluptuous woman. As he stared at it, it occurred to him that it looked much more like Evelyn's body. But when had it changed? It was never out of his sight! He glanced at the head, impaled on the pike in the corner; that was indeed Susan's. He felt slightly dazed. Even though he'd known what to do, what was expected of him, he had no idea what was happening.

The man in David's skin turned and left the room without speaking. Bertie wondered about him, started to ask the old man on the throne, but Tonatiuh spoke before Bertie could say a word. "I must go now, must leave here," he said. He sounded very tired. "Only twenty-four years left. A moment, just a moment." He got up slowly and walked out, the two warriors closing the door as they went. Bertie was left in the room with the headless corpse, wondering what to do now.

6

Danny no longer felt as if he were sitting in front of the stone looking in; he seemed to be spinning free in space. Below him, far away, he could see vague, hazy images. He could not make out what they were, but they were intensely interesting.

Realizing he was trying to see the images normally, he tried his heightened vision, and suddenly things began to make sense. He seemed to be in what he could best describe as a timestream, looking down on events, seeing them occur. It was as if each event he focused on was a movie, the individual frames all projected at the same time. He could scan them backward, forward, any way he wished.

There was one peculiar series of images in which his friends figured prominently, and he concentrated on it. In the first series, he saw Bertie; or perhaps it wasn't Bertie, maybe just someone who looked like him. He was a king, but his subjects were not humans. Instead, they were subhuman giants, slow and dull. Catastrophe befell his kingdom; he was struck treacherously from behind, knocked into the water and drowned. His assailant looked a great deal like John, the only other human Danny had seen in this series. The kingdom was then subject to a veritable plague of big cats, swarming like locusts, and when they had passed, the giant humanoids were all dead.

In the series which followed, John was the king, his subjects human. It was not the near paradise Tlillan Tlapallan had been during the real John's reign there, but it was a placid enough world. Then he, in his turn, was assassinated by a giant jaguar with obsidian eyes, a familiar image to Danny. As soon as he had died, great hurricanes ravaged the kingdom. When they calmed, no humans were left. A few monkeys scavenged for food in the ruins of the cities that had been erected.

Gradually, humans reappeared in the lands, and a new king was named. It was Frank Wasserman this time! His people were agriculturalists, creating huge farming communities. But he too died a violent death, struck from a hillside by a high wind. Danny could see the image of a smiling John, far away, removing the long-faced mask and laughing aloud as Frank hurtled to his death. As he died, the earth rumbled, and numerous volcanoes began erupting; the farm communities were buried along with the farmers under the ash and fiery lava raining from the skies. It took a long time for the kingdom to cool, and the only life Danny saw were birds flying to and fro over the ashes.

Now a queen came to power instead of a king, as the people returned to the lands. The queen was Evelyn, and her subjects were fishermen and seafarers, living near and off the bounty of the seas. A very high civilization rose under her benign rule. Great towers overlooked a mighty city, and envoys to all parts of the world went out in huge ships. Studies were done, knowledge collected. Then, it appeared that part of the knowledge forecast the end of this kingdom as well. He saw Evelyn crying in despair, while some of the subjects built colossal towers. But as she sat sobbing, the great cat, obsidian eyes glinting, was creeping up on her. It struck, and she was dead. Then the seas and rivers began to rise. Even the tower was not enough; the whole earth was inundated. He could see no life except the fish jumping on the uniform surface of a vast sea.

Eventually the waters receded, and the dry land reappeared. A new king came to power; Danny didn't recognize this man. He was bright, handsome, energetic, had a sunny disposition, but his world was one constantly at war, one kingdom fighting another. With a shock, Danny realized that time was unraveling rather fast now; the primitive spear and arrow wars gave way to knights in armor, then blue and gray uniforms, a German Stuka bombing a French town, nuclear bombs exploding in Japan, soldiers bogging down in the jungles of Viet Nam, in the hills of Afghanistan. He was very confused, scanned on forward. He saw the energetic king dying, apparently of disease; he couldn't seem to breathe. As he gasped his last, Danny saw a brief flash of John's grinning face, his mouth open and his cheeks pulled in as if he were sucking air. Then the kingdom shook with a series of huge earthquakes. All the edifices of this kingdom, he knew, were being destroyed. He scanned forward a bit, saw some of the creations of this fifth kingdom, saw them dying. New York. Moscow. San Francisco. London. Tokyo.

With a frightened gasp, he yanked himself away from the mirror. Glancing around, he found himself alone, sitting on the cushion. Down off the dais, he saw Cuecuex. His face white, he came down the stairs as fast as he could.

"The mirror," he asked. "What is it?"

Cuecuex looked at him with a surprised expression. "Why, it is the great tezeat. Only a powerful magician can use it. It tells the past and the future."

"A crystal ball. Scrying stone."

"Yes, of course."

"What did I see in it. Truth?"

"Always."

"Oh, no." For the first time he realized that Kathryn was not there. "Where is the lady that was with me?" he asked.

"She seemed to see something herself. She said she must go to meet her fate."

Danny just stared for a moment. He did not like the sound of that at all, considering what Evelyn had done at the ruined church.

"Where?" he cried, the visions momentarily forgotten.

Cuecuex indicated a passage leading out of the great hall. Danny ran for it.

7

For a long time after everyone else had left, Bertie remained in the room with the dead woman's body. He considered leaving, but he didn't know where to go. He was still in this state of self-doubt when Ihuimecatl came in.

"You forgot this," she said, holding up a leather sack. "I

don't know what would happen if we weren't around. Do you know the risks I had to take to get this to you?''

He stared, without comprehension. ''What is it?'' he asked. He really wasn't too interested. He felt listless, uncertain.

She rolled her eyes. ''Amazing. The chalchihuitl,'' she said. ''Do you think those two women drained their blood into a bowl for no reason at all?''

He took the bag; inside was a stoppered ceramic flask. Opening it, he peered down the neck. It was about two thirds full of dark blood.

''Evelyn's?'' he asked.

''Yes, and the other's. I got hers from the room where you left it sitting there. I swear, I can't understand you. Don't you know what's important and what's not?''

''I guess not. I don't see—''

''Well, take it! You know, I'll probably die trying to get back out of here. Toltecatl—well, Toltecatl didn't make it this far. We used bat forms to cross the river, and we didn't fly high enough. Cipactli caught him.''

''Toltecatl is dead?''

''Unless you want to go get him out of Cipactli's insides. If you do, get your foot while you're at it!''

''What?''

''You don't remember Cipactli taking your foot?''

''I guess—''

''Look. You have things to do if you're going to change anything, and so far, you haven't done much. You might as well have stayed up above and enjoyed those four brides while you had the time!''

Her words seemed to galvanize him to action. And though he couldn't believe that John or anyone else was going to return from the dead, he didn't want to take any chances. Taking the bag, and the pike with Susan's head attached, he hurried out of the room, leaving Ihuimecatl to try to get back as best she could. Once again, he had no idea where he was going, but now, his body seemed to know.

The hallway led him back outside, into an area less gloomy than before; now, there was vegetation. Trotting along a trail in an idyllic forest, he wondered vaguely how this vegetation could exist with no sunlight. It was a truly beautiful place, flowers blooming here and there among the stately trees. Soon, the trail was running alongside a creek which was clear and fresh. There were dense growths of reeds along the banks.

Up ahead, he heard voices. Slowing down, he took out his knife, hid the pike and bag in the bushes, and carefully approached the sounds, listening carefully. Female voices; apparently some women were down in the reeds, at the edge of the stream. He slipped down through the reeds until his feet were just in the water, then crept forward.

Suddenly he could see them. All his creeping was for nothing; his shock led him to step right out in the open, and they looked up at him as well. There were two women, both of them nude; they were nursing a child, who appeared to be about a year old, perhaps a little more. This was odd, because he felt sure it was the same child they'd delivered less than an hour ago! But that received little notice because of the identity of the two women.

Evelyn and Mayauel. Very much alive, caring for a baby!

"It's not possible," he said slowly, staring at Evelyn. "I killed you myself; I have a jar of your blood with me. It's just not possible." He looked at Mayauel. "And I understood you were dead too!"

"Oh, I was!" she said cheerily. "Nobody lied to you. It's just that, well, things aren't always quite what they seem around here!"

"That baby—" he began.

"You're right," Evelyn told him. "Same one."

"He looks like he—"

"Sure does, doesn't he?"

Bertie started to take a step forward, but Evelyn gave the baby to Mayauel, held up her hand. "No, I'm afraid not. Not here, not now. You keep your distance!"

He flared with rage. "I'll do what I please!" he snarled, and started to move toward them.

Evelyn was obviously ready for him; she extended her arms, palms down, and stiffened her pose slightly. He had time to realize she looked incredibly regal, standing there like that. Then the stream itself reversed its flow, built with amazing speed into a six foot wall of water, and smashed into him with terrific force. He was hurled backwards into the reeds, rolled over and over and nearly drowned. Finally the torrent subsided, and he climbed to his feet, choking and coughing. He walked back until Evelyn told him he'd come close enough again. This time he respected her wishes.

"Who are you?" he asked her.

"Evelyn Wasserman. You ought to know that. But I have another name, too. I didn't know it myself until after I'd died up there. Chalchihuitlicue. Lady of the Jade Skirt. Or turquoise skirt. Depends. But what the hell. Nice name, isn't it?"

He was dazed again, unsure of himself. "Chalchihuitl— Ihuimecatl called the bottle of blood a—"

"Yes, well, it is, of course. Anything precious can be symbolized by jade. You know the ancients considered it the most precious stone of all? So a container or source of the chalchihuatl is naturally a chalchihuitl. The words are so very close. And the meanings, too."

"What? I'm not following—"

"You don't know what chalchihuatl is, do you?"

"No. Well, I—"

"The precious water. Try and remember, it may help later on. Remember me, too. Think about it; it may come to you. You might even wake up!"

Wake up? he thought. All this can't be a dream, can it?

8

Fearing for Kathryn's safety, Danny sped down the hallway. As long as he could, he ran, but soon his wind gave out and he was forced to slow to a fast walk. Apparently he had been absorbed in the mirror for a long time, and she had a substantial head start on him. He had, for the moment, almost forgotten about everything else. Finding John was way down the list. He was far more concerned about Kathryn, Susan, and David.

Then the hallway ended at an open door. Cautiously, he passed through a little anteroom to another door, opened it, and stepped inside. He immediately saw the blood-soaked floor and his throat closed. On the stone was a body. He hesitated for a long minute; he wasn't sure he wanted to see who it was. But he had to.

His eyes took in the decapitated female body, the open abdomen, the bloodstains around the nipples and groin. Just like Evelyn. That body looked so terribly familiar to him, but he wouldn't admit it yet. Not without proof. Something. He saw the hole ripped in the chest, knew the heart was gone. The head was not there; he began looking for it, dreading what he would find. Searching the floor for it, his eyes fell on the mattress, and he saw the floral featherwork vest, the long skirt. Choking, he looked back at the body. He could keep it from himself no longer, and his eyes filled up.

He hurled himself on the cold, headless body, clutching it up in his arms as if he could restore life to it that way. "Susan," he moaned. "Oh, Susan, how can you be dead?" He let the body back down and fell over it. His tears fell on it, mixing with the dried blood.

9

Bertie's eyelids fluttered, and he came awake suddenly. He felt a moment of near-panic; unable to get anywhere even close to Evelyn and the child, he had withdrawn to a point where he could still hear them, laughing and talking in their reedy sanctuary, and waited. But he had fallen asleep. He hoped they hadn't moved; he was very uncertain about finding them again.

He opened his eyes and started to jump up, but was stopped by the sight of a smiling man crouching on his haunches in front of him. This man looked exactly like he assumed John would have looked at about age twenty.

"Glad to see you're awake," the man said.

Bertie looked at him suspiciously. "Who are you?" he asked.

"Oh, you know who I am, my friend. After all, you delivered me from my mother's belly. You don't remember?"

"You've grown rather fast—"

"Well, things can be strange down here, no doubt about it. Sometimes they move right fast. So we'd better get going, hadn't we? I mean, we have things to do!"

"What things? Go where?"

"First of all, we have to go to the east. Now, I know you planned to kill me as soon as you got the chance. But don't rush it, I can guarantee you'll get plenty of chances. A little later, if you still want to, I'm sure you can. After all, you've got the weapons. I'm unarmed, as you can see."

This was obviously true; the young John wore only his peaked ocelot hat and a loincloth. He had no weapons of any sort; his only other possession was the long-faced mask. Bertie was curious. John could have easily escaped to parts unknown while he was sleeping, but he hadn't. It was funny; it seemed like they had been close friends a long time ago.

John stood up, extended his hand. Bertie accepted the assist, got to his feet. He picked up the bag with the chalchihuitl and the pike with Susan's head still on it. John looked at it and smiled.

"She certainly was beautiful, wasn't she?" he said mildly.

John leading, they walked together down the trail in a direction opposite that from which Bertie had come. As they crossed a long valley, he could see mountains ahead; one of the peaks was far larger than any other, and the trail they were following led to the top.

"How are your memories?" John asked. "Anything coming back?"

"I don't know exactly what you mean," Bertie said.

"Well, for example, you remember the woman we killed together? The one with all the mouths and teeth?"

Bertie glanced at him. His face seemed open, guileless. "You know, that strikes a familiar chord, but I can't place it." He struggled to remember. All he had was a hazy image of a woman, a very strange woman with sharp-toothed mouths and eyes at her elbows, knees, wrists, ankles. He also could vaguely remember killing her, but he didn't know why. It had the feel of an old, childhood dream, cloudy and unreal.

"Well, I'm sure it'll all come back. Give it time. Meanwhile, we've got to get to Yohualtecuhtli. He's waiting for us, and we don't want him any more cantankerous than he usually is."

That name was utterly unfamiliar. "Who's that?" he asked.

"Yohualtecuhtli? Lord of the Temple of the Night. He has what we need this time, not Mictlantecuhtli. If we don't get there, none of this makes a whole lot of sense."

"It doesn't make a lot of sense anyway!"

John laughed. "I of all people should know how that seems! But a little patience, my friend. We've got to get through here, get around to the center. Four stops before that. If all goes well."

In relative silence they made the long climb up the mountain. On top was an open temple, much like the one which had predated the ruined church up above, as Bertie had seen in his visions there. Near the center of it stood Frank Wasserman, looking exactly as he had when he died. Bertie wasn't even terribly surprised to see him; after all, he'd already seen Evelyn, Mayauel, and John restored to at least some kind of life down here. He was forming a theory that these people could only die permanently if they died down here. And although his curiosity made him wait, he had no intention whatsoever of allowing John to return to the surface world alive. He was sure people could die here; Susan's head on his pike was proof of that. And she had shown no further signs of life.

Frank spread his arms in what was now a characteristic gesture, billowing the blue cloak out. He still looked inhuman, still had the fangs and voluted lip. John walked up in front of him and kneeled. Bertie had a momentary flash of anxiety. He thought the Frank-monster might kill John, and he reserved that for himself. But that didn't happen; instead, a gentle rain began to fall, only on John. It was dry where Bertie was standing.

Dropping his hands slowly, Frank took something from his cloak, gave it to John as if in solemn ceremony. It was a brilliant green jewel, hanging from a leather string. John put it around his neck.

"My thanks, o Tlaloc," he said in a hushed tone.

He got up and turned back to Bertie; the rain was stopping.
"Let's go," he said. "North now. Your country, old friend.
Any idea what you got waiting there?"

Bertie had no idea what he was talking about, and said so.

"Well, it's to be a surprise for both of us, then. But, we
have no choice, so let's do it."

With a jaunty step, he started down the trail again. It turned
to the left off the mountain and led into some pine woods that
looked like they belonged in the Arctic. But John had said they
were going north; it seemed appropriate. Bertie caught up with
him, and they went on down the road together.

After a while, they saw something up ahead in the mists; a
small stone pyramid, the trail ending at the base of a steep
stairway. His foot on the first step, John looked up. It was very
dark now, and they couldn't see the top, even though it was
not terribly tall.

"I guess we go up," John said, still straining to see.

"We could walk around it," Bertie pointed out. The base
of the pyramid was free of undergrowth, and the pines were
not so closely spaced as to present any kind of an obstacle.

John shook his head. "No, the path is here. You can walk
around if you wish, but I must go over it."

Bertie shrugged; it didn't really matter to him. As John
started up the stairs, he followed.

About halfway up, they could see the flat top; there were no
temples here. A lone figure was standing up there, and as they
got closer Bertie could see that it was a woman, facing away
from them. She was dressed in a long black robe, and she had
very long blond hair, almost white.

As soon as John stood on the top, she began to turn slowly.
Bertie was still a step or two down, but he could see her clearly.
She was very tall, over six feet, and very lovely, a sculptured,
almost cold beauty. She smiled at John, but somehow it didn't
seem friendly. Her arms were extended as if in welcoming.

"My beautiful man," she said to John. "I have waited for
you. Come to me now."

Again he shook his head. "I would only pass, my lady," he
told her. "I still have a long journey."

"But it can be pleasant for you if you stay," she insisted,
standing directly in his way.

"No, I cannot."

"You will not!" she spat suddenly, her expression becoming venomous. Her hands shot out of her sleeves, and as they came, they changed from human hands into bear's paws, armed with huge, sharp claws. Her face melted, a snout extended, resolved itself finally into the face of a bear, the eyes small and glowing dull red, like two tiny fires in the darkness. She was now all black except for the eyes and the light hair. In almost a reflex movement, Bertie put his burdens down and drew his flint knife, but the thing seemed not to notice him. It came toward John in a most peculiar way, the bottom of the robe not moving at all, as if it was rolling on wheels. It made a moaning sound, like a distant wind.

John stood his ground, although it was obvious the thing was intimidating him. "I would only pass, my lady!" he cried again. But the thing kept coming. Bertie could hear a grinding sound on the stone, as if it were immensely heavy, and he suddenly realized that it couldn't descend the stairs. It was trapped on top; all John had to do was back down. He cried out to him, telling him so.

"I can't do that!" he yelled back. The thing was getting closer, seemed to be getting larger as it came. But still he wouldn't back off. Bertie cursed. For whatever obscure reason, he didn't want to see John slaughtered by this creature, but he was not about to go up there and risk his life to prevent it. He backed down a few steps, exhorting John to do the same.

But he would not. The thing towered over him now, at least twenty feet tall, its clawed hands outstretched on either side, the bear face pointing down at his. The great jaws opened; saliva dripped from long fangs. As John looked up into the glaring red eyes, Bertie began to wonder why the thing didn't strike. John hadn't moved, and it was practically surrounding him. The wind-like moaning sound rose and fell in volume.

"I have no fear of you," John said, reaching out and touching the black robe. As soon as he did, the giant bear-thing vanished, and the blond woman was standing there. She stepped aside, her legs apparently moving normally under the robe.

"Pass," she said in an expressionless voice. John walked across the top of the pyramid and started down the other side. Cautiously, Bertie came back up the stairs and crossed the top. The woman did not even seem to see him.

"Really not a hard one at all," John said lightly as Bertie caught up with him on the descending staircase. "If they're all that easy, we'll have no problems."

The trail bent off to the left again and quickly they left the dark pine woods behind. They found themselves crossing a fertile river valley, where willows and similar vegetation predominated. The light seemed to Bertie like sunshine, but it came from nowhere in particular; he could see nothing resembling a sun when he looked up. There also did not seem to be a day-night cycle of any sort down here. Rather, it went by areas; some always twilight, like the pine woods; some always day, like this valley. He had not yet seen a true night area, if there were any. This made it seem like time was suspended here, and instinctively he felt that was the case. He imagined that they could spend weeks or months here with only minutes passing on the surface. John's rapid growth from infancy to manhood seemed to validate these ideas. Perhaps there was no one-to-one correlation, but in any case time here and time on the surface were not the same.

"How much do you know about the nature of the underworld?" he asked John as they walked, as if making idle conversation.

"How do you mean?"

"Well, some people who died on the surface are alive here, it seems—"

"That's not unusual. What did you expect, anyway?"

"I had no real ideas. What about people who die down here?"

"Any ordinary mortal who dies here is dead forever, irrevocably. That I do know. No doubt about it. But it seldom happens, you know."

This made Bertie sad; he was holding out a hope that Susan might come back, too. Helping her die had torn him apart, but there had been nothing he could do about it.

"Do you know, or remember, Ihuimecatl and Toltecatl?" Bertie asked.

"Yes, I remember them."

Bertie started to proceed with his questions, but that stopped him. He hadn't realized the implications when he asked; he'd been assuming that John remembered nothing of his surface life, since this was not physically him, but that answer implied otherwise.

He decided to go for it directly. "Exactly what do you remember?" he asked.

John stopped walking and looked at him, perplexed. "Why, everything, of course. Why shouldn't I?"

"Everything? Are you sure?"

"You mean, do I remember how you tricked me and my sister into sleeping together? Of course I do. How could I forget a thing like that? It's why I'm here!"

Bertie just stared at him, not knowing quite what to say next. He considered killing him now, if for no other reason than to end the awkward moment. Up until this moment, he'd had his doubts about this man actually being John. But now that doubt was erased.

"Aren't you angry about it?" he blurted finally.

John laughed. "The day may come, my friend, when I break you into a thousand pieces for it! Or you may kill me. Who knows? But we do what we must, and that day is not today. So let's go about our business and leave surface business on the surface. We have a long way to go in a short time, as you know."

He didn't know, but he was willing to leave it at that. He resolved, however, to keep a closer eye on the man. As for his plans to kill him, he could wait for a better time. Like when John was sleeping.

They continued to walk through the fertile valley until they came to an area where the maguey grew thick. Down among the plants was a little house with a thatched roof, and the path led them right to its doorstep. Evidently this was their destination, because John stopped here. No one was around.

The cottage had no door, but there was a little porch supported by two dried maguey roots, huge gnarly things, out front. They stepped under it, looked inside. A very neat little house, quite comfortable. There was a table in the middle of the room, a bottle on it and two cups. Dressed in a brilliant scarlet robe, a woman sat looking at them, her face in shadow. Both of them stepped inside without being asked, and looked at her face.

Bertie gasped. Out of the corner of his eye he saw John's smiling countenance crumble on seeing who the woman was.

"Nikki!" Bertie cried. "How in the hell—"

"Interesting choice of words, Bert," she said, getting up. He stared; it was indeed her, Nikki Keeler, prostitute extraordinaire.

"Nikki, it's good to see you," John said finally.

"And good to see you, my love," she said in a husky voice. "I've waited a long, lonely time for this. Always I've had to send you away, or leave you. But now it's different. We can be here forever, together. I'll never go away, and you never have to." She walked toward him, the red robe swinging open, revealing that she wore nothing beneath it. She kissed him, embraced him. But he was passive. He let her do what she wanted, but he didn't respond.

"Nikki," John said. "I can't stay; not now. I've got to finish my journey, you must know that!" Tears were filling his eyes, rolling down his cheeks.

"No," she cooed. "You can stay, don't you see? Think of it; we'll be together for eternity, here in the Western Valley. We will never age, never die. Eternity! All eternity!"

"Nikki, I can't!" he yelled.

Her eyes wide, she backed off.

"More than anything, I'd like to. But I have to meet Yohualtecuhtli. I have to!"

"I can't live without you!" she cried. "Not anymore! You have to, you want to, please, please—" She started to cry, bitter tears. "I waited so long. I did what I had to do—"

"I'm so sorry," John whispered. "You can't know how sorry—"

She didn't respond. Sitting back down at the table, she put her head down and cried into her arms. Finally she lifted her face to them.

Reaching into a little bin beside the table, she pulled out one of the familiar obsidian knives, laid it in front of her. "If you can't stay, then kill me before you go," she said. "I don't want to live anymore." Crying freely, John shook his head. "Then I'll do it myself!" she screamed. Quickly John turned and left the house, moving swiftly down the path.

Bertie looked at her questioningly; he'd had considerable experience with this, but the urge he'd felt with Evelyn and Susan was lacking. Nikki gave him an amused look and put the knife back in the bin. He glanced at John's receding figure only for a second, but when he looked back at Nikki, she wasn't there. He glanced around the little house, and saw no other exits. He was baffled, but he didn't have time to investigate. Running out the door and down the path, he caught up with John, who was walking along stiffly, his face a frozen mask. He didn't say a single word as they left the beautiful little valley.

Together they climbed up a little rise that took them out of the valley. On this ridge, they could see that the trail took them into an area which was virtually filled with the maguey; the growth alongside the trail was so dense they were forced to walk single file. After a while, Bertie saw their apparent destination; the trail ran straight into an odd stone structure and ended there. Viewed from the side, it formed a right triangle; at the front, the stone was carved to a peaked arch at the top, and bowed out at the middle of the sides. The stone faces around the opening were decorated with a raised rib of stone, curving to follow the contour of the opening.

"It looks like a stone vagina," Bertie commented.

"Sure does," John said. He went inside the opening, Bertie following him closely. Again, stairs descended at a steep angle, and they followed them down, further into the earth.

After a while the stairs ended at the doorway to a great hall. The far wall was high and straight with two long, descending stairways leading from it. The side walls were vaulted in, and seemed to glow at the top with a bluish light. On the floor was a variety of furniture, much of it curiously made. On the furniture and on the floor were numerous couples, all of them copulating in one way or another. It was a veritable orgy. In the center of this was a raised stone dais, a sacrificial stone, and another elevation just behind it on which sat an elaborate throne. On the throne sat Kathryn Phillips.

Slowly they walked across the floor, up to the throne. As they went, the couples paused momentarily to glance at them, then went back to what they were doing. They reached the dais, ascended the stairs. Kathryn, looking pale and nervous, waited for them.

"You're here," she said, unnecessarily.

"Yes," John replied. Bertie stood off to the side, watching. His eyes roamed over the couples on the floor. Many of the women were quite attractive.

"So what's all this?" he asked. Kathryn and John looked at him in a peculiar way.

"They pay me homage, as I understand is proper," Kathryn said. "Not that I understand much." She stood up. "I need something from each of you. Anything, it doesn't matter what."

John tore off a tiny piece of his loincloth, and Bertie did likewise, tearing his vest instead. They handed the pieces of cloth to Kathryn, who took them, one in each hand. She then ate them both. As she did, Bertie experienced an odd tremor.

"What the hell did she just do?" he asked.

Turning, John smiled at him. "Of course, you don't remember. She's the Eater of Sins. She has the ability to take them into herself and destroy them. Think about it; if you do, you'll realize what she's done."

Bertie just looked at Kathryn. One more thing of many he didn't understand. But he couldn't take time to think about it now.

She sat back down, rather heavily. "You know what you have to do?" she asked John, putting one foot on the seat of her throne and wrapping her arm around her leg; it pushed her skirt up so that her vagina was fully exposed to them. But she seemed totally unconscious of it.

"Yes," he replied. "But it's against my nature. I can't do it."

"He can. He has." She pointed at Bertie.

"I know, but it is a violation for me. I simply cannot."

She sighed. "But he will, as soon as he feels the need. Only moments now, I can tell. And you; if you don't act first, you'll be stranded here, and he'll go on, free. Besides, I'm asking you to. You aren't forcing me!"

Bertie started to ask what they were talking about; he was irritated at being left out. But the expression on John's face silenced him. He'd not been the same since they'd left Nikki's house in the valley. Bertie thought he might believe that Nikki had killed herself when he left, and he wasn't going to bother to relieve John of this. He had at least some guilt about the girl in Ohio, all the villagers, Evelyn, and especially Susan; why shouldn't John have some? Then he realized he wasn't feeling any of that guilt anymore; it had been lifted from him when Kathryn ate the little piece of his vest. But apparently it had not had quite the same effect on John. Or had it? For a moment, he'd seemed happy again. Now he looked totally miserable, his face twisted. But Bertie was only seeing him peripherally. There was something else; he was feeling an urge again, looking at Kathryn. The same urges he'd felt before, just before he'd helped Evelyn and Susan end their lives.

She glanced at him, then back to John. "You have to decide!" she cried, sounding almost desperate. "Quickly, or it'll be too late!"

"All right, all right!" he screamed suddenly. Bertie actually jumped. Kathryn got to her feet, stripped off her vest and skirt, and stretched herself out on the sacrificial stone. From somewhere she produced one of the obsidian knives and handed it to John. Bertie felt a pang of jealousy. He was more experienced, this was his area, his right! But she'd snubbed him.

"Don't you have to purify yourself?" he snarled at her.

She turned her head and looked at him. "No," she said. Then she looked back at John. "Quickly. Please, John. Hurry!"

John lifted the knife, holding it stiffly, awkwardly. Kathryn started to cry, her eyes closed tightly. Bertie was in a near frenzied state; he felt he had to do something. His eyes fell on a wooden sword, obsidian-edged, that leaned against her throne. He darted over, picked it up, and turned back to where John hesitated over Kathryn, his pose frozen.

10

With a conscious effort, Danny tore himself away from mourning over Susan's death. There was still Kathryn to think of, Kathryn who was hopefully still alive somewhere down here. He wanted to get to her, make sure she stayed that way. And, it was possible that David or John still lived. It made him feel horrible, leaving Susan's body like this, but there was nothing he could do for her. He held her cold hand for a moment, then left the room.

In the hallway outside, he stopped, used his heightened vision, and saw the wall of fog. He was about to make his snap turn when his concentration was broken by a figure rounding the corner in the hallway in front of him. In heightened vision, the figure looked incredible; a dead-gray, froglike body, hands like jaguar paws, and a face sort of like a shrimp. Shifting to his normal vision, he saw Ihuimecatl walking toward him.

"Well, well," she said. "Mr. Hudson. I must admit I'm surprised at your resourcefulness. I would have thought you dead by now."

Danny glared at her. "Where are my friends?" he demanded. "I'd bet money you've got some of them!"

"You'd lose your money. The only ones I've seen are the ones you call David and Susan, and they're both quite dead, I'm afraid."

Danny experienced another wave of grief. He had no feeling the creature was lying to him. David, sick as he was, had little chance separated from the rest.

"You killed him?" he snarled.

"Oh, no. He died on his own. Nice of him, I must say. Very cooperative."

Danny decided there was no use in trying to talk to the creature any further. It enraged him; he wanted to kill it, but he felt going after it with his knife was probably suicidal. He stood aside in the hallway to let it pass.

"Go on," he said. "Wherever you're going."

She smiled at him, looking for a moment like a coy young girl. "Oh, I'm not in a hurry to get anywhere. In fact, chances are I can't get back out of here alive. It isn't my place. Does that make you happy?"

"As a matter of fact, I'd enjoy seeing you dead!"

"Ah! We have something in common, then. I'd enjoy seeing you dead, too. And since Tezcatlipoca isn't here to tell me not to, I think I'll just do that. See you dead!"

Danny backed off a step or two, realizing he wouldn't have the time to concentrate on the wall of fog and get out of here. He was in a tight situation. Ihuimecatl started to advance on him, slowly.

"Now," she said. "Let's make this fun!" She grinned

broadly. "What can I get from your little head there?" She looked into his eyes. "Oh, that's a good one! The vampire. You got any crosses, any garlic? Well, too damn bad. But they wouldn't work on me anyhow!" She opened her mouth, and her canine teeth enlarged until she matched perfectly his mental image of a vampire.

He forced a grin. "You look ridiculous," he told her.

She laughed. "Hey, that's not bad! I like that. You're about to die, and you can say that! Better than I expected! I sort of thought you'd grovel and beg."

He gave her a scornful look, hoping the bravado would somehow dissuade her. He didn't feel like he could effectively fight. "Me, beg you? Good joke. But no chance, bitch!"

She stopped, actually hesitated. It's working, he thought; keep it up, keep it up. There was a look of doubt on her face, which passed after a moment. She started to come for him again. Backing off another step, trying to think of something else, he felt the quartz crystal in his pocket and pulled it out. He had a vague idea of trying to bluff her with it.

Now she really looked concerned, and hesitated again. He raised the crystal like it was a baseball, as if he were going to throw it at her. A look of real fear crossed her face, and she took a step back, the vampire teeth disappearing. Trying to press his advantage, he advanced on her, and she gave ground. Another step, and she turned as if to run. He made a motion as if he were hurling the crystal at her, although he didn't let go of it. At the same time, he felt an odd surge from his stomach, as if a liquid flow was traveling from there up his arm and into the crystal.

Turning halfway away from him, she grabbed at her side, an expression of agony on her face. Unbelievably, he saw blood gushing from between her fingers, staining her black cloak red. It was as if he'd shot her. She raised a hand as if to ward him off, staggered sideways down the hall.

He followed her, holding the crystal against his stomach. Then he raised it as if to hurl it again.

"No, please," she said in a choked voice. She turned to face him, made a supplicating gesture. "Please don't. Not down here. On the surface, I'll let you, I won't fight, I'll—"

"Murdering monster!" he cried, and made the hurling motion again. Her body jerked, and she stared down at her chest;

a red stain appeared in the center of it, spreading rapidly. She dropped to her knees, looked up at him briefly, then pitched forward on her face without another sound. A red pool spread beneath her, and her body within the cloak changed shape. With normal vision, he was seeing the froglike feet, the jaguar paw hands, the shrimp face. He smiled, put the crystal back in his pocket, and stepped over the body. A short distance down the hall, he stopped again, snapped to face the wall of fog, concentrated on Kathryn, and stepped through.

He found himself in another narrow hallway. Immediately ahead was an open doorway and a long, descending stairway. On the floor below him, he saw a number of couples engaged in various carnal acts. But immediately his attention was drawn to a frozen scene in the center of the room.

There was a throne, and a sacrificial stone. On the stone, he saw Kathryn stretched out, her eyes closed. John was holding one of the accursed obsidian knives, poised over her chest; and Bertie was picking up a sword from alongside the throne.

"Kathryn!" he screamed. "Get up, run!" She looked very tiny, almost doll-like, lying there. Her head snapped around as she heard his voice. He started down the stairs, as fast as he could.

"Danny!" she cried. "Oh, Danny, go back! It has to be! Please don't watch!"

"Nooo!" he shrieked. But he knew he wasn't going to get there in time.

John's paralysis broke, and he drove the obsidian knife into her left breast.

She screamed, her head lifting off the stone and her body going utterly rigid. But she made no effort to get up, no effort to stop him.

"Oh, please no," Danny said in muted tones. None of them could hear him. John was twisting and sawing with the knife, her blood was spraying out, her fingers clutching desperately at the air. He pulled the blade free, watched her blood pump out for an instant. Then he began working his hand into her chest, and her screams changed to moans.

Bertie stepped up beside the stone, lifted the sword, and struck downward, aiming at her neck. The force of his blow was such that the sword shattered after it passed through, sending pieces of wood and obsidian flying across the room. Her head rolled back off the stone and onto the raised dais. As John ripped her heart out, the room was echoing with the cries of the celebrants on the floor below, many of whom were obviously reaching their orgasms at that precise moment.

Danny took another step down; his knees were weak, and his emotions in turmoil; overwhelming grief and violent rage were twisted together. He saw Bertie run to get a jar or something out of a leather pack he had, hold it under the stream of blood from her open neck. For a moment, the blood looked like a bright red serpent, crawling from Kathryn's neck into the bottle. Finally it overflowed; Bertie capped it, put it back. He then picked up an object Danny hadn't seen before; a long pike with a human head on it. Susan's head. After pushing it down until the point broke through, Bertie added Kathryn's above it.

Another step, and another. Danny's fury mounted steadily as he watched John eat Kathryn's heart. If it was John; he looked very different, his eyes glowing red, his face very flushed. He had blood in his hair, turning it red, and in his beard. His whole head and upper body looked cast in red.

Danny was close enough; he took out the crystal, balanced it in his hand. "Payment time," he said. His rage had overtaken him, possessed him. He could think of nothing else as he aimed the crystal at Bertie's back, not like he'd done with Ihuimecatl, but pointing it straight at him like it was a flashlight.

"No!" a voice screamed. "Don't do it, you don't know what you're doing!"

He looked down and saw Maria standing on the stair below him, her eyes wild. She looked different, but he knew it was her; she looked now, under his normal vision, like she'd looked in heightened vision before. She was wearing a brilliant red cloak and sandals.

"This is not your affair," he told her, irritated at the distraction. He turned his attention back to Bertie and John, who seemed to be leaving together. As they headed for another stair on the same wall, which led to a different door, he aimed the crystal, began to concentrate.

Just as he reached a peak Maria let out an enormous howl, incredibly loud. He jumped, and his aim went awry. A full bolt of lightning burst from the crystal, striking the wall above

John and Bertie with a deafening thunderclap. A shower of stones and mortar exploded from the wall, raining down on the floor below, but missing the two men. They looked back at Danny with surprise and consternation and began to run, taking the steps two at a time. As he ran, Bertie dropped the pike on which the women's heads were impaled. For a moment he hesitated, as if he would go back. But he seemed to think better of it and ran on up the steps. Danny took aim again, but Maria began a peculiar, high-pitched, sustained cry that made it difficult for him to concentrate. He looked down at her.

"You're helping them," he said. The coldness of his voice surprised even him. He had no thoughts left, just the rage, the intent to destroy. "That means you're one of them." He swung the crystal down, aimed it at her.

Her expression changed from one of concern and concentration to one of terror. Lightning exploded again from the crystal, and she jumped into the air, amazingly high. The stairs exploded where she'd been standing. He looked up, saw her clinging sideways to the wall with her hands and the sides of her feet, like a giant spider. She ran up the wall, moving so fast he couldn't track her. He led her like he was aiming a gun, released another bolt, but she stopped and turned suddenly.

"Danny, please stop!" she panted. "I don't want to die down here, but you can't kill those two! Not at any cost!"

"I don't care about the cost!" he snapped. "I want to see those motherfuckers dead!"

"Danny, listen—" she started. He ignored her, took aim at Bertie again. He and John were getting close to the exit, and Danny meant to be sure they didn't escape. Marie hurled herself into the air, flying at Danny like a projectile. He didn't get the bolt off before she crashed into him and wrapped her arms around him, sending them both falling, tumbling through the air, off the steps. The floor was at least a hundred feet below.

11

As they ran through the door at the top of the high, dangerous stairs, Bertie was wondering where in the hell Danny Hudson had gotten that crystal. Shooting lightning bolts! Unreal. He wished he'd come across it first. He had no idea how Danny had known its powers, and could only assume somebody had told him. But regardless of that, Hudson was a dangerous man now. If he got half a chance, he'd kill him; he kept coming up with too many surprises. First the gun, then showing up here exactly at a crucial moment, finally the crystal. Bertie felt he should have killed him with Evelyn, back at the church; then he corrected himself. That would not necessarily have prevented him from showing up down here. He should be killed down here, Bertie thought, wishing he hadn't sent Ihuimecatl away so soon.

They slowed their flight and for the first time Bertie realized they were in a hall so low and narrow it might better be called a tunnel. There were no stairs, but the floor was tipped down like a wheelchair ramp, and they were headed back down. It was getting darker and darker as they went, the meager light supplied by a few torches along the wall. He glanced at John; there was blood all over him, and in this light he looked insane. Maybe in any light. Freed of the pressure of Danny's unexpected attack, Bertie was able to wonder why he had participated in Kathryn's death; it seemed so unlike him.

"John, why did you do that?" he asked directly. "Back there with Kathryn, I mean? I thought you were against that."

John turned to look at him, and Bertie felt the hairs on his neck stir a little. The man looked absolutely mad, his eyes literally smouldered. "You should know!" he said. "You, of all people! You've had a lot of experience with that, haven't you? Makes you strong, makes you feel good? You made it that way, damn you, and it didn't have to be!''

A surge of emotion came up in Bertie; he had no idea where it came from. He began to speak, listening to his own words as he did. He had no idea what he was going to say before he said it. ''You're wrong!'' he said vehemently. ''I didn't make it that way, that's just the way it is! You always try to get around it, and you always fail, don't you? Have you forgotten that it was you yourself who taught all of us the proper way to do it? So don't tell me it's such a fucking tragedy, because you know better!''

''It is a tragedy! It is! Every time!'' John screeched. ''On and on, over and over, blood, death, pain! Maybe I know what you say is true. Maybe I do, just now. But it is a tragedy. And maybe I can eliminate the necessity for it, at least for a while!''

''More power to ya,'' Bertie said lightly.

John glared at him. ''If Yohualtecuhtli wasn't waiting—''

''You'd what, old buddy?'' Bertie laughed at him. ''More blood, pain, and death?''

''Yours wouldn't be a tragedy,'' he muttered as he turned and continued down the tunnel, down into the darkness. Bertie laughed at him again. How the mighty do fall, he told himself. For some reason, John had been forced to kill Kathryn, and now he was down on the same level as everyone else.

For what seemed to be an endless time, they walked down the sloping tunnel. Finally, up ahead, was a doorway; it looked like it led outside. They stepped through it, and Bertie realized they were now in a true night world. The diffuse light, from an unknown point, had a character like moonlight. Ahead of them were two more pyramids, shaped like the ones up on the surface. These positively glowed, the left one black and the other intensely red. Bertie could see marvelously lifelike sculptures of huge serpents on top of them, each one the same color as the pyramid it rested upon. Then the one on the left moved its head and flickered a huge forked tongue. Bertie hesitated, but John was walking right toward them; he followed.

Directly ahead, between the pyramids, was an elaborate throne with a canopy over it. Above and behind it was an elevated platform accessible by stairs. A man sat on the throne, a most imposing figure, dressed in a dark blue cloak. He wore a very large, fancy headdress, and his face was jet black. His eyes glowed red, like John's did right now. Around the throne were a number of men and women, most of them sitting or kneeling. Many were armed. Bertie fingered the flint knife nervously, but followed as John marched up to the throne.

There was a rug or mat in front of the throne that resembled the skin of a black eagle; John knelt on it, bowed to the black figure. "I greet you and pay you homage, O Yohualtecuhtli, Lord of the Temple of the Night," he said. "And respects to the souls of the warriors, those who have died the death of flowers, and those women who have died that a warrior may enter the world."

Bertie remained standing, looking at John with some surprise. He no longer looked insane; once again he was the self-assured traveler he'd been in the pine woods. It was strange, Bertie thought. The pine woods seemed like years ago, a thousand miles away.

Yohualtecuhtli stood up. "You are welcome here. You have passed many trials to come to this place. I offer you what is yours. Take the mexquimilli with my blessings." He gestured, and one of the warriors walked around behind the throne, ascended the stairs to the platform. He reached for a bundle that lay there; as soon as he touched it, fire and sparks flared from the end of it. But he picked it up, brought it back to Yohualtecuhtli, who took it, held it reverently for a moment, then offered it to John. John dipped his head low and extended his hands. He didn't look up until the bundle was in his hands and Yohualtecuhtli had released it.

"I thank you, O Yohualtecuhtli, for my father, my heritage. But I crave yet another gift!"

The black man looked at him, his eyes narrow. "All else here is mine, and mine alone. What of mine would you have?"

"I would have the bones, my lord. The bones you hold for Mictlantecuhtli!" John said in a strong voice. He pointed to two bones lying beside the throne, one on either side. They appeared to be human ribs.

"No!" Yohualtecuhtli cried. "You may not take them!"

"I cannot, will not, leave without them," John said mildly.

"I could have the souls of my warriors destroy you where you stand!"

"Nevertheless."

"I could have these women tear you apart, scatter your pieces to the four winds!"

"Nevertheless."

"I could cause the red serpent to fill your body with poison, cause you to die in agony, agony you can't imagine!"

"Nevertheless."

"I could cause the black serpent to crush you, kill you slowly, take the breath of your life!"

"Nevertheless."

Yohualtecuhtli sat back down heavily. "A trial, then," he said, his eyes mere slits. "Pass, and they are yours. Fail, and you die in agony, and for all time!"

"Agreed, my lord."

Yohualtecuhtli leaned back on his throne and grinned broadly. He seemed to think he had the better of the situation, and Bertie could not help but believe he had. Bertie trembled; he wondered what would happen to him if John failed.

The black man reached down behind the throne and picked up a seashell; a queen conch. He tossed it to John.

"Sound it, make it sound," he said, still grinning. "Sound it, and the trial is yours."

Now John smiled, and Bertie could well understand why. He was, after all, a skilled trumpet player; it would be nothing for him to make a sound on a seashell! John brought it up to his lips, still smiling. Then his expression changed. The end was not cut off; the shell had its original sharp spire, just as the snail had formed it. There was no way to blow it.

John glanced over at Bertie, a worried look on his face. He rolled the shell over in his hands; there was no opening at all. It seemed hopeless. Yohualtecuhtli laughed out loud.

John was interrupted in his examination of the shell by an insect of some sort buzzing around his head. He swatted at it, but it was persistent. Finally he looked up, seemingly interested. The insect flew off a short distance, landed on a small bush, and John approached it, slowly and carefully. Wondering what he was doing, Bertie looked at it, saw that it was a large bee or wasp of some kind. He watched John hold the shell up to one side of it, then quickly knock it in with a swat of his other hand. Rolling the shell around, he caused the bee to roll deeper into the spiral twists of the shell. Continuing to roll it slowly, he walked back over and knelt on the eagle mat again, holding up the shell. The buzzing of the bee inside was focused by the flare of the aperture, and sounded quite loud.

"The shell sounds, my lord Yohualtecuhtli," he said.

The black man scowled at him. "It is not so, you do not blow it!"

"But you did not say blow it, my lord. You said sound it, make it sound. And as you can hear, it sounds!"

Yohualtecuhtli seemed to sink down in his seat somewhat. His scowl deepened. "Yes," he said finally. "You have won the trial. I give you the bones, and ten steps!"

"You are honorable, my lord," John said. He cupped his hand, spoke to Bertie. "Take ten long steps, then run like hell!" He reached down, picked up the bones, tied them into his loincloth. Then he turned, obviously ready to take the ten steps.

"There is one more matter," Yohualtecuhtli said. His tone sounded ominous. Lifting his hand, he showed them a spherical object apparently made of solid gold. He hurled it, seemingly weakly, but it hit John in the side of the head as he was turning, and he went down. Bertie watched the ball roll away, then of its own volition fly back to Yohualtecuhtli's hand.

"He hasn't taken a single step!" Bertie protested. He started to go to the prone figure, but saw that John was already stirring, trying to get up. Then he did; he rose to his knees, then stood straight. And at the same time, he was still lying on the ground, face down. The one standing looked at the other coolly, stepped away from him. Then the second one stirred, slowly climbed to his feet. Bertie blinked. Two of them? The second to get up had, once again, the wild red eyes John had immediately after Kathryn's death. The first looked to be the self-assured one; his eyes were very dark. The dark John, Bertie noticed, had the bones.

"Ten steps!" Yohualtecuhtli said, gesturing to the feather-crested warriors, who took bows off their shoulders and notched arrows to the strings. All three of them, Bertie and the two Johns, took nine long steps, then one more, and broke into a headlong dash for the entrance to a low, long building on the left of the throne and pyramids. The arrows flew; Bertie could hear them whistling around him as he ran. One thudded into the pack that contained the chalchihuitl. He gritted his teeth in anticipation of the one that would hit him in the back, but it never came. They made the doorway safely. All three ran down the hall it took them into, and after a while, they slowed down. The red John had an arrow through his ocelot hat, which he pulled out and discarded; and Bertie had one in his pack. The jar was not damaged, and he discarded this arrow as well. None of them were hurt at all.

This hallway was much larger than the previous one, and it led to another stairway, still going down. It seemed to go on forever, and it seemed to take them hours to get to the bottom. It was hot here, all of them were sweating, and there was very little light. They passed through a little anteroom at the base of the stairs and emerged into a dark, smoky, desert-like environment. Only cacti could be seen growing, and most of them were dead. A figure, dimly seen in the semidarkness, waited for them.

As they approached him, Bertie recognized him as the nameless man who wore David's skin, the one Tonatiuh had referred to as Xipe Totec. Eyes like furnaces looked out from the mask, and he held two huge obsidian knives, three times the size of the others Bertie had seen.

Taking a step toward the red John, he quickly seized his hair, pulling him over to a bent posture. He tossed one of the big knives to Bertie, who caught it gracefully by the handle.

"Make him your prisoner. Quickly now!" Xipe said. The voice sounded much like David's, but gravelly and incredibly cold, almost inhuman. The dark John looked at Bertie as if challenging him to do it. Good as anytime, Bertie thought. He grabbed the dark John's hair, pulled him over. Xipe gestured at his prisoner with his knife, as if he were about to stab him, but did not follow through. Following Xipe's lead, Bertie pulled the dark John along the path, which seemed to be descending into a valley. Actually, it was more like a pit; the way was quite steep. Seemingly from nowhere, a group of twelve women appeared, six on each side of them. They were all dressed as Kathryn had been, and they all resembled her somewhat. They walked along chanting, but Bertie could not understand the words.

"Who are they?" he asked.

"The cihuateteo. They belong to Tlazolteotl. Now shut up!" Xipe snarled at him. His tone and demeanor brooked no argument.

The path took them deeper and deeper into the pitlike valley and again it became very dark. The land here was sandy, like a desert, and only a few stones and dead plants dotted the dim landscape around them. It was quite hot already, and as they proceeded it got hotter. Wisps of steam or smoke could be seen rising from the sands at intervals. Far away on the right was a dull red, fiery glow, like lava from a volcanic fissure. On the left was a stark cliff face, composed entirely of obsidian. The glow and the solemn procession were both reflected in it, increasing the surreal effect of the place.

Bertie felt a heaviness he could not identify as they went down the slope. It seemed to him there was no going back from here; he felt a commitment to the darkness, the implied but restrained violence of this place. Several times he hesitated as if he would go back, give it up here; but the threatening attitude of Xipe Totec stopped him. This man was different; everyone else he'd met down here he'd felt at least equal to. But Xipe frightened him. There was an intensity about him than was unparalleled by any experience Bertie had ever had. He was glad that Xipe seemed to be an ally of his, not an enemy. And through it all, the women Xipe had called the cihuateteo walked calmly, chanting their unintelligible song, in a minor mode most appropriate to the surroundings.

Or was it unintelligible? He listened carefully for a while, and finally it began to make sense to him:

"He comes down, he descends, with precious water he descends.

"A jeweled bracelet, he descends.

"From the sorcerer's house,

"The dreamer comes down.

"From the quetzal land, from the land of plenty,

"The dreamer comes down.

"Shall he withhold thy due?

"In Mictlampa,

"Shall thy due be withheld?

"Maguey thorns, maguey thorns,

"Rest in his hands,

"He brings them down, he brings them down.

"To the well at the dark of creation,

"He brings them down,

"To the well of the red and black,

"He comes down, he descends, with precious water he descends."

Listening to the chant, Bertie was a little surprised to glance ahead and see the apparent end of this part of the journey. The path led into an imposing stone house, almost a cube, built of only a few massive blocks. Inside, he could see a reddish, flickering light. The cihuateteo lined up in two columns by the doorway as he and Xipe led their prisoners inside.

Within the block-like building, the only light was from a small fire in a brazier on the far side of the room. The floor sloped perilously down to a large hole, perhaps eight feet across in the center. Inside the hole was such a total blackness it seemed to draw the light into itself; indeed, Bertie could almost see the weak rays of light from the brazier flowing into the hole. It was oddly attractive to him. He felt an urge to hurl himself into it, to merge with this total, absolute blackness. It was as if the blackness in the hole was somehow alive, the hungry mouth of some horrifying creature that had to be fed. His emotions switched back and forth on him, not letting his mind settle; attractive/terrifying, soothing/repulsive.

At the edge of the hole, across from them, sat Frank and Evelyn. Both were dressed differently now; they wore long robes of red and black, and very elaborate headdresses. They seemed to be contemplating the hole, and did not immediately look up at Bertie, Xipe, and the two Johns as they entered. As they carefully made their way down toward the hole, Evelyn finally looked at them. She stood up and spread her arms.

"They have arrived at the chalchihuitl," she said reverently. The chalchihuitl? Bertie wondered. It seemed she was referring to the well, the hole. He'd thought the bottle he had so dutifully carried all the way down here was the chalchihuitl.

"And so it is," she said, not looking at him directly. "It is a double, a fragment, of the real one here. It will become one with it. Do you know what you must do?" Now she looked directly at him. He started to shake his head, but realized he did know. Gingerly he walked forward to the edge of the hole, took the chalchihuitl from his pack, and poured the contents into the greater chalchihuitl in the floor. As the red blood from the three women, miraculously not clotted, flowed from the bottle, the blackness in the hole seemed to move around, like it was excited, like it was living. It began to change color. A moment later it was as intensely red as it had originally been black. It glowed and squirmed, casting a circle of scarlet on the ceiling above. All their faces turned bright red in the light of the well.

Without speaking, Frank and Evelyn instructed Bertie and Xipe to seat their prisoners on opposite sides of the great chalchihuitl. They did so, and the two robed figures approached the two Johns, Frank going to the red John. They carried bone punches, like those that Evelyn and Susan had used in their final purifications, but far larger, perhaps eighteen inches long and a half inch thick. Pushing the legs of the two Johns down flat, they punctured each leg twice with these instruments. Each time they pushed a spike in, the red John grimaced and gave voice to a little cry, the dark John was impassive. But neither moved nor struggled. As the spikes came out, they were followed by arcing fountains of bright red blood, spraying high into the air; they had evidently been arterial punctures. As the streams fell, they formed an eight-sided pattern of pools of blood, evenly spaced on the floor around the glowing hole. Moments later, as the pools increased in size, they all began flowing into the hole, which glowed ever brighter and somehow became even redder.

While Evelyn stayed with the Johns, Frank got up and moved to a position high up on the sloping floor near the wall, midway between the Johns. Extending his arms, he pushed his hands out of his voluminous sleeves; to Bertie's surprise, they just kept coming until they were over the heads of the Johns, who were at least twelve feet away. He held his hands palms up, then tipped them at a forty-five degree angle; and water began to pour onto the heads of the Johns, a beautifully clear stream. Bouncing off the men's heads, it formed a similar pattern of eight pools, which looked black in the red light from the well. Immediately the water began running into the hole, and a great sunburst of eight black and eight red rays was formed around it. Inside the hole, the nexus of these rays was a maelstrom of red and black eddies, surging, foaming. Bertie could hardly stand to look at it, it was so intense, but he was forced to. It seemed to him that the well contained many things, or more properly many potentials; the black water and the red blood, opposite essentials in some way, unified in it, blended, two diametric opposites made into one whole thing, one perfectly harmonious structure. The glow was increasing in its brilliance, flooding the room with light; now the red and black eddies were no longer visible. As they came together, an incandescent white light formed in the center, bright as the sun. It coalesced into a ball, and slowly, majestically, rose out of the well. Slowly rotating, it hung there in midair, then began to rapidly darken, pulling its own light in on itself. It wasn't as if it were losing its energy; it was folding up, drawing in. This process continued until the white light was gone, and a small object which was every color and no color, prismatic, hung there in space. It was about as big as a baseball, spherical in shape.

Bertie looked around; he saw that the water had stopped flowing from Frank's hands, that he was withdrawing them, shrinking his forearms down to normal size. The blood had also stopped flowing from the legs of the two Johns, and the sunburst was only a trace of red and black streaks on the gray stone floor. The hole itself was back to the red color, and that was fading. Soon the inky blackness returned, and again the only light in the room was from the brazier, reflected a little in the prismatic sphere that still rotated, like a tiny, beautiful planet, in the air over the hole.

Delicately, Evelyn balanced herself on the edge of the hole and reached up for the ball. It moved toward her hand a little, and she caught it lightly, delicately. The two Johns, moving like mirror images of each other, got to their feet and started toward the brazier; behind it was an exit Bertie would have sworn was not there ten minutes ago. They went out, followed by Frank and Evelyn. She motioned for Bertie to follow them, while Xipe Totec turned on his heel and went out the way he'd come, leading the cihuateteo back up the path out of the pit. Carefully skirting the black hole, Bertie followed the other four out of the block building.

Behind the building was yet another low pyramid; atop it, yet another of the curving sacrificial stones. The dark John almost bounded up the stairs. From the top, he motioned to Bertie, urged him to hurry. Bertie ran past the red John, who just had his foot on the first step, and swiftly mounted the steps, to stand alongside his former prisoner. Slowly, painfully the red John mounted the steps. Frank and Evelyn waited at the bottom. The red John acted as if his legs had been damaged by the bloodletting, and acted as if he couldn't walk well. Twice he looked back, and twice Evelyn pointed insistently to the top. Finally he got there, stood on the other side of the stone. His wild eyes were now hopeless, resigned. He stripped away his clothes, and, like a sleepwalker, stretched himself out on the stone. The dark John gently took the huge sacrificial knife from Bertie's hand; Bertie hardly realized it was gone.

So familiar now, almost commonplace. The dark John held the knife above him, waited for a moment. He seemed to tremble a little, then plunged it down, striking the red John in his left breast, sinking it in until the point scraped on the stone beneath, a sound like a fingernail on a blackboard. The red John's body spasmed, but he made no sound; he just looked at the huge blade, fully four inches wide, piercing his chest. The dark John twisted it around almost viciously, but it was his face, not the other's, that showed the pain. A huge hole had been opened in the red John's chest, and apparently the heart itself had been pierced; another fountain of blood, thick as his wrist, spouted upward. On impulse, Bertie knelt beside the stone and caught the descending stream in his open mouth, swallowing frantically.

The dark John cast the knife aside and reached in, grasping the heart and ripping it out. He held it, dripping blood and squirming, over his head for a moment. Bertie saw that the prismatic sphere was rotating in the air again, right in front of them. The dark John offered the heart to it. A window of white light opened, cast a pencil-thin beam on the heart. The heart, still squirming, grew transparent and finally vanished; and as it did, the beam of light changed from white to red. Then the window closed, and the ball rotated placidly. Bertie looked around for Evelyn and Frank, but they were gone, nowhere to be seen. At the foot of the pyramid, a gaunt old man dressed in a long black robe, and an equally gaunt woman similarly dressed, stood as if waiting for something.

Bertie looked at the red John, still lying on the stone, and was astounded to see that the man wasn't even dead yet! He looked from one of them to the other, his gaze blank, showing no evidence of pain. But the dark John's face was contorted; he was chewing his lip, choking back cries of agony. Finally the rise and fall of the red John's mutilated chest slowed and stopped. His eyes remained open, staring at Bertie; the pupils widened to fill the irises. The red, smouldering look faded, and simultaneously the dark John's face relaxed. Taking the jewel Frank had given him from around his neck, the dark John slipped it into the dead man's mouth; then he removed the bones he had gotten from Yohualtecuhtli from his waistband and laid them on the stone, alongside the corpse. With great ceremony, he dipped his hand into the wound in the dead man's chest and sprinkled blood on the bones. Bertie could have sworn the bones wriggled a little as the droplets of blood fell on them. The living John smiled over at Bertie.

"The new man and woman," he said softly. "From my blood, taken from the body of my unintentional self. Assuming, of course, that I can hang on to them this time!"

"This time?" Bertie echoed, without comprehension.

"Yes. Well, of course, you don't remember. It isn't too surprising, you were already dead when I accidently blew them away while I was starting the sun. But then you were around when we decided that I had to go back—Xolotl and I—and I know you knew about Mictlantecuhtli breaking his word, and about the quail, and how I got killed down here, and—"

Bertie just stared at him across the body of the red John. "What in the fuck are you babbling about?" he demanded. To him, John's words made no sense whatsoever.

"Other days and other times, my friend," he replied with a laugh. "Right now, they're waiting for us." He turned, and Bertie followed his gaze, down to the figures waiting at the base of the pyramid. They looked back at each other, then unceremoniously hurled the body of the red John over the side. Arms and legs flailing about, it tumbled down the stairs and landed in an undignified heap between the two unmoving black figures. For several minutes, no one moved; the two black-robed figures gazed at the body, the living John and Bertie at them. Then, unbelievably, the body of the red John began to stir. He stretched out and turned his face back up to them. He had no eyes, just vacant holes where they should have been. Getting to his feet, the gaping hole in his chest more than obvious, he knelt facing the woman.

"Mictlancihuatl, I greet you. I am yours," he said. His voice sounded like it was coming out of a tunnel. He then turned to the old man: "Mictlantecuhtli, I greet you." Rising to his feet, he slowly walked away from them, flanked by the robed figures.

As Bertie stood and watched the trio go, John reached out, plucked the prismatic ball from the air, tucked it into a leather pouch Bertie had not seen before, and gathered up the bones and the massive obsidian knife. Bertie tensed; he didn't like the the idea of John being armed at all.

John laughed out loud. "No, eh?" he said. "Afraid I'd cut your throat when you're not looking? Well, my friend, let me put you at ease. It really isn't important, not in the least. Not now." He raised the knife almost threateningly; Bertie took a step backward, putting his hand on his own curved flint knife. John laughed again, and smashed the blade down on the stone. It shattered into a rain of black crystals, and he dropped the useless handle.

"Feel better now?" he asked. "You know, you're just too excitable. There is a time and a place for everything, and here and now is not the time and place for us to mix it up. We have to go up that path, up out of here. There is a sick little dog waiting for us up there."

"A dog?"

"A dog. Kind of a special dog." He laughed again. "After we find that dog, we'll be going to the Caves of Cincalco, and you may find things more interesting there. Just bear with me for a little while longer."

"You got it, John. You lead the way. I'm having a fascinating time, no doubt about it. Just try not to get me killed if you do yourself in along the way, all right?"

"Oh, I've no intention of it. None. You have your own appointment, you just don't know it yet."

Bertie decided he didn't like the sound of that. Every time someone around here had an appointment, it was with the stone and the obsidian knife. And everybody went peacefully; not a single person had to be held down. He didn't have the slightest intention of doing that, even if he felt it was necessary to some invisible greater goal, as the others had apparently believed. For Bertie, there simply was not, could not be, any greater goal than the well-being of Bertie, and that goal could not be served by lying on the stone and allowing someone to rip his heart out. No; he'd fight it, whoever or whatever. Even the

threatening Xipe Totec didn't instill that kind of fear in him.
He was, after all, the warrior, the warrior king of Tlillan Tlapallan, and he'd make that mean something, even in this crazy,
unreal world down here. He might die, but he'd sure take a lot
of his assailants with him. It was not for nothing that he was
also called Yaotl, the enemy, the—

He stopped himself. Yaotl? Where had he heard that name?
He could not remember. In fact, as he thought about it, he was
quite sure that no one in Tlillan Tlapallan, or here in the underworld, had ever referred to him by that name. It bothered
him; he was riding a wave of confidence and this thought just
came up and hit him, reminded him of how lunatic this whole
thing was. Dead people coming back to life, weird wells, magical happenings; he was taking them all as everyday events. He
experienced just an instant of sheer, unbridled terror, total
panic. He was in an impossible, unbelievable place, with no
way out! He began to sweat, but he put his hand on the flint
knife and his other side returned; all was again well, at least
for now. He hoped the other side would stay, Yaotl or whoever.
This was no place for Herbert North, computer programmer.

12

Danny felt Maria's arms around him as they spun helplessly
into space. He didn't have time to feel fear; it was too sudden.
There was nothing he could do except grab at her robe. Then,
with a jerk, her fall stopped suddenly. He slid out of her grasp,
and she grabbed for him wildly, caught his hand in hers. He
too stopped falling, looked up.

It was an unreal, impossible sight; the ball and toes of one
of her feet were touching the underside of the stair, sticking
there as if glued to it. Her robe hung open; he could see she
wore nothing beneath it. Her face was a study in strain as she

held his hand desperately, her arm stretched out as if it would tear away from her with his weight.

"Danny." She gritted. "You can do this! Concentrate, hurry! The fibers at your belly, grab the stair with them!"

He did as she said, saw himself as a luminous egg with weaving fibers extending from his navel. He tried to move them voluntarily; for a moment he couldn't. Then it seemed to come to him, and he tangled them around the stone of the stairway. Taking his weight on them, he relieved the stress on Maria's arm. It turned out to be surprisingly easy for him to regain the stair and sit down on it. For a moment, Maria just hung there like a bat; he could now see her fibers wrapped around her foot, holding it in place. Then she moved them, doubled her body up, and came up to sit beside him.

"You helped that bastard Bertie get away. Bitch," he said in a lifeless voice.

"Danny, I couldn't let you kill him. I couldn't. There are larger issues here, things you can't understand—"

He exploded into action. In a fraction of a second he was on her, driving her back into the stair. They slid down two or three steps, bumping. His hands closed over her throat, and he started to squeeze.

"I will not be told that shit again!" he screamed into her face. "I will not hear it! Will not! Not! Not!" He released one hand from her throat and slapped her violently across the face. "You'll tell me, you'll make me understand, or I'll kill you, bitch, bitch, monster! Tell me, Goddamn it! Tell me! Everyone I cared about is fucking dead! You are fucking well right I don't understand! You—you—" He faded off, his hand released her throat. She coughed once, staring at him, her eyes wide. The grief for Kathryn was hitting him, and he was blinded by his tears. He turned his face to the stone wall and pounded on it. "Why her too? Why her? She never hurt anybody. Why?" he sobbed.

Very tentatively, Maria touched his back. His eyes red, he turned to face her. "Danny, I—" she began.

"Why did you save me from the fall?" he asked her, his voice cracking and strained. "Wouldn't it be better for both of us if I was dead?"

"I don't want you dead," she whispered. "If you die, that's it. Over. It's the same for me. You may not believe this, but I would have let you kill me before I killed you. Even if I could, which isn't certain.''

"When anybody dies, it's over,'' he said. His voice had gone lifeless again. "Susan, Kathryn, Evelyn, probably David as well, Frank, Mayauel, Patecatl, Orizaba—''

"John?'' she asked him.

He stopped and looked at her. "Well, obviously it wasn't John I saw jump in the damn fire! Or else he's got a twin!''

"No, it was him you saw. And whether he has a twin or not, that was him you saw here, a little while ago.''

"That's not possible!''

"Are demons possible? Crystals that throw lightning? Monsters? This whole place? You? Me?''

He glanced over the edge at Kathryn's headless, bloody corpse, still lying on the stone. Again his tears welled up. "You can't tell me she can live again!'' he cried. "Look at her!''

"I will tell you that it's possible! You were told, Danny. Things down here aren't what they seem.''

"I know. We're in Hell. Sure we are.''

"You keep rejecting that idea. But, Danny, it's true. Maybe it isn't the classic Christian hell, but it is Mictlan! The land of the dead!''

"You mean the souls of dead people walk around down here?''

"Almost precisely. It isn't quite a soul, not as you think of them; at least not what I was taught, as a Catholic. It's better to think of it as a consciousness. And yes, the consciousnesses of the dead are down here; not all of them, but a lot. And they can form physical bodies here, that work here. They can't leave, of course. That kind of body doesn't work on the surface. But you have a rare experience, Danny. You are in the land of the dead, and you're still alive! Not many people ever do that.''

"So you're telling me Kathryn, or Susan, or Evelyn, their consciousness is still sort of alive here, can form a new body?''

"Yes, I'm telling you exactly that!''

"Bullshit. Anyway, you said she can't ever leave. Never go home. Just stay here, eternity—''

Maria looked at him directly. "You love her, my friend?''

"Yes, I did—I do—''

"Then would you rather be in New York without her, or be with her here? Here for all eternity?''

For Danny, this was no choice at all. "Here, of course," he said. Then he turned away. "But it isn't possible, it's crazy—"

"It is possible!" she insisted. "It does happen!"

He watched her face for quite a while. He truly wanted to believe her, but there were a hell of a lot of alternatives. She had saved his life; it was an undeniable fact. But she had also interfered with his attack on Bertie and John. And so far, she had not come up with a reason why. He still didn't feel he could trust her, not unless she had a better explanation. He was trying to formulate a question, nervously clinging to the hope that she was telling the truth, when he saw her eyes go wide again. She was looking past him; he sensed movement behind him and turned.

Of all the incredible creatures he'd seen down here, this was possibly the most frightening. On the other hand, it was a more normal looking animal; a bat, probably a vampire bat, to judge from its face. What was not normal was its size. It was at least thirty feet in wingspan, and it was rushing directly at him. He started to bring up the crystal, and realized for the first time he didn't have it. He'd dropped it when Maria had knocked him off the stairs. He could even see it, lying on the floor far below.

He had no more time to think about it before the bat was on them. Braking its flight, the huge wings curving in, its hind feet caught his shoulders in an iron grip. Too quickly for him to react, he was borne aloft, up near the ceiling. He could hear Maria yelling behind him as the bat carried him out of the room. He couldn't believe the thing could negotiate the narrow hall, but somehow it did, and soon they were out in the open, the floor of the underworld far below. Danny tried his heightened vision, everything. Nothing worked at all. He was absolutely helpless to stop the creature from taking him wherever it wanted to.

13

Bertie and John continued up out of the pit, but they remained in a desolate night-world of dead desert plants and rocks. Many of these boulders were carved into fantastic and grotesque shapes. More than once Bertie had caught a glimpse of one from the corner of his eye and whirled to confront what he thought was a menacing beast of some sort, only to find himself looking at an inert, harmless stone. He was becoming increasingly uncomfortable down here in this bottom world. He hoped they'd go back up a little higher soon, where it was more pleasant. But he liked the darkness, felt it was his element more than John's. It seemed he had an advantage in the dark.

They came across what seemed to be an encampment of some kind, a prepared campfire that had not been lit. Over it was a rack, made Indian-style, from which hung a large ceramic cooking pot. But there was no one around, no tents. John stopped here; Bertie trotted around among the nearby boulders, assuring himself there were no potential enemies lurking among them. He heard an odd sound, saw John looking at something on the ground.

When he came back, John was standing over a small dog; he had indeed found it. When Bertie got close enough, he could see that John had also been correct about it being sick. It looked up at them with pathetic eyes; three of its legs appeared to be broken, and one of its eyes was protruding and glazed. It had a variety of cuts and other injuries as well.

"He don't look too good," Bertie commented.

"No. He has suffered with me, throughout the trip, on a parallel journey. And he has had, if anything, a harder time of it."

"I don't think you can do anything for him now. Don't you think we should put him out of his misery?"

John looked at him strangely. "Yes, we should. In fact, we must. But it has to be properly done."

Bertie shrugged. Whatever. But he hated to see an animal suffer; that bothered him much more than seeing a human in agony.

Gently, John reached down and picked the animal up. It whimpered as he did so. To Bertie's surprise, he carried it over and put it in the cooking bowl, hanging over the unlit, but prepared, fire. Bertie saw water splash out as John dumped the dog in.

"What the hell are you doing?" Bertie asked.

John didn't answer; he stepped back from the pot. The dog laid its head over the side, looked at them, its tail wagging, splashing the water a little. Suddenly, with no warning, the fire roared into life.

"Goddamn it!" Bertie cried. "Not that way, you asshole!" He lunged forward, but John grabbed his arm, pulled him back. "No!" he yelled. "At least kill him first, for God's sake, man!"

But John held Bertie fast, and quickly the water was steaming, then boiling. The dog made pathetic sounds, but never barked. Bertie just stared at it; he couldn't believe John was being so cruel. The water in the pot was getting lower, and the dog was apparently dead. The skin down its back began to split open.

Bertie jerked his arm away from John's grip. "You are a bastard, you know that?" he snarled. John smiled at him, pointed at the dog; its body was splitting open like a butterfly's cocoon, and a misty, half-shaped form was rising slowly from inside. As he watched, the mist settled on the ground in front of them, rose to a height of about six feet. It shifted, changed, and became less misty, more solid. Finally it became human in shape, and a man was standing there in front of them, smiling. He was naked, and his penis was erect, pointing straight out. He smiled. Bertie was amazed; it was almost, but not quite, like looking into a mirror.

He then looked at John, and the man's face changed; now he looked like a beardless John. His erection dropped suddenly, and he made some odd movements with his hands. Suddenly he was wearing a long black cloak and a dog-faced mask hung off his belt.

"My brother. Welcome back," John said. He turned to Bertie. "This is Xolotl," he said. "Our twin, our double. And, I might add, a master magician!"

"Our twin?" Bertie asked, bewildered.

"All goes well then, my nagual?" John asked Xolotl, increasing Bertie's confusion.

"Yes, perfectly," the other told him. "I will go now to Cliff House and await your arrival there!"

"Excellent!" John responded. "We must, as you know, visit the Caves of Cincalco. But after that, no matter what the outcome, we will go to the House of the Red, to the Cliff House. I feel it, I know it will be well!"

"I, too, feel it will be well, my brother. Do not be long, for the dawn awaits!"

Xolotl stretched his arms out. As if only to exercise his power, he pointed to a boulder some hundred yards away; it glowed briefly, then exploded with a loud report. Smiling, he clapped his hands above his head and vanished before their eyes.

Bertie just stared at the space he'd occupied. He was glad the man was gone; he seemed to be coming down on John's side, and he was potentially very formidable.

"Now the caves, my friend!" John cried. "We must hurry!"

Again they started on down the path, side by side. Neither of them seemed willing to walk ahead of the other.

The path now led them up into some low hills, an area of open grasslands scattered with rocks. To all appearances they were out in the sunshine. There were few trees, but magueys dotted the hillsides, some showing the giant flower spikes. Ahead and above, the rocky outcroppings increased; this was the region they were evidently headed for.

Eventually the path turned into a rocky ledge. Above them was a rock face, not quite vertical; below, the gently sloping grasslands. It wound around the hill for a while, then terminated as it disappeared into the mouth of a cavern.

"The Seven Caves of Cincalco," John said softly.

"What's special about them?" Bertie asked him.

"Legend has it that corn—maize—came from here originally. You might have never realized it, growing up as you have this time, but maize is a very special food. Very special indeed.''

"This time?''

"Of course. As I was trying to tell you earlier, you've lived before, we all have.''

"Oh, you mean like reincarnation?''

"Yes, exactly.''

"I never really believed in any of that crap,'' Bertie said.

John stopped and looked at him, an expression of amazement on his face. "And how about now, my friend?''

"Well, who knows? Everything that's happened, I guess it's sure possible! I mean, it must be. Evelyn, Frank, Mayauel, you—you're all alive again, some way or another. But I'm not sure that's reincarnation, at least not like I understood it.''

"No, it isn't. That's resurrection, not reincarnation. All you've seen is resurrection here in Mictlan, and that's a little different.''

"How so?''

"Many people are resurrected here, in a sense. But it's not real. They can't return to the surface world, to ordinary reality. The bodies they have are kind of an illusion, a convenience to satisfy the mind. They won't work on the surface, they're not material enough. They're blown away by the winds, perceived by surface people as ghostly.''

"You mean Evelyn and Frank can't go back, say, to New York?''

"As they are now, no. They're dead. So am I. We are just ghosts, that's all.''

Now this was interesting. He'd been assuming all along that John was alive, and could go back up any time. Apparently not so. He had an attack of anxiety; a disturbing thought.

"What about me?'' he asked.

John laughed at him. "You're alive! You can go anywhere you want, do whatever you please. You, Danny, Susan, David, and Kathryn, you all came here alive. Of course, only you and Danny still are.''

"How do you know Danny is still alive?'' Bertie asked him.

"Oh, I just know. I imagine we'll be seeing him again, pretty soon now. But enough of this chatter. We have to go into the caves.''

They walked to the entrance to the cave; there was light

inside, but not much. As they started down the tunnel, Bertie felt a real concern about seeing Danny Hudson again. He had no idea where he'd gotten that damn crystal, but he surely was dangerous with it, and he had every reason in the world to want to see Bertie dead. He resolved to turn Danny into one of the ghosts at the first possible opportunity. Before Danny could get a chance to do it to him.

The tunnel widened out after a short distance. The rock formations here were as fantastic as they'd been down in the pit; huge stalactites and stalagmites, petrified waterfalls, and filigreed curtains of rock, in a variety of earth tones, ambers, and golds. A very beautiful place. And there were people in here, too. They encountered several of them; friendly, smiling men and women. Some of the women were cooking tortillas. Smelling them, Bertie realized he was hungry. He had no idea how long he'd been in the underworld, but he'd eaten nothing since he came here.

At last they entered a natural room, closed off at the back; inside were two throne-like wooden chairs, very artistically carved. One was covered with a mat of eagle feathers, the other with jaguar hide. John sat in the eagle chair, told Bertie to take the other. It seemed entirely appropriate to him.

"I'm sure you're hungry," John said. "I am too. The women of the corn will bring us food and drink."

"How can you be hungry?" Bertie asked. "Spooks don't eat!"

John smiled. "How many have you known? What makes you an expert?"

Bertie shrugged again. He wasn't; it just didn't seem logical. A young woman brought them identical plates: tortillas, cheese, corn on the cob. For a moment he regarded it suspiciously. Poisoned? Somehow it didn't seem likely. He took a small bite; it was delicious, and he dug in without further concern. They ate in silence, and afterwards Bertie felt much better. The women took the plates away, returned with two beautiful cloaks, one eagle, one jaguar, just like the chairs. Bertie and John put them on, then sat looking at each other for a moment.

A group of women came in, each carrying a large basket filled with flowers, and they began distributing them around the floor of the cavern. Soon the floor was practically covered with them, a riot of bright colors. This took quite a while, the women shuttling their baskets in and out. None of them said anything, but virtually all of them smiled richly at Bertie, who reclined on the Jaguar Throne, watching them work. After the floor was covered, a man carrying a cloth-covered tray came in. Dessert, Bertie assumed. He watched as John lifted the cloth, took from the tray a staff of gleaming hardwood, about thirty inches long. The end of it was carved into an eagle's claw, and the claw held a perfectly round ball of reddish wood, about seven inches in diameter. Bertie looked at it and tensed. It was much more of a war club than a staff. But his tension had been little more than a reflex; after all, the last time John had been armed—with the big obsidian knife, which was almost as large as a short sword—he'd smashed it on seeing Bertie's discomfort. Ever since then, Bertie had felt that he was in complete control.

"Still don't like to see me with a weapon, do you?" John said, hefting the club and grinning.

"No, I don't," Bertie said coolly. He waited for John to cast it aside, or break it.

"Back then, it wasn't time," John said, his grin growing wolfish. "Now, Tezcatlipoca, it is!" He got up off the eagle throne, came to the center of the room.

Bertie was totally stunned. He was being challenged! "That's not my name," he said weakly, remembering the name from the stele, back up in the pyramid.

"The Smoking Mirror. That's what it means, Tezcatlipoca. Didn't I tell you, back in my bedroom before you brought Xochiquetzal to me, that I wasn't the Smoking Mirror, that you were?"

"Who?" he asked. He still hadn't gotten up, he was too shocked. This was very familiar somehow, the whole scene; the flowers on the cavern floor, everything. What the hell was happening? His world had turned upside down in an instant.

"Get up and defend yourself," John warned. "Remember, you are also Itzacoliuhqui, Itzli,"—he paused and laughed—"maybe Mack the Knife, too! Don't just sit there! If you do, I'll spatter your brains all over the room!"

Still Bertie was too stunned to draw his knife. "Itzli?" he mumbled. "Itzaco—"

"Both mean knife, Yaotl. Quickly, man. Get yourself together!" With this he made a sudden lunge across the the room.

Bertie reacted, almost too late, rolling off the chair onto the floor, and the eagle club thudded into the back of it where his head had been. He scrambled to his feet, drew his knife. Holding it arc downward like the extended claw of some great cat, he faced John.

"Now that's better!" John cried. "Much better. The other way, you sitting there dazed, was not right, not good. You need to give a good account of yourself, Tezcatlipoca. Although you'll lose!"

Bertie was in a half crouch, John circling across in front of him. Peripherally, he could see the people of the cave gathering to watch. He feinted several times with the knife, and each time John jumped back. Bertie was amazed; he was quick as a cat. He tried another slash with the blade, and John's club caught his shoulder. It was a glancing blow, but he was off balance for a moment. It hurt like hell. He'd had no idea John was so strong, so agile.

Immediately John tried to press his advantage, but Bertie brought the knife up under him. John sprang up into the air, twisting his body, and came down off balance. Now Bertie tried to press in, the knife dancing, a thing alive. At this moment, he felt better, faster, and stronger than he'd ever been. But so was John; even while he was falling backward, he managed to pull in, twist aside, catch the blade with his club. But at last he went down, and Bertie pounced on him. He could almost see himself streak through the air, a spotted cat, obsidian eyes flashing.

Onto a serpent which twisted away again, its great fangs reaching for him. He slapped at it with his paw, saw he'd drawn a little blood. But it hit him again, in the ribs, the huge coiled body surging, yellow and blue plumes flying. The rattle made harsh sounds, and Bertie growled low in his throat, a coughing sound. The fangs came for him again, unbelievably fast, but he was quicker. He twisted away, struck with his claws, felt them engage and tear. Then the coiled body struck his head and he went flying across the floor.

On his back, Bertie looked up at John, who was bleeding from two superficial cuts, one on his forearm, the other across his chest. But still he smiled and circled cautiously. Bertie was sure he had a broken rib, and his head rang from the blow that had knocked him down. But he had the knife up and ready, forestalling John's attack. He felt an incredible exhilaration. The all-out battle, the opponents so well matched, here on a field of flowers in the sacred Caves of Cincalco. He'd been here before! He knew that now with a sudden, absolute certainty. And the last time, he'd won. He remembered clearly the winning strike, the curved knife cutting down across John's wrist, forcing him to drop the club. John surrendered then, became a prisoner. And then—then—what? Bertie couldn't recall. But he remembered the win, and it gave him confidence.

He came back up from the floor, onto his knees. Panting, he tried the same ploy that had worked on Toltecatl. But John was having none of it; he danced in, taking advantage instead, and planted another strike on Bertie's head. He twisted to avoid the full force, but it left him slightly dazed. Quickly, he got to his feet; as evenly matched as they were, he couldn't be at all dazed, it might tip the balance—

He didn't quite complete the thought. John had danced in again, as Bertie was balancing and turning. The full force of the club was coming straight at his head. Desperately, he twisted to avoid it, and knew he was going to succeed. But at the last instant John changed the direction of his blow, and the head of the club struck directly on Bertie's wrist. He felt the bones shatter, and he screamed; the knife fell from his hand onto the bed of flowers. He just looked at it, looked at the club cocked and ready in John's hand. No chance to get his knife, to try to fight left handed. None at all.

He knelt down, half expecting a lethal blow on his head, but defenseless against it. "You are as my own beloved father," he said in a loud, clear voice.

John took hold of his hair, not roughly. "You are as my own beloved son," he responded.

14

Spinning. Spinning like a miniature planet in a miniature solar system. Awareness was returning, awareness of the seventh, topmost cave of the Sacred Seven of Cincalco. Awareness of Chalchihuitlicue, Mayauel, and Patecatl, standing watching. And another; a living person. Here? Very strange, it had to be explained. Reach out a fiber of awareness, four consciousnesses bound up in one, touching the others, realizing the task. Awareness shrinking inward from its vast span, to the spinning shape high in the air over the floor of the Sacred Cave. Distilling the awareness down to a smaller package. What was of importance was here.

She slowed her spinning with conscious effort. Isolate, unify; a time to be constricted, just a little. Load some filters into place; events in the Himalayas, at the ocean bottom, were not of consequence. More filtration; but no, this wouldn't do. She willed her body to form. Like a small whirlwind, the spinning, iridescent shape dropped a point of itself down toward the floor. The remainder of the strange object followed the point, began to swirl around, disappear into a female form that glowed and pulsated. Eyes were formed; open them. Ears were adequate; listen to the vibrations. Activate the nerves, set the heart in motion, move the blood. Pull in the awareness, all inside except for the fibers. Close the boxes, control, solidify. Susan looked out through the eyes, saw Evelyn; Xochiquetzal looked through the same eyes, saw Chalchihuitlicue.

Susan's face turned from them as the body still rotated slowly. There was no back of her; as she came around, Kathryn's face was on the back of her head, Kathryn's body on the back of hers. Kathryn and Tlazolteotl looked out this pair of eyes, listened with this pair of ears. Rotation continued; consciousnesses separated. Now they were two, a Susan/Xochiquetzal side and a Kathryn/Tlazolteotl side. They pushed themselves apart, broke most of the bonds. Like a great two-headed coin spinning to a stop, they continued to turn, until finally the motion slowed and was no more. They felt each other, exchanged affection; their single heart fissured and divided, their bodies pulled away. Each consciousness took a step, and the backs of heads, the dorsum of torsos, formed from their misty connection. Another step; then two nude women, shining like the sun and moon, turned and looked at each other. Impossibly beautiful, a mere man would have died at the sight of them at that moment.

They rushed back together, embraced. Then, stepping apart, they looked at Evelyn/Chalchihuitlicue. Their glow, their flare, faded just a little, and they began to look more like humans.

"Welcome back," Evelyn said. "Feel okay?"

"Of course," Susan/Xochiquetzal said. She was fully aware now of her other self; it seemed impossible to her she could have lived all these years and not known. She was fully Susan, had Susan's memories, emotions, and personality; but she was also Xochiquetzal, Flower Feather, as Xolotl had told her so very long ago. Amazing that she hadn't recognized him. But, of course, he had been in the guise of Tezcatlipoca at the time. She glanced at Kathryn, knew exactly what was going on in her mind. She was reconciling her Kathryn Phillips personality with her much older self, Tlazolteotl. Naturally, the personalities were basically the same between Susan and Xochiquetzal, as they were between Kathryn and Tlazolteotl. But the twentieth-century American women were having to deal with the new awareness of their hundreds of past lives. They could not, however, dwell on this now; something of major significance was about to happen, and even they couldn't tell exactly what. Did it have to do with the living woman who stood there? No. Mayauel and Patecatl, who were as they were? No. It was coming, though, whatever it was. And then, there would of course be the matter of Xipe Totec to deal with.

They were in the south, the Place of the Tearing to Pieces, as Susan well realized. The Tearers were about; Cipactli, Ocelotl, Cuauhtli. But one was missing. She sensed his approach, heard his great wings.

From up out of the tunnel that led down to the sixth cave, a monstrous vampire bat sprang. Susan could feel the air from the massive wings as it moved toward them. It had something behind it; she couldn't see what yet. Hovering just in front of her, it swung its legs forward, and gently deposited what she knew would be the Heart of Humanity in front of her. How could she have forgotten? She'd been here many times.

The Heart of Humanity, still beating within the chest of Danny Hudson, turned to face her.

"Kathryn!" he yelled, his face lighting up. "Susan! Evelyn! And you too, Mayauel, Patecatl! You're all alive! Oh thank God, I thought I'd lost you all forever!" He rushed forward, embraced Kathryn. His arms flailed around, beckoning Susan and Evelyn in, and for a moment they all piled into a mass embrace. Danny was crying freely, his body shaking with joy and relief. He saw the living person, whose presence Susan didn't yet understand, and turned to her, motioned for her to come over to them.

"Maria, you were telling the truth!" he said to the red-robed figure. "I still don't understand, but I'm not sure I care now. I thank you."

"No thanks are necessary," she said. Susan still didn't understand. Danny was calling her Maria, but she didn't look like the Maria that had come to Mictlan with them. "And, let me correct you on one thing," the woman continued. "My name—at least what I go by—isn't Maria. My given name was Nicolasa Espinosa de los Monteros. But that was a long time ago; almost five hundred years ago. People know me now as Nikki Keeler."

"You're five hundred years old?" he asked.

She smiled broadly. "Almost. I age well, don't you think?"

In spite of everything, or perhaps because of it, Danny was a little dazed. "Nikki—John's Nikki?" he asked her. His head was swimming.

She smiled again. "The same. Or should I say guilty!"

"I guess I shouldn't be all that surprised," Danny said, shaking his head. "I'm carried here by a giant bat after hours and hours in the air, to meet with people I thought were dead. A five-hundred-year-old ought to be trivial!"

Evelyn took his arm. "Now, Danny, you need to keep your head. There's a few more things around here that are going to be really strange for you, and we need to get by them."

He looked at her, rather a pleading look. "No more deaths. I'm not sure I can take it."

"No," she said firmly. "None of us, anyhow."

For the first time, in the fire of his excitement at discovering these people alive, he realized David and Frank weren't about. He asked about them.

"Tlaloc—that is, Frank—is already up at Cliff House. We'll go there soon. As to David, well, that's one of the things we have to get you by."

"What did you call him? Frank, I mean?"

"Tlaloc. We have remembered our old names, Danny. I am Chalchihuitlicue, Susan is Xochiquetzal, and Kathryn is Tlazolteotl. Mayauel and Patecatl always went by their old names. But right now, I'm quite sure Xipe Totec will arrive any minute. And we have to be ready for him!"

Evelyn turned away from him, as if she was watching for someone. He looked back at Susan and Kathryn, who were standing side by side. Susan was now dressed, though he'd seen no clothes, and she'd been nude when he came in. But that was a minor mystery; he embraced the still-nude Kathryn again, just gazed at her. He didn't really care if they could never, as Nikki had said, return to the surface world. Here with her, that was good enough.

He started to ask about the mysterious Xipe Totec, but all heads were turning toward the entrance to the cavern. At some point, the great bat had silently departed; now a man was walking toward them. In a strange way he looked like David. But as he got closer, Danny realized with a jolt that he was wearing David's skin, just as David had worn the tanned skin above.

"David's still dead?" he asked. "Not back, like the rest?" That took an edge off the joy he felt.

Susan and Evelyn each took one of Danny's arms and guided him away. "Now, there are some things here you may not like. But not death. You've been through the worst. Wait it out, Danny. Keep control," Susan was saying. Kathryn, alone in the path of the advancing figure, glanced over at him, smiled and nodded.

Evelyn stepped out, spread her arms as if to stop the figure. He did stop, watched her; his eyes looked terrifying. She dropped her arms, crossed them over her chest, and began to speak:

"Xipe Totec, our lord, our awesome and terrible lord, you

fill our hearts with the nameless dread!'' she cried. Then she
began a kind of a chant, or song:

"You, the Night-drinker,
"Why must we beseech you?
"Put on your disguise,
"The garment of gold, put it on!
"My lord, your precious water descends,
"The cypress becomes a quetzal,
"The firesnake becomes a plumed serpent,
"And they have left me.
"It may be, it may be, I go to my death,
"I, Xilonen, the young corn,
"But my heart is precious,
"You shall yet see the gold there.
"They shall rejoice if it ripens early,
"As if a king was reborn.
"Let there be an abundance of the maize plants,
"Here, in these few places,
"Your servants turn their faces toward the mountain,
"Toward you.
"They shall rejoice if it ripens early,
"As if a king were reborn."

Again she spread her arms to the man. "Xipe Totec!" she
cried. "Our lord! We honor you, you who must suffer the agony of the springtime! But that day is done, O Xipe! Your day
of agony is past!"

He stopped in front of her. "My agony is never done," he
said. His voice, superficially like David's, was gravelly and
very harsh. Danny thought he was even more threatening than
Bertie had been, at his most extreme. Evelyn had been right;
he didn't like this. But he followed her instructions and waited.

Kathryn touched her hands to her groin. "Come into me,"
she sang to him. "Come into me!"

Xipe began to get an erection as soon as she said this. Danny
fought the impulse to try and stop this event from taking place;
he tried to keep trusting the women, they hadn't let him down
yet. He ground his teeth and watched, knowing what was going
to happen.

Kathryn lay down on her back, opened her legs. The dreadful figure came over her, his penis started sliding into her.

Danny wasn't enjoying this, but it was a hell of a lot better than the knives.

Once his penetration was complete, Xipe's body started to bend backward, as if he were hinged at the hips in the wrong direction. Kathryn had a look of ecstasy on her face as he sank deeper and deeper into her. With a start, Danny realized his entire body was liquifying progressively, flowing into his penis! She was absorbing him, drawing him into herself! Once started, the weird absorption progressed very rapidly. Like someone sucking up a pool of liquid, his entire body disappeared into hers. She lay there, her belly swollen as if she were very pregnant. A look of pain crossed her face, and a cloud of greenish mist emerged from her vagina, followed by a tiny face. A body, infant size, followed the face and head, surrounded by the green mists. She cried out once, and the infant, born facedown on the floor, stood upright, a column of the green mist around it. Before Danny's eyes, the infant grew. As he did, the mist was disappearing, seemingly helping to form his body. Only seconds later, he was fully six feet tall, adult; the mist was gone, and David stood there, looking rather blank. Danny could hardly look at him at all; he heard Nikki cry out, saw her avert her eyes. He was too beautiful to look at.

Evelyn was speaking, again a kind of a chant. "Cinteotl," she was saying, "born of Paradise, new and glorious. Cinteotl, from the Land of the Flowers. Cinteotl, he shines like the sun. Cinteotl, his mother is many colored as the quetzal. Cinteotl, from the House of the Dawn!"

David's blank look left him, and his glow diminished somewhat. Evelyn touched him, and clothing appeared on his body—brilliant, leafy green tunic and kilt, bright yellow hat, red sandals. He and Susan rushed together, embraced. Kathryn got up and walked over to Danny, clothing appearing on her body as she came.

"So tell me, Danny," she asked with a smile. "What do you think of my son?"

"Danny," David said. "It's good to see you again. Good to see all of you." He looked past them, down the corridor where the entrance to the cave was. Someone else was coming, running. Danny looked, saw a pretty young girl in a blue dress, her blond hair flying, her face streaked with tears. She looked to be about fourteen. David released Susan, and the girl ran into his arms. He held her like a father would hold his daughter.

"Danny," he said. "This is Xilonen!"

Danny nodded and smiled. He was now far past being surprised at much of anything. He thought to himself that if Jesus Christ walked in now, he wouldn't be shocked. But someday, he hoped, someone would fill him in on all this. He was utterly mystified.

Kathryn took his hand, smiled up at him. "We have to be going, Danny. I'm enjoying the reunion too, but we have to get up to Cliff House. They'll be waiting for us."

"You mean John?" Danny asked. John and Frank were the only ones missing; they'd said Frank was at this Cliff House.

"She does indeed!" Susan said. They started out, away from the cave entrance. There was an exit back there now. Danny knew it hadn't been there before, but he just followed them, and didn't ask a single question.

15

Up through the Seven Sacred Caves of Cincalco, John led his prisoner. Bertie did not try to escape from him here, even when he was released; it seemed better to wait for a truly good opportunity. At least, that's what he kept trying to tell himself. The fact of the matter was, he was bound in some odd way, unable to resist when John gave him some command, such as telling him to sit in a certain place. Internally, he fought against it, but it seemed to do no good. He had no will to escape, no will to fight back.

As they cleared the seventh cave, and emerged on the top of the range of rocky hills, Bertie could see the cave entrance, far below. But he could scarcely believe what he was seeing now. Either it hadn't been there when they'd been walking up into the hills, or in some mysterious way it had been concealed from his view; it was utterly impossible to miss. Rising from the top of these hills, and stretching as far as he could see in both directions, was a colossal black stone wall. The top of it could not be seen; it vanished into the clouds at a dizzying height. All up and down it, beginning at a height of about a hundred feet or so, were rooms of some kind, open on the side facing them; many of them were immense. On the lower levels, Bertie could see that there were passages between rooms on each level, some open to the side and some not. There was no obvious way to go from level to level, though. The rooms contained a variety of other constructions; the familiar flat-topped pyramids were particularly prevalent. Many people could be seen up there, moving about, executing indeterminate tasks. This was without a doubt the most incredible sight Bertie had seen down here.

John led him to a point about fifty feet from the base of the great wall, and sat down on the grass, cross-legged. He indicated Bertie should do the same.

"We await nightfall before we enter Cliff House," he said.

Cliff city, was more appropriate, Bertie thought. But he wondered about waiting for nightfall. There were no days and nights down here, and this was obviously a day area. He asked John about it.

"No," he answered. "Here, at Cliff House, the days pass normally. Wait, my friend, you will see."

And indeed, he was correct. Approximately two hours later, as near as Bertie could figure, the darkening of the landscape became obvious. Fires were burning in the rooms in Cliff House; the entire wall, as far as could be seen, was dotted with them. As darkness fell, a light having the quality of full moonlight was filtering down from above. Interrupted by clouds, it played over the face of the wall like weak searchlights. The moving pale light and the dull red fires created a very striking scene. For a long time, Bertie just sat watching it, engrossed.

Finally John got up, told him it was time. He was led toward the wall, toward a firelit opening he'd not seen previously. They went inside; the right-hand wall was covered with a thick layer of mist. Holding Bertie's hair, John walked right into it. They came out the other side, and Bertie saw immediately that they were walking the opposite direction on the next level. After passing through innumerable rooms, they came to another with a mist wall, and this took them up another level. For hours, this continued, until they had reached an incredible height. When Bertie looked over the open edge, the hills below looked like tiny bumps. He could see a whole panorama of the world they'd traveled through down there, but they were getting into the clouds, and soon all that was visible below was white mist, irregularly lit by the pale white light and the red of the many fires. Still they continued, ever upward. Bertie wondered how far it might go; there seemed to be no end to it. But after a while he began to notice something; the wall was no longer vertical. It had begun to lean backward, so that the view over the side was not a straight drop, but a very steep slope. At intervals among the multitude of rooms were ramps, smooth planes running down the slopes. Still no top was anywhere in sight. And still they continued, one mist-wall, one level, after another.

They had passed numerous people on the way up, but no one looked at them or spoke. All these men and women seemed very intent on whatever it was they were doing, and it seemed to be some kind of general activity. Virtually everyone was involved in some way with the fires. Either tending them, starting them, putting some kind of herbs in them, or carrying in fuel. Where they got the fuel, Bertie had no idea. An interesting feature was the starting of the fires; none were started from flints, or fire drills, or even matches. Always the flames were carried by torches from two other fires, lit simultaneously from these two; none were ever lit from one only. Of the dozens Bertie saw being lit, each one was being treated with a reverence. Once he saw a woman crying bitter tears over a fire that had gone out. It seemed they took their work very seriously.

Coming to a great room with a pyramid in it, they seemed to be at their destination, or at least at a stopping point. Three people came forward to meet them; Bertie was a little surprised. Frank Wasserman and Xolotl he pretty much expected, but the third was Eduardo. He'd had no idea the man was down here, and he wondered if he'd died up on the surface. There was another difference to this room, he saw now; one of the inclined ramps he'd been seeing was here a stairway. He looked up; he thought he could see a flat roof above them. The stair seemed to go through an opening in it, which was partially the source of the white light. Bertie felt a thrill of excitement. He was sure, somehow, that it was an exit back to the familiar surface world of everyday reality.

As the three came forward to meet them, Eduardo grinned broadly at John. "So, you are here, and well time enough!" he said.

"Why are you here, Eduardo?" Bertie ventured. No one had told him not to speak; he felt free to do so.

"Ah, Tezcatlipoca! Quite naturally, you haven't your full eyes, so you know me not! Let me drop this disguise, then!" His body and face seemed to fold in on itself, darken and shift. Moments later, Bertie was looking at the oldest man he'd ever seen. His face was lined by fleshy canyons, like folded fabric. But the black eyes within were somehow young. His clothes had changed too; he was wearing a robe and cape of dark, rich red. Although he'd never seen him before, Bertie knew who the old man was.

"The Old One of the Fire," he said slowly. "Huehueteotl, Xiuhtecuhtli!"

Huehueteotl grinned at him. "Yes, Tezcatlipoca, it is I. As always, I do not forget my duties!"

John took his hair again. "And now, my friend, it is the time." Six more people stepped from around the pyramid. Bertie recognized them; two of his Jaguar Knights, and the four village girls he'd made his wives. The girls were weeping as they came forward. They embraced him; the knights handed him the flutes he'd been playing that last night on the surface. He had a terrible feeling, looked up, toward the top of the pyramid. A black-robed, hooded figure stood there now; he saw the stone, saw the pale light glint on the obsidian blade. His knees went weak.

"No," he said, "No. I won't go, I won't, I—"

John looked him directly in the face. "Yes," he said firmly. "You will do what you must. You know that, you always have."

Bertie looked back in those eyes. He tried to say no again, but it wouldn't come out. He felt someone—Xolotl—cutting locks of his hair. Mechanically, he took off his clothes and cast them down. Once again, he embraced the four girls. Smiling at his knights, he held each one by the shoulders briefly. Then he started toward the pyramid, up the steep stairs, carrying the flutes.

Slowly, alone, he mounted the steps. Other people had gathered below, but he didn't look back. On the twenty-sixth step, he smashed one of the flutes, then continued upward, his face a mask. On the last step before the top, he broke the other flute. Finally, at the fifty-second step, he stood on top, in front of the stone, looking at the hooded figure. He could not see a face; it was in shadow. Silently, he lay down on the stone. It was more arched than the others, and he was stretched tightly backward. Spreading his arms and legs, he waited, looking upward at the roof of the underworld.

There was a touch of fiery pain on his left chest, just under the nipple. He looked down at the blade; it was in his skin, only about a half inch. A little blood flowed. His skin was so tight, stretched back as he was, that he felt his entire body might split open. There was pressure, more pain. The priest was pushing the blade in with incredible slowness. Minutes passed; the pain spread out through his chest. He looked again, and the blade was only an inch deep! He fluttered his hands; why didn't the man just push it on in, end this agony? He remembered how it had been with Evelyn and Susan, how he'd pushed the knife slowly into their bodies. But that was three times as fast as this, and they had wanted it that way; he didn't! But he was helpless to do or say anything. The priest worked the blade, slipped it into him a quarter inch more—so very slowly—so excruciatingly slowly!

The blade slipped into him just a little farther, and he felt a sudden heavy pain. Blood surged up into his throat, and he knew his lung had been penetrated. He swallowed and gasped for air. It took him a minute to accomplish even a breath. It seemed the priest was aware he was coming into danger of drowning in his own blood, and he pushed the knife in faster. When it was fully set, he began to twist it. The edges grated against Bertie's ribs, causing new flares of pain. Then the priest pulled the blade out, tossed it aside, and worked his hand into the hole, which really wasn't quite large enough. Bertie's body bounced and spasmed with this new pain. His consciousness centered on the pain, revolving around it. He felt the hand inside his chest take hold of his heart, and he waited for it to be ripped free. But there was a pause. The priest threw back the hood with his free hand, and looked into Bertie's face. Bertie looked back up at him, up into the face of Danny Hudson.

"How does it feel, bastard?" Danny asked him. His hand closed tighter on the heart; Bertie felt a great crushing pain. The hand was ripping, tearing; then it was coming out, and the pain was fading. So was the world. Through a haze, he saw Danny pull out his heart and hold it aloft, saw it jumping and surging in his hand. Then nothing.

The waiting group at the bottom silently ascended the pyramid and bore Bertie's body off, as if he were a fallen hero. This was the part Danny hadn't liked; he wanted to shove the body over without ceremony, as Bertie had himself done to so many of his victims. He was aware that Bertie was liable to come back to life like the others, but at least he'd denied him access to the surface, as his friends were denied it. Also, he'd given him a taste of the pain he'd been so willing to inflict. He felt a certain satisfaction with this, but no real joy.

He wondered about John; his feelings about the man had been heavily mixed since he'd stabbed Kathryn. But she herself had assured him that first, she'd practically had to force John to do it, and second, this was not exactly the same John that had in fact done it. Danny had not, of course, understood any of that at all. But his questioning had been interrupted by their appointment here, by the insistence of the group that he be the one to take Bertie's heart. He'd not been thrilled with the idea, but it did seem like justice to him. Nevertheless, he'd had to force himself at first to do it. But then it had gotten easier, and he wondered if killing and torture were always like that. Hard at first, easier and easier as you got into it. It was a disquieting thought. Glancing down at the obsidian blade he had used, he saw the bright redness of Bertie's blood on the black stone; and suddenly he knew one more meaning of his original vision, so long ago in New York City. One more of many, it seemed.

Down at the base of the pyramid, his friends were waiting for him, looking up at him expectantly. Bertie's body lay off to the side, his flint knife and the leather bag lying across it. Slowly, Danny descended, removing the black cloak, which had covered his shirt and pants, and tossing it aside. Kathryn was waiting; he certainly had more questions.

They embraced. Then he spoke: "You were telling me you

had to almost force John to stab you. Why in the hell would you do a thing like that?''

"The chalchihuitl," she said, indicating the leather bag. "It had to be filled, and I had to provide the final third. For two reasons, Danny. And in just a very few minutes, one of those reasons will be obvious. The chalchihuitl can only be filled with life's blood, the donor has to die in the filling. In John's bag is a little ball. It can only be made with the precious water of the chalchihuitl, life's blood. The chalchihuitl was emptied in the making of it, but if you look now, you'll see that it's full again! It's unique, very important. But just wait, you'll see!"

She pressed Danny's hand and released him, stepped away. Nikki came over to him, took his arm.

"We have to move away from this," she said. "We are living, not part of it. But don't worry. No harm will come to anyone."

Danny glanced around for the four brides and the knights. He saw that they were already ascending the stair, back to the surface world. Apparently their duties down here were finished.

As John stepped over to Bertie's body and lifted the leather bag off him, Bertie's eyelids fluttered, then opened. Danny was a little disappointed; so soon? Slowly, Bertie got up. But as he did, he seemed to come out of his body. The one standing was for a moment less physical, slightly translucent. Then he stepped away and it solidified. But his body, dead, still lay on the floor as well. The living body—or ghost body—took the flint knife from the corpse and put it in his belt. He grinned; the familiar sardonic, self-confident Bertie grin. He will never change, Danny thought. He still didn't trust Bertie, wished he didn't have that knife. Actually he would have preferred that Bertie remain dead.

Nikki led Danny off to the side; the others arrayed themselves in a semicircular arrangement; John in the center, Bertie on his left. Susan stood briefly on John's right, then moved to a position facing John. It was like a stylized dance; everyone knew their positions. The ancient man, Huehueteotl, had stayed outside the area. Now he stepped between John and Susan and stood facing John.

"The fires of the Temple of the Red are burning," he said

solemnly. "And the darkness is upon the world. It is the time for the lighting of the fire of the dawn."

He came forward, and John handed him a leather bag. Huehueteotl reached inside and brought out a ball, a dark sphere about the size of a baseball. Holding it aloft, he turned slowly until he was facing Susan. She raised her arms, spreading them as they went up; when they reached their zenith, her clothing, and the clothing of everyone else there except the old man, vanished. The one exception to this was Bertie's headband with the small mirror, and his belt carrying the curved flint knife. Otherwise, the entire assembly was now nude. Susan froze in her position, her arms extended.

Huehueteotl brought his arms down and held the ball near his face. He had taken on an awesome, imposing look; his eyes looked like holes in a furnace. He held the ball for a moment, then spread his hands apart from each other, keeping his wrists together. His palms stood at ninety-degree angles, and the ball rested in the V that was so formed.

There was a sudden rushing sound, a flare of brilliant blue light. The old man's hands looked as if they'd been turned into blowtorches. Blue flame, turning red at the top of a three-foot column, erupted from the junction of his hands, washing the ball in fire. Danny and Nikki were at least fifty feet away, but he could feel the heat like a warm desert breeze. The ball began to move in the rushing flames, to dance a little; finally it began to rise into the air. It started to rotate slowly as it went. Bouncing and spinning, it rose to the top of the fiery column. Here, in the red flames at the top, it hovered, a charred sphere. Then the fire began to die down, pull back toward the old man's hands. It fell into them, flickered a little, and died out. The ball still rotated in midair, no longer bouncing.

Leaving the ball, Huehueteotl ascended the pyramid and stood on top, his arms extended. Frank left his position in line and joined him there, standing one step below him, his arms out in the same manner. Again the old man's hands flared; a river of fire ran from them, spilling onto the pyramid and running down the steps. From Frank's hands, water flowed; and the streams of fire and water mingled, forming an odd substance Danny found hard to really see. It was, very simply, a fiery water, or a watery fire. It still flamed, yet sparkled cool, these apparent opposites united in some unfathomable way. He saw several little fluttering shapes above the two streams. Looking more closely, he realized he'd seen these before: the obsidian butterflies. Symbol, essence, of the union of opposites. He began to feel he was witnessing a true miracle, an event of vast significance.

His attention shifted to the rotating ball. It was changing now, a little window opening in it, as if it were a tiny spaceship. As it did, white light of unbelievable brilliance flooded out, scanning the assembly like a searchlight, illuminating each of them in turn. Danny found it difficult to look at it, but he forced himself; the window was beginning to rotate in the opposite direction to the ball's rotation, so that the sweeps of the beam were getting slower and slower. Finally, the speeds matched and the beam stopped moving. It was focused on Susan, directly on her stomach.

She closed her eyes, seemed to be in some kind of ecstasy. The pattern of light started to spread, wavered, then virtually exploded outward in all directions. It flared and danced, finally resolved itself into a bright, eight-rayed disk of light, its center on her belly. Initially the rays were white, but after a moment the clockwise edge of each ray became reddish. Simultaneously, the counter-clockwise edge became dusky gray. The red deepened to brilliant scarlet, the gray to inky black; and Danny was seeing once again his vision of the first day, back in New York, this time magnified in intensity a thousandfold.

The rays began to circle slowly in a clockwise direction. In the center, still bright white, an even brighter white dot formed. It grew, expanded upward, weaving as it went, leaving a light trail behind it. It began to look like the trunk of a small tree, growing out of Susan's middle, a tree of light. When it reached a point some six or eight feet above her head, it began to branch out, and the tree-like appearance was emphasized. Beads of light, like Baily's Beads in a solar eclipse, formed on the branches. A tree of light, with leaves and fruit of even brighter light. As the rotation of the black and red rays increased in speed, Danny looked up in the now-fully formed tree, saw a little green form up there, the green striking in contrast to the white tree on its black and red background. It appeared to be a hummingbird. It took to the air, its tiny green wings buzzing like a wasp's. Straight down it dived, straight at John, who opened his arms. The little bird flew directly at his chest and seemed to enter him. For a moment, a spot over his heart glowed green, then faded.

The tree of light began to shrink down, pull in, and after a few moments it was gone, just a bright spot in the center of the white disk; then even that faded. Still the rivers of fiery water flowed, still the obsidian butterflies flitted about. Now the light seemed to be coming from Susan, going to the ball; it began to pulsate, and the window opened a little wider.

John took two steps forward, stood directly under the ball. The window became wider yet; and the beam between Susan and the ball abruptly split. Part of it fell on John's midsection, so that there was a beam from the ball to Susan, and a similar beam from Susan to John. As soon as the beam touched John, the ball began to change. It was falling to pieces, little black particles falling to the floor. What was left, Danny couldn't look at; it was a miniature sun, brilliantly white, a captive star. And it was falling, descending, directly toward John's head.

When it touched him, his whole body was suddenly illuminated with the same light. The red and black sunburst from Susan was spinning now like a propeller, the beam pulsating, throbbing. The brilliance flooded down over John's body, and he stood there for several long minutes, his whole body formed of the star-material, a living sun in human form.

He began to move, turn; beams flashed out from him. They touched Bertie, Xolotl, David, Evelyn; all turned to stars momentarily, then back. Kathryn, Patecatl, Mayauel, Xilonen, all stars. Then Susan, perhaps the brightest star. She faded back, but the rayed disk remained. Finally Frank; he flared brilliantly, but different from all the rest; his light was bright blue, and he retained it longer, but it too gradually faded. Then Danny noticed a peculiar effect, as if his eyes were adjusting. John's brilliance hadn't faded, but his human body could be seen again. The rayed disk over Susan was becoming indistinct, fading way, but John had retained the fire from the ball, had given each of them, except for those who hadn't died, a little of it. Clothing reappeared on all the bodies; some of it not the same as before. John wore a magnificent headdress of blue, white, and green feathers. He turned as if presenting himself to the assemblage. His body appeared to be painted black, except for his face. Bertie was too, and he also had yellow and black horizontal stripes painted on his face.

The fire-water flow suddenly stopped. All of them except John looked up at the old man. He had given some silent signal for their attention; even Danny had been aware of it.

"Behold!" he thundered, his voice echoing through the darkness, seemingly loud enough to fill the entire underworld. "He is reborn, and his fire has been lit! Yea, he lives again; the Lord of the Dawn, the Plumed Serpent, Quetzalcoatl!"

Following John/Quetzalcoatl's lead, the assembled group began to ascend the stair, Nikki pushing Danny along behind them. He didn't protest; he was dazed, his mind churning. In single file, the group moved up the stairway. It appeared that only Huehueteotl was staying behind.

"Eduardo isn't coming?" Danny asked Nikki.

"No, his work on the surface is, for now, finished. This is his home, he'll stay here. And his name isn't Eduardo!"

"I still don't understand—"

"Yes, you do, Danny. You just won't let yourself believe it yet. But don't worry about it. There are still things to be done. Though I'm not entirely sure myself what they are."

"But Nikki, I thought they couldn't go back to the surface. I thought they'd be ghosts up there."

"That was before. What you just saw was the relighting of the fires of full life. They've all had their fires relit. As soon as we clear that doorway at the top of the stair, they'll have all been resurrected. Completely!"

"Resurrected?" Danny felt stupid. Perhaps, he thought, he wasn't asking the right questions. He'd adjusted to the notion that he had to stay down here to be with Kathryn, but now that had been turned on its ear. He was also wondering why Huehueteotl had called John Quetzalcoatl. He remembered the name. It was one of the principal gods of the ancient Mexicans. But also, if memory served, something else; a man, wasn't he, a great priest? But he didn't know much about this, wasn't sure. The main thing he did remember was that the Aztecs believed Cortez to be Quetzalcoatl, returning as prophesied to reclaim his kingdom. Naturally, they'd been bitterly disappointed. Cortez turned out to be a most greedy and brutal man, and had virtually destroyed the civilizations of old Mexico.

He remembered the visions he'd seen in the stone and was suddenly terrified. "Nikki, do you know what the tezeat is?" he asked.

"Surely," she said. "It belongs to Tezcatlipoca, and it's now in Huitzilopochtli's castle, where he lies dead."

"Yes, that's where I saw it. I saw things in it, terrifying things. A man there—he called himself an Eagle Knight—told me that whatever is seen in it is real. Past, present, future."

"Yes, that's so. Of course, only the most skilled naguals can see anything in it at all."

"I saw things in it, and I'm not—"

"Oh, yes you are. Destined to be one of the greatest, I'd hazard. You learned in ten minutes things that took me ten years!"

He let that go for the moment. "But Nikki, I saw the destruction of the world! Our world, the real world! And it seemed to me John had caused it!"

She gave him an odd look. "You saw the end of the Fifth Sun," she said. "One of Tezcatlipoca's suns. There is always destruction associated with the end of a sun!"

"But—"

The conversation broke off; Quetzalcoatl, in the lead, had reached the doorway at the top of the stairs. His body flared with a bright light as he went through, as did each of the others who had been resurrected. Danny was still not quite sure how to take that. Literally, it seemed; he'd seen most of these people quite dead.

Finally he and Nikki, last in line, passed through. There was no flare for them, nothing unusual at all, just walking through a door. He looked around; they were in another pyramid upper chamber, similar to the one where they'd encountered the taloned black monstrosity. In solemn procession, they passed through here, up another stairway, and out into the cool night air. They were out. All of them. And there was nothing ghostly about anyone. In fact, the only one remaining who looked different from the happy days of John's kingship was Frank, who retained his fanged countenance as Tlaloc. Danny looked at the eastern sky; it was a little before dawn. They went down the side of the pyramid and walked into the center of Tlillan Tlapallan, to the square. The entire populace was assembled there, waiting. It seemed they all knew about this. The recently returned group gathered at the east side of the square, Quetzalcoatl standing a little in front of the others.

He spread his arms to them, and a great cheer went up. Directly above his head, the morning star, Venus, was rising in the dawn sky; the sun was not far behind. He raised a bundle on high. Nikki told Danny it was the mexquimilli, the earthly remains of the last Quetzalcoatl. To Danny, this seemed to confirm that the name Quetzalcoatl was a title of some kind. As he opened the bundle, there was a flare of energy, and it seemed to Danny that the planet in the sky glowed just a little brighter. Probably illusion, he told himself. Quetzalcoatl discarded the bundle, apparently now only an empty tube, and stood silent, waiting for the dawn.

When the sun came up, its first rays fell directly on him, and the effect was incredible. He glowed golden, if anything more spectacular than when he had shone as a sun in human form in the underworld. The villagers were hushed, silent.

"Now what happens?" he asked Nikki.

"I don't know," she said. "There're always variations, and whatever they're planning to do now, it's new."

"New?" he asked. "I don't—"

She silenced him with a gesture, watching the others.

As Tezcatlipoca/Bertie moved to the north side of the square, Tlaloc/Frank took up a position directly opposite him. Quetzalcoatl moved to the west, the sun in his face, and Cinteotl/David took his place in the east. For a long time they stood like this. Danny could almost see some odd colors in the air. He tried his heightened vision, and the colors were clear; black in the north, blue in the south, red in the east, and white in the west. Little wavy bands of color connected the four men. Then the three women stepped forward, into the center of the square. Kathryn/Tlazolteotl knelt with her back to Cinteotl, Xochiquetzal/Susan with her back to Quetzalcoatl. Chalchihuitlicue/Evelyn remained standing, facing south.

Taking Danny's hand, Mayauel led him slowly, ceremoniously, into the center of the circle, pushing him gently to his knees between Kathryn and Susan, facing Susan; she herself remained standing in empty space, facing north. Two squares, an inner and an outer, male and female. In the very center, Danny. Patecatl trotted in; he carried an obsidian knife and the leather bag containing the chalchihuitl. Around the outer circle he went; each of the four men touched each item. Then in to the center. The bag he gave to Chalchihuitlicue, the knife to Mayauel. Danny watched the knife closely; he was beginning not to like this. Mayauel told him to stand up, remove all his clothes. He did so, liking it even less. Patecatl picked them all up, trotted back out of the square.

He then stood with Xilonen, Xolotl, and Nikki, watching. Nikki looked worried, and that didn't make Danny feel any better. It seemed he was about to be the last sacrifice. Should he mind? Wasn't it an honor? Perhaps it was, but he wasn't accustomed to thinking that way. He had friends and a new love, a lot to live for. He had an idea he'd reappear, conscious, back in the underworld, but he really didn't want that at all.

But it did not appear that they were giving him much of a choice in the matter. Susan smiled richly at him; she was so beautiful to him right now, it would be hard to deny her anything. He had no great altruistic feelings in terms of sacrificing himself; it was more that he was unable to resist the power of their personalities. They seemed to be focused on him, here at the center of the double square.

Susan put her hands on his chest, and he felt Kathryn do the same, both of her hands directly across from Susan's. Evelyn stood over them on one side, holding the bottle; Mayauel on the other, holding the knife.

"Behold!" Quetzalcoatl said suddenly. "Within the chest of this man, this special man, beats the Heart of Humanity! The soul and center, the crossroads, of the race of humans!"

Danny wondered how seriously he was supposed to take that statement. Him? Danny Hudson, the Heart of Humanity? If that meant anything like what it sounded, he felt it was ludicrous.

Quetzalcoatl smiled at him. As if reading his mind, he said, "No, my friend. It isn't ludicrous. The entire focus, the essence of the human race, is concentrated in you. You are, today, their representative here. You alone!"

So he, as the representative of humanity, was to be sacrificed now, like the others. They had all died; why shouldn't he? Still, he didn't really accept it, still tried to find a way to stop it. He didn't want to die, couldn't think of a good reason to just kneel here and let it happen. But a small voice inside him told him he was denying the understanding he did have.

"You do not want this honor, then?" Tezcatlipoca asked. "Well, there is another here, another suitable. Bring forth the woman called Nikki Keeler!"

Patecatl took her arm and brought her into the double square. He looked at Danny. "She can take your place if you so wish it," he said. "But you must formally ask that this be done. Then she will be your substitute!"

He looked at Nikki. Her head was down. Five hundred years old. A long enough life for anyone, surely. He'd not even lived half a century yet. Surely that was fair.

"There's no other way?" he asked.

"No other way at all. You and she are the only living humans who accompanied us in our voyage through the underworld," Tlaloc rumbled.

"It's your choice, Danny," Cinteotl told him.

Danny opened his mouth to speak. He could live, free! Nikki, she'd lived so long, she—

"No," he said finally. "I cannot. Patecatl, take her back. Let her live another hundred years."

Xochiquetzal and Chalchihuitlicue were crying now, but they were still smiling at him. Even now it made him feel warm, good. Not the worst way to die. He felt Tlazolteotl's fingers dig into his back a little, heard her sob, too. But somehow he knew she was smiling.

Chalchihuitlicue lifted the bottle as if to pour it, and Mayauel lifted the knife, the blade glinting in the sun. She brought it down, slowly, steadily. He hoped she'd do it fast, but apparently that was not to be. After what seemed like hours, the point touched his chest over his heart. She continued to push; his chest dimpled. There was a tiny pain, and a single drop of blood appeared next to the black stone.

And Mayauel pulled the knife away. She stabbed downward violently, deliberately missing him, shattering the blade against the stone in an explosion of black shards. Chalchihuitlicue began to pour the bottle over him. The red blood, the blood of the three sacrificed women, began falling toward his chest, where the single drop of his own blood still lay. When it touched him, it turned to a strange liquid; water, but water of a golden color. It seemed to stay with him, forming a pool around his knees. He felt an incredible flow of energy, like an electrical current, between the women's hands, front to back. The energy spread through him, filling him.

Finally, the two women took their hands away. He was unable to move; all he could do was remain there, kneeling in the pool of golden water. He felt different, like his whole body structure had been somehow rearranged. He wanted to ask what they'd done to him, but he couldn't speak. He was sure of one thing, however; he wasn't hurt, and he wasn't going to die, at least not here and now. The eight who had formed the square now moved close to him, then away to where Xolotl, Nikki, and the others were waiting. It was very strange. Danny was still as a statue, unable to talk or move, but so much was going on inside him he didn't really mind.

For a very long time after the ceremony was over, Danny remained kneeling on the square. He felt strong, he felt energized; ideas, concepts sprang into his mind apparently from nowhere, but soon he realized their source was himself. It was a unique mental state for him, and for the first time in his life, he felt completely in touch with all of himself. And that seemed to put him in touch with a great deal more, as well.

It seemed that Tlaloc/Frank was leaving, the first of them to do so. Danny wondered where he was going.

"He'll go to live on a mountain somewhere, it doesn't matter a lot where," Evelyn said aloud, exactly as if he had spoken to her. "He's not quite as human as the rest of us, Danny. But the Evelyn part of me will miss the Frank part of him." Her voice showed only a little emotion.

Danny was wondering about Tezcatlipoca, when he saw that he too seemed to be leaving. Still cocky, just like always, he waved to everyone, started off away from the square.

"Well, good friends, I'll likely be seeing you around soon," he said. "Probably as soon as we—"

But Quetzalcoatl did not even let him finish his remark. "Tezcatlipoca!" he cried. The other man turned, still smiling. But the smile left his face when he saw that Quetzalcoatl had put on his long red mask. "I told you," he said, his voice sounding hollow through the tubed mouth, "that the day might come when I'd break you into a thousand pieces for what you did!"

"No. My lord Ehecatl, I—" Tezcatlipoca said, backing away, his hands up defensively. Quetzalcoatl blew lightly into the mask; Danny could hear the soft puff. But it was Ehecatl that let the blast fly in the air. It was very controlled; the tented stalls in the square only ruffled as if in a soft breeze. But whirlwinds of terrific violence developed around Tezcatlipoca. He struggled frantically against them, but within a matter of seconds, his body started to be torn apart. The little tornado turned bright red, churning, now tearing the parts apart. Tiny pieces, none larger than a dime, flew off in all directions. Not one, not a drop of blood, landed on the square.

Finally the winds subsided. Tezcatlipoca's artificial foot sat there, the headband with the little mirror lying on it, the flint knife beside it. But the oddest thing was that his eyes still hung in midair. They didn't look like disembodied eyeballs; they still were lidded, the lids just couldn't be seen. They looked at each person in the assemblage, and Danny heard a voice in his mind, Bertie/Tezcatlipoca's voice, telling him, "Next time I'll win. Next time." Then the eyes were gone, and only the artifacts remained. The whirlwind Ehecatl had generated died down and disappeared; Quetzalcoatl took off his mask.

"Is he dead?" Danny thought. "Really dead? Forever?"

"No, my friend," Quetzalcoatl said. "He cannot be. Only his corporeal form is destroyed, and only for a short time. He will be back. You will doubtless see him many times in the futures to come. And eventually, unless you can accomplish something none of the rest of us have been able to do, he'll kill you too, send you back down to Mictlan. Chalchihuitlicue, who ruled the Fourth World, knows that from hard experience. But it is so, it always cycles. We always hope for a different result, and perhaps this time it will be different."

"What about the destruction I saw in the tezeat?" Danny thought. This thinking was just like talking.

"On the appointed day, Tonatiuh will die. I shall, I must, depose him. It is determined, it has now been written. It will occur. I will take Tonatiuh's breath, and he will die. The Fifth World will come to an end. It cannot now be prevented."

Danny stared; the man was talking about the end of the world! He started to protest in the mental voice he'd been using, but Quetzalcoatl raised his hand. "It is now time for us to leave Tlillan Tlapallan," he said. "At least some of us. Mayauel, Patecatl, Xilonen, Xolotl; you will stay, maintain the city, keep the entrances sound?"

"As always, my lord," Mayauel said.

"Then we will go. We must go to where we are not known for what we are, that nothing may interfere with the plan." His face softened "Nikki, you will open a gateway?"

She executed a very slight bow. "Of course," she said lightly, then frowned in concentration. Danny saw the wall of fog appear, visible even in normal vision. Susan, Kathryn, and Evelyn all ran up and kissed Danny as he knelt, still paralyzed, on the square. They were all crying. Quetzalcoatl walked up, stood in front of him, and smiled. He touched Danny's head, and he lost consciousness.

16

The sound of an alarm clock woke him, and he lay there staring at it without comprehension. Beyond, he could hear the hum of an air conditioner, and the sounds of traffic. The song of a police siren rose in pitch, passed, and died away. Danny still didn't move his body, just his eyes. He was seeing his own bedroom, his apartment in New York. What in the hell? He tested his fingers, his arms. All moved normally. Rolling out of bed, he went to the window, looked out. New York, summertime. Summertime? None of this was registering. His last memory was of being in the square in Tlillan Tlapallan, Kathryn and the others walking into the wall of fog, Quetzalcoatl touching him. It occurred to him that it might have been a dream; after all, he was just getting out of bed. But there was no way he could accept that. If so, where had at least three or four months of his life gone? If not, how had he gotten here?

He looked down at himself. He was nude, but that proved nothing; he always slept that way. But what was significant was that his chest was unmarked. No old scar over his heart, no prick where Mayauel had drawn a droplet of his blood with one of the sacrificial knives. For a moment he felt extremely dizzy, had to sit down. He could not seem to focus his thoughts.

When he finally was able to get up and walk around the apartment, he became even more confused. There was a *New York Times* on the kitchen table: June 30, 1987. Stale coffee, made not more than a day or two previously, in the pot on the stove. Anyone investigating this situation would have assumed that he'd occupied the apartment continuously for at least the last few weeks. The garbage hadn't been taken out. There were fresh coffee grounds in there, a darkened banana peel that looked maybe a day old.

They weren't real? he asked himself. Kathryn, Susan, David, all the rest? He remembered the Hallstens' phone number, lunged for the phone. He got a recording: "The number you have reached has been disconnected or is no longer in service." He slammed it down. There just was no way he could accept this. As quickly as possible, he showered, dressed, and went out into the streets.

And just as quickly discovered that the Hallstens' old apartment was vacant. The super told him the people who had lived there had moved away, that their name had been East.

He went downtown in a taxi next; he wasn't sure where Susan's office was, but he remembered David's. He went up, and asked. The answer he got was that no David Hallsten had ever worked there, no one had ever heard of him. He didn't bother trying to locate Susan's office. He knew the answer would be the same.

Sitting on a park bench, his head in his hands, he wondered if he should see a psychiatrist or check himself into a hospital. It was just impossible for him to believe none of it had happened. But it didn't seem as if he could verify anything. Then he remembered Tascan Acres, jumped up, and hailed a cab.

He had the taxi take him to the parking garage where he kept the seldom-used Chevette, drove it out to Long Island. Finally, at least a little verification. The dilapidated trailer was there, just as he'd remembered it. He stood in the office, looking at the couch, remembering the pile of blankets, the horrible face he now realized was a phantasm of Huehueteotl's face. But it didn't prove much, and he really wasn't interested in proving anything anyway. He wanted to find Kathryn and the others. The idea of returning to everyday life as he'd known it before he'd seen the red and black sunburst for the first time was untenable. He also believed that John—or Quetzalcoatl—did indeed plan to end the world, crazy as that might sound. The only person who could possibly prevent that was himself. And given everything he'd seen, he did not consider it outside the realm of possibility that Quetzalcoatl could and would do it.

He stood on the warm summer beach and looked out at the ocean, watching little sailboats out there. So very ordinary. But he didn't feel ordinary, not at all. And this was getting him nowhere. Then he remembered the technique of using the wall of fog to move around. He went to his heightened vision, and—yes!—he could see it, very dimly, off to his left. Some of his confidence returned. He concentrated, pushed, snapped around. But it kept rotating. For an hour, he stood there on the beach trying to stop it, but he could not. It just wasn't working for him. His face drawn and tight, his mind even tighter, he got back into his little yellow car and drove rather recklessly back to the city. In his apartment again, he made another effort to use the wall of fog, but it still didn't work for him. His heightened vision seemed to be operating normally; he just couldn't face the wall.

Finally he gave up, sat down heavily in a chair, and cried freely. He hadn't felt so bad, so utterly defeated, since he'd seen Kathryn killed. He could almost see her face; it was haunting him. In the periphery of his vision, he caught a glimpse of black and red; excited, he went to his heightened vision, saw it clearly. Over his bed, in the bedroom. He ran in, threw the sheets off. Nothing. Looking under the bed, he saw a large leather bag, clearly the focus of the vision. With trembling hands, he pulled it open.

And took out the beautifully crafted trumpet, touched the engravings of plumed serpents, the turquoise inlaid valves. He smiled. He'd find them. He didn't know how long it would take, and he didn't care. But he'd find them.

Epilogue

In an apartment in New York, six people sat around drinking coffee, talking. If someone were to walk in on them, look at them, he or she would not think that they were unusual, other than the fact that they were all remarkably attractive. What was unusual was what hung in the middle of the room; a hazy sphere in which could be seen the image of a man with bright blue eyes, holding a musical instrument much like a trumpet, but very ornate.

One of them, a very small woman with dark hair, wiped tears from her eyes. "I wish we didn't have to put him through this," she said.

"But we do," said Quetzalcoatl. "He isn't aware of what happened to him. And you well know he can't be. We have to wait."

"It just seems cruel, and it seems to me he doesn't deserve it," Xochiquetzal commented. "Besides, he and Tlazolteotl love each other. That shouldn't be denied."

"It won't be. Not for long. But right now, he's focused on preventing the death of Tonatiuh. He has to learn a few things first," Quetzalcoatl told her.

"At least it doesn't have to be bad for him," said Chalchihuitlicue. "Not like it was for us."

"Wait and see what he does with his Sixth World," said Cinteotl. "Next time around, maybe it'll be easier. That's going to be up to him."

Nikki looked from one of them to the other. "Perhaps he'll find the true sign, bypass all the crap," she said almost wistfully.

"Nobody would rather see him find the true sign than me," said Quetzalcoatl. "You think I get a kick out of killing billions of people? But it has to be—"

"I know, I know!" she sighed. "The race has to be reconstructed from the redeemed bones. But I still have my hopes. Maybe he can come to himself without dying. I doubt that, but maybe. He's clever. I think possibly he will find the true sign. He's going to spend a lot of time looking for us, you know. And we still have twenty-four and a half years before December of 2011. I have my hopes, Ce Acatl Quetzalcoatl!"